CW00337803

Cross
Hairs

Why everyone loves James Patterson and Detective Michael Bennett

'Its breakneck pace leaves you gasping for breath. Packed with typical Patterson panache . . . **it won't disappoint**.'
Daily Mail

It's no mystery why James Patterson is the world's most popular thriller writer. Simply put: **Nobody does it better**.'
Jeffery Deaver

'No one gets this big without **amazing natural storytelling** talent – which is what Jim has, in spades.'
Lee Child

'James Patterson is the **gold standard** by which all others are judged.'
Steve Berry

'Patterson boils a scene down to the single, telling detail, the element that **defines a character** or moves a plot along. It's what fires off the movie projector in the reader's mind.'
Michael Connelly

'James Patterson is **The Boss**. End of.'
Ian Rankin

The City of New York

POLICE DEPARTMENT
One Police Plaza
New York, NY 10038

Req #: 2014-PL-10945
File #:

PERSONNEL FILE

TO BE FILLED IN BY IMMEDIATE SUPERIOR:

Detective
MICHAEL BENNETT ☑

6 FOOT 3 INCHES (191CM)   200 POUNDS (91KG)
IRISH AMERICAN

EMPLOYMENT

Bennett joined the police force to uncover the truth
at all costs. He started his career in the Bronx's
49th Precinct. He then transferred to the NYPD's
Major Case Squad and remained there until he moved
to the Manhattan North Homicide Squad.

EDUCATION

Bennett graduated from Regis High School and studied
philosophy at Manhattan College.

FAMILY HISTORY

Bennett was previously married to Maeve, who worked as a
nurse on the trauma ward at Jacobi Hospital in the Bronx.
However, Maeve died tragically young after losing a battle
with cancer in December 2007, leaving Bennett to raise
their ten adopted children: Chrissy, Shawna, Trent, Eddie,
twins Fiona and Bridget, Ricky, Brian, Jane and Juliana.

Following Maeve's death, over time Bennett grew closer to
the children's nanny, Mary Catherine. After years of on-
off romance, Bennett and Mary Catherine decided to commit
to one another, and now happily raise the family together.
Also in the Bennett household is his Irish grandfather,
Seamus, who is a Catholic priest.

PROFILE:

☐ AMENDED REPORT

BENNETT IS AN EXPERT IN HOSTAGE NEGOTIATION,
TERRORISM, HOMICIDE AND ORGANIZED CRIME. HE WILL STOP
AT NOTHING TO GET THE JOB DONE AND PROTECT THE CITY
AND THE PEOPLE HE LOVES, EVEN IF THIS MEANS DISOBEYING
ORDERS AND IGNORING PROTOCOL. DESPITE THESE UNORTHODOX
METHODS, HE IS A RELENTLESS, DETERMINED AND IN MANY
WAYS INCOMPARABLE DETECTIVE.

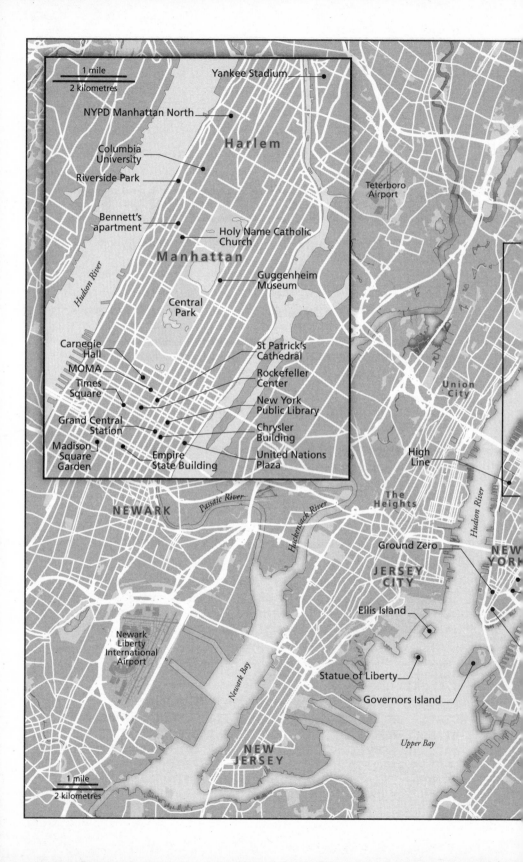

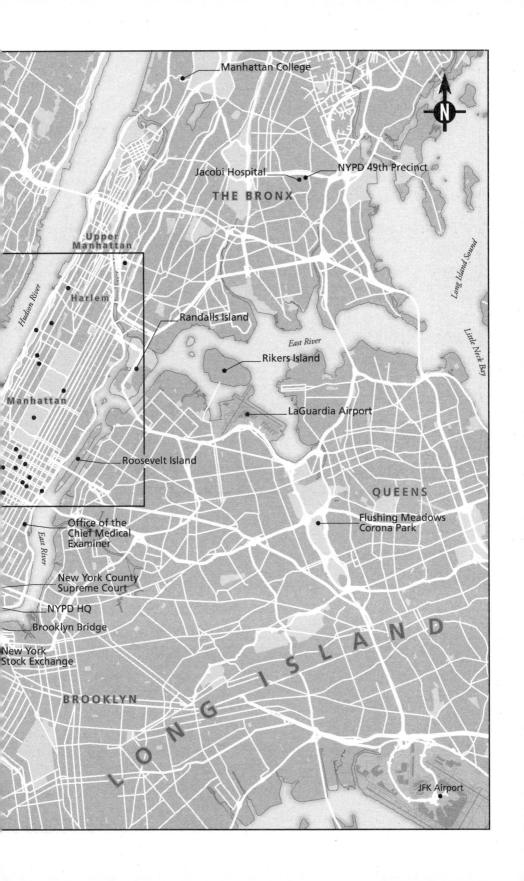

A list of titles by James Patterson
appears at the back of this book

JAMES PATTERSON

& JAMES O. BORN

Cross Hairs

C
CENTURY

1 3 5 7 9 10 8 6 4 2

Century
20 Vauxhall Bridge Road
London SW1V 2SA

Century is part of the Penguin Random House group of companies
whose addresses can be found at global.penguinrandomhouse.com.

First published by Century in 2024

www.penguin.co.uk

A CIP catalogue record for this book is available from the British Library.

ISBN: 9781529136432
ISBN: 9781529136449 (trade paperback)

Typeset in 12/17 pt Janson MT Std by Jouve (UK), Milton Keynes
Printed and bound in Great Britain by Clays Ltd, Elcograf S.p.A.

The authorised representative in the EEA is Penguin Random House Ireland,
Morrison Chambers, 32 Nassau Street, Dublin D02 YH68

www.greenpenguin.co.uk

John and Emily. Always proud of you.

Cross Hairs

CHAPTER 1

ADAM GLOSSNER HAD to work hard to conceal his smile, sitting on the edge of his three-year-old son's tiny bed. The little boy giggled as he squeezed the doll again. A shaky, recorded voice said, "Oh, geez. C'mon, Rick."

Brooke, Glossner's six-year-old daughter, snickered from the other bed.

Glossner said, "Are you sure you've never watched *Rick and Morty*?"

The little boy kept smiling and shook his head.

"How did Grandpa know you'd like this Morty doll?"

Jeremy shrugged his little shoulders and kept the huge grin on his face. From the other bed, Brooke said, "Grandpa is smart. He said that's why me and Jeremy are smart. It skips a generation."

Glossner couldn't keep from laughing out loud at that. His father often threatened to buy the kids a drum set if he didn't get

3

to see them enough. All Glossner could do now was hug his son and do the little ritual where he tucked the blankets tightly around him. Jeremy was an amazingly still sleeper. Glossner would often find him in the same position in the morning. The boy looked like a tiny mummy.

He stepped over to his daughter's bed and leaned down to give her a kiss.

Brooke said, "Daddy, can we go to the LEGO store soon?"

"Sure. What's my engineer need this time?"

"They have a new Star Wars collection. I just need one more TIE fighter."

"Wow. When did you guys go full science fiction on me?"

Brooke smiled and said, "We're not from the olden days. We grew up this way."

Glossner snorted. "Six whole years of growing up. Nothing like the dark ages I had to live through." He kissed his daughter on the forehead. "Once upon a time, I had to watch the commercials during Giants games. No fast-forwarding and no pausing either."

"Really? All the commercials?"

"Yep."

Glossner slipped out of the bedroom and down the hallway. His wife, Victoria, stepped out of their bedroom suite. She still could walk a runway as a model but looked like she was going out for a jog, in shorts and a T-shirt. She liked to sleep in the same clothes she intended to work out in the next morning.

"I love how Brooke lets Jeremy sleep in her room," Glossner said. "It'll be helpful when more siblings arrive."

His wife said, "You better not expect too many more kids. I'll be too old before you have the volleyball team you want."

He chuckled as he leaned down and kissed her on the cheek. "We've got plenty of time. Want to come out on the balcony with me?"

Victoria shook her head. "I have to give my sister a call, then I'm down for the count." As she turned to walk past him, she gave him a swat on the butt. "Not bad for a guy who doesn't have time to work out."

A couple of minutes later, Adam Glossner stood on his third-floor balcony, gazing out at the park in front of his apartment and the Hudson River beyond it. The air was cool but not uncomfortable. No snow so far this year, but that was always iffy before Thanksgiving. The wind was from the east, so he didn't catch that salty smell that came off the river. He held a snifter of brandy in his left hand. He'd given up smoking cigars in the evening when Brooke told him they smelled gross. He had to admit he felt better for it.

He could see the three closest buildings around a bend in Riverside Drive. Something caught his attention. A movement on one of the lower balconies. Then a boat on the river distracted him. He took a sip of the Rémy Martin Cognac and gazed back out at the river.

His brain didn't have time to process the sound of the bullet before it punched into the side of his head and sent him tumbling through the open French doors onto the Italian tile they'd just paid a fortune to have laid in their living room.

CHAPTER 2

I LAY IN bed, appreciating the dark bedroom. The apartment was quiet. With ten kids, that was rare. My wife, Mary Catherine, had been pushing both of us toward a healthier lifestyle. That included a couple of minutes of focused breathing and meditation every morning. This was my time to breathe and meditate.

I could hear Mary Catherine's light snore. It was cute. Not that I could ever tell her that. She had the belief that she never snored. As Trent once said to her, "You claim you don't burp. But I've seen you burp a couple of times. According to my debate class, that would negate your entire premise. Besides, everyone burps." That had earned my youngest son a stern look and a small portion of roast pork with rice and beans. It also put Trent on notice that Mary Catherine really didn't care for him pointing out her personal habits.

I was mature and experienced enough to know never to make a similar comment. I didn't care if Mary Catherine burped after a pepperoni pizza; I'd act like I didn't hear or smell anything at all. Maybe that was the secret to our very happy marriage. That or the fact that we'd been married less than two months.

Then my cell phone rang. As I picked up the phone, I saw that it was my boss, Harry Grissom, calling me at 6:01 a.m. There was only one thing he'd be calling about this early.

"Hey, Harry," I kept my voice low even though I knew the ring itself would've woken Mary Catherine.

"Sorry for the early call, Mike." Somehow his voice didn't sound quite as gravelly as it did during the day.

"What's up?"

Harry said, "This may shock you, but I'm calling because of a homicide."

"No, really? I thought you might want me to meet for you breakfast or maybe go for a walk."

I sat up in bed, then reached into my nightstand drawer and pulled out the little notebook I always keep there. "Where am I heading before breakfast?"

Harry gave me the address. I said, "Wait. Where?"

"I know. It's close to your apartment," Harry said. "You could probably walk there. We got a problem, though. The body was found a few hours ago, but someone screwed up, patrol got overwhelmed, and no one called us immediately. There's already media on the scene."

"That does make things trickier. I can't believe too many reporters are at the scene of a homicide. Even if it is probably some rich guy based on the address." I stopped and thought about it for a moment. I was careful when I said, "Harry, why is there already media there at this time in the morning?"

Harry said in a flat tone, "It's another victim of the sniper."

CHAPTER 3

THE ONLY KID I encountered during my attempt to escape the apartment quietly was Jane, who often got up early to study. Even by her standards, though, this was a little excessive. I gave her a kiss on the top of her head and headed for the door. A cop's kids know not to ask questions when they see their mom or dad leave early or in a hurry.

Just as I was passing through the door, Jane called out, "Be careful, Dad."

It put a smile on my face.

It took me longer to walk across the street and up to the parking garage where I park my NYPD Chevy Impala than it did for me to drive the few blocks to the crime scene. But the entire trip gave me a little time to think. The media had been playing up the story of two people shot from long range almost a month apart. I think it was the *Brooklyn Democrat* that came up with a catchy name: the Longshot Killer. It was easier to appreciate a good nickname for a killer before you met the victim's family. For now, I respected someone's poetic license.

This was the only victim in Manhattan. The first, Marie Ballard, had been a single grandmother in Queens. The next one was Thomas Bannon, a fireman who lived on Staten Island. I was already racking my brain, trying to find a pattern to the killings.

Every homicide detective tends to note homicides with similar details. You never know when it might reveal a serial killer. I wasn't even sure if I was up for another major investigation after my past few months. But I learned a long time ago that neither the NYPD nor the public cares one bit how tired I am or what kind of mood I'm in.

I pulled up next to a parked patrol car. I recognized the patrol officer but couldn't think of his name as he waved to me. After a dozen steps, I stopped for a moment. I sucked in a deep breath like a free diver attempting a hundred-foot dive. Then I listened to the sounds of the city just waking up. I never know how frantic my life might become as soon as I dive into a homicide investigation. I like to savor my last moments of relative calm.

I noticed half a dozen reporters and three cameramen hovering near the entrance to the building. A young female patrol officer stood by the door, blocking the media people.

One of the reporters stepped right up to the officer, trying to intimidate her. He said in a loud voice, "I live in the building. I demand you let me in."

The young cop let a smile slide across her face. She said, "I'm sure you do. In your mind. But I expect it's more likely you live in a studio somewhere in Queens. I'm just basing that on what reporters at your shitty station are paid."

I let out a laugh.

Before I got any closer, I heard someone call my name. It was Lois Frang from the *Brooklyn Democrat*. She had a decent reputation among the cops for honest reporting and being a straight shooter. I knew she'd worked at one of the big newspapers years ago but left under a cloud of some kind. She seemed to get a charge out of racing around the city, writing about some of the more lurid crimes. She also seemed to love working for the small Brooklyn newspaper. Even if the little paper had more ads than articles.

Lois said, "Must be big if they brought you in on this, Detective Bennett."

"C'mon, Lois, no one's bringing in anyone. It's a homicide in Upper Manhattan. If you'll recall, my assignment is to the Manhattan North Homicide unit. I'd get called no matter the circumstances."

"Can you give me any insights?" Lois had pulled a small pad from her purse, which looked more like a duffel bag.

"The best insight I can give you is that cannabis stocks might be a good investment."

"Very funny. Anything about this homicide?"

"Technically, we don't know it's a homicide yet. Until I get up there and look around it's still a death investigation."

"Cut the shit, Bennett. We all know he was shot at long range. Why do you think everyone's out here at this ungodly hour? We want to pick up details about the latest victim of the Longshot Killer."

"Did you come up with that name, Lois?"

She beamed for a moment. "Why, yes, I did."

"Well played. Descriptive without being too campy. You could give lessons to the *Daily News* or the *Post* about variety and imagination when naming a killer."

"Thanks, Bennett. It would be an even better story if you could give me a few details."

I shrugged. "Don't know what to tell you, Lois."

"We heard the victim was well-known."

I shrugged again. I honestly didn't know anything yet except the victim's name: Adam Glossner.

CHAPTER 4

THE APARTMENT WAS on the third floor, so I took the stairs. When I stepped through the stairwell door on the third floor, the scene was exactly as I had expected. Cops, medical examiner workers, and tenants all milled around the open door to an apartment. A few doors down, sitting in a chair that looked like it came from the apartment, was a distraught doorman. Several crime-scene techs were getting their equipment ready, and a uniformed patrol sergeant kept nonessential workers and gawkers away from the door.

The sergeant looked up and said, "About time someone from Homicide showed up."

I smiled at Sergeant Leslie Asher and said, "We show up as soon as we're called."

"Touché." She smiled and said, "I already sent the imbecile who didn't call you home. What we got isn't pretty."

"Talk to me, Leslie."

"The victim is forty-one-year-old Adam Glossner. Some kind of hedge-fund manager. His wife found the body about two hours ago, when she realized he wasn't in bed. She said he'd been headed out to the balcony when she went to bed around nine. It's a single bullet hole visible on the right side of his head. Looks like he sort of bounced off the French door frame and fell on the floor. The two kids are with the wife in one of the neighbors' apartments. There, you're up to date."

I stepped into the apartment and let the videographer and photographer do their job before the crime-scene techs moved in. The body was still on the floor where it had been found. Someone from the medical examiner's office was waiting outside to take Mr. Glossner.

I paused and said a quick prayer for Adam Glossner's soul. My grandfather always tells me how important it is to take every life seriously. By extension we must take every death seriously. This isn't a ritual I treat lightly. But I wish I didn't have to do it so often.

I felt a pang of sorrow for the victim's children. I've seen too many kids grow up without parents due to homicides. A murder can have ripples in a family for generations.

For a long moment, I stared down at the body and its blood that had seeped onto the gorgeous tile floor. The dark blood clashed with the white tile. It was my deepest hope that Glossner's wife had been able to get the kids out of the apartment without them seeing the remains of their father.

I could see exactly what Sergeant Asher had been talking about. It was clear Glossner had been standing on the balcony when the bullet struck him. I could picture him spiraling through the door and onto the pristine tile.

I looked out the open French doors. The apartment was on a bend in the road that allowed a view of the balcony from at least five different buildings. I tried to get an idea where the shot had come from. I was at a loss. My boss, Harry, had texted me that he already had cops canvassing the area. Maybe someone heard or saw something.

I walked through the apartment by myself. I could see the family had built a life here. Young kids, good job, the American dream. I hoped the victim had had enough sense to appreciate his family and situation. I'd seen many a Wall Street financial manager work so hard they forgot they had a life outside of lower Manhattan.

The other thing I realized as I stared at the wound on the right side of Adam Glossner's head: I was not used to homicides like this. I generally dealt with killers who get up close and personal. Even with firearms. Most people feel more confident the closer they get.

Clearly that wasn't true of this killer.

CHAPTER 5

I'D GOTTEN A decent sense of the crime scene. Now it was time to toughen up and do my least favorite assignment in a case like this: interview the grieving. I nodded to the crime-scene techs filing into the victim's apartment as I walked out and then down the hallway to the neighbor's place.

The door was open. I saw a young female patrol officer sitting on the couch next to Victoria Glossner. The officer had a little boy in her lap as the mom rocked back and forth with a girl I judged to be about six years old.

Mrs. Glossner was a very attractive, fit woman of about thirty-five, probably six or eight years younger than her husband. I don't even notice teary, bloodshot eyes anymore on this job. But I saw how she clutched her daughter and how both the kids looked completely confused. It hit me like a sledgehammer. I remembered talking to my kids when their mother was dying of cancer.

We'd had months to prepare for the eventual shock. What do you do when your whole world changes in just a moment?

The patrol officer looked up and saw me. I nodded. Then I tilted my head to the left and the sharp young officer stood up with the little boy still in her arms. She said to the little girl, "Let's see if we can find something for you guys to drink."

Mrs. Glossner released her daughter to walk with the officer into another room. I sat across from her in an antique, uncomfortable chair. I introduced myself and told her how sorry I was. It wasn't an act. I am always sorry in a situation like this.

She said she was okay to talk. "I watch so many of the police reality shows that I know how important the first forty-eight hours of a homicide investigation can be. I don't know what I can tell you. But I'll answer any questions you have."

I handed her a tissue from a box on the table next to the couch. She nodded her thanks and dabbed at her eyes. She explained to me that she had gone into the bedroom around nine and had talked to her sister on the phone for about forty minutes. Afterward, she'd quickly drifted off to sleep. Her husband had not come to bed by that time.

I asked, "Is it usual for him not to come to bed at the same time as you?"

She nodded. "He liked to clear his head. He loved to look at the river from our balcony. He did it almost every night. He usually came to bed somewhere between ten and eleven." She sniffled and looked like she was about to sob again. Then she gained control of herself.

Victoria Glossner said, "It's just not fair. We had so many plans. We'd been through so much. We were talking about having another baby. How could this have happened?"

I asked all the usual questions. The ones about her husband's friends and associates. If she knew of anyone who might want to harm him. I held off on the questions about potential drug use and gambling. It's surprising how often one of those two vices is behind a homicide in an area like this.

She answered no to all of those questions.

I said, "You said you'd been through so much; was it anything that would've made someone angry enough to do this?"

She quickly shook her head and said, "Just some rough spots in his business. Nothing we were too worried about now. That's what I'm saying. Our life was really good. Or at least about to become really good." She started to cry. Then it turned into a flood of tears.

I waited silently, wanting to expand on what sort of business problems Adam Glossner had been experiencing. Before I could speak again, a tall, well-dressed woman came to the door.

When a patrol officer tried to stop her, she snapped, "I'm going in to get my daughter and I don't care who doesn't like it."

The officer looked at me, and I just nodded. As the new woman marched toward the couch, Victoria Glossner looked up and then moaned, "Oh, Mom. Thank God." She jumped up and hugged her mother.

Her mother said, "Get the kids, and let's go to my apartment. We need to get you and them away from here."

Victoria said, "I was just answering a few questions for this detective."

Her mother didn't even bother to look in my direction. She said, "That can wait until later." Then she took her daughter by the hand and started calling for the kids.

They were all out of the apartment in less than a minute.

CHAPTER 6

VANESSA WRIGHT, A new detective with our squad, brought me the neighborhood canvass summary. She wasn't quite my height of six foot three, but she stood well over six feet and could look me in the eye as she gave me the report.

Vanessa said, "We tried to hit all the buildings to the north, where we think the shot came from. Now we'll swing south for a building or two. Does that sound thorough enough for you?"

I said, "Vanessa, I know you haven't been in our unit for too long, but I'm not used to getting a professional report without some kind of a prank." I saw her wide grin and beautiful, straight teeth. I added, "Someone told you to prank me, didn't they?"

"I won't say who, but it *was* suggested that I should tell you everyone went to get breakfast and would start again sometime around lunch. I knew better than to even joke about that."

I smiled and nodded, letting her know I wasn't an officious

prick. I like pranks and I've played plenty during my career. Instead, I asked her about the canvass they had just completed.

Vanessa handed me a sheet of paper and said, "A couple of people thought they might have heard something. Maybe a pop or a bang sometime around 10:15 last night. One elderly man in a building to the north said he'd only talk to the boss. Claimed he had important information."

Even the neighbor next door to the Glossners hadn't heard or seen anything unusual. It wasn't until she heard a commotion in the hallway this morning that she even looked out and saw the police officers. She knew Mrs. Glossner and the children. "That's why she took them in while everything was going on."

As we came out the front door of the building, I saw Lois Frang still standing there. I had to admire that kind of persistence. She yelled out, "What do you got, Bennett?"

I called back, "I have a slight sciatica problem and arthritis in my hip!"

"When am I going to get a straight answer out of you?"

"When I've got something worth saying."

Detective Vanessa Wright led me to a building nearby, to the third-floor apartment of Walter Cronin, the elderly man who'd claimed to have information. When he opened the door, he was clearly happy to see Vanessa again. Despite having asked to talk to the boss, he didn't care too much about me either way.

I said, "I heard you have some information that might be useful, Mr. Cronin." I spoke a little louder than I normally do. I don't know why — I just assumed an elderly man would have poor hearing.

"You bet I do." He motioned us all the way into his lovely apartment. The eighty-six-year-old retired dentist had apparently had a very lucrative practice. After he made us sit on the sofa, he pulled out a notebook and said, "I've been detailing the shenanigans going on with this building for years. The fees this place charges are outrageous. There's so much fraud going on I don't know where to start."

I held up my hands and said, "Excuse me, Mr. Cronin, but we're not here about fraud. We're in a homicide unit. A man across the street was shot from somewhere around here. The killer used a rifle."

"Yes, yes, yes, I know. I was just trying to give you some bonus information as well."

"Do you have any information at all about the shooting?"

"Aside from hearing the shot before I fell asleep last night, I don't know anything."

"You're sure you heard a gunshot?"

"You're too young to remember this, but we used to have a draft in this country. I did two years in the Army and heard plenty of gunfire. I know the sound of a high-powered rifle when I hear it. There are no car backfires anymore. There were no sonic booms. Just a single gunshot, not long before I fell asleep. Probably around 10:15 or 10:30."

"Did you investigate the source of the gunshot?"

"Why on earth would I do that? I don't have a gun. What happens if I find a man with a gun? I doubt you're the right man to look into the fraud of this building anyway. Investigate the gunshot." Mr. Cronin just shook his head as I finished up my notes.

CHAPTER 7

AFTER THE CRIME scene was secured and I'd done all I could to talk to relevant witnesses, I headed to the office. I knew there'd be a lot of questions from my bosses, and I had names and information I wanted to pass on to our squad's criminal intelligence analyst. His name is Walter Jackson, and he's an absolute wizard with computer databases. Give Walter a name and a few minutes, he can tell you every neighbor they've ever had as well as their cell phone carrier, their main bank, and what credit card they use.

I took the elevator up in the unmarked building that housed Manhattan North Homicide. It had been my home within the NYPD for so long I couldn't imagine reporting to a precinct or to One Police Plaza.

It's always comforting to see my lieutenant, Harry Grissom, sitting in his office with the door open. He oversees three staff assistants, two criminal intelligence analysts, and nine detectives, plus a rotating group of detectives trying to get broader experience. And he does it all without losing his temper, getting frustrated, or being petty. In short, Harry Grissom is an awesome boss.

I gave Harry a quick rundown on what I'd learned.

Harry stared at me across his desk without saying a word. It lasted maybe five seconds, but it felt like a week. This is why I never play in Harry's poker games. He seems like he'd be unbeatable.

Absently smoothing his mustache, Harry asked in a quiet tone, "How did the wife seem?"

"The usual. Distraught, near shock. She answered a few questions before her mother swooped in and told me I could talk to her later."

"Did she say anything useful?"

"I did get an odd vibe. It's hard to describe. It's more about what she didn't say. It felt like she wasn't telling me everything about their current circumstances. I don't know if it was a marital strain or something else. But I'll have it in my head if I need to talk to her again."

"You think she was unhappy with her husband and figured a way to have someone shoot him, do you?"

"I don't think so. But maybe. I guess it's possible. Although it did cross my mind that if someone was really smart, they could use the cover of the sniper to have a person shot from a long distance. But I don't think that's the case here."

Harry gave me a folder with some information on the other two homicides involving the sniper. Harry said, "I heard someone call the shooter 'the Longshot Killer.' I guess that's as good a nickname as any."

Harry told me to grab the complete reports off the computer and said I could consider myself the lead detective on all three cases. That might not make me too popular with the other homicide detectives already working them, but I knew better than to say anything. Harry doesn't much care for whining or complaints. His philosophy is simple: *We've got a job to do, so let's go do it.*

Frankly, it does make the work environment here in our off-site office much more pleasant without people bitching constantly about everything.

Harry said, "What kind of help do you need? Besides the usual analytical assistance and help with interviews?"

"I'm glad you asked. As I was standing on the balcony where the victim was shot, I realized I don't know much about snipers. I'm pretty good with figuring out trajectories and bullet wounds inflicted from a drive-by a few feet away, but these long-distance angles and the whole sniper mindset is new to me. Do you think we've got anyone who can help me with that sort of stuff?"

Harry chuckled. Or as close to a chuckle as he ever came. "Mike, this is the NYPD. We got someone who can help you build a plane. Leave it to me."

CHAPTER 8

LESS THAN AN hour later, Harry Grissom forwarded an email to the whole squad. Someone new was going to be around the office for a while. Command staff was sending over Rob Trilling, a sniper from the Emergency Service Unit, to help me on the case. He'd be on temporary duty until we made an arrest, or until I didn't need him anymore. That was about all I could ask for.

As a trained investigator, I like to have as much information as possible before I start anything new. That includes knowing who I'm working with. As soon as I had the chance, I went over to Walter Jackson to get the scoop on this sniper from ESU.

As I stepped into Walter's office, he turned his computer screen slightly so I could see a photograph of a mountain with someone working at the top of it.

I said, "Okay, I'll bite. What's that?"

"Mount Rushmore just as they were starting construction on the monument." A huge smile spread across the big man's face. He had to add, "The beauty of the mountain was un-president-ed."

I groaned. Then I said, "Aren't your daughters making you put a dollar into a jar for every pun you make?"

"Not anymore. I made them another bet. I told them if they could keep a straight face and not groan or laugh at my latest pun, I'd keep doing the pun-jar payments."

"So I take it they lost that bet?" I asked. "Since you're going to tell me anyway, what was the pun?"

"What happened when two artists had a competition?"

I shrugged.

"It ended in a draw."

I gave him a look, not a groan, and said, "Okay, I'll admit that was pretty good." I could envision his little girls giggling at that one. "But the real reason I stepped in here was not to hear more of your puns. I need some information."

"On your new partner?" It wasn't really a question. It was a statement, and it made me realize how transparent I could be.

All I could do was smile and say, "Yes, that's exactly what I'm looking for."

"I was curious myself. Vanessa was the last one to come on the squad, and we vetted her like she was going to the White House. The weird thing is, I can't bring up this guy's NYPD personnel records, but I did get into his military record. I have a contact with DOD who forwarded his electronic file to me."

"Why can't you get his NYPD records?"

"That's like asking me why we don't get HBO on the squad TV. I don't know the specifics; I just know we don't have access to them. This guy Rob Trilling's file is locked. But I know he's on an FBI task force, so that might have something to do with it."

"I thought he was on our ESU as a sniper."

"A couple of quick phone calls to my contacts tells me he hasn't been in ESU since midsummer and has been over at the FBI fugitive task force since then." He turned the screen a little more and motioned me to sit in the chair in front of his desk. He brought up the electronic file he'd received from the Department of Defense.

Before I could even understand what we were looking at, Walter let out a whistle. He said, "Damn, this guy has seen some shit. An Army Ranger. A tour in Afghanistan. He even received a Bronze Star for protecting a medical unit under ambush."

"How the hell did he end up in New York?"

Walter shrugged, never taking his eyes off the screen.

I said, "Was he a sniper in the Army?"

"You'd think, right? I don't see where he was sniper qualified. But if you look at his last fitness report, it lists his rifle and self-defense skills as 'outstanding.'"

"Is that outstanding compared to the general population or compared to other Rangers?"

Walter whistled again and said, "I'm betting it's against other Rangers. That makes him a certified badass." He looked me in the eye and added, "You won't like this part."

"What?"

"Rob Trilling is only twenty-four years old."

"Then how long has he been with the NYPD?"

Walter said, "I told you, I can't get into his NYPD file. But if he was in the Army and is only twenty-four, he can't have been with us for very long."

A voice just outside Walter's office said, "A little over nineteen months."

My head snapped toward the door, where I saw a dark-haired young man dressed in a nice button-down with a blue tie that looked like the one I'd worn to my prom.

The man said, "Hi, I'm Rob Trilling."

CHAPTER 9

I TURNED AND stared at the young man standing just outside Walter Jackson's door. It wasn't just that Rob Trilling had surprised us in the middle of discussing his service record. It was that he *did* look incredibly young. He looked like he could've been one of my kids. Age-wise, he actually could have been.

It was quite a blow to an active cop who tries not to think of himself as getting older.

It was Walter who saved me. While I just sat there with my mouth open, Walter slid out from behind his desk and extended his hand. I was still trying to get my head straight and say something intelligent. I couldn't even really judge Trilling's height because six-foot-six Walter towered over him, like he did over most people.

Finally I stood and introduced myself.

"Nice to meet you, sir."

"Please call me Mike."

Trilling nodded but didn't say anything else.

I said, "We'll be working together."

"Yes, so I've been told."

"I'm looking forward to it. I could use a perspective on long-range rifle shots." I took a moment to study the young man as we all stood there. I guess I'd expected him to say something in response, but he just stood there quietly.

Walter suggested I introduce the new guy to the lieutenant and the other detectives on the squad. It didn't take long to walk him around the office. I noticed he had extremely good manners and didn't say much. He used "sir" and "ma'am" a lot but generally waited for people to ask him questions before he said anything.

When all the introductions were done, I led Rob Trilling to our conference room. I shut the door so we would have some privacy. I brought over a folder with reports giving a broad outline of all three cases and what had been determined so far about where the shots had originated.

I tried to put Trilling at ease and said, "Can I get you some coffee?"

"No thank you, sir."

"Call me Mike."

Trilling just nodded again. He wasn't at attention, but it was close. There are a lot of former military members who continue their public service as officers with the NYPD, but it's usually not this easy to spot them. They typically slip into a more relaxed, civilian mode. This guy seemed like he was still a Ranger.

"Why don't you tell me about yourself?"

"Not much to tell. I was in the Army and now I'm with the NYPD. That sums things up pretty well."

"Are you from this area originally? I can't place your accent."

"I'm from just outside Bozeman, Montana."

"How on earth did you end up in New York City?"

The young man just shrugged and didn't say anything.

I stood there in awkward silence with this twenty-four-year-old former Army Ranger. After almost a minute of dead air, I had to say something.

I said, "Look, I moved us in here so we could have some privacy. I'm getting the sense that you don't like the idea of working on this case with me. Talk to me, cop to cop. Nothing either of us says will leave this room. What's going on?"

It took almost a full ten seconds before Trilling looked me in the eye and said, "It feels like I've been assigned here so you can keep an eye on me. I don't need a babysitter."

"No one said you did."

"That's the problem with the NYPD. No one says *anything.* They move you around or send you someplace new, but no one ever explains why they do it."

"I'm not sure I follow."

"The military lets you do your job. If you screw up, they tell you. Here, it seems like they dance around issues, and it doesn't help with accomplishing the mission."

"What do you think our mission is?"

"To protect people."

I couldn't argue with that.

CHAPTER 10

I SAT AT my desk after Rob Trilling had left. I was at a loss. My initial meeting with my new partner had been a little tense and awkward. Altogether less than spectacular. Less than encouraging, even. Veteran cops have a natural inclination to want to help younger cops along. Pass on some advice, maybe a few decent quotes. It makes you feel like you've done your part.

Rob Trilling was not making me feel that way. He'd seemed happy to scoot out of the office and grab the gear he needed from the FBI task force. I'd told him we'd start early the next morning. I hadn't given him a time on purpose. I wanted to see what his idea of "early" would be, what kind of a work ethic the young man had.

But he'd left me with a number of questions. Questions that made me uncomfortable but I had to get answered. You can't be with one agency for as long as I have been and not have a list of contacts that could fill up three phones.

I wasted no time jumping on my phone. I was able to reach exactly who I was looking for. Sergeant Alane Eubanks was an old friend who was now working as some kind of liaison to the federal agencies and a task force coordinator. It was a desk job after she'd been ambushed by young men claiming to fight fascism. They'd fired sixteen shots at her and hit her three times. The three bullets had put Alane in the hospital for more than two months. She'd fought her way back on the job. The shitheads had taken a generous plea offer and were now in jail upstate.

Alane sounded like her usual cheerful self when she answered the phone. "Bennett, you old dog, how's it hangin'?"

I couldn't hide my smile, hearing her sound like her old self again.

Alane made me fill her in on the family. She's one of the few people who can remember the names of all ten of my kids. I remembered how Alane once told my daughter Bridget that the next time a particular boy started to pester her, she should punch him right in the nose. No boy is going to admit that a girl clocked him hard in the face, Alane said. But she'd left out one detail: she'd forgotten to tell Bridget not to do it in front of a teacher. Bridget may have scared away a bully, but she spent a week in detention for it. Secretly I was still proud of her.

After we made it through the family roundup, I was finally able to ask Alane, "How are you feeling now?"

"Not bad. Few aches and pains. One of the bullets damaged my bladder and I feel like I have to pee all the time. I guess it's better than the alternative."

I set her up for one of cops' oldest jokes. "What's the one thing you never want to hear anyone say again?"

"'It comes with the job.' I swear to God I will punch the next asshole who thinks being shot is part of a cop's job description." Every cop hears that every time they're punched in the face or stabbed or shot. Then Alane said, "So what prompted this call out of the blue?"

"I got assigned a new partner named Rob Trilling. Most recently he was over at the FBI fugitive task force."

"The really young guy? I remember him. Good-looking too."

"That's him. I was just wondering if you had any insight into why he's been shuttled around even though he's been on the force less than two years."

"The FBI says he's a real go-getter. They like him."

"He made it sound like he had been sent here as a punishment." I noted the long silence on the other end of the phone.

Finally Alane said, "I know they pulled him from Emergency Service a couple of months ago and sent him to the FBI. Our command staff had put him into ESU without the usual time in grade, and enrolled him in sniper school immediately. He got moved to the FBI without much notice."

"Do you know why?"

"No, not really."

"Can you guess?"

Alane had a slightly harsher tone when she said, "You're the devil, Michael Bennett. I'm trying to be a professional."

"And I'm trying to make sure I'm not being saddled with a problem partner who could get me killed."

She started slowly. "Okay, this is only conjecture. Command staff must be worried about him for some reason. Either some kind of complaint or a weak allegation against him. It's easy to shuttle someone off to a simple task force. Looking for fugitives. What could go wrong?" There was a pause before Alane asked, "Why the hell is he working in Homicide?"

I explained the case and his expertise.

She said, "That makes sense. He'd be the right guy to talk to. I can tell you, all his assessments are very good. But you know how people around One Police Plaza get nervous and overreact about every little thing."

I really did know.

CHAPTER 11

I MISSED DINNER but somehow managed to make it home before everyone was asleep. When you have ten kids, it takes a while to greet everyone properly.

I finally found myself alone in the kitchen with Mary Catherine. The fertility treatments had become a little less jarring to her physically. She looked good and seemed to have a pretty reasonable handle on the household. I felt bad that I hadn't been more help. Some people might say it's crazy to try for an eleventh kid. I understand that. But with ten adopted kids from my first marriage, I also understand Mary Catherine's desire to have a baby.

I filled her in on my first conversation with my new partner. I tried to paint a realistic picture. She picked up that I was concerned the meeting had been tense.

Mary Catherine said, "Invite him to dinner. That way you get to see a different side of him, and he gets to meet your wonderful family. Including your beautiful new wife."

I chuckled. "Having someone over for dinner seems to be the Irish answer to every problem."

"Because it tends to solve every problem. No one can be upset over a good brisket with onions and carrots."

"Let's give it a little more time. I'm not ready to give up an evening to this guy just yet." Then I did a little math and realized I'd only said hello to nine children. I looked at Mary Catherine and said, "Where's Jane?"

"Juliana said she's at the library working on something super-secret."

"Sounds like her."

From the dining room table, where she was drawing with crayons, Chrissy yelled, "I bet she has a boyfriend."

Mary Catherine was quick to point out that my youngest daughter should mind her own business.

Chrissy innocently said, "Isn't my sister my business?"

I stepped out into the dining room and kissed the top of Chrissy's head. "That's a pretty good answer. Is that what you think Mary Catherine meant by her comment?"

Chrissy shook her head and said, "Nope."

I glanced into the kitchen to see Mary Catherine smiling. We are definitely on the same sheet of music when it comes to raising these kids.

I went back to the kitchen and nibbled on the kids' leftovers. I guess that's a dad thing, no matter how gross everyone thinks it is. There were no other immediate problems on the horizon with the kids, so I decided to venture into a slightly more controversial topic.

"When is the next appointment with the fertility doctor?" I asked. Now I knew to keep my voice a little lower.

"Day after tomorrow. And we may get some concrete information one way or the other."

"Have you given any more thought about when we should bring it up with the kids?"

Mary Catherine looked at me and shrugged. "Trying to find the right time with at least a quorum of the kids has been hard. I think I'd rather wait till we have some real news. No reason to get them excited—or upset—by spilling the beans too early."

"What do you mean 'upset'? None of them would be upset by a new baby in the house."

Mary Catherine gave me a look like I was an eight-year-old trying to use physics for the first time. "It's hard to tell how people might react to big news like a new baby. I'm thinking specifically of Chrissy, and maybe Shawna, because they're the youngest. Chrissy's used to being treated like the baby of the family. I don't know how she'd react to being replaced in that role."

"We've raised those kids right. I guarantee they'll support any new addition."

"I hope you're right. I agree that we've raised them to support one another and the family as a whole. But you know that doesn't mean there aren't some squabbles every once in a while."

Thank God I'd found a woman who understands dynamics like this much better than I do. Tough family discussions like these make me realize the relative safety of work once in a while.

CHAPTER 12

I HAD A quick goodbye with the kids and Mary Catherine as I rushed out the door before 7:00 the next morning. I wanted to set an example for my new partner, so I arrived at work at about 6:50. I had plenty to do around the office anyway.

I stepped into the quiet squad bay, glad to see a light on in Walter Jackson's office. I needed a little time with Walter, the earliest riser on our squad. I don't know that anyone has ever beat him into the office. I'd have to hear a few puns, but I'd get a lot done.

I felt a twinge of anxiety about mentoring Rob Trilling. He was so young yet had more experience than I had in the military and in combat. That could sometimes translate to a good police career, but sometimes it didn't. I had seen it go both ways. The strict discipline of the military helps with the transition to police work. But the job requires an incredible amount of flexibility. I was worried about whether he'd be open enough to listen to my suggestions. Most people think cops are trained to investigate. That's not untrue—they do go to classes for it—but the real learning happens on the job. What worried me was that there was nothing Trilling had done with the NYPD that told me he understood investigations. Sure, he had moved into Emergency Service quickly and they had obviously wanted to take advantage of his military background. But working patrol and a fugitive task force wouldn't prepare you for homicide investigation.

I shuffled toward Walter's office with a list of things I needed. I could hear Walter's deep voice and assumed he was on the phone. I heard him laugh about something. Then, just outside the door, I stopped.

Walter wasn't on the phone; he was chatting with someone in his office.

I stepped through the doorway and was surprised to see Rob Trilling laughing and nodding his head. They both looked up.

Walter said, "Mike, you didn't tell me the new guy could hold his own with puns." He looked at Trilling.

No one can resist Walter, so Trilling said, "I love the way the Earth rotates. It really makes my day."

Walter almost fell out of his chair laughing. I smiled and nodded. It was a lot more than I had gotten from the young officer.

I avoided asking what time Trilling had arrived. He'd obviously gotten here before me, and I didn't want him to think I really was keeping tabs on him. It was clear the young man had some drive and ambition. I liked that.

I looked at Walter and asked for the backgrounds on each of the victims in the case.

Walter said, "Rob's already got them all. He even showed me a few more public records databases we can access for free. Just another way to look at things."

Trilling kept his mouth shut, as usual. He looked up at me and shrugged. He finally said, "A little trick to supplement the FBI info on fugitives. They never look too far into social media or anything like that."

I nodded and mumbled, "Good. You ready to head out to Queens? We gotta go look at the site of the first shooting. We're also going to have to come up with a list of potential snipers who live in the greater New York City area. There can't be all that many."

Trilling said, "Military snipers are relatively rare. I was a Ranger, but not a sniper with the Army. The NYPD also put me through the weeklong sniper class."

"Why? You could already shoot."

"A lot of people grow up with guns and are really good shots. That doesn't mean they'd be good snipers. There's a lot more that goes into sniping. Tactics, movement, and decisions on the ground are just as important as having good shooting skills."

"Do you think the list is a good idea?"

"I think we can use it, but I wouldn't depend on it. I talk to guys at the VA all the time. I'll see if they have any ideas."

I nodded. "Sounds like we do need to get you over to look at the first crime scene. I've never read a good account of exactly where the shot could have come from."

We were in my car and headed to Queens a few minutes later.

CHAPTER 13

IT WAS STILL pretty early, so we stopped at a little café on Kissena Boulevard in Queens, not far from the address where the first victim of the sniper was killed. I was hoping to use a little quiet time to get to know Trilling better and maybe smooth over our rough start.

We sat outside at a tiny table with our coffees and breakfast sandwiches. I sprang for both of us, hoping it might loosen up the young former Army Ranger. After five minutes of sitting there silently, sipping coffee and watching people stroll by on the wide sidewalk, I realized Trilling wasn't going to say anything unless I started the conversation. He seemed quite content to keep his mouth shut unless compelled otherwise. Normally, I'd consider that a great characteristic in a relatively new cop. In this case, I needed to try and reach him.

Out of the blue I said, "Where do your folks live?"

It was as if he had to gather his thoughts even on a simple question. It took a full five seconds before he said, "My mom still lives just outside Bozeman. I don't have any contact with my dad."

I would've liked to explore that more, but his tone made it clear that was all he was going to say about it. Instead, we were interrupted by a young, pudgy guy walking by, wearing the uniform from one of the local grocery stores. His name tag said, CHIP.

Chip stopped near our table, looked right at me, and said, "What's coffee run these days? About five bucks?"

I just nodded.

Chip said, "And you probably have at least ten cups a week, right? That's fifty bucks a week. That's about twenty-five hundred dollars a year. Think about it! In the last twenty years of coffee drinking, you would've saved enough to buy a decent boat."

Trilling looked at the man. "Do you drink coffee, Chip?"

Chip seemed psyched to say, "Not at all."

Without missing a beat, Trilling asked, "Where do you store your boat?"

That flustered Chip, who decided he was in over his head. He kept walking down the street.

I smiled and filed the interaction away, realizing there was a lot to this young man that I hadn't seen yet.

It was about eight thirty in the morning by the time we pulled up in front of a nice single-family home with a small front yard and a beautiful garden in a raised patch by the front door. The place was tidy but could've probably used a new coat of paint and maybe someone to pressure clean the walkway and front door.

I'd been a little disappointed by the lack of details about the victim, Marie Ballard, in the reports from the homicide detective, but I knew that her two adult children and one grandchild still lived at the address.

Trilling and I stood on the sidewalk for a moment as I let him soak in the neighborhood. I was about to tell him where they'd found the victim's body, but he beat me to it.

Trilling said, "I looked through the crime-scene photos. She had been gardening and was found at 5 p.m. in that raised bed just under the bedroom window. That means"—he looked up and down the street—"most likely the shot came from that direction."

We took a couple of steps into the front yard when the door opened and a muscular young Black man stepped out onto the porch with a baseball bat in his right hand. He slapped it into his left hand to show us it was heavy and he meant business.

CHAPTER 14

I WASN'T HAPPY to see a man using a baseball bat in such a menacing way. But I wasn't panicked either. The young man was about Trilling's age but a little bulkier. I knew from reports his name was Duane Ballard, and he was the victim's son.

Duane was still a good thirty feet from us. I was more interested in how Trilling might react. If he drew his gun, I'd be a little concerned. I know there's no rule about cops retreating to safety instead of defending themselves, but retreating isn't a bad tactic either. Certainly not in a nice neighborhood like this where crime isn't the central problem.

Trilling stayed absolutely still. He gave no reason for the son to get more upset. I was impressed.

I pulled out my badge and identified myself.

Duane eased up. He set the bat on the small porch with the handle leaning against a brick wall. We cautiously worked our way up the walkway, and he came down the three steps to meet us.

He said, "I thought you were more reporters." He looked at Trilling, then at me. "I guess neither of you look too much like those douchebags who try to get photos inside the house or take pictures of my sister and her baby."

I said, "I'm glad we passed your test."

Duane said, "Y'all doing anything to find my mom's killer? You're the first cops I've seen in a month. Once that fireman in Staten Island was shot, it was like you forgot about us. Even the media attention all shifted to him. Now some rich dude in Manhattan gets shot and I figured you'd ignore us."

"We're trying to narrow some things down."

"I'm not even sure I want you guys at our house. No one from the NYPD has shown much interest in solving the murder of a single Black woman."

Now Trilling stepped toward the young man and spoke for the first time. I tensed, hoping he didn't try to do this the hard way.

Trilling said, "Man, I'm so sorry about your mom. I don't know what I'd do if I lost my mom."

I hadn't expected that.

Trilling stepped even closer to the young man. "You staying in touch with friends and family? That can drop off when you're grieving. It's really important."

Duane tried to answer but got choked up. He just nodded as he looked down at the ground.

I was surprised to see Trilling scoot to the side of the man and put a comforting arm around his shoulder. He said in a low voice, "Now, can you walk us through what happened? Maybe you could tell us what you think the other cops have been missing."

Duane started slowly. He sniffled and wiped his nose on his arm. But he showed us how he'd walked outside to find his mother lying in the garden with blood pouring out of a hole just above her right eye. He hadn't heard any shots or seen anything suspicious. I knew all this already from the reports, but I think it was good for Duane to let it out again.

"Someone killed her while she was just out here tending her favorite plants, like she did every single weekend at that time." Duane looked off as he remembered his mother. "She was nice to everyone. And everyone loved her."

I watched as Trilling followed the young man across the yard to the garden. Standing in front of the house, his eyes tracked from every position, and I realized he was looking at the crime scene from an entirely different perspective than I did. I didn't know what this young officer knew about investigations, but it sure looked like he understood long-range shots. I still didn't know how he'd ended up with the NYPD, but I was suddenly grateful we had people with his expertise in our ranks. Officers with this kind of specialized experience are what make the NYPD so effective.

Trilling said to Duane, "Give us a few minutes to walk down the street and we'll come back and talk to you. I'm sorry we disrupted your morning."

Duane nodded and stuck his hand out for Trilling to shake.

Trilling shook, then started walking away from the house, and I had to quickstep to catch up to him. Now I felt like the trainee as I trailed behind Trilling. We finally slowed down about four houses away from the victim's house.

Trilling looked at the corner of one house and the thick bushes all around it. "The sniper fired from right there, under the bushes."

I looked and didn't see anything specific. "Okay, you're going to have to explain that one to me."

"Because that's where I would've shot from. This house is empty."

I hadn't even noticed.

"There's a clear view to the victim's house, but no one would see the shooter. He could have been lying under those bushes for hours. And a single shot fired is very difficult to locate just by the sound." Trilling's head swiveled in every direction. "Really, there's nowhere else the sniper could've shot from."

I looked up and down the street and decided to take Trilling's word for it.

CHAPTER 15

AN HOUR LATER, Rob Trilling did almost the exact same thing when looking from the balcony of Adam Glossner's apartment. The doorman, whom I'd already interviewed, had walked us up to the apartment but refused to come inside. He believed the apartment had bad karma and he didn't want it rubbing off on him. Victoria Glossner and the children were still at her mother's place.

Trilling stood on the balcony as I explained what the forensics people had told me about how they thought the body had fallen into the apartment. Trilling leaned on the railing. He pointed to a building down the street to the north, just visible from the balcony. The little curve in the road gave the other building a perfect view of this balcony.

Trilling pointed and said, "The killer shot from that building. Probably from the second or third floor."

"Again, you're going to have to walk me through your reasoning," I said. "I interviewed an elderly man in that building who thought he heard a gunshot the night Glossner was murdered. He couldn't tell me much else."

Trilling took me a little too literally and we left the apartment and started walking to the building. I don't know why I was still a little skeptical after my new partner's impressive review of the first crime scene. Once again, he didn't say anything as we walked toward the building. When I thought about it, I realized he didn't say much most of the time.

When we walked up to the front of the building, I was surprised to find the door propped open by a stool. There was no doorman. I called out but got no answer. Trilling walked right past me to the stairs and went up to the second floor. It was almost like he was in a trance.

I followed my partner up the concrete stairs to the second floor. He turned and walked to the front corner of the building and didn't hesitate to knock on the door of apartment 2A.

When we got no answer, Trilling tried the door handle and found it unlocked. Before I could even object, he'd opened the door and stepped inside.

The place was completely empty. Not even any furniture.

Trilling walked through the apartment to the balcony. The sliding-glass door was open an inch. He grasped the door high up on the frame, in case there was any forensic material we could get from the door handle, and slid it back.

As soon as he stepped onto the balcony and looked toward Adam Glossner's apartment, Trilling said, "This is definitely where the shot was taken."

I stepped out onto the balcony behind him but couldn't

picture exactly what he was talking about. I could see the building where the Glossners lived, but I didn't understand how Trilling was so certain the shot had come from here.

Then we heard a sharp voice from behind us, in the apartment. I turned to see a heavyset, middle-aged man holding a bucket. It had to be the super.

In a thick Russian accent he said, "The realtor has to show the apartment. You can't just walk in."

I badged him and identified myself.

The Russian superintendent said, "That badge don't give you no right to walk in any apartment you want."

"We tried to find someone when we entered the building. Your front door was propped open."

"Don't give me no excuses. I hate the cops. You guys don't do nothing."

Trilling turned to the man and said, "This is a crime scene. You're going to step out of this apartment and wait until we're done processing the scene. Your shitty security allowed someone to enter in here and shoot someone in the building down the street. That's on you. So you can take your attitude and shove it up your ass. We've got a job to do."

I knew I was smiling as I stared at my new partner, but I couldn't help it.

We didn't wait long for the Crime Scene Unit, but unfortunately they didn't find much to help us. They couldn't find any fingerprints on the doors. They took some DNA swabs but weren't hopeful.

I turned to Trilling and said, "Let's start putting together a list of potential snipers and see if any tips came in from the hotline."

Trilling said, "I have an appointment."

That was all he said, and then he was gone.

CHAPTER 16

IT HAD TAKEN a meeting of the minds from our squad to come up with a decent investigative plan for the Longshot Killer. (Even our lieutenant was using the nickname.) My idea of putting together a list of snipers in the greater New York City area wasn't realistic. But I did still think that if we coupled that idea with tips coming in on a phone line, we might get lucky and connect an unknown sniper to the killings.

We'd already gotten a lead involving a guy who lived up in Newburgh but had been traveling back and forth to the city. The tip said he'd trained as a Navy SEAL.

That's why in the early morning the next day I picked up Rob Trilling in front of the Three-Three in Washington Heights. It was the precinct closest to the George Washington Bridge so we could race up Route 9W to Newburgh, about a ninety-minute drive north.

When he hopped into my Impala, I asked Trilling if he knew anyone from the Three-Three. All he did was shake his head. It wasn't a surprise he didn't know anyone at the precinct. Usually you actually have to speak to people before you get to know them.

We found the guy in Newburgh quickly, and it took only about a minute of talking to him to realize he was a straight shooter, so to speak. He had washed out of SEAL training, but he had worked with the shore patrol afterward. Now he was some sort of half-assed, unlicensed private investigator. He'd been trying to find a missing husband and was able to show us a couple of receipts and reports that convinced me he was telling the truth.

I couldn't face another hour-and-a-half ride without any conversation. I engaged Trilling immediately as we got back in my Chevy.

I said, "Those SEALs can really shoot well. Don't you think?"

Trilling *did* think about it for a moment. The silence stretched close to ten seconds, then he said, "They're good with a lot of different weapons. Only a few SEALs are sniper certified. Most of them are trained to move and shoot."

"How well do Rangers stack up against SEALs or other special forces with long-distance shooting?"

"It doesn't really work like that. Every unit and situation has different dynamics. I'm proud to have been a Ranger, but I would never denigrate any other position in the military."

"Okay, I'll make it more personal. How well can *you* shoot from a long distance? Maybe that would give me a baseline and I could figure out something about our killer."

That must've made sense to Trilling. I saw him smile. I realized it was probably the first time I'd seen it.

The young officer said, "We're about twenty minutes from West Point and it's hardly out-of-the-way on our drive back down to the city. One of my old platoon leaders has a six-month assignment to the academy. He could get us on one of their rifle ranges and I could show you. Maybe it'll give you some insights as to what goes into a shot like that."

I liked that idea, and I also liked the opportunity to see the military academy at West Point up close. Trilling made a call, then turned to me and said, "Captain Hawks said to drop on by and he'd work out the details."

I noticed an even broader smile on my new partner's face.

CHAPTER 17

DOING THE MATH, I realized Trilling had been only twenty-two years old when he left active service and joined the NYPD. I knew from his service record he was now a sergeant in the Army Reserve. But someone thought highly of him. As we pulled up to the front gate, a tall Black captain stood right by the inspection point.

Trilling jumped out of the car and saluted the captain as he approached, then they gave each other a big hug. I didn't even want to think what these two might've gone through together to forge such a strong bond.

Trilling led the captain over to my car. "Detective Michael Bennett, this is Captain Isaiah Hawks. He was just a lieutenant when he ran my platoon in Afghanistan. He's also one of the most trustworthy men I've ever met."

Captain Hawks gave me a big smile and stuck out his hand,

saying, "Is Trilling causing as much trouble at the NYPD as he did in the Rangers?"

Trilling certainly hadn't learned interpersonal skills from the friendly captain. I just grinned and said, "He's been a great resource on this sniper case we've been working."

The captain let out a laugh. "We're just grunts. We don't know shit about snipers." I wasn't sure what the inside joke was, but I laughed along with the two of them.

I parked my Impala, then jumped into a Toyota pickup truck along with the captain and Trilling. Hawks gave a quick tour as we drove down toward the ranges. The campus really was spectacular. He pointed out historic and beautiful spots, like Washington Hall with the giant parade field in front of it. But I was mainly interested in seeing Trilling on the range.

We rode past ranges for all sorts of ordnance. Range 1 was called Argonne, after the US Army campaign of World War I, and was for hand-grenade training. Range 3, called New Orleans, was the combat pistol range. We drove all the way out to range 11B, called Normandy. This was a long-distance range for rifles.

Captain Hawks took a hard-sided case from the rear of the truck. He opened it and pulled out a rifle equipped with a short scope on the top rail. The captain handed the rifle to Trilling and said to me, "This is an M4, the Army's main infantry rifle."

We stepped back while Trilling readied the rifle to fire and stretched himself out on the ground. He moved with authority and speed. This was clearly a weapon he was comfortable with. I was starting to suspect that Trilling might be more comfortable with rifles than people.

When Captain Hawks and I were out of Trilling's earshot, the captain turned to me and said, "I worry about him. Is he doing well with the NYPD?"

"I've only worked with him a few days. To tell you the truth, he's awfully hard to read."

The captain chuckled. "That won't change. The one thing I could count on was Rob Trilling doing the right thing."

"How do you mean?"

From the firing station, Trilling yelled out, "Eyes and ears, the range is hot!"

The captain handed me a tiny packet with earplugs inside. Then he also handed me heavy plastic goggles.

Trilling looked over his shoulder at us to make sure he could fire. Then he looked through the scope and paused.

The captain said, "We have a paper target set up at two hundred yards. He's going to zero in the scope on a metal target about a hundred yards downrange."

Trilling fired once. Then he turned the knobs on the scope. He fired a second time and then sat up. "I need a minute to tighten a few things."

The captain nodded, then turned to me. "He's meticulous. That's an example of doing the right thing. You won't ever accuse Trilling of being sloppy. But more importantly, he follows the mission. For instance, when we were in Afghanistan, the fighting was being done mostly by Afghans with our support. One day Trilling was security on a medical call for an IED victim. Not far from the Pakistani border near FOB Fenty in Jalal-Abad. Turns out it was an ambush. A medic and a Black Hawk crew member were hit immediately. They were grounded with insurgents firing from several nearby buildings. Trilling didn't wait for orders or reinforcements that would be too late to help. Instead, he slipped off to a side street, flanked the shooters, killed two and captured three more.

"He was standing with the prisoners near the building when a squad of Afghan soldiers rolled up in an old deuce and a half. The leader of the squad marched up, gave a short bow of appreciation to Trilling, then kicked the closest prisoner. Trilling knocked the Afghan squad leader off his feet, stood between him and the prisoners, knocked out two other soldiers with some kind of martial arts moves, then held the rest at gunpoint until US troops arrived and flew everyone out.

"Once Trilling knows his mission, nothing will stop him."

I was almost in shock at the story. Then Trilling yelled again. "Line is hot!"

He fired once more. I could hear the ping of the bullet hitting a metal target downrange. Then he shifted slightly in his prone position and fired a steady stream of a dozen shots.

He stood up, showed the captain that he'd removed the magazine from the rifle and that the chamber was empty. He said, "Let's take a look."

As we strolled downrange, the captain explained that the range wasn't in official use so there was no one on hand to run the target back.

Trilling said, "Remember, this was just a scoped rifle, not a true sniper rifle."

It didn't matter. All the bullet holes were basically in the center printed on the paper target.

I got the idea and looked at Trilling in a new light.

CHAPTER 18

I FELT I might understand my new partner a little better now. It took some serious concentration to have the sort of shooting skills Rob Trilling possessed. I had to look past his reserved nature and quiet demeanor. It was almost unsettling. But on the ride back from West Point, he was a little more animated and interested in talking. Maybe it's because I'd let him take me into the world he knew so well.

Before we were even halfway back to the city, Walter Jackson called with a new tip that had come in, one he thought was pretty good. Walter had done the background himself. It was for a Marine veteran named Anton Hobbs, who'd had several violent outbursts and been referred to mental health officials three different times by NYPD officers responding to his apartment in Harlem. The tipster said the guy was sullen and surly.

I had a feeling that one of Anton's nervous neighbors had

made the call. Of course, that was just a guess, but a guess backed up by years of experience dealing with this kind of thing.

Walter had retrieved a fitness report on Anton from his contact at the Department of Defense. The report said that the former Marine had excellent rifle skills even if he wasn't officially a sniper. I wasn't sure what that meant in relation to my criminal investigation, but Anton was someone we could talk to. It was also another chance to evaluate how Rob Trilling dealt with the general public, one of the single most important skills a New York police officer could develop. He'd certainly impressed me so far, but I knew firsthand that not everyone had those skills.

We went to the address Walter had given us, an apartment in a six-story building. Anton's mother answered the door and told us he'd moved out a few months ago to his own apartment a few blocks away. She said her son visited her frequently at this address. That narrowed down who had called in the tip on the former Marine.

The middle-aged woman held me by the forearm and said, "My baby's not in trouble, is he? He gave so much to this country, and he's not gotten a lot back."

That was a lot of pressure. Anton's mother was the sort of sincere, hardworking person who could keep a whole neighborhood from spiraling down the drain. Young people would usually listen to a woman like this, and her tone and manner told me she'd been putting out a lot of fires in this neighborhood for many years.

I said, "We just need to ask him a few questions. I don't think you have a lot to worry about. And I promise we'll be careful and respectful."

The woman said, "You have kind eyes. I believe you. Don't let me down."

We drove two blocks east to an apartment building almost identical to the one we'd just left. Maybe it was a little more run-down. As we stepped out of the car, I had an uneasy feeling. This really could be *the guy*. It's easy to get complacent in this job, but I've learned to listen to my gut feelings.

I took a good look at the building and this time I noticed several apartments with plywood instead of windows. There were some broken bottles along the sidewalk. No one was looking out for kids around here. There was nowhere to play safely.

Walking up to the third-floor apartment, I saw that the floor of the stairwell was covered with trash. Empty Gatorade bottles; ice cream wrappers; old, soggy magazines; and fast-food containers from every possible chain.

There was no one in the third-floor hallway as we emerged from the stairs. I found the Marine's apartment just about in the middle of the hallway.

I knocked on the door.

We heard someone inside call out, "Go away."

I spoke to the door after identifying myself. "Anton? We just need to talk to you for a few minutes."

From behind the door, Anton said, "Am I under arrest?"

"No, sir."

"You have a search warrant?"

"No, sir."

"Then I stand by my earlier comment. Go away. Right now."

I was at a loss. We needed to talk to this man, but he was right: we had no legal paperwork on him. I noticed Trilling writing something on his business card. Then he leaned down and slid it under the door.

Trilling motioned me away from the door and we then stood

down the hallway silently. I didn't even ask Trilling what he had written on his card.

About forty-five seconds later, the door opened, and a tall Black man pointed at Trilling. He said, "You the one who slid the card under the door?"

Trilling nodded.

Anton said, "You can come in. Tell your buddy he has to wait."

CHAPTER 19

I REACHED OUT and held Rob Trilling's arm for a moment. I said in a low voice, "I'm not sure I want you alone in a room with that guy."

"I'll stay alert and keep him in front of me at all times. We need to talk to him, and this is the fastest, most efficient way to do it."

"I'm gonna wait right here. Make sure he doesn't lock the door. If I hear anything out of the ordinary, I'm coming through fast."

"I hope so."

Anton waited at his open door, not even trying to hear what we were saying. He kept glancing up and down the hallway. I wasn't sure what to make of that.

Finally I just nodded, and Trilling stepped into the former Marine's apartment. The door closed behind them.

Aside from being nervous about Trilling inside the apartment, I didn't mind waiting in the hallway. Although the wait was a little longer than I'd expected. I nodded hello to residents who hurried past me nervously. One young lady muttered something about the police. It didn't sound like a compliment.

After a little while, a small boy popped out of the apartment I was standing next to. He looked at me and said, "Why are the police here?"

"Why do you think I'm the police?"

"You're white and you're not collecting rent."

I had to laugh at that. I said, "I'm waiting for my friend, who's just talking to someone in another apartment."

"He talking to Anton?"

"As a matter of fact, he is."

"That won't take long. Anton don't say much."

"Neither does my friend."

The door to the Marine's apartment opened, and I was surprised to see Trilling chatting amiably with Anton. The man who'd wanted to be left alone now laughed at something Trilling said, then slapped him on the back like they were old friends.

Trilling and the Marine shook hands and Anton shot me one last suspicious look before he shut the door.

We took the stairs back to the ground floor. Trilling said, "He's not our man. He had a plane ticket showing he was out of town during the Staten Island shooting, and he was at a group therapy session the night before yesterday, when Glossner was shot in Manhattan. I'll follow up with his therapist to get the details, but I could tell this guy hasn't shot anyone in New York."

I asked, "What did you write on your business card that convinced him to open the door?"

"Just my Ranger background and the date I deployed. I also wrote down that I understood. That's what most people want to know: can you step into their shoes and understand their circumstances."

If Trilling knew that, he'd already discovered one of the most important lessons of being a good cop: understanding where people are coming from and having some compassion.

Maybe I'd been a little harsh in my initial judgment of the former Army Ranger.

CHAPTER 20

I DROVE TRILLING back to the Three-Three to pick up his car. When I pulled into the lot, I was greeted by a couple of cops I'd met over the years, as well as a few of the precinct's administrative people who knew me from past assignments.

Trilling sat silently as I shook hands and gave hugs to the people walking past the car. It was a little like dealing with a surly kid. He clearly didn't care about meeting anyone new. I tried to make introductions a couple of times but then sort of gave up when he barely acknowledged the other person.

I considered calling him out on the rude behavior. Something told me that a guy with Trilling's good manners would take being called "rude" to heart, though, so I decided to keep my mouth shut instead. I felt like we had made some progress today with our interpersonal relationship. I had to weigh the risk-to-reward ratio of calling him out on something as petty as not being friendly enough.

Once we were alone, standing between my car and his, I said, "I was very impressed with how you handled the Marine. I'm glad you're on the case and I hope you feel the same way."

As usual, I had to wait for some kind of response. Unlike what I've seen before with a lot of young cops, Trilling didn't spend any time getting puffed up with the praise and bragging about how he handled the situation. Trilling just smiled, nodded his head, and mumbled, "Thanks."

I was starting to appreciate my new partner, quirks and all.

I glanced over at the Ford Taurus he was driving. "Is that an NYPD car?"

Trilling shook his head. "The Bureau said I could keep it from the task force since I was only working here temporarily. I haven't been assigned a car by the NYPD."

That made sense. Officially, Trilling was still a patrol officer. Based on what I'd observed so far, though, it was clear to me he'd make detective pretty quickly. That was another one of the reasons I wanted him to start meeting people at different precincts. Contacts are what separate good detectives from great detectives. Knowing where to go to get information or who to ask for help. That is stuff absolutely no one can learn in the Police Academy.

I checked my phone for the time and discovered that it was earlier than I'd thought. I gazed out over the parking lot and surrounding streets. Traffic still wasn't too bad. "We got another couple of interviews we might be able to knock out quickly."

Trilling turned from his car and said, "Sorry, I have an appointment." That was all he said before he climbed into his Ford Taurus and pulled out of the lot.

I was still standing there, just staring at the rear of his car as it disappeared down the street. It wasn't often you saw a junior officer blow off a senior detective with a line like that. Especially twice in two days.

I couldn't make too big of a deal about it. There *were* a couple of interviews to knock out, but I was also supposed to meet Mary Catherine in two hours at the fertility clinic. I'd planned to give Trilling a present by cutting him loose a little early. Apparently it wasn't early enough.

I decided to swing by my apartment and act as chauffeur to my wife.

CHAPTER 21

THE APPOINTMENT AT the fertility clinic was un-eventful. I listened, but beyond that they were still monitoring all aspects of Mary Catherine's treatments, I didn't really understand everything that was going on. The important thing was that Mary Catherine did. She had already scolded me for asking too many questions and making our appointments go longer. That's why I held my questions until after we were free of the confines of the upscale clinic in Midtown Manhattan.

After the appointment, Mary Catherine and I decided to sneak in a quick, private dinner since my grandfather, Seamus, was looking after the younger kids tonight. The Bennett clan is definitely an Upper West Side kind of family. Between our apartment, Holy Name School, and all of the kids' extracurricular activities, it felt like we were rarely east of Columbus Avenue.

Tonight we ventured a few blocks north of 72nd on Second

Avenue on the Upper East Side to a place called Up Thai. I liked the ambience of the narrow little restaurant. It looked more like a popular bar than anything else. I saw several plates of appetizers strung out among the young couples and professionals crammed in at the bar. Mary Catherine and I were in a corner at a tiny table just for two. It was a nice change from needing a giant table just for thirteen.

I said, "Is this what quiet feels like?"

She giggled, then said, "Is this what conversation is like?"

I smiled. It did feel like we spent a lot of time at home either giving orders or shouting for someone's attention.

Mary Catherine said, "What should we do about Fiona's struggles with algebra? Maybe a tutor?"

"I'd recommend we discuss it tomorrow when we're not on a date."

"That's a fine idea." She smiled and said, "How's your new partner?"

"He's still odd and I definitely don't want to discuss him. Either now or tomorrow." I gave her a grin to let her know I was kidding. Sort of.

Mary Catherine replied with a spectacular smile herself. "You're right, Michael. This one time I'll admit to being incorrect."

"Wrong?"

"Ha! Don't push it. I'll only admit to 'incorrect,' or maybe poor timing."

I reached across and took her hand on top of the table. We started to chat about everything. The kids, our life, our future. There really was no way to compartmentalize our lives when we shared so much.

We both sat appreciating the moment. I gazed across the small table at my wife's beautiful face. Her light hair—which was varying shades of strawberry blond—framed her cheeks and brought out the blue in her eyes.

Mary Catherine said, "We Irish have a saying about love."

I cut in. "Don't the Irish have a saying for everything?"

"As a matter of fact, we do. The first one is, never interrupt someone when they're trying to be romantic." She gave me what she liked to call her Irish glare. It felt more like a loan shark's threat.

When Mary Catherine was certain I'd learned my lesson, she continued. "Love is like a friendship caught on fire."

I just sat and thought about that. It captured us perfectly.

Mary Catherine said, "And a baby would only make the flames grow."

I guess Mary Catherine had no lingering doubts whatsoever about having a baby. There was no hesitation at all.

CHAPTER 22

ROB TRILLING DIDN'T like leaving his new partner so abruptly to handle his personal business. But he hated to miss appointments, and he'd barely made the one today.

At least now he was on his own time and not responsible for anyone but himself. It hadn't taken long for Trilling to learn that a cop, like a member of the military, rarely had time when he or she was completely "off duty."

Trilling had considered going home and getting some rest. But he knew that was a foolish idea. He was lucky to doze off for an hour a night without taking some kind of medication. And the fact that he required stronger and stronger medication was starting to scare him. Lying awake in bed wasn't the way to relieve his anxiety. But he could definitely feel the lack of sleep catching up to him.

Trilling hesitated at a curb. Maybe he was paranoid, but he

didn't really want anyone to know where he was going or what he was doing. That's why he figured it was safer to park farther away and walk to the building he needed to reach.

It was just getting dark, and he could feel a stab of hunger in his stomach. He tried to eat at places he trusted. He didn't know Midtown that well and decided he could find something healthy to eat at home later. It was tough to stay healthy *and* stay on a budget in New York City. No matter how many times his mom had warned him it would be almost impossible to live comfortably in the city, he was still surprised at the prices. A hamburger in this neighborhood could cost as much as a hardcover book. Trilling considered that his only serious vice: collecting books. His mom let him store half a dozen boxes at her house in Bozeman, Montana. He had another hundred or so books stashed around his apartment.

He started walking the four blocks to the bar he was looking for. The walk gave him a chance to think. To clear his head. Something he was able to do in Montana easily. New York City had proved to be a little more of a challenge when he wanted some space and perspective. He found that was a problem with a lot of New Yorkers: they had no perspective. They just assumed the rest of the country was good with whatever they thought was right. After living here for almost two years, he kinda understood both sides of that problem.

When Trilling first moved to New York, all he'd thought about was his time in the military. Now it felt like most of his time was spent contemplating the politics and landscape of the New York City Police Department. He was starting to warm up to his new partner, Mike Bennett. The detective was intimidating even if he didn't mean to be. The guy was an absolute legend in the department. He'd caught some of the most high-profile killers the city had ever seen.

It wasn't Bennett he was so concerned about, though. It was the police department itself. This latest move to pull him off the FBI fugitive task force had thrown Rob for a loop. He didn't mind being assigned somewhere else temporarily. But there was one fugitive case he did not intend to give up. A real dickwad named Lou Pershing had gotten under his skin.

Pershing was wanted for drug trafficking, but Trilling's interest came from interviewing the fugitive's former girlfriend: an attractive young lady who now wore a glass eye because Pershing had punched her so hard during an argument, he'd popped her real eye. Back in Montana, a guy who did something like that would've been beaten by the other citizens. Trilling had decided after meeting Pershing's poor girlfriend that he was going to bring this man to face a judge no matter what.

Pershing had been arrested several times over the years, but age and some effort on his part had changed his appearance drastically. All Trilling had to go on was a blurry photograph that the girlfriend had provided, and reports that Pershing had a tattoo on his right biceps of a Muslim being hung. Maybe it had something to do with his employment as a contractor in Iraq and Afghanistan.

Trilling found the little bar he was looking for. To say it was a hole-in-the-wall was an insult to holes everywhere. It literally looked like some sort of storage area in the corner of a building. There were no markings over the door and only a little sign on the wall that simply said, MUG AND BOTTLE. This was where Lou Pershing was supposed to hang out. Rumor had it that the bar was also where business off the grid was conducted. Its location was relatively convenient for anyone from the Bronx all the way down to SoHo. A good central spot.

Rob Trilling had been here twice before, looking for Pershing. Even for this expensive neighborhood, the mediocre drinks were wildly overpriced to make up for the small number of patrons who came through the place. Everyone paid without complaint because they needed an establishment like this that they all knew and trusted.

The place was busier than Trilling had ever seen it. Over a dozen patrons. Most of them rougher-looking, middle-aged men. Three attractive women were sitting with a man in a dark corner. A couple of men were watching a hazy TV, trying to keep up with some soccer match in Europe. A few younger men played darts, and the rest were chatting quietly at the bar or one of the few tables. And one guy in the back who could be Pershing. He had a thick, untrimmed beard and hair slicked back with some kind of product.

Trilling made it a point to not even look the man's way as he eased toward the bar. He wished there was a mirror at this dive so he could covertly look at his suspect, but there was just a bare concrete wall with no decorations behind the bar. He couldn't risk a direct confrontation here, especially in case the man wasn't Pershing.

The pretty bartender didn't fit with the place. She was chatting with a tall guy at the end of the bar and showed no interest in seeing if Trilling wanted a drink. That was fine with him. After his childhood, he barely drank more than a single beer when he went out. It had been tough in the Army, but now he just avoided invitations to go out with people from the NYPD. Easier that way.

CROSSHAIRS

As Trilling stood at the bar, something whizzed past his left arm. He looked down at the noise it made as it thunked into the bar itself. He had to squint to make sure what he was really looking at: a dart was buried deep in the mahogany.

It definitely had been intentional.

CHAPTER 23

ROB TRILLING STARED at the dart that someone had thrown dangerously close to his arm. It was a cheap green plastic dart with a brass head. The attractive bartender glanced at the dart and then at him but didn't say a word.

Trilling worked hard to maintain his composure and not snap his head around. That would give too much satisfaction to whoever had thrown it. He turned his head slightly and looked instead at a framed poster leaning against the wall. In the reflective glass of the frame, he caught a glimpse of two young men laughing at their handiwork. They were both about his age, with a little more muscle and weight than him. He knew guys like these in the military. A lot of time at the gym, the rest of the time bothering people.

Trilling turned his head slowly and smiled at the two men. They were both still smirking. He firmly gripped the end of the plastic dart with his fingertips and jerked it from the wood.

He stood there, watching the men in the poster frame while he held on to their dart. He wondered if it would interfere with their game to be missing one of their darts.

Then he heard a voice behind him say, "Little help?"

Trilling glanced over his shoulder at the two men. He didn't say a word.

The taller of the two, a guy with shaggy hair and a half-assed goatee, said, "That dart don't do you much good unless you're going to clean your fingernails with it. How about tossing it back to us."

Trilling didn't hesitate to wing the dart as hard as he could at the table in front of the two men. The man with the shaggy hair and goatee was leaning on the table and the dart landed pretty close to between his hands. That wasn't what Trilling had intended, but he'd let it ride. That was as good a throw as he was going to make. He risked a quick glance to the back of the bar to make sure the man who might be Pershing was still sitting alone. He was.

The shaggy dart player stood up straight, showing that he was a good six foot two. "Think that's funny?"

Trilling smiled and let out a laugh as he said, "Yeah, kinda funny."

"How'd you like it if I shove that dart up your ass?"

Trilling kept his broad smile. "Your mom tried to do that last night. Can't you think of anything new?"

He let the man rush him. It was almost like when he used to wrestle with his brother. The man was slow and cumbersome. With the smallest of movements, Trilling stepped aside and grabbed the man's right arm. Facing the nicest part of the lounge—the mahogany bar—Trilling guided the man's head directly into the wooden bar top. The resulting thud was the only sound from the encounter.

Trilling felt the man's legs go weak and shoved him so that he landed on a stool in a dazed lump.

Now he gave a hard stare at the man who'd been playing darts with the groggy one.

The second man lifted his hands and backed away to show that he wanted nothing to do with this.

Trilling scanned the bar one more time to make sure his potential fugitive hadn't walked out. Clearly no one here cared if there was a fight going on or if a semiconscious man was sitting on a stool. Only a few people even looked up.

Trilling's eyes darted to the rear of the bar.

The table where his suspect had been sitting was empty.

CHAPTER 24

IT WAS A nice surprise when Mary Catherine and I got home to find that all the kids had already eaten and were just finishing up the dishes. I'd like to think my grandfather had something to do with it, but I knew Ricky would have done the cooking, while Seamus was sitting at the end of our long dining table, teaching the twins which hands would win in poker.

My grandfather may look like a kindly old priest, and he is, but he sowed a lot of oats before taking his late-in-life vows.

I was still feeling great after a wonderful meal with my wife. My resilient and understanding wife. The one who wanted to have a meeting to discuss the possibility of bringing a new baby into the family. God, I hoped she was right about a family meeting.

I spent a few minutes chatting with my grandfather, which drew the attention of a couple more of the kids.

Seamus said, "What an easy task it is to babysit these angels."

I cocked my head. "Okay, that doesn't sound like you. What's wrong?"

"Nothing, my boy."

"I can make someone squeal on you if I have to."

"Are you always a cop?"

"Cop, parent—not that different. Now spill."

My grandfather leaned in a little closer. "Bridget may have caught me finishing off your cabernet."

"Not the last bottle of the 2019 Caymus."

"That's just it, boyo. I didn't realize it was the last bottle until it was gone and I couldn't find any more." He gave me a smile like a kid who'd been caught in a fib. I just laughed. No one could get angry at an elderly priest who was still mischievous.

When Mary Catherine and I decided we were ready for the family meeting, six of the kids were already in the dining room: the two oldest, Juliana and Brian, who were both starting to find their way in the world as young adults but still living at home for the moment, thank goodness; Eddie and Trent, our younger boys; and Bridget and Fiona, the twins.

I had to call in Shawna and Chrissy, finishing their chores in the kitchen, and Ricky, playing on his phone in his bedroom.

I started counting heads and got to nine, but before I could ask where Jane was, the front door burst open and she rushed in, apologizing for missing dinner.

Mary Catherine said, "Where were you? Holy Name has been closed for hours."

Jane looked at Mary Catherine, then at me. "I said I was sorry. I'm working on a project and have to spend some time at Butler Library up on the Columbia campus. Sister Mary Margaret worked it out so I have a Columbia ID and everything so I can use the library."

I said, "What's the project about?"

A sly smile spread across Jane's even features. Then she said, "Can I keep it a surprise? I think you'll like it."

How could a father deny a request like that? Plus, she was using her sweet tone, not her disillusioned teenager tone. It was enough to convince me.

I turned to the room and raised my voice in a mock shout, saying, "We're going to have a family meeting!"

The only one who seemed happy about that was Chrissy. "Do I get to vote?"

I said, "Everyone gets to vote. Except, as always, my vote and Mary Catherine's count as two each." That earned a few groans and comments from the older kids, who started to make excuses and wander off.

Without confronting anyone individually, Mary Catherine clapped her hands one time. Everyone froze like we were in a *Twilight Zone* episode. In reality, it was just years of conditioning: when the kids heard Mary Catherine give that single hard clap, they knew they'd better listen.

Mary Catherine said, "Your father doesn't ask that much of you. One meeting to clear something up will help us all. Everyone take a seat at the table."

I stood there dumbfounded as, without another word, each child sat down around our long dining room table. Mary Catherine hadn't raised her voice. She hadn't even issued a threat. That was power. There's no way I could've done that.

I took a breath and started telling the kids about our appointments with the fertility clinic, what the doctors had told us, and that we hoped Mary Catherine might soon be pregnant. I finished by saying, "We were hoping to get your honest reactions to this news."

There was dead silence.

My heart sank.

Then Brian started to clap. The others all joined in. Shawna and Eddie added a couple of shouts and hoots. It was a shower of applause.

Juliana was the first to speak. She looked at Mary Catherine and said, "I was worried you were sick. I knew you were going to a doctor, and you seemed so tired. This is great news."

I let out my breath. Juliana was the oldest and remembered the early days of Maeve's, my first wife's, cancer diagnosis. I should've been more aware of that.

That opened the floodgates. The twins jumped up from each side and hugged Mary Catherine. Suddenly our dining room echoed with raised voices and squeals of surprise.

Then I noticed one kid wasn't joining in. At the middle of one side of the table, sitting quietly and looking like she was about to cry, was my youngest, Chrissy. The baby of the family.

I said loud enough to make everyone calm down, "Chrissy, tell me the truth. How do you feel about this?" I was anxious about her reply. One unhappy kid could sour this whole endeavor.

Chrissy's head snapped up like she hadn't been paying attention. She said, "I just, I mean, I..." She started to cry and tried to wipe her eyes on the sleeves of her blouse.

I felt disappointment lurch through me. Mary Catherine's smile fell right off her face.

Then, through her tears, Chrissy wailed, "I'm so happy I can't stop crying. I'll finally have a little brother or sister! This is the best day of my life."

I was correct; we had raised these kids the right way. Next thing I knew we were in a giant hug around Mary Catherine.

CHAPTER 25

ROB TRILLING DIDN'T want to make it obvious that he'd been watching the man in the corner. He knew the guy hadn't gone out the front door, so he must've slipped out the back. Trilling didn't burst through the back door and race into the alley looking for him. Instead, he eased away from the semiconscious man on the stool and casually strolled toward the rear door.

Out of sight of the bar patrons, though, Trilling picked up the pace, sprinting down the alley and onto the street. He'd like to say it was his keen instincts that led him to turn a corner and catch sight of the man he thought might be Lou Pershing, but that wasn't true. It was just luck. The same way luck could determine who survived the battlefield.

The suspect walked with a determined pace, but Trilling had no problem staying half a block back. He had to remind himself he was on his own and couldn't call in help. All he had to do was see the disgusting tattoo on the man's right biceps and he'd have his best fugitive arrest.

Trilling followed the man onto the 6 train, but almost lost him when he got out of the subway at 116th Street. East Harlem was an unfamiliar neighborhood for Trilling. The crowds in Midtown made it easy to blend in, but here there wasn't nearly as much foot traffic, and he found it much more difficult to stay unnoticed.

Trilling watched as the suspect met a wiry Latino man. The Latino man introduced the suspect to a young woman. She looked *really* young. Dressed in knee-high boots and a skirt too short for the cool temperatures.

No matter what happened, Trilling decided he couldn't ignore this. He watched as the Latino man walked away and the suspect and woman continued north to a questionable-looking building that resembled an old-time SRO—single-room occupancy. Trilling had heard places like this were all over the city thirty years ago but rare now. The nine-story building looked run-down and had no style. Trash blown from the street gathered around a few dead bushes at the entrance.

Trilling raced half a block just as the suspect and the young woman entered an elevator. He flew up the stairs, jumping out of the stairwell at each floor to see if the elevator had stopped there. He kept pushing himself to the next floor. All the way to nine.

Trilling burst through the stairwell door in time to see the suspect step into a room twenty feet away from the elevator. He took a breath and sprinted to the closing door. He blocked it from locking.

There was no turning back now.

The man turned as Trilling pushed completely into the room.

Instantly Trilling realized how formidable the suspect was up close. He stood a little over six feet and had to have forty pounds of muscle on Trilling.

"What the hell?" the man said in a gravelly voice, reaching down with his right hand and grabbing a pistol from his beltline. He had it out and aimed at Trilling's nose in an instant. Trilling didn't think he had ever seen someone draw a pistol so quickly.

There was at least six feet between them now and Trilling knew he couldn't act without taking a .380 slug in the face.

He stayed in place and raised his hands slightly. Then he looked past the suspect to the frightened girl in a corner of the room. He said in an even voice, "You okay, miss?"

The young woman was obviously flustered but managed to nod. She wore a stylish knit cap, and her light-brown hair framed a pretty face.

Trilling knew he needed the suspect to move closer to him if he had any chance of disarming him.

The man was smarter than that and didn't move. He said, "You got three seconds to tell me who you are and what you want."

"Otherwise you'll shoot me?"

"We got a genius on our hands."

He still didn't move any closer.

The man said, "Who the hell are you?"

"My ID is in my front pocket. Do you want me to reach for it or do you want to take it? I don't want to risk you getting nervous with that gun." He could see the man weighing the pros and cons of each option.

Trilling had no intention of telling the man who he was. He just needed him to get about three feet closer.

CHAPTER 26

ROB TRILLING STOOD with his hands raised, ignoring the SIG Sauer P230 .380-caliber pistol and instead looking closely at his suspect. Based on the blurry photo he'd been given, he really couldn't tell if this was Lou Pershing or not. The guy seemed to be a little better built than any of the descriptions of Lou Pershing, but the bushy beard was the biggest impediment to identifying him.

Trilling wondered briefly if the man would show him his right biceps if he asked nicely. That was the most efficient way to handle this situation.

The suspect growled, "Do you have any idea who I am?"

Trilling kept a positive attitude. "Yes. Yes, I have an idea that you're Lou Pershing."

"Who?" The man stepped closer.

That was helpful, but Trilling wished the suspect would come another foot closer. He decided to make use of his training both from the Army and the NYPD. He wanted the man distracted. Thinking about something other than shooting him. Trilling said, "Are you saying you're not Lou Pershing?"

The man shook his head and started to say, "I'm not—"

As soon as he started speaking, Trilling lunged forward, slapping the pistol away, then pivoted and swept the man's legs with his right leg. The bigger man seemed to levitate for a moment then hit the floor with a tremendous thud.

By chance, the man's arm swung past Trilling's face. A metal snap on the cuff of the jacket caught Trilling under his eye, causing a moment of pain. But it was outweighed by the satisfaction Trilling felt as he casually leaned across the man and snatched the pistol, disarming him. He dropped the magazine, pulled the slide of the pistol, and ejected a single hollow-point .380 bullet. It made almost no sound when it hit the thin carpet.

Trilling looked up at the girl again and said, "It's okay. I'm not going to hurt you or anyone else. I just need to check something with this man."

The girl nervously nodded. Her right hand trembled.

He looked back down at the man on the floor. He said in a casual tone, "I need to get a look at your right arm. Slip off your jacket?"

The man looked up at him and grunted. "I ain't taking off nothing."

Trilling shrugged and said, "Suit yourself." He reached into the front pocket of his Wrangler jeans and pulled out the Gerber pocketknife he'd carried with him since he was twelve. Including his time in Afghanistan. He flicked the three-inch blade open with his right thumb.

The suspect's eyes were wide with terror. He didn't say anything. A slight mewling sound creeped out of his throat.

Trilling wasted no time stabbing the knife near the man's right shoulder. With two quick movements, he severed the sleeve without leaving a scratch on the man's arm. He yanked the sleeve off and stared at the man's biceps, partially covered by a T-shirt.

Trilling jerked the sleeve of the T-shirt all the way up even though he now knew he wasn't going to see anything. He stared at the man's arm, which had no tattoo at all. In frustration, he rolled the man to one side and pulled out a wallet from his rear pocket. He checked the man's ID. Albert Craig from Jersey City. *Shit.*

Trilling stepped away from the man on the carpet. His hand came up and touched his cheek under his eye where the man's jacket had struck him. It was a little tender but nothing serious. Then he turned his attention to the girl, now sitting in the single chair.

Trilling said, "How old are you?"

"Twenty-two."

Trilling gave her a good look. The way he'd looked at his sister when he'd catch her coming in late and she'd given some lame excuse.

Without further prompting, the young woman said, "Eighteen."

"Is this meeting consensual?"

The girl said, "What does that mean?"

"You agreed to meet this man voluntarily?"

This time she nodded. "Yeah, for two hundred bucks."

The man on the carpet said, "You going to tell me what the hell is going on?"

"Sorry, building security. I'm going to take your gun and you can get it back from the doorman when you leave. You might not want to mention this to anyone since you're carrying an unlawful firearm within the city limits."

The man nodded but didn't say anything.

Trilling took the elevator to the lobby. It was still empty as he calmly ambled through, disassembling the pistol in his hands as he walked. He dropped the slide into a garbage can on the sidewalk. He dropped the main body of the pistol down a storm drain and kept walking.

He'd find another way to locate Lou Pershing. He had the name of a Pershing associate who might even be a decent suspect in their sniper case.

CHAPTER 27

I GOT INTO the office early again. As soon as I walked through the door, I realized it still wasn't quite early enough. The first thing I heard was Walter Jackson's deep voice and then a chuckle. I knew exactly who was in there talking to him this morning.

I stepped into Walter's open doorway and said to him and Rob Trilling, "I hope you two are doing something constructive this early in the morning."

Walter said, "You mean in addition to sharing puns and jokes?"

"I'm sure they're hysterical."

Walter was grinning like a little kid. He looked over at Trilling and said, "Go ahead, tell him yours."

"It doesn't look like he's in the mood for puns, Walter."

Walter didn't miss a beat. He looked at me and said, "I have a friend who was raised in England. Over there, they call elevators

90

lifts. We, of course, call them elevators. I guess we were just raised differently."

I'll admit it was cute. I'll also admit it took me a moment to get it. I gave him a pity smile and hoped to move on to business.

Walter, now looking deflated at my response, said, "Rob gave me a potential suspect's name and I've been seeing what we can come up with. Mostly making connections through public records and rental agreements. I'm waiting for confirmation on a couple of things."

I turned to Trilling and paused. There was a tiny cut on his left cheek and his eye was slightly swollen. It almost looked like he had a black eye. I said, "Did you get the shiner at your appointment yesterday?"

Trilling absently reached up and touched his cheek. He said, "I was trying to hang a bookshelf in my apartment. It came loose and smacked me in the face. Nothing to worry about. I'm fine."

He let the whole dig I gave him about his appointment slide.

I decided to let it go. Instead, I said, "Where'd you get the name?"

"He's an associate of a fugitive I was looking for at the FBI. They both are former military and worked for contractors in Afghanistan. The name I have is William Hackford. On some promotional bio he created for their company, Hackford mentioned that he was sniper certified. I'm not sure who certified him or if it's legit, but I thought it was worth a try."

"You're not just looking for a way to find your FBI fugitive, are you?"

I'd been teasing, but for a minute I thought Trilling wasn't going to answer. Then he said, "It wouldn't be a bad thing if we caught the fugitive, Lou Pershing, too. I thought this guy might be a decent interview for us."

That was a good answer. It's hard to argue with a guy who's doing things for the right reasons. It made me think of the Army captain he'd introduced me to at West Point. Captain Hawks had told me Trilling stayed on mission no matter what. Not a bad thing.

Walter started printing out a packet of information for us. He said, "This Hackford guy's got a decent criminal history. Three assaults and one charge of carrying a concealed weapon. The victims dropped the charges in every case. I know some of the military contractor companies will overlook a criminal history if it gets them a motivated worker.

"And he's been ticketed twice in the last month right here in the city. I don't see a home address or even a contact phone number for him, but looks like his name is on the lease to a warehouse up in the Bronx." He handed a folder across to Trilling. "Here's everything I have as well as a Google satellite photo of the warehouse."

I felt a surge of excitement at a new lead. It was hard to tell if Trilling was excited or not, but he jumped up from the chair and moved pretty quickly.

CHAPTER 28

WE TOOK MY Impala north all the way to the New York Botanical Garden. I didn't spend a lot of time in Bronx Park near the Rose Hill campus of Fordham University and was surprised how unfamiliar the area looked to me. Trilling kept a sharp eye out and found the string of older warehouses on a short block at the very north end of the Bronx. None of the warehouses was more than three stories tall, and it didn't look like they were being used much nowadays.

I took a moment to survey the street as we sat in the car. A good cop should know who might be around. I noticed Trilling doing the same thing—although I got the impression he was looking for bad guys more than he was for innocent bystanders we potentially needed to get out of the way. Either way, there was no one around.

At Hackford's warehouse, we nonchalantly took the outside

stairway to the main door. It had to open onto the second floor. I tried the door, which was locked. The two windows in the front had been frosted over from the inside. We found an alley that cut behind the warehouses and tried the rear door at the top of a rickety wooden staircase. It was also locked.

Trilling put his ear to the door and, after thirty seconds, turned to me and said, "I hear noise. There're people inside."

"Think we can use a ruse to convince them to let us inside?"

"I'll bet you lunch they won't even answer the door if we knock."

I didn't give him a chance to back out of the bet. I knocked politely and we waited. Then I pounded on the door with my fist. Still nothing. I turned to Trilling and said, "What d'you think?"

Trilling said, "I don't think you're hitting the door hard enough."

I stepped to the side and said, "Be my guest."

Trilling didn't say a word as he stepped in front of the door. Then, in one smooth motion, he lifted his right leg and kicked the door right next to the handle and dead bolt.

The door flew open, smashing into a wall behind it. Trilling slipped inside before I could say anything. I followed my partner, half expecting to be confronted by an outraged business owner. Instead, there was no one near us. I could hear faint noises coming from another room.

We carefully walked next to the wall toward where we heard noise. When we came to an open door, we saw a catwalk above a main floor that trucks must use to load whatever was held in the warehouse.

Before we stepped through the door, Trilling tapped me on the shoulder and pointed to the far corner of the main warehouse room. There were four or five women working near some tables, all wearing what looked like white surgical clothes. Their faces were covered with N95 masks, but dark hair spilled out and down their backs.

The floor of the warehouse was covered with row after row of heavy, empty shelves. There was a line of cots with blankets on them against the far wall. There was also a refrigerator and microwave by a door. The only activity was in the far corner.

I ducked back behind the wall and leaned in close to Trilling. "I don't see William Hackford. I don't even see any men in that group."

"But you see the drug operation, right?"

"I see what *looks* like five women processing drugs. But if I got on the stand and said that, without going down to check, a defense attorney would rip me in half. That's after we were arrested ourselves for B and E after explaining how we entered without authority."

Trilling nodded, then said, "They got a lot of room here for not much activity. You think they plan to expand?"

"I think the whole idea of this warehouse is that they don't have to worry about noise or anyone paying attention to what's going on here."

Trilling looked over my shoulder. He nudged me to step out onto the walkway. We crept along together, gathering a better view of the operation with every step.

Then I heard a gunshot.

CHAPTER 29

I'D LIKE TO claim it was my police training or my lightning-fast reflexes that saved me from getting shot. The truth is, my new partner, whom I didn't completely trust yet, grabbed me by the arm and jerked me flat onto the catwalk.

I was panting as we hit the wooden walkway. Now I was lying on my belly alongside Rob Trilling. The young former Ranger showed no stress or anxiety. He could have been playing a game with his buddies.

I said, "What the hell? That asshole didn't even offer a warning. Whatever they're doing in the corner is a big deal."

I could just see the far corner of the warehouse floor. The women who'd been working at the tables were now all cowering in the makeshift kitchen. I couldn't see the shooter on the floor of the warehouse. At least not without exposing my head.

I turned back to Trilling as I fumbled for my phone to call for help. Trilling was still as calm as if he were waiting in line. He said, "I'm going to flank him." He was up and moving before I could tell him to sit still and wait for backup.

I scooted back from the edge of the catwalk with my phone in hand. I took a couple of breaths to slow down my heartbeat and tried to *remember* some training that might save my life.

When the dispatcher picked up, I kept my voice low so as not to attract the shooter. In a harsh whisper, I identified myself by name and ID number. "We are in a warehouse in the Bronx and taking fire from an unknown assailant." It took me a moment to recall the address and I barked it out in my hushed voice.

The dispatcher was really sharp, and I heard her already clearing the air to call out, "Officer needs assistance."

Then another bullet ripped through the walkway, about three inches from my face. I sprang to my feet but couldn't see the shooter below me. I knew I had to move. Every footstep felt like a signal of where to aim. I slid to a stop behind some crates piled on the catwalk. I hoped that whatever was in them was enough to stop a bullet.

At least now I could see the entire floor of the warehouse. I finally caught a glimpse of the shooter as he darted from underneath the catwalk and lost himself in some shelving in the middle of the floor.

Then I noticed Trilling two rows away from the shooter. He looked up at me and I pointed past him and held up two fingers to tell him where the shooter was. I saw Trilling crouch down, trying to look under the shelves to locate the shooter.

Then Trilling stood up and put his back to the shelving unit next to him. He started to push. He squatted lower and braced his back against the lowest shelf as he pushed with his legs.

It took me a moment to realize what he intended. I didn't think it was a good idea. The wall of shelves he was pushing tipped dangerously away from Trilling. Then the whole thing tumbled into the next wall of shelves, which immediately started knocking the shelves into the next row.

The noise was unbelievable. It sounded like a freight train had flipped in my living room. I raced to the first ladder coming down from the catwalk to the warehouse floor. I landed and scanned the area in front of me. There was dust in the air as thick as fog.

As I ran toward the toppled shelves, Trilling stepped out of the rubble, holding a man in an arm bar.

Trilling casually said, "Can you collect his pistol? It's about twenty feet down the aisle."

CHAPTER 30

TRILLING AND I turned the prisoner and the pistol over to detectives from the local precinct. The Narcotics guys couldn't believe they had just made a seizure of sixteen kilograms of heroin right at the edge of the Bronx.

For as much noise and damage as we'd caused inside the warehouse, it had had no effect whatsoever outside the four walls. No one had heard the gunshots or the deafening sound of the shelves crashing, or had seen anything unusual.

That was exactly why William Hackford had rented this place. There was no one around to see or hear anything. God knows how much heroin had run through it in the eight months Hackford had leased it.

I looked over at Trilling, who was trying to comfort the five women who'd been working with the heroin. They were all Pakistani and had been smuggled into the US by associates of

Hackford. The women looked amazed that a police officer could be so friendly.

I'd learned that three of them spoke broken English and two could understand basic phrases. They all seemed to be in their twenties. I noticed they all had pronounced forearms, which I assumed had something to do with the work they had been completing every day for the last eight months.

Our suspect was already off the premises. When Trilling brought him out of the rubble of the shelves, I handcuffed the man. Then I said, "NYPD, you're under arrest." I read him his rights immediately and then told him, "You get extra credit if you cooperate with us right now."

The smirk he gave was all I needed. I'd never talk to this asshole again. I didn't care if he had evidence that would bring down the Gambino crime family. That one look told me he assumed he'd be getting out quickly. That someone was going to come up with a boatload of money to get him out on bond, then out of the country. At least that's how I took it.

Some Homeland Security agents showed up for the women. Trilling intercepted them and said, "None of these women are under arrest. They were here under duress."

A tall Black agent, about forty, nodded and said, "That's how I understood it when we got the call."

"So you won't treat them like prisoners?"

"Technically, they're not free to go, so they *are* prisoners."

That seemed to get to Trilling. He looked at me and wiped his face with his bare hand.

Trilling said, "Where will you house them?"

"What are you, writing a book?" The agent turned to his partner and said, "How long till the van gets here?"

Trilling looked like he was getting desperate. "Do they get to see a judge?"

"They sure do. Depends on the roster, but probably not tomorrow — maybe the next morning, first thing, at the annex near the federal building where they hold immigration hearings. The hearings are open to the public."

Trilling rushed back to the women and explained what was going on and that everything would be okay.

Not only did I appreciate that my new partner had saved my life but I also appreciated how he was dealing with these poor women.

Maybe it was time to *show* my appreciation for his talents and attitude.

CHAPTER 31

IT TOOK SOME effort to convince Rob Trilling to come to my apartment for dinner. I had to assure him several times that it would be no bother for anyone in the family. He still seemed unsure, so I told him to do it as a favor to me. Not that he owed me any favors. In fact, he had just kept me from catching a 9mm slug in the head. If anyone owed favors, it was me.

We had a brief conversation before reaching the apartment. I told him, "I've got sort of a big family. Just to let you know."

"Walter said you had a lot of kids."

I smiled. "No specific number?"

"Nope."

"Good. Care to make a guess?"

As always, Rob Trilling looked thoughtful before he answered. Then he said, "Six?"

"Not a bad guess." I didn't commit to anything besides that. I don't often get the chance, but I love to surprise people with the sheer size of my immediate family.

On the way to the apartment, Trilling insisted we stop so he could buy flowers for Mary Catherine and a bottle of wine. He took my suggestion and picked up a bottle of Wirra Wirra Catapult shiraz. Seamus loved the Australian wine, and it wouldn't break Trilling financially.

Once in the elevator to our apartment, Trilling turned to me with a very serious look on his face. "I'm sorry, I have to ask."

"Ask what?"

"How do you live in a building like this? Does your family come from a lot of money?"

I laughed out loud at that. "The quick story is that my first wife, who died of cancer, inherited the apartment from an elderly man she used to take care of who had no other family. He loved her like she was a daughter. He even set up a trust to pay the taxes. Trust me, that's crucial—my entire NYPD salary might not cover the taxes on this place." Obviously the answer satisfied Trilling's curiosity. I had to add, "Why, were you worried I was on the take?"

Trilling shook his head. "That never crossed my mind. Too many people have told me what a great cop you are. You don't get a reputation like that if there was ever any suspicion about your honesty."

It was the closest he'd ever come to giving me a compliment, so I took it with a satisfied smile.

When I finally opened the door to our apartment, the shock on Trilling's face was priceless. Mary Catherine stood with nine of the kids, looking like they were in a receiving line for a wedding. Only Jane was missing, I assumed off working on her secret project. My grandfather, wearing his tab-collar priest shirt, stood next to Mary Catherine, grinning.

Trilling introduced himself first to the crowd, then more formally to Mary Catherine. He just stared at everyone for a moment, trying to take it all in.

For her part, Mary Catherine almost swooned at the beautiful flowers and wine that my handsome young partner presented to her.

Trilling made it a point to shake hands with each of the children. I noticed Juliana lingered and chatted for a moment. She clearly approved of my new partner. Maybe I hadn't realized Trilling wasn't that much older than her.

It's tough to think of your kids becoming adults right before your eyes. Juliana had been doing an internship at Holy Name for a sociology class she was taking at City College. It just felt like she was still at the family school.

Then Trilling found himself face-to-face with my grandfather. Seamus made a show out of sizing up Trilling. The young officer fixed his gaze on my grandfather's collar.

Seamus grinned at the attention. He said, "Are you a man of faith, Rob?"

"Yes, sir. I even attended the first Methodist grade school in Bozeman."

"So you're not a Catholic?"

"No, sir." Trilling paused and finally worked up the nerve to say, "I'm a little confused. If you're Detec...I mean Mike's grandfather, how can you be a Catholic priest?"

I waited for the answer, hoping Seamus didn't lay it on too thick. I was still cultivating this shy young man. Maybe bringing him here to the entire brood was a mistake. My family is a lot to take in.

My grandfather smiled, clapped Trilling on the shoulder, and said, "I entered the priesthood quite late in life."

"May I ask what you did first?"

"I owned a bar."

"Really?"

Seamus put on a serious face, placed his right hand in the air, and said, "Swear to God."

Both men started to laugh at that.

CHAPTER 32

WE WAITED FOR Jane, who burst through the door just as Ricky's pot roast was ready to come out of the oven. Ricky has a talent for mixing cheap red wine, onion soup mix, and Campbell's mushroom soup in a way that would make even vegans want to dig into the meat. It's phenomenal.

Rob Trilling seemed comfortable at the table, though that might've been because Juliana made it a point to sit right next to him. I noticed them speaking quietly whenever they had a chance.

My grandfather opened with a prayer, as usual. "Dear God in heaven, thank you for the many blessings you've given us and for our special guest tonight. Although not a Catholic, he assures me he is a man of faith." The old priest had an impish grin.

Trilling smiled at the comment as well. Maybe he wasn't as stiff-necked as I'd thought.

Mary Catherine asked him a series of casual questions that any CIA interrogator would have envied. I think as soon as she saw Juliana sitting next to him, she wanted to find out everything she could about Rob Trilling.

Mary Catherine was a master. She kept it flowing and never got him overwhelmed. I learned more about the young man in three minutes than I had in the days we'd been working together.

After the initial round of questions, Mary Catherine moved into follow-ups. "How on earth did you end up in New York City from Bozeman, Montana?"

"I spent my first eighteen years in Montana. Then after four years in the Army, I was looking for a change. Plus, my sister and her kids don't live too far away—they're about an hour or two from here, up in Putnam County in a little town called Ludingtonville." He gave the group a charming smile and said, "I used to think Bozeman was a big city."

Mary Catherine asked, "What do you do when you're not slaving away for the NYPD?"

"That's another reason I moved here. I'm finishing up my degree using the GI Bill and a couple of grants that Columbia got to help veterans with their education."

I broke in. "You're taking classes at Columbia University?"

"So far, just one class a semester, except last spring when I took two."

Jane said, "I just came from Butler Library at Columbia." She leaned forward as if in a courtroom. "How does a Columbia student get a black eye?"

I liked how she sounded like a prosecutor about to spring a trap.

Trilling took a moment, as usual. "I was trying to put one of my heavier textbooks on a high shelf and it slipped out of my hand and hit me in the face."

I noted that his excuse for the black eye had changed from when I asked him about it this morning. Clearly he didn't want to talk about how he came by the injury. On the bright side, he was not a particularly good liar. That is a trait I appreciate in people. Good liars can manipulate you and lead you anywhere. Bad liars are usually basically honest people.

Trilling turned to Ricky and said, "This is the best pot roast I've ever had in my life. And our beef in Montana was as fresh as it could be."

Ricky beamed at the recognition from an outsider.

My grandfather said, "How do you like working for the NYPD?"

Trilling hesitated.

I noted it and assured him, "Everything said at this dinner table stays at this dinner table." I looked around at everyone's heads nodding.

Trilling sat up straight and said, "I'm still adjusting. I thought it would be a lot more like the military. Turns out, every unit has a different agenda and different ways of completing that agenda. I like the work. I like continuing my public service. I'm still getting used to the politics."

Mary Catherine said, "Michael says you've been a great help on this case. At least the department is using your military experience."

"I wasn't a sniper in the Army. We practiced with rifles a lot, but like I've been telling Mike, there's a huge difference between a military sniper and someone who can shoot well."

"That's saying something, from a guy who can shoot *very*

well," I said. The conversation moved on from putting Trilling on the spot, and dinner was capped with ice cream for dessert.

I was surprised Trilling was willing to stay after dinner. He played video games with the boys for a few minutes, then continued to chat quietly with Juliana. It reinforced how young he actually was. He was much more comfortable with my kids than with me.

But I continued to gain appreciation for this quiet young man.

CHAPTER 33

I STROLLED INTO the Manhattan North Homicide office the next morning feeling pretty good. Rob Trilling had been a huge hit at dinner. I also felt like I understood the young man much better. Now all we had to do was catch some nut who could shoot long-distance, whom no one had ever seen, and who seemingly chose his victims at random. And we had no leads. Easy.

Harry Grissom was in early this morning as well. I could hear him talking to someone in his office. I was afraid the person might be from One Police Plaza, so I tried to scoot past the lieutenant's door without saying good morning. It didn't work. I heard Harry say, "Mike, come on in here for a second."

When I stepped through the door into Harry's office and saw who was sitting in the chair opposite his desk, I'll admit I was surprised to the point of being shocked. Lois Frang from the *Brooklyn Democrat* was chatting pleasantly with my boss.

Harry said, "Why didn't you ever introduce me to this lovely woman?"

Lois smiled. She had me and she knew it.

Harry said, "You know, she's the one who came up with the nickname 'the Longshot Killer.' "

"Really?"

I hadn't seen this kind of glow around Harry since the last time the Jets made the playoffs. That had been a while ago. He said, "Anything new we can give her?" He turned his head to look at Lois.

I caught Lois's satisfied expression. The reporter had Harry eating out of her hand.

I said, "Not a lot of leads. We're working on it."

Now Lois said, "C'mon, Bennett, at least give me something I can write about."

"I don't know what to tell you but the truth. We really don't have a lot of good leads. It's not particularly exciting and probably doesn't play well in a newspaper column. But that's exactly what's going on."

Lois said, "I tried speaking to some of the victims' families. But no one is talking. At least not to me. The second victim, Thomas Bannon, the fireman from Staten Island?"

I nodded, interested in hearing what she had to say.

"His family is a real piece of work. A couple of them are firemen too. Classic close-knit Irish Catholic city workers. And they don't like outsiders coming into their neighborhoods."

I said, barely concealing my grin, "I'm not sure I can relate to a close-knit Irish Catholic city worker and his family." I did like Lois's insight on the second victim's family. By coincidence, that's where I was heading today. I wanted to talk to the firefighter's widow and see if I could find out any details from her that other detectives had missed.

Harry's glare told me my time bantering with the reporter was over.

I took that opportunity to head in to speak with Walter Jackson. I could see a light on in his office and wondered if he had anything new for us to look at since yesterday. When I knocked on his door, I found the big man involved in a detailed search of records for one of the other detectives. Even so, Walter handed me a folder with all the information on the firefighter's family that I'd asked for yesterday.

He also passed along a new lead on a woman who supposedly worked out at a gym in the Bronx every day around 2 p.m. The woman, Wendy Robinson, was a former Army sergeant who had been part of a special program bringing women into the ranks of snipers. Someone had called in a tip about her and how she'd occasionally brag about shots she'd taken in Afghanistan. The caller said the way she talked about shooting people made them uncomfortable.

I took the folder. It was as good as any lead we had now.

CHAPTER 34

I SAT AT my desk, looking through the folder Walter Jackson had given me and feeling a little uneasy because Lois Frang was still sitting in Harry Grissom's office. Every couple of minutes I heard Harry's cackle. That was not common.

Rob Trilling walked in carrying coffee and donuts for the entire squad. That's a classy move that everyone remembers. After setting down the donuts and coffee, Trilling marched directly to my desk and sat in the chair across from me. He had a serious look on his face.

I said, "When you said you were going to appointments, I didn't realize you were taking a class at Columbia."

"That wasn't the appointments. My class is at night."

That was it. He offered no further explanation about his appointments and why he left in the middle of the day. I decided it was something I'd deal with if it became more of a problem. I was more concerned about the dour expression on Trilling's face.

I said, "What's wrong?"

"That obvious?"

"Even for you who's a sourpuss, as my grandfather likes to say."

Trilling hesitated, then said, "I need to be up-front with you, but I don't want to get anyone in trouble."

I said slowly, "I'm listening."

"Juliana texted me this morning and asked if I wanted to hang out sometime in the next week or two."

It took a moment to digest what he'd just said. My voice was louder than I'd intended when I blurted out, "My Juliana?"

Trilling nodded.

"What did you tell her?"

"Nothing. I haven't replied yet. I thought I should discuss it with you first. Even if she is legally an adult, I'd never come between a father and a daughter."

"I appreciate that, but I'm not crazy about my daughter dating a cop. Though you're right, I try not to dictate to her or Brian what they have to do. They're both old enough and smart enough to make their own decisions."

Trilling thought about that. Then he said, "I'll decline her invitation. That way you don't have to seem like the bad guy. It also avoids any stress in your family."

"I appreciate your mature approach."

"I appreciated you inviting me into your home last night. Your family is so different from mine. I only have one brother, one sister, my mother, and my grandfather."

I noticed he didn't mention his father at all.

Trilling said, "I especially enjoyed speaking with your grandfather. My grandfather raised me. He had a little car lot in Boze-man. But he always had time for my brother, sister, and me. Now he kind of splits time between my sister's house and my mother's house. He's still in good shape physically at seventy-two, but he's been diagnosed with early onset dementia. He has good days and bad. It's scary."

I understood. I worried about my grandfather every day. Every grunt or sigh from him set me on edge because I was afraid it was the start of some terminal ailment. But I couldn't imagine Seamus ever losing that sharp mind of his. That would just kill me.

I tried to cheer up my new partner. I put on a smile, leaned over, slapped him on the shoulder, and said, "You ready to go to a resort?"

"What do you mean? Where is there a resort?"

"Staten Island, my boy. It's an island, so it's kind of like a resort. And we've got people to talk to."

CHAPTER 35

LOUISE BANNON, WIDOW of the sniper's second victim, Thomas Bannon, lived in a nice neighborhood, Dongon Hills, off Hylan Boulevard on Staten Island. The GPS said traffic was bad, even for New York, so we came down through Brooklyn and took the Verrazzano-Narrows Bridge over to the island.

The Bannon house was a cute 1960s two-story. The tricycle turned on its side in the front yard immediately broke my heart. Even with the sun shining and the temperatures comfortable, I felt gloomy when Rob Trilling and I walked up to the house.

As I knocked on the wooden door, I noticed that someone spent a lot of time on the porch. There were stacks of magazines next to a comfortable rocker and a little heater tucked in the corner.

A woman in her late thirties with frizzy brown hair came to the door. A cute toddler and a little girl about five years old stood behind the woman, staring out at us.

I held up my badge and identified myself and Trilling. Louise Bannon didn't say anything for a few seconds, then finally said, "Do you have news on Tommy's killer?"

"No, ma'am. We're working the case and just wanted to talk with you about any details we might've missed."

"You're not even the original detectives. I haven't heard shit in three weeks." She opened the door and shook her head, muttering something about the NYPD.

I knew this wasn't the time to make apologies or excuses. Everything would be forgiven if we could find the killer. To do that we had to ask questions, and I needed her to be open to answering questions. So I kept my yap shut.

After the rough start, we chatted with Louise to get background on her husband. I didn't really learn anything new. He'd been with the FDNY for twenty-one years. He had numerous commendations and was well thought of generally. The whole family had connections to the Fire Department and Staten Island. Thomas Bannon's brother was a paramedic and their father had retired as a captain.

Even Louise Bannon's family was tied to the department. Three of her four brothers were with the FDNY. The fourth worked at a machine shop just a few blocks away from the Bannon house.

After the usual questions, I came in a little hotter with "Did your husband have anyone who could be angry with him? Anyone who felt he did them wrong?"

"Tommy was a good guy. Everyone liked him."

"He didn't have any vices, did he? I mean ones that might draw some attention. I'm not trying to insult your husband's memory, just hoping to find some lead that will catch this shooter."

"But the way you asked that question tells me you are willing to smear Tommy's reputation." Now she set the toddler on the floor and told him to go play with his sister. Louise looked at me and said, "Vices? We all have vices. I don't see what this has to do with your investigation. Tommy was a good guy," she repeated.

Then her phone rang. She pulled it from the outer pocket of the loose cardigan sweater she was wearing. I heard her mumble answers to a couple of questions, then say, "No, the cops are here right now. They're starting to piss me off."

When she looked up at me after ending the call, it was clear she had no use for the police. Louise Bannon said, "Do you have any questions that will catch my husband's killer?" She folded her arms and started to tap her right foot.

I felt like I'd hit a nerve when I asked about vices. It was hard to tell in a situation like this. I turned to Trilling, hoping the charming young man might find a different approach.

Trilling said, "Mrs. Bannon, you read about this latest case in the paper, right?"

She nodded.

"Did your husband or you know either of the other victims? The first one or this latest one?"

She shook her head.

Trilling hit her with a series of decent questions. He was trying to find a connection between her husband and anyone else on the case. I liked the way he was thinking. It was the first time I had seen his natural investigative sense.

I heard two cars screech to a stop in front of the house. Then heavy footsteps on the porch. The front door burst open. Four men, all in their thirties, and all of a decent size, rushed into the room.

I looked up and said, "You must be Louise's brothers."

The tallest one, still in his FDNY uniform, growled, "And if you upset our sister…"

Louise said, "They're asking about Tommy's vices. Making it sound like it was his fault he got shot."

One of the brothers was dressed in a mechanic's uniform with grease smeared across the front and the name LIAM on an embroidered name tag.

I stared at the man, who looked like he was unpleasant in the best of times. "You're not a firefighter like your brothers?"

"Eat shit."

"Oh, I get it. You're too eloquent for the FDNY."

Maybe I should have left the juvenile comments for another time.

The mechanic growled, "We're gonna fuck you up."

CHAPTER 36

I'D NEVER HAD anything like this happen at a *victim's* home. I certainly didn't want this interview to turn ugly. That didn't change the fact that I was standing in the living room of Louise Bannon's house, facing her four brothers, who looked like they were ready to make a physical statement.

The tallest brother, the one in uniform, turned his hips. He looked like he knew how to punch. The two other brothers, presumably the other firefighters now off duty, were heavier and built more like wrestlers. They squared off against Rob Trilling.

The brother in the mechanic's uniform cracked his knuckles as he stared at me.

I said in an even voice, "Don't let this get out of hand, fellas."

The brother in uniform said, "Why not? If the NYPD takes as long to investigate this as it has my brother-in-law's murder, I'll be an old man before anyone comes for me. Maybe it's time you arrogant cops feel a little of the pain the rest of us put up with."

I stole a quick glance over at Trilling. He didn't look concerned. Then again, he never did. One of the brothers facing him said, "I kicked a cop's ass a few years ago."

Trilling smiled and said, "Oh, I doubt that." It took a moment for that dig to sink in. The tubby off-duty firefighter dropped lower, like a defensive lineman ready to knock down a quarterback.

The two brothers facing me took their cue. The tall one in uniform threw a wild roundhouse swing at my head. I juked to the side and then planted a good left directly in his solar plexus. It was the best punch I'd thrown in years. All the air went out of him as he sank down to his knees, trying to catch his breath.

Both of the brothers facing Trilling lunged at him at the same time. Trilling seemed to barely move. He guided one brother into the other, then stepped to the side. It took them both a moment to clear their heads, then, incredibly, they lunged at him exactly the same way.

This time Trilling let one pass him completely, then struck the other brother in the head with his elbow. When the first brother turned to charge him again, Trilling delivered a perfect side kick, right in his lower ribs. The brother bounced off a floral couch that had seen better days and tumbled onto the hardwood floor.

The mechanic charged me with his head down. All I did was bring my knee up as hard as I could, and I caught him right in the face. He stumbled and fell on the floor with a whimper.

Now both Trilling and I backed toward the door. Louise Bannon stood in an archway, staring at her four brothers sprawled across her living room. She cut her eyes to me and said, "I guess they went a little overboard."

I said, "What should we do about it? They assaulted us."

The tall brother had started to catch his breath and come up off his knees. He was clearly the smartest of the group. I suspected he was probably the oldest brother, and the spokesperson. He said, "We're frustrated. We don't hear nothing about Tommy's murder. Then two cops we don't know just show up out of the blue and start interrogating our sister about his life. Maybe we did get a little carried away."

I thought about it for a moment. I didn't like the idea of hitting these guys with an assault charge. At the very least, a couple of them would lose their jobs. I had everyone's attention as they stared at me.

I said, "If we go by old-school rules, I can let this slide."

The mechanic, using his bare hands to try and stop the blood pouring out of his nose, said, "What kind of old-school rules?"

"If no one has to go to the hospital, no one has to go to jail."

We backed out of the house and walked down the pavers to the street.

Trilling said, "I'm impressed. I knew you were smart, but I didn't know you could tussle like that."

"I *can* do it, I just don't like to."

Trilling glanced back at the house, then said, "Real nice folks, you New Yorkers."

I chuckled at that. Then I said, "Ready to head up to the Bronx for what I hope is a calmer interview?"

"I'll meet you at the office at one. I have to run to an appointment right now. Sorry."

All I could do was stare at him. Just when I'd thought I had Rob Trilling figured out, I realized I was wrong.

CHAPTER 37

TRUE TO HIS word, Rob Trilling walked into the office at 1 p.m., just as I finished my Lenwich turkey and provolone sub.

I was still annoyed about our morning workout session with the Staten Island firefighters. I asked, "Did you eat?"

"Not hungry."

A few minutes later, we were both in my Chevy Impala, headed north to the Bronx to interview Wendy Robinson. The tipster had said that Robinson worked out daily at a hybrid boxing-wrestling gym.

The Bronx had evolved over the years. There was a time when people were uneasy going to the Bronx, but in recent years local activists had brought in a number of grants and set up programs for kids. People who don't live in disadvantaged areas often have a hard time grasping the connection, but as a cop, I know how valuable youth programs can be to deterring crime.

We drove through Kingsbridge Heights, looking for the gym. We had to stop for a few minutes in front of the community center while some news crews interviewed a tall, good-looking Latino man. He was dressed in a nicely cut suit and seemed familiar.

Trilling shook his head and muttered something.

I said, "What's with you?"

Trilling pointed at the man speaking to reporters. "You know who that is?"

I took another look and shook my head.

"That's Gus Querva. I looked for his brother, Antonio, on a homicide warrant out of Baltimore. Antonio is supposed to be hiding in the city somewhere. The whole family is a bunch of dirtbags. They organize the gangs up here in the Bronx and then put on the front of trying to help the neighborhood. The whole time they're squeezing businesses for protection money. They haven't helped the neighborhood, they've ruined it. Guys like that make me sick to my stomach."

I rolled down my window to see if I could catch what Querva was saying. He was talking about programs for kids, bringing qualified teachers to the area. I didn't hear anything I could disagree with.

And just like that the impromptu news conference was over. I noticed Trilling's eyes track Querva as he stepped away from the microphones. It was one of the first times I'd seen actual emotion in Trilling's face. Maybe the captain I'd met at West Point was right: Trilling did have passion.

I drove past the community center slowly and let Trilling stare at his nemesis as Querva walked and spoke with several reporters trotting along with him.

I said to Trilling, "We can't fix everything."

"Then what's the point?"

I had to think about that for a few seconds. I felt like I was back in my philosophy classes at Manhattan College. Finally I said, "The point is to do the best we can with what we have. There's another side to the law-and-order equation. People have to work with us. People have to want things to get better."

"That's why things always stay the same. Bullies bully, thieves steal, and no one's willing to do much about it."

CHAPTER 38

IT TOOK LONGER than I'd expected to find the gym where Wendy Robinson worked out. The reason we couldn't find it was because the gym had absolutely no advertising. There weren't the usual bay windows where you could look in and see people getting fit. There was no sign on the door or on the side of the building.

We had parked and were walking down the sidewalk when I saw a homeless man sitting on the steps of a closed business. I thought I could take a moment to show Rob Trilling one of the tricks of being a detective in New York City: make use of all available information. Homeless people generally spend their time outside. Usually that's in one neighborhood. That makes homeless people experts on who comes and goes and who belongs in certain neighborhoods.

It was hard to tell how old the man sitting on the steps was. Somewhere between forty-five and sixty-five. His gray hair was cut short, but his beard traveled the length of his chest almost to his belly button.

Trilling whispered to me, "He's holding a leash. Make sure there's not a dog that could surprise us."

I appreciated Trilling's sense for detail. He wasn't wrong. But somehow I didn't see a German shepherd jumping out from behind the steps at us. Still, we approached carefully.

I smiled and gave a wave to the man as we approached. I said in sort of a loud voice, "Hello. How are you today?"

The man nodded and said, "Pretty fair, today. That's not the way it always is."

Trilling casually leaned around the steps to see what was at the end of the leash. Then he jumped back a foot.

It was the first time I'd seen Trilling agitated and it was obvious in his voice. He said, "That's not a dog. That's the biggest rat I've ever seen in my life."

The homeless man started to cackle. He pulled on the leash. I was astonished to see a huge rat scurry out onto the sidewalk. The leash ended in a harness that went around the rat's back and chest. It was probably made for a Chihuahua or poodle, but it seemed to fit this super rodent pretty well.

The homeless man reached down and stroked the rat. It was clear the rat enjoyed it, and it snuggled up closer to the man's leg. The man said, "Nothing to be afraid of, Nigel."

Trilling said, "You named a giant rat Nigel?"

"I originally was going to name him Cecil, but it just didn't sound right for a rat."

I wasn't sure if the homeless man was just having fun with Trilling. Either way, it was good for someone from Bozeman, Montana, to get a different view of New York.

I asked the man if he knew where the gym was, and he pointed to the building across the street. We were making progress. When I saw how closed off the building was, I decided to show the man Wendy Robinson's photo. I had her New York driver's license photo and the description from the tipster who'd said she was tall and athletic-looking. The man nodded and said, "She's in there most days. But she's done something with her hair. It looks funny now."

I chatted with the man for a few minutes, partly as a way to conduct surveillance without drawing attention but mostly because I was interested.

The man said, "You know all those sad stories about businessmen who lost everything or veterans who ended up on the street?"

Both Trilling and I nodded.

"I ain't none of that. I started drinking beer and really liked it. When I was twenty-eight, I got a job at the port, then hurt my back. The pills they gave me mixed pretty good with beer, and I discovered I had no interest in going back to lifting heavy things off boats. A year later I'm living with my mom. Two years after that she kicked me out. I've been on the street sixteen years. No rules, no one telling me what to do, and no schedule. Aside from freezing my ass off in the winter, I do all right. Me and Nigel are making it together."

When I looked up from the homeless man, I noticed a woman coming out the side door of the boxing gym. She fit the general description of Wendy Robinson except her hair was dyed red and blue. There was some white on the tips in the back. Then I realized she was trying to wear a US flag as a hairstyle.

Trilling noticed her at the same time as I did. I stood up and reached in my pocket to find any loose bills to give the homeless man. Before I could come up with a five, I noticed Trilling hand the man a ten-dollar bill.

My new partner was starting to make me smile more and more.

CHAPTER 39

WENDY ROBINSON HAD a fast stride. Even at six foot three, I had to scramble to catch up to her. A detective learns early in his career not to call after someone. Especially someone who could be a suspect. If I shouted, *Hey, Wendy Robinson, I need to talk to you!* she could easily break into a sprint and I might never see her again.

It was Rob Trilling who made the smart move. He called out, "Sergeant Robinson, is that you?"

The woman stopped and turned. I saw she had a pretty noticeable shiner on one eye. "Do I know you?"

Trilling said, "I'm Rob Trilling, 75th Ranger Regiment."

"Nice to meet you, but how did you know who I was?"

Trilling pulled his badge from the inside pocket of his windbreaker. "I'm with the NYPD now. I was wondering if you had a few minutes to talk to us."

"What's this about?" She tensed, then looked up the street to see if anyone was closing in on her.

It made me think we might be on the right track. The little action of turning her head and bending her knees told me she was thinking about running. That meant she was a legit suspect.

Trilling said, "We have a few questions about your rifle skills we'd like to ask you."

That had a profound effect on the former Army sergeant. Instead of looking to flee, she turned to face us fully and said, "Ask away."

I tried to put her at ease by introducing myself, then said, "I guess my first question isn't necessarily official. How did you get the black eye?"

A smile spread across her face. "You don't work out at a boxing gym without taking a few knocks once in a while." She looked at Trilling and said, "Why does it look like *you* have a black eye?"

"Nothing interesting. Just clumsy."

"Why on earth do you want to talk about my rifle skills? Is the NYPD that desperate? I have an arrest for disorderly conduct and feel like I've already performed my public service."

I appreciated the way Trilling took over the interview, sensing a connection with Robinson. He put her at ease by chatting with her about their shared military service in the Army. Not only did I learn some of Wendy Robinson's interesting background but I also saw a different side of Trilling. He was relaxed and friendly. They made inside jokes that both of them laughed at.

Finally Trilling asked her how she became sniper certified in the Army.

It seemed like the question energized Robinson. Now she pulled me into the conversation. She had an expressive face and talked with her hands as well. "I applied for every interesting school that came available. It turned out they had a special program where they were testing out female snipers." Now she looked directly at me and said, "There's a big precedent in history for female snipers. Especially during World War II with the Russians."

Robinson explained to us how she passed every test they threw at her, physical and mental. "It felt like every sergeant along the way assumed I was going to fail. Everyone thought I would be on a bus back to Fort Belvoir or some other base to wait out my time. But I fooled them all. And along the way I became addicted to serious exercise." She looked back at me and repeated, "Now will you tell me why you're interested in my rifle skills?"

I respected her frankness. I decided to match it. "Will you tell me why you were going to run when you realized we were the cops?"

There was a slight hesitation. Just enough for me to notice and leave a little spark in my brain. "Isn't everyone nervous around the police? You've got a good eye to pick up on the fact that I thought about running. Just an instinct."

I nodded and said, "Fair enough. And we're interested in your rifle skills as part of our investigation into the series of murders by a sniper." I purposely decided to leave out the part where someone she apparently knew had phoned in a tip about her.

Robinson's eyes got wide and she said, "You think I might be the Longshot Killer? That is so cool."

"I'm assuming you wouldn't think it was cool if you were really the killer."

She cocked her head, a lock of blue hair tumbling into her face. "I don't know how to answer that because I'm *not* the Longshot Killer. I suspect that if I was the Longshot Killer, I'd still find it kinda cool you *thought* it was me."

"I'm pretty sure you're telling me you're not the sniper who's murdered three people here in the city."

She gave us another big smile. "I like the way you frame questions. You're correct. I am saying I am *not* the Longshot Killer."

I opened my notebook and showed her a single-sheet printed calendar, each day in the last two months clearly laid out in its own individual square. It was an old trick I'd learned before there were calendars on phones and tablets. I had circled the night Adam Glossner had been shot on the balcony of his Upper West Side apartment.

I said, "Can you tell me where you were this night?" I tapped the circled date with my finger.

Robinson studied the calendar carefully, then looked up and said, "I was in a study group. I'm enrolled at City College. Math is giving me some problems."

"Can you give me some names and phone numbers of the people in your study group?"

She shrugged. "Truthfully, they're all so much younger than me that I haven't bothered to get to know any of them. I know a few first names, but that's it."

I went through the same exercise with the other two dates. As I suspected, they were too far in the past for her to remember where she was.

We all chatted for a few more minutes. We made sure we got her current address and cell phone number.

Wendy Robinson looked at me and said, "You must have a lot of experience. And you seem like the kind of guy who has fun in life." Then she looked directly at Trilling and said, "You don't need to call me just for questions. You can call me anytime."

I enjoyed seeing Trilling blush.

CHAPTER 40

NOT LONG AFTER our interview with the interesting female sniper, I pulled into the parking lot of One Police Plaza. Surprisingly, there was someone else at headquarters we could interview about our sniper case.

As we climbed the steps toward a side entrance, Rob Trilling smoothed out his hair and flattened his windbreaker against his shoulders. He said, "I'm uncomfortable here."

"Join the club."

"Shouldn't we be wearing ties?"

"The only people who wear ties here are the people who *want* to work in this building. We're just coming in to talk to this guy, Joseph Tavarez."

Trilling said, "Do you really think an NYPD officer could be the sniper?"

"First, I always try to keep an open mind. Second, if we make a case on someone else, the defense is going to ask if we checked other potential suspects. This will show that we're diligent. Third, and most important, it wouldn't hurt to get another perspective on the case from a guy who was an actual sniper with the NYPD."

"Why is this guy working an admin job if he's a qualified sniper?"

I stopped in the doorway and turned to Trilling. "He took a shot as a sniper about two years ago. A guy with a gun was holding a convenience store cashier hostage. All the negotiations had failed. The robber had been surprised by a patrol officer who happened to pull in front of the bodega just as the robbery was going on. The robber was more and more frantic and drew blood from the victim's temple by pressing the barrel so hard against her head.

"Tavarez got the green light and made a phenomenal shot. The cashier was saved and the robber had a bullet in his brainpan."

"So what happened? Did Tavarez freak out and ask to be on desk duty?"

"They had to pull him off the street because of a lawsuit from the robber's family, pressure from the media, and insurance liability. It sucks that he did his job perfectly and still got punished for it."

I let Trilling think about that as we worked our way through the maze of hallways and secure entrances of the NYPD headquarters. I nodded hello to half a dozen people who passed us in the halls. After all these years, I still didn't like getting caught in this building.

We found the unit where Joseph Tavarez was assigned. The

unit was basically comprised of nine intelligence analysts handling information, similar to Walter Jackson's job, with Tavarez
and a lieutenant running the whole thing. As I understood it,
Tavarez's job was to review intelligence reports to see if there
were crimes that needed to be investigated or referred to other
agencies. Not a job I'd care for at all.

When we walked through the door, I saw the pool of analysts
working in cubicles and a man with dark hair, wearing civilian
clothes, working at a desk over to the side. He looked up and
noticed us, stood from his desk, and walked over to us.

The man said, "You're Michael Bennett."

"Have we met?"

"Are you kidding me? I'd know you anywhere. If not from the
newspapers, from some of the NYPD news briefs. I'd recognize
you before I'd recognize the commissioner." He stuck out his
hand and said, "Joe Tavarez. Nice to meet you."

"You're just who I wanted to talk to."

CHAPTER 41

THE FIRST THING I noticed about Joseph Tavarez was how similar he seemed to Rob Trilling. Not only in his demeanor but also in his appearance. He was ten years older but had the same lean frame and short, dark hair as Trilling.

I introduced Trilling.

Tavarez said, "I know your name too. You're on ESU, right? You came on after I was reassigned."

Trilling nodded. "Yes, sir. I'm not assigned to the unit at the moment. I'm working with Detective Bennett for the time being."

"Don't sweat it. There are worse assignments."

The two of them chatted comfortably for a few minutes until Tavarez looked at me and said, "I know you didn't come by here just to keep me company. Is there something I can help you with?"

I let Trilling explain what we were working on.

Tavarez said, "The Longshot Killer? You guys are working on

the most interesting case I've seen in a long time. I've been following it closely in the media and in homicide reports. You know, the exciting part of police work."

I decided to handle this sensitive part of the interview. "We have to eliminate potential suspects. You were a sniper in the Army, and according to Trilling, military snipers are rare. You were also a sniper with the department. So I've got to ask you where you were on a couple of dates."

Tavarez just eyed us silently. Clearly he didn't expect to be considered a suspect. Even the way I'd worded it, by telling him we were *eliminating* suspects, didn't ease the insult. He was a guy who'd spent his whole life in public service and it looked like the only reward he'd gotten was a shitty job at headquarters and now someone suggesting he was a potential killer. I gave him some time.

Tavarez said, "I'll talk to you, even though we both know it's never a good idea to talk to the cops. This is bullshit."

"No one is accusing you of anything. You know all the hoops we have to jump through. I'm just trying to be thorough." Then I did the calendar trick with him. He said he'd been off duty for the most recent murder, at home with his wife. He gave us her phone number.

"You can call Cindy right now to make sure I don't try to coordinate my story with hers." Joe still had a touch of annoyance in his voice. "I'll give you her office number too. She works over at the FBI as an analyst. Kinda what I'm doing here. In fact, I know I have a similar schedule to FBI intake analysts because I got a buddy of mine from the service a job over there, and we have almost identical schedules. I work ten hours a day, two evening shifts and two day shifts a week."

I said, "Was your buddy a sniper in the military too?"

"Looking for another suspect?"

"No, just curious."

"His name is Darnell Nash. He was my spotter in Iraq. He might not have been a certified sniper, but he's really good with the rifle. He lost a foot to an IED."

"Sorry to hear that."

Trilling asked, "Why is your buddy an analyst if he has military experience? Clearly he must have a college degree or the FBI wouldn't have hired him."

"An FBI analyst's job is not too bad."

Trilling and Tavarez started to talk about different veterans' groups and causes they were involved in. I respect the bond military people feel toward one another.

As soon as we said our goodbyes and were heading to another unit in the headquarters building, I made a quick call to Cindy Tavarez to verify what her husband had told me about his alibi. She backed it up, and even provided a few details about what they'd had for dinner and watched on TV.

CHAPTER 42

I TRIED TO advise Rob Trilling about the importance of making contacts everywhere he went. That included headquarters. There's no way a detective can know all the things that are needed in big cases. Between electronic surveillance, witnesses, forensics, and so forth, it's just too much for any one person. That's why it's important for a good detective to know who to call if he or she has questions.

Trilling was so quiet and reserved, I worried that establishing that kind of network might end up being one of the hardest aspects of the job for him.

I turned to go up to the fourth floor and meet Rebecca Swope, one of the sharpest analysts at headquarters. She also had a direct connection to every college and school in New York. We needed to verify a few things.

As we started up the stairs, I heard someone coming down from the third floor. As we turned for the next flight, I saw the wide figure of my old friend Greg Stout. Greg was a little overweight but liked to tell everyone that he felt it was important his body match his surname. And he was known for being a resourceful and determined investigator. That, coupled with his writing abilities, had moved him up through the ranks to sergeant in charge of major investigations. He also had a joke for every possible occasion.

As soon as he saw me, Greg broke into a wide smile and said, "Mikey boy, what brings you to the king's castle? Someone figure out your degree in philosophy is bogus?"

"My biggest fear, but that's not the issue today."

"How's that big beautiful family of yours?"

"All good. And yours?"

He shrugged.

I knew not to ask any more questions. Stout was frustrated by his twentysomething slacker son who believed every wacky conspiracy he read on the internet.

Stout changed the subject. "Seriously, why are you here? We want to escape, and you come here willingly?"

"Need some expertise and I'm headed up to see Becky Swope."

"If she can't figure something out, no one can." He turned his attention to Trilling and said, "Who's this?"

"He's working on the Longshot Killer case with me. Greg, this is Rob Trilling. Rob, this is Sergeant Greg Stout."

He patted his belly and said, "No jokes. I'm the only one allowed to make jokes around here." Then he took another look at Trilling and said, "God damn, how old are you? You even made an arrest yet? I mean, for anything."

Trilling stayed silent. In fact, he did a pretty good job of ignoring Stout altogether even though it was just the three of us in the stairwell.

Greg looked at me and said, "Seems a little touchy. Maybe he needs to learn some manners."

Now Trilling spoke very evenly. "Where I'm from, manners are something we use every day. With everyone. My grandpa told me to ignore loudmouths."

That was it. Trilling didn't have anything else to say. He continued to ignore the sergeant but looked at me like he was waiting to see what I was going to say. Obviously Trilling followed his grandfather's advice. And he was pretty efficient too.

I said, "Lay off, Greg."

"What's the matter, rookie can't defend himself?" When that didn't get Trilling's attention, Greg Stout reached out and flicked Trilling's ear.

Trilling moved so smoothly I barely noticed as he swept the sergeant's legs out from under him, then held his arm to ease Stout's drop to the metal landing in the stairwell.

Trilling calmly looked at me and said, "I'll meet you up on the fourth floor." Then he started taking the stairs casually, one at a time.

I helped my friend to his feet. He wasn't hurt. Trilling had made sure he wouldn't be.

Greg Stout said, "He really *is* a little touchy, isn't he? I was just joking around."

I looked at him and said, "You were out of line. He's not a rookie anymore. And he's starting to impress the shit out of me. He could've dropped you on the floor like a sack of potatoes. But he grabbed you and eased your fall. It was as good a message as I've ever seen sent."

Greg Stout gave me his goofy grin. "Everything you're saying is right. I guess I deserved that. I'm glad the kid went easy on me. The last thing I need is back problems."

I said goodbye and started up the stairs to catch my partner.

CHAPTER 43

REBECCA SWOPE WAS tucked in her own office with the only sign on the door saying, INVESTIGATIVE SUPPORT. Other analysts and detectives worked in the same squad bay, but the only reason anyone ever seemed to come up here was to talk to Becky.

She'd spent a decade developing contacts at every local college from NYU and Columbia to some of the lesser-known private colleges on the outskirts of the city. There was no registrar she couldn't call and get a straight answer from about something. The trick was to catch her when she wasn't overwhelmed by other detectives looking for similar information.

I stood in her doorway for a moment as she worked on her computer. She raised her eyes and smiled. I didn't know her age, but I knew she had adult children. One of them worked at the NYPD garage as a technician.

Becky said, "I got the name you sent me and checked with City College."

"And?"

"Wendy Robinson was enrolled there but only took one class, two semesters ago."

Rob Trilling stepped into the doorway next to me. He was frowning and I knew why. We'd both bought a lie.

I said, "Becky, this is my partner, Rob Trilling."

Becky said, "Trilling? I don't know that name yet, but if you're working with this guy, I'm sure I'll start seeing it in reports in no time."

Trilling said, "I just started working with Detective Bennett a few days ago, ma'am."

Becky let out a laugh. " 'Ma'am'? I'm not used to good manners from most of these guys. I'm going to take a wild guess and say you're not from New York."

"No, ma'am. Montana."

"I love Montana. We took our kids there on vacation probably fifteen years ago. We had a great time. I hope it's nothing like the TV show *Yellowstone*. That makes the locals seem awfully violent."

"Like everywhere else, we have some problems. But don't worry. It's nothing like that show."

Becky got back to business. "Walter Jackson ran Wendy Robinson's name past the Department of Defense. He told me to give you this folder with everything in it. It shows she's not at City College anymore, and it's got a summary of her military fitness reports."

Trilling stepped forward to take the folder Becky handed across her desk so she didn't have to reach too far.

I said, "Anything interesting?"

"Oh, your suspect, Wendy Robinson, saw a whole lot of trouble in the service. Her fitness reports say she had anger issues and she did not work well with people who annoyed her. Which apparently was about half the Army. She has impressive reports on her determination in training, her fitness level, and her participation in some special sniping program. But I wouldn't call her warm and cuddly."

"I didn't get that impression either when we met. But she outright lied to us. That makes her a decent suspect."

Trilling asked, "Why would she lie about something as simple as a study group?"

"Exactly. She could've given us any number of different alibis. She could've said she was home alone and we would never have been able to disprove it. But I'm thinking we surprised her. And now we've got to track her down again." I looked at Becky and said, "Thank you for all this help."

"No problem at all. But in return you need to tell Walter Jackson my price: the next time we're together on a training, he can't tell me puns for a solid eight hours."

"That's a deal."

CHAPTER 44

I CAME HOME that evening absolutely exhausted. After leaving One Police Plaza, Rob Trilling and I had run down every lead we could find on Wendy Robinson. We talked to one former landlord who wasn't particularly happy with the fist-sized holes she'd left in his apartment. She wasn't even connected to the address she had given us.

Trilling said he'd run by the gym where Robinson worked out to see if he could find anything. That was fine with me. My day was over. A few hours with my family and a decent meal would do wonders.

Or so I thought.

As soon as I stepped through the apartment door, I could hear high-pitched yelling that had to be coming from one of the younger girls.

I hurried through the entryway to the dining room. Bridget

and Fiona had squared off with Jane across the dining room table. The usually calm Jane looked ready to spring across the table and crack someone's head. Bridget, normally much more interested in arts and crafts, was screaming that Jane had violated her civil rights.

I could already tell that this was a story I was not particularly interested in hearing. But I was a dad. That left no room for me to just walk away.

I said in a loud voice, "Everyone to a neutral corner." That at least got the girls' attention and stopped the screaming. They all turned and stared at me like I'd interrupted a debate. Then I asked, "Where's Mary Catherine?"

Jane spoke first. "She took Ricky and Shawna to the Museum of Natural History so they could do some kind of report."

That made sense. There's no way these girls would ever get into a fight like this with Mary Catherine around. I made everyone take a seat. As usual, the twins, Bridget and Fiona, sat right next to each other. Across the table, like opposing counsel, Jane sat by herself.

I said, "Does someone want to tell me what this is all about?"

Jane took a breath and said in a reasonably calm voice, "I think it's best if we handle this ourselves."

"Somehow I doubt that. Plus, I'm not sure if my medical insurance can cover what you guys might do to each other." I gave Fiona a hard look. It's wrong to say, but she is always the first to crack in any situation like this. A lot of people talk about knowing which parent to ask permission for different things. The flip side of that coin is that most parents know which kid to question when there's an argument. In this case, my basketball star Fiona was the weak link.

She cracked even faster than I'd expected. She blurted out, "Bridget and I were just fooling around. Jane's the one who freaked out when we took her little notebook. She pulled my hair." Fiona pointed to a few strands of hair on the table. It didn't seem that serious, but it backed up her comment.

I didn't even have to turn my head toward Jane before she started on her defense. "Dad, I told you, I have a big project! It's driving these two nuts that I won't tell them what it's about. So they grabbed my notebook. I'm sorry we were so disruptive when you came through the door."

"Wow. That's a good explanation." I looked at the two younger girls. "Is what Jane said accurate?"

Both the girls nodded their heads. It was satisfying to see my girls tell the truth. Especially after I was already feeling bad about having bought a lie from Wendy Robinson and wasted my afternoon. Then we heard the front door open.

Bridget said in a low voice, "Please don't tell Mary Catherine." The other two girls were nodding their heads vigorously. Was *I* the pushover? Was my new wife the disciplinarian in our family? This was something I'd have to think about.

I looked at Jane. "I appreciate your honesty. The only thing I'll ask is that you guys find a less aggressive way to work out problems. Also, I need you to keep your phone on all the time when you're out of the house, Jane."

"Dad, when I'm in Columbia's library they're really strict about us keeping our phones off and not using them."

"They're probably strict about turning the volume down. But you can answer texts."

Mary Catherine came in and gave me a hug and a kiss as Ricky and Shawna raced by with a quick "Hey, Dad!" But my wife's Irish sixth sense took only a second to read the temperature of the room. She said, "What's wrong?"

I smiled and said, "Not a thing, now that you're home."

I noticed the three girls' smiles as I covered for them. I didn't like to lie, but this one seemed like a good cause.

CHAPTER 45

I WAS AT my desk the next morning before seven. One minute later I was bothering Walter Jackson. I'd given him Wendy Robinson's name and told him we couldn't find her anywhere. That was usually enough for our super analyst to come up with a few addresses no one would think of.

Before I could say a word, Walter asked me, "Do you know why the man who invented the Ferris wheel never met the man who invented the merry-go-round?"

I just shook my head.

As usual, Walter couldn't contain his wide grin. He said, "They traveled in different circles."

I chuckled and tried to be polite as I asked about Wendy Robinson's information.

Walter handed me a sheet of paper with a few more addresses.

He said, "The address up in Brewster is her mother. I think that might be a good place to start."

I lost track of time as I went through notes and answered phone messages. Trilling still hadn't shown up when I broke out of my tunnel vision. I dialed his phone but got no answer. A few minutes later, he sent a text. I'm at an appointment. Then I have to run by my apartment. I'll meet you at the office.

Trilling's lateness was the sort of thing that an administrator like Harry Grissom should handle. But I didn't want to get my new partner in trouble. I just wanted to find out what the hell was going on with him. On the other hand, it was closing in on noon, and I wanted to get on the road and talk to Wendy Robinson's mother in Brewster. It would take about an hour to get up to the little town near the Connecticut border.

I decided it was time for bold action. I found Trilling's home address in Queens and headed over there to catch him when he came home. According to his text, he was headed there before the office. This way we could save some time.

It wasn't hard to find his apartment building after I came over the Queensboro Bridge. It was a two-story building just off Northern Boulevard. I slipped into a spot on the street nearby.

About twenty minutes later, Trilling pulled up in his FBI-issued Ford Taurus. He didn't seem shocked to see me.

All I said was "We need to talk."

Trilling nodded. He said, "Wait here. I'll be right back." A couple of minutes later he was back on the sidewalk with two Miller Lites and a bag from a local deli.

Trilling said, "Sorry. Apartment's a mess. I'll share my roast beef sandwich with you if you don't tell anyone about having a beer in the middle of the day."

I took the beer and half a sandwich. We leaned on the hood of my Chevy. I was a little curious to see how a young man would decorate an apartment in Queens but decided to worry about it later. "You ever going to tell me where you disappear to?"

"Is this a private, off-the-record conversation?"

I nodded impatiently. I wanted answers and then we needed to get back to work.

"And you want to know about my appointments."

I nodded silently.

Trilling took a few moments. He let out a sigh and finally started slowly. "I see a therapist at a VA outpatient center in Manhattan. I've been having a few problems adjusting to civilian life, and my therapist is concerned I have a form of PTSD. I talked to the NYPD medical staff and told them what was going on. That's why I was pulled out of Emergency Service. It's also why they shipped me over to the FBI fugitive task force. They thought it would be a good place to hide me so no one would ask questions."

I tried to process what he was telling me. As a member of a large government agency, I knew that this sounded plausible on every level. If I told someone on the street about this, they'd laugh and say it was part of a prank. But I could see the anguish on Rob Trilling's face. Now I understood why he was skeptical about the NYPD.

Trilling said, "I'm not ashamed of having issues after combat. Just feel like it's my business and it shouldn't be advertised."

"It is absolutely your own business. Sorry I ambushed you at your own apartment. Just needed some answers. Why didn't you tell me sooner?"

"I don't know. You just seem to have it all together. Great

reputation, beautiful wife and family. Maybe I didn't think you'd be able to understand."

"I don't pretend to understand PTSD. But I understand people trying to do what's right. Both for themselves and for the community. We could work it so our schedule isn't as rigid. You can make your appointments easier."

Trilling looked at me and said, "If we're being completely honest, I didn't have a therapy session this morning."

"Are you comfortable telling me where you were?"

"Immigration court. I sat in on the hearing for the five women we rescued from the warehouse in the Bronx."

"And what did you learn?"

"That no one gives a damn about human smuggling."

CHAPTER 46

OUR RIDE TO Brewster, New York, was uneventful. Somehow I'd hoped that by Rob Trilling telling me about his PTSD and treatment, communication would open up between us. But I was starting to realize that Trilling's natural state was quiet and thoughtful. It didn't do much for a ride through the Putnam County landscape.

Calling the area "rural" was like saying Shaquille O'Neal is tall. This was what we city dwellers would call the middle of nowhere. It looked sort of like the area where I imagined Ted Kaczynski had once lived. Quiet, isolated, and, to a New Yorker like me, a little on the creepy side.

The mailbox on the main road had the name Robinson handwritten on it, and the address matched what Walter Jackson had given me. Wendy Robinson's mom, Bev Robinson, had lived at this address for more than thirty years.

A long driveway seemed to wind up the heavily wooded lot. I thought a driveway like that would've led to a mansion. Instead, what stood at the end was a modest, one-story, middle-class house landscaped with manicured ornamental bushes and well-trimmed grass. It was the sort of place you'd expect a teacher or a mechanic to live in.

Trilling asked, "What do we do if Wendy is here?"

"We question her."

"I mean, tactically, one of us should stay by the car."

He was right. I try not to argue with anyone who's right. Trilling stood at the rear of the car as I walked up the short path, onto the porch, and knocked on the front door.

As I waited, I looked down and saw the doormat. It said, ALL WHO ENTER THIS HOUSE ARE LOVED.

A woman in her sixties with short gray hair answered the door with a smile. I could tell right away that she was Wendy Robinson's mom by her eyes. They were almost exactly the same as Wendy's.

I introduced myself and showed her my ID. Trilling stood by until I gave him a signal.

Mrs. Robinson didn't ask the usual *What's this about?* She knew what this was about. From this small but important detail, I could tell the cops had been here about Wendy before. Mrs. Robinson invited us inside, and I motioned for Trilling.

I waited at the front door for him. As he stepped onto the porch and saw the welcome mat, he smiled and asked, "Are we sure this is the right place?"

It was true. Wendy Robinson had warmed to us but hadn't exactly given off "love everyone" vibes. I said, "Kids don't always reflect their parents' traits."

Trilling said, "Thank God. Otherwise, I'd be in prison too."

I did a double take at this revelation from my partner, but he didn't elaborate.

Mrs. Robinson called out from the kitchen, telling us to make our way to the living room. She put on a pot of coffee for us without even asking. That was old-school polite.

The interior of the house was exactly as I'd expected: neat and orderly to a fault. It took us a moment to settle onto the couch with a low coffee table in front of us.

Mrs. Robinson came in and said, "What has my Wendy done now?"

I had told Trilling I wanted him to start the interview. When he said, "Mrs. Robinson—" she interrupted and said, "Call me Bev."

Trilling gave her a charming smile, shook his head, and said, "I'm sorry, ma'am. I'm afraid I can't. I have too many memories of my mom pinching me for not using proper manners."

She smiled and said, "Good boy."

"That's what my mom would say." He paused for a moment, then said, "Why do you assume we're here about Wendy?"

"I have four daughters. Each exceptional in their own way. But only one of them draws the attention of the police. She can be a wild one. She joined the Army to avoid a battery charge. You're not the first police who've made the trek up my driveway to talk to me about my daughter. I'm afraid I haven't seen her in over two months. And I'm afraid I'd rather not know why you're looking for her. I just want to make sure you won't hurt her."

We assured her it was in everyone's best interest for us to find her daughter. We checked to make sure we both had the right phone number for Wendy. Then we even asked Mrs. Robinson to call Wendy herself, to see if she could figure out where her wayward daughter was staying. Just like our calls, she got no answer.

Mrs. Robinson said, "Last time she was here was to practice with a rifle. There are no other houses around, and she said there were no ranges in the city."

Both Trilling and I leaned forward. Mrs. Robinson didn't know where Wendy's rifle had come from, but she told us it wasn't here at the house. Then she took us into the backyard and pointed out to us where a large old sheet of plywood was propped up against some trees in the distance.

As we walked toward it, I saw groupings of bullet holes in four different parts of the four-by-eight-foot sheet.

Trilling said, "Wrong caliber. These holes are likely made by .223s. We're looking for maybe a .308."

"That doesn't mean she only has one rifle."

We couldn't find any bullets to dig out of trees for forensic examination, but we told Mrs. Robinson that we might be back.

She walked us to our car, where I handed her a business card with both of our cell phone numbers. She agreed to call us if she heard from Wendy. Then Mrs. Robinson said, "Can you help her?"

"She may not need help. Right now we just want to talk to her. She lied to us, and we need to know why."

Mrs. Robinson shrugged. "You can never tell with Wendy. At one time, she wanted to be a teacher. She even took a few classes at City College. But she's content to take on odd jobs around the city and exercise at that gym of hers."

Once we were in the car, I turned to Trilling and said, "Doesn't your sister live close by?"

"Yeah, Ludingtonville. About ten minutes from here."

"We can count that as our lunch break if you want to visit."

He didn't answer immediately. He was even more thoughtful than usual. Trilling turned to me and said, "You introduced me to your family. I guess I should introduce you to mine."

CHAPTER 47

ROB TRILLING'S SISTER lived in the middle of the tiny town of Ludingtonville, in a nice two-story house that was kept in good order. A Dodge Ram 1500 pickup truck with Montana plates sat in the driveway.

Trilling casually said, "My mom and grandpa have been here visiting for a few months. They're helping my sister with the kids because my brother-in-law is a long-haul trucker."

He said that his mom, who was named Mona, and his grandfather, Chet, would be there watching his sister's toddler and infant while she worked as a bookkeeper at an auto-parts store in the next town.

A woman I took to be Mona Trilling opened the door as we walked up the driveway. I don't know why it surprised me to realize that she was only a couple of years older than me. She had black hair and wide, dark eyes. She hugged Trilling like she hadn't seen him in years, instead of only six days ago, which he had just told me was when he last came up to visit.

Trilling's grandfather, Chet, came to the door behind Mona. He was a distinguished-looking older man, just under six feet tall with neatly trimmed gray hair and clear, dark eyes.

Chet asked, "Who's this, Rob?"

Trilling said, "This is my partner, Michael Bennett, Pops."

"Partner in the Army?"

"No, Pops. I work for the police now."

The old man smiled and nodded.

They welcomed us into the living room. I chatted with Mona Trilling about the differences between New York and Montana. She told me how happy she was that two of her kids had ended up living near each other, so she could visit both of them at the same time. I gathered that Trilling's older brother was running the grandfather's car dealership back in Bozeman.

I said, "It's nice that you and your father can drive across the country together to visit your children."

"Oh, Pops isn't my father. He's my former father-in-law."

"From what I hear you take really good care of him. I just assumed he was your dad."

"No, but we're close. After my husband left, Pops stepped up and really helped with the kids. I don't know how much Rob has told you, but his father was not a good man. Anyway, Pops has always been very kind to me. And I intend to stick with him through the troubles I know are coming. Right now it's just a little memory glitch. We've been told it'll get much worse and he'll start to act erratically. That'll be tough on Rob. He loves his grandfather."

I just sat there silently. That hit me hard. I couldn't imagine my grandfather, Seamus, having those issues, even though he was almost ten years older than Pops. I listened to the banter between Trilling and his grandfather. In short snippets, you couldn't tell there were any problems at all. They joked with each other. The elderly man brought up incidents from years before with perfect clarity. And it all made me a little sad.

Learning that Mona looked after an ex-in-law, I started to understand my new partner a little better. Apparently everything I'd seen on the job where he cared so deeply was no act. He had learned lessons about looking after other people, and I could see exactly where he'd picked up those traits.

Trilling and his grandfather went to the rear bedrooms to check on the napping children. As soon as they were out of the room, Mona Trilling turned to me and said, "Is my boy doing all right in the big city?"

"Everything I've seen says he's caught on to life in New York pretty well."

"You have no idea how I worried about him the whole time he was deployed. When he told me he was leaving active duty, I felt such relief, I didn't know what to do. Then he goes and joins the New York City Police Department and I start to worry all over again."

"He's got a good head on his shoulders. And he knows how to take care of himself. I wouldn't worry too much."

"Do you know if he's dating at all? I don't want him to be lonely. He brought a young woman by in September for a visit. They were coming back from some weeklong VA retreat in Albany. Her name was Darcy and I think she worked for the VA. She seemed like a nice young lady, but I never heard anything more about her. And Rob is so private, I hate to ask him direct questions about his dating life."

I thought about my own daughter texting Rob Trilling to ask him out. I looked at Mona and said, "I think Rob will be okay. We're working a lot of hours right now while we're on one case. Like every job, we have busy times and slow times. He'll have time to figure out what he wants to do and who he wants to date."

That seemed to satisfy his mother. Just then, Trilling stepped from the hallway, holding an infant, while his grandfather held the hand of a toddler.

Chet looked right at me and asked, "Who's this?"

My heart broke a little bit for the whole family.

CHAPTER 48

BEFORE WE'D EVEN driven back to the city, Walter Jackson had texted me a new possible address for Wendy Robinson. Rob Trilling insisted we look for her right now.

Trilling said, "I'm just thinking about the groupings we saw on the plywood behind her mom's house. Robinson knows what she's doing with a rifle. I don't like being in this gray area where we don't know how strong a suspect she is."

"You'll get used to it in Homicide. It feels like everyone's a suspect sometimes. Let's run by this address in the Bronx and see what we can find out."

"I'll tell you the truth, I hope she's not the killer. I know what it's like readjusting to civilian life. She might just be having a few problems. She seems like she's trying to straighten her life out."

"By lying to us and ignoring her mother?"

Trilling didn't respond. If I'd never met him, I would've said he was brooding.

We found the address Walter had given us and sat in my Chevy down the block from the building. I casually said, "Where do you think she keeps the rifle she used up at her mom's?"

Trilling thought about it. "If I were her, I'd have a place to keep it up in Putnam County. It's too hard to move it around in the city without people noticing."

We'd been sitting on the apartment building for only about five minutes. I was trying to think ahead and wondering if we needed assistance. When a cop does a surveillance like this, they never know when it will end. I've been on surveillances that lasted more than twenty-four hours.

My thought processes were shut down when Trilling tapped my shoulder and I looked up from my phone. Wendy Robinson was walking out of the apartment building, carrying an oversized gym bag.

I said, "Could you hide a rifle in a bag like that?"

"If the rifle broke down, you could. The oversized bag is good camouflage." Trilling started to shift in his seat and reach for the door handle.

I said, "Hang on just a minute. Let's follow her and see where she's headed. Maybe we'll learn something. If we start to lose her, we'll end the surveillance and interview her on the spot."

We waited until Robinson was almost at the end of the block, then Trilling and I hopped out of the car. He jogged up the block when we saw her turn at the end of the street. I remained behind her while Trilling crossed the street to follow her from another angle.

We followed the former Army sergeant six blocks. It only took a minute for me to realize she was headed to her boxing gym. I sent a quick text to Trilling so he could get ahead of her.

I started to catch up to her when she reached the block where her gym was located. I noticed the homeless man with the pet rat, Nigel, sitting across the street, keeping an eye on the entire neighborhood.

I saw Trilling a block ahead of me. Then I hesitated. Wendy Robinson walked right past the entrance to the gym. Trilling picked up on it and stayed out of sight as he casually walked on the other side of the street.

He met up with me as she turned on the far side of the gym.

Trilling said, "What's the plan?"

"We stay on her. Now I *need* to know what she's up to."

We hustled around the building in time to see our suspect speak to a tall man wearing sweats, then follow him through a door at the rear of the building.

Trilling and I walked up to the door. He gave me a questioning look, so I shrugged and tried the handle. We both walked through the door with confidence and were surprised to find ourselves in a warehouse crammed with dozens of people. No one paid us any attention. I worked my way through the crowd and saw that a square area on the floor was being lined with heavy mats.

When I looked across the open area, I saw Wendy Robinson taking off her sweatshirt and flexing her arms and shoulders. The tall man she'd walked inside with stepped onto the mat across from her.

Trilling inched up next to me. "What the hell is going on?"

I was about to say I wasn't sure. Then I heard the ding of a bell and Robinson rushed out onto the mat to meet the man in the sweatsuit. There was no introduction or announcement. She just started swinging.

CHAPTER 49

WHEN WENDY ROBINSON stopped her wild swings and squared off against her opponent, I took a closer look at the man she was bare-knuckle fighting. He was well over six feet tall. He had some bulk to him as well. I figured him to be around thirty-five years old. He had a long, droopy mustache that reminded me of Harry Grissom's impressive facial hair.

Trilling started to step past me, his instinct to stop something like this too strong to ignore. I put my hand out and caught him by the chest. I leaned over and said into his ear, "This isn't her first rodeo. Give it a minute before we do anything stupid."

"We can't let this keep going."

"We can't fight the forty people in here either."

Trilling nodded but didn't look happy about my decision. We both turned and watched the fight. Robinson knew how to move. The tall man landed one glancing blow off her shoulder. Then

166

she stepped to one side, cocked her right arm back, and caught the man on the side of the chin with her bare fist.

I could tell by the way his head snapped that the fight was over, even before I saw his eyes roll back in his head. Then he dropped to his knees and fell face forward to a round of cheers from the entire crowd.

Wendy Robinson had hardly broken a sweat. She checked to make sure her opponent was okay. Several men from the crowd had him sitting up and were checking his eyes. The man gave her a thumbs-up and she turned to walk away.

Trilling and I intercepted her as she was headed into the crowd to watch the next fight. As soon as Robinson noticed us, she turned on the ball of her foot and tried to cut through the crowd to the rear door.

Trilling raced ahead and was waiting at the door.

Once I reached the door, we all stepped outside into the relatively quiet alley behind the gym-warehouse. The place was a perfect camouflage for these illegal fights. Even from inside the gym you couldn't tell there was a rear warehouse section of the building.

We stood on either side of Wendy Robinson as I said, "You haven't been enrolled at City College for almost two years. You lied to us."

She smiled. "I lie to everyone. I have to just to stay sane. My mom wants to know my every move. The VA wants to make sure I stay on my meds. And cops asking questions just makes things worse. I didn't want to tell you I was involved with these guys. You'd shut them down."

I said, "So it's like the movie. First rule is not to talk about it."

"What movie?"

"Fight Club."

She just gave me a vacant look. "Our first rule is to make sure no one gets hurt. It just adds a level of realism to our training, and the owner of the gym makes a little extra from people coming to watch the fights. The VA would never sanction this sort of therapy for PTSD. I swear to God it's the only way to deal with living here."

I said, "Now that I know your alibi is bullshit, I need to know where you were the night Adam Glossner was shot on his balcony." That was the date we knew she had lied about.

She made a sour face and said, "C'mon, guys. You can't figure it out? I was right here. I'm here two or three nights a week. Your detective abilities don't seem that sharp to me."

I looked at Trilling and he nodded as he went back inside to verify her story. He'd find the manager easily enough.

I looked back at Robinson. "We visited your mom. She seems very nice."

"She's the best. Except she expects everyone to live their lives the same way she has. I don't want to end up in a little town with a house full of kids running around."

"Where's the rifle you used at her house?"

Another smile slid across her face. "So you're saying I shouldn't confide any criminal activities to my mother. She showed you my little range, didn't she?"

"To be fair, she didn't know why we wanted to talk to you."

"The rifle belongs to one of my buddies who lives near my mom. I just wanted to feel a rifle against my shoulder for an hour or so. It's too expensive to shoot anymore. Ammo costs a fortune. I liked it a lot better when the government provided me with bullets." She gave me a sly smile. She wasn't worried about a homicide charge.

After a while, Trilling came back out. "Robinson's story checks out. The manager even showed me some video. He says she's a regular and never causes any trouble."

Robinson did a little curtsy. "That's me, just a good little girl." She pointed at the building. "I guess you could say this whole thing is my anti-anxiety drug. Please don't shut us down."

"Answer your phone if I call you again and we won't bother this place. Ignore me and I'll make a call that shuts this place down for good. Do we have an understanding?"

She held out her right hand and shook mine. "You have my word." She turned to Trilling and stuck her hand out again. When he reached to shake it, she pulled him close and planted a kiss right on his lips. "That's just to show I'm serious about my work."

Watching Trilling blush never got old.

CHAPTER 50

I'M USED TO calls in the middle of the night. Every homicide detective is. The only thing that surprised me about this one was the caller. Instead of Harry Grissom calling to give me an assignment, it was my sometime partner, Terri Hernandez, directly from a scene in the Bronx. Usually Terri handled the homicides up that way. Then she dropped the bombshell: it looked like the sniper had struck again.

Mary Catherine was just conscious enough for me to give her a kiss on the forehead as I slipped out of the bedroom and then the apartment. Traffic was light at this hour. I was on the scene in the Highbridge area, half a dozen blocks north of Yankee Stadium, in about ten minutes.

Terri met me in front of a nice apartment building. She gave me a quick hug and asked about the kids. It doesn't matter the situation; you still know who your closest friends are.

Similarly, before I even asked about the specifics of the homicide, I asked after her sisters, Christy and Sylvia.

Terri smiled and said, "My dad is getting used to the idea of their goofy white boyfriends. Sylvia's boyfriend loves heavy metal music and has a dog named Ace, after one of the members of Kiss."

Thinking of how that would go over with Terry's Cuban-born father made me smile. Then I got serious. I said, "What's the story here?"

"Someone used a rifle to shoot a community activist named Gus Querva. The doorman found him about an hour ago. My rough estimate is that he was shot around eleven o'clock from somewhere to the north of the building. It looks like Querva was walking in the front door when the killer took the shot."

I considered that for a moment, then asked, "Is this the same Gus Querva who some people claim is part of a gang that terrorizes the Bronx?"

Terri gave me a sideways glance and said, "Whoever told you that wasn't from any of the precincts around here. We got a very specific memo saying we weren't supposed to talk to anyone about him. We weren't sure if it was because of all of his efforts building youth centers or if the feds were working some kind of big case on him."

Terri had already covered the bases on this homicide. She had people out canvassing the area, talking to doormen, and looking for video surveillance. She asked, "Where's your new partner?"

I was more than a little annoyed to notice that Trilling hadn't shown up yet. I had texted him after I got the call from Terri but had gotten no answer. I looked at Terri and shrugged.

She said, "What's with these guys with no sense of duty?"

"That's not Rob Trilling. He's all about duty and responsibility. But I don't know where he is right now."

A couple of local TV news trucks came down the street and stopped just outside the police perimeter. I figured one of the doormen had made the call. They'd learned there were some perks to tipping off the media to things like this.

A green Toyota Camry rattled to a stop behind one of the news trucks. I couldn't help but smile when I saw Lois Frang pop out of the beat-up car and start marching toward the perimeter. When she waved at me, I felt obliged to walk over and talk to her.

I said, "Tell me who tipped you guys off. I'm just curious."

Lois let out a quick laugh. "No one ever gives *me* tips. I work for the *Brooklyn Democrat*. What could I give them in return? I rely on a good old-fashioned police scanner. It catches your general traffic, and I could tell something was going on."

"You were up listening to a police scanner at this hour?"

"Insomnia. It's either a gift or a curse." She looked past my shoulder and said, "I thought it might be the sniper again. Seeing you confirms it. Can you tell me anything?"

"Not much." In the silence that followed we both heard the TV reporter next to us practicing his introduction.

"We're at the scene of a murder, possibly committed by the sniper who has been terrorizing the city. The victim is Gus Querva, the man responsible for bringing countless youth centers and community advancements to the Bronx."

Lois snorted.

"What's funny?"

"These journalism-school grads who believe anything that's fed to them. Everyone with half a brain knows Gus Querva was able to live in a building like this by running a protection and extortion racket. There's hardly a bodega in this part of the Bronx that doesn't pay one of Gus's crew a cut every week just to be left alone."

I nodded and made an excuse as I headed back to find Terri Hernandez. I checked my watch and called Rob Trilling. I told him to call me as soon as he got my message.

I thought about how upset Trilling had been when he saw Querva talking to the media. He'd said the same things about Querva that Lois Frang just had. I felt a sharp sting of anxiety in my stomach as I thought about my partner's comments regarding our latest victim.

CHAPTER 51

ROB TRILLING SHOWED up at the crime scene in the Bronx at almost exactly seven in the morning. All his new partner said when he arrived was "You need to live next to your phone when you're working in Homicide." Trilling nodded, knowing more would be coming later. He'd had his ass chewed by professionals in the Army. So far, no one in the NYPD scared him too much.

Trilling tried to make sense of the scene and what each of the team members was doing. Uniformed police officers kept the media and gawkers behind the police line. Crime-scene techs took photos near the front door where the body had fallen. Detectives were searching for potential witnesses. And Trilling took it all in. He wanted to understand how a smart guy like Mike Bennett could figure out the details that led to an arrest. He knew that was always the key to any mission: details.

Trilling stepped over to Bennett and asked, "When did the M.E. take Querva's body?"

Bennett stopped what he was doing, turned to face Trilling, and said, "How did you know the victim was Gus Querva?"

"It's on the news. I heard it on my way over here." Trilling didn't like the look Bennett gave him. He stayed put while Bennett started to march through the crime scene, checking on each person doing a specific task.

Trilling wanted to be close to Bennett so he could learn how this shit was done properly. He caught up to Bennett and started to follow him around as he talked to a couple of potential witnesses, including Querva's girlfriend. The former Miss Colombia had been asleep in their apartment. Apparently the doorman had an excused absence for a couple of hours, then came through the rear door, so he didn't notice the dead man by the front door. As soon as he'd found the body, he called 911.

After the initial round of tasks was completed, Bennett turned to Trilling and said, "Let's go sit in my car for a few minutes. It's quiet and I need to think." His Chevy was parked almost in front of the building. Its close proximity to the crime scene discouraged anyone from walking up and talking to him when he was sitting inside. Trilling could understand why he needed to get away from everyone's questions for just a few minutes.

Once they were settled in the car's front seats, Bennett turned to him and said, "We have something we didn't have before."

"What's that?"

"The canvass turned up a coffee shop employee who saw someone walking by with what they thought was a musical instrument case. At least we have a description now. White male, about six feet tall, with short, dark hair. The description that fits maybe five hundred thousand people in the greater New York area."

"I even fit that description." Trilling noticed Bennett didn't say anything.

"You going to be okay working on the homicide of a guy like Gus Querva?" Bennett asked. "You told me you thought he'd ruined the neighborhood and was just putting on a show for the media."

Suddenly Trilling felt like someone was tightening a vise on his chest. He'd never had anyone question his integrity before. In the service, if you completed your mission, no one harassed you.

"It almost sounds like you're trying to accuse me of something. Go ahead and ask me anything you want."

"I just did. Can you work the case?"

Trilling nodded.

"Where were you that you didn't answer your phone?"

Trilling was silent. He stared at Bennett for a moment, then said, "Do I need an alibi? Sure you want to ride around town with me?"

"Making smart-ass cracks right now doesn't help anything. I texted and called you and got no answer. Where were you?"

Trilling didn't need someone looking at him the way Bennett was right now, grilling him over a missed phone call. All he could say was "I was at home, sound asleep. No fancy excuses. I screwed up and I know it."

Bennett sat silently, looking out the windshield. "For a guy who got to sleep last night you look like shit."

Trilling nodded. He knew he had bags under his bloodshot eyes. He could tell Bennett was exhausted. Maybe too tired to pick up on some details of the crime and the shooter.

Trilling said, "I'm here now. Let me take some of the burden off you. What do you need done right now?"

Bennett took a deep breath. He was thinking hard about something. Finally he said, "Coordinate the canvass of the neighborhood. Extend it two blocks south. Maybe someone else saw the man with the large instrument case. Maybe we'll get lucky and he'll be on a security video somewhere." Bennett looked at Trilling. "And tell me exactly where you think the shooter fired from. That's what you're an expert on, right? We'll send a forensics team to you when you find the location."

In the Army, a superior officer would usually tell him, *Dismissed,* when they were done with giving orders. Trilling had the good sense to know when he'd been dismissed whether someone said the word or not.

CHAPTER 52

IT'S SOMETIMES HARD for people to comprehend what goes into a police investigation. I had two things going for me: experience and a really good team. I never took Walter Jackson for granted. He saved me hours of work on every homicide by finding where witnesses lived and worked. Other detectives conducted canvasses for witnesses and checked for other vital information. But the initial period after a homicide is always hectic.

This one was particularly difficult for two reasons: it was the fourth in a string of killings, and I had a disturbing thought in my head about my partner. I just couldn't ignore his very specific comments about Gus Querva. And the fact that Trilling hadn't been around last night made me consider some terrible possibilities.

I made it a point for us to take a break at noon. I'd been on the clock longer than a regular workday and saw no end in sight. I needed some food and made Trilling stop with me at a small sandwich shop in the Bronx.

We were able to grab a tiny table for two in the corner and a bit of privacy. The place was busy enough that our voices didn't carry.

I wiggled on the hard, wooden chair, trying to get comfortable. Trilling stared down at his tuna salad like he was dreading having to speak with me.

Finally I said, "Tough night and day. This is what a homicide investigation looks like immediately after the body's discovered."

"I'll admit, I didn't expect it to be like this. Your phone has rung at least thirty times."

"That was before I put it on silent. I always update Harry Grissom. It's the bosses from One Police Plaza that I tend to ignore. There's always a lot of information thrown at us right after we get the call of a body being found. It never really changes." I waited, hoping Trilling might say something to put me at ease. I was out of luck.

After a few minutes of silence, I said, "Can we talk frankly? I don't really have time right now to beat around the bush."

Trilling smiled and said, "I've never been around you when you *did* have time to beat around the bush."

"Do you want to say anything to me? Do you have any more details you can provide about why you never answered my call?"

It took longer than usual for Trilling to answer. When he looked up at me, I noticed his eyes were bloodshot. He suddenly looked older as well. Then Trilling said, "I don't know what to tell you." He shook his head and kept looking down at his plate.

"Tell me what's going on. Why you look like you've been running from aliens all night. I just want to understand."

Trilling slowly nodded. "I get it. And I can see why you're looking at me funny after what I said about Gus Querva. The truth is, I've had a few issues since coming back from Afghanistan. The worst issue is sleep disturbance. My counselor at the VA got me a prescription for a drug that really puts me out. I mean, I lose eight to ten hours of consciousness. They call it 'sleep.' I call it a coma. Then I wake up feeling weak, tired, and confused. So I can't honestly tell you exactly what I did last night. I started the night lying in my bed, and I woke up in my bed. I've learned from past experience that doesn't mean I didn't do something in between. Once I made a meal when I was asleep. The next morning, I thought someone had broken in and microwaved the Stouffer's lasagna and garlic bread that was sitting on my kitchen table."

"Have you told the NYPD medical staff about this?"

"They know I'm under treatment by the VA. They've been in touch with my counselor. I stay on my schedule for appointments and even have been to a couple of their weeklong retreats. My counselor, Darcy, is the one who came with me to visit my mother. We were on our way back from Albany in September. I let my mom think it was more than just a counseling retreat. That way she didn't keep asking me if I'd met any nice girls in the city."

I appreciated his honesty as I considered everything he had said. But it didn't ease my concerns. I still had that funny feeling in the pit of my stomach. The one that always made me nervous. The feeling that everything was about to be turned upside down.

CHAPTER 53

WE CLEARED UP all the immediate interviews and leads related to the murder of Gus Querva. Rob Trilling looked so rough, I told him to go home. As soon as I said it, I knew ordering an insomniac to rest and sleep was like telling a heroin addict, *Just stop using heroin.* But Trilling didn't complain. He said he was going to do his best.

I called Mary Catherine. She sounded tired.

I said, "Is the fertility treatment getting to you?"

"I don't know, Michael. I thought I was past it."

"Is there anything I can do for you?"

"No, darling, I'm just a little tired. And you've been working since the middle of the night. Is everything okay with you?"

There was so much I could've gone into. Instead, I said, "Just finishing up the last few things for the day. You sit tight and I'll grab dinner on my way home."

Forty minutes later, I barely made it through the door as I juggled four large pizzas in one hand and a dozen roses in the other. The grateful look on Mary Catherine's face made the effort well worthwhile.

Despite a deep-down exhaustion, I enjoyed hearing about the kids' day. It sounded relatively uneventful. Fiona appeared to have finally figured out algebra, Trent used parts from four different computers to make a working one at Holy Name's computer lab, and Brian helped install a giant AC unit on top of a warehouse in the Bronx.

Chrissy was very sweet, making Mary Catherine sit at the table while she rushed around and brought her pizza, then a drink, then moved the roses closer to her on the table.

I noticed Jane huddled with my grandfather at the end of the table. They were looking at a sheet of paper and whispering back and forth like middle schoolers who had just been passed a note.

I waited until after dinner to casually slide next to my grandfather on the couch. He had just gotten his good-night kisses from the younger girls and was patiently watching the boys play a video game. I took the quiet moment to do some subtle investigative work.

"What were you and Jane discussing at the dinner table?"

"I'm not allowed to catch up with my great-granddaughter during dinner?"

"That's not what I said. And I'm too tired to play your crazy word games tonight. Jane's been acting a little secretive and I want to make sure everything's okay. So do you care to tell me what you were talking about?"

"You know that I love you, my boy. This whole family is what keeps me feeling young. That's why I'm sorry to disappoint you when I cite priest, great-granddaughter confidentiality. I'm afraid it's one of those immutable laws of nature that wasn't designed to be broken by an old sinner like me."

"Do you ever peddle this crap down at the church?"

"Every day. Why do you think the monsignor always looks so confused?"

I had to laugh at that and appreciate how my grandfather kept the kids' secrets. Everyone needed someone they could talk to without fear. Maybe that was where I was letting Rob Trilling down. Maybe he wasn't comfortable being completely honest with me. I shook that thought out of my head.

I said to my grandfather, "I just worry about the kids growing up too fast."

"I wouldn't worry about Jane, my boy. She's more likely to be the city's youngest mayor than she is to do something stupid."

"Some people would say running for mayor *is* stupid."

My grandfather smiled. "That's because only stupid people usually run for mayor. Jane will break that trend."

CHAPTER 54

I'D BEEN CAREFUL once I got into the office. The morning had been a blur. I had some serious anxiety about my new partner, but I couldn't just start suggesting he could be responsible for a series of murders. Life doesn't work that way. Once I said it, it could never be taken back. And that would follow Trilling the rest of his career. Assuming, of course, he *wasn't* the Longshot Killer.

I could've used some help from Walter Jackson, but I didn't want to involve him. I gave Trilling a detailed list of things to do on the case. Checking security videos, re-interviewing a few witnesses, and generally tying up his entire day. He didn't bat an eye at the long list of assignments.

Now I found myself in Midtown Manhattan. Trilling had told me he came to an off-site VA clinic here. That wasn't too hard to track down. I recalled that he and his mother had both told me that his counselor's first name was Darcy. A name just uncommon enough for me to think I could find her.

The clinic was on the third floor of a commercial building just a tad on the run-down side, with cheap carpet and scuffed walls. Not high-end enough for law firms and architects to rent office space.

I walked through the door marked VETERANS AFFAIRS, with the *s* faded off the end of the nameplate. In the small waiting room, I found an empty reception desk with a note that said, "Be back in twenty minutes." I had no idea how long the receptionist had been gone, so I sat in one of the five mismatched chairs available. In front of me was a coffee table with magazines I barely recognized. The best I could find was a *Sports Illustrated* that was about four years old. I wondered how many coaches the New York Jets had gone through in that time span.

One of the four doors leading to reception opened, and a young man dressed in a T-shirt and ratty jeans stepped out, followed by a pretty woman in her early thirties with short brown hair. I caught a break when the young man said, "Thanks, Darcy. I'll see you next week."

As the man headed out the door, I stood up. Darcy turned to me and said, "Can I help you?"

"I wasn't sure how long the receptionist would be gone so I waited."

"She's been gone about two and half years. We haven't gotten funding for a new one. I wrote that note myself about six months after she left. Pretty good, right?"

I already liked her. I pulled out my badge and introduced myself.

Darcy cocked her head and said, "And you want to talk to me?

I haven't run afoul of the law since I was a graduate student at Boston University."

I smiled and said, "Couldn't get into City College, huh?"

That made her laugh and put her at ease.

"I was hoping I might talk to you about one of your clients."

"I'm afraid I can't discuss any of my clients with the police. I need their permission, and there would be some paperwork with the VA."

"I understand all of that. And I'm not trying to pressure you. I'm just trying to assess the situation in my office. One of my coworkers told me he comes to see you, and I have some concerns about his psychological stability. I'm worried about him." I could tell by the look on her face Darcy knew exactly who I was talking about. But she was a pro, so she didn't let anything slip verbally.

"I can tell you that the majority of my caseload isn't any threat to anyone. They're just trying to adjust to life back here after being deployed. Our focus here is assimilation. We're trying to keep veterans from withdrawing. That's why so many vets end up homeless. This is one way to try and stop that. All I do is let them talk. I would think you were perfectly safe working with anyone under my care."

I liked her even more. Darcy was trying to help me without betraying any confidences or breaking any rules. "Do you prescribe medications?"

"No, but I'm supervised by a psychiatrist. She can write prescriptions as needed."

"Would some of those prescriptions be for serious sleeping pills?"

"I'm not giving anything away by saying most of my clients have issues sleeping through the night. The most common symptom of PTSD," Darcy said. "As far as the drugs go, I'm a counselor, not an MD. I have a general idea of what each drug does, but I'm certainly no expert."

The door to my right opened and a tall woman in her fifties with a giant ball of bleached-blond hair stopped in the doorway and stared at me like my fly was down.

Darcy jumped in quickly. "Dr. Hendrix, this NYPD detective was just asking about the symptoms and treatment of PTSD. Can you give him any insight?"

The doctor looked annoyed. Clearly Darcy was used to dealing with her on a regular basis. She seemed to have developed techniques of distraction, much like coaxing a reluctant cat into a carrier.

Dr. Hendrix snapped, "Which drug? We prescribe a huge array depending on what the client needs."

Darcy spit out a long, six-syllable pharmaceutical name. I knew immediately she was surreptitiously telling me which drug Trilling had been prescribed. She was able to do it without violating any trust or confidence.

The doctor frowned and said, "That's a very strong sedative. It's also one we prescribe regularly."

I said, "Can you give me an idea of the side effects?"

"It does have a tendency to make the user hazy in the morning for the first twenty to thirty minutes. It's also not uncommon for the user to perform activities while under the influence of the drug."

"What sort of activities?"

"Usually activities related to their everyday lives. They cook. They clean their apartment. I had a carpenter once who built an entire pigeon coop on the top of his apartment building over the course of a month and never realized it."

I asked, "These can be complex activities that the user of the prescription does during the day?"

"That's what I just said." She looked at Darcy. "Several of your clients take it. Even the young cop. The one who sits and doesn't talk? That one worries me with his sullen attitude."

Darcy all but cringed. She recovered quickly and said, "I know who you mean." It was her way of shutting up the psychiatrist.

Dr. Hendrix asked, "You have a case involving the drug?"

I just nodded, trying not to give anything away. The statement from the psychiatrist alarmed me. Her description of the powerful side effects, and their potential impact on Trilling's behavior, sent a chill through my body.

I started to formulate a hypothetical question that might shed more light on my concerns, but I was cut off.

The doctor looked past me toward the exit. "I'm sorry. I have some errands to run. Doesn't the NYPD have someone on staff who can answer these questions?" She didn't wait for an answer. She marched past us and out the door without another word.

Darcy just looked at me. She handed me her business card.

I looked down and saw her last name was Farnan. I said, "Thank you, Ms. Farnan. You've been a big help, and I won't tell anyone I was here."

"I'll keep it quiet too, for now. Can you keep me in the loop if there's anything specific that's worrying you? Of course, I have no idea who, exactly, you're talking about." She had a friendly, mischievous smile.

"I promise. And I hope it's nothing. But I have to be thorough."

CHAPTER 55

I KNEW MY next stop was going to be tricky. I had a love-hate relationship with the Federal Bureau of Investigation. I'd worked with them closely in the past, but always with my good friend Emily Parker. I hadn't had much contact with the FBI since her murder in Washington, DC, a short time ago.

I managed to score a fifteen-minute appointment with Robert Lincoln, the ASAC, or assistant special agent in charge. Usually the ASACs were the ones who actually ran the FBI offices in big cities. The special agent in charge was more likely to meet with the other law enforcement agencies and the media when required. Lincoln and I had butted heads on several different cases over the years. He was exactly what most cops disliked about the FBI: pompous, secretive, and patronizing. The trifecta of pissing off people trying to do their jobs.

But I'd learned that Lincoln was personally overseeing the

fugitive task squad Rob Trilling had been previously assigned to while the squad supervisor was out on extended medical leave. So it gave me an excuse to come find out some information.

My escort was a young man named Jason, who led me through the maze of hallways at the New York office of the FBI to a solid door with the nameplate ROBERT LINCOLN on it. Jason knocked on the door softly and opened it carefully. I saw Lincoln sitting behind his enormous oak desk. He didn't even bother to look up. He mumbled, "Thanks, Jason. You can have a seat, Detective."

I still wasn't sure how I wanted to handle this. I didn't want to get Rob Trilling in trouble. Not if he wasn't doing anything wrong. I thought I'd figured out a way to talk to the ASAC and still accomplish that goal.

Finally Lincoln looked up at me. He was in his late forties or early fifties and still looked fit. I knew there weren't that many high-ranking Black agents with the FBI, so despite our differences, I realized he had to be somewhat on the ball.

All he said was "What can I do for you, Detective?"

"Thank you for letting Rob Trilling come back to the NYPD temporarily to help us on the sniper case. I thought I should give you a quick update that we've tied the latest shooting to the other three. We don't have any specific leads yet, but I wanted to let you know you can call me anytime if you have questions. Or if you'd prefer, I'll come here to your office and brief you."

"I'd *prefer* not to have a twenty-four-year-old police officer on our fugitive task force. I took him as a favor to one of your assistant commissioners. As far as your case goes, I'm not surprised the NYPD hasn't come up with anything. This sniper seems a notch above the level of killers you typically deal with. I have some analysts looking at different information to decide if we're going to get involved or not."

I knew Lincoln said that just to stir the shit. Contrary to public opinion, the FBI couldn't just step in on any case. It would cause too many problems with a major department like the NYPD. I let it slide.

I said, "I was told that the supervisor of the fugitive squad has been out for several months with some sort of medical issue. They said you're overseeing the group."

Lincoln nodded. "Yeah, the supervisory special agent has serious back problems. He might go out on a medical. Is there something specific you want to know?"

"Just doing an evaluation on Trilling. Did he do a good job for you?"

"Surprisingly, yes. I don't usually expect much from local law enforcement. But he seemed to be sharp and determined, even if he's awfully young."

"Anything negative?"

"You understand, supervising a single squad is a sideline for me. I have the entire division to look after. I didn't see or hear about anything that Trilling screwed up, if that's what you're asking. Now, if you'll excuse me, I have actual work to do. Not that I would expect someone from the NYPD to understand that."

Robert Lincoln would never know how much it took for me not to respond to a snotty comment like that.

CHAPTER 56

YESTERDAY, ROB TRILLING had found the sniper's perch one block south of the building where Gus Querva had been shot. Trilling had talked to the crime-scene tech who'd taken the most photographs. The photos were detailed and showed the wound just above Querva's right temple. Trilling admired the shot from a professional perspective.

After looking at the photos, Trilling determined where the body had been found, then stood in that spot and looked down the street in each direction. That's when he knew exactly where the shot had come from. A nice recessed doorway to a small office building was perfect. Trilling got crime-scene techs to photograph it. He didn't ask for any DNA swabs of the area.

Trilling liked working alone and consulting with the crime-scene people as needed. He didn't feel like he was just tagging along behind someone as he usually did with Michael Bennett.

Not that that was a bad place to be. He appreciated how the seasoned detective had gone out of his way to explain how investigations worked and how everything came down to details. There were no shortcuts in a homicide investigation.

Today, Trilling checked security footage from the shops and buildings around the crime scene. He'd just finished looking at the fifth security recording. He was able to find a short clip of a man carrying a long case right after the shooting. The man walked past a camera in an electronics store. The image wasn't clear enough to identify the man, but Trilling could see that he was around six feet with short, dark hair. He didn't appear overweight or really skinny. Pretty similar to the description given by the coffee shop employee.

Trilling wanted to prove to Michael Bennett that he could conduct a professional investigation even if he wasn't sorry that the victim was dead. Gus Querva and his buddies had run roughshod over parts of the Bronx. The media focused on Querva's PR moves, especially the money he'd shelled out for community centers. The irony was, he had taken the money *from* the community before he'd put it back *into* the community. Not one major media outlet seemed to ever question how he'd made his money.

Just thinking about the situation made Trilling angry.

As he was going over his assignment notes, Trilling got a text. He looked down at it immediately. He was surprised to see it was from Michael Bennett's daughter, Juliana, asking if he had time to call her.

Trilling sighed and made the call right then.

Juliana's cheerful voice immediately made him perk up. She wanted to go to lunch. When he said he didn't have time, she settled for ice cream. She gave him a place on the Upper West Side that was on his route back to the office.

As Trilling walked down the block toward the ice cream shop about twenty minutes later, he wondered why he was doing it. No question Juliana was a beautiful, intelligent girl. But the hassles this could cause in his already strained relationship with Michael Bennett outweighed the benefits.

Just as he considered turning around and texting Juliana that he couldn't make it, she spotted him and waved from a table in front of the shop. She wore a simple jacket over jeans and a colorful blouse. Her brown hair bounced on her shoulders as she waved. He couldn't turn around now even if he wanted to.

Trilling ordered two chocolate sundaes. As they sat in the cool autumn air, Juliana peppered him with questions about his personal life. She sort of sounded like his mother.

No, he wasn't dating anyone. Yes, he was eating enough. Yes, he was taking a break from work when he needed to. At least that's what he told her.

Then Juliana asked, "How is it, working with my dad?"

"Educational. He'd be a good teacher."

"I guess he would be. I never thought of it like that. But he does handle ten kids pretty well. That's not something everyone can do."

"It looks like he's done a great job with your family. I can barely keep my own schedule straight let alone keeping track of ten other people's schedules too."

"Mary Catherine gives him a lot of help. She's been part of our lives for a long time now. My youngest sister, Chrissy, even developed her own little Irish accent for a while, not long after Mary Catherine joined the family." Juliana paused and turned serious as she said, "How's the case going?"

Trilling just shrugged. He was tired of telling people they had no leads.

A giant smile spread on Juliana's face. She was almost bouncing in the seat when she said, "Do you want to surprise him and come to our apartment for dinner again tonight?"

Looking into Juliana's warm brown eyes, it was hard for him to make a rational decision. After a full ten seconds, Trilling said, "I don't think that would be a good idea right now."

Juliana didn't ask for any explanation. Trilling had a hard time reading the look on her beautiful face. He couldn't tell if she was angry, hurt, or okay with his answer. Trilling's experience with women was limited. This was another puzzle he'd have to learn how to solve.

CHAPTER 57

I HEADED OUT of the FBI building, still smarting from Robert Lincoln's comments about the NYPD. I passed a squad bay marked INTELLIGENCE ANALYSTS and decided to take a risk. I remembered the analyst at One Police Plaza, Joe Tavarez, telling me that his wife, Cindy, worked a similar job here at the FBI. I slipped into the room, and a woman at the first desk looked up and saw my law enforcement visitor's badge. She asked if she could help me.

"I was hoping to see Cindy Tavarez. I don't have an appointment. I just wanted to say hello." The woman led me to an inner office that held six more analysts.

Cindy stood up and greeted me as I approached her desk. She said, "Detective Bennett? I thought I recognized you from all the newspaper articles over the years. Glad to meet you in person." She had a warm smile.

"Just wanted to make sure no one was upset we were verifying Joe's alibi. I told him we were just trying to eliminate anyone with his kind of skills." Cindy seemed okay with my explanation and invited me to sit for a minute.

As we were chatting, a younger man walked by, and Cindy said, "Darnell, this is Michael Bennett with the NYPD. He knows Joe." She looked at me and said, "Detective Bennett, this is Darnell Nash. He was Joe's spotter in the service."

I shook the young man's hand. "Joe said he had a friend who worked over here."

Nash said, "I would've followed him on to the NYPD if I hadn't gotten a little careless and stepped on an IED." He lifted his left pant leg to display a titanium prosthetic. Then he said, "If it wasn't for Joe and Cindy, I never would've landed this job. I thank God every day for them."

"You got a lot more analysts in one place than us. The NYPD tends to scatter them among the squads."

"The FBI does too. I'm still new to this, and they thought it would be best if I worked down here in intake until I was up to speed on everything. Cindy makes sure I don't get in too much trouble. Plus, I like the 4/10 schedule. Do you ever work joint cases with the FBI?"

I hesitated, then said, "Occasionally. I used to work with an agent named Emily Parker."

Nash said, "I'm sorry. I heard about her murder. It's shocked all of us to the core. I didn't know her personally, but I've heard great things about her."

"She was great. She made working with the feds easy. Sometimes it feels like a lot of your agents didn't get that memo."

Nash handed me his business card. "I'd like to work with other agencies. Especially the NYPD. I met one of your guys working on a task force. Rob something."

"Trilling. He's working with me for the time being."

"We vets tend to stick together. I hope he's doing well."

I just nodded.

Cindy Tavarez excused herself.

When she was gone, Nash asked me in a quiet voice, "Working anything interesting right now?"

"That depends on how you define 'interesting.' I met a man with a pet rat named Nigel. That was interesting."

"I meant case-wise."

I shook my head. "I never think of people being murdered as interesting. Just a job that needs to be done." A job I needed to get back to right now.

CHAPTER 58

THE NEXT MORNING at nine o'clock, I was surprised when Rob Trilling still hadn't come through the office door. I had a lot I wanted to discuss with him. Some of it was professional, some was personal. All of it was starting to eat at me badly. I couldn't be around anyone else. I pretended to be going over reports at my desk so I didn't have to hear any of Walter Jackson's corny puns. Even if they usually made me smile. On rare occasions, I don't *want* to smile. I want to be grumpy. I think that's in the Bill of Rights for fathers. Certainly for fathers of more than three children.

Trilling rolled into the office about 9:30, carrying a stuffed equipment bag and an armful of notebooks. He dropped it all at the desk he'd been using next to mine.

He didn't wait for the question. Trilling said, "Sorry I'm late. The FBI's rotating cars and I had to return my Ford."

"Did they give you a replacement?"

"They said I get a new one when I come back to the task force. I only had about five minutes to clean out the car. I don't like to turn in equipment that's not spotless."

That was definitely a military attitude. I wasn't sure I'd ever seen it as a police attitude. Sometimes it felt like the goal of some detectives was to see how much garbage they could leave in a car they had to turn in.

Trilling looked at me and asked, "Something wrong?"

I looked in every direction to make sure no one had wandered into the squad bay. It was empty, aside from us. Trilling took the chair next to my desk.

I said, "Were you going to tell me about your date with Juliana?"

"It wasn't really a date. It was ice cream in the afternoon. And it was over before four o'clock. There was really nothing to it. I swear to God."

There wasn't a lot to argue about in that reply. I dropped the subject and instead asked, "Did you come up with anything interesting yesterday?"

Trilling said, "Here's a still taken from security video of a potential suspect. I think this is the same guy the coffee shop worker saw after Gus Querva was shot." He laid a four-by-six-inch photo on my desk.

I picked the photo up and studied the grainy image. It wasn't something we could use in court to identify an individual, but at least it gave us a general description. What immediately struck me was that the man with the case looked like Trilling. I felt a ball of ice in my stomach.

Trilling stared at me with his usual silent intensity. He said, "Tell me what you're thinking."

I admitted, "That this could be you. Same height, same hair, same build."

"Maybe I should hang out with Juliana more often so she can provide me with an alibi."

I looked up at Trilling's face. I couldn't tell if he was joking or not. I knew that *I* wasn't in a joking mood at the moment.

CHAPTER 59

ROB TRILLING AND I managed to work together during the morning. We searched through NYPD records and reports having to do with shootings over the last twelve years. The time period was dictated by how long the reports had been computerized. For anything older, we'd have to look at paper files. We were hoping to find a similarity to an earlier shooting. Anything that might help the case.

My mind wasn't completely on the task at hand. I kept finding myself glancing up at Trilling, working at the desk next to mine. It seemed crazy to even think about an active police officer being a vigilante serial killer.

He didn't act like a vigilante. He seemed to be working hard on the case. The fact that he'd so willingly handed me that photo of a potential suspect made me hesitate. If I'd committed a crime and there was a photo of me walking away from it, I don't think

I'd show it around the squad. The flip side was that he might've realized I would probably see it at some point anyway. Bringing it to my attention himself looked less suspicious.

This sort of circular reasoning tied my stomach into a knot. Why couldn't life be simpler? The fact that my daughter had a crush on this young man only made things more confusing.

I thought back to the day I went to Trilling's apartment. The day he'd explained to me about visiting the VA and the appointments he kept having to leave work for. He had been careful not to let me into his apartment. At the time, it had struck me as a little odd. Now it was just one more piece of the puzzle that made me anxious.

What was my next move? Go to Harry Grissom and explain my concerns? Wait till there was another killing? There were no good answers. Harry would be required to relieve Trilling of duty. If no more evidence came in, there was nothing else we could do on the case. And Trilling would be left in limbo, his career shattered. Even if he came back on duty, no one would trust him.

My phone rang. It was a switchboard number so I couldn't see who was calling. I answered curtly, "Bennett."

"Hello, Detective. Robert Lincoln here."

As if I needed to hear his name once I heard his baritone voice. "What can I do for you?"

"You might want to come over to the office. One of our agents was cleaning out the car your man Trilling turned in today."

"And why should I care?"

"The agent found an empty .308 bullet casing. Could that be the same caliber your sniper keeps using?"

I was shocked into silence. That never happens. Then I blurted out, "Where did they find it?"

"Stuck in a gap in the carpet in the trunk."

"Maybe it's just the casing from when he was at the range."

"That's for you to decide. I was just giving you a courtesy call, in case you wanted to place the casing into evidence and have forensics performed on it. Seems like an odd coincidence that an officer working on a case like yours would have a casing like that."

"I'll leave right now and be at your office in the next thirty minutes."

Lincoln chuckled. "Somehow I thought that's what you'd say."

CHAPTER 60

MY TRIP TO the FBI proved to be anticlimactic. Maybe I was reading more into ASAC Robert Lincoln's comments. He was busy and couldn't see me. At least that's what the flunky he sent to meet me said. The agent just handed me a .308 rifle casing in a clear plastic bag. He told me there'd be a report on where it was found and recovered coming to me in the next few days.

I still wasn't ready to just run Rob Trilling into the ground. I called a sergeant on the NYPD Emergency Service Unit. His name was Jeff Mabus. I'd met him at training over the years. He was also one of our defensive tactics instructors. He had a reputation for brutal honesty, exactly what I needed right now.

He agreed to meet me in the back lot of One Police Plaza. My request for the location had as much to do with my tight schedule as my hoping to avoid the command staff so I didn't have to update them on the sniper case. What would I say? *The young officer you sent to help me might be the sniper.* I doubted that would go over well with anyone.

Mabus was about my age and dressed in 5.11 cargo pants and a tight NYPD T-shirt. I guess if I looked like him, that's all I'd ever wear too. Even in cool weather like this. He wore a ball cap over his bald head. A scar from some fight years ago ran across his neck and chin.

We greeted each other and Mabus said, "I slipped out of a training class. Figured if a guy like you from Homicide needs to talk to me, it's more important than learning how to fall properly when someone shoves you." He looked around the parking lot, then at me and said, "What can I do for you?"

"The first thing is that you tell me this conversation is private and unofficial."

Mabus took a moment, then said, "Hard to say okay to that without knowing what you need."

That was the veteran, intelligent answer.

I said, "It's about Rob Trilling."

Mabus was quick to say, "He's not on ESU right now. Last I heard he was over at the FBI on some task force."

I paused, then looked at the lean ESU sergeant and said, "It's about Rob Trilling. But it needs to be off the record."

Reluctantly, Mabus said, "Okay, I won't say a word to anyone. I like Trilling. Is he in trouble?"

"Truthfully, I'm not sure."

"He was a good ESU member. At first, I was annoyed they waived some of the rules to get him on the team so quickly after he signed on with the PD. But he turned out to be a good team member and a pretty good sniper. Never complained. Worked hard. Paid attention in training. His military background was a real positive."

Now I was more hesitant. This had seemed like a better idea when I left the FBI office. Finally I asked, "Do you know the last time Trilling shot a rifle? Specifically, a .308?"

"I can check. But I can tell you for a fact he hasn't been on an NYPD rifle range since early summer. I don't think there's any way he would've fired a rifle since then. I'll double-check our training records and confirm with you."

"When can you confirm it?"

"God damn, this isn't some minor policy violation, is it?"

"I'd rather not say yet."

"I respect that. Like I said, he's a good kid. He gave up a lot for the country. Cut him some slack if you can."

"I hope I can."

CHAPTER 61

I DROVE BACK to the Manhattan North Homicide office slowly. Just trying to give myself a few minutes of quiet to digest everything I'd learned today. My first thought was that it could all be explained. A crazy coincidence.

Somewhere in my brain, I wondered how a sniper who'd been so precise and careful could leave such an obvious piece of evidence for someone to find. The answer was simple: he made a mistake. Everyone makes mistakes. Even the sharpest former military man. The only people who don't make mistakes are in the movies. It didn't make things any easier and I felt a little sick thinking about it, but at least I could wrap my head around it.

Before I even found a parking spot outside our building, Jeff Mabus texted me to confirm that Rob Trilling hadn't officially fired a .308-caliber rifle in seven months. Well before the time he had the FBI car. *Shit.*

The squad bay was fairly empty. Trilling was out on an assignment. I noticed Harry Grissom sitting in his office. I walked in without fanfare, sat on the hard wooden chair he kept in front of his desk, and laid my entire concern out to him. Everything, including the comments Trilling made about Gus Querva, his absence on the night of Querva's murder, my research on the drugs the VA had prescribed him, and, finally, the empty casing the FBI had found in his vehicle. I even told him about verifying Trilling's training records to see when he last shot a .308 rifle.

Harry bit his lower lip. Something he only did when things had slipped from bad to horrible. He sucked in a deep breath and said, "You were right to come to me with this."

"Harry, I looked at this a half a dozen ways. Tell me I missed something obvious. Something that might clear this whole thing up. I keep asking, *Why Trilling?*"

"Because life works out that way sometimes. But we gotta notify the right people. And we've got to do it right now. No delays."

"But if it's not true, the gossip will cripple Trilling's career."

"And the answer is to let a potential killer run around the city?"

Questions like that were hard to answer. No, we couldn't let a potential killer go free. I sat there silently, considering everything that was about to happen. I knew the NYPD could move swiftly when they wanted to. They'd want to get in front of this before there were any accusations of a cover-up.

Harry leveled his eyes at me. He said, "If you had this much on someone you didn't know, would they be considered a good suspect?"

"Yes."

"You like this kid."

"It's kind of tough to call a war hero a 'kid,' but yes, he seems like a good person."

"And you don't want him to be the killer."

"No."

"Tough shit. You're a homicide detective. You go where the evidence and witnesses lead you." Harry picked up his phone. Then he looked at me and said, "Stand by. Whatever we do, we're going to need your input."

CHAPTER 62

THE BAD NEWS from headquarters arrived in the form of Detective Sergeant Dennis Wu. The Internal Affairs sergeant had been on the force about ten years and no one would ever think he was a veteran cop. He wore glasses that made him look like a banker or stockbroker, his usual Brooks Brothers dark suit, and a colorful tie chosen to distract people he was interviewing.

He strolled over to my desk, smiling. "Hey, Bennett, how's it going? I mean, besides your gigantic fuckup?" He let out a laugh and then mumbled, "Classic."

I let him go into Harry's office, confident my lieutenant wouldn't put up with much bullshit. After two minutes alone with the IA sergeant, Harry called me into the office.

When I stepped through the door, Dennis Wu said, "Let's see if I can fix this mess with a good interview."

Harry said, "We don't know if it's a mess yet. We're still trying to figure things out, *Sergeant*."

I smiled. The way Harry had emphasized "Sergeant" was a chance to remind the IA investigator how the rank structure worked.

Dennis said, "From what I've seen, it looks like he's good for it." He glanced around Harry's office, then out to the squad bay. "I thought off-site offices would be nicer than this."

I said, "I thought an IA sergeant would be more professional. Maybe if you'd spent more than a few months in patrol you'd have a better understanding of how things work."

Dennis Wu took off his glasses and nodded. "Is that a shot at me for being moved from patrol to translate a Mandarin wire for the FBI? Clever. So what? I only did a month in the bag. I did five years at the FBI, a few years in general investigations, and I've been in IA for three years. I think I have a pretty good handle on how things work around here."

"What about having concern for a fellow cop?"

"I do worry about cops. And the very few bad cops we have give us *all* a bad name. So why don't we cut the shit and start to focus on the case."

He was right, so I nodded in agreement.

Wu asked, "Did you put the .308 casing from the FBI into evidence?"

"I did, and it is going to the lab for every possible test the Ballistic Information Network can do on it."

"NIBIN?"

"Yes, we've entered the casing into the national ATF database. It'll only be useful if a casing from the same gun was used in another crime. Most shootings with rifles are AK rip-offs or .223s. The local drug dealer doesn't have a .308 lying around."

"And no one ever collected an empty casing from any of the scenes we could use for comparison?"

"There were none."

Wu looked annoyed, like someone had dropped the ball. "And this is not a caliber Officer Trilling has fired in the normal course of his job for at least seven months, is that correct?"

I nodded. Then I started to say, "He's a good —"

Wu held up his hand to cut me off. "I don't deal in good or bad. Can Officer Trilling shoot a rifle well?"

"Yes."

"Are you judging that from range scores on his training sheets?"

"No. He showed me at a range in West Point." I told him the story.

Wu said, "You went on a tourist trip to West Point during work hours? Why would you waste time like that during a serial killer investigation?"

"I wanted to see what went into setting up a long-distance shot. Trilling knew someone at the academy. We had access to a convenient long-distance range. I didn't consider it a waste of time. I consider talking to *you* a waste of time."

Wu smiled. "That statement makes me question your judgment about what is, or is not, pertinent to this investigation. Do we need to replace you with a competent detective?"

Harry Grissom stepped in at that point. "I make those decisions, Sergeant. Don't make threats to officers under my command. Not now and not in the future. Especially to a senior detective who's done more in the last year then you've done in your whole career."

All Wu said was "Duly noted, Lieutenant."

Dennis Wu made a few notes in a leather-bound pad. He

gathered his thoughts and basically acted like Harry and I weren't in the cramped office with him. Then he looked directly at me and said, "I'm going to need you in the interview for your knowledge of the sniper case. Will you be able to help or is this too personal?"

That stung a little bit. It sounded a lot like what I'd said to Trilling after Gus Querva was shot. Then I thought of Juliana. What was her relationship with Trilling? I looked at Wu and nodded. I didn't trust myself to speak.

Wu said, "Command staff wants this done today. No delays, no excuses. We're not NASA. We go on time." He looked at Harry.

Harry knew what the look meant and said, "I texted Trilling to come back to the office. He should be here any minute."

I was still standing by the door inside Harry's office. Wu sat in the spare chair. We just stared at each other for a moment. Then I gave the IA sergeant a little smile. There's nothing more insulting than a smile during a disrespect contest.

Harry didn't even know he was breaking up anything when he said, "Trilling just walked in."

Wu asked Harry if we could use his office for the interview.

Harry said, "I think I should be here."

Wu shook his head. "We might need you to take action if things go bad. It's best if you wait in the squad bay."

I thought it was best if Harry was in the other room to block inquiries from command staff. My stomach tightened when I saw Trilling walk toward Harry. Trilling was actually smiling for a change. That made it worse.

Harry said, "This is Sergeant Wu from Internal Affairs."

The smile dropped off Trilling's face. He looked over at me like a kid who'd just gotten dress shoes for Christmas. He suddenly realized that I really did suspect he was the sniper.

CHAPTER 63

I WATCHED ROB TRILLING'S every movement. It was the first time I'd seen him unnerved in any way. Who wouldn't be? Even a relative newcomer like Trilling had heard of Dennis Wu. He realized this was serious and didn't know what to do. I'd be in the same boat.

The Internal Affairs sergeant was polite and offered Trilling a hard wooden chair in front of the desk. Wu grabbed a plastic chair from just outside Harry's office and sat across from Trilling. That left me with the chair behind the desk. It was Wu's way of telling me I was only there to provide information, not to participate in the interview.

As soon as he closed the door, Wu turned to Trilling and said, "You have the right to remain silent."

Trilling stiffened in the chair and blurted out, "Am I under arrest?"

Wu didn't change his polite demeanor. He said, "No, you are not. I just like to be thorough and careful."

I knew that was bullshit. It was an old IA tactic to read Miranda rights at the beginning of an interview. Even if no one was in custody. It tended to scare people and knock them off balance.

When Wu was done reading the Miranda rights, Trilling said, "What's this about?"

Trilling looked at me, but Wu answered. "What do you *think* it's about?"

Trilling didn't say a word. I was used to the new partner's silence, but I wondered how Wu would react. He waited it out a lot longer than I thought he would. Finally Wu said, "The sniper investigation. I'd say you have some explaining to do."

Trilling turned again to face me. He still didn't say a word. His expression said it all.

After another stretch of silence, Dennis Wu said, "Officer Trilling, do you have an alibi for the night Gus Querva was shot? Or any of the shootings?" Wu only waited through a little silence before he added, "Just so we can be sure you're not the..." He paused for a moment. "What's the media call him? The Longshot Killer."

Trilling finally spoke. "Why don't you ask my partner? I told him where I was."

Wu looked down at his notes and said, "Yes, you said you were home asleep. A single guy alone in his apartment. That's a tough one to verify."

I saw a definite change in Trilling's demeanor. He was no longer uneasy. He was angry. He had a slight twitch in his left eye and a vein in his left temple pulsed. I leaned forward slightly in my chair to get my feet under me in case things turned crazy.

Trilling glared at Dennis Wu. My anxiety level started to

rise. I knew Trilling was remarkably quick and well trained. I let my hands drop to the arms of the chair, ready to jump.

Wu must have realized the changes as well. He shifted his tone completely. He took a friendlier approach and assured Trilling again he was not under arrest. Wu said, "I'm just trying to give you a chance to tell your side of the story. It's a good time to do it. No media, no crowds, just us."

Trilling spoke through gritted teeth. "I already told you my side. I was home asleep."

"So you expect us to believe that a dedicated guy like you, who's done nothing but serve his country and community, wasn't bothered by all the praise a guy like Gus Querva was getting from the media?"

Trilling sat stone-faced.

Dennis said, "Praise of a guy like that doesn't help the mission, does it? The mission is to serve and protect. What better way to protect than by eliminating a predator?"

Trilling started to answer. Then he stopped himself. He calmly said, "I need to speak to an attorney." His right hand dropped and rested behind him.

I tensed, worried that he was going for his pistol. When he moved his hand, I realized he had taken his pistol and holster off his belt. He stood up and tossed it onto Harry's desk. Then Trilling plucked the ID badge from his inside jacket pocket and pulled his police credentials from inside the jacket. They all hit the desk next to the pistol.

Trilling paused like he was waiting for someone to tell him he couldn't leave. When no one said anything, he turned on his heel and marched out of the office, through the squad bay, and out the door.

Dennis Wu looked at me and said, "I think that's all we need. He's good for the shootings."

I stared at the sergeant.

Wu ignored me. And continued. "As of this moment, Officer Trilling is suspended, is an official suspect in the sniper case, and you're going to make the charges stick."

"You can't be serious. All he did was ask for his attorney."

"He asked for an attorney because he had no more weak excuses. What are you upset about? You did a great job." Wu saw I wasn't happy with the situation. He said, "I had orders to convey to you that the brass wants this cleared up immediately. Command staff said you were the right guy to do the investigation quickly and efficiently."

"You can tell the brass that it's going to take a little while to clear this up. I've got a lot of background to do. No one wants to charge the wrong person with this crime."

Dennis Wu smiled. "You put together the homicide case, and I'll take care of the Internal Affairs aspects. But make no mistake, I'm going to tell command staff we have our man."

"And *I'm* going to conduct an unbiased homicide investigation."

The Internal Affairs sergeant said, "That's good. Use that line with the media after you arrest that redneck prick."

CHAPTER 64

I WASTED NO time after Dennis Wu's interview of Rob Trilling. I didn't sit at my desk and pout. I didn't try to convince myself that Trilling was guilty or innocent. I looked at what I knew so far and what I needed to find out. There was a mountain of information I had to decipher. And I needed to do it right away. The NYPD might be telling me to keep it quiet, but I knew how things worked: eventually someone was going to make a comment that got into the media. That meant I only had a limited amount of time.

I used a contact at the FBI to gain access to any reports Rob Trilling wrote while he was working on the task force. I didn't go through the ASAC, Robert Lincoln. I may have hinted to my contact that Lincoln had approved it, but I didn't have the energy or the time to put up with that condescending jerk right now. I explained it had to do with a performance evaluation.

So I was sequestered in a room on the first floor of the New York field office with a stack of reports on the table in front of me. If I wanted copies made of any reports, the FBI was going to make a log of what I copied. They even had someone sit in the room with me while I went through the reports. They didn't seem to trust anyone.

Trilling had been busy during his brief time at the FBI. He was out looking for fugitives every day, even on the weekend a couple of times. And it looked like he usually got who he was looking for. I saw the name Lou Pershing and remembered that he was an associate of the asshole William Hackford we'd arrested at the Bronx warehouse. The guy hadn't yet weaseled out of federal custody yet, mainly because of the amount of heroin found in the warehouse. Like Trilling had said, it was almost as if no one cared about the human trafficking violations, though Hackford had been charged with that as well.

I was looking through a surveillance report from a couple of months ago on a house in Queens. The resident at the house was the mother of a fugitive the FBI had been looking for. I saw the address and felt an icy shot through my system.

I quickly pulled out my phone and brought up a map program. The house he'd been surveilling was only two blocks away from the house of the sniper's first victim, Marie Ballard. It could be a coincidence, but it made me uneasy.

Now I raced through report after report, focusing mainly on the addresses. Trilling had been in Staten Island and Midtown Manhattan. Neither of the surveillances was that close to the shootings, but they did show Trilling had been in the area.

I took a deep breath and tried to figure this out. Of course, on a task force like this, he'd always be riding all over the city, looking for fugitives. But I kept going back to the address in Queens.

I tried again to get into the head of the shooter. I'd been trying since the case was first assigned to me. Why were these victims targeted? What was different about them? Was it completely random?

I had copies made of the most relevant reports. The young woman who was assigned to sit with me looked like she wouldn't care if I told her the case involved the kidnapping of the president. She just filled in the number of each report I had copied and had me sign the bottom of the log.

I needed to bounce a few things off Walter Jackson before he left for the day.

CHAPTER 65

WALTER WAITED FOR me at the office after I texted him. He liked coming in early so he could be home at a decent hour to spend time with his daughters. I know what it's like to fight for time with your family. I hated taking him away from that. But if ever there was a case that was important to me, it was this one.

As soon as I walked in the door, Walter said, "I don't need to be home early today. I already gave my wife a present."

I was confused but managed to ask, "What'd you give her?"

"A little model of Mount Everest." He paused, and when the smile came over his face, I realized what he was doing. "She asked me if it was to scale. I told her no, it's just to look at." His belly laugh lifted my spirits.

I grinned, then quickly got Walter up to speed. I said, "I can't believe the victims are just random choices. But looking at them, I can't find a pattern. It's driving me crazy."

Walter opened a folder on his computer. I could see it held newspaper and internet articles. Some had been scanned, so I could see the headlines. Others were just electronic files in small fonts.

Walter said, "You know I always keep every media report about a case someone on the squad is working. It helps me keep an open mind about cases. I find that occasionally reporters will see something or interview someone that we didn't. They may not know the significance of what they saw. Maybe you'd want to look through these files?"

"Have you seen anything that would be of interest?"

"I haven't had time to do anything but save the articles. But they're from a wide range of media. From straight-up newspaper reports, like the articles Lois Frang has been writing for the *Brooklyn Democrat,* to business journalism covering Adam Glossner's company. There's a lot in there right now."

I had Walter email the files to me so I could look through them.

Walter said, "By the headlines, the media is portraying each of the victims as a hero in their own right. A single mother, a firefighter, a family man, and a community activist."

"The question is, how accurate are those portrayals?"

"You know how the media can twist things to their own narrative. And no one likes to talk badly about crime victims or the dead. Hell, even if someone like O. J. Simpson died, some sports reporter would be talking about what a great running back he was and leave out the double murder and armed robbery. It's just a way to get readers interested." Walter added, "Look at Gus Querva. The media's about to anoint him a saint. But no one's talked about how he extorted businesses and is a suspect in four different homicides."

I thanked Walter for his information and for giving me the chance to just run ideas by him. He had a good head on his shoulders, and sometimes that's all you need to see something more clearly.

I had to find time to read Walter's media reports. That meant I'd have to steal some time away from my family. Just like most cops.

CHAPTER 66

I GOT HOME late and scrounged a few leftovers. The kids had already dispersed to do homework and other projects. Trent and Ricky tried to make it look like they were studying, but I knew they were on their phones playing a game together. I didn't have the time or energy to comment.

Mary Catherine knew I had a lot to do and gave me some space. I was looking down at my iPad, which was usually reserved for watching movies or following New York sports teams. Tonight I was using it to read the files Walter Jackson had emailed me.

I saw what he meant about no one wanting to say anything negative about the dead. Each of the victims was painted in the best possible light. The first victim, Marie Ballard, had worked at the Housing Authority for over twenty years. She also had raised two children by herself—Duane Ballard, the young man we spoke to the day Trilling and I went to the house, and his younger sister. As far as I could tell, she'd done a good job raising the kids.

The firefighter, Thomas Bannon, had coached Little League baseball on his days off.

The *New York Post* shared four different photographs of Adam Glossner with his wife and kids. Anyone would be moved by those family photos.

Most of the articles about Gus Querva were glowing. Only Lois Frang at the *Brooklyn Democrat* was brave enough to mention that Querva had done prison time for strong-arm robbery and had beaten his first wife so many times she fled and stayed at various women's shelters until she could move out of state.

The last thing I read was an older article from a financial journal. It talked about the company Glossner had run, Holbrook Financial. There was a photograph of Glossner at a conference table with six other professionals, but nothing about his family.

Mainly, the article talked about a fine the company had recently paid due to a complaint from the Securities and Exchange Commission. There wasn't much else I picked up from the article other than the attorney's name at the SEC: Chloe Lewis.

Then someone said, "Hey, Dad, can I talk to you?"

I looked up from my iPad to see Juliana standing next to me. "Of course. You can always talk to me." She slid onto the seat beside me. Her eyes looked a little bloodshot. "What's wrong, sweetheart?"

"Did you and Rob have a fight?"

"Why do you ask that?"

"I was texting with him, and his last message said he couldn't talk to me for now until you and him got something straight." She wiped her eyes with her finger. "Was it a fight about me?"

"No, sweetheart, it has nothing to do with you. But it could be a pretty big deal. Maybe try not to have any contact with Rob until we resolve it."

"Can you tell me what it's about?"

"I wish I could. But it has to do with work, and I'm not allowed to discuss it." That may have been the truth, but the look on my daughter's face made me feel like shit for saying it.

I didn't like how threads of this case were getting entwined in every part of my life. Maybe I'd get some clarity tomorrow. I try to keep my work and home lives separate. This whole situation with Trilling blurred that line.

I couldn't focus with the kids that night and slept in fits. All I kept thinking about was whether Rob Trilling could be the Longshot Killer.

CHAPTER 67

ROB TRILLING DIDN'T exactly wake up. He just sort of transitioned from lying in his bed, unable to fall asleep, to standing up and moving around. Even if he didn't have sleep issues, he wouldn't be able to get any rest now anyway. His whole world felt like it was crashing in around him.

He had no idea how seriously the NYPD was looking at him. His ex-partner, Michael Bennett, was probably working the case right now.

Trilling needed some friendly human contact. Some lively conversation. He wasn't going to find that in his apartment. At least not with his current roommates.

He got dressed quickly and slipped out the door. The cool early morning air invigorated him. The feeling wore off before he reached the sidewalk. Without even thinking about it, Trilling hopped on the subway. He was hoping to catch Darcy Farnan at the VA off-site counseling center in Midtown.

There were only five people on his train as it rolled toward 42nd Street. Sitting by himself in the back of a subway car wasn't any way to get his mind off his troubles.

Two men stepped onto the train at the next stop. They were both in their mid-twenties, trying to look cool. Light shirts in the cool weather to show they were tough. Maybe it would be okay on the subway, but the wind in the city would cut right through them. Trilling went back to feeling sorry for himself.

A few minutes into the ride, raised voices caught Trilling's attention. When he looked up from the rear of the car, he saw the two men without jackets were standing over a pudgy guy who'd been typing on his phone.

One of the men looked down and said, "Nice phone you got there."

The other man said, "Give it here. I wanna take a closer look at it."

The seated man was older, maybe forty, with wire-rimmed glasses and a heavy parka like he was in Wisconsin.

This was the shit that drove Trilling crazy. That bullies like this would just take things away from people because there was no one to stop them. A bullet in the head might stop them. Maybe a good thrashing on the subway would too.

Trilling sat up straight and watched the confrontation for a moment more. The man meekly handed his phone to one of the bullies. The bullies just turned and went back to their seats with it, satisfied with their effort.

Trilling stood up and held the overhead rail. He tested its strength to see if he could pull himself up and kick if he had to.

He realized it was a little theatrical and decided that his heart wasn't in the effort anyway.

He watched silently as the bullies got off at the next stop with the man's phone.

Three stops later, Trilling left the subway car. He didn't even give a look of concern to the man whose phone had been taken. Instead, as soon as he came up onto the street level, Trilling called Darcy Farnan at the VA. But he got no answer.

Trilling wasn't sure what he'd say to her anyway. That all he was trying to do was help the people of New York? That his meds and lack of sleep had caused too many problems for him, and he needed more serious therapy?

Maybe it was just as well Darcy didn't answer.

CHAPTER 68

I'D ALREADY BEEN to the office and was out running down leads when my cell phone rang. I was surprised to see that the caller was Lois Frang. I debated picking it up. I really had nothing I wanted to tell her about. But I also knew that she'd met Harry Grissom for breakfast once already this week. If I didn't answer, she might call Harry. I decided to make it a quick conversation.

"Hello, Lois. What can I do for you on this beautiful morning?"

"Wow. That's the best greeting I've ever got from someone at the NYPD."

"Part of our new directives. Spread sunshine, then worry about solving crimes."

"Between you and Harry Grissom, I'd say you guys are working overtime on the sunshine part."

"Was there something specific you needed today, Lois?"

"I'm trying to follow up on some rumors that I heard."

My stomach tightened. Had a rumor about Rob Trilling already slipped out of the NYPD? I didn't even want to think about that.

Lois said, "It's about the second victim in the Longshot Killer case. The fireman named Thomas Bannon. I thought about talking to his family, but I heard they're a closemouthed bunch. You know how the Irish Catholics can be."

"I know all too well."

"Do you know Bannon's family?"

"We've met." I flexed my hand, which had been sore since I'd punched one of the brothers who'd assaulted us at Louise Bannon's home. I added, "What's the rumor?"

"That Bannon was a pervert. That he'd been caught downloading child pornography on a FDNY computer."

"You're not going to run a story like that, are you? It doesn't do any good for anyone."

"I'm not sure where I'm going with it. But I was hoping you might verify the rumor."

"I've never heard anything about that." Even as I said it, I realized I wanted to check this rumor out. It might also explain why Bannon's in-laws and widow got so bent out of shape when I just asked a few simple questions.

Lois said, "I need to hear it verified from a reliable source. Any ideas who might talk?"

"I thought you and Harry Grissom had breakfast yesterday. He's a pretty reliable source."

"We had breakfast today too."

"Did he say anything about the case?"

"Zilch."

I chuckled. "He's a puzzle, that one."

"And I'll figure him out one day. But now I'm looking for someone to quote. Even anonymously."

"That doesn't sound like it's directly related to our case. You couldn't get Harry to comment?"

"As I understand it, you and Harry have been friends for twenty years. Have you ever known him to talk about a case or police work with someone other than another cop?"

"Good point. I rarely see Harry talk to anyone about anything. You should consider yourself privileged."

"He's a lovely man. But now I feel like you're trying to distract me."

"Not really. I've honestly never heard that rumor, and I'm up to my eyeballs with other things to worry about."

All I got was a quick thanks as she hung up.

If Thomas Bannon did download child pornography on a city computer, why was there no mention in any NYPD report? Just one more thing to add to my list.

CHAPTER 69

I HAD NEVER visited the offices of the Securities and Exchange Commission. There's not a huge call for it when working homicides. The first thing I noticed was that the SEC was not among the agencies in the Jacob K. Javits Federal Building just east of Broadway but in the American Express Tower just west of the 9/11 memorial.

This luxurious skyscraper was a far cry from the near-slum conditions of the VA off-site office. The lobby bustled with well-dressed professionals who might take clients to lunch in the array of restaurants on the second floor or show off the unobstructed western views of the Hudson. Not bad for a government office.

I took the elevator up to the fourth floor and easily found the SEC offices. I marveled at the art reproductions on the walls and realized this was one of the few government agencies that actually *brought in* money. The fines the SEC levied on hedge funds and banks who'd skirted the law were legendary.

The polite receptionist took my name and then led me down a hallway. I'd called ahead for an appointment and was surprised I could get in so quickly. The receptionist tapped lightly on a solid wooden door, then opened it for me.

I stepped into the wide office with a view to the north. A young woman behind a giant desk was on the phone but waved me into a chair. I took a moment to look around the office and saw the attorney's personal touches. A full-sized movie poster of Marvel's *Avengers: Endgame* dominated one wall; degrees from NYU, including a law degree, hung on the wall directly behind her.

As soon as she hung up the phone, the woman stood to shake my hand. "Chloe Lewis. Nice to meet you." She had a warm smile that put me at ease.

After we chatted for a few moments, Chloe Lewis said, "What, exactly, can I do for you, Detective?"

I explained that I was investigating the murder of Adam Glossner. I asked her about the article I'd read concerning his company paying huge fines.

The attorney shook her head. "I can't believe they let him get away with just paying fines. Not to speak ill of the dead, but Glossner personally raided several accounts, and if everything had gone right, no one would have ever caught him. He also hid interests in two different companies that he pushed to clients. I referred the case to the FBI. I assumed they'd go after him, not settle without even an indictment."

It was an old story. Not just with the FBI but with most law enforcement agencies. With limited resources and manpower, if a case could be resolved quickly, that was usually the route taken.

Chloe Lewis said, "I guess I just expected more from the FBI. They're nothing like how they're portrayed in movies and on

TV. They let Glossner write a few checks and that was it. I hope he developed an ulcer at the very least." She cringed, then looked at me and said, "I'm sorry. Is that wrong? I mean, with him being dead."

"Did you kill him?"

"No, of course not."

"Then I wouldn't worry about it." I liked her relieved giggle.

The attorney went through a few other issues on the case. I wasn't really listening toward the end. All I could think about was that two victims, Adam Glossner and Gus Querva, may have both had criminal backgrounds. And I needed to look into the rumor Lois Frang had brought up to me about the firefighter. It was the only thing I had at the moment.

CHAPTER 70

I TOOK A moment before I walked into the fire station on Staten Island. After my last encounter with the local firefighters, I wanted to think this through. Despite everything, I would've felt more comfortable if Trilling were with me. Having him around was sort of like having your own superhero walking the streets of New York. My pistol was on my right hip. To be on the safe side, I also had slipped a collapsible ASP baton into my front pocket and a slim container of pepper spray into my jacket pocket. I didn't think I'd have to use them. But I like to be prepared.

The fire station where Thomas Bannon had worked was not far from his family's house. I'd been in dozens of firehouses over the years, and truthfully, aside from a few structural differences, they all looked and felt about the same to me. Big cavernous buildings to hold the fire engines. Echoes from every corner. Millions of dollars in equipment stacked along the walls or in cabinets. And a few easygoing firefighters cooking or doing chores.

This station was no different. The first two firefighters I saw were engrossed in polishing some equipment. They looked up at me but soon returned to what might have been a power saw.

I continued into the administration area, where I found four firefighters sitting in comfortable chairs in a semicircle facing the captain, a tall, fit woman in her mid-forties who was leaning on a counter. It almost looked like they were holding an encounter group.

I waited at the rear of the room until the captain looked up and saw me. I was in an all-weather jacket with no visible police insignia. But the captain was sharp. She said, "Can I help you, Detective?"

I walked closer to the group, men and women in their twenties and thirties, including one man who had to be over six feet tall. All eyes were on me, and I felt a definite hostile vibe.

I had an idea how she knew I was a cop. In my most polite voice, I said, "I was wondering if I could talk with you in private, Captain."

"That's not necessary. We have an open-door policy in this station. Anything you say to me, I'll say to them. In fact, since we're all gathered here, this is the perfect place to talk."

She was a cool customer. Clearly the Bannons had talked about their scuffle with me and Trilling at the Bannon residence. I decided I had to plow ahead. If I went through official FDNY channels, it could take time. I was starting to feel like I had a real break in this case. I wasn't going to ruin my momentum.

I cleared my throat and said, "I'm—"

The captain cut me off. "We know who you are. We also know what you're doing here. Louise Bannon already told us about your run-in with her brothers. We also know the nasty rumors

that have been floating around about Thomas Bannon. Am I
pretty close to why you're here?"

All I could do was nod slowly.

The captain said, "But he's dead. So the rumors don't mean
anything and have nothing to do with why he was murdered.
What none of us can understand is why you're trying to smear
the reputation of a true hero, instead of trying to find the shit-
bird coward who shot him."

That comment was greeted with a round of nods and approval
from the other firefighters.

The captain looked at the giant man I had noticed as soon as I
stepped in the room. She said, "Russ, why don't you show the
detective out. And I'm telling you right now you don't have to
take any shit from him at all."

When the man stood up, I realized I had underestimated his
height. He was more like six foot eight, and probably weighed
three hundred pounds. The vast majority of it muscle. All the
other firefighters seemed satisfied with the way this situation was
being handled. It made sense. If this guy knocked the crap out of
me and I filed a complaint, no one else would be in trouble. If I
caused a scene here, not only would I have to deal with multiple
firefighters, after it was all over, but also they could get their story
straight and make it look like I was lying.

I went willingly with Russ. He didn't grab me by the arm or
shove me. He just pointed me through a side door, blocking my
path back to the open engine bay where I'd entered.

As soon as I stepped outside, I realized exactly what Russ had
planned for me. There was a little grassy area between the fire station
and a furniture store. No one would notice the empty patch unless
they walked around the building. That could be bad news for me.

I turned and faced Russ. All I could say was "You're big."

"I know." He showed a little satisfaction with that statement.

I said, "I don't want any trouble."

"No one ever does."

I said, "You know the old saying 'The bigger they are, the harder they fall'?"

"Yep. Just more fake news."

"I think it'd be better if you just sat down and avoided the fall altogether. Less chance of injury that way."

Russ said, "I'm going to enjoy knocking out a few of your teeth. Why would I sit down?"

"So you don't run into a wall or twist your ankle tripping over something when you can't see."

The giant man said, "What the hell are you talking about?"

That's when I casually pulled my left hand out of my jacket pocket. The can of pepper spray was easily concealed in my palm. I sprayed Russ in the face and stepped back. I'd expected a shout of agony, but the low register and volume were surprising. I watched the giant firefighter stumble around in the grass. I stepped forward, holding his arm as I kicked his feet out from under him.

I said, "Easy does it, big fella," as I eased him to the ground and left him whining and holding his eyes. I made sure he was safe in the grass. "Just sit here for a while and the stinging will go away."

He managed to speak through the sniffles. "Really? How long till it stops?"

"An hour. Maybe less."

Russ moaned as a long string of snot flooded from his nose.

I'll admit I had to keep from smiling as I hustled around the building to my car.

CHAPTER 71

AFTER MY ENCOUNTER session with the giant fire-fighter on Staten Island, I raced directly to One Police Plaza. Essentially, the firefighters had confirmed the rumors. There's no way they would have reacted like that if there wasn't some fire behind the smoke. Their crude attempt at scaring me off only pushed me to find out exactly what the hell was going on.

Once inside headquarters, I didn't make my usual rounds to say hello to my friends and check in with old partners. Instead, I went directly to a specific analyst who had helped me on cases a dozen times before. His name was Neil Placky, and he had one of those minds that could remember and interpret seemingly insignificant details. All good analysts have that same trait. But Neil had a University of Pennsylvania education to augment it. A fact that he worked into virtually every conversation.

As soon as I stepped into the main analytic room, several

heads turned to look at the door. Once they established that I wasn't anyone of note, everyone went back to work. Everyone except Neil. He stood up from his desk at the front of the room and waved me over.

We shook hands and caught up. But I'll admit I gave him the abbreviated version. Basically, "Everyone's fine." Then I laid out parts of the case I was working on. Mainly, the rumor FDNY firefighter Thomas Bannon had downloaded child pornography on a city computer.

I could tell by Neil's silence that there was meat to this rumor.

After a quiet moment, I gave Neil a hard look and said, "I can't tell you how important this is. Not only to a homicide investigation but for the NYPD as well."

Neil let out a long sigh. He said, "C'mon, Mike. Don't do this to me. I have very explicit instructions not to talk about this."

"I already know Bannon was downloading child pornography. That fact was confirmed by other means. I just want to understand, if everyone knew about it, why wasn't there an investigation? Could it lead to someone taking the law into their own hands?"

It looked like a light went on in Neil's eyes. He now understood exactly what I was asking and why. He said, "We never talked about this, right?"

"I was never even here."

"That's not gonna fly, because every analyst in this room just saw you walk in and talk to me. But we're just catching up. Two old friends. I remember when I was at Penn, I had an ethics class. Thank God I slept through most of it."

"You don't have to give me evidence, just tell me what happened so I understand."

"Okay. We did receive a complaint that Thomas Bannon had downloaded child pornography. Apparently, an administrator who was at the fire station observed it. To avoid a conflict of interest, the NYPD referred it to the FBI. All I know is there was some issue with the chain of custody of the evidence and they cut a quick deal for no prosecution if Bannon retired immediately. His paperwork was in when he was shot. That's all I know."

"While I have you in the right frame of mind, let me ask you about the first victim of the sniper. She worked for the Housing Authority."

Before I could say anything else, Neil asked, "Marie Ballard?"

I stared at my friend. Just by coming up with the answer without knowing the exact question told me everything I needed to know.

I said, "Were there allegations against her?"

"We got a referral from the Housing Authority inspector general. She'd used over a hundred thousand dollars in city money to pay personal expenses. This was over the course of at least nine years."

"And nobody caught it until recently?"

Neil just shrugged. "We referred that one to the FBI as well. That's how I knew her name so quickly. I heard that the mayor had called the FBI directly to keep it quiet. She was on a repayment plan to keep from going to trial." Neil was now speaking in a very low tone. Almost like we were in church. But he was smart enough to know he had pointed me in a new direction in the case. I'd finally found a link between all four victims. They had each committed crimes for which they weren't being prosecuted.

And Rob Trilling would have had access to all those reports while he was at the FBI.

CHAPTER 72

ROB TRILLING HAD to do something to get his mind off his worries. He didn't think it was right to go visit his family up in Putnam County. They shouldn't have to be around someone who felt as low as he did. He didn't even want to think what his negative vibes might do to his niece and nephew. He needed to get out and do something useful, maybe volunteer for a few hours. Usually food banks and soup kitchens posted when they needed people, but Trilling decided to help the community in another way.

He looked down at his phone. There was a text from Juliana Bennett, asking if he was okay. He messaged her back, saying, As good as can be expected. Hope to be able to talk to you about it soon. He didn't risk saying anything else. The last thing he wanted to do was hurt a young woman who'd been nothing but nice to him. Trilling didn't have any idea what her father was saying about him. It didn't matter. He intended to keep on doing the right thing.

He slipped out of the apartment with the idea to look for his fugitive, Lou Pershing. Trilling had searched internet forums having to do with mercenaries and off-the-grid nut jobs. Even if they called themselves "military consultants." Although there was a lot of extraneous crap on the internet, Trilling was able to find a few mentions of Pershing. A few new mentions of Marisol Alba had popped up too, a woman with a phone number that had been linked to Pershing when Trilling was still at the FBI. Intel had said she could be his current girlfriend and she lived in a rented brownstone apartment in Brooklyn. Maybe Pershing would be there too.

Trilling rode the F train into Brooklyn and got out at Carroll Street, then walked south toward the area called Red Hook. He liked not worrying about a car and where to park, though he didn't particularly care for walking. Not that he minded the exercise; it just felt boring to him. He found himself looking at the address about forty minutes after he got off the train.

There was a vacant house a few doors down and across the street. Trilling found a comfortable place on the porch to sit where no one could see him from the street and he could watch the house where he thought Lou Pershing might be living. He appreciated parents walking children home from school and joggers hustling along the sidewalks under the canopy of trees. Somehow this didn't feel like the kind of place a guy like Lou Pershing would live.

Not long after nightfall, Trilling noticed a single light in the upstairs of the house. The way it moved told him it was a flashlight. That looked like someone trying to keep a low profile.

Maybe Pershing and his girlfriend had turned off the electricity so people would think they'd moved away.

Having scouted the area, Trilling was able to walk unseen across the street and down to Pershing's building. He slipped into the building's entryway. It took only a little effort with his pocketknife to slide the single lock from the doorframe.

He creeped through the ground floor and made his way upstairs without making any noise. He paused at the top of the staircase near where he'd seen the light and lowered to a crouch to listen for sounds within the apartment. His plan was simple: grab Pershing and leave him tied up in front of the nearest precinct. He didn't care about getting credit for an arrest. He just wanted to get an asshole like Pershing off the street before he hurt anyone.

Trilling realized he was in the weeds on this one. But if he was already going insane, one more crazy act wouldn't mean much. He stood up and heard his knee pop. When he stepped around the corner, he froze.

The point of a knife pressed against his throat.

CHAPTER 73

IT WAS AFTER dark by the time I arrived at my apartment on the Upper West Side. I had been so busy all day that I'd lost track of life in general. I'd skipped lunch; I hadn't checked in at home like I usually do; I'd jumped from interview to interview. And as soon as I walked through the door, it all hit me at once. I thought I might collapse. But something wasn't right. Some vibe in the apartment felt off.

I stepped through the foyer and still didn't see anyone. I heard some movement in the living room, but no one had come to greet me. That was unusual. One of the big advantages of having ten kids is that there is always someone interested in meeting you at the door.

When I came through the dining room and into the living room, I had to stop and take in the scene. Mary Catherine sat on the couch, propped up on a mountain of pillows. Her feet rested on an ottoman. A TV table was positioned in front of her. All the kids—and I mean every one of them—turned and faced me, grinning like they were posing for a photograph.

I couldn't keep a smile from spreading over my face. "What's this all about?"

Chrissy stepped forward. "We decided it was International Mary Catherine Day. We want to show her how much we love her. And how happy we are about trying to have a baby."

I was speechless. A tear ran down Mary Catherine's left cheek. We really had raised these kids the right way.

I said, "Ricky, does this mean you're making something extra special for dinner?"

My son shook his head. Then he looked across at Chrissy and said, "Jane and I are the official servers. But Chrissy and Shawna are making dinner." The four of them broke off from the group and headed into the kitchen.

Bridget and Fiona took my hands and led me to the couch next to Mary Catherine. They set me up pretty much the same way. Only without the ottoman. They used a chair to put my feet up.

After a couple of minutes, Ricky and Jane walked out with plates. Each plate was covered by a bowl, and they made a show of revealing the meal to us: hot dogs on buns, with mustard, plus a handful of potato chips and a pickle.

Jane whispered to me, "Chrissy counts the pickle as your vegetable serving."

I said, "It looks delicious."

Chrissy came out of the kitchen still grinning and said, "They're even your favorite kind of hot dogs."

"Nathan's?"

Chrissy looked crestfallen. She said, "No, all-beef Ball Park franks."

"I love those too."

Then Shawna said, "We even have the perfect movie for everyone to watch. You don't have to move or anything."

Jane said, "We picked the movie through a democratic process."

Trent moaned, "A really long democratic process."

Jane gave her brother a dismissive look, then added, "We each listed five movies, then we picked three out of that whole group. We kept voting until we came up with *The Princess Bride*."

Mary Catherine beamed. "Brilliant."

It was exactly what I needed. It got me out of my head and only thinking about what was most important in life: my family.

CHAPTER 74

ROB TRILLING STOOD as still as possible. He was afraid to even swallow. He could feel the knife tip dig into the skin of his throat. The idea of his blood spilling onto the floor kept him from doing anything stupid. At least anything more stupid than breaking into a building to find a fugitive while he was suspended from the police force.

Trilling felt a slight tremor in the blade. Whoever held the knife was nervous too. He hoped they weren't nervous enough to make a mistake. In the dim light he couldn't tell who was standing against the wall with the knife to his throat.

Then a woman's voice said, "Who are you?" She had a slight accent.

"I'm Rob. Who are you?"

"What do you want here?"

Trilling decided he had nothing to lose. He said, "I'm looking for Lou Pershing."

"Why?"

He was going to say, *To arrest him,* but at the last moment said, "To turn him over to the authorities."

"You're a bounty hunter?"

"I guess." He felt the knife move away from his throat. Trilling sucked in a deep lungful of air. Then the flashlight turned on and he saw an attractive woman with long, dark hair that needed to be washed. She held a butcher knife with an eight-inch blade.

Trilling said, "Are you Marisol?"

She nodded.

"No power?"

"I have power, but I didn't want to risk Lou thinking I was home. He's been gone a few days, and I'm just trying to get out without him seeing me. I was going to go to Los Angeles, but I can't come up with the money."

When Marisol turned, Trilling noticed bruises around her neck and swelling around her left eye. He felt anger welling up inside him. How could men act like this?

Trilling made a split-second decision. "I know a place you can go where you'll be safe. Pack a small suitcase. Just the stuff you really need."

"I'm wearing everything I really need. Can you actually get me out of here?"

Forty-five minutes later, Trilling and Marisol stood in front of a women's center in Manhattan. Trilling had learned about the center while on patrol his first week with the NYPD.

He stayed with Marisol while she answered a few simple questions from the woman who ran the facility.

As he stood up to leave, Marisol gave him a hug. She whispered, "Thank you," into his ear.

The director said, "I wish every cop paid attention like you do, Officer Trilling. I'm glad you know to bring women here."

"One last thing," Trilling said to Marisol. "Do you by chance have a recent picture of him? The one I have is blurry, and I could really use a better one."

Marisol fumbled for her cell phone. It took her a minute. "I may have deleted them all." But then she stopped, turned her phone for Trilling to see finally a clear image of the man he was determined to find.

"Thanks." He left the center feeling like his head had cleared a little bit. He hoped to find Pershing soon. If for no other reason than to stop him from terrorizing his girlfriends.

252

CHAPTER 75

I WAS IN the office early again. Despite the great evening with my family, where Mary Catherine and I were pampered like a rich lady's French poodles, I still had an anchor in my stomach when I thought about Rob Trilling.

As usual, the only other person in the office was Walter Jackson. I gathered my notes and went in to talk to Walter, the walking computer whose ease in finding the smallest detail in a case matched his ability in coming up with puns.

I stood in Walter's doorway, waiting for him to stop focusing on the computer screen. He looked up and grinned. "When I heard someone else in the office, I knew it had to be you. Are you holding up okay?"

I shrugged and said, "I'm trying to treat this like any other case. Be thorough and fair. That's what they used to drill into us at the academy." I tried to get a glimpse of his computer screen to see what Walter had been focusing on. "What was that you were reading?"

"A story about glass coffins being all the rage, but I don't know. All I can say is: remains to be seen." He kept a neutral expression for almost five seconds, then his grin came back. That was also about the time his pun clicked in my brain. I smiled and nodded. It wasn't bad, but my mind was elsewhere.

Walter picked up that I wasn't in the mood to joke around. He turned in his chair to fully face me. He said, "Tell me what you found out so far."

I told him about the victims and their criminal pasts. I said, "It's not just the NYPD. The Securities and Exchange Commission also sent a referral to the FBI for Adam Glossner. That means whoever's getting the information is getting it from the FBI."

"And your boy Trilling had been working at the FBI since around the same time the sniper started shooting people." Walter paused and looked at me. "I like him personally too. None of the rest of you ever come up with puns for me. But I can't dismiss him as a suspect because of my personal feelings."

"Neither can I."

"Your theory is sound. He's got the skill, the opportunity, and possibly the motive. I didn't want to mention it, but he's wrapped a little tight. He could have a serious vigilante streak in him. Straight arrows like Trilling hate it when people beat the system. Maybe it pushed him over the edge. Call it whatever you like. PTSD, morally driven, or just plain crazy. Look at how pissed he was about the gang leader, Gus Querva, being treated like a saint. I think he's good for the shootings."

I said, "I know. It's a simple theory to follow. Rob Trilling took exception to people getting away with crimes. I've seen it before, but not to this extreme."

Walter said, "Why does a simple theory make you nervous?"

"Because it is so simple, someone from headquarters could run with it without any follow-up. I think we owe it to Trilling to take it a little more seriously."

"So, what do you do next? Wait for him to snap and maybe shoot a bunch of people at once?"

That made me stop. All I could think was *Holy shit, what if that really does happen?* The thought scared me to my bones.

I hung my head. "I guess I've got to go over to the FBI again. That could be messy."

"Or at least unpleasant. Who can you call over there? That ASAC who has it in for you?"

I shook my head. "I'm not sure. I used to call my friend Emily Parker. She always worked miracles." It hurt to even think about my dear friend.

Walter mumbled, "She was a smart woman. That was a big loss to us all."

Instead of answering, all I could do was nod. I sat there silently, considering my options. Then I had an idea. Possibly a really good idea.

I spun around and aimed for my desk as I thanked Walter. It was still too early in the morning to try this idea, but I knew what call I'd be making as soon as the clock struck eight.

CHAPTER 76

THE OFFICE WAS still mostly empty when I called Roberta Herring. Roberta and I had worked together in the Bronx decades ago, back when we were both rookie patrol officers. I tried to teach her patience and she tried to teach me to use my gut feeling more. The irony is that she left the NYPD and worked her way up the ladder with the Department of Justice Office of the Inspector General. It was about the only agency with any oversight over the FBI. It also forced Roberta to be patient with every case. Investigations into wrongdoing at the FBI were never undertaken lightly and always took far too long.

Roberta picked up on the second ring. I could almost feel the smile as she said, "Mike Bennett, calling me before 9 a.m. My guess is that you need help, or you miss me so badly you couldn't wait until I was a little more settled behind my nice cushy desk."

"Both." We laughed together for a moment. We weren't only

old friends; we were also *good* friends. We didn't need any pretext to call each other, and we didn't need excuses when we called to ask for help. Roberta had helped me through some of the most difficult times imaginable. Hell, Roberta had stood as godmother to my second youngest, Shawna. She had been just about the only choice. Often people just assume that because Shawna is Black, we chose a Black woman as her godmother. That never once played into our decision.

We quickly caught up with each other's lives since I'd last seen her in Washington, DC, where not long ago she'd helped me look into Emily Parker's murder. Then Roberta got right to the point. "What's this call really about, Mike?"

I held nothing back. I told her about the case, Rob Trilling, how even my family loved him. Every detail I could think of. I waited in silence. Maybe longer than I thought I should. Then I realized from the sound of keystrokes that she was looking at her computer. I heard a couple of um-hums and ah-ahs.

Roberta said, "I can see all these referrals you're talking about. None of them are restricted. None of the cases seem particularly high concept or unusual. We both know the city of New York experiences a great deal of fraud. We also know people from all walks of life download child pornography. I'd be surprised to find a serious hedge-fund manager who didn't bend the law."

"So you can find the cases that quickly on the computer?"

"And that means anyone in the New York field office could do the same."

I felt disappointment. I couldn't quite place it at first. But I now realized just how much I didn't want this theory to be possible. Trilling had gone off the rails. I couldn't ignore it. Walter's concern about Trilling snapping popped into my head.

Then Roberta said, "What I'm missing is the psychological makeup and assessment of...What's his name? Rob Trilling?"

"I gotta say, Roberta, he seemed like a really decent young man. I'm afraid Juliana has a little bit of a crush on him. On the flip side, I could see him having a self-righteous streak. He thinks things should be done a certain way. He believes in a mission for the police department. I can imagine him taking things too far. I just don't want it to be true."

"You say he's an Army vet."

"Yeah."

"Sniper?"

"No, a Ranger. From what I gather, a really good one."

"We can't eliminate this being a result of some form of PTSD."

"I've considered that. It doesn't change the fact that he needs to be stopped."

"Does he go to any kind of therapy or counseling?"

"Yeah, I spoke to his VA counselor. She's not all that worried about him."

"Of course she isn't. That's *our* job. And it's a much tougher job when a suspect is likable."

I thought about that, then said, "I guess that's where my doubts spring from."

"Have you started writing the arrest affidavit? That was what always made cases real for me. When I had to put the facts in order and hand it to someone who knew nothing about the people involved. They could read the facts and see that a crime had been committed."

"I've got a few more things to tie up. But I intend to start working on it this afternoon. I'm still piecing together information on the last shooting. The neighborhood activist with a criminal background, Gus Querva. Aside from being a public figure with a dark past, I don't see where the FBI was investigating him."

Roberta typed away for a moment more, then said, "I see it."

I started taking notes on another nail in Rob Trilling's coffin.

CHAPTER 77

I WAITED ON the phone while Roberta Herring checked and rechecked every file she could find connected to Gus Querva.

Then Roberta told me to hang on while she set down the phone. I could hear her on her office phone calling someone to confirm what she'd found on the computer. I had to smile when I heard her tone. Whoever she was talking to must've asked why she was interested. Roberta said, "I'm interested in everything the FBI does. It's my job. I'm not sure what you don't understand about that." There was a pause and then she said, "Thank you for your assistance."

Hearing Roberta Herring dress down someone like that, especially someone in the FBI, made me smile. She'd been a great partner when we worked together in the Bronx. She couldn't stand to see hungry stray dogs, so she always kept dog food in the patrol car. She'd take the dogs back to the precinct and hold them in a back room until she could find someone to adopt them. It worked well until a lieutenant looking for something stumbled upon the makeshift kennel. He would've let things slide, except he'd stepped in a big puddle of dog urine. After that, Roberta kept the dogs she found at a Department of Water facility at the edge of our precinct. One way or another, she always gets what she wants.

She came back on the line, apologized for the wait, and said, "There *was* an official investigation by the FBI into Gus Querva's activities. The New York office had a RICO investigation that included drug distribution, extortion, and murder. The case went on for almost a year until someone blabbed and two key witnesses were murdered. That incident, coupled with the high-profile charity work Querva had been doing, led the US Attorney to decide not to proceed with the case partly for public perception."

"Could Trilling have been able to see those reports?"

"The case was restricted while it was active, but it was closed about two months ago. He would've been able to see the reports. The FBI is weird because they protect the reports like gold but, like in any other agency, everyone talks. Someone must've let something slip. Looks like your boy Trilling cleaned up their mess."

"Roberta, don't make it sound like he's doing a public service."

"You telling me you don't get a little discouraged with the way the courts just spit people out? That's why every cop loved that old Charles Bronson movie series *Death Wish*. Charles Bronson got to do what we dream about doing: killing some of these thugs who prey on people."

"Except this isn't a movie and Rob Trilling isn't Charles Bronson. I'm worried about him as much as anything else. Now I have a definitive link between the four victims. Each had been in the FBI system. Maybe that was enough to throw Trilling over the edge."

Roberta said, "Keep me in the loop, and call me if you need any more help. I'm not sure the ASAC in New York, Robert Lincoln, would appreciate you poking around."

"I guarantee you Lincoln wouldn't appreciate me doing anything."

CHAPTER 78

ROB TRILLING HAD spent the day leaning against a light pole in front of the little dive bar where Lou Pershing was supposed to hang out. The one fugitive he wanted to catch was still out of reach. Hell, Trilling wasn't technically allowed to even *look* for Pershing right now. But he couldn't concentrate on other things knowing this asshole walked free. Technicalities wouldn't stop him from keeping the city safe. It's how he lived with himself.

In reality, Trilling was doing everything he could not to think about his own problems. The alternative to looking for a dangerous fugitive was to lie around his apartment and feel sorry for himself. That wasn't in his nature.

Trilling credited his grandfather with a lot of his attitude. Chet used to tell Trilling and his brother that no matter how low they felt physically, they could always still accomplish something.

So on the few occasions when Trilling was sick and had to stay home from school, his grandfather would make up simple assignments to occupy his mind. Rob would read the entire newspaper, every story, then answer his grandfather's questions. It didn't sound like much, but Trilling knew it helped build his memory and reading skills.

Every time he stopped thinking about Lou Pershing, even for a moment, a feeling of dread washed over him. Trilling felt like his career was already ruined. What would happen if they charged him with murder?

A couple of times he'd even considered the possibility of fleeing. He had options. He could work overseas as a mercenary. Not his first choice. He could go back to Montana and get lost in the wilderness. The idea of not seeing his family again depressed him. So here he was, doing the best he could.

Just then his phone rang. Trilling looked down and saw that it was Darcy Farnan from the VA. He answered it quickly.

Darcy said, "Rob, I saw you called yesterday. Is everything okay?"

"No. Not by a long shot."

"I'm on my lunch hour now, and it's the only free time I have all day. Are you anywhere near Midtown?"

Trilling glanced up at the dive bar's doors, making his decision instantly. "Yes, I'm in Midtown now."

Darcy hesitated, then said, "Rob, there's something I need to tell you."

Trilling didn't like how she'd said that. A quick flash of nerves ran through him. He said, "Why don't you wait till we see each other in person."

"That's probably for the best."

Trilling asked, "Where would you like to meet?" Then he glanced up and froze in place.

He couldn't believe what he was seeing. Lou Pershing, in the flesh, walking out of the bar. How had Trilling not noticed him go in?

Darcy was still talking when Trilling ended the call and stuffed his phone into his front pocket. He fell in behind Pershing, who didn't seem to have a care in the world.

Trilling hoped to change that very soon.

CHAPTER 79

I'D HOPED TO get a little more unofficial background on Rob Trilling's NYPD career so had put in a call to Yvette Morris, a respected patrol officer who'd worked with him in the Bronx. When I got a call back, she told me that she was in training at One Police Plaza today, so I agreed to meet her for coffee in lower Manhattan.

Yvette sat across from me at a tiny café off Church Street. She was in training clothes, which consisted of a T-shirt and 5.11 cargo pants, plus an oversized windbreaker, which covered anything that showed she was an officer with the NYPD. She was about thirty years old, with a soft voice and demeanor, which were incongruent with her hard-edged look of a veteran cop: fit, tall, and with her hair cropped close to her head for practical purposes. She literally inspired confidence.

After we chatted for a few minutes, Yvette said, "I can't imagine why Detective Michael Bennett wants to talk to me."

I said, "This conversation has to be completely confidential. It's about Rob Trilling." I noticed her smile immediately falter. I said, "What's wrong?"

"You're in Homicide still, not IA, right?"

"Yep. Trilling is temporarily assigned to my squad."

"I'm not sure what you want, Detective. Rob is a hard worker."

"I agree."

"Smart, compassionate to victims. He has real potential."

"I sense some hesitation." I noticed how she looked around the café and leaned slightly closer to me.

Yvette said, "He's quick to anger. I mean, he goes from zero to sixty in an instant."

"How so?"

"He won't get in trouble for this, will he?"

I said, "Believe me, any trouble Trilling gets in will be of his own doing."

Yvette took a moment to gather her thoughts. Then she said, "Rob hates to see people beat the system. We arrested a guy for dealing meth twice in one day. The perp got cut loose without any bond the first time. You'd have thought the guy killed the president by Rob's reaction. After we arrested him the second time, Rob walked the perp through booking and then showed up in court on his own time to tell the prosecutor not to release him again."

I nodded. That sounded like Rob Trilling.

Yvette said, "Another time, at a domestic, I saw how Rob hated bullies. The wife and baby were crying, but there were no outward signs of violence. The wife didn't want to press any charges. The husband didn't seem to care one way or the other. Rob led him out of the apartment and downstairs. Supposedly the guy tripped and fell the last flight. He never made a complaint, but it still worried me.

"And then there was a concerning incident of a foot chase of a robber who stole a woman's purse at knifepoint, then shoved the woman into the street, where a taxi nearly ran her over. Rob tackled him hard. Too hard. Broke the guy's jaw and hand in the fall. It made me nervous."

I said, "Did you report these incidents to anyone? This is no comment on you. I'm just curious."

"I didn't have anything solid. No one complained. And he only seemed to react this way to the worst suspects or the ones not facing any punishment. Rob's quirky that way."

I found myself nodding. I wasn't happy to hear anything she had to say. I was almost distraught. But it helped me make up my mind. For a moment I pictured Trilling in prison. The irony wasn't lost on me.

CHAPTER 80

TRILLING FOLLOWED PERSHING east on foot. He thought about calling someone or stopping the fugitive right now, but he wanted to see who Pershing talked to. With Pershing's partner, William Hackford, being held on federal drug and human trafficking charges, there was no telling who Pershing was working with now.

Trilling walked on for a few minutes, assessing his target. Pershing was a big man, over six foot two with broad shoulders. Watching him made Trilling angry, unable to stop thinking about the marks on Marisol's neck or the glass eye Pershing's former girlfriend now had to use.

Trilling had a vague memory of his father. It was really the only memory he had of the man. When Trilling was about four, his father slapped his mother. Hard. Then stormed out. He'd seen his father twice since that incident, but the only thing that had

stuck in his mind was the slap. He had no idea where his dad was
now. He'd heard rumors. A cowboy in Idaho. Shot by a jealous
husband in North Dakota. In jail in a couple of different places.
Trilling just assumed it was jail.

Pershing took a corner into a maze of alleys. They were really
more like walkways into different businesses. Then Trilling lost
him. The fugitive just seemed to vanish.

Trilling looked in every direction. Nothing. Then he started
jogging toward the river, which seemed the most likely path
Pershing would've taken. Trilling had only taken a few steps
when he saw a flash out of the corner of his eye. From around the
side of the building a garbage can lid glanced off his head. Trilling ducked and missed the full impact, but it still knocked him a
little woozy.

He stumbled back against the brick wall of a building. When
he looked up, Lou Pershing was standing in front of him with a
three-foot piece of rebar in his hand.

Pershing said, "Who are you?"

"No one."

Pershing let out a little laugh. "Don't sell yourself short, kid.
I'm tough to find. I'd say you look a little like a cop. Or you will
when you grow up." He looked up and down the alley. They
could've been in the Arctic for all the people they saw right now.
"Why are you following me?"

Trilling said, "You're a smart guy — you should be able to figure it out."

Pershing slapped the rusty piece of rebar into his left hand.
"I'm going to break both of your arms and both of your legs.
Teach a cocky bastard like you a lesson."

"I may be cocky, but I knew my dad. I didn't like him. He was a piece of shit who beat his wife, just like you. But at least I'm not a bastard." Trilling canted his body. He'd taken on larger men in his life.

Pershing swung the rebar. Trilling dodged it, then delivered an uppercut. It landed perfectly. Trilling felt a crunch as the punch to Pershing's jaw drove his teeth into his head. Blood spurted from Pershing's upper lip.

Pershing stumbled backward, swinging the rebar wildly. It brushed across Trilling's front, the rough end of the steel rebar tearing open his shirt and breaking the skin of his chest.

They both paused for a moment as each man warily watched the other. Trilling noticed Pershing was panting.

Pershing said, "Let's cut a deal."

Trilling wasn't about to negotiate with scum like this. He raised his left fist. When Pershing tried to block it, Trilling threw a front kick, catching Pershing in the gut.

Trilling heard the air rush out of Pershing and knew he had the advantage. He threw a second kick to almost the same spot.

The blow knocked the remaining air out of Pershing and made him drop the rebar. It clanged on the shoddy asphalt in the alley.

Trilling swung his right hand in a big arc, catching Pershing in the face again. The larger man stumbled back to the wall, but somehow he stayed upright.

Trilling unloaded with half a dozen more punches, until Pershing slid to the ground. He fell on top of Pershing, still throwing punches, then stopped mid-punch. What now? He felt like a dog who'd finally caught the car he'd been chasing. Trilling considered delivering the fugitive to the FBI. That wouldn't work. Too much explaining.

Then he came up with a plan. A plan he didn't like but that made sense.

He stepped away from Pershing. The fugitive was barely conscious, with blood from his nose and cut lips running down his face. Trilling reached for his phone. There was only one person to call.

CHAPTER 81

I WASN'T FAR from downtown when my phone rang with the piano solo from "Layla," the ringtone my kids had installed for me a while back. I was shocked to see Rob Trilling's name on the screen. I thought about not answering the call. I wouldn't take a call from a suspect in any other homicide investigation. I decided to risk it.

I kept it simple. "Hello."

"I'm in an alley. I need you to come here right now." Trilling gave me a couple of cross streets. Then there was silence on the line.

I said, "I'm a few minutes away. I'll be right there." I don't know why I agreed to meet him in person. But something told me it was important. Maybe he'd say or do something that would help me with the case.

Traffic wasn't overwhelming and it was all right turns. I

wondered if I should call Harry Grissom and let him know what was going on. He'd be worried I was talking to Trilling, but at least someone would know where I was. If there was a problem later, a dispute, at least I'd have a boss who knew what was going on. Then I thought about Trilling. The tone of his voice hadn't made me think it would be a trap, or that he was trying to trick me somehow.

I double-parked my Impala and gave a quick wave to an electronics store owner who shouted at me. I raced into the alley and realized it was actually a maze of alleys. I called out, "Rob, Rob!"

I heard him call back, "Over here."

I hustled toward the sound of his voice. I found Trilling sitting next to a big man who was bleeding from a couple of different spots. The man was conscious but not moving too much.

I stared at the scene, and when I didn't get an explanation, I said, "What's this?"

Trilling said, "I told you I'd been looking for the fugitive who was partners with the guy who shot at us in the Bronx."

"The guy who had the Pakistani women to help process heroin?"

Trilling gave me a little smile. "I guess you're not so old that your memory is going completely." He looked over at the man on the ground. "This jack-off is Lou Pershing. He's supposedly the brains of their operation. He's also wanted for heroin distribution and some weapons charges out of Boston."

I stared at the bloody man. Then at Trilling. This was not normal. The sick feeling grew in my stomach. I'd been so focused on trying to find a way to exonerate Trilling that I'd missed his real motivations. He had an intense hate for lawbreakers. By the looks of Pershing, we were lucky we didn't have another homicide on our hands.

Trilling said, "This is your collar now. You've got a major federal fugitive in custody."

"I can't just stroll into a precinct with this mope."

Trilling let out a laugh. "Like anyone in the NYPD is going to turn away the famous Michael Bennett. Or are you too busy trying to pin some more murders on me?"

"Rob, listen…"

Trilling didn't want to hear it. He just turned and walked away.

CHAPTER 82

I TURNED ROB TRILLING'S fugitive, Lou Pershing, over to a patrol sergeant I knew named Chris Zuelie. He was thrilled to claim the arrest. I was still uneasy about the whole event. Trilling was unpredictable, by my estimation. I had to write an affidavit on everything I'd learned about the sniper case, then see what happened from there.

My phone rang. It was Harry Grissom. I answered it, "Hey, what's up?"

Harry jumped right into it. "There's been another shooting."

"Shit." I said to Harry, "Give me the address and I'll head over there."

"No. Keep working on your affidavit and close out any leads you have. I'll supervise our own squad detectives on this and get you the important details."

I blurted out, "I saw Trilling a few hours ago."

"Doing what?"

I explained it all to Harry. When I was finished, Harry said, "That doesn't sound good." Harry had a gift for understatement.

"Do you know anything about the new shooting? Victim? Witnesses?"

Harry said the victim was named Scott Dozier. "He's a twenty-six-year-old white male who dropped out of Rutgers. He's got a couple of arrests at protests. One of those antifa folks. He tried to light a patrol car on fire with two cops inside."

"I remember that."

Harry said, "Yesterday, a judge gave him five years' probation. Today, the kid was shot outside his apartment on the Lower East Side."

"Shit." That did sound like something that would get under Trilling's skin.

Harry asked, "What's wrong?"

"That's where I saw Trilling."

I told Harry a few more details of what I'd found and what I was working on. My mind raced with the possibilities. I'd found a pattern among all five victims: each had committed crimes but wasn't being prosecuted. At least we now had a potential motive. Any homicide detective would be excited about that.

As I was about to hang up, Harry said, "One more thing."

"What's that?"

"Dennis Wu is already involved in the new shooting."

"Why?"

"He just showed up. I don't have control over Internal Affairs. Something tells me the guy wouldn't listen if someone told him *not* to get involved."

My phone beeped. I looked to see who was calling, then said

to Harry, "Wu is trying to reach me. I'll call you back in a little bit." I switched over to Wu's call. Before I could even speak, I heard Dennis Wu's voice say, "Bennett, have you heard about the latest shooting?"

"Harry was just filling me in."

"Why aren't you at the scene? What are you, on vacation?"

"I'm trying to finish the affidavit on Trilling. Isn't that what you and command staff want?"

Wu said, "I got something you can add to the affidavit."

"What's that?"

"I came straight to Trilling's apartment after I heard about the shooting. The fat Armenian super said he saw him leave early this morning and he hasn't been back since. Sounds like our boy is on the prowl."

"Could be." I didn't know what else to say. Trilling actually had been on the prowl. That's how he'd found Lou Pershing.

Wu said, "I'm gonna enjoy arresting this prick. Hurry up on that affidavit."

My mind pictured the buttoned-down IA sergeant trying to physically handle Rob Trilling. I doubted he and I together could do it.

CHAPTER 83

IT WAS EARLY afternoon by the time I stepped through the doors of the FBI office in Manhattan. This time, instead of talking to ASAC Robert Lincoln, I linked up with the personnel director, Francesca Scott. All I needed to do was look at Rob Trilling's time sheets, to see if he had been working during any of the sniper murders. I wanted to see if there was any pattern with his work hours as they related to the shootings. I had a warrant in hand, but the director greeted me cheerfully with a big smile and said if I reviewed the file with her I didn't need court orders.

Francesca Scott's office was well located—in terms of reducing my risk of running into someone I didn't want to talk to—on the main floor at the front of the building. We chatted as she led me down a short hallway.

She said, "You're kind of a celebrity, Detective Bennett. I've read your name in the papers a dozen times over the years. I didn't think you would do something as mundane as look at time sheets for an evaluation."

I said, "Rob Trilling is working in our unit. They just wanted me to see what kind of hours he was working over here. You know, the usual."

She had a charming laugh. "I've been the personnel director here for nine years. Everything is usual. I'm happy to get a chance to talk to someone from outside the office. My husband works for ConEd as a supervisor. My conversations with him aren't much more interesting than the conversations around here." She had a twinkle in her eyes that I appreciated.

At first, she wanted me to review the computer-generated time-sheet reports. I explained I needed to see the original, handwritten time sheets. I left out the part where I wanted original signatures because I might need them as evidence.

The personnel director turned her attention to her computer as I started to look through the file of Trilling's time sheets. I flipped through his initial paperwork and noticed that the time sheets were not in chronological order. Great. Luckily there weren't too many of them. Trilling had punctually turned them in every two weeks, and his supervisor at the FBI had signed them.

Then I found a leave request, for an entire week in September.

That made me recall a comment Trilling had made about being at a VA counseling retreat in September.

All I could do was stare at the slip for a moment. Thomas Bannon, the firefighter from Staten Island, had been shot in the middle of that week. This really did change things quite a bit. If Trilling had been out of town at a VA retreat, he couldn't have shot Thomas Bannon.

I had to move quickly. I didn't want to make it seem urgent to Francesca Scott. She'd been nothing but pleasant and helpful. I eased from my chair and asked if I could take a couple of the time sheets as well as the leave slip.

I was out the door as quickly as I could be without making it look urgent or obvious.

CHAPTER 84

I KEPT TABS on the latest shooting. No one had found any witnesses. Nothing to point to a new suspect. Great. It seemed to be typical for this sniper case. Dennis Wu's call had told me Rob Trilling was really in the NYPD's sights. That was no surprise. I couldn't waste any time. I had to verify that Trilling had been in Albany when Bannon was shot. I had to do it in person. And I had to do it right now. By this time tomorrow, Trilling could be at Rikers.

As I headed to my car, I called Walter Jackson.

Walter said, "I'm working on leads from the last shooting."

"Anything useful?"

"Zilch. You still running down other leads?"

I explained what I'd learned at the FBI. I said, "I have to be certain. I'm not sure how else to verify this newest lead from the FBI personnel office. If he was actually in Albany at that time, Trilling can't be the sniper."

Walter had a brilliant suggestion: he was going to expedite getting Trilling's credit-card records from the last three months. He'd already submitted a warrant, like he did on most homicides. It's amazing what credit-card records can confirm. I can't tell you how many cases I've made because I could refute alibis with credit-card receipts.

A few minutes later, I was still in my car when my phone rang again. It was Walter Jackson. His contact with Mastercard had been able to help him immediately.

I said, "I'm guessing you wouldn't have called me so quickly if you didn't find something in the credit-card records."

"That's why you're a detective. You're correct. I have a credit-card receipt from a Holiday Inn in Albany. I'm going to text you all the information, as well as the PDF of the receipt. It looks like Trilling was at the hotel for five days. Thomas Bannon's shooting occurred on the second day of Trilling's stay."

My heart started to beat faster. "I told Harry I was working on the last details of the affidavit. Tell him I'm on a decent lead and will fill him in later. Call me if anything else happens."

"You're not driving to Albany right now, are you?"

"I'm headed into the Lincoln Tunnel as we speak. I hope to be on I-87, headed north, not too long from now."

I felt another pang of guilt for not being at the shooting scene. It's tough to ignore when you're a homicide detective. Like a chef using Hamburger Helper, it just didn't seem right. But clarifying this issue about Trilling couldn't wait. I had to prioritize my anxieties.

I couldn't help pushing my Chevy Impala a little harder once I hit the interstate. I wasn't used to open roads or being able to drive fast in a car. Manhattan is far from Utah's Bonneville Speedway.

I called Mary Catherine to let her know that I wouldn't be home until very late. I didn't go into details. I wasn't even sure what the details were yet. I just knew that I couldn't let this lead wait another day.

I rolled into Albany just about two and a half hours after I'd entered the Lincoln Tunnel. I hoped someone at the hotel could help me even though I hadn't bothered to get a warrant.

The next few minutes could mean a lot to this case as well as to Rob Trilling.

CHAPTER 85

AS I ROLLED up to the address Walter Jackson had given me for the hotel, I realized it was not a Holiday Inn. It was, in fact, called Holliday's Tavern and Inn. It was a fair bit shabbier than most Holiday Inns. It had two long rows of rooms that stretched off the road with the center part of the property holding a restaurant and conference rooms. The dark-green paint looked like someone had slapped it on in the mid-1980s and hadn't touched it up since. The make of cars in the parking lot told me the hotel's biggest attraction was its relatively low rates.

I parked next to a beat-up Ford F-150 pickup truck. As soon as I stepped into the lobby, I could smell a musty odor that would make me worry the place was infested with mold. But I wasn't here to give a review. I was just hoping someone would give me information without needing a warrant. Clearly I had raced out of the city without worrying about legal documents or roadblocks to the investigation. All I could think about was Rob Trilling.

I paused at the empty front desk, avoiding hitting the bell on the counter. I didn't want to annoy anyone I was about to ask for help.

Three men in their mid-thirties stood in the small lobby, not far from reception. I wondered if they were military; all three were in good shape, two of them well over six feet tall, and the shorter one had a Marines emblem tattooed on his forearm. We nodded a silent greeting to one another as I looked around the lobby. After waiting for a little longer at the desk, I called out, "Hello," to the open door behind the counter.

Fifteen seconds later, an older woman shuffled out of the office until she stood behind the desk. She had long, wild gray hair and glasses hanging from a beaded strap around her neck. She looked down at a folder in her hand and didn't even notice me.

I cleared my throat.

The woman looked up at me, startled. "You must be some kind of ninja. I didn't even see you there." She glanced over the desk to see if I had any luggage.

I said, "My name is Michael Bennett. I'm a detective with the NYPD."

The three men nearby all looked over at me as the woman reached a hand across the counter. As we shook, she said, "Margaret Holliday, with two *l*'s. My friends call me Maggie."

I smiled. "That explains the sign."

"I've had a couple of cease-and-desist letters from a hotel chain I won't name. The only thing I ever conceded to was adding 'Tavern' to our title. Other than that, I've run this place for thirty-two years. And I always support the police. I don't think people realize how dangerous your job is. What can I do for a detective from the big city?"

"I was wondering about a veterans' group that met here not long ago. Do you remember that at all?"

"Of course I do. Obviously I support the military too. The VA has encounter groups here at least once a month. I have the perfect conference room for them. Our rates are cheap, and they work around our busy times. Like I said, what can I do for you?"

"Could I look at your registration log?" I slipped her a piece of paper with the exact dates and Rob Trilling's name.

She read the note and said, "I know Rob Trilling. He's here every few months."

Maggie started to type on the computer sitting on the counter. After a moment, she looked up and said, "Got it right here. He was here for four nights and then we let the VA guys stay through the whole day for free—that way they complete a five-day course of some kind and don't have to pay as much."

"Any chance I could see the original registration card with a signature on it?"

That made her pause. "What kind of detective are you?"

"A tired one."

"I like a good sense of humor. Now give me the straight answer."

"Homicide."

The tallest of the three men said, "Hang on, Maggie."

The hairs on the back of my neck tingled. I suddenly had a feeling that I was in for a repeat of my firefighter interviews. I couldn't understand why people wouldn't mind their own business.

The man looked at me and said, "You got a warrant?"

"I'm sorry, who are you?"

"David Klatt. I'm here with the VA and we all know Rob Trilling."

Now I purposely took a step away from the front desk and turned to face the three men fully.

The other tall man in the group said, "Why are you looking at Rob's work here? He does a great job."

"I'm not looking at anything to do with the VA." I tried to stay calm as the men circled me. Each one of them looked like they knew how to fight.

Maggie, the clerk, hadn't left the front desk. She stared at the four of us, no one saying a word.

I said, "Guys, if you're gonna kick my ass, let's take it outside." I needed to buy some time to think. I had a hard time reading the expressions on the three men's faces.

Finally Klatt said, "Kick your ass? Why would we do that? I'm an attorney. I asked about a warrant."

The other tall man said, "I'm an accountant. I haven't been in a fight since basic training."

I looked at the shorter Marine.

He smiled. "I'm an unemployed house painter. I'll kick your ass if you want, but I'm mostly looking to get my faulty key replaced by Maggie."

I turned to Maggie at the front desk. "You confirmed Rob Trilling was here at the time in question. If you could do me a favor and hold the signature card, I'll get a warrant and come back later."

She gave me a cheerful smile. "Sure thing, Detective."

I nodded to the three men. I had to get back to Manhattan and figure things out.

CHAPTER 86

I GOT HOME from Albany late that evening and my effort to be engaged with the kids quickly fell flat.

My mind was racing with the hope that Rob Trilling was not our sniper. But the newest shooting still made me doubt my findings. I'd heard that when Dennis Wu found Trilling at his apartment building hours later, Trilling had refused to speak to the Internal Affairs sergeant. I didn't blame him. From his perspective, there was no upside. Dennis made no secret of the fact that he was trying to pin everything on Rob Trilling. It was still a bad look for Trilling, because without any other suspects, all the attention was focused on my former partner.

The kids and Mary Catherine realized I'd had a long day when I dozed off in the chair in the living room.

I sprang awake the next morning and tried to make amends by preparing a giant breakfast. No one would be at the VA until nine o'clock anyway. I pulled out all the stops. Pancakes, eggs, bacon, and ham. Plus a whole wheat English muffin for Mary Catherine and a bowl of Lucky Charms for Chrissy.

It didn't take long for all the kids to start wandering out to the dining room. Nothing I couldn't handle. Their plates were already made. I realized if the whole homicide investigation thing didn't work out, I might have a second career as a short-order cook.

A few hours later, I was waiting at the VA office when Darcy Farnan walked in. She did a double take when she saw me in the lobby. She turned to a young man with long, stringy hair walking with her and said, "Can you give me a few minutes with this man, Peter?"

The young man nodded, then turned back to his phone. Darcy gave me a quick nod with her head to get me to hustle into the office. As soon as the door was closed behind us, she said, "Please don't tell me anything has happened to Rob Trilling."

"No, it might be just the opposite. I need to confirm something with you."

"I'm sorry, but the same conditions apply as before. He has to give me permission to talk to you. I almost told him you'd been here, but he never met with me after we spoke."

"I get it. I'm not trying to get you to violate any rules or ethics. But I think I can help him. And I already have a lot of the information I need." I gave her the briefest of thumbnails of what I was doing. I explained that Trilling was a suspect in some murders but that I'd gone to Albany, and it looked like he might've been out of town during one of the murders.

Darcy smiled for just a moment. She brushed some hair out of her eyes. "Like I said, Detective, I'd need Rob's permission to confirm that he was at a VA retreat in Albany as both a facilitator and a participant. He would tell you that he was at the hotel the entire time with me and nine other veterans. He would probably also tell you that I saw him every single day." She couldn't hide the smile.

I said, "At some point, probably fairly soon, after Trilling gives you permission, I'll have to ask you about this again."

"After I get his permission, I'll tell you anything you want to know about the week. Even the side trip he and I took to visit his family in Putnam County. I mean, if we really did that." This time she gave me a wink.

CHAPTER 87

I WANTED TO see if there was some way to confirm that Rob Trilling was at his apartment on the night Gus Querva was shot. Things were moving quickly now, and I decided to forgo the surreptitious route and talk to Trilling directly. I had a few more questions to ask him.

I drove directly to Trilling's apartment. The small, older building was just as I remembered from my previous visit. I didn't buzz him. I knew the apartment number and was able to enter the building when another tenant came out. I walked inside and up to the second floor. The stairway's banister was missing six spindles and its carpet was clean but fraying down the center—in need of enough repair that the building was obviously not run by a corporation. I checked apartment doors until I found Trilling's and knocked. I could hear someone moving around behind the wooden door. Maybe more than one person. I hadn't pried much into Trilling's personal life, but I sort of assumed he didn't have a girlfriend. At least that's the impression I'd gotten from my daughter Juliana.

I waited about fifteen seconds, then knocked again. I called out, "Rob, it's Mike Bennett. I gotta talk to you for just a minute." I heard some more rustling in the apartment. Now it sounded like there were half a dozen people in there.

The door opened about two inches, and three separate safety chains caught it. I took a step to the side to look into the apartment. All I saw was a veil of long brown hair.

Without thinking, I called out, "Juliana?" I couldn't see her face. She moved away from the door quickly. I took a step back from the door. Maybe, somewhere in the back of my head, I was considering kicking the door in. You never know how you'll react if you think your child is in some sort of dangerous situation. This time I called out a little more forcefully, "Juliana!" I really couldn't tell if it was my daughter inside or not. But no one was speaking to me, and I was starting to get nervous. I rechecked the number on the door to make sure it was the right apartment. There was no mistake. This was Rob Trilling's place.

This time I called out, "Rob, are you in there?"

The brown hair appeared at the door again. This time I could see a little of the young woman's face. It wasn't Juliana. She said, "Rob not here." Her accent was thick, but I could understand her.

"When will he be back?"

"I say Rob not here." Her voice had risen in volume. I couldn't tell if she was angry or frustrated that I wasn't listening to her.

I said, "Look, I really need to talk to Rob."

There was a long silence. I reached for the door and grabbed its edge so she couldn't close it easily. Then I felt a sharp pain shoot through my hand. I jerked it away from the door. I had a gash across my index and middle fingers. Blood started to seep between my fingers and down the back of my hand.

I mumbled, "What the…"

A four-inch blade popped out of the opening in the door. The hand tightly gripped the knife, pointing it right in front of my face. I could see her knuckles turn white from the pressure.

This time, speaking slowly and concentrating on each word, the woman said, "I say Rob not here. Go away. Go away right now."

"I'm Mike Ben…"

The door slammed shut and the dead bolt twisted into position.

I went outside, wiping the blood from my hand with a paper bag I'd found in the hall. It didn't look like the wound needed stitches. But I didn't intend to put my hand on that door again.

As I walked toward my car, a heavyset man with the thickest mustache I'd ever seen looked over at me. He was cleaning out some buckets with a hose. I guessed he was the super Wu had spoken to. I went over to talk to him, and he confirmed that he'd run the building for nearly sixteen years.

I explained that I was Trilling's partner at the NYPD.

"I love having a cop in the building. Especially one like Rob. Very levelheaded, that one."

I didn't need Dennis Wu to tell me the super's nationality. I could tell by the super's accent he was Armenian. He could've been a commercial for hardworking Armenians in the US. He probably wore size 45 work pants to fit his belly. But he was friendly, and I decided to not waste the opportunity to talk to him. I said, "The girl in his apartment didn't sound like she spoke much English."

"She has not been there long. I've never spoken to her. I seen her walk out one day and that was it. They're a little loud now and then. Sounds like a soccer team from the apartment underneath. But I said something, and Rob told me they would try to keep it down."

I looked up and noticed several cameras around the building. "Looks like you have a pretty good security system."

The super smiled. He had a gold crown on one tooth. "No one can come or go without my system recording it. Haven't had anything stolen in three years. That's got to be some kind of record here in New York."

It didn't take any effort at all to convince him to show me his security system. The system was everything the super had said. Four cameras on the building periphery, two cameras in the lobby, and one in each hallway and stairwell. Very impressive.

I said, "Can I test it out?"

"What do you mean?"

"Let me pick a day and I'll count how many times I see Trilling."

The super was intrigued to have a law enforcement professional evaluate his system. He took a moment to show me how it worked on a simple Windows operating system.

Of course, I immediately went to the night Gus Querva was shot. The super stood over my shoulder.

I scrolled through the video taken by the cameras in the lobby until I saw Trilling enter.

The super pointed and said, "There, there — you see him?"

I nodded. The time stamp said 6:05 p.m. He would've just been coming from the office. Then I fast-forwarded through the lobby cameras. And I kept fast-forwarding, looking to see when he appeared again. I didn't see him until 7:05 the next morning.

The super said, "You can't really tell much from that."

"Let me see if I can find him on the other cameras." And that's what I did. I raced through the cameras in the stairwell and in the hallway by Trilling's apartment. He never came out of his apartment.

I turned to the super and said, "How long do you keep these videos?"

"All saved on the cloud. They always keep them for at least one year."

I convinced him to let me burn a copy of the single day onto a DVD. I explained that it could be a good training tool about what to look for on surveillance videos.

The super slapped me on the back as I was leaving. He said, "You seem like you would be a good partner to Rob. He's a good boy. I worry about the way people treat police. I worry about Rob."

All I could say was "I worry about him too."

CHAPTER 88

IT WAS STILL midmorning when I left Trilling's apartment. The phone rang and I saw it was Harry Grissom. I didn't know what bad news was waiting for me, so I hesitated to answer. That's a terrible place for your mind to be, especially if you're a cop working on a major case.

Harry didn't even bother with the greeting. All he said was "I just got an official notice of suspension on Trilling."

"Shit. I guess it means they intend to go after Trilling hard."

"It says that personnel interviewed him yesterday. Did the admin and read him his work rights. That sort of shit."

"What time yesterday? I was with him in the morning and Wu couldn't find him later."

There was a pause and I knew Harry was studying the document on his computer screen. Finally Harry said, "Looks like it started at 10:15, until 11:05."

"What time did the antifa guy get shot?"

"God damn, I must be getting old. Shooting happened at 10:50. Get over to personnel and figure this out."

"On my way."

It felt like only a few minutes later I was walking through the doors of the NYPD personnel department at One Police Plaza. I heard someone call from the other room and found Sharone Baxter-Tate sitting behind a wide, cluttered desk.

She had a brilliant smile and ushered me to the seat in front of her desk. I explained that I wanted to talk to her about Rob Trilling.

"Seems like a nice young man. Sorry to see he was suspended. I never see the reason. I just have to inform them of their rights and what they can and can't do while suspended. I'm guessing he had some kind of a personal issue. Maybe he drank too much?"

"No, nothing like that."

"Moonlighting without permission?"

"Nope." I really hadn't come here to answer her questions. Before she could ask another, I said, "I just want to verify when Trilling was here and how you keep track of the time when you're interviewing someone."

Sharone said, "I talked to him in the morning."

"Can you be more specific?"

She reached into her desk and pulled out a worker's rights form. "See, there is a space for the start and ending times of the interviews. I look at that clock right behind you and write down whatever it says. Yesterday I started the interview with Officer Trilling at exactly 10:15 and ended at 11:05. I didn't round up or round down. He was right on time for his meeting, and I noticed we finished our chat at 11:05."

I checked the digital clock on the wall against the time on my phone. They matched. I looked at Sharone and said, "And you were here with him the entire time?"

"I'm required to read the documents aloud so no one can claim they didn't understand what was going on. It almost always takes forty-five to fifty minutes."

I was already up and out of my chair, heading for the door, as I thanked Sharone Baxter-Tate. "I'll get back to you and explain everything one day soon. Please keep all that original paperwork secure."

I didn't hear her response as I hustled out the door.

CHAPTER 89

I'D GATHERED A fair amount of evidence that pointed to Rob Trilling *not* being the Longshot Killer. I still wasn't sure what to do with the information. In the back of my mind, I was worried command staff might relieve me and put someone else in to investigate the sniper. They would have a fair argument. I had now prioritized actively looking to exonerate Rob Trilling over the rest of the case. That's not exactly what homicide detectives do.

Walter Jackson called me while I was still at One Police Plaza. "The report on the casing found in Trilling's car came in and I'm emailing it to you now."

I opened the email on my phone and quickly read the report while Walter was still on the line. The report said there was no usable DNA or fingerprints on the casing. Not even a partial print.

"Who wipes a bullet down before they put it in a rifle?" I

thought about it and said to Walter, "Unless the casing was planted." I paused, trying to wrap my head around the possibility that someone might have tried to frame Rob Trilling for the sniper murders.

Walter asked, "Who would do something like that? *Why* would they do it?"

"Good questions. I have no answers." The frustrating part was that I knew I had all the information in my head to figure this out. I just needed to organize it and then worry about articulating it.

I thought about it for a few moments, then said, "One key question for me is, where did someone plant the empty casing in Trilling's car? It would've had to be in the FBI parking lot or possibly even the NYPD parking lot near One Police Plaza. If we could figure out where it happened, it might lead us to the more important question of *who* planted the casing." I added, "Maybe someone was trying to take the heat off themselves. That means we might have to consider another suspect who works in law enforcement."

"That means your original theory could still be true. The killer could be a straight arrow who doesn't like the fact that criminals are not being punished."

"And it has to be someone with access to police files and the inner workings of a criminal investigation."

Then it hit me. How could I have been so focused on one suspect? There was another suspect. Another sniper. Also a cop. I recalled speaking with the former NYPD sniper now on desk duty: Joe Tavarez.

CHAPTER 90

I DIDN'T SHARE my epiphany with Walter Jackson on the phone. I trusted Walter completely. But I didn't want to put him in an awkward position. If I ended up accusing a different person after first suggesting it was Rob Trilling, the fallout could be harsh. Especially if I was wrong. Command staff could move me to some distant precinct to write traffic tickets until I retired. I didn't want Walter to catch any of the blowback, so I didn't tell him what I was doing.

This was going to be a difficult concept to sell. After accusing one cop, I was now saying I was wrong. And I would be accusing a different cop. But I wasn't sure if there was any alternative.

In fact, if I wasn't careful, I could end up ruining the reputations of three different cops on this case: Rob Trilling, Joe Tavarez, and me. I slipped back into personnel to speak with Sharone Baxter-Tate again. It took me about five minutes to verify that Joe

Tavarez had been off duty during each of the five sniper murders. That in itself didn't mean anything. And I recalled talking to his wife, Cindy, some days ago, to verify his alibi for one of the nights in question. She had backed him up, with details about what they'd had for dinner too.

Then I texted Sergeant Jeff Mabus, the ESU supervisor I'd talked to about Trilling. He was on his way to One Police Plaza and agreed to meet me in the back parking lot at the exact same spot where we had spoken last time.

Today, Mabus was dressed more like an NYPD officer. He wore a blue, long-sleeved T-shirt with an NYPD insignia on the chest. He still looked impressive physically.

We both leaned against an unmarked Chevy Tahoe the ESU team used to move around the city unnoticed.

After a quick greeting, I wasted no time. "How well do you know Joe Tavarez?"

"I know him pretty well since we were on the team together for about three years. Very stable and reasonable guy. Why? Are you going to pile on him like everyone else? He saved a young woman's life by making an incredibly difficult shot and hitting an armed man before the perp could kill the victim. Now he's being punished, rotting away as some kind of analyst for doing the right thing—exactly what he was supposed to do as a sniper on the special-ops team."

"I'm not disputing that. I'm just trying to piece together some information. What kind of rifle did he use when he made the shot?"

Now Mabus gave me an odd look. "It was a Remington 700, the SPS Tactical. Why?"

"Because I am trying to figure a few things out, and you're the guy with the knowledge to help me. Was Tavarez angry he was relieved of active duty?"

Mabus considered this question. Finally he said, "Who wouldn't be? You train for one job, do it right, and still get crucified for it. And it's not just Tavarez. Any police sniper who takes a shot is treated about the same way."

I wasn't sure what to say. Now wasn't the time to get into political discussions, and Mabus had a point. "Can police snipers do anything to change that policy?"

Mabus shrugged. "You know the saying: There are two things cops hate. The way things have always been done, and change."

It was an old saying but absolutely true. I made a few more notes, then asked a question I knew the answer to. "What caliber does that Remington 700 take?"

"Either .300 or .308."

That last one matched the casing found in Trilling's FBI car.

CHAPTER 91

HARRY GRISSOM WAS meeting with another homicide detective when I got back to the office. I wanted to burst in and start telling him everything I'd figured out, but I restrained myself. I went back to my desk and started looking again through all the reports, trying to find something I had missed. Key during a good investigation is keeping an open mind. It's a lesson I had to relearn almost every time I started to look at a mysterious death.

As soon as Harry was free, I burst into his office. I laid out exactly what had happened and who I had talked to.

Harry considered everything as he stroked his long gunfighter's mustache. Then he looked up at me and said, "Joe Tavarez could've had access to FBI investigations through his wife. That would explain Adam Glossner and Gus Querva, who were not under investigation by the NYPD."

"So you don't think I'm crazy?"

"That remains to be seen. But you've laid out a logical argument on this investigation. Even with Tavarez's wife alibiing him for that one night. Was she just protecting him? As a responsible supervisor, I can't ignore it all. These findings are going to throw Dennis Wu into a tizzy."

Harry gave me a little smile. I wasn't sure if it was because he liked the idea of aggravating the Internal Affairs sergeant or his use of the word "tizzy."

Harry said, "How do we make the case on Tavarez? He's got to be pretty smart the way he threw the blame onto Trilling. And his wife could be actively helping him in his crusade. We have no physical evidence or witnesses. We don't even have anything that can put Tavarez in the area of the shootings."

"I can try and get all of that through interviews and investigation. It might take some time."

"I don't see command staff giving us much time. They won't railroad Trilling on the killings if we convince them Tavarez is our man, but they won't want to wait either."

I said, "What if we set a trap?"

"What kind of trap?"

"I'm not sure. I just thought of it this second. But I think we'd need Trilling to help us with this trap. It makes sense to use a sniper to catch a sniper."

"What if it's not Tavarez?"

"If we set up a trap right, it won't matter. He just won't show up. No one is hurt and we can decide where to go from there. Do you think you can get Trilling back on duty?"

Harry was already picking up the phone. I knew that meant yes.

I had a new list of priorities. After getting Trilling back, I intended to focus completely on Tavarez. It was like starting the entire case over again.

CHAPTER 92

IT DIDN'T TAKE long for Harry Grissom's clout to be obvious. The first sign that he'd stirred the pot at headquarters was Internal Affairs sergeant Dennis Wu storming into the office and throwing daggers at me with his eyes. A few minutes later, Inspector Lisa Udell arrived in full uniform like she'd been called away from some sort of public ceremony. There were two points on Lisa Udell that no one could argue. She looked impressive in her dress blues. If you were in the right, she'd back you every time.

The two visitors huddled with Harry in his office. Walter Jackson joined me at my desk. We supported each other like two siblings waiting out an argument between their parents.

Walter said, "There's a strong set of personalities crammed into that office."

"At least they're actually communicating." Then some voices were raised. It turned into a series of shouts.

I said, "That's not Harry yelling."

"How can you tell?"

"Because Harry doesn't shout."

Walter looked at me and said, "I guess you're right. Given your ability to stir people up, I would've heard a lot of shouts over the years."

I just shrugged. Walter was right. I could stir people up.

The office door opened. Harry leaned out and motioned me into the office like they were on a coffee break.

As I stepped inside, Inspector Udell said, "Hello, Bennett."

I smiled and said, "Inspector. Nice to see you." I glanced over at Dennis Wu.

He said, "Is it nice to see me too?"

"Of course. It's always a pleasure to deal with a representative from Internal Affairs." I was surprised that earned a smile from Wu.

Harry said, "We've been discussing the Rob Trilling situation. Inspector Udell says we can reinstate him."

The inspector chimed in. "Should be easy. No one even realized he'd been suspended. There's no official notice yet."

I couldn't help myself. I looked at Dennis Wu.

He shook his head and said, "Sounds like another Bennett screwup to me."

Inspector Udell turned to face Wu. "Screwup? Are you some kind of moron? Bennett followed the evidence that was available. He did what he thought was right. He investigated, then corrected a mistake." The inspector turned toward me. "Drove to Albany on a hunch. You can't teach that in the academy." She paused, then looked back at Wu. "Besides, as I understand it, you were at Trilling's apartment when he was sitting in personnel right inside One Police Plaza." The inspector shook her head in disbelief.

Dennis Wu said, "Fine, he's fucking Columbo." He stared at me. "What's your plan?"

"I need to talk to Trilling first. Make sure he'll still work with me. I wouldn't blame him if he told me to hit the road."

Wu said, "Is that an option? Because I don't want to work with you."

Inspector Udell said, "That can be arranged."

Wu said, "You need IA on this. You know it. We gotta keep this quiet until this caper is over."

Inspector Udell nodded. Then she looked at me and said, "What are you waiting for? Get your ass moving."

CHAPTER 93

I FOUND MYSELF back at Rob Trilling's apartment building, feeling a little uncomfortable about the awkward conversation I was about to have. It can be tough to look someone in the eye and tell them you really believed they were a killer. And the way Trilling held his feelings inside didn't put me any more at ease.

I stood in front of his building and rang the buzzer for Trilling's apartment. I looked at the two Band-Aids on my fingers. I wondered if the girl with the knife and the long brown hair was home. The one I'd thought was Juliana at first. I'd say it was none of my business, except my daughter *is* my business. That was an issue I might bring up later. For now, I was on an apology tour.

Trilling's voice came through the intercom and I asked if I could come upstairs.

Trilling paused, then said, "The apartment's a mess. I'll meet you out front in a minute."

I walked over and waited by my car. A couple of minutes later, Trilling strolled out in jeans, a jacket, and cowboy boots.

I said, "I've never seen you wear boots before."

"Is that why you're here? To talk about my fashion choices?"

I got right to the point. "No, I'm here to tell you you're no longer a suspect in the Longshot Killer case. And you're no longer suspended."

Finally, after almost a full minute, Trilling said, "What happened? Have you found the real sniper?"

"I think so." I explained everything about how I thought Joe Tavarez could be the sniper, including my theory that someone had planted the .308 casing in Trilling's car. I even went into my trip to Albany.

Trilling never interrupted me. When I finished, he said, "Darcy Farnan confirmed the trip?"

"Not exactly. She wouldn't say anything officially without your consent. But I can guarantee you she's on your side and wants things to work out."

Trilling looked off into space. When he was done thinking, he turned to me and said, "Darcy's the best." He paused, then added, "You drove all the way to Albany?"

"Yep."

Trilling smiled. "That's smart. And I appreciate it."

"You're cleared to come back. If you want to work on our squad again."

Trilling just looked at me. He didn't say a word. I was starting to get used to that. I decided I could do the same thing. Then he just nodded and said, "When can I start?"

"Right now, if you're up to it."

A woman with short, dark hair walked past us. She gave us a quick look. Something about her seemed familiar to me.

Trilling interrupted my train of thought. "What's the plan for Tavarez?"

"The best I've got right now is that we send a memo or report through the analysts' room. We make sure it's forwarded to the FBI as well. In it, we'll talk about an unnamed cop who's cooperating so he can skate on a whole slew of charges. Then we'll see if Tavarez bites."

"Sounds risky."

I said, "I like the plan sounding risky rather than sounding crazy."

"No, it's crazy too."

CHAPTER 94

I MADE IT home in time for dinner. I needed a respite from the craziness of this investigation. Rob Trilling and I had discussed the case. His initial anger had given way to understanding. I think his outlook could've best been described as "logical." He understood duty and honor. That meant he understood I had been duty bound to investigate the possibility that he could have been the sniper.

I'd considered asking him to come home with me for dinner again. I knew Juliana would've been thrilled. But I didn't know what the story was with the woman at Trilling's apartment, and it wasn't something I wanted to get into with him just yet. He and I both needed to focus on our incredibly dangerous plan to trap the sniper.

It was so nice to listen to the chatter around the table. Trent leaned in from the far end of the table to say to me, "I have some puns for your friend at work."

"Walter?"

"Is that Mr. Jackson? The great big guy?"

"That's him. I'm not sure I want to start the precedent of *me* telling *him* puns. But I'd definitely like to hear yours. Whatcha got?" I smiled at my son, who looked about to burst with excitement.

Trent said, "Hear about the butter rumor? Don't spread it." He got a couple of chuckles from the older kids, and Mary Catherine gave him a mercy laugh. The lack of a big reaction didn't dissuade him. "I've got another." He looked around the table to make sure he had everyone's attention. A true showman. "I had a photographic memory. But I didn't develop it." That one got a better response.

Chrissy and Shawna jumped in with some basic riddles. Shawna's was the best, asking, "Why did the rooster cross the road?" She didn't wait for any guesses. "To prove he wasn't a chicken."

We all had to giggle at that one. I never knew my kids were so talented with jokes. I never really felt this way waiting for a pun to come from Walter Jackson. Then Jane cleared her throat and waited until everyone was looking at her. She glanced over at my grandfather, who nodded his encouragement.

Jane said, "I know I've been sort of secretive lately and hiding out at the library a lot. I've been getting tutoring and doing research for a speech I've been asked to deliver at Columbia because of my performance in Debate Club. It started last month and just sort of snowballed from there. I was jealous of Trent when he spoke at the mayor's office, and it spurred me to work harder and do well. The speech is going to be this Friday night. I hope everyone can make it."

My second oldest daughter is not prone to showing off, but she was clearly quite satisfied with her announcement. She sat with a smile on her face as she glanced around the table. Then, with perfect delivery, she said, "You may all applaud now."

Mary Catherine was quick to say, "Sounds like we have a great Friday night plan. Dinner, then we hear Jane rock Columbia." She focused on Jane. "What are you talking about?"

Jane just smiled. "I was told I could talk about anything, so I'll just tell you it has to do with our family. I'll let you guys wonder about it until Friday. There has to be some mystery in our lives."

The laughter and celebration were almost enough to take my mind off the sniper case.

CHAPTER 95

IT WAS AMAZING how much we accomplished with everyone working together. This hodgepodge team of homicide investigators, Internal Affairs investigators, analysts, and even an inspector had created a fake cop with a history and a court schedule.

I hated to admit it, but Dennis Wu had designed a realistic scenario in the fake memo. On the surface, the memo was only meant to warn law enforcement of unusual activity near one of the NYPD off-site buildings in lower Manhattan. The memo had just enough information to tease Joseph Tavarez and make him act. It basically said that a corrupt officer who was cooperating to avoid indictment would be meeting at the off-site building around 2 p.m. The extra cops were supposed to transport the bad cop to a hearing at 4 p.m.

We'd made sure the memo came through Joe Tavarez's office

around 5 the previous evening. We wanted to also be sure that Tavarez saw the memo that night because his schedule had him listed as off duty today until 4 p.m.

Rob Trilling was trying to catch up on as much as he could and peppered me with questions. We were now set up in an NYPD surveillance vehicle that no one would notice. A beat-up hatchback. From it, we could see the off-site building where the fake cop was supposed to enter and leave. We could also see some of the surrounding buildings.

Trilling said, "How many people do we have out here?"

"For a big case, this is an absolute skeleton crew. Terri Hernandez and a couple of the detectives from our squad are on the perimeter. We have a special team led by Jeff Mabus of four ESU members for the takedown. I think Dennis Wu is lurking somewhere. We're all on the same secure radio channel."

Trilling said, "Are we trying to limit the possibility of a leak by only using a few people?"

"You're starting to catch on. This is nothing like fugitive cases or patrol, is it?"

"I never would've been able to put this together."

"After today you will."

Trilling said, "Where's the lieutenant on this surveillance?"

"He's inside our trap building. He's going to move the curtains and turn some lights on and off to make sure the sniper sees someone in the building. We purposely didn't put a surveillance team on Tavarez so he wouldn't get hinky."

"Get what?"

I grinned. "It's a word old-school cops use to mean suspicious. One of the problems with surveillance is if you're following someone with some experience, they often spot the tail."

"Words are a little like fashion. Their popularity rises and falls with different generations."

"That's pretty smart. Did your grandfather teach you that?"

"Modern Theories of Society, Columbia University." He gave me a decent, smug smile, then cocked his head and said, "I'm curious. Do you also call marijuana 'Mary Jane'?"

I laughed out loud at that one. Trilling sounded like one of my sons when they broke my balls. It was also possibly the first joke I'd ever heard him crack.

I said, "I'll try to work on my vocabulary. I'll admit I cringe when I hear older people try to use street slang. I guess that's why I use out-of-date terms."

Maybe he *was* becoming a New Yorker.

CHAPTER 96

THE SURVEILLANCE STARTED to drag on. I'd been on dozens of stakeouts like this. Even ones where the suspect acted hinky. I'll admit, I might not have been worried, but I could feel my nerves. There was a lot that could go wrong with this plan. Even though I wasn't in command, everyone knew it was my idea. The whole thing was my case. And I'd already made one major error on it. Thank God I'd been able to figure it out and correct it.

Trilling said, "If Lieutenant Grissom is inside our fake office, where are the ESU guys?"

"In an unmarked Chevy Tahoe a few blocks away. We're the main team watching the fake office."

Trilling sat up in his seat quickly. He moved, trying to see a building across the street. "I got something."

I looked toward the older apartment building. "What do you see?"

"It's tough from this angle, but I think a man walked into that building via the front door, carrying a case of some kind. I didn't get a good look."

I put it out over the radio and said we'd keep everyone updated. It's a good idea that everyone knows what others are seeing during a surveillance.

Harry came on the radio. "Everyone stays in place until we hear something more definite from Mike."

I hit the Transmit button when he was finished. "It's the building to the south and west of you. Trilling thinks he saw a male walk through the front door with a case of some kind. We don't have a perfect angle from here." My heart was starting to beat faster.

Now Terri Hernandez came on the frequency. "I'm looking right at the building now. I can see in the lobby through the front door. There's no one visible from here."

Trilling said, "Should I get out and walk past the building? Or maybe try to get inside?"

"Let's give it a minute. I want you out of sight. As long as Harry is staying away from the windows, the sniper doesn't have a target. I'm sure the ESU guys are getting ready and can move anywhere we tell them to go." It was easy to advocate patience but much harder to practice it. My first instinct was also to get out of the car and go to the building myself. But if Tavarez had scoped out the area and was watching from somewhere else, we'd blow the whole surveillance.

Trilling twisted in his seat. He almost shouted, "Look, on the second floor! Looks like a community balcony."

I followed his line of sight and saw that the narrow balcony had some plants. Then I saw something move. I only got a glimpse, but it did look like a man with a rifle. And from the front of the balcony, he was aiming directly down on our fake office.

Just as I grabbed the radio from the console of the surveillance car, someone rapped on the driver's-side window. It was enough to make me jump. When I turned, I almost said, *What the hell*, out loud.

Leaning down, looking into the car, was our suspect, Joseph Tavarez.

CHAPTER 97

I STARED AT Joe Tavarez with my mouth open. I had to blink my eyes a couple times, wondering if I was dreaming. *What the hell?* It really was Joe Tavarez standing on the driver's side of our car.

I turned quickly to Rob Trilling. "Keep watching the balcony. See if you can confirm what the man has with him. It may not be a rifle."

Tavarez signaled for me to lower my window.

I held up my hand and reached for the handheld radio we'd been using on surveillance. "Hold, hold." I gave it a moment for everyone to focus on their radios. Then I said, "Terri, can you confirm what the man on the balcony is holding?"

Terri Hernandez came on the radio. "Stand by."

Joe Tavarez crouched down so his head was even with mine. I finally said, "Tavarez, what the hell are you doing here?"

"I came to help. Not as a sniper, just as a cop."

I could only continue staring at him in disbelief. A thousand thoughts rushed through my brain.

Tavarez said, "I saw the memo. Then I saw the Emergency Service memo about detailing some ESU members to this operation. I figured out exactly what you were up to. When I saw you sitting in the car, I knew I was right. I know what you're doing."

"Right about what?"

"You're trying to catch the sniper."

The radio crackled and I held up a hand to Tavarez again.

Terri Hernandez came on the air. "I have a male in a dark hoodie. He's crouched low and some plants are blocking his face. He's definitely looking toward our off-site building."

"But you don't see a rifle?"

"Not at the moment. I saw what I was pretty sure was a rifle a few moments ago."

"Keep a sharp eye. Everyone else, hold your positions until we verify a few things."

I turned my head to face Tavarez outside the driver's-side window. "I still don't understand what you're doing here, Joe."

"You think the sniper is someone in law enforcement, don't you? I knew this would need to be kept quiet and you couldn't use many cops. I'm not officially on duty until 4 p.m. Consider me just an extra set of eyes."

Now, from my right side, Trilling said, "I see him clearly at the near end of the balcony. He's scanning the area."

I barked at Tavarez, "Get down!" I didn't want him to give away our position.

After a moment, Trilling said, "Now he's changed positions and I can't see him."

Tavarez came level with the window again. He said without prompting, "You don't understand what it's like to be sidelined."

Trilling chimed in, "I do."

I said, "I can appreciate that, Joe, but you didn't think this through."

Terri Hernandez came on the radio. "I see him. Suspect is holding a scoped rifle. No question."

Just as I held the radio up to acknowledge Terri Hernandez, our windshield in the surveillance vehicle shattered. My brain registered the sound of the gunshot at about the same time that glass sprayed into the car.

I ducked low in the seat as the rest of the windshield dropped onto the dashboard.

Trilling bailed out of the car instantly. It took me a moment, then I yanked the latch to the door, but it didn't open easily. I realized that Tavarez was huddled against the car and I had to bark, "Joe, move away from my door!"

Tavarez scrambled to the rear wheel.

I tumbled out of the car onto the asphalt, then scuttled back to the protection of the vehicle. My hand hit something wet in the road. Blood. I looked up and saw the bullet had struck Tavarez in the ear. I blurted out, "Joe, you're hit."

"No shit. It's just my ear. I'm okay." He reached up and touched his ear gingerly. "God damn, that was too close."

I started to call out on the radio when I realized I'd left it in the car. Before I could open the door and reach for the radio, another shot rang out.

I did what every cop under fire does: I crouched down for cover and wished I had more.

CHAPTER 98

I WASN'T THE only one trying to find shelter behind the surveillance vehicle. Joe Tavarez and Rob Trilling were both huddling near the rear of the vehicle. I noticed Trilling had stayed calm and kept surveying the street for a safe path to get to the building where the sniper sat.

After another shot, I risked opening the driver's door to reach in and snatch the radio off the seat. I heard radio traffic, someone already asking what had happened.

I shouted into the radio, "Shots fired, shots fired! Shooter is on the balcony!"

Jeff Mabus, in charge of the ESU team, came on the air. "We're moving as a group into the lobby. Too dangerous to split up."

Terri Hernandez said, "I can cover the front door."

Trilling called to me from his position at the rear of our car. "I'll cover the back."

I saw him low-crawl from the car until he was covered by another building. Then he started to run.

I glanced over at Joe Tavarez, who had his Glock pistol trained on the roof. His ear poured blood onto his shoulder, but he held his position.

I said, "Joe, we gotta stop the bleeding from your ear."

"It can wait. We can stop this asshole right now if we keep our cool."

I said, "Joe, that's someone who read the memo. Someone in the analysts' room or maybe the FBI. Do you have any ideas who it could be?"

Tavarez peered up at the balcony like he might recognize the man with the rifle. Then he snapped his fingers, leaning back slightly as he turned to me. "Son of a bitch."

I said, "What is it, Joe? Who's up there?"

Another shot rang out. It was from a different position on the roof. The bullet ripped through the car's side window. It hit Joe Tavarez in the center of his back and exited through his chest.

Tavarez toppled onto the asphalt with a thud. Blood immediately spread across the street.

I quickly reached out and grabbed him by the arm to drag him back behind the car. I checked his pulse. It seemed futile, but it felt like he might still have a heartbeat.

I grabbed the radio and called out, "Officer down, officer down! We need medical help!"

Harry Grissom came on the radio. "How bad is Trilling?"

"He's not the officer down."

"Who else is there with you?"

I didn't want to confuse things. I just said, "Harry, stand by." I heard sirens. Help was coming. I saw a woman and two kids step out of a building across the street. I screamed, "Police! Get back inside!" The woman gathered up the children and stared at me and Tavarez lying on the ground. I shouted again, "Get back inside!" The woman turned quickly, fumbled with the door handle, then shooed the kids inside and followed them.

I felt again for a pulse on Joe Tavarez's throat. Nothing. He was definitely dead. I stayed low just in case the sniper was still up there, looking for a new target. When I peeked over the rear panel of the car, I saw no movement on the balcony or the roof. The radio was quiet.

After a minute, I saw Harry scurrying along the street toward me. He stayed low behind parked cars. I heard him on another radio channel, directing arriving cops, setting up a perimeter and generally keeping things running.

Harry slid in next to me and looked over at Tavarez's body. Harry said, "That's Joe Tavarez."

"I know."

"Then who the hell has been shooting?"

"No idea."

Harry checked Tavarez again for any signs of life. When he was done, he just shook his head. Then he said, "Where's Trilling?"

"Covering the back door of the shooter's building."

Jeff Mabus came on the radio. "The balcony is clear at the end of the second-floor hallway. No one on the roof either. No sign of the shooter anywhere."

Terri Hernandez said, "He didn't come out the front."

I had to use my cell phone to call Trilling. We had shared the radio in the car. As the phone rang, I realized he could be in danger. Each ring made my heart pound harder. I mumbled, "Answer. Answer."

Then he did. Thank God. Trilling said, "I haven't seen anyone in the rear of the building."

"Keep your eyes open. He's on the move. Watch for Mabus and his guys."

"Roger that."

I looked over at Harry, who summed up the situation. "That did not go well at all."

"You should've been a poet."

CHAPTER 99

I SAT ON the curb, a few feet from Joe Tavarez's body. I watched the paramedics slowly pull a tarp over him. Even the wide tarp couldn't cover the giant pool of blood on the asphalt. Rob Trilling plopped down on the curb next to me. I didn't feel like talking. Trilling made the perfect companion.

We sat in silence as Harry Grissom spoke with the four-person ESU team.

I was in shock. Seriously. The only thing I could do was think about how Joe Tavarez gave his whole adult life to service, only to be benched and then killed for trying to help. Sometimes this job didn't make any sense at all to me.

Trilling put a reassuring hand on my shoulder. I just wanted to go home. I wanted to spend time with my family. But I knew that wouldn't be in the cards for me today. There was still way too much to do.

A shiny new Dodge Charger rolled to a stop across the street. Trilling said, "Someone from command staff?"

I watched for a moment, then said, "Worse. It's Dennis Wu."

The Internal Affairs sergeant was the only one at the scene dressed in a suit and tie. He looked at all the flashing lights from the emergency vehicles and shook his head. As Wu walked past me, he said, "Looks like you're oh for two, Bennett. Excellent job, as always."

I felt Trilling start to rise in anger. I grabbed his arm and pulled him back to the curb. I said quietly, "Wu's right. Let it go."

After a few more minutes, Harry Grissom came over and leaned against the car we'd been driving. "I guess we can write off Joe Tavarez as a suspect."

I knew it was Harry's way of easing me back into reality.

He said, "We have to figure out who else, exactly, saw that memo back at headquarters. It might take some time." Harry let out a sigh, then said, "Why don't you and Trilling make notification to Cindy Tavarez, Joe's wife. I know you'll be sensitive to the moment, but maybe she'll know something. Anything. Maybe she mentioned the memo to someone."

I nodded. Harry was doing me a favor by getting me away from the scene and Dennis Wu.

Harry gave us his car since our surveillance vehicle was shot to pieces. I turned down Trilling's offer to drive. The FBI office wasn't too far from here. I took one more look at the body covered by a tarp. I wondered what Joe Tavarez had been about to tell me just before he got shot.

I said a prayer for him.

CHAPTER 100

I PULLED HARRY'S car into someone's reserved spot in front of the FBI. Rob Trilling and I were inside the building a few seconds later. The expression on the receptionist's face when I identified myself made me pause.

The young woman said, "You're here about Cindy Tavarez, right?"

"How'd you know that?"

She held up a long, slender finger as she spoke to someone on the phone. We only had to wait a minute to see who the receptionist had called: Assistant Special Agent in Charge Robert Lincoln.

Lincoln didn't bother to greet us at all. Not even a nod. He walked right up to me and said, "We've already informed Cindy about her husband. One of the NYPD officers on a task force told me about the incident and I didn't think we should withhold that from Cindy." Then he folded his arms across his chest and stared at me like I was going to refute his reasoning.

I said, "I appreciate your thoughtfulness. We'd like to ask Cindy a couple of important questions. We don't feel like it can wait."

"Why?"

I hesitated, the natural instinct of any cop to not share details of a case before it's finished. "It appears that someone from either the NYPD or the FBI is the Longshot Killer. Or at the very least fed him information. We need to know if Cindy mentioned to anyone today's covert operation we had going on. I think this is an important issue for both of us."

Lincoln took a long moment to consider the situation. I couldn't get a read on his facial expression. After a full twenty seconds, Lincoln made a decision. He looked at Trilling and me and said, "This way."

We followed him up the stairwell and through a maze of hallways until we were in the analysts' common room. Cindy Tavarez sat on a long brown couch with two women, one on either side of her. She held a soaking-wet paper towel and used it to wipe the tears from her eyes.

We hung back until Cindy looked up at us and burst into a new set of sobs. Her two friends, who had been comforting her, moved from the couch so I could sit down. I sat quietly while Cindy first asked me a few questions. I told her everything I knew. When I thought she was calm enough for me to continue, I hit her with my big question.

"Who saw the memo about the NYPD operation to take an indicted cop to court?"

Cindy sniffled. "We all did. It was one of the more interesting memos to come through the office in a long time. We all looked at it and speculated about what was going on. When I talked with Joe about it last night, he told me his theory that it wasn't what it looked like. He'd seen some other memo about using four Emergency Service members in plain clothes. He thought it was some kind of operation to catch the sniper." Cindy blew her nose into the wet paper towel.

I couldn't help but glance around the room as she spoke, wondering who else could be a suspect. No one jumped out at me.

CHAPTER 101

WE WAITED WHILE Cindy Tavarez composed herself on the couch. Another analyst, an older woman named Rochelle Lynch, joined us. I got the impression that Rochelle was a senior analyst. She also had a clear head. I gave the two of them a moment to discuss the issue and to look through a printed-out roster of analysts.

I noticed that ASAC Robert Lincoln hadn't gone anywhere. He stood back and let us conduct the interview, but he clearly wanted to be in the loop. That made me nervous as ever with the FBI.

I felt jittery, like I had to do something. Anything. That happens in homicide cases when things take weird turns and you're not sure how to proceed. Joe Tavarez showing up at a trap we'd set intending to catch him definitely qualified as a weird turn. I wanted to figure out who the Longshot Killer was and stop him right this minute.

Rob Trilling started to make notes next to the names Cindy and Rochelle were going through. All the analysts had been with the FBI for years. A couple of the younger ones weren't in the office yesterday. When they came to the name Darnell Nash, both women paused.

I said, "That's the guy who served with Joe in the Army, right?" Before Cindy even nodded, everything clicked into place. I remembered Joe telling me that Darnell may not have been a sniper in the service but that he could shoot really well.

I blurted out, "Is Nash here?"

Rochelle Lynch answered. "He's in the building. I noticed he came in a couple of hours early, but that's not unusual. Sometimes analysts take care of personal business and make up for it with extra time."

I sprang up from the couch and looked at Lincoln. "Can you call Nash, get him to come here without scaring him?"

Lincoln started to speak, then something outside caught his eye. He did a double take, said, "Too late. He's definitely scared." He pointed out the window.

I stepped forward and saw Darnell Nash getting into a white Ford Focus, then backing out of the parking spot.

I spun and almost yelled to Trilling, "Nash is trying to run! Let's see if we can chase him down."

Lincoln kept a calm tone as he said, "You'll never catch him if you parked out front. My car is the second from the door. Follow me."

We didn't hesitate to fall in behind the FBI assistant special agent in charge.

CHAPTER 102

I'D ALWAYS ASSUMED Robert Lincoln was a little older than me, but you couldn't tell by the way he moved. He raced through the maze of halls and had to wait for us to catch up when he bolted down a flight of stairs.

We burst out into the same lot where I'd seen Darnell Nash jumping into a Ford Focus. I followed Lincoln to a brand-new Chevy Tahoe. I hopped into the front passenger seat and Rob Trilling slid into the back seat.

As he started the SUV, Lincoln said, "The only reason Nash even has a car in this lot is because he's handicapped. He's missing the lower portion of a leg. Besides, I doubt he wanted to walk around Manhattan with a rifle."

I said, "The one time I talked to him, he told me he'd stepped on an IED."

Lincoln said, "That's more than I know about him. Aside from meeting him on his first day and saying hello in the hallway, I've never really interacted with Nash. I can't tell you if I think he's good for the shootings or not. But he's certainly not helping himself."

I had to grudgingly admit I was impressed at how Lincoln remained calm even as he peeled out of his parking spot, darted through the lot, then spurted out onto the street. Amazingly, he soon managed to get Nash's Ford Focus within sight.

I could tell by the way Nash was driving that he wasn't trying to evade us. He didn't even know we were behind him. That was a testament to Robert Lincoln's ability and experience. He had to have been some kind of great street agent years ago to be this smooth behind the wheel. Maybe I'd misjudged the guy.

I saw the Focus turn and said, "Did you see him turn right?"

Lincoln kept an even, calm voice as he replied, "I see him. I see him. And I'm going to pull an old Baltimore police trick." A block before where we'd seen Nash turn, Lincoln took a right down a narrow side street. The move paid off when at the next block Lincoln paused and we saw Nash drive right past us.

Lincoln said, "He may not know anyone's following him, but he's being careful. That kind of round-the-block turn is one of the oldest counter-surveillance tricks in the book." He let one more car pass and fell in behind the Focus again.

Lincoln stayed cool as he said, "Nash just signaled to turn left." He glanced over his shoulder and slid into the left lane. Then he suddenly jammed on his brakes and muttered, "Dammit. Busted."

Nash had purposely stopped instead of turning to see if any cars were following him. Not a bad move for a guy who wasn't a full-time drug dealer. Now we were stuck and he'd clearly seen us.

Darnell Nash punched the gas and squirted around the corner. By the time Lincoln brought the Tahoe around, we could see the Focus making a crazy U-turn and heading toward the East River.

Lincoln leaned down and flipped a switch that activated the hidden blue lights at the top of his windshield. His siren started to blare from under the hood. We made the U-turn as easily as Nash. Confused drivers tried to move out of our way, but we were stuck in heavy traffic.

Once we were moving east, Lincoln called back to Trilling, "There's a lockbox directly behind your seat. The combination is 2-5-8-1. I assume you know how to operate an AR-15."

I caught the quick smile slipping across Trilling's face. Now we were playing a game that he understood.

CHAPTER 103

I ABSOLUTELY HATE high-speed chases. I'm not crazy about the FBI either. Now I found myself in a high-speed chase with an FBI agent.

I don't like the feeling of being a passenger during a car chase. Despite what people see on police shows, high-speed chases are relatively rare but wildly dangerous. It seems like someone always gets hurt: either the suspect fleeing, the cops chasing, or some innocent bystander.

Darnell Nash took a left turn and then another right. Lincoln got on the radio and started calling for help.

After a few moments, Lincoln said, "He's headed toward the Battery Tunnel."

I had to brace myself as Lincoln took a right turn a little sharply. For a moment, I thought we might be tipping over. If it weren't for the heavy traffic, we would've caught the underpowered little Ford easily. I had no idea where Nash was headed.

We came out of the tunnel on the other side of the river with a sprawling construction site to our right. It looked like a giant bomb had hit South Brooklyn. Half of the site was filled with cranes and machines working in a pit far below street level as construction workers laid the foundation for a huge new building.

I heard Trilling ask from the back seat, "Where'd he go?"

Lincoln slowed the Tahoe and cut off its lights and siren. Heavy traffic continued, but I didn't see any sign of the Ford Focus in the lanes up ahead.

Trilling asked, "What's that over there?" He pointed between the two front seats. I followed the line of sight from his finger to what I now realized was the Ford Focus. All I could see was a little of the trunk and roof, but it looked like it was parked on the far side of the construction site.

Lincoln said, "He tried to avoid lane closures and cut through the site. Looks like he got stuck." As Lincoln exited the highway and turned onto a street running alongside the site, he got on his car's radio and again called for any FBI agent in the area to come over and help.

I looked across the construction landscape and realized there was no way to drive across there easily. But we might make it on foot with fewer delays.

Lincoln pulled over and we all jumped out of the Tahoe. No one needed to tell us to take cover immediately. Based on some of Darnell Nash's previous shots, there was no question he could hit one of us from across this hectic construction zone.

Trilling held the AR-15, which had a short scope on it. He

checked the magazine and made sure the rifle was charged. On either side of Trilling, Lincoln and I crouched behind a mound of construction debris. A broken plastic pipe stuck me in the ribs.

Lincoln said, "I'm afraid we're trapped here until more help arrives. I wouldn't recommend trying to move from the safety of this cover."

Trilling was looking through the scope at the far side of the construction site. He said, "I see him at the base of the pylon on the left side of the site. It doesn't look like any of the construction workers have even noticed him."

Lincoln asked, "What's he doing? He should be trying to get away."

"Just standing there. I think he's seen the Tahoe and he's looking for us on the site."

I said, "He knows we're not going to take a shot at him for just standing there. We can't say the same thing. We can't just sit here. He may decide to shoot one of the construction workers instead."

Trilling, still looking through the scope of the rifle, said, "I'm open to ideas."

I said, "Good, because I have a plan."

CHAPTER 104

ROBERT LINCOLN, Rob Trilling, and I crowded together behind construction debris. I peeked around the edge of the pile and across the site. The site had workers spread out as well as working in groups. Not an ideal situation.

I said, "I'll cut around to our right and try to stay out of Nash's sight all the way across the construction zone. You should be able to see me most of the way. When I get to the far side, I'll see how hard it'll be to charge him."

Once I started explaining my plan out loud, I realized it had some serious flaws. The biggest one was the risk that I might be shot in the head.

Lincoln said, "You won't even make it that far. That's exactly what he's waiting for us to do."

"I don't see any other choice. I'm concerned that he's going to get agitated in a minute and just shoot a construction worker."

Lincoln said, "I'm going to make a fake run to the left. I'll draw his attention. That's when you go." Before I could even respond, he sprang to his feet and started jogging toward the left side of the site.

I was seriously reassessing the FBI ASAC. My initial impression that Lincoln was an administrative geek could not have been more wrong. This guy had balls the size of Trenton.

Trilling scrambled back to his position where he could see Nash. He looked through the scope for a second, then called out, "Nash has got his rifle up! Take cover. Take cover."

Lincoln reacted quickly. He ducked down and jumped to his left. Just as he landed behind a heavy concrete block, I heard the report of Nash's rifle. My head snapped to the left, and I could see dirt and dust kicked up by the bullet just a few inches from where Lincoln was crouching.

That was my signal. I sprang up and started racing to my right with my body bent in half, trying to keep whatever I could between me and Nash.

I saw some of the construction workers on the east side of the site start to panic. Lincoln was on the run again and shouting for the workers to take cover.

I followed suit and started yelling the same thing on my west side of the construction site. Most of the workers just stared at me as I scurried past with my head low. They hadn't heard the rifle shot over the sound of the heavy machinery.

Nash fired again. I wasn't sure where the bullet was aimed. But the construction workers on my side of the site heard it this time. They all scrambled, desperate to find cover.

I sprinted onto an original stretch of sidewalk that skirted this half of the giant lot, giving up some cover for speed. When I was about a third of the way around the construction site, I saw a woman lying on the sidewalk behind some kind of metal container, holding a toddler in her arms. I slid in next to her like a base runner trying to beat a play at home plate.

She was crying as she held a little girl close to her chest.

My badge was hanging around my neck, so she realized I was a cop. I asked, "Are you hurt?"

She shook her head. Her black hair flew in every direction as a gust of wind hit our position.

I said, "You'll be safe here. Just stay right in this position. I've got to run to the far end of the site."

As I tucked my legs under me to get a running start, the young woman reached out and grabbed my arm. "Please don't leave us alone." Her voice was shaky.

I gently moved her hand. "Trust me. You stay right here and this will all be over in a couple of minutes."

"Do you promise?"

"Swear to God."

I did a quick peek over the top of the container. I didn't see anything except running construction workers. I stuck my head up a second time to get a better look. It was about then that Robert Lincoln jumped up on the other side of the site and waved his arms.

I couldn't take my eyes off him. Then another shot rang out from the far end of the construction site. Lincoln went down. It looked like he'd been hit. I shook my head, wondering what had just happened. But he'd bought me two seconds to scramble up and start running again.

I made it another thirty yards down the sidewalk. Now I could look to my left and see the area where Nash was hiding. I saw the flash from the barrel of his rifle. But he was shooting downrange.

Then I heard another rifle shot. It had a different sound. I looked over my shoulder in time to see Trilling fire the AR-15 a second time. Whatever he was doing to make Darnell Nash keep his head down was working. I decided to grab a lot of real estate with an all-out sprint.

By now, most of the workers were either off-site or hiding in safe positions. That might make my job a little easier.

I stopped behind a post a little wider than a telephone pole. It looked like the post was used to guide the big trucks as they backed into the site. As I took a second big gulp of air, a bullet struck the post just above my head.

Instinctively, I dropped to the ground. Not that it did me any good. The next shot hit the ground only an inch from my right leg. Dirt and debris flew up onto my chest and face.

I didn't need a third shot to tell me this wasn't the place to take a break. I did a burpee back onto my feet like an Olympic athlete and continued to run hard to the end of the construction site.

Now it was Trilling's turn to fire again.

CHAPTER 105

I'D MADE IT all the way to the far corner of the construction site when Rob Trilling fired again twice. Not quite a double tap but two shots in quick succession. I saw them both impact a pile of rubble in front of Darnell Nash.

I could only see Nash intermittently. Occasionally his head popped up or he moved back enough that I could see him behind the pile of debris. He was a little farther from me than what I'd originally thought. And it was all open space between us. As soon as I started moving in Nash's direction, all it would take would be a casual turn of his head and I'd be in deep shit.

Trilling took another shot, which made Nash duck down and cover his head. I realized it was time.

I couldn't afford to hesitate. I just started running hard. And I mean *hard*. My long legs covered a lot of ground, but it didn't mean I wasn't terrified the whole time. I wondered whether I could cover the distance before I took a .308 round in the face.

As I got closer, I could see around the beam that had blocked my view before. Nash had his rifle up, resting on a wooden truss. He was focusing through the rifle's scope and didn't notice me racing toward him until the last second.

For the record, the last second is always the most important one in a situation like this.

As soon as Nash noticed me, he turned to point his rifle, but I was already leaping off my feet and sailing through the air. My shoulder knocked the barrel of the rifle before he could point it at me. I hit him with the full force of my body weight. We slammed backward into a fifty-five-gallon drum filled with something liquid. We hit the sealed barrel hard enough to make the liquid slosh inside.

Now we were in a close-quarters scrum. It felt like we were in a pit even though we were just on the shale-and-gravel ground. Somehow the rifle ended up between us, pointing almost straight up in the air. It was wedged between a couple of boards, and we both reached for it at about the same time.

Nash got his hand around the trigger guard, so I wrapped my arm around his. I'd rather have him locked against the rifle than punching me in the face. As we wrestled, the rifle went off. It was shocking to hear the sound of the high-powered rifle so close to my head.

I raised myself off the ground into a squat. Now I had my hand around the barrel of the gun and ripped it from Nash's grasp. I let the momentum carry me and tossed the rifle twenty feet away.

Then I squared off against Nash.

CHAPTER 106

I WASN'T PARTICULARLY happy about fighting a younger man, a former Marine who looked like he'd stayed in pretty good shape despite his titanium leg. The way Darnell Nash had his body turned told me he understood the basics of a fistfight.

But I had experience. I'd been in actual street fights. People had tried to stab me, hit me with pipes, slash me with broken bottles, and once someone even tried to choke me with a garden hose. Nash had learned to shoot in the military and worked a desk job at the FBI.

We circled each other for a moment. I'd gotten the rifle out of Nash's hands. That was the most important thing. Now it was more of a waiting game until someone came to help.

Then I realized the mistake I'd made. Nash had maneuvered so that he was now between me and his rifle. I couldn't waste any time. I reached for my Glock, locked in the holster on my right hip.

Before I even had the pistol fully clear of the holster, Nash lunged toward me and slapped it away. Somehow I initially managed to hold on to the gun. Then his punch to my solar plexus knocked me for a loop and I let the pistol drop out of my hand.

It hit several empty fifty-five-gallon drums and disappeared between them. When I looked up, Nash was smiling. He knew he had the advantage now.

I ducked a wild right hand and immediately threw a low kick, hoping to take out his knee.

Nash lifted his leg, so I struck his lower leg, his prosthesis made of titanium. The shock that went through my system was incredible. It was like someone had hit me with a TASER on the foot. I limped back a few feet and decided to take another tack. I said in a loud voice, "Is this what you want to do? Fight a cop doing his job?"

That brought Nash up short. He just stared at me for a moment. Then he shook his head. "You're right. I don't want to fight you. I just want to get away. Considering all the help I've given the NYPD the last few months, I think you might let me go."

"You've misread the situation. And me. You're wrong. Nobody appreciates what you've done the last few months."

"The cops and courts aren't doing anything to help people. Killers are let out on bond. No one cares when poor people have their money stolen by fraudsters. I still think you'll let me walk. I'll even leave my rifle over there." Nash turned his back to me.

He'd made a decent point. It's tough to be a cop. I got it. I still only let Nash take two steps before I tackled him. When I tried to yank his wrist behind his back so I could cuff him, Nash did a little spin move on the ground and we ended up face-to-face again. Then he bit me on the hand.

Before I could react to the bite, he headbutted me. My nose started to pour blood. Then Nash squirmed out of my grip. He took two steps toward the rifle on the ground, but I was able to reach out, grab his ankle, and yank him back toward me.

He was strong and I was a little woozy. I needed help but couldn't reach my phone. We grappled like wrestlers until somehow I found my arms around Nash with my hands locked behind his head in a modified full nelson.

Once Nash had stopped struggling in the powerful hold, I looked up and saw FBI ASAC Robert Lincoln step around the pile of debris where Nash had hidden. Lincoln had a nasty gash on his head and blood had soaked into his white shirt. He turned away and I heard him say in a calm voice, "I've got eyes on Bennett. He's got Nash."

As Lincoln took control of Nash and cuffed him, I sat on a toolbox to catch my breath.

A few seconds later, Rob Trilling stepped around the same pile of debris, cradling the AR-15 Lincoln had given him. He took in the scene with Nash lying face down on the shale-rock ground and me sitting a few feet away. Trilling looked at me and said with a deadpan delivery, "See? I told you I wasn't the shooter."

CHAPTER 107

AS SOON AS we took Darnell Nash into custody, I wondered when politics might jump up and slap me in the face. I was surprised that Robert Lincoln didn't object when I announced we needed to take Nash to One Police Plaza to be interviewed. In fact, the FBI ASAC asked if he could come along.

The NYPD headquarters houses some operational units as well as most of the administrative offices. It's not set up for prisoners or interviews, but I figured this would qualify as a special circumstance. It wasn't hard to slip in through a back door with the prisoner and commandeer an empty office.

Rob Trilling made sure Nash was comfortable. He grabbed him a bottle of water and a package of crackers with peanut butter. Usually officers try to be aware of prisoners' needs. It can come back to haunt a detective later if the prisoner complains about being mistreated and giving a confession under duress. In this case, I thought it was one military veteran looking after another, no matter what the circumstances.

Lincoln took a seat in the corner while Trilling and I sat in sturdy metal chairs across a table from Nash. Lincoln had been very good about accepting the fact that the NYPD was the lead on this case. The fact that the suspect was an FBI employee didn't even come up. This guy was surprising me at every turn today.

We got some background and read Nash his Miranda rights. He didn't try to deny anything. I wasn't a psychotherapist. I didn't want to get into the reasons why he did what he did.

After a few minutes, I asked, "Are there other victims we're not aware of?"

Nash didn't answer immediately. Then he shook his head.

"So Marie Ballard was your first victim?"

He nodded.

"And the antifa activist your last one?"

That made Nash laugh. "There's no way I'd ever consider that scumbag a victim. He tried to murder two cops by burning them. Have you seen his rap sheet? Domestic violence, arson, theft. I'm sure his parents are proud."

Nash looked directly at Trilling. "Sorry I shifted the blame to you by planting that casing in your car. I knew why you'd been called back to the NYPD. I also realized your background would make you a tempting suspect. I hated doing it to a fellow vet. I apologize."

Trilling didn't say anything. He gave Nash a little nod.

Nash said, "I was so tired of not contributing. After the Marines, everything seemed sort of pointless. This gave me a sense of accomplishment. I know you all think I'm a nut and you can't believe I'd do something like this, but you'll see I was right.

When we start letting people get away with crimes so easily, society goes to hell."

Nash said, "I didn't realize that was Joe Tavarez earlier today. Joe was like a brother to me. I saw movement by the car and realized I'd stepped into a trap. I was just trying to get away. I knew if I shot someone, it'd throw the whole operation into chaos, and I could slip away. It hasn't hit me yet that I shot my best friend." He looked down and shook his head. "I'll never be able to look Cindy in the eye again. Hell, the list of things I'll never do again is really long."

He turned and glanced at Robert Lincoln behind him in the corner. Then he looked back at both of us. "Any chance you could leave me alone in here for a while? It'll save the taxpayers a lot of money and me a lot of embarrassment."

I shook my head. After all the time I'd spent on this case and all the heartache I'd gone through, I couldn't believe I actually felt kinda sorry for this guy. He was rational enough to know he'd ruined his life along with so many others.

I felt a little sad being in on the interview. I wished we could save a veteran like this. Smart, educated, and dedicated. Maybe a little too dedicated. It is times like this when I wish I had more answers.

CHAPTER 108

INTERVIEWING AND ARRESTING Darnell Nash, and everything that went with it, took us into the evening. When I got home, Mary Catherine and the kids had already huddled around the TV. They looked like a group of fans watching a sporting event, but they were actually watching a live NYPD news conference about the sniper investigation.

No one even glanced away from the TV when I stepped into the apartment. Contrary to the scoldings I'd gotten as a kid—that I would ruin my eyes by sitting too close to a TV— my grandfather was positioned about three feet from the screen. The kids were grouped around him in rows, with Mary Catherine at the center of the back row. Naturally she got to sit in the recliner with everyone else either leaning on it or sitting on the floor.

I made my way across the living room, then slipped through

the kitchen to come into the living room behind the crowd. I eased up to the rear of the group without anyone noticing me.

On the screen, the NYPD public information officer provided background on the case from a podium in front of a US flag, a New York City flag, and a blue, green, and white NYPD flag. Behind the PIO was the usual NYPD brass. I saw a few faces who'd actually been involved in the case. Inspector Lisa Udell again looked impressive, standing next to the police commissioner. A little farther back, I noticed Harry Grissom wearing a fairly sharp suit and looking less grizzled than usual.

Ricky, sitting next to my grandfather, said, "Where's Dad? It was his case. Why isn't he at the news conference?"

That's when I said in a good, clear voice, "Because I'd rather be here with you guys." It was true. Harry had asked me if I felt up to attending the news conference. I had politely declined, citing the fact that I had been in a gun battle today.

The kids sprang off the floor and swarmed me like piranha around a bloody cow leg. Or whatever happens down in the Amazon. Mary Catherine was particularly agile, coming out of the chair and spinning around to hug me. I wondered if there was any event in life that would ever equal the feeling I have when my whole family embraces me.

I waved off questions about why I was home so we could watch the end of the news conference. Most everyone went back to their original places in front of the TV. Except for my grandfather, Seamus. He stood next to me and wrapped a bony arm around my shoulders and gave me a squeeze. He said in a low voice, "This city needs to thank God it has someone like you around."

A murmur of excitement rippled through the kids as Harry Grissom stepped to the microphone and gave a quick recap of the actual arrest. He left out a lot of detail, which I was glad to avoid discussing with my family. Most cops never want to let their kids know the kind of danger they face every day.

Harry opened up questions from the media. There looked to be about twenty reporters and seven or eight cameramen all wedged into an area in front of the podium. I smiled when the first person Harry called on turned out to be none other than Lois Frang of the *Brooklyn Democrat*. Suddenly I realized why Harry looked so dapper and cleaned up. He had a new girlfriend. I'm sure he'd never use that phrase or even admit it, but it was clear the way he was gazing at Lois from the podium that she was more than just a reporter for a little-known newspaper in Brooklyn.

Lois asked, "This seems like quite a complex case. Did any one tip or piece of info break the case open?"

Harry straightened at the podium and leaned toward the microphone. "We found multiple pieces of evidence that allowed us to assemble information leading to the arrest of Darnell Nash. I'd like to acknowledge not only NYPD personnel but also FBI personnel, who helped us narrow the focus of our investigation."

That was the most politically correct statement I had ever heard Harry Grissom make. But it was true. The damn FBI had saved my bacon today. And I wouldn't be forgetting it anytime soon.

CHAPTER 109

AFTER THE NEWS conference, we all settled down to a modest feast of sloppy joes and a Greek salad. I could tell by the awkward pairing of cuisines that our resident chef, Ricky, had not prepared the meal. He was a little bit of a nut when it came to the dining experience. He always insisted that every side dish complement the main dish. But when you regularly feed thirteen hungry people for dinner on an NYPD detective's salary, cheap meals like sloppy joes are essential.

Brian hurried into the kitchen. A few seconds later he walked out holding up a bottle of champagne. Not the ritziest and not the nastiest of champagnes. He had a broad grin on his face as he said, "Dad solving this case means we can finally pop the cork."

It was Korbel, and it sounded like a fine idea to me, so I gave him a little nod.

Brian was prepared, with a dishrag around the collar of the

bottle. He pointed the bottle at an angle and worked the cork slowly. It still made the good popping sound. Brian managed to catch the cork in his hand and avoid spilling any of the champagne.

My grandfather stood up and took plastic champagne flutes from a bag sitting on the dining room table. That's when I knew the entire incident had been preplanned. The place got boisterous fast. The kids all politicked for some champagne. We settled on letting anyone over the age of twelve have a sip and anyone over sixteen a small glass.

I held two plastic glasses, each filled halfway. I turned to Mary Catherine and offered her one, but she held up her hand. I knew it had to do with her fertility treatment. So I gave it to my grandfather, who gladly threw it down with gusto.

Now I could focus on my sloppy joe dinner. I couldn't believe how much better I felt listening to the chatter around the table. It made me wonder what it'd be like to be around the house full-time. Retirement was just around the corner if I wanted it to be.

It didn't help that Seamus sat next to me. About midway through dinner he said, "You doing okay, boyo?"

"I am now."

"We haven't seen much of you lately."

"It was a big case."

"Technically, every homicide is a big case. Don't try and tell me that a family in the Bronx is any less grief-stricken than a family in Tribeca when a family member is murdered."

"You know I don't feel anything like that. I don't think I'd even talk to someone who thought that was true. This investigation was complicated. That's what made it a big case."

"You've got a big family too. They need you more than the police department does."

I nodded without responding. This was a recurring theme. What I think a lot of people have to deal with in life: finding the right balance.

After dinner—and a dessert of pound cake made by Chrissy and Shawna, with serious oversight by Juliana—we played a few hands of Go Fish using three decks of cards.

About an hour later, as soon as we were able to name Bridget the Go Fish champion, Mary Catherine gave me a subtle signal that it was bedtime.

CHAPTER 110

IT HAD BEEN a remarkably long and stressful day. I knew Mary Catherine was constantly tired from her treatments, and wrapping up a big case was always draining. We said our good nights to the wild mob that is our family, then headed to our bedroom.

The sheets and the pillow under my head felt like heaven. I could still hear the kids talking in the hallway and around their bedrooms. The boys had a habit of shouting to one another from the bathroom to their bedroom. Still, there was something comforting and normal about the noise.

Mary Catherine snuggled up close to me in bed. She said in a soft voice, "I don't know what's better, a family get-together or being so close to you in bed."

"Definitely bed. None of those annoying kids around."

She let out a gentle laugh and draped an arm across my chest.

Mary Catherine said, "Also, I'm not loud or whiny, and I change my underwear every day."

I snorted at the shot at Trent, Eddie, and Ricky, whose hygiene practices were still evolving. Much like any adolescent boy's. "I'm glad you have a goal, like changing your underwear every day. I think you're doing great at it."

Mary Catherine gave me a little bite on the shoulder.

Then I turned so I could look her in the eye and said, "How are you doing? I'm sorry I've been a little scarce. Seamus reminded me at dinner."

"He's a good conscience. And he's been a huge help. All the kids adore him, and he's still the only one who's heard Jane's complete speech."

I asked, "And what does he think of it?"

"You know your grandfather. He never lets out a hint. It must be all the practice he's had keeping confessions to himself."

I smiled at the idea that one had to *practice* to keep quiet.

Mary Catherine propped herself up on her elbow. "I have a secret I've been keeping for a couple of days."

"Oh, yeah?"

"Yeah." She twisted in bed and grabbed something out of her nightstand. She turned and held out her hand.

Just as I was about to ask, *What's this?* I took a closer look and saw the pink plus sign in the middle of the white plastic handle. It took only a moment to click in my brain exactly what I was looking at. My eyes shifted from the pregnancy test to my wife's beautiful face.

All I said was "Really?"

Mary Catherine nodded vigorously. She said, "I still have to confirm it with the doctor next week. That's why I haven't said anything to anyone else yet."

I tried to grasp this news. I didn't even go into the future implications, like being the oldest father at graduation. Or teaching a kid to drive when my eyesight was failing. Looking at Mary Catherine, I realized how happy she was. Maybe it was partially because she didn't have to go back for any more fertility treatments. But it was much more than that. There was actual joy on her face. And the idea of a new baby rumbling around the house made me ecstatic.

Mary Catherine looked at me. Finally frustration overcame her, and she said, "Well? What do you think?"

"Hallelujah!"

"And you'll keep it a secret?"

"From the kids?"

"Anybody."

"This is big news. I might blurt it out."

She smiled. "You Bennetts just love telling good news."

"And kissing beautiful women." I planted a kiss on Mary Catherine's lips.

Her smile was contagious. So were her giggles. Then we laughed and hugged and I had to say a quick prayer of thanks.

CHAPTER 111

WHEN I WOKE up the next morning, it felt like a new age had dawned. We were having a baby. I wanted to gently shake Mary Catherine awake and shout that we were having a baby.

We were having a baby, my nightmare case was over, and Jane was speaking at Columbia University. I wanted to pinch myself. Just to make sure I wasn't dreaming.

As I flipped pancakes, Fiona shuffled into the kitchen wearing big pink bunny-shaped slippers that Seamus had bought her. She looked at me and said, "What are you smiling about?"

I turned and kissed her on the forehead. "You'd be smiling too if you had kids like mine."

Fiona screwed her face up and said, "You're weird."

"But happy." I put a little singsong in my voice.

Fiona shook her head and shuffled out of the kitchen.

I took the kids to school. We even made it on time. I gave a quick wave to Sister Sheilah. Oddly, for all of my ups and downs with Holy Name's senior nun, whom I had known since my own first day of kindergarten, I badly wanted to tell her about Mary Catherine's pregnancy. But I restrained myself.

Forty minutes later, I strolled into the Manhattan North Homicide office still in a phenomenally good mood.

Rob Trilling was at his desk. He looked up and right away said, "What put that smile on your face today?"

"Just the way things are rolling." We chatted for a few minutes, then I went over some notes from the case with him.

Trilling looked at me and said, "Robert Lincoln called me from the FBI. He said I could come back on the fugitive task force whenever I wanted."

"You don't like it here? I understand if you don't like the way the sniper investigation unfolded."

Trilling shook his head. "I already told you. I understand what it's like to do your duty no matter what. You did what you had to do. That's not the issue." He had an agitated expression on his face that I couldn't interpret. Finally he said, "I have a problem I need your help with."

Coming from Rob Trilling, that made me nervous. When a guy like Trilling says he has a problem, the chances are it's fairly serious. It could be anything. I nodded and said, "All right, what's bothering you?"

"I need to show you in person. Can you take a quick ride with me?"

I nodded and followed Trilling out of the office. It was a new adventure.

CHAPTER 112

I QUICKLY REALIZED that we were headed toward Rob Trilling's apartment, but I didn't ask any more questions about the "problem." If he wanted to show me something, I'd see it first before I made any comments.

Instead, as we drove, I came clean to him about my earlier visit to his apartment and speaking with the building's super. I also told him about going through the security tapes, looking for when he left the building during one of the shootings.

At a stoplight, Trilling turned to look at me and said, "You snuck into my apartment building and tried to get George to rat me out?"

I instantly felt like a shithead. I hated that Trilling interpreted it that way. I started to say, *I just wanted to verify that you were* not *the sniper.*

That's when Trilling started to laugh. Maybe the first time I'd heard him really laugh out loud. He said, "Relax. I appreciate how you went about the case. I'm just messing with you."

Now I was shocked speechless. I heard Rob Trilling laugh *and* he pranked me, all in the same day? Unbelievable.

When we arrived at the building and walked up the stairs to his second-floor apartment, Trilling turned to me and said, "I'm a little surprised you haven't figured out my problem already, if you looked through those security videos."

He opened the door to his apartment and ushered me inside. I heard low murmurs and conversation as the door opened, but it all stopped the instant I stepped into the darkened apartment.

A TV mounted on the wall was playing some kind of kids' program that spelled out simple words like "cat" and "run."

Five women all turned and stared at me at the same time. One was in the kitchen, two were watching the TV show, and the other two appeared to be doing yoga. They were all in their twenties with dark hair and features. I recognized one of the women. She'd walked past us while Trilling and I were outside the building speaking by his car.

I looked at Trilling and he understood my question instantly.

"They're the women from the heroin operation in the Bronx. I went to their immigration hearing after we busted that William Hackford asshole who shot at us. They were going to send them to some sort of facility unless someone agreed to take responsibility and sponsor them."

"And that someone was you?"

Trilling just shrugged.

"I hope you understand that with ten kids still at home, I can't take any of them."

"That's not what I was asking. We're actually getting along all right. The girls know to be careful when they leave, and George, the super, thinks it's just one girl living here. They all look similar enough that he thinks they're all the same person. They're on a walking routine so each of them gets out of the house for at least an hour a day and they keep the place absolutely spotless."

"So this is why you were so vague about your alibi. And why you never wanted me coming inside."

Trilling nodded.

"And it was one of these young ladies who told me you weren't home, and when I tried to get more information, she cut my fingers with a knife."

Trilling cringed a little. He looked at the woman in the kitchen. "Ayesha told me about that. I figured it was you. She speaks the best English of any of them. But they're all improving every day."

I looked toward the tiny kitchen. The young woman working at the counter waved at me with a paring knife in her hand. She had a big smile. I didn't know if it was a smile of apology or a smile telling me never to come near her again.

Trilling introduced me to the other women, who all had Pakistani names except the youngest. She called herself "Katie." I didn't ask why.

Trilling explained his biggest problem was the cramped living quarters and that he was running out of money buying food for everyone. It took one call to my grandfather to find some agencies willing to help out with the food.

Trilling told me he didn't mind if the women stayed with him a while longer. He felt like their brother taking care of them.

I realized just how happy I was that we were able to figure out the sniper case and keep a conscientious young man like this out of trouble.

CHAPTER 113

FINALLY FRIDAY NIGHT had arrived. Jane's world debut as an orator. It had taken a near-Herculean effort to get everyone ready on time and dressed appropriately. Part of it was because it'd been since Mary Catherine's and my wedding that everyone dressed in their finest clothes, and the kids, especially the youngest ones, seemed to have been using some sort of special growth hormone.

Basically, everyone wore some version of their Sunday church clothes. Ricky's blue blazer from Holy Name had undergone a slight alteration—Mary Catherine had carefully removed the emblem from the front pocket. The blazers were only for special occasions at school, so we weren't worried about putting it back together anytime soon.

Columbia University's main campus is located in the Morningside Heights neighborhood, bordering Harlem above the

Upper West Side. Jane had been with the other speakers at Havemeyer Hall since about five o'clock. I was excited about her speaking in this particular venue because it was the most filmed classroom in the world, showing up in movies like *Spider-Man* and *Ghostbusters*. And on more TV shows than I could count.

The historic hall was four stories of classic stone and brickwork. The classroom's interior had a much more modern feel. The hardwood paneling reminded me of a courtroom, with a gallery super-sized to hold hundreds of people.

We stuck together in the lobby while we waited to catch a glimpse of Jane. People were coming and going in all directions. I kept a close eye on Shawna and Chrissy. Mary Catherine called everyone together like a quarterback in a football huddle. She spoke in a low voice, but there wasn't one kid there who didn't understand exactly what she was saying.

"No video games, no loud talking, and no whining." All the kids nodded. Mary Catherine added, "And have a good time." She looked up at me and Seamus and gave us a wink.

Jane came through with a group of other young people. She stopped for a moment and spoke to her brothers and sisters. She gave Mary Catherine a hug and blew me a kiss from across the crowd. She smiled and gave my grandfather a thumbs-up. He returned it enthusiastically.

As we turned and the first set of kids started to file into the lecture hall, I had to take a deep breath.

My grandfather slapped me on the back and said, "You okay, boyo?"

"Great. Trying to ground myself so I don't look like a fool. I'm just so proud of all these kids."

"Now you know how I felt so many times with you. From

basketball games to the NYPD academy graduation, I know exactly what you mean."

I couldn't believe the compliment my grandfather had just given me. It made the wave of emotion that much more intense.

The twelve of us filled up an entire row with only one empty seat left over at the far end. I heard some of the comments from other people about the size of our family. Nothing I wasn't used to. We were pretty remarkable.

The first three student speakers were from different high schools across the city. Two of them talked about the environment and what we needed to do to save the Earth. One young man from Regis High School talked about the benefits of volunteering in the city and all the opportunities the work can bring.

I still had no clue what topic Jane had chosen for her speech.

My second eldest daughter stepped confidently to the podium. My heart pounded and I felt my face flush. I was both thrilled and terrified—I knew I'd think whatever she said or did was great, whether she was happy or not with her performance.

Jane looked very mature, thanking the university and Sister Mary Margaret, her English and debate instructor. I looked down one row to see Sister Mary Margaret sitting with a couple of the other nuns from Holy Name. She had to wipe a tear from her eye. So did I.

After Jane finished all her introductions and thank-yous, she looked over the podium to the row of seats filled by our family. She pointed us out and introduced us to the crowd, saying, "My immediate family. I have nine brothers and sisters, plus my father, my stepmother, and my great-grandfather. And if you can't tell by looking at us, all ten of us siblings are adopted. Proudly. Purposefully. My father was born here in the city. I have a sister who's Hispanic, a brother and a sister who are Black, and a great-grandfather who was an immigrant from Ireland. I'd say that qualifies us as New Yorkers as much as anything else." That earned a few snickers from the crowd.

"When I was researching this topic, my great-grandfather pointed me to an unfamiliar quote. 'Happiness is having a large, loving family...in another city.'"

That brought a roar of laughter.

Then Jane threw in, "That's from someone named George Burns. A great philosopher, according to my great-grandfather."

That earned laughter from anyone old enough to know that George Burns had been a comedian.

"I don't know if most people have an idea of what adoption is like. But my brothers and sisters and I are closer than most blood relations. We're all from different backgrounds. In fact, I think I was adopted from Scandinavia."

Seamus leaned into me and said, "She's killing. She's as good as Denis Leary."

Jane continued. "Our family is a microcosm of the city. Each of us is different, but in order for things to run smoothly, we all have to work together." She looked directly at me and beamed. "My father made sure each of us understood the importance of democracy. We vote on important issues. I have to admit that my father gets two votes, so he straddles the line between democracy and dictatorship." She had the crowd eating out of her hand.

"It's all the things my siblings and I have in common, not our differences, that are important. Just like the people who live in the city. We have to look past our personal prejudice to try and understand people with different perspectives.

"It's not only the different perspectives from my family that help me, it's also the love and support they give me. The fact that every single one of them is in the audience tonight means so much to me. It also means that I can look out into the audience at any event where I speak and know that when my family is present, I'll always get applause from at least a quarter of the attendees." She paused politely for the chuckling and laughter rippling through the audience.

Jane said, "We yell and argue, then compromise. It's how we keep moving. No one hates someone for their opinion. No one ignores the others. Just like New Yorkers, we're a big, wonderful family.

"As Maya Angelou said, 'I sustain myself with the love of family.'" Jane made it a point to look quickly but directly at our entire row. "In closing, I want to look at my family and say, 'You mean more to me than anything else. Thanks for always supporting me.'"

Mary Catherine used a tissue to wipe her eyes then blow her nose. Next to me, my grandfather did the same, only not nearly as quietly.

The crowd applauded. Loudly. First our entire row stood up, then a number of others followed our example. I couldn't hold it in any longer and I started to cry.

Jane came off the stage and joined the family. She sniffled as she said, "You guys are the best. I couldn't imagine anything better than tonight."

Then I said without thinking, "I can think of one thing." When everyone turned to me, I said, "Mary Catherine is pregnant." I avoided her scowl as I looked at the astonished faces of my family. A cheer rose up. We huddled around Mary Catherine, everyone giving her a hug.

Jane ended up next to me near the end of the line. She looked at me and said, "Really, Dad? You had to tell us tonight? On my night?"

"I'm sorry, sweetheart, it slipped out."

A smile swept across her face. "I know, and I love it. More material for a future paper." She hugged me.

I was having a pretty damn good day.

ACKNOWLEDGMENTS

The authors appreciate the insights Palm Beach County Sheriff's Deputy Mike Hansen and NYPD Lieutenant John Grimpel gave on this book.

ABOUT THE AUTHORS

James Patterson is one of the best-known and biggest-selling writers of all time. Among his creations are some of the world's most popular series, including Alex Cross, the Women's Murder Club, Michael Bennett and the Private novels. He has written many other number one bestsellers including collaborations with President Bill Clinton and Dolly Parton, stand-alone thrillers and non-fiction. James has donated millions in grants to independent bookshops and has been the most borrowed adult author in UK libraries for the past fourteen years in a row. He lives in Florida with his family.

James O. Born is an award-winning crime and science-fiction novelist as well as a career law-enforcement agent. A native Floridian, he still lives in the Sunshine State.

Have You Read Them All?

STEP ON A CRACK
(with Michael Ledwidge)
The most powerful people in the world have gathered for a funeral in New York City. They don't know it's a trap devised by a ruthless mastermind, and it's up to Michael Bennett to save every last hostage.

RUN FOR YOUR LIFE
(with Michael Ledwidge)
The Teacher is giving New York a lesson it will never forget, slaughtering the powerful and the arrogant. Michael Bennett discovers a vital pattern, but has only a few hours to save the city.

WORST CASE
(with Michael Ledwidge)
Children from wealthy families are being abducted. But the captor isn't demanding money. He's quizzing his hostages on the price others pay for their luxurious lives, and one wrong answer is fatal.

TICK TOCK
(with Michael Ledwidge)
New York is in chaos as a rash of horrifying copycat crimes tears through the city. Michael Bennett investigates, but not even he could predict the earth-shattering enormity of this killer's plan.

I, MICHAEL BENNETT
(with Michael Ledwidge)

Bennett arrests infamous South American crime lord Manuel Perrine. From jail, Perrine vows to rain terror down upon New York City – and to get revenge on Michael Bennett.

GONE
(with Michael Ledwidge)

Perrine is back and deadlier than ever. Bennett must make an impossible decision: stay and protect his family, or hunt down the man who is their biggest threat.

BURN
(with Michael Ledwidge)

A group of well-dressed men enter a condemned building. Later, a charred body is found. Michael Bennett is about to enter a secret underground world of terrifying depravity.

ALERT
(with Michael Ledwidge)

Two devastating catastrophes hit New York in quick succession, putting everyone on edge. Bennett is given the near impossible task of hunting down the shadowy terror group responsible.

BULLSEYE
(with Michael Ledwidge)

As the most powerful men on earth gather for a meeting of the UN, Bennett receives shocking intelligence that there will be an assassination attempt on the US president. Are the Russian government behind the plot?

HAUNTED
(with James O. Born)

Michael Bennett is ready for a vacation after a series of crises push him, and his family, to the brink. But when he gets pulled into a shocking case, Bennett is fighting to protect a town, the law, and the family that he loves.

AMBUSH
(with James O. Born)

When an anonymous tip proves to be a trap, Michael Bennett believes he personally is being targetted. And not just him, but his family too.

BLINDSIDE
(with James O. Born)

The mayor of New York has a daughter who's missing. Detective Michael Bennett has a son who's in prison. Can one father help the other?

THE RUSSIAN
(with James O. Born)

As Michael Bennett's wedding day approaches, a killer has a vow of his own to fulfil . . .

SHATTERED
(with James O. Born)

After returning from his honeymoon, Michael Bennett discovers that his former partner is missing. After everything they've been through, he will never give up hope of finding her – he owes her that much.

OBSESSED
(with James O. Born)
Detective Michael Bennett must discover who's
murdering young women in New York – before
his eldest daughter is targeted.

They run the most in-demand private investigation agency in New York City.

But who really are the detectives who call themselves Holmes, Margaret and Poe?

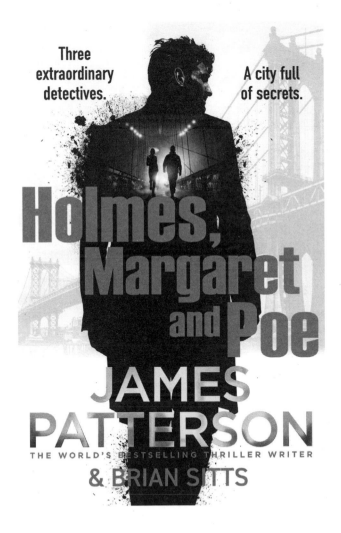

Three extraordinary detectives.

A city full of secrets.

Holmes, Margaret and Poe

JAMES PATTERSON

THE WORLD'S BESTSELLING THRILLER WRITER

& BRIAN SITTS

OUT NOW!

Also By James Patterson

ALEX CROSS NOVELS

Along Came a Spider • Kiss the Girls • Jack and Jill • Cat and Mouse • Pop Goes the Weasel • Roses are Red • Violets are Blue • Four Blind Mice • The Big Bad Wolf • London Bridges • Mary, Mary • Cross • Double Cross • Cross Country • Alex Cross's Trial (*with Richard DiLallo*) • I, Alex Cross • Cross Fire • Kill Alex Cross • Merry Christmas, Alex Cross • Alex Cross, Run • Cross My Heart • Hope to Die • Cross Justice • Cross the Line • The People vs. Alex Cross • Target: Alex Cross • Criss Cross • Deadly Cross • Fear No Evil • Triple Cross • Alex Cross Must Die

THE WOMEN'S MURDER CLUB SERIES

1st to Die (*with Andrew Gross*) • 2nd Chance (*with Andrew Gross*) • 3rd Degree (*with Andrew Gross*) • 4th of July (*with Maxine Paetro*) • The 5th Horseman (*with Maxine Paetro*) • The 6th Target (*with Maxine Paetro*) • 7th Heaven (*with Maxine Paetro*) • 8th Confession (*with Maxine Paetro*) • 9th Judgement (*with Maxine Paetro*) • 10th Anniversary (*with Maxine Paetro*) • 11th Hour (*with Maxine Paetro*) • 12th of Never (*with Maxine Paetro*) • Unlucky 13 (*with Maxine Paetro*) • 14th Deadly Sin (*with Maxine Paetro*) • 15th Affair (*with Maxine Paetro*) • 16th Seduction (*with Maxine Paetro*) • 17th Suspect (*with Maxine Paetro*) • 18th Abduction (*with Maxine Paetro*) • 19th Christmas (*with Maxine Paetro*) • 20th Victim (*with Maxine Paetro*) • 21st Birthday (*with Maxine Paetro*) • 22 Seconds (*with Maxine Paetro*) • 23rd Midnight (*with Maxine Paetro*)

DETECTIVE MICHAEL BENNETT SERIES

Step on a Crack (*with Michael Ledwidge*) • Run for Your Life (*with Michael Ledwidge*) • Worst Case (*with Michael Ledwidge*) • Tick Tock (*with Michael Ledwidge*) • I, Michael Bennett (*with Michael Ledwidge*) • Gone (*with Michael Ledwidge*) • Burn (*with Michael Ledwidge*) • Alert (*with Michael Ledwidge*) • Bullseye (*with Michael Ledwidge*) • Haunted (*with James O. Born*) • Ambush (*with James O. Born*) •

Blindside (*with James O. Born*) • The Russian (*with James O. Born*) • Shattered (*with James O. Born*) • Obsessed (*with James O. Born*) • Crosshairs (*with James O. Born*)

PRIVATE NOVELS

Private (*with Maxine Paetro*) • Private London (*with Mark Pearson*) • Private Games (*with Mark Sullivan*) • Private: No. 1 Suspect (*with Maxine Paetro*) • Private Berlin (*with Mark Sullivan*) • Private Down Under (*with Michael White*) • Private L.A. (*with Mark Sullivan*) • Private India (*with Ashwin Sanghi*) • Private Vegas (*with Maxine Paetro*) • Private Sydney (*with Kathryn Fox*) • Private Paris (*with Mark Sullivan*) • The Games (*with Mark Sullivan*) • Private Delhi (*with Ashwin Sanghi*) • Private Princess (*with Rees Jones*) • Private Moscow (*with Adam Hamdy*) • Private Rogue (*with Adam Hamdy*) • Private Beijing (*with Adam Hamdy*) • Private Rome (*with Adam Hamdy*)

NYPD RED SERIES

NYPD Red (*with Marshall Karp*) • NYPD Red 2 (*with Marshall Karp*) • NYPD Red 3 (*with Marshall Karp*) • NYPD Red 4 (*with Marshall Karp*) • NYPD Red 5 (*with Marshall Karp*) • NYPD Red 6 (*with Marshall Karp*)

DETECTIVE HARRIET BLUE SERIES

Never Never (*with Candice Fox*) • Fifty Fifty (*with Candice Fox*) • Liar Liar (*with Candice Fox*) • Hush Hush (*with Candice Fox*)

INSTINCT SERIES

Instinct (*with Howard Roughan, previously published as Murder Games*) • Killer Instinct (*with Howard Roughan*) • Steal (*with Howard Roughan*)

THE BLACK BOOK SERIES

The Black Book (*with David Ellis*) • The Red Book (*with David Ellis*) • Escape (*with David Ellis*)

STAND-ALONE THRILLERS

The Thomas Berryman Number • Hide and Seek • Black Market • The Midnight Club • Sail (*with Howard Roughan*) • Swimsuit (*with Maxine Paetro*) • Don't Blink (*with Howard Roughan*) • Postcard Killers (*with Liza Marklund*) • Toys (*with Neil McMahon*) • Now You See Her (*with Michael Ledwidge*) • Kill Me If You Can (*with Marshall Karp*) • Guilty Wives (*with David Ellis*) • Zoo (*with Michael Ledwidge*) • Second Honeymoon (*with Howard Roughan*) • Mistress (*with David Ellis*) • Invisible (*with David Ellis*) • Truth or Die (*with Howard Roughan*) • Murder House (*with David Ellis*) • The Store (*with Richard DiLallo*) • Texas Ranger (*with Andrew Bourelle*) • The President is Missing (*with Bill Clinton*) • Revenge (*with Andrew Holmes*) • Juror No. 3 (*with Nancy Allen*) • The First Lady (*with Brendan DuBois*) • The Chef (*with Max DiLallo*) • Out of Sight (*with Brendan DuBois*) • Unsolved (*with David Ellis*) • The Inn (*with Candice Fox*) • Lost (*with James O. Born*) • Texas Outlaw (*with Andrew Bourelle*) • The Summer House (*with Brendan DuBois*) • 1st Case (*with Chris Tebbetts*) • Cajun Justice (*with Tucker Axum*)• The Midwife Murders (*with Richard DiLallo*) • The Coast-to-Coast Murders (*with J.D. Barker*) • Three Women Disappear (*with Shan Serafin*) • The President's Daughter (*with Bill Clinton*) • The Shadow (*with Brian Sitts*) • The Noise (*with J.D. Barker*) • 2 Sisters Detective Agency (*with Candice Fox*) • Jailhouse Lawyer (*with Nancy Allen*) • The Horsewoman (*with Mike Lupica*) • Run Rose Run (*with Dolly Parton*) • Death of the Black Widow (*with J.D. Barker*) • The Ninth Month (*with Richard DiLallo*) • The Girl in the Castle (*with Emily Raymond*) • Blowback (*with Brendan DuBois*) • The Twelve Topsy-Turvy, Very Messy Days of Christmas (*with Tad Safran*) • The Perfect Assassin (*with Brian Sitts*) • House of Wolves (*with Mike Lupica*) • Countdown (*with Brendan DuBois*) • Cross Down (*with Brendan DuBois*) • Circle of Death (*with Brian Sitts*) • Lion & Lamb (*with Duane Swierczynski*) • 12 Months to Live (*with Mike Lupica*) • Holmes, Margaret and Poe (*with Brian Sitts*)

NON-FICTION

Torn Apart (*with Hal and Cory Friedman*) • The Murder of King Tut (*with Martin Dugard*) • All-American Murder (*with Alex Abramovich and Mike Harvkey*) • The Kennedy Curse (*with Cynthia Fagen*) • The Last Days of John Lennon (*with Casey Sherman and Dave Wedge*) • Walk in My Combat Boots (*with Matt Eversmann and Chris Mooney*) • ER Nurses (*with Matt Eversmann*) • James Patterson by James Patterson: The Stories of My Life • Diana, William and Harry (*with Chris Mooney*) • American Cops (*with Matt Eversmann*) • What Really Happens in Vegas (*with Mark Seal*)

MURDER IS FOREVER TRUE CRIME

Murder, Interrupted (*with Alex Abramovich and Christopher Charles*) • Home Sweet Murder (*with Andrew Bourelle and Scott Slaven*) • Murder Beyond the Grave (*with Andrew Bourelle and Christopher Charles*) • Murder Thy Neighbour (*with Andrew Bourelle and Max DiLallo*) • Murder of Innocence (*with Max DiLallo and Andrew Bourelle*) • Till Murder Do Us Part (*with Andrew Bourelle and Max DiLallo*)

COLLECTIONS

Triple Threat (*with Max DiLallo and Andrew Bourelle*) • Kill or Be Killed (*with Maxine Paetro, Rees Jones, Shan Serafin and Emily Raymond*) • The Moores are Missing (*with Loren D. Estleman, Sam Hawken and Ed Chatterton*) • The Family Lawyer (*with Robert Rotstein, Christopher Charles and Rachel Howzell Hall*) • Murder in Paradise (*with Doug Allyn, Connor Hyde and Duane Swierczynski*) • The House Next Door (*with Susan DiLallo, Max DiLallo and Brendan DuBois*) • 13-Minute Murder (*with Shan Serafin, Christopher Farnsworth and Scott Slaven*) • The River Murders (*with James O. Born*) • The Palm Beach Murders (*with James O. Born, Duane Swierczynski and Tim Arnold*) • Paris Detective • 3 Days to Live • 23 ½ Lies (*with Maxine Paetro*)

For more information about James Patterson's novels, visit www.penguin.co.uk.

STRATEGY IN ADVERTISING

Matching Media and Messages to Markets and Motivations

Second Edition

Leo Bogart

 NTC Business Books
a division of *NTC Publishing Group* • Lincolnwood, Illinois USA

Contents

Preface

Strategy is the art of deploying available resources to attain objectives in the face of active opposition. In a competitive economy, the success of a company often hinges on its ability to master the strategy of advertising. This mastery in turn depends on the company's ability to assemble and to apply information. Advertising professionals today deal with a greater volume of information than ever before. In every substantial advertising agency and department, specialists are now at work systematically setting forth their knowledge, inferences, and guesses on consumer interests and purchasing habits, the effects of repeating advertisements, the relation between information, attitudes, and buying action. The computer has given the advertiser a remarkable capacity to apply this kind of knowledge to the ever more complicated problems of the marketplace.

Advertising is inevitably a powerful economic force in any complex industrial society where production capacity exceeds effective consumer demand. But advertising is more than an economic force; it is also a profound influence on culture, values, and the quality of life. Directly, it provides us with constant stimulation, reminders, judgments, and guidance, not only about what products we ought to own but about the kinds of people we ought to consider attractive, the kinds of places we should want to live in, and the standards we should observe in our dress or way of speaking. Indirectly, advertising strongly influences our great mass media; their shape, substance, and style—in fact, their very survival—are all profoundly affected by the fact that they are themselves products in a market where the advertiser is the customer.

The assumptions that enter into advertising decisions thus have consequences that go far beyond advertising itself. Not all advertisers operate by the same rules, of course; but bit by bit, as knowledge replaces conjecture about the process of communication, more and more advertisers come to work from the same basic assumptions. Most of these assumptions, let us hope, are sound and solidly rooted in evidence, and in this book I have tried to set them forth systematically. But the greatest obstacles to effective advertising strategy are assumptions that are faulty and that because of their widespread acceptance create complacency on the part of business managements and advertising practitioners alike. These questionable assumptions waste the advertiser's money; they also lead to judgments that cause our mass media to be different from what they otherwise might be and perhaps to fall short of their true potential.

Systematic inquiry is the only way by which evidence can replace conjecture, true or false. Research can transform into science judgments made on the basis of art or intuition. As our information accumulates and our sophistication grows, will we ever get to the point where the scientific aspect of advertising becomes all-inclusive and the aspect that is art unimportant? I don't believe this can ever happen, because no advertising problem is ever exactly like any other. The scientific method may and should be used to approach subjects that are in at least some respects outside the domain of science (and I believe communication is such a subject), but it will not always lead to solutions. Advertisements may be *evaluated* scientifically; they cannot be *created* scientifically.

I shall have little to say in this book about how to write good copy, design good layouts or produce good commercials. These are highly specialized subjects in themselves; I do not believe they readily lend themselves to generalization, because they involve elements *unique* to the particular product and its manufacturer: its name, packaging, and physical attributes, its established competitive position, its existing reputation and advertising history.

This book deals rather with the *generic* characteristics of mass communication that lend themselves to marketing purposes. It focuses sharply on media strategy: how much money to spend, where, in what kind of message units, with what frequency, directed at what targets. Over these matters the advertising strategist can exercise rational controls. But the symbolic content and style of the advertiser's message may be even more important than the means of communication he uses.* The idea behind his ad, original or banal, is at the very heart of strategy, and this idea cannot come from a book on "how to do it."

Since the first edition of this book appeared in 1967, a considerable amount of research has accumulated on advertising and how it works. Although this is reflected in a substantial expansion of this text, I cannot say that it has caused me to alter my underlying thesis, which is that the process of advertising communication is vastly more important than the numbers that track its reach, frequency, and cost.

Although advertising is a much bigger business now than it was then, it has not undergone any radical transformations of the kind that can be discerned on the horizon in 1990. The spread of cable into two out of every five American households is merely a harbinger of greater changes yet to come as we move into the twenty-first century. The world of communication will be changed by teletext and videotex, by direct broadcasting by satellite to the home, by high-definition and low-power localized television, and by computer-controlled ink-jet printing that will eventually permit the publication of periodicals customized to the needs of the individual reader. Such developments are bound to alter the forms and techniques of advertising, as well as the present balance of advertiser and consumer support of the mass media.

---

*"He" and "his" are used in a neuter or generic sense throughout this book. Obviously both women and men are objects of advertising and participants in making advertising decisions.

Individual broadcasters and publications deliver different quantities of viewers, listeners, and readers, and charge different prices accordingly for ads of different sizes and lengths. Still, every message is important to the advertiser who runs it, and to the medium that carries it, and it becomes part of the total communications environment in which individual media choices are exercised. Naturally, if audiences increased at the same rate as advertising, there would be an equilibrium. But they haven't, and there isn't.

From the standpoint of communication, the number of advertisements to which people are exposed is more important than the number disseminated. Exposure requires that viewers and listeners be present and tuned in when commercials come on the air or that magazine and newspaper readers open to the pages on which ads appear. Between 1967 and 1982, the number of messages exposed to an average person increased overall at about one-fifth the rate of the number of messages disseminated by advertisers. But there is quite a difference in what has happened to print and broadcast media. In those years, there was a jump of 78 percent in the number of television commercials the typical individual sees each day and of 53 percent in the number of radio commercials he hears. Magazine ads were up 27 percent, newspaper display ads only 5 percent. The increase is greatest in broadcasting, because, as we shall see, more commercials have been crowded into the same amount of air time.

If we go back even further, the changes in both dissemination and exposure are even more dramatic, reflecting the expansion of the television broadcast day in the early 1960s, the growth in the number of stations on the air, and the spread of television into a larger proportion of households.

The process I have been describing has serious implications both for the economics of advertising and for advertising strategy and research. The increase in the opportunities for exposure to advertising would not in itself be noteworthy if those opportunities continued to be translated into persuasive communication at a constant rate of effectiveness. There are two reasons why this cannot be.

One is that the sheer volume of inconsistent and contradictory information represented by competing advertising messages is bound to create its own confusion. It is easier to learn one new fact a day than to learn ten and easier to learn ten than a hundred. It is easier to reach for a Coke than to decide whether to reach for a Coke or a Pepsi.

The second reason why advertising effectiveness cannot stay constant is that the time people spend with media, and thus with advertising, has changed very little in the past 15 years, so more and more units of information must be squeezed into the same sack.

All advertisers are more or less consciously aware of this process. It is summed up in the cliché that advertising must work harder than ever today to make a sale—a profound thought that I first heard expressed when I entered the business in 1948.

To compensate for declining efficiency, many advertisers have turned from media schedules that reach undifferentiated mass audiences to those that reach specific segments of the public. Thanks to the computer, the notion of selective targeting has become established advertising doctrine.

The switch from universal to selective, and therefore smaller, media normally requires the use of more individual vehicles, thus increasing the total advertising message flow. But it does not commensurately increase the number of advertising impressions received by an individual consumer. Thus media specialization tends to enlarge further the disparity between diffusion and exposure.

The use of specialized media is intended to make advertising more efficient and more powerful. That objective would be served if ads printed or broadcast were always being converted into meaningful communication at the same rate. But more choice means that a reduced proportion of the total advertising output is actually delivered. Thus the aggregate effect is to lower the impact.

With the inexorable growth of cable and new forms of telecommunication, and with the steady proliferation of specialized periodicals, the gap will widen further between the number of messages disseminated and the number of messages actually placed before the public. If this threatens to weaken the economic productivity of advertising, it only heightens the importance of making the most out of each ephemeral moment of contact with potential customers. That can only be done by wisely crafting the advertising plan, since it does no good to exhort the creators of advertisements to become more creative. While methods, institutions, and statistics will change, the basic principles of good advertising strategy will, I believe, remain valid, and they are the main preoccupation of this book.

In judging what I have to say, the reader must be alert to the fact that I held a job with one advertising medium, which naturally has competitive problems with the rest. However, while I have indeed drawn heavily on studies I directed at the Newspaper Advertising Bureau,* this book reflects my own time and my own personal opinions.

Leo Bogart

---

*Formerly called the Bureau of Advertising of the American Newspaper Publishers Association.

Acknowledgments

Some sections of this book have appeared previously in *Advertising Age*, the *Harvard Business Review*, the *Journal of Advertising*, the *Journal of Advertising Research*, the *Journal of Marketing*, the *Journal of Marketing Research*, *Management Review*, the *American Psychologist*, and *The Conference Board Record* and are used with the publishers' permission.

I am deeply indebted to Marie Thornton for her conscientious labors in typing, filing, assembling, and indexing the manuscript and to Joan Walters Lent for her similar struggles with the first edition. I appreciate Richard Hagle's editorial aid, and I have had indispensable help from Ann Brady, Susan Hyer, Randi Levine, James Conaghan, and the late Mary Saxton Lehr and both help and encouragement from my wife, Agnes Bogart.

L.B.

It is far easier to write ten passably effective Sonnets, good enough to take in the not too inquiring critic, than one effective advertisement that will take in a few thousand of the uncritical buying public.

Aldous L. Huxley, *On the Margin*

We would spare no effort in the organization of good advertising. Neither should we economize on advertising, because expenditures for it are repaid a hundredfold.

M. Argunov, in *Sovietskaya Torgovlya* [Soviet Trade], February, 1966

Introduction

Advertising is a growing business, already transformed in the few years since this edition of *Strategy in Advertising* last went to press. Over the years, it has outpaced the American economy and made rapid advances around the world. In the United States of 1990, it involves the spending of some $133 billion, more than the gross national product of all but a handful of nations. It provides employment to hundreds of thousands of people.

Advertising is an unusual business because it deals in communication, which unarguably is an art form. Those who prepare advertisements must work to meet deadlines and timetables to which the creative muse is not always responsive. A continuing preoccupation of the managements who run advertising enterprises has been the problem of how to foster the artistic temperament and at the same time harness it within the budgetary and scheduling constraints that business requires.

In this book I have tried to apply scientific method to the art of advertising, but without any illusion that advertising is a science itself. My interest is in the ideas that underlie professional practice. I have tried throughout to use statistics as indicators and for comparative purposes, rather than as facts worth noting in themselves. Changes come so fast that statistical data become obsolete as quickly as they are set down. The significant trends to watch are in the social environment, in the structure of marketing institutions, and in the mass media experience.

The Changing Society

The changes in advertising's social environment have already had enormous repercussions on the markets that advertising serves and on the living patterns to which advertising must be responsive. They have produced and will continue to produce a society with greater capacity to consume and with a penchant for consuming differently than it did.

Social change creates new patterns in housing, transportation, savings and investment, entertainment, dress, diet, and drink. Product innovation is spurred by the growth of the consumer economy and by its growing complexity. Changing aspirations are reflected in new tastes and styles. New niches open up in the market. The demand for new products accelerates. Second homes; eating out; the rise of wine, soft drinks, and tofu; the decline of liquor, coffee, and meat; the introduction of single-service packaging and home security systems; the burgeoning of the health club, health maintenance and nursing-home industries—all these are manifestations of the developments in society. Speculation about changes still in the offing is itself a growing business.

The trends now under way do not represent any sharp discontinuity from what went on before. The character of the American people has been changing continually since the country's beginnings. The evolving age distribution of the population reflects changing rates of family formation occasioned by wars and depressions, subsequent baby booms, and grandbaby boomlets. It also reflects medical technology in the form of birth control techniques and life-extending drugs and surgical methods. As people live longer, the work force becomes a declining part of the population and faces greater economic burdens. At the same time, the growing numbers of active elderly look for new styles and meanings for their lives.

Age distribution affects the structure of families, which are formed later now that outside work has replaced housework as the norm for women. When women work, income and consumption power go up, self-image changes for both sexes, and the patterns of household maintenance and leisure activity also change. There are fewer children and new complexities to the care of children in dual-career families. Families have been getting smaller. More people live alone (partly because they are living longer, partly because the divorce rate has gone up as a result of the heightened instability of family life). With growing social acceptance of premarital sex and of homosexuality comes an increase in the number of nonfamily households.

The rising productivity of the American economy has led to increases in real income, and the changing nature of the job market has fortified the traditional impetus toward ever higher educational aspirations and achievements. Rising education and income levels have accelerated personal mobility and reduced insularity and regionalism. The Advertising Council warns that by the year 2000 two out of three Americans could be illiterate, suggesting that a majority of those now alive will be dead or amnesic by that time. Actually, there has been and will continue to be a steady growth in the proportion of young people who finish high school, go on to college and add to the productive skills that fuel the nation's economy.

But personal consumption levels continue to be lowered by the social burden of poverty. Racial and ethnic minorities make up a growing proportion of the entire population and constitute majorities in many large cities. Caught up in a clash of cultures and the aftermath of rapid social change, the urban underclass has experienced an intensified alienation that manifests itself in disorganized families and in repeat patterns of dependency and delinquency. This has had profound effects on everyone else's living habits and has weakened the traditional function of cities as catalysts of civilized human contact and as market centers.

Media audiences change as the population does. Changing family structure has put increased time pressures on everyone, so that media exposure more commonly concurs with other activity, including other media activity (reading with the radio or TV set on). A better educated, more mobile public is by definition more resistant to persuasion, more concerned with acquiring information, more interested in product comparisons. It responds to new themes and images.

Advertising, like other marketing institutions, is inextricable from the changes in its social setting. But advertising is also an important force for change. It has fed the voraciously expanding appetite to consume goods and services, an appetite that has not been matched by commensurate increases in productivity, and that must share some blame for the national deficits in trade and in the federal budget.

The Changing Economy and the Economics of Advertising

The American consumer economy has been changing too. Manufacturing represents only half of it, and services will continue to become an even bigger part of the total. The service sector represents not merely the expansion of existing industries (like insurance or food service) but also the creation of vast new industries (like computer software). While cobblers and barmaids are in service trades, so are security analysts and genetic engineers. The general trend, matching the demographic developments already reviewed, seems destined to move the mainstream of the American public into more of a white-collar lifestyle.

This trend carries important implications for advertising. The advertising-to-sales ratio for service businesses has always been considerably less (2.7% among the 100 leading advertisers in 1984) than for manufacturing businesses (4.4%). The implication would seem to be that advertising will get a decreasing percentage of a growing gross national product.

In the minds of consumers, and in the preoccupations of the advertising business itself, advertising is dominated by the major packaged goods brands. Their big budgets and high visibility reflect the large advertising-to-sales ratios common in product fields where real brand differences are negligible. It seems inherently easier to build a brand image around a tangible piece of merchandise than around an intangible service.

Services may be more likely than goods to find their markets among limited target groups of consumers rather than among the mass public. They commonly deliver benefits that require extensive explanation and are not easily summarized in a single catchy phrase or visual symbol. These attributes may carry implications for service advertising's comparative use of print and broadcast. They also bear on the selection of appropriate units of advertising space or time. Advertisers who try to maximize targeted reach and frequency within a defined budget now tend to take the advertising unit for granted. If they turn more and more to long and demanding messages, frequency may have to give way.

Although in the late 1980s advertising's growth did not keep pace with the consumer economy, this appears to be part of a recurring cycle rather than an indication of continuing decline. One explanation advanced for the diminishing ratio of advertising to sales is the growing emphasis on sales promotion. The last few years have seen substantial growth in sales promotion budgets, either aimed directly at consumers, like coupons and premiums, or intended to heighten a brand's visibility in the retail store through incentives and allowances paid to the trade.

As companies expand into each other's traditional territories, the number of new brands and line extensions continues to grow, and competition intensifies for the limited amount of shelf and display space at the point of sale. Marketers' attention shifts from the struggle to influence the consumer to the primary battle to get products into the stores in the first place. Sheer presence and the visibility that can attract consumers sometimes appear to count for a lot more than any amount of preconditioning through advertising. Trade promotions offer direct or indirect incentives to retailers to put the product where it can be bought.

Much consumer promotion takes the form of spending for coupon advertising in newspapers, magazines and the mail. Coupons delivered through these media produce immediate sales effects when they are redeemed, but the advertisements in which they are embedded refresh the favorable awareness of the brand among many more readers who never tear out or cash the coupon. In any case, statistics on nonmedia sales promotion expenditures have been considerably overstated, as McCann-Erickson's authoritative analyst, Robert J. Coen, points out. Consumer and trade promotions together will amount to no more than $15 billion in 1990.

The objective of sales promotion is to move merchandise quickly, rather than to change purchasing habits or brand attachments as advertising does. When promotions are used by one brand in a product category, they also tend to be used by the competition, so they rarely have more than short-run effects on market share.

The short-run results may be precisely what more and more marketers are after. The compensation of brand managers is linked to short-term indicators of sales gains rather than to the long-term profitability of their brands. In the 1980s, corporate America became increasingly preoccupied with the quarterly balance sheet as an indicator of success, and building for the future took second place to appreciation of stock value as management's primary goal.

The ratio of long-term to short-term effects is different for advertisements with different objectives. In fact, it varies with every advertisement. It is always difficult to determine how much of the value of advertising represents the accumulation of impressions and reminders that occur over an extensive period of time, and how much represents the immediate stimulus to buy.

As this book points out, advertising has generally been regarded as an investment rather than as an expense. This became more than a merely philosophical issue by the late 1980s, as the advertising business faced proposed tax legislation, at the federal, state, and local levels. (It successfully forced the repeal of a tax on advertising in Florida.) Central to some of the proposals was the idea that some proportion of a firm's advertising budget should be considered a long-term investment rather than a current operating expense. The proportion thus designated would be wholly arbitrary, of course. Ironically, the advertising establishment, in insisting that advertising was a routine cost of doing daily business, was contradicting its historical position that advertising must be considered an investment whose returns are paid back over the long haul.

The Concentration of Market Power

Power in decisionmaking is increasingly concentrated, both among advertisers and in agencies. The late 1980s saw a spate of mergers and acquisitions, inspired by the new forms of high-interest, high-risk financing that were generating excitement in the financial world and transforming much of American industry.

Leading executives in manufacturing, retailing, and the agency business expect the big to get bigger, for fewer companies to account for a growing share of the total. The process of concentration seems irreversible, without a major shift or upheaval in national economic policy.

In the new climate of Wall Street, a company's principal assets often lay in the consumer consciousness of its established brands—a consciousness created by its sustained advertising over the years. Giant cash-rich tobacco companies like Philip Morris and R.J. Reynolds sought diversification to balance their vulnerability to restrictions and attrition of their cigarette sales, and bought out major food companies who were already leading advertisers. The top five national advertisers (Philip Morris, Procter & Gamble, General Motors, RJR/Nabisco, and Grand Met) now account for about a fifth of all national spending in consumer media. These giants are formidable forces in the media marketplace, with agencies more than ever attentive to their interests and impulses.

All this brings changes in power relationships. Big advertisers can exert their market power to extract advantages in rates and positions. As corporations got bigger, they spent more money to advertise, and inevitably used the power of their big budgets to bargain from strength. At the same time they demanded what they considered to be greater rationality and accountability in the way their ad money was spent.

Growing concentration of power over advertising budgets brought with it an increased pressure on advertising rates, as the massed weight of billings, both in supercorporations and in superagencies, was brought to bear in a tightening cost squeeze. Media that had traditionally kept firmly to their published rates were being required to negotiate. Media were encouraged to "add value" in the form of merchandising support or special ad positioning that might formerly have commanded a price.

The trend in media buying followed that of corporate mergers—the art of the "deal" triumphed over more considered strategies. By 1990, advertisers were spending as much money on program syndication as they spent on cable ($1.25 billion). Program syndication involved bartering programs, including their commercials, for air time. Stations could turn around and sell open commercial time to local advertisers. Such syndication sales are usually based on flexible "ceiling and floor" arrangements that provide compensatory "make-goods" or even cash rebates, if a program does not generate the expected audiences. The growing impulse toward cost-savings often worked at cross-purposes with the goals of scientific media planning to which lip-service continued to be paid.

The life and death of periodicals and programs, the waxing and waning of advertising creative fashions, and the accepted methodologies of advertising research seem likely to be determined increasingly by what the Big Boys want. Moreover, these Big Boys, ruling over expanded empires, are besieged by more requests for appointments; more literature floods their in-boxes. They have less time to listen to new presentations and read new research reports. The brilliance of the deal-makers at the top of the corporate pyramid isn't always matched at the working levels where advertising decisions are made.

Advertisers and their agencies would indignantly reject the charge that they are given to the use of formulas in their media judgments or advertising research techniques, but it is difficult for them to avoid this. The management of every major corporation is today wrestling with the question of how it can reconcile its inherently bureaucratic operating style with the entrepreneurial spirit required to be innovative and competitive.

Consolidation in Retailing and in Media

The merger trend affects retailing as well. Here too, the rationale for mergers and bigness lies in the economies of scale that come with centralized purchasing and planning. Central planning is dependent on formulas: what works in El Paso must work in Mankato. With the application of the Universal Product Code (described on page 356) and other scanner-produced data, fixed criteria can be applied to determine whether or not an item should be kept on the shelf. As the major retailers' market share expands, so does their power to dictate terms, both to manufacturers and to media.

Turmoil has resulted from the high-interest borrowing required to float buy-outs. A notable example was the Canadian Campeau Corporation, which acquired major retail groups, notably Federated and Allied, that included some of the country's best-known department store chains, and then proceeded to bankrupt them in the process of paying off its debt. The managements of companies caught up in this game were under mounting pressure to produce short-run profits by cutting costs, and advertising budgets were in many cases among the first to feel the knife. Major groups of stores with names long familiar to consumers have been merged with other groups and in some cases, eliminated overnight.

Mergers and acquisitions were also highly visible in media organizations, the most noteworthy case being the creation in 1989 of Time Warner, a $10.6 billion combination that included almost the entire gamut of media except for daily newspapers.

More and more newspapers were owned by multi-media companies.

Giants like Capital Cities/ABC, Gannett, Times-Mirror, CBS, and News America have steadily expanded their holdings in both broadcasting and print. This has affected the way media are sold. Companies like Gannett, Times-Mirror and News America have studied ways of selling an assortment of media through a single sales force, thereby switching the underlying rationale for an advertising buy from the medium to the market.

Changing communications technology has created ambiguities between broadcast and print and between video and film, spurring media conglomerates to multiply and diversify their holdings. U.S. media were to a growing degree elements of international empires like Rupert Murdoch's News Corporation, Germany's Bertelsmann, and France's Hachette, which move capital, people, and editorial and programming ideas back and forth across frontiers, as a by-product of the enormous development of international trade and marketing. The increasing internationalization of the media and advertising businesses were fostered by high expectations for the start of the European Community in 1992. It brought along some easy talk about global advertising, the idea being that there were cost savings in the universal application of the same visual materials, and the same marketing plans. But this ran into the inescapable fact that competitive conditions as well as the social climate of consumption differ greatly from country to country. International advertisers like the soap, oil, and electronics companies have by now well explored the opportunities and discovered the limitations of using the same creative symbols and slogans in more than one place.

The Changing Agency

Agencies have also been caught up in the drive toward consolidation. The top four groups of agencies (Saatchi and Saatchi, Interpublic, WPP, and Omnicom) represent a third of all U.S. agency billings. By 1989, the J. Walter Thompson Company, with billings of $1.79 billion, no longer had the country's biggest domestic billings. In fact it ranked number nine. The number one position was held by Leo Burnett, with $1.95 billion in U.S. volume. Thompson itself was merely a subsidiary of WPP, a British-based advertising conglomerate constructed through financial skills, rather than advertising genius. WPP, which took over the Ogilvy and Mather group of agencies in 1989, was the world's biggest group of advertising agencies, with billings of $16 billion ($8.3 billion in the United States), followed by Saatchi and Saatchi, also British-owned, a $15.75 billion company whose financial stability increasingly came under question.

"A lot of the fun has gone out of the business," said Bob Jacoby, former chairman of Ted Bates, after he deposited $110 million as his share of the agency's sale to Saatchi and Saatchi. Fun is what the agency business has been, and what makes advertising successful. Can large agencies create great advertising? Of course they do, every day, but the job is tougher for them than it used to be.

Even if there were no agency takeovers and mergers, the process of corporate conglomeration would have affected the agency business. Giant agencies dealing with giant conglomerates inevitably are faced with client conflicts. This may open the way for newcomers and change both the organizational structure of the agency business and the client-agency relationship. The superadvertiser has so much at stake that it becomes more inclined to think it knows best, less inclined to listen to the agency's advice. Advertising research represents sensitive marketing intelligence that becomes a pawn in the game. Competitive considerations make clients more inclined to concentrate it in-house, more reluctant to leave it within the agency's control. Where agency research, at least in its heyday a quarter-century ago, tended to be catalytic, eclectic, and cosmopolitan, corporate research styles tend to be insular, linked to the company's internal politics and dependent on favored research suppliers for intellectual stimulation.

The growth of the superagencies arose in part as a way of redressing the imbalance of power, by confronting the gigantic client with a force that could withstand intimidation. The first person to understand this was Marion Harper, Jr., who became president of the McCann-Erickson agency in 1948 at the age of 31, and created the Interpublic Group of companies at the close of the decade. Harper died poor in 1989, in self-imposed exile to avoid his many creditors. When I worked for him, over thirty years ago, the agency had Chrysler in its stable of big accounts. Chrysler was known as a difficult and demanding client, resistant to research and sluggish in its marketing posture. That year (1958), the automobile business was in a deep recession and Chrysler was hurting very badly.

Along with many of the other executives of the agency, I was sent out on a special project to interview automobile dealers around the country and to find out how they felt about the state of the market and about automotive advertising in general. We thought we were working on a project for Chrysler. But that's not what our boss had in mind. He used the results of that crash study to build a presentation to General Motors in a pitch for the Buick account. When he announced the resignation of the Chrysler business, it sent a shock through many of us. We felt it was unseemly and improper. The agency was supposed to work at the client's behest, not the other way around.

It was customary in this volatile business for clients to fire agencies, but never the reverse. Harper showed that this could be done. He positioned the agency as an independent force. And by acquiring Marschalk & Pratt and later a stable of other agencies under the umbrella of Interpublic, Harper made it clear that he envisioned a marketing world in which it was possible for an agency, through separately managed subsidiaries, to handle competing accounts. This is the principle on which most of the superagencies are based today, and it is in part a response to the declining number of major corporate clients, along with the increase in the number of their separate subdivisions.

Agency mergers appeared to promise a means of reducing administrative expenses and thus of meeting the client's demand for cost reductions. Some advertisers tried to break down the established fifteen-percent commission structure, preferring to buy extra marketing services as needed or to supply them through their own staffs, thus limiting the agency's functions to the basics of creating and placing ads. The commission system had developed in the days when the advertising agent represented newspapers in remote locations and collected his share of the money before transmitting the rest. Nearly a hundred years ago, when agencies became responsible for choosing among media and for writing and designing the ads, their function became differentiated from that of the media representatives. The advertising agency was now expected to act in the client's interests. The set commission structure encouraged creative ingenuity because it held out the promise of reward commensurate with the growth of the client's business.

With the coming of radio, the creation of advertising and the management of media selection became more complex, more technical, and more specialized, and the structure of agencies changed accordingly. In the era before marketing became a well-known term and an accepted discipline, the agency worked in close harness with the client's management and sales department to set sales objectives and to plan new product introductions.

The stock in trade of the account executive (the huckster, the man in the grey flannel suit) was his ability to command the client's confidence. His wise counsel and good fellowship, even his bottomless thirst for lunchtime martinis, had to appear indispensable.

To fit their expanding role, agencies developed specialized departments for research, for sales promotion, for merchandising, for public relations. The fifteen-percent commission no longer proved adequate to meet the client's growing demand for more services. Agencies began to charge extra for them and even to set up subsidiaries that could charge special fees above and beyond the commission without raising questions in the client's accounting department.

As the cost of marketing services continued to grow, it was inevitable that more and more corporations felt they could operate these functions internally, without the need to use an agency. Corporate marketing staffs appeared and expanded, corporate media departments and house agencies proliferated. Corporations developed their own sales promotion and public relations facilities. Clients tended to deal directly with outside research services themselves and to rely increasingly on syndicated and prepackaged research. Retailers lagged behind manufacturing and service corporations in this process, but they took much the same route.

The construction of gigantic managerial structures in the agencies brings with it new dangers from formularized thinking. It also threatens the quality of the creative environment in which great advertising ideas must be generated. The superagencies continue to command the greatest resources and can offer the greatest rewards for talent, but their very size and system is not always congenial to the blithe and iconoclastic spirits who can produce the kind of ads that penetrate consumer resistance.

The Rising Tide of Messages

And the real challenge to the advertising profession is to create ads that can stand out. Over a century ago, a commentator wrote, "The names of successful advertisers have become household words where great poets, politicians, philosophers, and warriors of the land are as yet unheard of; there is instant recognition of Higg's saleratus and Wigg's soap even where the title of Tennyson's last work is thought to be 'In a Garden' and Longfellow understood as the nickname of a tall man."

Today, Higg's saleratus is hardly a household word, while Longfellow and Tennyson are remembered and even read. Which merely supports the theme of this book: that the depth and intensity and meaning of a communication is not touched by popularity contests.

The volume of messages disseminated has been growing at a much more rapid rate than the number to which people are actually exposed. Just between 1967 and 1986, the number of TV, radio, magazine, and newspaper advertisements disseminated in the United States increased by 133%. The number of TV messages alone increased by 257%, with more channels and shorter commercials. The number of TV messages to which the average person is exposed grew 128% in that period; the total number of messages by 73%. But the human capacity to absorb and make sense of this swollen flow of attempted persuasion hasn't changed one iota in those twenty years. In this welter of communications, the messages that stand out do so not because of their cost or number but because of their character.

The number of ad messages disseminated will double in the next dozen years, in the opinion of a panel of 250 top marketing executives whom I queried shortly after this book was last printed. They believe that the proliferation of specialized media vehicles of all kinds will continue. A majority of agency executives also expect the fifteen-second commercial to become the standard TV unit, thereby doubling the inventory of positions and increasing competitive pressure against other media. A greatly increased output of advertisements must make it harder for any individual message to penetrate the Babel of competing and contradictory messages.

Specialization and audience fractionation would seem to indicate increases in real advertising costs. This in turn would reduce the efficiency of advertising relative to other forms of selling and promotion and might affect the ratio of advertising to the total consumer economy. Miraculously, the 250 advertising leaders think that consumers will also be exposed to double the number of messages as at present. This is impossible. When the choice of channels goes from ten to twenty, we can still only watch one at a time.

If consumers raise higher protective barriers of inattention against the overload of messages with which they are burdened, this will build the importance of the creative element in advertising and thus of research that offers guidance to the writers and producers of ads.

By 1989, 39% of prime-time network commercials were the short fifteen-second variety, though they represented only 6% of all spot announcements. Psychologist Herbert Krugman points out that "perception precedes perceptual defense," so that the viewer is "captive" for the first few seconds of any commercial, during which a kind of orientation takes place that governs the decision as to whether to keep on paying attention. With shorter commercials, this preliminary orientation takes up a greater proportion of the time, leaving less for the actual advertising message to take effect.

The shortening of commercials, and the consequent multiplication of their numbers, led to a drop in recall scores, as shown by Burke Research studies commissioned by the Newspaper Advertising Bureau, and described on page 178. Fifteen-second commercials had not yet become prevalent when the most recent of these studies was conducted in 1986, and the recall of the "last commercial" seen in prime time was 7%, the same as in 1981. Recall, however, was lowest in the age groups that did the most viewing. In fact, recall levels were almost three times as high among people aged 18–34 as among those over 65, although the younger people watch 42% fewer hours of television, on average. And the shorter commercials, as might be expected, were less well remembered. Indexing recall of the average sixty-second commercial at 100, the thirty-second ones averaged 43, the fifteen-second ones 30, and ten-second commercials came in at 11.

Since production costs have been escalating, commercials tend to be aired over and over again, which means that they are recalled because of their familiarity rather than because of the impact they make. In 1965, 31% of those who recalled a commercial said they had seen it previously; by 1986, the proportion had doubled, to 61%.

Even more important, however, was the fact that commercials embedded within a cluster had only 28% the average recall level of the opening commercial. (The last commercial had 85%.) In Australia, a study by D. Bednall and M. Hannaford has also recently found that isolated commercials are better recalled than clustered commercials. As the number of fifteen-second commercials increases, more of them will obviously have to be placed in the middle of a commercial pod.

Commercials are not the only aspect of television that is changing fast. With cable in 57% of all households and VCRs in 66%, more and more viewers had remote control devices that enabled them to switch channels and zap commercials. According to a survey made by Florida State University's Edward Forrest and Barry Sapolsky, 36% of remote control owners and 75% of VCR owners regularly fast-forward past commercials on playback.

With the growing number of programming choices available, the networks' share of the television audience continued to drop, falling to 62% in prime time in 1989. Yet television, on-air and cable, continued to increase its total share of advertising budgets, especially from local advertisers.

Television is not the only medium undergoing great change. By 1990 there were twenty national radio networks on the air, appealing to distinctive musical tastes. The preceding year saw the start-up of 255 consumer magazines, each vying for a different definable sliver of the audience. Media were being created to fill what were perceived to be "niches" in the market that certain advertisers might want to reach, rather than as expressions of an editorial or programming vision.

A few years ago, the rise of new forms of telecommunications might have been at the top of everyone's list of trends to watch. But the home computer market has grown slowly, and experiments with videotex have thus far evoked a disappointing response. The 250 experts I questioned are skeptical about the advent of interactive telecommunications within the next 25 years. It is obviously not essential for such systems to achieve saturation before they begin to have an impact on the established forms of marketing. Catalog merchandising and telemarketing have already made substantial inroads into conventional in-store retailing. The diversion of even a small amount of additional business into computerized home shopping would further affect retailing profitability and practices, including advertising practices. The pricing economics of retail and national advertising are interrelated, and changes in retail advertising would have different repercussions on newspapers and radio than on magazines.

Although videotex and teletext may not emerge as competitors for existing media, as initially feared, they will produce valuable new ways of assembling information, including market-related information that could take on some of the functions of advertising.

As pay TV continues to accumulate larger audiences, it may begin to accept advertising as a way of limiting rate increases to the subscribers. Should that occur, it would mean a new source of competition for the networks. While cable broadens viewing choices and accelerates audience fractionation, the VCR reverses the tendency for viewing to become more individualistic as sets spread around the home. In the VCR household, the family huddles together as of yore in the living room to make sure it gets its money's worth from the rented movie cassette. In the offing is high-definition TV, which should make commercials more compelling and vivid.

The New Problems of Measurement

Technological changes in the media pose new and difficult problems of accurate audience measurement. The proliferation of media complicates the task of planning, placing, and evaluating the performance of advertisements. Twin tendencies toward media specialization and toward target marketing have created a growing need for market and audience data based on ever larger samples, to permit statistically significant comparisons among subgroups of the public. Like the feckless search for the Holy Grail, marketing managements have embarked on a quest for the Single Source, a fountainhead of data on both media and product consumption. The latest buzz phrase making the rounds was "single-source data." This refers to the dream of getting all the information on what individuals buy and on all their media experiences from one giant research service, so that cause and effect can clearly be measured.

Getting lots of different kinds of information from a panel of respondents is an excellent way of doing experiments, in which elements can be changed and the consequences tracked. But the idea of the "single source" goes beyond this legitimate purpose. It has the ambition of encompassing the whole range of projectable information on the consumption of products and communications.

Presumably this would end the deplorable present necessity of putting together the data derived from different research organizations, with all the inevitable inconsistencies that result. The underlying premise is that the quality of information you can get from a single source is equivalent to what can be obtained from specialized studies, each trying to learn as much as it can about one subject.

For the reasons explained in Chapters 11 and 12, the quest for a single source is destined to founder on the hard realities of information-gathering, as it becomes ever more difficult to gain the cooperation of a representative sampling of the public. Just as a smaller number of companies sponsor, place, and disseminate a growing proportion of all advertisements, so a smaller number of organizations account for a growing share of the research that is used to evaluate media.

In 1989, syndicated research on local newspaper audiences became a monopoly of Scarborough Research, a subsidiary of a Dutch media conglomerate, VNU, which also acquired Belden Associates, the leading supplier of customized newspaper audience research. Far more significant was the monopoly that Dun & Bradstreet's A.C. Nielsen Company established over national television ratings in 1988, after a British company, A.G.B. Research, gave up its effort to break into the U.S. market.

A.G.B.'s brief presence had forced Nielsen to accelerate the conversion of its national ratings (and local ratings in New York and Los Angeles, in 1990) from the audimeter method described in Chapter 11 to the People Meter. This device is an electronic version of the viewer diary. Individuals in a national sample of 4,000 households are identified by a key-numbered push-button, and are reminded by a light on top of their TV set to indicate their comings and goings from the room whenever the set is on. A report from the network-sponsored CONTAM (Committee on Nationwide TV Audience Measurement) noted that two-thirds of the households originally asked to join the People Meter panel refused to do so, and that the characteristics of these noncooperators could not be determined because they refused to cooperate!

Since the People Meter ratings averaged about 10% lower than those obtained by the earlier method, their adoption at first occasioned considerable anguish on the part of the networks, but the adjustment was eventually made, and the broadcasters prodded Nielsen to measure visitors to the household and to account for out-of-home viewing.

It was evident from experimental research that family members often became somewhat lackadaisical in fulfilling their assigned button-pushing, and that the originally contemplated two-year life for the sample was much too long. Nielsen, working through the Sarnoff Laboratories of SRI, proceeded to experiment with the engineering of a "passive" People Meter that would automatically detect the presence of particular individuals in the family (and distinguish them from large dogs), thus making button-pushing unnecessary. Meanwhile, Arbitron, Nielsen's leading competitor in local ratings, was working with a French company called Telemetric and with the MIT Media Laboratory to develop its own passive meter system. Arbitron had already introduced its own (interactive) People Meter and planned to have it in 20 markets by 1995. In Denver, Arbitron's ScanAmerica subsidiary was linking audience information with purchasing information obtained by a scanning xxx Strategy in Advertising

rod that consumers are asked to wave over the items they bring home from the supermarket, to produce measurements of advertising effects.

A passive People Meter would solve the problem of measuring viewers who left the program, but not the problem of inattention. Research by Television Audience Assessment found that half the audience leave the room during the course of a typical program, most of them repeatedly. Two out of five gave the program full attention.

At the University of Massachusetts, Daniel E. Anderson and Diane E. Field placed video cameras in the television rooms of 100 households, photographing both the set and everything going on in the room at the same time. The room had no one in it 15% of the time. And among the people who were in the room, only three out of five were watching television with their eyes on the set at a typical moment in the program.

Accurate measurement of television audiences was hampered by the practice of "hyping" during the "sweeps" weeks when local ratings are taken. The problem was not limited to local stations. Networks also schedule specials and miniseries during these crucial periods, in an attempt to expand their audiences.

While these developments suggest that advertising research has more on its plate than ever before, the research function in the larger agencies has progressively atrophied. This seems to reflect in part the cost-cutting impulses of publicly-held companies concerned with the bottom line and short-run profits. Partly it reflects the increasing reliance on syndicated research readily available on the desktop computer of every corporate manager. Partly it reflects the tendency of many clients to develop their own in-house capabilities for both market research and, in many cases, media analysis and planning.

The changes I have just described seem important and vivid as I comment on them at the start of a new decade, but they will have given way to others as you begin to read this book. Although the advertising business is in perpetual motion, the principles of intelligent advertising strategy are durable. I can't guarantee success to those who follow them, but those who don't are unlikely to find it.

Leo Bogart
New York

Chapter 1
Advertising on the American Scene

At noon on a summer day in 1916 a media representative called at the J. Walter Thompson agency and found that his luncheon date was tied up with a client and would not be able to see him. He was about to leave, he told Sidney Dean* years later, when he found himself being clapped on the back by the normally aloof Commodore Thompson himself. To his amazement, Thompson invited him to lunch at the Duane Hotel across Madison Avenue and even bought the first round of drinks. He then made a gleeful announcement: "Congratulate me, Joe! I just sold the business to the Resor boys. They don't know it, but the advertising agency business has seen its best days!"

Two-thirds of a century later, 75 billion dollars were being spent annually on advertising in the United States (58 billion through consumer publications, broadcasting, and posters);** the "agency business" was handling over 20 billion dollars worth of accounts; and the J. Walter Thompson agency alone was doing business worldwide at the rate of $1.2 billion a year!

Advertising billings in the United States have expanded 26-fold since World War II. Not all of this expansion has been converted into greater advertising pressure on the individual consumer. But even when we adjust for inflation and for the rise in population, the growth of advertising as an economic and social force stands as one of the most remarkable developments on the American scene in recent years.

Every day, 12 billion display and 184 billion classified advertising messages pour forth from 1,710 daily newspapers, billions of others from 7,600 weekly

---

*Sidney W. Dean, Jr., a former vice president of the J. Walter Thompson agency, to wnom I am indebted for this anecdote.

**In 1983, about $75 billion was spent on advertising in the United States, or $443 per adult. Of the total, daily newspapers represented $20.3 billion ($2.75 of it in national advertising); television $16.1 billion ($11.9 billion national); magazines $3.9 billion (87 percent national); radio $5.2 billion (about $1.3 national); and outdoor and transit advertising about $900 million (about $600 million national). The remainder represented weekly newspapers ($1.4 billion); industrial, farm, and trade publications ($2.6 billion); direct mail ($11.6 billion); telephone yellow pages ($4 billion), and other miscellaneous forms of promotion. Cable television, included in the television totals, received less than $400 million.

newspapers, and 6 billion more each day from 430 general magazines and 10,500 other periodicals. There are 4,658 AM and 3,367 FM radio stations broadcasting an average of 2,600,000 commercials a day; and 844 television stations broadcast 330,000 commercials a day, redisseminated by 5,000 cable systems. Every day, millions of people are confronted with over 500,000 outdoor billboards and painted bulletins, with 1.5 million car cards and posters in buses, subways, and commuter trains, with 40 million direct mail pieces and leaflets, and with billions of display and promotion items.

The main source of messages to the consumer is not within advertising mass media at all, but at the point of sale. We are subjected to more product ideas and impressions from packages and store window displays than we get from television commercials or magazine ads.

The signs that identify shops are a form of advertising. Matchbooks, calendars, and a host of other commonplace objects carry advertising messages that are hardly ever out of sight, though they are generally out of mind because we absorb them not as active communications but as part of our visual environment.[1]

Advertising and the business climate

One reason why more advertising messages are disseminated per person today than was the case only a few years ago is that there are more new products than ever and an increasingly competitive business climate. Throughout the world, the marketing function has become increasingly important to corporate managements, and the attention paid to advertising has grown correspondingly.

Because advertising is at the white-hot center of marketing competition, perhaps no other aspect of American business management undergoes so many

---

The widely used McCann-Erickson estimates of advertising expenditures include a factor that covers the non-media operational costs of advertising departments and classify all direct mail as national advertising. Actually, 30 percent of direct mail is business to business advertising; of the component addressed to consumers, only one-third is national. This means that while McCann-Erickson reported that national advertising represented 57 percent of total expenditures in 1983, it was only 40 percent of the advertising in consumer media. About 85 percent of *national* consumer advertising investments were made in the four major media. Of this four-media total, television received about 61 percent of the investment, magazines 18 percent, daily newspapers about 14 percent, and radio 7 percent.

In addition to these advertising investments, the public spent vast sums to purchase newspapers ($6.7 billion in 1982) and magazines ($3.8 billion) and to buy and maintain radios and television sets ($28.5 billion). The advent of new electronic media further increased the public contribution to the support of the American mass media system.

In 1982, $6.8 billion was being spent on home video. Of the total, 37 percent went for basic cable services; 28 percent for pay cable; 14 percent for VCRs and other home recording devices; 6 percent for subscription TV; 4 percent for prerecorded video cassettes; 2 percent for video discs; 6 percent for blank tapes; 1 percent for video disc players; and 3 percent for multipoint distribution systems. Cable's revenues from subscribers amounted to $3.3 billion in 1981, compared with $129 million from advertisers. About 85 percent of cable advertising accompanies satellite-delivered programming, and only 15% of it originates in local cable systems. Of U.S. households, 15 percent also had an electronic video game at home.

fluctuations in its focus of attention from year to year. There is a ceaseless search for new formulas to make better use of the advertising expenditures that business finds so hard to evaluate. Fads and fashions are characteristic of advertising as they are of any field that is fraught with an intense competition of ideas and a constant outcropping of new pressures from unpredictable sources.

In advertising, fashions center on key phrases, often ones arising from the vocabulary of research—motivation research, operations research, "demographics" ("demos"), "psychographics," "positioning," "target marketing." Perhaps because it was vaguely associated with sex, the motivation research of the 1960s got more general publicity than most advertising fads and left an indelible impression on advertising's words and illustrations. It reawakened interest in the Great Creative Idea as the heart of successful advertising.

When American business was reorganized in the postwar years, marketing emerged as a major function which coordinated hitherto separate specialties: product development, sales promotion, merchandising, advertising, and market research. Great emphasis was placed on the integrated marketing plan that attempted to reduce selling to the same cut-and-dried assemblage of budgets, quotas, and completion rates that occur in manufacturing. Contrary to the assumption of the planners that customers could be "manufactured," creative people in the business continue to be attracted by the old P. T. Barnum concept of advertising as the creation of dreams and fantasies.

In contrast to such technical marketing specialties as market research or distribution planning, advertising is one of the most familiar phenomena in modern society. Its very familiarity leads business decision makers to deal with it in commonsense lay terms and with an illusion of knowledgeability that they would hardly assume on other specialized subjects. The businessman who fancies himself an advertising expert is not only the bane of professional advertising men, he is also responsible for much of the wasted effort that a surprising proportion of advertising expenditures represents.

Advertising and society

The importance of advertising in American life cannot be measured either by the sheer number of individual advertising messages disseminated or by the substantial expenditures these represent, whether in actual dollars or as a percentage of consumer sales. It is also necessary to consider the power and influence of advertising institutions and leadership in the business community and—at election time—in politics.*

Political campaigning has been transformed by television, which has made candidates for national and state office into highly visible personalities whose charm and debating skills often count for more than their positions on public issues. A new breed of "campaign consultants" has emerged as specialists in the "packaging" of candidates for television; they have adapted product advertising

---

*An advertising agency with a political assignment uses the standard operating procedures and terminology of the trade. On one occasion, a meeting of the "product group" of an agency planning a pre-election advertising campaign was interrupted by the unexpected appearance of the "product," the governor of the state.

techniques to the creation of political "images" and "sales points" crystallizing the traditional rhetoric.[2]

More than in politics, however, the significance of advertising is expressed by the ubiquitous presence of its symbols and slogans throughout the culture. The historian (and Librarian of Congress) Daniel Boorstin has equated the emergence of advertising in the mid-19th century (along with brand names) with the rise of the "Consumption Community," a peculiarly democratic institution in which "the material goods that historically have been the symbols which elsewhere separated men from one another have become, under American conditions, symbols which hold men together."[3]

As a subject of conversation, advertising can generate strong emotions, pro and con. For several generations advertising has been condemned by intellectuals because of its frequent use of the cliché in language, illustration, and concept and because of its occasional appeal to irrational motives and vulgar tastes. Within the academic community everywhere, though perhaps less in the United States than in Europe, there is also an essential cynicism about advertising's economic usefulness that reflects a sense of malaise about the place of the intellectual in the business system. Charles Horton Cooley, a pioneer social psychologist, once wrote that "only a somewhat commonplace mind will give itself wholeheartedly to the commercial ideal."[4]

The great economist Thorstein Veblen described advertising as "parasitic." The social philosopher Marshall McLuhan called it "a very powerful aggression." The historian Arnold Toynbee called it "an instrument of moral, as well as intellectual, mis-education. Insofar as it succeeds in influencing people's minds, it conditions them not to think for themselves and not to choose for themselves. It is intentionally hypnotic in its effect. It makes people suggestible and docile. In fact, it prepares them for submitting to a totalitarian regime."

To this Mandarin disdain has occasionally been added an aversion on ideological grounds. Orthodox Marxism regards advertising as a visible manifestation of the evils of capitalism, just one of innumerable techniques by which the workers and peasants are exploited by monopoly interests. For those who share the Marxist revulsion against the social waste involved in economic competition, it is easy to focus on advertising as the most blatant, vigorous, and overt manifestation. These strains of negative criticism persist in America today long after Communist economists have revised their theories and practices about the law of supply and demand, long after marketing principles and advertising's utility have been accepted as part of the natural order in the Soviet Union and other socialist countries.*

---

*Soviet advertising specializes in such exhortations as "Drink Tea" (without an exclamation point). An electric billboard on Moscow's Gorky Street sometimes flashes the words, "Advertising Advertising Advertising." The newspaper *Evening Moscow* publishes a popular advertising supplement twice a week; TV ads appear periodically in 15-minute blocks.

V. Tereshchenko, writing in Moscow's *Literaturnaya Gazeta* (translated in *Atlas*, May 1968, pp. 46-49), makes the obligatory observation that "abuses, cheating the consumer, fierce competition are facts of life in the U.S.," but he acknowledges that "whether we like it or not, advertising has always existed in its rudimentary form" and that "American advertising has its own test-proven technique which, I think, merits serious attention."

In such Soviet-bloc countries as Hungary and Rumania, marketing and advertising have become respectable fields of activity. An advertising conference I attended in one communist country included very practical discussions of market planning, advertising department operations, and showings of ads and commercials. These workaday efforts alternated with theoretical papers by party functionaries who warned that advertising must avoid petty bourgeois tendencies and advance the interests of the toiling masses.

The thesis of one such paper was one with which many Western critics of advertising would agree: advertising serves a useful economic function if it is *informative* for the consumer. Advertising that appeals to reason and facilitates more *rational* consumer choice helps promote the sale of desirable goods and services. Advertising is harmful when it appeals to emotion and plays on unconscious motives to persuade people to buy things they do not need. Incongruously, following this sermon, a collection of commercials was shown, with jingles chanting the merits of apparently identical brands of shampoo and canned peas.

Later I asked the speaker whether economic productivity was increased by competition among enterprises producing similar products, like shampoo and canned peas. He agreed that this was so. Was it, then, economically desirable for a firm to try to make its brand or company name familiar to the consuming public? Yes. Could this kind of familiarity be a desirable end in itself even if the consumer was given no other information about the product? He thought for a minute and then gave his official answer: "Unofficially, yes."

This short conversation gets down to the essential issue that both defenders and opponents of advertising must confront. Once we accept the principle of competition among firms producing what is essentially the same commodity, it follows that advertising—perhaps not all, but certainly a good deal of it in that product class—will be noninformational, except for the very fundamental information that the brand exists. When brand image represents the only distinctive feature the advertiser has to sell, he is more likely to use irrelevant and nonrational appeals and to rely on gimmick techniques to capture attention and heighten identity. These are precisely the appeals and techniques that invite criticism and censure. In practice, the factual and nonrational aspects of advertising content are very difficult to separate. To the extent that socialist societies rediscover the economic incentive value of competition among enterprises, they must become more tolerant of noninformative advertising content. As Nikolai Naumenko, the head of the Soviet Union's largest advertising agency, Soyuz Torgreklama, puts it, "We don't reject the emotional method, but we use it very carefully with the most noble purposes."[5]

The innumerable appeals of advertisers simultaneously clamoring for attention are constant reminders of the incessant claims that are made on all of us by the many complex relationships of an impersonal and mechanized society. When once we look at these appeals coldly and objectively, when once we question their meaning and value, many of them appear monstrous or ridiculous.

But the fatuous, absurd, and exaggerated symbols through which some advertisers metaphorically proclaim the virtues of their products are rarely a subject of dispassionate examination by the average citizen of contemporary America. They are accepted as part of the landscape.

Does anyone really believe that Clairol products have "The Power to Make You Beautiful," that the 24K Mastercard "Works as Hard for Your Money as You Do," or that "Us Tareyton Smokers Would Rather Fight than Switch"? Of course not; yet no one is indignant at these widely proclaimed statements because no one assumes they are to be taken at face value.*

The Western visitor to a communist country who is appalled by the countless identical plaster casts of Lenin and the sloganeering drivel adorning places of public assembly inevitably wonders how intelligent people can live seemingly normal lives in the presence of so massive and continuous an assault on their intelligence. A Pole whose company cafeteria had been festooned with a banner reading, "To Socialism through Collective Eating!" once gave me a convincing answer. He compared the political inanity in question and his own reaction to it with the animated stomach action depicted in TV commercials for analgesics, which American viewers similarly "accept" with complete aplomb. The intimation is that neither type of message really influences people directly, though it may have a more subtle effect as part of the environment.

Advertising is one of a modern society's most visible aspects. Its character reflects the state of the civilization from which it springs. The same moral standards prevail in the creation of advertising as in the ordinary conduct of citizens. Most of the rules and regulations (legal or otherwise) that generally apply to the conduct of business carry over to the conduct of businessmen as advertisers. In short, advertising and its values are interwoven with the whole fabric of society.

Individual advertisements for any particular product provide scant basis for assessing the overall social usefulness of advertising as an institution. The dramatic cases of "bad" advertising in recent years are more often those which involve misleading illustrations of permissible claims than those which involve fraudulent claims *per se*.

Depicting a product in a print illustration often requires artifice. Unretouched photographs, especially in color, rarely conform to the reality in the eye of the live beholder. With television, a whole new dimension has been added. A literal depiction, transformed into the two dimensions of the picture screen, can convey a misleading impression of how a product performs, while a contrived demonstration can come closer to the literal truth.

A shaving cream commercial that showed loose sand being shaved instead of sandpaper (as represented) was, in the producers' minds, not a deliberate deception but an attempt to dramatize a real though minor product advantage: "softening" power. Similarly, Campbell's Soup and its agency, BBDO, came under fire for placing colorless glass marbles in bowls of soup photographed for commercials so that the chunks of meat and vegetables would be visible, in defiance of gravity. In the world of hyperbole, exaggeration, and nonsense—which is the

---

*Daniel Yankelovich, addressing the 1982 Advertising Research Foundation Conference, recalled an airline commercial he had seen recently: "It showed a couple in Miami. The husband was calling his boss at home while lying in an easy chair in the sun. His wife was eating a chicken leg which she broke in half. The man said gleefully to his boss that they couldn't come back because his wife has just broken a leg."

everyday milieu of some kinds of advertising expression—the borderline between the cute and the crooked is often difficult to trace.

How does the public feel about this? Fifty-one percent (in a national sample of 4,010 adults interviewed in 1976 and 1977)[6] say that half or more of all advertising messages are deceptive in intent. (By way of comparison, 36 percent also think this is true of half or more of the statements by government leaders.) But only 27 percent of the "deceptive" advertising messages are considered "very" or "extremely" difficult to see through. People are twice as likely to think that such ads deceive the public at large than think they deceive them personally. However, this self-confidence on the part of the public may not really be warranted. In 1981 Herbert J. Rotfeld and Kim B. Rotzoll interviewed 100 adults about five nationally advertised brands. Forty-nine percent believed legitimate product claims, and 39 percent believed what a panel of law students and marketing professors agreed were puffs. The researchers concluded that "once they are communicated, facts and puffs show similar probabilities of being noted as true."

Many moral problems in advertising arise with regard to those product categories where brands are actually very much the same or differentiated to such a very minor degree that consumers are unable to distinguish them, as in blindfold tests. Of course, the very notion of a brand name implies some differentiation, since names, even in sound and appearance, carry different connotations, different psychological values for different people. To make its brand stand out a little more from the rest, however, each company is forced to take such minor utilitarian differences as exist and convert them into what appear to be large psychological differences. Small variations in packaging, ingredients, or other secondary attributes are exaggerated and stressed by copywriters and artists to distinguish the product from its competitors.

It is in the zeal to differentiate that many of the so-called ethical problems of advertising occur. Yet this very differentiation being sought is a visible sign of freedom and one which the social critics of advertising often reject too easily and thoughtlessly. In communist countries during the Stalin era, one of the most depressing features of the topography for a visitor from abroad was the stores labeled "meat" or "bread" or "men's clothes," all with identical signs and identical window displays and with none of the cheerful variety that is present in the brand displays of merchandise in a free market economy.

The aspect of advertising that may be most vulnerable to criticism is actually one which is rarely associated with ethical problems; that aspect is its relation to the aesthetics of the mass media. Advertising has helped create tolerance for kitsch in taste and for cant in ideas. It has helped devalue the coin of communication by developing a massive, unthinking tolerance for nonsense and vulgarity. While individual ads and commercials are often brilliantly witty, far more tend to blunt our sense of humor. We are forced to take for granted too much that is ridiculous.

However, advertising can hardly be assigned the responsibility for the deficiencies of public taste. The intimate relationship between the institutions of advertising and the control of the mass media has indeed governed much of the shape of popular culture. But, while advertising people need not be proud of the cultural values reflected in much of American broadcasting and the popular publications, neither can they be wholly blamed for those values. *Reader's Digest*, that greatest of all middle-brow magazines, built its formula for success on the public taste long before it accepted advertising. And motion pictures, which decades ago explored and exploited every inanity on which television programming bases its nightly fare, similarly depended directly upon pre-existing tastes as reflected at the box office—and not on corporate decisions in the advertising industry.

Social critics often speak of the billions spent on advertising as though this money represented a single lump sum that might better be spent to destroy slums and build schools. But the economy at large has no advertising budget. The sums spent are an aggregate of separate decisions made by many hundreds of thousands of individual enterprises to whom advertising represents an essential cost of doing business.

At the other extreme from the critics are those who proclaim the sacred virtue of advertising as the mysterious catalyst of the entire free enterprise system and who regard even minor criticisms of advertising as an attack on the entire structure of capitalism. (At one convention I attended, the opening invocation asked that the gathering be blessed by "the Great Advertising Salesman in the Sky.")

How Americans feel about advertising: the AAAA studies

Advertising comes in for periodic investigation by Congressional committees and federal agencies, but at the same time it enjoys an extremely high level of public acceptance. In spite of occasional specific criticisms and a prevailing suspicion of Madison Avenue "city slickers," the American public, according to many opinion surveys,[7] has put its seal of approval on advertising as a part of the business system.* The most elaborate examinations of how people consciously react to advertising have been made for the American Association of Advertising Agencies (the AAAA) in 1964 and 1974. Raymond A. Bauer of the Harvard Business School,[8] who directed the first study, concluded that 41 percent of the people interviewed could be classified as generally favorable toward advertising; 34 percent had mixed attitudes; 11 percent were indifferent; 14 percent were unfavorable. Those in the unfavorable group were likely to report seeing or hearing annoying and offensive ads. They also tended to overestimate the pro-

---

*A national survey made in 1983 for *Advertising Age* by Selection Research, Inc. found that 93 percent of the public agree that advertising is an important part of the American economy and way of life; 90 percent agree that it is a highly professional occupation, and 53 percent would like their children to be employed in the business. Only 9 percent rate the overall quality of advertising as poor. Still the same study found attitudes toward advertising to be highly ambivalent. A majority (59 percent) of the public enjoy and "feel good about" the advertising they read, see, or hear. But the 32 percent who disagreed with that statement represent a substantial chunk of opinion. So do the 18 percent who call it misleading. While 49 percent of the public agree that advertising is generally honest and trustworthy, 44 percent disagree.

portion of a typical television hour that was taken up by advertising.[9]

The AAAA study was repeated among another 1,800 people in 1974 by a research team that again included Raymond Bauer, as well as Rena Bartos and Theodore Dunn.[10] Again, among a list of 11 subjects, advertising was the least talked about, and it was not high among those people who thought these matters required attention and change. A majority expressed favorable feelings toward advertising, less than toward the press, but more than toward labor unions, big business, and the federal government. Slightly more people felt they could not depend on what advertising said than felt they could, but advertising still enjoyed greater credibility than unions, business, and government.

However, overall attitudes toward advertising became somewhat less favorable between 1964 and 1974.[11] A majority felt that advertising is essential, that it results in better products, helps raise the standard of living, and provides desirable economic support for the media. But a majority also agreed that advertising persuades people to buy things they shouldn't, that it insults the intelligence, and that it fails to present a true picture of the product advertised[12] or to result in lower prices.[13]

The consumer benefits of advertising, its credibility and its entertainment value, were found to be the key determinants of consumer attitudes; the role of advertising as a social force and the question of manipulation were also significant issues. Of far less importance were TV "commercial clutter," the actual content of television programs or ads, and advertising's support function for the media. However, the public overwhelmingly understands that the rich choices provided by commercial television are made possible by the very advertising for which they express such distaste. (In a 1974 Roper survey, 84 percent agreed that having commercials on TV "is a fair price to pay for being able to watch it."[14])

The AAAA researchers identified four "nonissues," which turned out to be unrelated to consumers' attitudes: advertising to children, political advertising, and the social and economic roles of advertising. The 5 percent most strongly critical of advertising appeared to be people who were also negative to other social institutions. An additional "mostly unfavorable" group tended to be "upscale and intellectual." At the opposite end of the scale, the 8 percent who were completely favorable and the 29 percent "mostly favorable" tended to congregate at the bottom of the social heap and to be older than average.

Criticisms of advertising on the part of the general public are echoed within the business itself. A survey among advertising and agency people in 1973 found that 22 percent of them "were either highly critical or downright antagonistic toward the industry.[15] Another 45 percent found cause to be critical but, at the same time, tended to be favorable toward their profession." Media people were most critical; product managers and marketing directors least so. One senior art director called advertising "an extremely necessary evil." An agency president said, "Most consumer advertising is parochial and inept, insulting to the reader/viewer, the work of the immature adman with no marketing background, the effluent of a pot session."

Asked what they would do if they had a chance to select a career all over again, 25 percent of the agency people and 33 percent of those with advertiser companies said they would go into advertising, though other choices included 'househusband," being a rich man's son, and "motherhood and marriage to a millionaire." Not surprisingly, then, when *Advertising Age* queried 162 ad executives in 1978, over half thought that the effectiveness of advertising had declined in the preceding five years, while only a fourth thought it had increased.

Advertising practitioners rarely take as aggressive a public stance against members of their own fraternity as did Al Ries, president of Ries Capiello Colwell, in a full-page "open letter" ad in the December 21, 1970, issue of *Advertising Age* addressed to the makers of Alka-Seltzer. He said, "In this day and age, there seems to be something wrong with spending $23 million to sell some $60 million worth of product . . . that is mostly sodium bicarbonate and aspirin . . . No wonder the advertising business is under attack." In his rebuttal, Walter Compton, president of Miles Laboratories, makers of Alka-Seltzer, noted that "while the measured media figure for Alka-Seltzer is credited to a public source, it is materially overstated" and that the product contains "other essential active ingredients."

Reacting to ads—not just to advertising

The way people feel about advertising in general reflects their reactions to individual ads. A 1980 Gallup poll conducted for the National Advertising Review Board found half (50 percent) of the public reporting that they had wanted to complain about a specific advertisement. Twenty percent mentioned misleading or deceptive ads, 15 percent objected to seeing women's personal products advertised on TV, 12 percent referred to ads that insulted the intelligence, 8 percent complained about something that was uniquely objectionable in a specific ad, 7 percent complained of something offensive or in poor taste, 6 percent to sexual innuendoes, 5 percent to whiskey or beer advertising, 2 percent to cigarette ads, and 2 percent to ads for sugar or "junk foods." A variety of other products, like toys, intimate apparel, and deodorants, were named by 1 or 2 percent each. Eight percent claimed that they had actually complained about the ad they objected to, but of these only one in five complained to the advertiser, and even fewer to the medium.

A special feature of the 1964 AAAA study was that the people sampled actually added up all the ads they were aware of during half a day with the aid of hand counters that they carried around with them. Bauer called the figures resulting from this procedure a measure of "sensitive attention" rather than "exposure." The respondents also filled out cards with their detailed reaction to unusual ads. The readings on the counters and the number of cards filled out were then doubled to project a full day's response. The average person recorded 76 ads a day; 12 of them (or 16 percent) were considered sufficiently singular to warrant classification on the cards. Of the 12 ads so categorized, 4.4 were considered informative, 4.2 enjoyable, 2.8 annoying, and 0.6 offensive.

In general, ads were considered "informative" because of the information they gave on a product. "Enjoyable" ads were categorized as such largely because of their technique. "Offensive" ads were largely judged so because the product itself was considered in bad taste or uninteresting to the respondent. "Annoying" ads were reported seen or heard too often, exaggerated, or boring and monotonous.

The method used forced the participants to interrupt their normal media experience in order to record their advertising impressions. The effects were inevitably less disruptive for the broadcast media than for print (in which ads are scanned or read as part of a whole communications environment rather than as isolated units). This gave heavy emphasis to TV commercials among the advertising singled out for special and for critical mention. The method may have had another effect: when someone knows he is being used as a guinea pig, his media habits may be affected as well as his exposure to advertising. Even in 1964, the average person was exposed to far more ads in a day than the 76 recorded in the AAAA study. However, the proportion of these exposures that create a significant reaction must be far less than the 16 percent that were written up by the respondents. Presumably, many hundreds of additional messages went "unseen" and unrecorded.

Two lessons about the public's response to advertising are immediately suggested. First, constant repetition of ads for inoffensive products may induce a boomerang effect opposite to the advertiser's intention, especially when, as in broadcasting, there is no easy way to avoid the advertising message. (Getting up from one's chair requires an effort.) Automotive and cereal ads were most often criticized as annoying because they were seen or heard too often. Drug ads, however, were more often classed as annoying because of their exaggeration. Coffee, tea, and cocoa ads were often classified as annoying because they were boring or monotonous. Individual advertisements that are repeated often may be repeated, literally, *ad nauseam.*

A second lesson of the study is that many objections to advertising actually reflect a dislike of the product it is selling. Eight times as much criticism of "annoying" ads was directed at the advertising as at the product advertised. However, among ads classified as "offensive," a much higher ratio of criticism was directed at the product (one-fourth as many references as to the ad itself).[16]

For such sinful products as beer and cigarettes, the advertising presentation received only about two-and-a-half times as many mentions as the product itself. For wholesome products—soaps and detergents, cleansers and polishes—criticism of the presentation was seventeen times more frequent than criticism of the product. An unusual proportion of favorable mentions was given to pleasant product categories like canned and packaged goods, cereals, and baked goods.

The study seems to suggest that people harbor a certain amount of resentment at being subjected to information that carries no useful meaning for them. The resentment may be of a very low level. Most of it probably rises to the level of consciousness only under artificial conditions of exposure, such as those called for by research in which the individual is asked to play the role of advertising critic. Negative opinions are inevitably voiced with disproportionately high frequency when people are asked to play critic.

As a matter of fact, much or most advertising can never be meaningful or interesting to any one person at any one moment of time. There are bound to be ads for products we do not use, some for brands with which we have had poor experiences, and some that we may look at down our noses. The puritan's rejection of cigarette or beer advertising carries with it a *heightened* sensitivity to such advertising. But for most people, most ads are received with great tolerance when they manage to penetrate into awareness. Americans approve of advertising in practice as well as in principle.

In 1981, there were 29,612 brands advertised in magazines, television, network radio, and outdoor advertising.[17] Hundreds of thousands of local businesses were similarly trying to impress their identities on the consumer. The enormous expansion in the volume of advertising messages represents only one aspect of the twentieth century information explosion. A more complex society demands more and more specialized knowledge. In the United States, the demand for information reflects the steady rise in education, and the increasing complexity of technology,* along with the increased purchasing power to pay for transistor radios, second TV sets, and magazine and newspaper subscriptions. The diversification of interests creates more differentiated occupational, avocational, and social roles, and new media spring up to serve the special needs of hot rodders and art collectors.

Paradoxically, the enormous growth in the overall volume of advertising complicates the problem of measuring its effects. The more highly competitive the climate, the more advertising works defensively and at cross-purposes. The consumer now has a harder job in differentiating information that is useful to him from the "noise" of advertising that is irrelevant to his needs or interests. Advertising is perceived selectively. It is also perceived differently at various stages of the purchasing process. Because of the variety of forms that advertising assumes in each of the different media, the number of advertising messages disseminated every day provides few clues as to how many come within the average person's range of vision or hearing,[18] or how many actually make a conscious impression on his mind.

The American public is engulfed in an ocean of words, spoken and written, informing, persuading, importuning, cajoling, demanding. The process of scanning, filtering, screening, and squelching the words we don't need is one in which most people are unconsciously engaged every moment of the waking day.

Human beings have developed unconscious defensive reactions to the information explosion and to all the irrelevant messages that assault our senses. We defy their intense stimulation by being indifferent or oblivious, by discriminating in the attention we give things to cope with the vastly increased output of ideas and facts. Education gives people a better capacity to sift information at the same time that it makes for a bigger supply of information to sift.[19]

We handle excess information by automatically and subconsciously ranking the stimuli with which we are bombarded. The sound of an automobile horn to which we pay no attention on a street crowded with traffic will startle us when we hear it on a country road.

Television and radio newscasts and newspaper and news magazine columns may for weeks and months resound with the names of Indonesian cabinet ministers, Brazilian generals, and Saudi princes. Yet most of this information fails to register with the general public, which dutifully exposes itself to it in massive doses each day.

---

*Over the long run, shorter work hours and more leisure time have also been factors, but these have not changed significantly in the past half-dozen years.

Mickey Mouse and Frankenstein's Monster are figures of far greater renown and familiarity to most people than the names of their own legislators. A Gallup poll some time after the first announcement of the hydrogen bomb found that only half the public knew what it was and 30 percent had never heard of it.

When we consider the extent of public ignorance on matters of far greater concern than the merits of competing brands on the market place, the fact that much advertising goes unobserved or unregistered by the consumer is far less remarkable than the fact that so much appears to be remembered.

The consumer is somewhat like an Indian in a forest who hears and sees a thousand things at once, but who brings his attention to bear only on the particular crackle and the particular bent twig that tell him what he needs to know.

Notes

1. The distinction between advertising and other forms of promotion is in fact a very difficult one to make. In 1982, about $5.5 billion were being spent on point-of-purchase displays alone.

    Russell D. Bowman of John Blair Marketing distinguishes consumer and business advertising media from such forms of sales promotion as direct mail, point-of-purchase display, premiums and incentives, meetings and conventions, trade shows and exhibits, printing and audiovisual expenses, coupon redemption, and other miscellaneous forms of promotion. Of the grand total of $102.6 billion in 1981, 38 percent was advertising, by this definition, and 62 percent promotion, compared with a ratio of 42 percent to 58 percent in 1976. Thus, nonadvertising forms of promotion have been growing at a faster rate than advertising has. *Marketing Communications*, August 1982, pp. 5-8.

2. For discussions of this phenomenon, cf. Harold Mendelsohn and Irving Crespi, *Polls, Television, and the New Politics* (Scranton: Chandler, 1970); Thomas E. Patterson and Robert D. McClure, *The Unseeing Eye: The Myth of Television Power in National Politics* (New York: G. P. Putnam's, 1976); and Thomas E. Patterson, *The Mass Media Election: How Americans Choose Their President* (New York: Praeger, 1980).

3. Daniel Boorstin, "Welcome to the Consumption Community," *Fortune*, September 1, 1967.

4. Quoted in Richard Hofstadter, *Social Darwinism in American Thought, 1860-1915* (Philadelphia: University of Pennsylvania Press, 1945), p. 121.

5. *The New York Times*, January 30, 1977.

6. Franklin Carlile and Howard Leonard, "Caveat: Venditor!" *Journal of Advertising Research*, (August-September, 1982) 22, 4: 11-22.

7. The relevant polls for the period between the Great Depression and the Vietnam War have been reviewed and digested in Stephen A. Greyser and Raymond A. Bauer, "Americans and Advertising: Thirty Years of Public Opinion." *Public Opinion Quarterly*, 30, 1 (Spring 1966): 69-78.

8. *Cf. The AAAA Study on Consumer Judgment of Advertising*, American Association of Advertising Agencies, May 1965. This research was initiated by two AAAA researchers, William Weilbacher and Donald Kanter, and conducted by the Opinion Research Corporation.

9. A national telephone study made in 1980 for the Marcshalk Company among 509 adults and 102 teenagers found that 25 percent rated TV commercials "not very enjoyable," and 25 percent "not at all enjoyable or entertaining." Five percent said they were very enjoyable and entertaining, and 47 percent "somewhat." As usual, better educated respondents showed a more negative response. Commercials were liked primarily for being amusing or informative and disliked as being childish, insult-

ing to the intelligence, or exaggerated. Sixty-six percent agreed with the statement that commercials are repeated too many times. About a third of the respondents admitted that they would be inclined to use a brand if they enjoyed a commercial for it, once they had decided to buy the product.

10. Rena Bartos and Theodore F. Dunn, *Advertising and Consumers: New Perspectives* (New York: American Association of Advertising Agencies, 1976).

11. There is other evidence that public support for advertising underwent decline in the 1970s. William D. Wells, in studies at Needham, Harper and Steers, found that 60 percent of the population agreed that "advertising insults my intelligence" in 1975. But by 1980, the proportion had risen to 66 percent.

   A 1978 survey of 1,087 people by the Opinion Research Corporation found that 53 percent considered advertising "in general" believable, and 44 percent called it unbelievable. Compared with a similar survey in 1964, a growing number (71 percent) agreed that advertising frequently seeks to persuade people to buy things they don't need or can't afford. Two out of three approved of the practice of corrective advertising when false or misleading claims had been made in the past. And three out of four agreed that TV networks should be required to carry counter-advertising from public groups. (But 85 percent also believed that companies should be allowed to rebut statements made by TV newscasters.) In a 1983 Gallup survey, 9 percent rated the honesty and ethical standards of advertising practitioners as high compared with 64 percent who gave that rating to clergymen, 51 percent to dentists, and 29 percent to funeral directors.

12. In 1971, almost two-thirds of the American public felt that the issue of "advertisers making false claims" was a serious moral problem, but the same proportion gave this answer ten years earlier (from a survey made by Opinion Research Corporation for the Newspaper Advertising Bureau).

   A survey of 500 college students in the early 1970s found that little more than a third thought that advertising was necessary at all, and over half thought that advertising insults the intelligence. Thomas F. Haller, "What Students Think of Advertising," *Journal of Advertising Research* 14, 1 (February 1974): 33-38.

13. In 1966, an R. H. Bruskin national survey among 2,540 adults found that two out of three believed that advertising influences prices, but they were evenly split between those who think advertising raises prices and those who think it lowers them. (The lower income, less educated people were most likely to think it raises prices.)

14. This was echoed in a 1982 study conducted by John D. Abel of Michigan State University among 5,000 television viewers in 10 cities where public television stations had begun to run regular commercials experimentally. Between one-half and three-quarters of public television viewers were favorable to the practice as a way of sustaining the programming they wanted.

15. *Anny*, March 2, 1973, pp. 8-9.

16. A similar conclusion emerged in a recent study in which TV viewers evaluated 524 prime-time commercials through a mail survey. Dislike was related to the product itself; the evaluations of commercials as entertaining, warm, personal, or relevant were related to the advertising. The informativeness of the commercials was associated with product type and with certain characteristics that could be defined at an early stage, such as whether they were hard or soft sell, whether or not they posed a serious problem. David A. Aaker, Donald E. Bruzzone, and Donald G. Norris, "Viewers' Perceptions of Prime-Time Television Advertising and Characteristics of Commercials Perceived as Informative," Cambridge, Mass.: Marketing Science Institute, 1981.

   And a 1981 survey by the Home Testing Institute found that 70 percent of the public consider feminine hygiene product advertising "in poor taste," compared to 18 percent who call cosmetics or perfume advertising in poor taste. Fifty-one percent consider laxative advertising in poor taste, and 50 percent consider advertising for bras and girdles in poor taste. Curiously, 48 percent consider advertising for jeans in poor taste.

17. As measured by Leading National Advertisers.
18. A commonly used "guesstimate" is 1,500 a day.
19. Better educated people read more newspapers on a given day and read them more thoroughly and intensively. But they actually spend *less* time with each newspaper that they read because they read more efficiently. *Cf.* Leo Bogart, *Press and Public* (Hillsdale, NJ: Lawrence Erlbaum Associates, 1981).

Chapter 2
Is All This Advertising Necessary?

The most commonly heard kinds of complaints about advertising in our own society are remote from the Marxist criticisms of its economic and social effects, which were mentioned in Chapter 1.

As we have seen, objections to advertising very often mask objections to what is advertised. To meet these objections would require limitations on production, distribution, or pricing of products that are now legally available, like cigarettes or deodorants.

Business has for years faced restrictions on making or selling merchandise adjudged injurious to public health or safety. There are, at the state and local levels, bans on the sale of fireworks. At the federal level there have been orders to cease manufacture of patent medicines with dangerous side-effects or of foods processed under poor sanitary conditions. Efforts at outright prohibition—of liquor, in the case of our Great Experiment, or of other drugs, in our current practice—represent the ultimate in consumer protection. Such restrictions are often hotly debated and difficult to enforce, even when they enjoy wide public support.

Measures that are today rather widely accepted (forbidding the sale of liquor to minors, requiring health warnings on cigarette labels, setting official standards for automotive emission systems) have been opposed at their inception as unwarranted interference with the right of a maker to sell his product and of a buyer to buy it in a free market. A conflict may arise between the consumer's immediate interest as an individual and his interest as a member of the public at large. The price of a car has to go up when seatbelts are added as standard equipment. The price of soft drinks must be raised if bottles are taxed to cover the social cost of disposing of them. People who say they want product improvements are in practice often unwilling to pay the necessary added cost.

Even when there is a hazard to public health and safety, there is bound to be resistance to any limitation on the right to make and sell goods. There is even more resistance to any restrictions on copy claims or media to promote goods that are legally made and sold. Such restrictions have sometimes been imposed voluntarily rather than by government edict; for example, the liquor industry has a traditional ban on broadcast advertising, while the ban on broadcast advertising of cigarettes was imposed by Congress.

A different order of complaint about advertising represents objections to specific ads that are aesthetically offensive or vulgar and to those whose claims or presentations are false, misleading, or unfairly competitive. Another set of concerns relates to advertising that might be unpersuasive to most mature adults but that can coerce vulnerable sectors of the population.[1] For example, under the Carter administration the Federal Trade Commission proposed restrictions on advertising to children. Indeed, the evidence supports the view that advertising is especially effective among children, even though they develop a generalized distrust of it as they grow older. This distrust is apparent among about a fourth of the pre-eight-year-olds and three-fourths of those over ten, but they find it hard to apply this attitude in evaluating specific ads and claims.[2]

Advertising is the most visible aspect of marketing. As it has become a more significant part of the sales function, increasingly replacing the personal selling of the past, the irritation that consumers occasionally feel toward an unsatisfactory product tends to be deflected from the individual salesman or merchant to the corporation that manufactured it.

In our acquisitive society the average person surrounds himself with more and more possessions to cherish and worry about, more things that go wrong and that he cannot fix. As the homeowner copes with the insides of the washing machine, the lawnmower, the hi-fi, and the dispose-all, he is not only the victim of the service man; he also becomes the adversary of the companies that made and sold him these things.

Cheating, misrepresentation, overpricing, and shoddy workmanship have been an unfortunate but incidental aspect of commercial relationships since the Stone Age, and there is a self-evident need for proper social disciplines to keep them to a minimum. But should such episodes of individual malfeasance be regarded as part of a pattern, in fact as *the* normal pattern of business behavior?

Most social criticisms do not really concern the basic function of advertising. Both moral and statutory laws discourage fraud. Transgressors can be brought to account, but their individual derelictions have very little to do with the whole system of advertising in which deception and coercion must be considered the exception rather than the norm. Case-specific criticisms tell us nothing about the essential character or value of advertising techniques or institutions as such.

Fairness, full disclosure, and correction

During the 1970s, the rise of consumer activism and of government moves for consumer protection was prompted by the feeling that business needed more surveillance than was provided by existing law. The FCC's* fairness doctrine, with its principle of free rebuttal time, was extended from the domain of partisan politics in news and public affairs programs to the realm of advertising. Cigarette commercials, before the ban, were matched by unpaid-for antismoking commercials. Now corporate institutional advertising on public issues has been faced with the same kind of demand for free compensatory time for industry's opponents. Some consumer advocates have demanded that the doctrine be further extended to include "controversial" *products* like toys, cereal, or gasoline.

---

*Federal Communications Commission.

The broadcasters argued that while the advertiser would be held to the FCC's "rigorous standards of truth telling," the counter-advertiser would face no such restrictions. A spokesman for WMAR-TV in Baltimore contended that "It is difficult to conceive of a single advertisement which has been shown on any television station which would not come under the content of any or all of the . . . aspects of the proposal."[3]

The fairness doctrine was invoked in objecting to an Advertising Council campaign on behalf of the National League of Families of American Prisoners and Missing-In-Action in Southeast Asia. Another organization of servicemen's relatives produced its own counter-advertisements, thus inhibiting stations from donating time for the Ad Council messages.

In Dayton, Ohio, the United Appeal was attacked by a citizens' group on the grounds that "corporations do not give their fair share, and that the governing board of United Appeal is controlled by business leaders without representation of factory workers, poor people, and youth." The FCC agreed that this charity campaign did indeed involve a "controversial issue of public importance."[4]

Another development moved well beyond government restriction of the advertiser's right to say anything he wants to say about his product, or to present it as he chooses, in any medium that suits his purpose: "Full disclosure" means that the advertiser must advertise what is wrong with his product as well as what is good about it. In addition, he may be required to devote a decreed percentage of his future advertising to correct past misstatements.

The Federal Trade Commission first raised the issue of corrective advertising in a suit against the Campbell Soup Company in 1970.* The idea was that misleading ads continue to exercise an effect for some time after they are run and that any advertiser guilty of deception should be prevented from reaping any of the resulting sales benefits. Corrective advertising was intended not only to compensate for ill-gotten gains but to redress the competitive balance in the market after an offender had improved his position through deception.

At the height of these efforts, Thomas Dillon (then chairman of BBDO, Campbell Soup's agency) observed, "No one can write something that gives both sides of a picture in all its ramifications--except attorneys, and that kind of language is not communicative to the ordinary person. To avoid that kind of writing, you reach the point where you say virtually nothing about the product. The FTC has everyone so nervous about accurate depictions that if you do a commercial for a bathtub cleanser, you have to have eighteen kids take a bath to produce a realistic ring."[5]

Surely nothing can be more offensive to an advertiser than to take back what he has previously said or to say unpleasant things about his product at his own expense. If cigarette ads are required to publish a health warning, or if tire ads and bread ads are required to deny the advertiser's past claims, does this not represent effective counter-advertising, against the advertiser's interests? Not necessarily. The value of much advertising lies as much in its reinforcement of

---

*The research budget of the FTC's Bureau of Consumer Protection rose from $800 in 1971 to a million dollars 10 years later, a large percentage increase to what is still a trifling sum relative to the scope of the agency's activities.

the consumer's familiarity with the product as in the explicit information contained in the ads. When the FTC required Excedrin and other advertisers to advertise corrective statements, many consumers failed to understand them, making the effort somewhat counterproductive.[6] Clever technique can make the retraction of past sins seem like a strong affirmation.

The FTC required one baking company to spend a fourth of its media budget for a year to retract its copy claim that people could lose weight by eating its brand of bread. But why a fourth, and why a year? These decisions came from guesswork, not from knowledge. How long-lasting is the residual effect of a misleading advertising claim? How long can the advertiser reasonably be expected to run a correction? Does an ounce of self-criticism equal an ounce of the original misstatement? Or is it worth more? Or less? Clearly, the answers to these questions must be specific to the product and the claim, but advertisers and government alike are in the dark when answers are required.

At one point there was a proposal before the Food and Drug Administration to limit product claims to such approved terms as "antiflatulent" and "antiemetic" which, subsequent research showed, were unfamiliar to all but a small fraction of the public. (One respondent described an antiflatulent as a bust-development product; another said an antiemetic was a person who disliked doctors.)[7]

Faced with sharp challenges to its free-wheeling traditions, the advertising business responded by setting up a self-regulatory procedure in 1971 through the National Advertising Division of the Council of Better Business Bureaus and the National Advertising Review Board. The objective is to review complaints from the public and to render judgments before government agencies become involved. In its first 10 years of operation, the NAD processed 1,734 complaints, many of them brought by competitors rather than by consumers.

Forty-seven percent were found to be groundless, and 52 percent led to some kind of corrective action. The effect of these activities coincided with a change in the political climate that sharply reduced goverment attention to advertising in the early 1980s.

Advertising and the media system

Thus far, we have looked at complaints about advertising that relate to the ads themselves or to the products they sell. A more troublesome set of objections relates to the influence of advertisers over media content. There are recurring instances in which media present publicity and puffery in the guise of disinterested information. It is charged that media censor themselves to avoid offending advertisers and thus deceive the trustful public. A more subtle and compelling argument is that the array of media content available represents advertisers' choices—or choices made on their behalf—rather than a selection made in the public interest; the consequences are considered disastrous for both public opinion and popular taste.

If the dependence of media upon advertising support has socially undesirable consequences (and the argument must begin by asking "compared to what?"), does this represent a fundamental flaw in advertising? Not really, since in democratic societies, media are structured and funded in a variety of different ways. Cross-national comparisons show substantial variations in the mix of advertising among media, even where total advertising is high. In Germany, for example, television advertising has been deliberately kept to a minimum by government policy, and in Finland, it is banned altogether.

The British subsidize the BBC through license fees; we subsidize magazines through our low second-class postal rates. Sweden taxes advertising and provides a newsprint subsidy for smaller newspapers. In some countries, the reader pays most of the cost of the newspapers he buys. In the United States, the advertiser does, and we restrict advertising of certain products from broadcast media by custom (contraceptives), voluntary choice (liquor), or law (tobacco). We take it for granted that broadcasters should seek to maximize audience size as a prerequisite to gain advertising revenues, but around the world, broadcasting systems are managed with varying emphasis on this criterion of success.

All this variation suggests that while changes and reforms might be made to reduce the dependence of media on advertising income, these changes would have more to do with the evolution of social policy toward the *media* than with the functions of *advertising* itself.

The objections to advertising's influence on the media, like the objections to specific advertised products and ads, fall under the heading of social criticism; they do not relate to the economic function of advertising, nor to the important issue of noninformational advertising.

Advertising and the economy

American advertisers were spending $75 billion in 1983 to promote their products and services. Is all this advertising necessary? It probably isn't, but it is pretty much an inevitable consequence of the economic system we live with, which is married to a political system that most of us like.

In evaluating the economic effects of advertising, we may take the standpoint of the individual consumer, of the brand or the firm that manufactures it, of the product class or industry, or of the entire economy. In classical economic theory, all these interact. That is, if we want to go along with Adam Smith rather than with Karl Marx, a consumer benefit is translated into greater consumption, greater profit for the successful firm, increased sales volume for the product category, and greater efficiency for the whole system through economies of scale in production and distribution. Product innovation is stimulated by advertising, creating new markets and expanding old ones, with consequent benefits for the consumer.

Where economists disagree with this description, they generally seek to demonstrate that advertising raises rather than lowers the cost of goods.

The old socialist critique of capitalism rests on the Marxist theory of surplus value. The theory is that there is a gap between the actual contribution that a worker makes to the value of a product and the return he receives from his employer. That gap represents an unearned increment that the employer can extort by virtue of his power over the means of production.

Applied to consumer marketing, a similar theory of surplus value would hold that there is a gap between a product's market price and its "true value"— represented by the cost of raw materials, labor, overhead, and a reasonable return on investment. The market price that the consumer must pay also includes unnecessarily high costs of promotion and a profit inflated by the absurdly high psychological value which that same expensive but skillful promotion has placed upon the product.

The cost of goods and labor for a lipstick may be $1.05; another $1.20 may be spent to promote it. (Why does the lipstick manufacturer spend as much as he does to advertise? Only because the experience of the marketplace tells him he has to.) The lipstick is sold to the retailer for $3.60 and to the consumer for $6.00. The pricing mechanism being what it is, one can uncontestably say that to the lady who buys it, the $6.00 is fair or at least an acceptable value. But her assurance that $6.00 is an acceptable value reflects the $1.20 worth of advertising that gives the simple material product its overtones of fantasy. Fantasy is inseparable from the whole subject of consumer marketing, and fantasy is not amenable to cost accounting.

In the words of two economists, Isaac Ehrlich and Lawrence Fisher, "Advertising affects the demand for goods because it lowers the gap between the market price received by the seller and the full price borne by the buyer—a gap that exists because of the buyer's cost of obtaining information about the characteristics of varieties of products and sellers, and the cost of adjusting to disappointing or imperfect purchases. . . . Advertising reduces the time price of consumption."[8]

Advertising may work to lower retail prices by making consumers more alert to the prices of advertised brands as they shop around.[9] But this very process puts the brand advertiser in a better bargaining position with retailers and thus may raise the price the manufacturer can charge. In an (unpublished) analysis of "The Advertising-Promotion Balance," William Moran concludes that advertising weight heightens the likelihood of repeat purchase for a brand. Since brand loyalty makes the brand less vulnerable to competitive price promotions, its price can be set at a higher level, thus increasing its profitability.

Evidence can always be found in individual case histories to counter the thesis that advertising raises prices. For example, an analysis of eight Quaker Oats brands and their average price per pound showed that the higher the advertising budgets, the lower the unit price of the product.[10]

The focus of attention in this kind of discussion (as I suggested in Chapter 1) is generally placed on parity products characterized by high advertising-to-sales ratios and a low level of informational content. What is a parity product? The archetypal illustration might come from a campaign for blended whiskey that ran some years ago. The advertising agency copywriter on the account was simply unable to find a single good copy point to distinguish his client's product from any of its competitors. Having sought in vain for evidence of superiority, he came up with a slogan that the client loved and that ran for years. It was persuasive without being in the least deceptive. The slogan was "If you can find a better whiskey, buy it."

The first criticism of this kind of advertising for the sake of name registration is that it is economically wasteful and unproductive, that it adds to the cost of goods without providing any commensurate tangible benefit in return in the way of facilitating more rational and efficient consumer choices. The result is a misallocation of economic resources.

Although this criticism takes the form of an economic demonstration, its most devastating impact occurs when it is translated into *social* terms. In this form, the argument is that advertising corrupts and debases human *values;* it creates a preoccupation with material goods and exploits irrational and neurotic motives to promote products that serve little genuine purpose. (John Kenneth Galbraith suggests that advertising creates a consumer who "reliably spends his income and works reliably because he is always in need of more.")[11] Advertising changes social priorities by encouraging expenditures for individually consumed articles and services at the expense of public goods that must be consumed in common. It persuades consumers to buy things they don't need instead of devoting a larger part of their productive labor and income to the social purposes that everyone needs; clean air and water, crime prevention, the arts, efficient public transportation, preventive medicine, and the like.

How can this come to pass? Nicholas Kaldor argues that since advertising is supplied jointly with goods and services, consumers are forced to "buy" more of it than they want or need as a by-product of their intended purchases. The result is that the whole economy spends more on advertising in the aggregate than it should.[12]

A related argument is that advertising contributes to the growth of monopoly and thus to economic inequities as well as to higher prices. Advertising enhances the power of the dominant firms in product fields characterized by minute differences among brands and in which advertisers compete in symbolic terms rather than through significant product improvement.

The advertiser of a parity product must differentiate it from competitors by promoting image rather than information about product advantages.* Thus it is often suggested that the sheer weight of his advertising, rather than its content, becomes a prime determinant of his market position. Critics argue that the leaders can set up the biggest budgets and hire the outstanding talent to manage their schedules and create their ads. As they swing their weight around, they can buy advertising most efficiently, outspending and outmaneuvering their competition and progressively increasing their market share.

Advertising and corporate power

Does heavy advertising lead to corporate concentration? A former assistant attorney general in charge of the Antitrust Division of the Department of Justice, Donald F. Turner, has argued strongly that it does. Since there exists "a significant correlation between the proportion of industry sales devoted to advertising and the average profit rates which were earned,"[13] Turner maintained that "what has become important is not so much the context of an advertising message, but rather the mere fact that it has been advertised." He suggested that "to the extent that consumers are unable to evaluate the relative merits of competing products, the established products may have a considerable advantage and it is

---

*To illustrate the challenge in doing this, by 1982 there were 225 different brand styles of cigarettes on the U.S. market. "Product differentiation" is the term that economists use to describe consumers' perceptions that brand differences are meaningful and real when, in fact, the product attributes are virtually the same.

this advantage that advertising messages tend to accentuate." Since large firms enjoy the advantages of volume discounts from media, Turner insisted that advertising works in the direction of monopoly and should be controlled or limited.

A strong rejoinder to Turner came from a prominent economist, Jules Backman. Analyzing the evidence, Backman concluded that "the assumption that large companies will continually increase their share of the market because of their financial resources is not supported by experience." He refuted Turner's argument about the advantage enjoyed by the established brand by pointing to the successful introduction of many new brands. Backman's statistics disputed the charges that advertising leads to concentration, price inflation, and excessive profits. For the 125 largest advertisers in 1964, less than one-tenth of the difference in rates of return could be explained by differences in the percentage of sales that had been spent on advertising.[14]

As for the charge that advertising makes much out of minor brand differences, Backman asked,

> What is the alternative in a competitive economy? Shall we allocate special sectors of the market to different companies as is done under cartels? Or shall we prohibit the introduction of new brands which are not "genuinely new products," however that term is to be defined? Clearly, there are inefficiencies inherent in the competitive process. These must be incurred if the benefits of competition are to be realized.[15]

Still, a more recent review of the evidence by Willard F. Mueller and Richard T. Rogers reiterates the argument that the large budgets required for television advertising create barriers to entry and thus play "an especially potent role in increasing concentration of consumer goods industries."[16]

An imposing effort to prove the point that advertising leads to economic concentration has been made by William S. Comanor and Thomas A. Wilson, who conclude that a firm's ability to dominate advertising in its product category leads to increasing market share, monopoly profits, and barriers to the entry of new competitors.[17] However, Comanor and Wilson's data base, analytical procedure, and conclusions have all been rejected by a number of other economists.[18] Henry Grabowski, for example, points out that Comanor and Wilson may be reversing cause and effect; though the two are linked together, sales can explain advertising rather than the other way around.[19] He reports from his own analysis that "with the exception of a few advertising-intensive categories, advertising had an insignificant effect on consumer demand" for "fairly broad aggregate categories." This negates the thesis that advertising in general changes consumers' priorities. But those few advertising-intensive categories that are exceptions to the rule are probably the very ones that attract the lightning bolts of the critics.

What are these types of goods? Phillip Nelson seems to suggest the answer: the lower the "utility value" of a product (that is, the less good it really does for the consumer), the more heavily it will be advertised and the more likely it is to become a repeat purchase.[20] Nelson's analysis "assumes that consumers are able to determine the utility of a brand after enough purchases of that brand." In fact, defenders of advertising commonly insist that the product itself must warrant the repeat sales on which most manufacturers of heavily promoted goods depend. Advertising may induce a first trial, but an unsatisfactory or inferior product will not be bought again. This assumes that consumers are consciously aware of product performance—a questionable assumption for many low-interest items or where the shopper is not the ultimate user.

Nelson observes that an advertising message can provide direct information about the brand and also the indirect "information" that because it is advertised it is a good buy. The direct information, he argues, requires no repetition of the message once it has been remembered, while the indirect information must continually be reinforced.* (Since he defines all advertising as informative by his starting premise, he avoids the distinction between rational and nonrational persuasion that is crucial for the Marxist critics I mentioned earlier.)

Moreover, even if advertising cannot in the long run make unacceptable products look good, does it not make acceptable products that are heavily promoted seem preferable to equally acceptable products that aren't—and for no good reason? The fact is that consumers do seem to develop "brand loyalty" to identical samples of beer identified only by key letters in taste tests.[21] People prefer to reduce risk by buying a widely advertised brand or one they had used before rather than relying on other kinds of information like word of mouth or government reports.[22]

Dick R. Wittink, in an analysis of territorial variations in market share over time for a heavily advertised, frequently purchased brand, found that its price elasticity (that is, its ability to get away with a price increase) increased when its share of advertising went up within the product category.[23] Wittink infers that the more a brand advertises, the more likely it is to be considered by the consumer. But the consumer will actually buy it only when the price is considered reasonable, and thus increased advertising will increase price sensitivity. Thus his evidence refutes the theory that advertising allows a firm to charge excessively high prices and hence discourages competition.

Reviewing the economic literature on advertising and market power, Mark Albion and Paul Farris conclude that while advertising and profitability appear to go together, the evidence does not clearly indicate which comes first.[24] Similarly, they find it hard to interpret the very spotty evidence on advertising and concentration, which also shows a positive relationship.

Some research supports the view that advertising increases sensitivity for consumer prices, and other research shows it decreases sensitivity for factory

---

*How much "direct" information does advertising contain? Alan Resnick and Bruce Stern analyzed the content of 378 television commercials broadcast by the three major networks in 1975. Half of them communicated "information" in terms of 14 criteria like price, quality, performance, and components. The proportion classified as informative ranged from 40 percent of the commercials for personal care products to 75 percent for institutional advertisements. (Alan Resnik and Bruce L. Stern, "Information Content in Television Ads," *Journal of Marketing*, 41 [January 1977]: 50-53.)

prices. Thus "advertising increases the market power for the manufacturers, selling the product to retailers," but "it decreases any monopoly power the retailer might have in selling the product to consumers." Albion and Farris conclude that while advertising may contribute to economies of scale in production, the results vary widely from case to case, and the resulting cost savings "must be weighed against the cost of advertising itself." They disagree with the idea that larger firms have lower advertising-to-sales ratios than smaller ones because of economies of scale. "Firms within an industry often compete in totally different market segments (branded and unbranded) with different market strategies." Advertising is especially important for low-involvement products bought in self-service outlets, where advertising is the primary source of consumer information. They find it similarly difficult to draw any definitive conclusion about the part that advertising plays in new product introductions, apart from the fact that they do lead to higher expenditures. Advertising can do little to offset the decline of a market, though it may help to accelerate a growth trend that is already under way. "There is no convincing body of evidence that advertising always, or even usually, increases the amount of brand loyalty in industries. Other aspects of the marketing mix, especially product quality, are much more influential."

Advertising pressure and brand position

In 1921, the economist Frank Knight made a classical case on behalf of the economic function of brand name advertising on behalf of similar products:

> If people are willing to pay for "Sunny Jim" poetry and "It Floats" when they buy cereal and soap, then these wares are economic goods. If a certain name on a fountain pen or safety razor enables it to sell at a 50 percent higher price than the same article would otherwise fetch, then the name represents one third of the economic utility in the article, and is economically no different from its color or design or the quality of the point or cutting edge, or any other quality which makes it useful or appealing. The morally fastidious (and naive) may protest that there is a distinction between "real" and "nominal" utilities; but they will find it very dangerous to their optimism to attempt to follow the distinction very far. On scrutiny it will be found that most of the things we spend our incomes for and agonize over, and notably practically all the higher "spiritual" values, gravitate swiftly into the second class.[25]

In how many product fields does the consumer's choice reflect the belief that brand differences are real and important, rather than the attitude that all familiar brands are acceptable? In the latter situation, can we assume that the informational content of the message is totally meaningless and that the only residual value of the advertising is the reminder that the brand exists? To the degree that this is true, advertising is a means of registering the brand name rather than a means of competitive persuasion. This suggests that nonsense is accepted as such by the consumer, with no particular resentment. If this is so, it would appear to support the proposition that the sheer volume of advertising pressure in dollars is directly translated into sales. That proposition is untenable.

A demonstration that advertising expenditures are not directly linked to product visibility can be drawn from a series of national surveys conducted between September 1976 and February 1977 by R. H. Bruskin Associates. Between 16 percent and 82 percent of the public correctly identified the advertising slogans currently used by 18 major brand advertisers. The familiarity of the slogans related strongly to the length of time they had been advertised but not to the money to advertise them.[26] (Incidentally, there was 16 percent identification of the then-current Coca-Cola theme, which had been supported with $31,000,000 in advertising since its introduction earlier in 1976, while Coke's old slogan was identified by 59 percent.) Slogan identification is, of course, nothing but a means to an end. However, the results do not support the viewpoint that advertising pays off generally in proportion to the budgetary weight behind it.

The frequency of consumers' exposure to brand advertising for parity products may be determined roughly by the amount of their television viewing, since TV receives over half of all national advertising in the major media and three-fourths of packaged goods advertising (food, soaps and cleansers, toiletries, beer, and cigarettes). Unaided awareness of leading brands of laundry products (among women in 1967) and of gasoline (among men in 1969) and beer (among men in 1975) was measured in three studies by the Newspaper Advertising Bureau. The data do not suggest any clear-cut linkage between brand awareness and advertising volume for the brand, nor between brand awareness and frequency of exposure to advertising.[27]

Familiarity with a brand is not automatically translated into an increased disposition to buy it. Small differences in purchase propensity between heavily exposed and lightly exposed consumers may translate into substantial shifts in sales volume. Examination of the figures for individual brands suggests that some have produced sharp increases in awareness among people likely to have had a stiff dosage of their advertising. Other brands appear to be coasting on the sustained promotions of earlier years. Yet overall, the evidence suggests that brand preferences are distributed very similarly among people who have had little or no exposure and those who have had a great deal.

Is the explanation that even the supposedly "unexposed" have some fleeting contacts with those brands, and that these contacts occur randomly in the same proportions as among the more heavily exposed, with each brand's advertising canceling the effects of each other's? Advertising exposure for any given brand is an index of its visibility in the market place. This reflects its sheer physical distribution, which in turn is a function of its market share. (Supermarket buying committees, which rigorously limit the number of items stocked as well as the shelf space per item, necessarily start with the best sellers and work their way down the list.)

What of the contention that advertising, apart from its ability to boost the sales of a given brand, also has a cumulative effect on behalf of a whole class of products, modifying and manipulating consumer desires? If heavy advertising by a particular industry can successfully change consumption patterns to its advantage, one might expect that this would lead to increased sales for the product category, and hence to an even larger share of *all* advertising.

Competitive brand gasoline advertising in Europe was examined by Jean-Jacques Lambin in the days before the oil embargo and the hike in prices.[28] He found that total industry advertising had negligible effects on total consumption, though advertising for individual brands had a statistically significant effect on their market share, both short and long run. Although individual advertising efforts seemed to have a positive effect on profits, for the industry as a whole advertising investments yielded a loss rather than a profit and might better be reallocated "to other promotional purposes."

An analysis by the Metra Consulting Group examined the relationship between cigarette consumption and advertising in the United Kingdom over a 20-year period.[29] A variety of statistical methods were used to analyze data, quarter by quarter, with proper controls for pricing changes and other extraneous variables. No significant relationship was found between total consumption and the total volume of advertising, which varied considerably over the measured period.

Advertising can induce trial of new products and build a market for them. It may, for example, have created a demand for deodorants among men. But in the case of established products, with a well-ingrained pattern of use, advertising seems to have the effect of maintaining and occasionally shifting the shares of competing brands rather than of stimulating total consumption.

Changing advertising/sales ratios

Advertising is 2.2 percent of the Gross National Product. As a percentage of all expenditures on personal consumption, advertising has shown wide swings in the past twenty years. From a high of 3.8 percent in 1963, it fell to 2.8 percent in 1975 and has since risen to 3.4 percent in 1983. Similar fluctuations may be found in the percentages that advertising represents of the gross sales volume of retailers and manufacturers. As a percentage of gross sales by department and specialty stores, advertising was 2.4 percent in 1965, 3.1 percent in 1967, down to 2.2 percent in 1971, and back up to 2.7 percent in 1981. Advertising-to-sales ratios for all manufacturing companies fell from 1.42 percent in 1961-62 to 1.25 percent in 1972-73, the two most recent reports from the Internal Revenue Service.

Advertising-to-sales ratios are, of course, highest among parity products, and consumer packaged goods (which include a high concentration of parity products) represent a declining share of all advertising. In 1967, food, toiletries, soaps and cleansers, beer, and cigarettes represented 48 percent of all national advertising in the measurable media. In 1982, they represented 34 percent. And national advertising has itself been growing at a slower rate than the local sector. This is especially interesting because critics of the noninformation aspects of advertising are generally tolerant of local ads, which tend to be highly specific and factual. In any case, it is hard to reconcile the trends with the proposition that the power of advertising is persuading consumers to spend more and more of their incomes on products they don't really want.

Have these trends had any visible effect on industry concentration ratios? Between 1963 and 1970, advertising-to-sales ratios fell from 5.0 percent to 3.8 percent for the major cigarette companies and from 13.2 percent to 10.9 percent for the leading soap companies. Yet in that period (before the ban on their broadcast advertising and during a period of extraordinary brand volatility) the four leading cigarette companies increased their share from 80 percent to 84 percent, while the four leading soap companies' share fell from 72 percent to 70 percent. The monopoly thesis is not easily demonstrable.

Some manufacturers may have concluded that the ever-increasing number of advertising messages has brought them up against the perceptual threshold beyond which consumers can no longer absorb new impressions. Does this, then, mean that firms will increasingly turn to alternative means of promotion as a substitute for advertising? Economic principles would suggest that such alternatives will be tested and pursued if their payoff is greater.

Setting limits on advertising

Determining the economic effects of advertising is, as the preceding discussion suggests, no easy task. Michael Porter comments, "Explaining the variation in advertising rates among industries is an extremely difficult problem, leading generally to low coefficients of multiple determination and low levels of significance of coefficients in careful studies. And even statistically significant coefficients are often difficult to interpret unambiguously because they can support more than one hypothesis."[30]

Lester Telser reported in 1964 that there was no consistent relationship between monopolistic tendencies in an industry and the prevailing advertising-to-sales ratios.[31] More recently, Stanley I. Ornstein has analyzed IRS data for a substantial proportion of U.S. industries. The total volume of advertising by the industry, or by the average firm in it, was not related to concentration, and there was no support for the hypothesis that advertising represents a barrier to entry.[32] James Ferguson, in a comprehensive examination of the evidence on advertising and competition, concludes that "there is both an inadequate theoretical and an inadequate empirical basis for any public policy based on the presumption that advertising decreases competition."[33]

Paul Farris and David Reibstein examined data on advertising, prices, and profits for 227 consumer goods companies over the period 1971–77.[34] The most profitable brands were those of high quality and those that maintained the most consistent advertising and pricing strategies. Relative to competition, heavy advertisers charged higher prices, and the highest prices of all were charged for brands that combined high product quality with heavy advertising. The relationship between advertising pressure and price was most evident for products at a mature stage of their life cycles and for businesses with high market shares. It was least applicable to new products in which there was still volatility and confusion in competitive pricing. Products that cost more than $10 (and that thus represented "high risk" for the consumer) also showed a weaker relationship between advertising and prices. Even though it is hard to prove that advertising in general leads to monopoly, to higher prices, or to the creation of demand for products that have no real utility, critics like to point to those product classes where advertising expenditures are exceptionally high. They sometimes go on to suggest that the total amount of advertising for those products should be limited at some arbitrary cutoff point, defined either at a percentage of gross sales volume or at a percentage set in relation to advertising for all products and brands.

Some years ago, the British Monopolies Commission sought to demonstrate that such heavy advertising represented an unwarranted and uneconomic exploitation of the consumer. Under government pressure, Unilever and Procter & Gamble each agreed in 1967 to market a soap powder and two detergent powders at wholesale prices 20 percent below their comparable main brands, but without sales promotion or advertising support. After two years of this experiment, the reduced-price brands held the identical 20 percent market share they had at the outset. (By contrast, higher priced new enzyme products introduced in 1968 managed to capture 25 percent to 30 percent of the market within one year after launch.)[35]

But limiting advertising for a few particular brands is very different from limiting advertising for a whole product category. Suppose, in the British case, the government had banned *all* advertising for laundry soap and detergent powders. Would this have made sense without also banning advertising for *all* soaps and for bleaches, water softeners, and similar products? The aggregate promotional effect of all advertising in a product category is competitive with that of all other categories for its share of total consumer spending. Any government body that determined that people should spend less money on detergents, sleeping pills, soap, or cosmetics could limit the market much more effectively through discriminatory taxation than by regulating any one particular form of sales promotion.

Limitations on the volume of advertising would simply divert sales pressures into other forms of merchandise and promotion—from market research to push money—directed to the same purpose and perhaps more difficult to regulate. The cigarette industry's diversion of funds out of broadcast advertising into premium offers and auto races represents just one example. Advertising and other promotional activity are hard to disentangle. Cooperative advertising and coupon advertising are often paid out of promotion rather than advertising budgets.

Regulations and controls of advertising have to be based on generalizations. That is, you have to be able to assume that you are dealing with a class of events in order to subject such events to regulatory proceedings. But generalizations about advertising performance are hard to come by.[36]

Even Comanor and Wilson, whom I mentioned earlier, come up with qualified answers, and considerable product class variations when they review the evidence of advertising's effects on market share. In a more recent paper (with Arthur Kover and Robert Smiley), Comanor retreats to the position that the intensity of advertising can raise barriers to entry "at least in *some* industries and for *some* period of time" (my italics). He and his co-authors conclude that "the major problem, both for the process of allocating resources toward advertising and for research towards understanding this process, arises from our inability to measure the effectiveness of advertising."[37]

As a matter of fact, the percentage of national advertising accounted for by the leading company or companies in a product field varies widely. It may be necessary for a firm to register a minimum amount of visibility or acceptablity through advertising pressure. Still, it is difficult to state with any precision at what point such a barrier to entry is transformed from a minor obstacle to an impenetrable wall.

The perils of generalization

Why is it so hard to generalize about advertising? It is because its unpredictable creative element cannot be programmed. Looking at advertising volume strictly in terms of dollar investments gives us no real clue as to its yield. In a remarkable series of experiments conducted for Anheuser-Busch, Russell Ackoff and James Ernshoff found that the highest level of sales improvement occurred when advertising pressure was reduced by 50 percent. In areas where advertising was completely eliminated, sales did not decline until a year and a half had passed.[38]

In econometric studies of advertising, it appears to be tacitly assumed by both critics and supporters that creative quality may be considered a constant. Its variability is assumed to be random and to fall within about the same range that could be expected in product performance or in entrepreneurial talent from firm to firm. This assumption is critical, and also mistaken.

The striking inconsistency in advertising productivity must lead us to conclude that the yield from advertising is not significantly related to its sheer volume of expenditure or to its ratio to sales. Different advertising messages for the same product vary tremendously in persuasive appeal and power, as copy testers have long known. And many advertising messages are forgotten very rapidly.

If only a small proportion of ad messages are remembered, this implies that an incredible amount of waste must occur in advertising communication. A message that is not consciously remembered may still have substantial effects, since its echoes may be reinforced when it is repeated and evoked when the consumer confronts the product at the point of sale. But messages that are poor in memorability or inadequate in persuasive content are more likely to be nonproductive, underproductive, or counterproductive for the advertiser and for his product field, and thus serve no useful economic function. What can be the social benefits of this unproductive advertising, which fails to produce sales effects commensurate to its cost and, therefore, results in no increased economic activity?

So—is all this advertising necessary? Well, yes—and no.

1. It is impossible to conceive of a competitive market economy in which advertising does not play a part. Advertising is one of a variety of forms of selling and promotion. The advantages of size to an advertiser parallel advantages of size in other realms of merchandising, distribution, and sales. There is no logical or reasonable way of restricting one aspect of promotion without restricting all other ways. This would mean the end of competition and the economic advantages and political freedoms that go with it.

2. In many instances and in many aspects there may be legitimate reason to criticize the economic and social effects of advertising. But these instances must be dealt with on their own specific terms. A knee-jerk

defense reaction to any attack on any aspect of advertising is just as witless as knee-jerk hostility. The economic effects of advertising are not subject to universal generalizations.

3. A growing percentage of all advertising is informational in character. A declining proportion is represented by national advertising in product fields characterized by minor performance differences among brands. This trend should continue as we have increasing product differentiation in the market place and more rapid growth in the consumption of services than of goods.

4. The misallocation of resources that results from overspending by certain advertisers is probably small relative to the misallocation that arises from inadequacies of advertising content and scheduling. The greatest waste in advertising is in the many messages that fall wide of the mark.

Notes

1. One paradox of the consumer movement is that it involved precisely those elements of the population that are *least* likely to be exploited. A landmark study by sociologist David Caplovitz (*The Poor Pay More* [New York: The Free Press, 1963]) established the notion that "the poor pay more," at least when the poor were residents of Harlem buying furniture and appliances on credit. Clearly, people of lower income and education, disadvantaged people, are less likely to be in a position to comparison shop, to withstand high-pressure salesmen, or to read the fine print in a warranty or installment payment contract.

On the other hand, the businessman who sells to slum dwellers faces a higher rate of pilferage and defaulted payments on goods received. The higher cost of doing business in poor neighborhoods presents particular problems to large retail chains. They must advertise their prices on a citywide or regional basis and thus in effect must tax their rich customers in order to sell to their poor ones at the same price. The result has been that many chains have simply closed their stores in poor neighborhoods, thereby reducing the competition for the local merchant who often charges as much as the traffic can bear.

Conversely, the upper class customer is not only better able to cope with product claims and to study the label, he also buys in larger quantities and thus more economically; he is more apt to buy store brands instead of similar national brands. Awareness and active use of unit pricing, we have found in New York City, is concentrated among the better-off and better-educated, who need it least. (Unit pricing means that the exact price per standard weight unit must be posted for packaged goods that come in different size cartons and bottles. The research mentioned was done by the Newspaper Advertising Bureau.) As a social phenomenon, the demand for consumer protection is heard most loudly not at the end of the social scale where the need for protection is more needed, but at the opposite end.

2. Children who watch advertising for cereals and candy more than the average also are heavier-than-average consumers of those foods. Moreover, viewing ads for specific brands of cereal relates directly to consumption of those brands. Among adolescents, heavy TV viewers are more likely to think that people need or use highly advertised products like proprietary medicines, mouthwash, and deodorants, and they also tend to express a preference for advertised brands. (Charles K. Atkin, "Television Advertising and Socialization to Consumer Roles," in David Pearl, Lorraine Bouthilet, and Joyce Lazar, eds., *Television and Behavior: Ten Years of Scientific Progress and Implications*

for the Eighties, Vol 2 [National Institute of Mental Health, 1982].)

3. *Broadcasting*, February 28, 1972, pp. 24–26.

4. Thomas Asher, "Smoking Out Smokey the Bear," *More*, 2, 3 (March 1972): 12–13.

5. *Business Week*, June 10, 1972, p. 49.

6. Jacob Jacoby, Margaret C. Nelson, and Wayne D. Hoyer, "Corrective Advertising and Affirmative Disclosure Statements: Their Potential for Confusing and Misleading the Consumer," *Journal of Marketing*, 46, 1 (Winter 1982): 61–72.

7. Samuel Thurm, "Uses and Abuses of Research in Washington," Paper presented to the Advertising Research Foundation Conference, New York, 1982.

8. Isaac Ehrlich and Lawrence Fisher, "The Derived Demand for Advertising: A Theoretical and Empirical Investigation," *American Economic Review*, 72, 3 (June 1982): 366–88.

9. Robert Steiner, "Does Advertising Lower Consumer Prices?" *Journal of Marketing*, 37, 4 (October 1973): 19–26.

10. Kenneth Mason, "How Much Do You Spend on Advertising? Product is Key," *Advertising Age*, June 12, 1972.

11. John Kenneth Galbraith, *The New Industrial State* (Boston: Houghton Mifflin, 1967).

12. Nicholas Kaldor, "The Economic Aspects of Advertising," *Review of Economic Studies*, 18, 1 (1949–1950): 1–27.

13. Speech before the Federal Bar Association, June 2, 1966, Washington, D.C. The same argument was taken up in testimony before the Senate Antitrust Subcommittee in September 1966. John Blair, the committee's Chief Economist, analyzed the degree of economic concentration in various product areas involving consumer goods heavily advertised on network TV. He reported increases in the 4 leading companies' share of market in 25 product areas. In 11 other consumer fields concentration declined, although the 4 leading companies were heavy users of network television.

14. Jules Backman, *Advertising and Competition* (New York: New York University Press, 1967).

15. Speech before the Association of National Advertisers, October 24, 1966, Colorado Springs, Colorado.

16. Willard F. Mueller and Richard T. Rogers, "The Role of Advertising in Changing Concentration of Manufacturing Industries," *Review of Economics and Statistics*, 62 (February 1980): 89–96.

17. William S. Comanor and Thomas A. Wilson, *Advertising and Market Power* (Cambridge, Mass.: Harvard University Press, 1974).

18. Harry Bloch finds that Comanor and Wilson's positive association between advertising-to-sales ratios and profits is entirely due to the fact that they used the accounting procedure of treating advertising as current expense rather than as an investment. (Harry Bloch, "Advertising and Profitability: A Reappraisal," *Journal of Political Economy*, 82, Pt. I (March-April 1974): 267-86.) The positive correlation between profit rates and advertising intensity is also labeled an "accounting artifact" by economist Harold Demsetz. Cf. "Accounting for Advertising as a Barrier to Entry," *The Journal of Business*, 52, 3 (July 1979): 345-60.

19. Henry G. Grabowski, "The Effects of Advertising on the Inter-Industry Distribution of Demand," *Explorations in Economic Research*, 3, 1 (Winter 1976): 21-75.

20. Phillip Nelson, "The Economic Consequences of Advertising," *Journal of Business*, 48, 2 (April 1975): 213-41.

21. J. Douglas McConnell, "The Price-Quality Relationship in an Experimental Setting," *Journal of Marketing Research*, 2 (August 1968): 300-3.

22. Ted Roselius, "Consumer Problems of Risk Reduction Methods," *Journal of Marketing*, 35 (January 1971): 56-61.

23. Dick R. Wittink, "Advertising Increases Sensitivity to Price," *Journal of Advertising Research*, 17, 2 (April 1977): 39-42.

24. Mark S. Albion and Paul W. Farris, *The Advertising Controversy: Evidence on the Economic Effects of Advertising* (Boston: Auburn House, 1981). *Cf*, also Stanley I. Ornstein, *Industrial Concentration and Advertising Intensity* (Washington, D.C.: American Enterprise Institute, 1977).

25. Frank Knight, *Risk, Uncertainty and Profit* (Boston: Houghton Mifflin, 1921), p. 262, quoted by Michael Schudson, "Criticizing the Critics of Advertising: Towards a Sociological View of Marketing," *Media, Culture and Society*, 3 (1981): 3-12.

26. There is a strong (+.57) rank-order correlation between the length of time the slogan had been advertised and the degree of its familiarity. There is a substantial (−.49) *negative* rank-order correlation between the amount of national advertising behind each brand in 1976 and the amount of slogan identification early the following year. When total advertising since the introduction of the slogan is used as the measure, the rank-order correlation with slogan identification is nil (+.07).

27. Leo Bogart, "Is All This Advertising Necessary?" *Journal of Advertising Research* 18, 5 (October 1978): 17-25. Joan Geiger also found no difference in brand choice between heavy and light viewers. *Cf.* "Seven Brands in Seven Days," *Journal of Advertising Research* 11, 5 (October 1971): 15-22.

28. Jean-Jacques Lambin, "Is Gasoline Advertising Justified?" *Journal of Business*, 45, 4 (October 1972): 585-619. Expanding his research, Lambin analyzed econometrically the sales records for 108 brands of various products in eight European countries. He concluded that advertising has only limited power over brand preferences, since a 1 percent increase in ad expenditures yielded only a 0.1 percent short-term increase in sales or market share, or a 0.25 percent increase if long-term effects were allowed for. Moreover, incremental increases in advertising yielded diminishing returns. Lambin also concluded that advertising has hardly any ability to differentiate brands artificially, compared with real differences in product attributes, price, or quality. He confirms the oft-demonstrated observation that small brands have a higher advertising-to-sales ratio than leading brands and thus a higher ratio of advertising share to market share. Advertising-to-sales ratios are volatile for individual brands, even though they may be stable at the company level. Lambin examined 35 brands in 13 different product classes and found that in 14 cases the expenditure on advertising did not cover its own cost. However, for the average brand, there was a return of $1.80 in incremental revenue for each $1.00 additional spent on advertising. He found no indication that intensive advertising was associated with monopoly power and profits. Jean-Jacques Lambin, "What Is the Real Impact of Advertising," *Harvard Business Review* (May-June 1975): 139-47.

29. *The Relationship Between Total Cigarette Advertising and Total Cigarette Consumption in the UK*, London: Metra Consulting Group Limited, October 1979.

30. Michael E. Morter, "Optimal Advertising: An Intra-Industry Approach," in David Guerck, ed., *Issues in Advertising: The Economics of Persuasion* (Washington, D.C.: American Enterprise Institute, 1978).

31. Lester G. Telser, "Advertising and Competition," *Journal of Political Economy*, 72, 6 (December 1964): 537-62.

32. Stanley I. Ornstein, *Industrial Concentration and Advertising Intensity* (Washington, D.C.: American Enterprise Institute, 1978).

33. James M. Ferguson, *Advertising and Competition: Theory, Measurement, Fact*, (Cambridge, Mass.: Ballinger, 1974). *Cf.* also Richard Schmalensee, *The Economics of Advertising* (Amsterdam: Elsevien, North Holland, 1972). Still another review of the literature by J. A. Hennings and H. M. Mann also finds no demonstration of causality in the positive

associations between advertising-to-sales ratios and market concentration and between advertising-to-sales ratios and profitability. Advertising intensity appears to precede concentration, largely because it is linked to the number of new products a firm introduces. As new products are introduced, Hennings and Mann suggest, the consumer's existing product information becomes obsolete. Advertising becomes correspondingly more valuable to him as a source of new information, and, therefore, sales become increasingly dependent on advertising. (J. A. Hennings and H. M. Mann, "Advertising and Oligopoly: Correlations in Search of Understanding," in David Guerck, ed., *Issues in Advertising: The Economics of Persuasion* [Washington, D.C.: American Enterprise Institute, 1978].)

34. Paul W. Farris and David J. Reibstein, "How Prices, Ad Expenditures, and Profits are Linked," *Harvard Business Review*, 57, 6 (November/December 1979): 173-84.
35. George Polanyi, *Detergents: A Question of Monopoly* (London: Institute of Economic Affairs, 1970).
36. To illustrate: In 1969, the Federal Trade Commission analyzed the advertising-to-sales ratios of 97 food companies in product lines where four firms account for 40 percent of the market. When advertising-to-sales ratios averaged 1 percent, net profit averaged 6.3 percent. But at a 35 percent A/S ratio, profit rose to 8.5 percent. When the four firms had 70 percent of the market, net profit was 11.5 percent with an A/S ratio of 1 percent, but profit rose to 13.7 percent at an A/S ratio of 3 percent. The conclusion was that the sums required to advertise heavily acted as a barrier to new products seeking to enter a market. Frank M. Bass reanalyzed the results and noted that the report had aggregated data taken from firms in industries with varying internal structures, different profit yields, and different market characteristics. In only one third of the cases was there actually a strong link between profitability and the advertising-to-sales ratio. In fact, the FTC's conclusion applied only to manufacturers of candy, chewing gum, baked goods, and cereals. (Frank M. Bass, "Profit and the A/S Ratio," *Journal of Advertising Research*, 14, 6 [December 1974]: 19.) As Charles Ramond later pointed out, these are products sold to children. Thus they are able to command only a brief brand loyalty, and they are characterized by frequent introduction of new brands. (Charles Ramond, "The Profitability of Advertising: An FTC Study Revisited," Paper presented to the American Marketing Association, January 30, 1975, New York City.)
37. William S. Comanor, Arthur J. Kover, and Robert H. Smiley, "Advertising and Organization," in William Starbuck, ed., *Handbook of Organizational Design*, Vol. 3 (Amsterdam: Elsevier, 1978).
38. Russell L. Ackoff and James R. Ernshoff, "Advertising Research at Anheuser-Busch, Inc. (1963-1968)," *Sloan Management Review*, 16, 2 (Winter 1975): 1-15.

Chapter 3
Deciding How Much to Spend, and Where

The chewing gum magnate, William K. Wrigley, once likened advertising to a locomotive: "It is needed to get the train moving forward. When the train is moving at full speed, most passengers don't even realize it's there. However, detach the locomotive from the train and everything else will soon come to a grinding halt."[1] John Wanamaker made a similar observation: "To discontinue an advertisement is taking down your signs. If you want to do business you must let the public know it. I would as soon think of doing business without clerks as without advertising."[2]

Advertising's functions obviously look very different in the eyes of the individual entrepreneur than they do from the broader perspective of economists and social critics on which I have focused in the first two chapters. The ultimate purpose of *most* advertising is to sell.* A sales objective must be achieved through a devious route. Along the way, advertising has many intermediate aims: to identify the product, to catalog its attributes, to surround it with the right emotional aura, to inform people of its virtues, to remind them of its existence, to persuade them that it merits use, to reinforce their favorable predispositions against forgetfulness. In preparing an advertising campaign, there is often great confusion as to exactly which of these different purposes is intended. Yet the size of the budget, the selection of media, the media-scheduling strategy, the copy theming, the creative form of the advertising message, and every other aspect of advertising depend for their success upon a clear definition of aims.

Retail and national advertising objectives

Although the layman often indiscriminately lumps all forms of "advertising" together, the term encompasses innumerable subspecies, each with its own characteristics, techniques, and objectives. To begin with, there is a generic distinc-

---

*There are exceptions to this. Public relations advertising may be basically concerned with the company's survival or its freedom to achieve corporate goals, and these vital functions may have nothing to do with sales.

tion between the advertising placed directly by manufacturers to promote their products or services and the advertising placed by retailers to bring in business.

The so-called national* advertiser doesn't think in terms of a specific ad, as the retailer usually does. The retailer tends to be mainly concerned with the return on investment in today's advertising here and now. Yet, like the national manufacturer, the typical retailer advertises on a continuing basis and must be concerned with the cumulative effects of repetitive advertising. While particular ads stress different items with different selective product appeals, the whole continuous progression of ads serves to create and build the store's reputation. No one item in any one ad can attract all of the readers, but at the same time that the retailer directly appeals to some of the customers with any one ad he is subtly influencing all of them. Retailers have become increasingly aware that the design and visual style of their advertising, the selection of models (in art as well as in photographs), the nature and price range of the merchandise depicted—all combine to produce the impression that consumers have of the store itself. As marketing concepts have taken hold in retailing, major retailers have turned to advertising agencies to create campaigns for them that are directly comparable in their long-term perspective to the national advertiser's effort to build favorable awareness of a brand.

Classified advertising in the newspaper represents, perhaps in its purest form, communication for business purposes via the mass media. The reader who seeks out classified ads is highly purposeful, as purposeful, in fact, as is the advertiser who has a specific house to sell or car to trade. The people who see the ad, by definition, include those with a strong buying interest, who are represented within the total audience of the newspaper in much the same proportion as in the population at large. However, not all of those who look at a classified ad are people who are actively in the market. On any given day, 53 percent of newspaper readers look at classified advertising, and these large numbers include many who are checking out their own net worth (or their neighbors') or simply engaging in a little fantasy of upgrading or changing their condition. Yet inevitably this kind of browsing can lead to an unanticipated shopping expedition or job application.

Retail display advertising in the newspaper (where over half of all retail advertising runs) is also aimed at the people with potential interest in the product advertised, but at a broader group than those with the avid concern of the classified ad reader. The retail ad's position within the body of the paper lends itself to casual perusal by a great many people who would not trouble to turn to a classified listing of the same merchandise. Such advertising plays upon the vague, unformed, tentative buying interests which, in enormous variety, are latent in the minds of most people at any given moment.

A person who is in the market for a coat, dress, or living room sofa is apt to shop the retail ads in a purposeful way, much as the prospective purchaser of a house will look through the classified ads in the real estate section. But the bulk of the people whose attention alights on the typical retail display ad or who

---

*"So-called" because manufacturers with only regional distribution are normally grouped under this heading.

happen to hear a retailer's commercial are people who have, at the moment, only the most nebulous interest in the product.

For the national advertiser, the probability of catching readers, viewers, or listeners who are actively in the market for his product is more remote. He may hope to reach people who are actually on the verge of a specific brand purchase decision, but at any moment in time such persons will represent but a fraction of those within reach of his message. His main objective in advertising is to lay a foundation for the purchase decision when the time comes.

About one-fourth of retail advertising is actually paid for by national manufacturers through the means of cooperative allowances. (The manufacturer's share of the total ranges from 10 percent for discount store advertising to 50 percent for supermarket ads.) These allowances are intended to give the retailer an incentive to promote a manufacturer's wares, not only in the retailer's ads but in his internal display and promotion.

For many manufacturers, cooperative advertising is considered as more a sales or promotional expense than as advertising, since the company—though it furnishes copy, artwork, and other materials—loses effective control over the end product. Since the average retailer is less skilled in advertising techniques than the average manufacturer and his agency, "co-op" ads sometimes present a hodgepodge of products from different companies.

However, cooperative advertising gives the manufacturer the positive advantage of associating his merchandise with stores of fine reputation that the customer respects. For an unknown or little-known brand or for a new product, this may be a substantial advantage indeed. There is also a practical advantage for the manufacturer: under the less expensive bulk rates paid by the large retailer who advertises fairly continuously, the same amount of newspaper space may usually be bought for a single ad at less cost than the national advertiser would have to pay if it bought directly through its agency.

As much as two-thirds of the funds manufacturers set aside for cooperative allowances go unused. Partly this is because of retailers' reluctance to add their own money to what manufacturers make available, and partly it is because they want to present consumers with a balanced picture of their merchandise assortments rather than emphasize the merchandise for which advertising funds happen to be on hand.

Retail advertising serves a number of distinctive purposes. The average person thinks of a retail ad as one designed to sell those particular products that the store has on sale. Most retail advertising does represent this kind of specific promotion of individual items, which the store hopes to sell within the next few days at a gross profit that will more than pay for the cost of the ad itself.

Retailers expect such advertising to have a direct pull, to sell more of the product than usual. However, merchants normally do other important things at the same time they advertise a product, like reducing its price and displaying it prominently within the store. It is therefore very difficult in practice to determine how much of the extra sales come from the advertising and how much from other aspects of the promotion. Any store in a good location, with an established reputation and clientele, is going to draw customers in the normal course of events and is going to sell any item featured in the store.

The direct value of a promotional ad is that it draws some customers who might not otherwise be shopping in that store on that day. Once in the store, they will not necessarily buy the advertised product, no matter how much the ad may have attracted them. The item may not live up to the promise in the ads; the store may not have the right color or size; the customer may not get the proper level of attention and service.

But if the customer is in the store, whether or not he buys the item, there is a strong likelihood that he will buy *something*. (A study made by the Newspaper Advertising Bureau in association with a large department store found that two-thirds of the women interviewed who had bought a product after seeing it advertised also bought one or more other items in the store. Another similar study found that women attracted by promotional ads bought 1.3 unadvertised items for every advertised item they bought. And in yet a third study we found that customers who had come to the store because of an ad spent the same amount of money on other items as they did for the advertised merchandise.)

It follows from all of this that a major objective of every promotional ad run by a retailer is to generate store traffic, because an ad that brings customers to his store will result in the sale of merchandise that is *not* advertised. Among people exposed to the advertising who are not immediately impelled to visit the store and shop for the product, the advertising serves an extra purpose: it reminds them that the store carries this particular kind of item. The illustration, the description, the pricing of the articles—all go to create or strengthen identifications which, over the long haul, bring customers to that store for that type of merchandise.

Promotional ads run by retailers for individual products or product assortments therefore carry an institutional burden. Straightforward institutional advertising, moreover, represents an increasingly important part of retail advertising. Big chains like Kroger's and Sears have joined ranks with those individual department stores that have long run advertising to extol their intangible merits—service, quality controls, style sense, pricing policy, concern for the individual customer. Stores run large ads to commemorate holidays, to welcome visiting celebrities, to honor new buildings and civic accomplishments, and even to congratulate their competitors. This kind of celebration of the store's identification with its community represents institutional advertising at a level that must inevitably affect sales results, but to a degree that is impossible to trace.

For the national manufacturer, institutional advertising for general public relations purposes may also take the form of a "special"—as in the televised sponsorship of national political conventions. Often, however, it is carried on over a period of years and with great consistency. "Grants" in support of public television programs have provided large corporations with an inexpensive form of sponsorship and high visibility with an influential and elite audience. The maintenance of an established, consistent schedule of institutional or public relations advertising may give a company a strong pedestal from which to launch its harder-hitting product promotional campaigns. If there is a clear and strong identification of product brand names with the company name (as is true of General Electric but not of General Foods), however, corporate advertising and brand advertising are hard to distinguish.

Advertising objectives for the established product

The communications task of advertising a product that has been around for a while and of which people have an impression, whether or not they have actually used it, is essentially different from that involving a new product. The promotion of an established product may represent a continuing effort to maintain an established market position. It may also be a special event, closely tied to activities of the company's sales department. Such a particular effort may be in support of a trade deal involving extra financial incentives to the retailer to stock the product or to give it extra shelf or display space.* It may be backup for a consumer deal involving price-off labels, coupons, or premiums.

In many packaged goods categories, such consumer promotions represent a fact of normal advertising life and occur at predictable intervals and must, more-over, be built into the year's advertising plans right from the beginning. But special promotions may also represent a company's response to an unexpected competitive development, and the advertising schedule and budget required to support them may have to be created at the expense of the planned advertising program.

For the established brand, advertising pays off in profitability even when it does not increase unit sales. Since it reinforces the consumers' sense that it is different from its competitors, they are willing to pay more for it. William Moran points out that the greater the probability of repeat purchase, the higher a brand's market share will be.[3] But at any given level of brand share, the higher the rate of repeated purchase, the more profitable a brand can be, since it is less vulnerable to competitive activity. Thus a brand that is perceived as distinctive will also be more profitable. While sales promotions (normally involving price reductions) encourage customers to switch brands, advertising for packaged goods products works to counteract this by encouraging consumers to stick with the brand they know and thus to raise the chances of repeat purchase.

Depending on its past history, an existing product may be thought of as unpopular or unsuccessful by those who have never tried it themselves. It may carry negative associations in the case of those who have tried it in the past but found it unsatisfactory. In either case, the communications objective is to remind these people that the product exists and to present it in a light different from the one in which it may have been cast before.

An additional and important job to be done in advertising an established product is to reinforce among past and present satisfied users their existing favorable opinion of the product. They must be given reasons and arguments to support what might otherwise be no more than an emotional tone of relatively low charge.

This task must be approached differently for an established product with a dominant market position and for one with a minor share. It must also be different for a product that is gaining momentum, one whose share is stable, and one that is losing ground. The notion of a product "life cycle" is commonly

*A typical supermarket carried over 14,000 items in 1980 compared with 6,000 twenty years earlier.

accepted in marketing theory. It is generally agreed that in their "youth," products should receive a relatively high advertising investment, while in their "maturity" this should be reduced, and in their "old age," virtually eliminated, since they can continue to eke out sales based on their past reputations. But the analogy to a living creature does not always fit, and the homilies about advertising objectives and expenditures may be counterproductive. Clever advertising may give an ancient and enfeebled brand a new injection of youthful vitality. A rising new product may be stopped dead by the advent of a superior competitor. Regardless of its past history and its competitive position, every product must call out to potential purchasers and tell them or remind them why it deserves to be bought.

The term "reminder advertising" applied to transit ads, small print ads, and outdoor advertising properly refers only to advertisements that communicate nothing more than the name or picture of the product itself. "Reminder advertising" describes a technique rather than an objective. Any ad reaching someone who does *not* already know the advertised product obviously does not come as a reminder; any ad reaching someone who *does* know the product is a reminder to some degree, depending on the new information it contains.

Advertising objectives for the new product

Established products rarely make spectacular case histories. Much of the lore in advertising concerns new products that achieve success through a brilliant slogan, theme, or concentrated effort—Lestoil, Mr. Clean, Alberto VO^5, Miller Lite, Merit. Such campaigns attain greatness in the annals of advertising when they manage to put a product's name into common currency and transform that familiarity into actual trial use, repeated use, and, finally, established brand position.

Over 6,000 new items are introduced into American supermarkets every year. For the companies that make them, each one is a new venture; for the consumer, it may or may not be seen that way. The definition of a "new product" is a matter of some confusion. A product may be wholly new in the sense that it does something that no existing product has managed to do up to that point. (An example of this might be video games or personal computers.) Or it may be a substantial improvement on an existing product (like color TV).

Most new products, however, are far less novel. They merely represent minor variations in products already on the market, improvements in some cases, in others a difference merely in size, packaging, or name or a slight variation in the secondary features. The allegedly high failure rate of new products largely reflects the luck of this type of new brand entry into an existing competitive market rather than that of major product innovations.

A substantial part of new product development occurs under the labels of existing brands. Kellogg's new varieties of dry cereals and Campbell's new varieties of canned soups maintain these companies in strong positions of market leadership, where innovation plays a vital part. It is the generic brand name, rather than any subvariety of the product, that maintains continuity in the public mind. Ivory Liquid and Bayer's Children's Aspirin are examples of line extensions. But although a familiar brand name (like Rave Home Permanent) can be successfully carried over to a related new product (Rave Hairspray), it will create problems if there is an incongruity in the application. "If you liked Vicks VapoRub, then you'll love Vicks Mouthwash, right? Wrong."[4]

In the dry products grocery field, manufacturers' advertised brands (as opposed to private store labels, wholesaler brands, and nonadvertised brands, mostly of the local or regional variety) account for 18 percent of the brand choices available, but for 74 percent of the sales.[5]

Ninety-five percent of the sales of such brands in 1965 came from labels that were on the market four years earlier, leaving only 5 percent of sales from newer brands. Moreover, in the four-year period checked, the existing brands chalked up a 13 percent gain. Apart from this evidence that new brands are not quite as important as they are sometimes thought to be, it should be noted that almost all the money invested by manufacturers in new brands comes from profits made on existing products.

The advertising budget pressure required to support a new product introduction is sometimes mistakenly equated with the number of messages that must be delivered or even that must be delivered through a particular medium whose indispensability is taken for granted. For example, Foote, Cone & Belding's David Berger analyzed 14 introductions of new grocery products during the 1970s. He concluded that for a TV-advertised brand, an acceptable (60 percent) level of high brand awareness required 2,500 Gross Rating Points* in its first three to six months. "Below 1,000 GRPs, the likelihood of high awareness is nil."[6] But such an emphasis on sheer "tonnage" omits a crucial element: the quality of what is being communicated.

W. K. Kellogg once explained how to get into the cornflakes business: "To build production facilities, X million dollars; to get consumer acceptance, three times as much."[7] However, things may have changed. Kenneth Mason of Quaker Oats once reported on the first year's advertising budgets and sales figures for seven new products introduced by his company.[8] The one with the largest budget ($6 million) produced sales of only $8 million. The one with the smallest budget ($1.1 million) produced sales of $11 million. But this doesn't prove that it pays to advertise as little as possible, because the second most heavily advertised new brand (at $4 million) produced $28 million in sales. The creative element, the product attributes, the competitive pressures, the pricing policy, the choice of distribution channels—all may have made the difference.

Smashing success stories in advertising are very few and very far between. For established brands on the market place, the struggle for survival is keen and never-ceasing. For new products, it is even more desperate. It expresses itself at every step of development, starting with the initial debate over the packaging, the name, and the ingredients to be used in the product. Even after a product has been successfully test marketed, it takes a hard fought battle to get distribution through retail buyers, wholesalers and buying committees, and the innu-

*A Gross Rating Point is 1 percent of a population (people or households) reached in an audience measurement over a designated period of time, regardless of the number of exposures. In the case of spots, GRPs are computed by averaging the ratings of the adjacent programs.

merable other guardians of the gates to consumer access and consumer awareness.

The new product marketer must traverse a dark and intricate labyrinth before he sees the light of day and gets his product out where people can buy it. Throughout this whole initial process of product planning and introduction, advertising appears as only one of many elements that the marketer must confront.

The brilliance of a planned advertising campaign can never be used to presell it to the trade. The company salesman calling on his accounts takes pains to mention the *size* of the advertising budget for the product. He emphasizes how much money is being spent for the product within the local market. He may stress the use of prestige media which the retailer believes in or which the company believes the retailer to believe in. But rarely (if ever) will he say as he opens his promotion kit, "We've got a great new slogan, a great new unique selling proposition, a great new research-engendered shortcut to the consumer's libido!"

Within the market, brand share for established products does not undergo rapid or dramatic shifts from month to month, from one store audit period to the next, or even from year to year.*

With new products the story is different because they have no place to go but up or out. A new product must, by advertising, fight its way into the public's awareness and into a sector of the established market. It must work quickly to get past the initial months of heavy investment and learn to stand on its own feet within the designated pay-out period.

In the case of a new product, the advertiser's objective is twofold. He must create a sense of awareness or familiarity that permits his brand to be anchored as a significant reference point in the consumer's mind. Then he must create from scratch a favorable or positive set of associations that will cause the product to be tried, perhaps even preferred.

If the product has sufficient intrinsic interest, an announcement that is sufficiently striking and vividly presented can accomplish both purposes: arresting the consumer's attention and familiarizing him with both the brand name *and* the product story at the same time. Typically, however, the new brand faces a real problem in making the consumer aware of its existence. There is no purpose in registering copy points if the product itself lacks clear identity in the consumer's mind.

For this reason, it often makes sense for an advertiser to build awareness and recognition for his product before he launches into a full-fledged exposition of its virtues. A decision to proceed in this way has implications for the choice of media as well as for the types of messages to be used at each stage of an introduc-

---

*Store auditing is the most widely used system for measuring changes in a brand's market position. Audits involve the use of a sample of retail outlets in which, at periodic intervals (usually of two months), a count is made of all merchandise on the shelf or in inventories and a record is kept of all shipments received since the last audit date. For each measured brand, initial inventory plus shipments minus stocks on hand equals sales for the audit period.

tion. "Familiarizing" the consumer is sometimes done with small-space print ads or with outdoor or transit ads that have high visibility. Sometimes it is done with large and dramatic "announcement ads" or with a concentrated "blitz" of television advertising. Such a schedule is designed to place the product name, however fleetingly, before the largest possible number of people. Later, a full product story can be directed at the best prospects through a different media strategy.

The initial advertising push for a new product must bear a disproportionate part of the load in meeting the marketing objectives for the whole first year. It has to be strong enough to provide substantial support for the salesmen during the selling-in period. It must help achieve a high level of distribution. It must make the product generally familiar. It must establish the brand's identity and its principal points of advantage in people's minds. It should create trade "excitement"; it must often tie in with merchandising premiums, sampling, or other incentives to get the consumer to try the product. All these things must be done at once. Is it a wonder so many new products never make it?

Peckham's formula

James O. Peckham has analyzed the relation between advertising and sales for hundreds of new grocery, toiletry, and proprietary drug products, using the A. C. Nielsen Company's vast resources of store-audit data.[9] Peckham used share percentages rather than actual dollar figures in measuring both advertising and sales. Share percentages do not take into account the element of leverage that is introduced into the total consumption of a product category as new brands are introduced or as existing brands step up their advertising on special promotions. According to Peckham, over a four-year period there was a 35 percent increase in the total volume of consumer sales in 12 product groups with new or improved brands. In 32 more stable product groups the gain was only 20 percent.

Between the early 1960s and 1978, Peckham analyzed shares of advertising and shares of market for 64 *successful** new brands of food, household products, proprietary drugs, and toiletries. Over their first two years of life, these brands spent at a rate that gave them an advertising share 60-70 percent greater than the market share they achieved by the end of this period. This spending was not an "in-and-out affair," but was consistently maintained, and it was not "front-loaded" as is often the case with new products. (While a heavy introductory budget may create awareness of the brand, it generally takes many months to build the retail distribution required to guarantee sales success.) Those brands with the highest share of sales also had the highest share of advertising.

Peckham's evidence covered a variety of products, distribution situations, and promotional plans, so there is no way of inferring how an advertising investment should be scheduled or spread out. In one case, a substantial proportion of it *was* spent in the first few introductory months. In another case, there was a slower buildup to a peak. Once at a peak, sales were sustained at the same level in some instances but not in others.

---

*He attributes their success to "a demonstrable consumer 'plus' both recognizable and merchandisable, developed with the benefit of adequate consumer product studies and thoroughly market-tested in the crucible of actual sales conditions at the retail store level."

Peckham advances a "Formula for Marketing Success" that stresses introductory offers to both consumers and the trade, "sufficient advertising over a 24-month period to produce a share of advertising about one and one-half times that of the share of sales you plan to attain," and "enough advertising in subsequent months to maintain [the product's] share modestly ahead of its sales position."* The question of how much that "enough" will turn out to be is best answered the way Abraham Lincoln answered the question of how long a man's legs should be—long enough to reach the ground.†

Although Peckham stressed that the average successful new product has an advertising share one-and-a-half times its eventual sales share over a *two-year* introductory period, his individual case histories also presented convincing evidence of the lack of any consistent *short-term* relationship between share of advertising and share of sales on a national basis. Here are just a few illustrations:

Food Brand Epsilon. This company made a real effort to "buy" the market. Its share of advertising climbed steadily, reaching 82 percent of the total within eight months. As late as 18 months after introduction it was spending half the advertising dollars in its field; it was spending a third of the dollars 10 months after that. While its sales share first rose steadily and touched 31 percent within a year after introduction, it was down to about a fifth of the market six or eight months later and then held at that level.

Toilet Goods Brand Beta. This brand's history is almost a perfect model of what every advertiser dreams about. The product was introduced slowly and selectively with very limited advertising support. In its first eight months on the market its share of advertising did not go above 3 percent nor did its share of sales reach 1 percent. About a year after introduction, a massive advertising campaign was launched, raising the advertising share to nearly 30 percent of the total corporate budget for a six-month period. Then advertising was slightly reduced, reaching the 23 percent level two years after the product's introduction; nevertheless, sales share showed a consistent and steady increase during this same period and was over 12 percent at the two-year mark.

Toilet Goods Brand Theta. This brand got off to a fast start. Six months after introduction, it had a 5 percent market share, and it held on to that 5 percent

---

*To the smaller manufacturer who wonders where the money will come from to maintain his advertising pressure at a level one-and-a-half times as great as his sales share goal, Peckham suggests a selective concentration on the parts of the market that the bigger companies are neglecting.

†In the course of a new business pitch, Don Grasse reports that an agency president had promised he would personally devote a major portion of his time to make sure the client received the agency's best effort. After mulling over the decision, the dubious head of the client company telegraphed, "Exactly how much of your time do you intend to spend on our account?" Hoping to avoid a firm commitment, the agency president wired back, with a slight misquotation, "As Lincoln said—as much time as it takes to make sure the pants are long enough to reach the ground." The return wire from the client ended the exchange: "Not interested in Lincoln quotes—wire exact percentage."

share for the next year and a half. During that same period, advertising came and went in the form of successive campaign waves: 12 percent share after two months, down to 6 percent after four, up to 12 percent at eight months, down to 3 percent in the following six-month period, then up to 9 percent and down to 2 percent again. Here, obviously, is a classic demonstration that short bursts of advertising pressure, with periods of inactivity in between, can produce sales results that are smooth and consistent. They do not reflect the saw-tooth pattern of the advertising curve itself. Yet sales curves just as smooth resulted in other cases from advertising pressure steadily maintained at an even pace.

These were success stories, but the case history of a failure bears out the general point about the lack of a consistent short-term advertising-sales relationship.

Toilet Goods Brand W. Share of advertising for this product built up to 5 percent within four months and remained at that level for another four months. During this period the brand share hovered just above the 1.5 percent level. Advertising was cut back sharply (a year after introduction it was practically nonexistent). Then a sudden short-run advertising promotion raised the advertising share back up to 3 percent. This had no effect on sales share, which continued on a slow but steady downward course after the brand's first six months on the market. (Peckham's diagnosis of this particular case is that the advertising promised more than the product could ever deliver in actual performance.)

Peckham stresses the distinction between *share* of advertising and the advertising/sales ratio. He refers to "the fallacy of attempting to link advertising expenditures to product sales on a ratio basis." He cites as an example the sales of one brand that increased 47 percent during the second year, although the percent of sales spent for advertising declined to 5 percent. "Since 10 percent of one brand's sales may be more in actual dollars than 50 percent of another brand's sales, obviously the brand with the smaller sales volume must have a higher percentage in advertising or go completely unnoticed by the majority of consumers."

Since "it is readily apparent that sudden increases or decreases in advertising expenditures alone, during a given year, do not prompt similar responses in sales except in a minority of cases," Peckham is pessimistic about the chances of finding an ideal ratio of advertising to sales. He states: "The net conclusion seems to be that the methods used to encourage product growth must be tailored to the individual product and to the market in which the product is competing."[10]

Setting advertising goals

Peckham's analyses emphasize that a company must outspend its competition for every point of market share it hopes to win for a new product. For years, agencies have encouraged their clients to think of advertising as an investment rather than as an expense, since the term *investment* suggests a continuing pay-out over a period of time rather than a recoverable short-run cost. Economist Joel Dean points out that "advertising is now book kept and budgeted as though its benefits were used up immediately, like purchased electricity." The result is that advertising is thought of as a current expense and as part of the operating budget. He suggests that advertising and other forms of promotion belong in the capital budget, since "the hallmark of an investment is futurity."[11]

Regardless of how his "bookkeepers" handle the matter, the typical advertiser is constantly preoccupied with the question of what return he is getting on his advertising "investment," maybe because he is apt to think in conventional cost accounting terms. He would like to be able to say that for a given number of dollars spent on advertising he got back a specific dollar return in sales. But this assumes that advertising is a discretionary expenditure rather than a fundamental cost of doing business, like the cost of raw materials or of labor.

Every business has expenses that are necessary, yet whose amounts are fixed by the laws of supply and demand in only the most general way. Executive compensation is one example of an expense that can rarely be justified in precise terms. The board of a large corporation may pay its president $300,000 a year on the premise that this is what it takes to attract a man of the ability required. How could the board prove that the salary should not be $310,000 or $290,000 a year? If the figure were substantially increased or lowered, judgment would dictate at some point that it was unreasonable, unrealistic, or out of line. But where would that point be?

This kind of judgment about expenses is made in business all the time, and the sense of it is rarely questioned. It is really much like the kinds of judgments that people make in their personal spending.

In the imaginary world of early classical economics, the consumer was expected to make rational choices about the comparative utility of his various purchases. Today we are more willing to acknowledge that Economic Man's rationality is often modified by subjective and irrational notions about what is of value to him.

To ask about the return on advertising is somewhat like asking the reader, "Did the last $200 suit you bought really give you $200 worth of satisfaction? Might you not have been better off with a different suit at the same price or with a $150 suit and $50 worth of shirts and furnishings?"

Advertising is as essential to the functioning of a business as clothes are to the consumer. The answer to the question of how much advertising is needed must therefore be "just the right amount; not too much and not too little." There can be no general laws. Only judgment can prove the answer to the advertiser who is unwilling to experiment with his own product. As the old story goes, a horse trained to work without eating will eventually die. A product that has no promotion or advertising to nourish it must eventually die too, but no one can predict just exactly when this will happen.

"DAGMAR"

In his book, *Defining Advertising Goals for Measured Advertising Results*,[12] Russell H. Colley attempted to clarify the "corporate management approach to the advertising investment." His work has been highly influential because of its sponsorship by the Association of National Advertisers (the ANA). Over 20 years later, a study by the Advertising Research Foundation found the DAGMAR model still being applied by "most companies" to define strategy and copy research objectives.[13] PACT (Positioning Advertising Copy Testing), a "Consensus Credo representing the views of (21) leading American Advertising Agencies," proclaimed in January 1982 that "the industry recognizes (as exemplified by the landmark DAGMAR study of the ANA) that the goal of advertising is to achieve specified objectives."

As his title implies, Colley is out to show advertisers how they can *measure* the return they are getting on the money they spend to advertise. He concludes that "to measure the accomplishment of advertising, a company must first have a clear understanding of the specific results it seeks to accomplish through advertising." This means distinguishing advertising objectives from the more general marketing objectives. For example, Colley distinguishes the *corporate* objective of making a profit from the *marketing* objective of selling goods and the *advertising* objective of creating brand preference.

Colley makes a futher distinction between long-run advertising objectives and "goals." In his lexicon, "goals" are objectives that are specific as to time and degree—e.g., earning 10 percent on invested capital in a given year, or achieving a given brand share or a given brand preference among a certain number of housewives.

He offers the following illustration of an advertising goal that could be "based upon research studies and tests": "To increase among 30 million housewives who own automatic washers the number who identify brand X as a low-sudsing detergent and who are persuaded that it gets clothes cleaner—from 10 percent to 40 percent in one year."

To set so specific a goal implies that a benchmark piece of research has been done to measure acceptance of the message before the start of the advertising campaign and that a similar study will be made afterwards. "Thus," says Colley, "with defined goals and measured results, we have a basis for both copy and media evaluation. Does copy approach A get the message through to more people than copy approach B, does medium C do a better job at lower cost than medium D? Is the copy theme or major media used for several years beginning to get a little tired? Or is the public just beginning to catch on?"

Colley concludes that current sales are not a final yardstick of advertising performance except under one of three conditions, none of which frequently prevails among nationally advertised products: (a) advertising is the single variable in sales; or (b) advertising is the dominant force in the marketing mix; or (c) there has been an immediate pay-out, with sales closely following the ads, as in mail order or (he says) retail advertising.

Apart from the carry-over effect of today's advertising on tomorrow's purchases of big-ticket items, Colley points out, "the consumer who switches today to a brand of cigarette, toothpaste or coffee because of advertising may continue to use the brand and pay dividends to the advertiser for several years to come."

Colley concludes that to define advertising goals, information based on research, experience, and judgment is needed regarding the merchandise, the markets, the motives, the messages, the media, and the measurements in question. Moving from this fine alliterative sequence, Colley says, "Information must be translated into strategy, strategy expressed in terms of goals. Measurement then becomes feasible." He cites four stages of commercial communication—awareness, comprehension, conviction, and action.[14]

Colley begins quite correctly by rejecting the "hard" evidence of sales results as a criterion for advertising effects because, as he points out, too many marketing forces might interfere with the cause-and-effect relationship. Then he dashes on, courageously assuming that major changes in attitude and awareness can be created by the typical advertising campaign and that these changes can be measured in a clear-cut way.

Colley provided the "broad outlines" and left it to the technicians to fill in the "operating details."* Happily, figuring out "how to do it" was beyond his concern. It is not surprising that during the 1970s the attention of advertising researchers appears to have shifted in other directions. Tremendous difficulties of research design and experimentation must be overcome in judging whether a particular set of goals has actually been met. And research of quite a different kind is required to determine whether the goals are realistic in the first place.

Setting the budget total

Hershey's chocolate was long cited as an example that proved the rule; it was a company with a strong market position that did no consumer advertising at all. But in the 1960s, Mars and other competitors used television effectively, and Hershey lost its first place in the candy-bar field. Hershey started advertising in 1970, cut its budget in 1973 after a rise in the price of cocoa, and lost market share again. Subsequently, its ad budget went from under $2 million to $46 million in 1981.

Every year, many words are written and spoken about how to determine the advertising budget. Most of them are ignored in practice. (Kirk Parrish, president of Lanvin-Charles of the Ritz, suggests that "setting advertising expenditures by the use of left-over funds . . . is not an unusual business practice.")[15] One tack is to take a fixed percentage of expected sales derived from past experience with the product (or from the record of competitive products) and peg the advertising budget to that. An advertising "allowance per case" (of merchandise) may be used as the basis of calculation. This procedure can be highly conservative in its effect if the decision on each year's budget is set exclusively in terms of the previous year's showing rather than in terms of future expectations and forecasts.

Another textbook approach (the "task method") is to start with the media schedule required to do the desired job and then calculate what it costs. The next step, which the texts sometimes ignore, is to cut this (generally ambitious) figure back to fit somebody's judgment of how much the company can afford in relation to all its other manufacturing and sales expenses, its overhead, and its profit goals.

---

*The dragonfly on the nose of the hippopotamus suggested that his host learn to fly, and instructed him by flapping his wings. "How can I do it?" asked the hippo. "I've given you the broad outlines of the idea," said the dragonfly. "Surely you can work out the operating details." This summarizes the agency-client relationship.

The task method of budgeting arose in a pre-broadcast era. This method afforded the advertiser a considerable degree of freedom because of the variety of ways in which print media can be scheduled. In an epoch of large-scale expenditures on network television, the task method lost a good deal of its flexibility. The advertiser who is considering possible participation in a network "package" buy that covers a share of both production costs and air time costs has only a yes or no choice. The inflexibility of these media costs is incompatible with the task method theory that the advertiser should spend whatever is needed to do a particular job.

Essentially, setting the advertising budget is not very different from any other business investment decision. The firm looks at the total market for the product field and assesses its potential for growth. It examines its own competitive position, seeking to evaluate realistically the attributes of its product, packaging, pricing, and distribution relative to what other brands have to offer.

Budgeting practices of 54 of the top 100 national advertisers were examined by Charles Patti and Vincent Blasko in 1981.[16] They concluded that there had been an increasing trend toward the use of quantitative methods involving objective and task-setting and less reliance on arbitrary judgment.

Andre San Augustine and William F. Foley interviewed two executives in each of 25 leading firms in consumer advertising and 25 leading industrial advertising firms. Among the consumer advertisers, half based their budgets on a percentage of anticipated sales, and 30 percent based them on what was affordable. Among the industrial advertisers, about a fourth used each of these methods, and a third took what was simply described as an "arbitrary" approach. In a number of cases, financial and advertising executives within the same company differed in their descriptions of the budgeting procedure![17]

A change in corporate management can lead to remarkable changes in advertising practices. At Campbell Soup, the advertising budget was cut by 24 percent to assure a continued increase in profitability during the 1974 recession. A new president, Gordon McGovern, raised the ad budget by one-third in 1982, changed the theme, and managed to increase profits by 16 percent.

During a 1970 strike at General Motors, each division reduced its advertising expenditures at a different rate. The car makes that cut their advertising most showed the greatest sales losses.[18] In general, ad budgets tend to be cut when profits are down and to be reinforced when profits are good.[19] Still, many companies have learned that this is a shortsighted policy, and in recent recessions, national advertising has continued to show real growth. Norton Simon Inc. boosted its spending by 38 percent during the 1982 recession. Avis raised its budget from $13 million to $22.5 million and regained market share from 23 percent to 26 percent.

Advertising requirements can be clearly stated only in relation to the total sales and marketing effort, including promotion, display, and publicity.* All the judgments a company makes must be based on the best available evidence, which

---

*In the packaged foods business, advertising and sales promotion expense averages 30-40 percent of gross margin, and about equal amounts are spent to advertise to the consumer and to provide incentives for the trade.

may not be very good at all.* How this can be done systematically has been outlined by Robert Weinberg.[20] Weinberg begins by positioning the company in its four simultaneous environments: economic, internal, competitive, and institutional. Company net profits depend on such factors as general business conditions, the level of industry sales, competitive activity and the company's own reactions to it, and the tax structure.

Weinberg points out that the additional sales the advertiser seeks to create by advertising ought to be *profitable* sales, which return more than they cost to create: "The relative merit of a given *increase* in advertising or sales promotion expenditure may often depend on what fraction of the *incremental* profits generated will remain available to the company after taxes."

In actual practice, Weinberg points out, it is unlikely that a company can increase its ultimate profits through an expansion of its share of market without, at the same time, changing its cost structure and the net profitability of its total sales. This profitability is bound to be weakened by "the actions required to increase the company's share of the market ... advertising, sales promotion, new customer development, new market development and related expenditures." Thus, he concludes, "the key question in formulating an optimal competitive strategy is that of determining the most profitable trade-off" between an improved share of market for the company and a lower ratio of net profit to company sales.

However, the company's optimal market share depends on its current market position and on the intensity and effectiveness of competitive activity, which are beyond the company's control. The intensity of competition will reflect both the consumer demand for the product and the production capacity of the company and the rest of the industry. It does not always pay to advertise when the objective is to win more of an existing market share at the expense of the competition. This is just one reason for the constant stress on new product development by American business. Apart from the objective of gaining an immediate competitive advantage, there is always the hope that through a change in the product itself additional sales may be gained by expanding the circle of consumer demand.

In recent years, there has been increased use of advanced statistical methods involving computerized "models" that permit rapid processing of both real and hypothetical data. Thus, corporate planners can forecast the consequences of changes in conditions both within and beyond their control. The Ogilvy & Mather agency has used a model developed by Hendry Associates as a way of relating alternative levels of advertising expenditures, pricing changes, and different strategies of promotion and distribution to probable outcomes in terms of

---

*One company president told Sidney Dean that a full-dress sales forecasting session (replete with charts and statistics) he had just attended reminded him of a wartime experience he had in the Aleutians. A meteorologist noticed an Eskimo building an igloo with double-thick walls and, impressed by the natural instincts of this primitive man, asked him how he was able to predict that the winter ahead would be a hard one. "I *know*," said the Eskimo, "I see the white man has laid in extra big coal piles this winter." The company's market analysts were not amused by this analogy.

sales and market position. Another model called Dialogue is used by some advertisers to analyze the relationship between advertising and sales based on historical data.

One example of this practice is the case of Totino's frozen pizza, a Pillsbury product. As Malcolm McNiven explains it, the goal was to double profit and increase sales volume 30 percent. Specific objectives were set to improve product quality, distribution, and brand preference. Advertising was expected to increase consumer awareness, trial, and repeat purchase, and advertising strategy was changed accordingly. To reckon the effect on sales of different levels of investment, an advertising elasticity coefficient was calculated through a computer model using data on sales, advertising, distribution, profits, and consumer behavior for the brand and its major competitors.[21]

As I shall point out in Chapter 13, computer models, of necessity, incorporate the same judgments that enter into seat-of-the-pants decisions, but they require these judgments to be explicit and thus permit a more systematic and informed appreciation of what they imply.

There is a considerable difference between the advertising investment decision for an established product and the decision for one about to be introduced. For a new product, the decision is at once more difficult and more simple because it is part of a whole series of interrelated policy decisions as to how the product will make its debut.

A new product is commonly taken through a rather elaborate process of research and laboratory development, starting with tests of the acceptability of the "concept" itself. This makes it possible to check consumer reactions to the product, packaging, and copy theming and to get some indication of the potential rate of purchase before major investments are committed. In market tests, advertising schedules can be compared, using different levels of expenditure, different mixes of media, and different copy themes.

In the case of an established product for which no major changes are contemplated, the most common procedure is to plan strategy on the basis of what was done the previous year, with appropriate adjustments for inflation, growth expectations, and competitive changes. An advertising investment and media strategy that has produced successful growth in the past is normally not abandoned without compelling reason. Most manufacturers and their advertising agencies have a tendency either to maintain the same investment policy or to reinforce the strategy they have been using.

A decline in sales or brand share is always likely to produce a shift in advertising strategy. This may take the form of a change in the ratio of advertising budget to sales or a change in the mix of media, in the campaign scheduling, or in copy theming or art style. Not uncommonly it also leads to a change of agencies.

Market tests of expenditure levels

It is common practice today for companies to arrive at an advertising-to-sales ratio by test market experiments in which budget levels are varied and sales results or attitude changes compared. As I shall emphasize later, this kind of study is hard to do well, and it is difficult to avoid inadvertently testing media and copy at the same time that budget levels are being evaluated.

Of 69 experiments with advertising weights found by David Aaker and James Carman in a comprehensive review of the literature, there were only 11 in which a reduced advertising treatment was compared with the original weight.[22] Five of these experiments ran for two years or more and had the potential to detect long-term effects, and four of these five showed that a reduction in advertising appeared to have no long-term effect on sales. Among the remaining 58 experiments, 57 percent suggested that existing advertising levels were at or above the optimum, and 43 percent suggested that an increase in advertising expenditures would not result in substantially increased sales. Still, some of the notable experiments are worth mentioning.

In the previously cited application of operations research methodology by Russell L. Ackoff and James R. Ernshoff, Budweiser Beer was able to cut its TV advertising budget in half without losing sales by changing the scheduling of its commericials to "pulsing," with on-again, off-again "bursts" of messages.[23] Advertising expenditures went from $1.89 a barrel in 1962, when the company had an 8 percent market share, to 80¢ a barrel in 1968, when its share was up to 13 percent.

The Missouri Valley Petroleum Company conducted a three-year experiment in which a large number of cities were divided into three test groups and a control group. As reported by Charles H. Sevin, one test group received half as much advertising as normal while the other two got twice and three times as much.[24]

This company found that reducing advertising by 50 percent had neither a favorable nor an unfavorable effect on sales compared with the control group. In the double power group, sales at company-owned outlets increased 17 percent the first year, 23 percent the second year, and 36 percent the third year over the base. However, in the group receiving tripled advertising power, the increases were 16 percent the first year, 11 percent the second year, and 16 percent the third year. "Thus company officials expected, within certain limits, that a doubling of advertising would actually foster a greater sales increase than would a tripled advertising schedule."

Can such a conclusion actually be drawn? The more disappointing record in the triple power markets may simply illustrate the difficulty of controlling for competitive activities, distribution conditions, and market idiosyncracies that inevitably beset the advertising tester.

From the experience of the Milwaukee Advertising Laboratory, G. Maxwell Ule describes a case where extra advertising input was applied against half the market.[25] The results in the second of four test periods showed a fourfold increase in the extra sales volume generated, compared to the first. In the third test period, the effect was reduced by about a fourth, and it fell again by a third in the fourth period studied. This case shows what Ule calls the "principle of diminishing returns through time" but also a continuing net gain, on balance, in the area with extra advertising.

In another notable study, a DuPont product that is sold only through a relatively short season[26] was tested, using different advertising expenditure levels in separate parts of the country: the same level of expenditures as the base period, and two-and-a-half and four times normal. Within each area, three test markets were selected in which the product's market share was either comparatively high, middle, or low. In the areas that were to receive above-normal expenditures, additional advertising was placed in local media over and above the national network TV schedule. Therefore, the media mix was inevitably varied as well as the total budget.

As reported by Sevin, "The results showed a range in profit contribution per dollar advertising of 2.5 to 1 as between the highest and lowest areas. Accordingly, parts of the advertising budget were experimentally reallocated from some of the least profitable territories to the most profitable ones." In other words, the conclusion from the published evidence appears to be that the effect of increased advertising expenditure weight could not be divorced from the overall marketing conditions in each area.

In yet another experiment reported by Sevin, a manufacturer varied the level of television and newspaper expenditures in a number of different sales territories and compared the resulting sales and profits. On both these scores there appeared to be an inconclusive set of findings with regard to the media mix. Total sales went up 3.5 percent when advertising expenditures were doubled in both newspapers and TV. But because of the cost of this advertising, the profit actually went *down* 15.5 percent.

When the budget was cut in half in both media, the sales went down 1.5 percent but the profit went up nearly 7 percent. "Accordingly, marketing management adopted the experimental results on a national basis. TV and newspaper advertising expenditures were reduced by 50 percent in almost all territories for this particular product. Long-run profits of this product were soon increased substantially."

Over a hundred studies of the return on increased advertising pressure were examined by Julian Simon and Johan Arndt, under the headings of the "physical" and "monetary" aspects of the effort.[27] They concluded that from the standpoint of *physical* exposure (ad size, commercial length, number of exposures, etc.), there were diminishing returns from increased pressure. Similarly, they found diminishing value from increased *monetary* expenditures; as budgets went up, the incremental return on the advertising investment tended to go down.

No one can quarrel with experimental methods of arriving at the "right" level of advertising expenditure—as long as the research is done properly. But the assumption that less advertising may be more efficient carries with it an immediate question as to whether the message is right and whether the right combination of media is being used. The advertising planner may still be reduced to conjecture and to judgment when he tries to answer that question.

What should the advertising/sales ratio be?

We saw, in looking at "Peckham's Formula," that a brand's share of total advertising in its product class is a totally different matter from the percentage of sales it spends on advertising. In most industries, the top brand spends less on advertising in proportion to total sales than is true of its competitors. The smaller firm has the problem of maintaining high visibility for its brand on a lesser budget. At the same time, the smaller firm is usually unable to earn the same volume discounts from the media that permit economies for the larger advertiser, and it is less likely than the larger company to win the most favorable positions for its ads or commercials. For the same reasons, a brand manufactured by a multiproduct company starts with an advantage over a competitive brand made by a one-product company.

Brands that have a two-to-one lead in market share over their closest competitor have an advertising-to-sales ratio that may be as low as half the industry average. In 1982, 723,000 Buicks were sold, at an advertising cost per car of $67, while 179,000 Chryslers were sold at a cost per car of $569. Unilever U.S. markets products at the same prices as Procter & Gamble. But this larger firm, with its gigantic sales volume and advertising power, can put greater promotional support behind each case of soap it sells, at a lower cost per case, and create, in total, greater pressure on the minds of consumers. In 1982, Procter & Gamble, spending a total of $726 million in advertising to create $12.3 billion in sales, had an advertising/sales ratio of 5.8 percent. Its smaller competitor spent $305 million on advertising to create $2.9 billion worth of sales, or an A/S ratio of 10.3 percent.

The ratio of advertising to sales for the leading 100 advertisers in 1982 ranged from 0.6 percent in the office equipment industry to 8.3 percent for toiletries and cosmetics. The average for the 100 advertisers was 4.3 percent. (Being the 100 biggest, they naturally spend more on advertising than the average company in absolute dollars, either because they are big or because they are concentrated in consumer product categories where heavy advertising is the norm.)

Of substantial interest, however, is the variation among individual companies in the same category. Among food companies, the range was from 6.4 percent for Norton Simon Inc. to 2.0 percent for Dart and Kraft. In the toiletries field, Noxell was high with 18.9 percent, while the Beecham Group and Revlon were both at 4.8 percent. American Motors had the highest ratio in automotive, with 2.5 percent, Volkswagen of American the lowest with 0.6 percent. In tobacco products, Philip Morris and Batus spent 4.3 percent, American Brands 1.1 percent. Among pharmaceutical companies, Richardson-Vicks had the highest ratio, 11.6 percent; Pfizer the lowest, 1.9 percent. While the pattern is confused by the fact that in an age of conglomerates, different companies have different mixes of products, it is quite clear that active competitors are advertising at very different levels.

The ratios of advertising and promotion to sales for a large array of industries are estimated annually by Schonfeld and Associates, a consulting firm. For liquor, they found the proportion in 1980 to be 10 percent; for cosmetics and toiletries, 8.8 percent; for drugs, it is 7.8 percent; for beer, 6.5 percent; food, 3.3 percent; soap and detergents, 6.5 percent; cigarettes, 6.3 percent; household appliances, 2.5 percent; motor vehicles, 1.7 percent; airlines, 1.6 percent; movie producers, 10.7 percent. The differences are also marked among different types of retailers; for department stores, 2.9 percent; grocery stores, 1.1 percent; furniture stores, 7.8 percent; appliance stores, 4.7 percent.[28]

What determines the ratio of advertising to sales? Paul Farris and Mark

Albion summarize the evidence by noting that it is not related to the level of concentration in an industry or to its market growth.[29] It goes up with the number of brands in a market and goes down with the size of the market, the company's market share, purchase frequency, and the size of the item's typical price tag.

Farris (with Robert Buzzell) examined data from PIMS (Profit Impact & Marketing Strategy), a research data base that includes pooled information from over 1,500 businesses, regarding their marketing and competitive characteristics, strategies, and financial performance. Farris and Buzzell restricted their analysis to 281 consumer products manufacturing companies and to 789 industrial product manufacturers that spent at least .01 percent of sales on advertising and promotion. The ratio of advertising and promotion to sales was highest for products that were standardized, had many end users, involved a small purchase amount, offered auxiliary services of some importance, sold through intermediaries rather than directly to consumers, and priced the product at a premium (probably for a product of premium quality). The ratio was also high where the manufacturer had a high margin per dollar of sales and a relatively small share of market and where a high proportion of sales came from new products. But to set advertising budgets in this way involves methods that, in the authors' words, "require money, time, and data that are often not available."

The relatively high percentage of sales income spent on advertising in certain product fields (toiletries, for example) is often cited by critics of advertising as a cost passed on to the consumer. (One such critic, Harry J. Skornia, estimates that a typical family is "taxed" 1.5 percent of its income for broadcast advertising alone.[30]) Actually, A/S ratios are generally found to be high precisely in those categories that are characterized by a strong fashion or style emphasis and frequent introduction of highly competitive new products with their inevitably high advertising investments. The advertising "tax" may be the price the consumer pays for his own interest in innovation, which, at the same time, advertising stimulates.

Allocating the budget

A shift in advertising strategy almost always produces an increase in sales. When an advertiser switches from one combination or mix of media to a radically different one, his sales usually get a shot in the arm. But the immediate effect of such a policy is generally short lived, and sales quickly resume their former position or else dip lower.

Why does a change of media add to sales in the first place? The answer might well be that the advertiser is benefiting *both* from the delayed impact his messages had on the audience he reached with his former media schedule and *also* from the effect of his new campaign on people he previously wasn't reaching. As his new media strategy continues, the effect of his earlier media mix becomes more and more tenuous and finally dies out altogether, at which time the effect of the new campaign begins to take over.

A number of case histories from the Milwaukee Advertising Laboratory document the notion that when advertising strategy changes, the resulting effects diminish over time.[31] In one instance, an experimental increase in advertising produced a proportionately much sharper increase in sales, but a subsequent further increase in advertising was accompanied by a drop in sales. And when advertising was maintained at this level, the sales curve returned to a point only slightly above the level at which the experimentation began. In yet another case, the advertiser varied his media strategy but kept the same budget level. One strategy produced a steady gain in incremental sales over a 12-week period, but in the subsequent 20 weeks there was no change in the margin of extra sales gained by this strategy over the other.

An analysis of expenditures in 1981 and 1982 shows that there is an annual turnover of about one out of every four national and regional advertisers in magazines, nearly the same proportion in spot television and of about one advertiser in every six in newspapers. This turnover represents leaving a major medium *altogether* and usually reflects an important shift in advertising policy, without an important change in budget.

Some years ago I analyzed the measurable media expenditures of ten leading U.S. advertisers over a three-year period. In the last year studied, these companies spent, in the aggregate (for all their products), 6.5 percent more than the previous year. One of them was spending 51 percent more and one was spending 12 percent less. This same wide range of variability is found when we compare the previous year's budgets with those of the year before, making the average rate of increase highly misleading.

When we go beyond these figures and examine the expenditures of these advertisers on individual media, we find even more striking variations. Here are just a few illustrations:

In one year, Company A's budget was up 1.5 percent—almost unchanged from the previous year. But it gave up a third of its budget to enter network TV. This meant that it virtually eliminated newspaper supplements and cut its budget for business publications by nearly half, its budget for newspapers by a fourth, and its budget for magazines by a fifth.

In the same year, Company B, already in network TV, decided to greatly increase its effort in that medium. But it did so by raising its total ad budget by 80 percent, so that TV, while drawing about the same proportional share, was actually getting much more money. It put substantially more effort into newspapers, but raised magazines only slightly, so that their share was nearly 30 percent less than before. The next year the company cut its advertising slightly, but at the expense of print media, actually raising its share for TV.

Company C raised its budget by 12 percent, but tripled its expenditures in newspapers, cut supplements by one-half and slashed its network TV commitments from 40 percent to 30 percent. The following year its ad volume went up 25 percent, but the budget for supplements increased fivefold, while the other media maintained about the same balance. The scheduling of budgets within these media showed similar fluctuations.

Few competing brands spend their advertising media dollars in exactly the same proportions. The variability in media strategies among leading national advertisers is reflected in the proportions of their 1981 budgets devoted to just one medium, spot television. Among the four top airline advertisers, spot television got 29 percent of the spending from United Airlines, 11 percent from

Eastern. Of the four top automotive advertisers, Toyota put 42 percent in spot TV, General Motors 4 percent. General Foods gave it 22 percent, Dart and Kraft 43 percent. Of the four top manufacturers of soap and cleansers, Lever put 27 percent of its dollars into spot, Clorox 12 percent. In toiletries, Johnson & Johnson spent 3 percent in spot, Warner-Lambert 24 percent. If the list were extended beyond the top four in each category, it would show even more of a range. And if brands, rather than corporations, are compared, the variability is greater still.

It is apparent that companies with rather similar marketing objectives spend rather different proportions of their available budgets on advertising and distribute their advertising dollars according to different strategies. Yet it is unusual to find a product category in which they use radically different mixes of media. Regardless of whether or not they end up with the same media mix, most advertisers appear to operate under rather similar assumptions in devising their strategy for the same product.*

Generalizations *are* possible: Beer advertisers go for TV sportscasts. Automotive advertisers rely very heavily on prime time network television, large newspaper advertisements, and prestige-building color ads in magazines. Many food advertisers use magazine color heavily for appetite appeal and service suggestions. They use TV to show how easy it is to prepare their products and how grateful the children and the husband are to the housewife. Detergent and soap advertisers make strong use of daytime network TV and rely on spot television to concentrate against their key markets. Appliance and tire advertisers rely heavily on cooperative dealer-placed advertising in the newspaper, along with network TV (for product demonstration) and magazines.

How drastically can a company change its advertising strategy? It is usually held in check by counterpressures to stay in line with what its main competitors are doing, both in the overall level of advertising expenditures and in the choice of media. Competitors must contend with similar problems in allocating their promotional expenses. In evaluating media capabilities, competitors and their agencies are apt to start from similar premises and make comparable judgments.

If an advertiser keeps his media schedule in a constant state of ferment, should he not benefit by the constant change in his audiences? He would probably run a new danger of confusing people by the rapid shifts of messages and creative techniques. His various campaigns might only confound and contradict each other in the consumer's mind.

In advertising, as in every other aspect of business, there are cautious companies and companies that are willing to take risks; there are followers and leaders; there are operating styles that are consistent and others that are quixotic. At the point when all corporations proceed from the exact same premises in

---

*This was vividly illustrated when a marketing problem was set forth for a group of four well-known media directors as part of a AAAA program. All of them were given the facts in the case and asked to prepare a media plan. While the four plans differed in detail, they were highly similar in the selection of media and in the outline of the suggested schedule. A repetition of the same project at a subsequent meeting with a different panel of experts produced very similar results for a different product.

determining how much advertising money to spend and where, there will no longer be any reason to advertise.

Notes

1. Quoted by John A. Howard and James Hurlbert, *Advertising and the Public Interest: A Staff Report to the Federal Trade Commission* (Chicago: Crain Books, 1973).
2. Quoted by Ralph E. Dyar, *News for an Empire* (Caldwell, Idaho: Caxton Printers, Ltd., 1952), 187.
3. William T. Moran, "Information for Advertising Budgeting," Paper presented to the General Electric Customer Communications Council, October 31, 1978.
4. Thomas W. Peterson, "The Line vs. the Brand," in Earl L. Bailey, ed., *Product-Line Strategies* (New York: The Conference Board, 1982).
5. James O. Peckham, Address to the Grocery Manufacturers of America, November 9, 1965, New York City.
6. Paper presented to the Advertising Research Foundation, May 1980, New York City.
7. Quoted by Nariman K. Dhalla, "Assessing the Long-Term Value of Advertising," *Harvard Business Review* (January-February 1978): 87.
8. Kenneth Mason, "How Much Do You Spend on Advertising? Product is Key," *Advertising Age*, June 12, 1972.
9. Peckham's work was originally presented in speeches before the Grocery Manufacturers of America, November 9, 1965, New York, NY, and before the Advertising Research Foundation, October 4, 1966, New York, NY. It was most recently brought up to date in his report, *The Wheel of Marketing*, (Scarsdale, NY, 1981).
10. *Nielsen Researcher*, No. 1, 1965.
11. "Does Advertising Belong in the Capital Budget?" *Journal of Marketing*, 30, 4 (October 1966): 15-21.
12. New York: Association of National Advertisers, 1961.
13. Benjamin Lipstein and James Neelankavil, *Television Advertising Copy Research Practices Among Major Advertisers and Advertising Agencies* (New York: Advertising Research Foundation, 1982).
14. Unfortunately, most of the examples offered in this widely quoted book are theoretical ones, illustrated with "before" and "after" campaign changes that are rarely encountered by research under normal conditions in the market place. However, a series of case histories using the DAGMAR approach (most of them involving before and after consumer surveys) were subsequently collected by Roy H. Campbell and published by the ANA. (Roy H. Campbell, *Measuring the Sales and Profit Results of Advertising: A Managerial Approach* [New York: Association of National Advertisers, 1969].)
15. T. Kirk Parrish, "How Much to Spend for Advertising," *Journal of Advertising Research*, 14, 1 (February 1974): 9-11.
16. Charles H. Patti and Vincent Blasko, "Budgeting Practices of Big Advertisers, *Journal of Advertising Research*, 21, 6 (December 1981): 23-29.
17. Andre San Augustine and William F. Foley, "How Large Advertisers Set Budgets," *Journal of Advertising Research*, 15, 15 (October 1975): 11-20.
    For a detailed look at budgeting procedures, cf. Richard J. Kelley, ed., *The Advertising Budget: Preparation, Administration and Control* (New York: Association of National Advertisers, 1967). Malcolm A. McNiven, ed., *How Much to Spend for Advertising* (New York: Association of National Advertisers, 1969). Julian L. Simon, *The Management of Advertising* (Englewood Cliffs, NJ: Prentice-Hall, Inc., 1971). The Conference Board, *Some Guidelines for Advertising Budgeting* (New York, 1972).
18. According to an analysis by Robert Buzzell and Michael Baker, Marketing Science

Institute Research Briefs, February 1972.

19. Mark Albion and Paul Farris, *op. cit.*

20. Weinberg is a mathematical economist, formerly with IBM and Anheuser-Busch, who became a marketing consultant to the brewing industry. His paper, "Developing an Advertising Expenditure Strategy," was prepared in 1962 for an ANA symposium.

21. Malcolm A. McNiven, "Plan for More Productive Advertising," *Harvard Business Review* (March-April 1980): 130-136. "Elasticity" refers to the relative impact of increasing advertising budgets to different degrees.

22. David A. Aaker and James M. Carman, "Are you Overadvertising?" *Journal of Advertising Research*, 22, 4 (August-September 1982): 57-70.

23. Russell L. Ackoff and James R. Ernshoff, "Advertising Research at Anheuser Busch Inc.," *Sloan Management Review*, 16 (Winter 1974): 1-17.

24. "What We Know About Measuring Ad Effectiveness," *Printer's Ink*, July 9, 1965: 47-53.

25. Address before the 12th Annual Conference of the Advertising Research Foundation, October 1966, New York, NY.

26. This condition simplified the problem of measuring advertising results, since there was no reason to assume that there would be carry-over effects during an extended period. Malcolm McNiven was an outstanding figure in this type of difficult experimentation during his tenure as advertising research manager of DuPont. DuPont ran another interesting experiment, summarized by Sevin, in which it was found that sales of Teflon-coated cookware increased most dramatically when a high level of advertising expenditure (in TV) was maintained, not only through the fall months but during the winter period as well. When advertising was low both in the fall and in the winter, there were 25 units sold per 1,000 housewives. When it was high in the fall and low in the winter, the number of units rose to 32 units. Low fall and high winter advertising doubled sales from 25 to 49, but a high fall and high winter combination brought sales from 32 per 1,000 to 70 per 1,000.

27. They also found no evidence to prove or disprove the role of advertising as a barrier to market entry. Julian L. Simon and Johan Arndt, "The Shape of the Advertising Response Function," *Journal of Advertising Research*, 20, 4 (August 1980): 11-28.

28. *Advertising Age*, August 17, 1981. A 1954 study, conducted jointly by the University of Illinois and *Advertising Age*, analyzed the percentage of sales devoted to advertising by 2,325 companies in 70 business classifications (the average was 2.5 percent). Among the 27 firms in the cosmetics and beauty aids category, the range was from 0 percent to 38 percent. In the proprietary medicine category, the proportion ranged from 0.1 percent to 49.3 percent in 1954. In the gasoline and oil field, it ranged from 0 percent to 18 percent. For small appliances, it ranged from 0.8 percent to 45 percent. In the beer, wine, and liquor category, it ranged from 0 percent to 65 percent. Although no more recent study has been done on so comprehensive a scale, there is no reason to believe that the variability has lessened in the past three decades.

29. Paul Farris and Mark S. Albion, "Determinants of the Advertising-to-Sales Ratio," *Journal of Advertising Research*, 21, 1, (February 1981): 19-26.

30. *Television and Society*, New York: McGraw-Hill Book Company, 1965.

31. G. Maxwell Ule, Address before the Annual Conference of the Advertising Research Foundation, October 1966, New York City.

Chapter 4
Advertising Strategists in Action

Just as war is too important to leave to mere generals, advertising investments in many companies are too large and too important to leave to the advertising department or agency. Top managements are often involved not only in approving plans but actually in shaping them. In many large companies served by a number of advertising agencies, advertising departments have increasingly taken on major responsibilities for planning functions that the agency traditionally performed in the past. As agencies' operating costs continued to mount, advertisers built their own research and media staffs and budgets and became more intimately engaged in the details of advertising evaluation. But while a comparatively small number of large corporations employ the specialized talent required to develop sophisticated advertising strategy, the typical advertiser relies on the agency's knowledge and skill to do the job, with the company's own advertising director supervising and acting as liaison with individual brand managers.

A business executive who has not come up through the marketing route is likely to be concerned with the overall effectiveness of advertising before he turns his attention to the detailed questions of advertising strategy. To the extent that he is called on to review particular advertising recommendations, he probably thinks first of all in terms of his rather general opinions about the media that the advertising agency recommends and next in terms of the broad question of what to say about his product and how to say it: sales appeals and themes, copy, layouts, the choice of models or broadcast personalities. He seldom grapples with the tricky problems of how to buy and distribute his units of advertising in any given medium.

In the past, when business executives have evaluated media, they have been inclined to make three common errors:

1. They don't pay enough attention to the *quality* of communication through each medium.
2. They exaggerate the intensity of the public's experience of the mass media.
3. They assume that advertising comes through at a level of interest and emotion that is somehow comparable with the information or entertainment content that audiences seek in a medium.

Media decisions are often made on the basis of cliché judgments. Each medium is typically considered to be endowed with certain characteristics in its manner of communicating: radio is thought of as a companion, TV as a device for demonstration, newspapers as a way of making announcements, general magazines as colorful showcases. Such generalities are then, for simplicity's sake, applied as though they operated across the board.

Actually, each medium provides an enormous number of subvarieties of media experience. Each encompasses many vehicles, and every vehicle evokes different kinds of audience response under different circumstances. Finally, different segments of society typically use media in different ways.

Impressing the dealers

Any advertiser is subject to pressure from his own organization and dealers as well as from rival media whenever he departs from the conventional media strategy of his product field. One of the perennial bugaboos in the advertising business is the notion that dealers or distributors insist on a certain type of advertising media strategy. Their opinions on this subject are generally supposed to be based on "mother-in-law" surveys or on their own media habits, which they naively identify with those of the average man. According to this theory, national advertisers must use the particular mix of media that their dealers approve and demand.

Both the individual chain-supermarket manager and the chain buying committee are generally impressed by the weight of advertising and promotion behind a product; they consider this when one or the other is deciding whether to stock a product and how much shelf space to give it. But no grocery retailer can possibly keep in mind the full array of advertising plans that backstop all the competitive products he sells. In spite of this, many advertising campaigns are run to conform with the real or imagined specifications of dealers. Thus the advertising objective is to assure optimum distribution or display rather than to sell to the consumer directly.

Underlying the faith of many national advertisers in the dealer's judgment is the assumption that somehow the retail merchant is in the best possible position to judge the effect of a specific advertising campaign. The principle behind this is that the dealer is close to the "true" results; his satisfaction with a campaign is determined by the jingle of the cash register as the contented customers respond to successful advertising strategy. In point of fact, most retailers are actually just as uncertain about the sales effects of specific ads and campaigns as manufacturers are. Perhaps this will change as electronic systems like the supermarket laser-beam checkout scanner universally provide instantaneous sales records item by item. But the time required to analyze the resulting data is prodigious, and it is hard to see how the necessary procedures could be applied routinely to the vast array of advertised brands and items.

The advertiser's concern with the sensibilities of distributors and dealers may be based on the common notion that the merchant is an active student of the advertising for the brands he sells. Clearly, such a notion is erroneous in the case of the storekeeper or store manager with thousands of branded articles for sale. But it is even untrue in the one industry where the relation between retailer and manufacturer is closest and exclusive. In a study of 785 car dealers,[1] only 7 percent were able to answer the question, "Do you know the approximate breakdown of the factory advertising budget for newspapers, magazines, television, radio, outdoor, direct mail?"

In spite of this widespread ignorance of how their factory's advertising was distributed, three out of five dealers reported that the factory's use of the media was "about right." There were only small differences in this proportion between the dealers who knew how the factory was advertising and those who did not. This is in keeping with what many studies in other fields have shown to be the tendency of most people to believe that those whom they accept as authorities are making the right decisions and doing their jobs well.

Of course, in the advertising business, authority does not always enjoy automatic respect. The talented but impossible vice president of promotion for a major network once submitted a routine ad to the network president. Instead of getting a routine OK, as Jay Eliasberg recalls, the ad came back with a note saying, "Let's discuss." Infuriated, the creative man rushed up and into the president's office, where he was in the midst of a meeting with another network V.P. Interrupting their conversation, the promotion director handed the president a felt pencil and a pad and said, "Here, if you think you can do a better job, go ahead! *You* write the ad!" The other vice president spoke up indignantly, "You can't talk like that to the president of the network!" "Like hell I can't," said the promotion director. "Well, I'm not going to sit here and listen to this," came the answer. The loyal vice president rushed to the door and with a violent gesture wrenched the doorknob, which came off in his hand. The three sat in the office for half an hour, waiting for a locksmith to let them out.

Who decides?

Advertising decision makers at any level of authority do not represent a cross-section of the consuming public they set out to persuade. They are geographically concentrated in a few big centers (45 percent of all U.S. agency billings are placed in New York, 13 percent in Chicago, 6 percent in Los Angeles, 5 percent in Detroit). They are above average in income and education. Their media habits are atypical. For one thing, they are far less avid viewers of television than the general public. A survey of 513 advertising executives made by the Psychological Corporation in 1965 found that average viewing time on the day prior to the interview was one hour and a quarter, exactly half that of the average person, according to national television viewing surveys at that time.

It is obvious that while the advertising decision maker may be a conscientious student of the media, he is not an ordinary reader, listener, or viewer. This makes it all the harder for his own subjective judgments to be dissociated from his sober professional ones.

How is the advertising decision of how much to spend and where made? This question can provoke highly contradictory answers within the same organization. There is a wide gap between official procedure and actual practice both in companies and agencies. There is also often considerable disagreement among people holding various functions and titles regarding the importance of the roles they play.

Periodically one or the other of the advertising trade publications surveys executives in companies and agencies to find out who is involved in advertising decisions. Invariably there are discrepancies among the reports given by different individuals within the same organization and between the agency on the one hand and the client on the other. These discrepancies reflect more than mere differences in viewpoint; they also reflect the fact that different individuals and departments have key roles to play at different *points* in the decision-making process.

David Stewart, a former president of Kenyon & Eckhardt, analyzed the progress of a media recommendation made to a national advertiser and found that "counting agency and client executives, the recommendation had to pass through 54 different hands."[2]

Among 197 consumer advertisers responding to a 1982 survey by *The Gallagher Report*, 25 percent had their budgets prepared by the advertising agency, 35 percent by the vice president of marketing or marketing director, 22 percent by the advertising manager, and 18 percent by the vice president/advertising or advertising director. In almost every case, the budget had to be approved by the company's chief executive officer, though this may often be little more than rubber-stamp approval.

Advertising planning in different product fields ranges from the orderly to the disorderly. This variation reflects whether or not the business is subject to fluctuations resulting from product innovation or from competitive promotion, merchandising, or other sales activity.

A business whose sales are relatively even and stable from year to year, like the insurance business, is able to lay out its plans well ahead of time. The toiletries business, in which companies must respond quickly to competitive product introductions, may experience radical shifts of advertising strategy within short spans of time.

Big advertisers like Procter & Gamble and General Foods generally have strong ideas about how their very large advertising investments should be made and strong economic motivation to coordinate the media buying to support their different brands. They have a corporate philosophy about media and how they are to be used. They generally have a corporate policy regarding media concepts and about research concepts and techniques as well.

An advertiser like General Motors or P & G is bound to be a major account, if not *the* major account, for every agency on its list. In 1982, a depressed automotive year, GM's eight U.S. agencies billed nearly $3.3 billion. Procter & Gamble's ten U.S. agencies (all but one different from GM's) billed $4.2 billion that year. (Even when an agency has only a minor product or modest billings from such a big advertiser, it always lives in hope of more, of showing the client what a great job it can do.)

This often means that the practices and preferences of the big advertiser may be adopted as standard operating procedure or as the preferred services of all their agencies. Once adopted, or once the investment has been made to use a certain service on The Big Account, it is not surprising to find further use being made of it on *all* the agency's acounts. Thus the leverage exerted by the large advertiser is even greater than it might at first appear to be. Nine companies account for one-fourth of all the spending in network television.

The advertising buying pattern for the various media depends not merely on the advertiser's own timetable, but on the production schedules of the individual media themselves. Monthly magazines, for instance, require a lead time of nine weeks between the advertising deadline and the publication date, and frequency rate discounts encourage advertisers to commit themselves to long-term schedules rather than to buy ads one at a time. Newspapers are most flexible from an advertiser's standpoint in that they are comparatively easy to get into and out of on short notice, and advertisers can generally earn discounts as their volume accumulates through the year.

The extent to which top company management itself becomes involved in the advertising media decision depends upon the importance of advertising within the total corporate budget. There are few companies indeed where top management does not make at least an overall review of the allocation of advertising strategy by media budgets. But there are many companies where decisions made by the advertising department are, for all practical purposes, final and where the corporate management merely exercises a formal approval or veto power.

In still other companies, particularly those dominated by a single strong personality, the head of the firm may interject himself into even the most picayune details of the media scheduling or creative strategy in an advertising campaign. His influence may be felt in television programming, even extending to the question of what quiz show contestants should win or lose. (The same attitude is not unknown within the agency business either. At one top management meeting, the assembled potentates were warned by their Supreme Leader, "This is not a democracy. Any good ideas that any of you have become my ideas from now on.")

There is also great variation in the respective importance of the agency and of the company's own advertising and sales departments. In some instances, advertising strategy is set by the company down to the finest point of media selection and schedule building; the agency merely executes the orders. In other cases, the agency may function as the company's advertising department, or a company department may exist merely to review and approve plans worked out in detail by the agency.

Between these extremes is the pattern of give and take that characterizes most agency-client relations. The client comes up with a general statement of direction he wants to pursue; the agency implements these informal directives by preparing a media proposal as part of an overall advertising plan. This in turn the company's advertising department scrutinizes and modifies in a manner that may range from authoritarianism to democratic partnership.

The different ways in which agencies function in part reflect variations in the status of the corporate advertising director. In many instances, the agency principals have a close personal relationship with the management of the client company. They are accepted as equals and confidants. Where there is such a close relationship, the corporate advertising director may be regarded almost as a clerk, as someone who attends essentially to details and deals with his opposite number in the agency, the account executive. In such a situation, the latter is also likely to be a person of subordinate status.

In other cases, the advertising director wields real life-and-death power over the agency. The same little drama is played out lower on the scale of power, between the account executive and the advertising director, with the higher-ups maintaining a detachment that reflects disinterest or snobbery or both. Consider this episode, recalled by Don Grasse:

> A young man recently given his first account assignment chaired an all-day presentation for his client, covering the next year's advertising and marketing plan. Present for the meeting were the presidents of both the client organization and the agency. The very nervous account executive somehow got through the day, and after the meeting those present retired to the company president's office for refreshment and discussion before they left on the long trip home. During the discussion, the young account executive glanced at his agency president and to his horror spotted him napping. Scared to death, he stole a look at the client to see if he had noticed his leader asleep. He was relieved to see that he was dozing, too.

In 1968, *Advertising Age* published a dozen case histories involving ethical issues confronting practitioners of advertising and invited its readers to choose the proper course of action. In most of the cases, the readers responded with a clear-cut ethical choice, but in the following case they divided exactly 50-50:

> You've just landed a $3,000,000 advertising account and now you've been asked to deliver a speech before the local marketing execs' club. You use the occasion to promote your "hot, creative shop." You tell of your agency's expertise and cite examples of skills that led that big account into your agency. You know that the agency has such skills.
>
> Q. Should you go on like this when you know in your heart that your new client is your old college roomie, just elected president of his company?

Within the corporate structure, the advertising department may be an autonomous operation with considerable prestige and authority, reporting directly to top management. Or it may be one of a number of subsidiary staff functions reporting to a general marketing or sales management which exercises strong professional control over advertising plans.

Most big companies today use the brand manager system in which a single marketing executive heads up all aspects of planning a brand's production, sales, and promotion as though he were running his own little business. In such a setup, the advertising department may be merely a coordinating, liaison, and contact operation. The actual decisions in this instance are made by the brand manager, who looks on advertising as merely one of a whole panoply of tools with which he works (including merchandising, promotion, pricing, packaging, and display). To the extent that the brand manager is responsible for the advertising budget and advertising strategy for his brands, the advertising department is reduced in status from a strategy-making unit to a service arm.

Where a strong sales management views advertising primarily as a weapon to support the sales force, the allocation of advertising budgets may be largely determined by the definition of sales districts and by the varying nature of dealer or distributor demand.

Within the advertising agency, there are also variations in the division of responsibility between the account group and the specialized departments that may have a voice in the major decisions. Sometimes, discussions over high principle may even lead to personal acrimony. At one agency, recalls Ted Giletti:

> A particular copy supervisor took a violent dislike to an account executive who was always well dressed in Brooks Brothers clothes. Our copy supervisor got the exact style, color, and size of hat that the account executive wore. He then went to Brooks Brothers and ordered two hats identical to the original in all respects, including initial and size tags, except that one hat was ⅛ size larger and the second was ⅛ size smaller than the hat worn by the account executive. Frequently the copy supervisor would substitute either of these for the regular hat. After some time, the account executive mentioned to several of us that he was having trouble with his head and was going to consult a specialist. On some occasions his head was smaller and on other occasions it was larger than normal. His hat would fit correctly some days and was too small or too large on other days. We finally told him when there was a visible sign of a nervous collapse.

In a large agency, an associate media director works closely with the account group in preparing media strategy. His recommendations may or may not be significant in the overall determination of how the advertising budget should be divided. There is always give and take between the account group and the media department, just as there is between the client's advertising department and the agency. Plans are usually discussed informally before they are officially presented.

Almost always a precedent exists in previous practice as a starting point for media strategy. By and large, the account group sets the broad dimensions for budget allocations by media, but it does so within the limits described by the media department as realistic requirements for each medium to be used with the desired weight and coverage. Once the general outlines have been set, it is the function of specialists within the media department to prepare detailed plans and estimates based on specific media vehicles, the frequency of ads or commercials, and the size units to be employed. A major fixed budgetary commitment to a single medium like a network television show or a monthly ad in a magazine may set restrictions on the way in which other media can be used. The opinions and predilections of the creative department often dictate the choice of a medium that is considered comfortable or appropriate to the creative approach.

Extraneous business considerations also sometimes force media decisions.

Since the beginnings of advertising, space has been bartered for advertisers' goods and services. In the infinitely complex media world of today, barter takes on far more sophisticated forms than some free meals at a restaurant in exchange for an ad. Barter specialists engage in elaborate deals, exchanging broadcast time for credits that can in turn be translated into a variety of items. The catalog of one big barter house, Pepper and Tanner, was nearly as big as Sears in 1969. As the *Wall Street Journal* described it (September 4, 1969):

> From the catalog, a station manager can order a fur coat or a Florida trip to be used as a quiz show prize or a sales incentive for his advertising salesmen. He can order a brand new television camera for the station or an airplane for traffic reports, or he can lease a new Cadillac for himself. ... A bottle of men's cologne that retails at $5 costs only about 25¢ to make, but it can be traded for a $5 commercial spot. The spot can then be sold to an advertiser for, say, $3—which is $2.75 more than it cost Pepper & Tanner.

Buying broadcast time

Negotiation of TV programming arrangements falls under the jurisdiction of the media director in some agencies. In others it comes under a unit of the creative department which also has charge of talent and production management for commercials and in some cases for programs offered to stations as part of a syndication or barter arrangement. Needless to say, the creative department may exercise strong influence on overall media planning within the agency, for it represents the agency's coveted link to show business.

Since the value of time on the air diminishes to zero if it has not been sold to an advertiser at the time of broadcast, time rates have always been flexible and negotiable, both for spot and network buys. The negotiating pace was stepped up in the late 1960s and early 1970s with the rise of independent time-buying services. These sought to replace the traditional agency media-buying function on the grounds that this could be done more economically by specialists who wielded greater clout in their last-minute deals with the stations. Buying of spot TV and radio entails intense bargaining, with the original asking price tumbling progressively as air time approaches. In such bargaining, the total budgetary weight of the advertiser, or the media-buying organization, may be a significant factor. Rate cards have virtually disappeared in the broadcast advertising sales business, and prices are adjusted to meet demand, just as in trading for any commodity. The prevailing practice among time buyers is to concentrate with one individual station representative at a time in a particular market and not spread business among a number of representatives. (The strategy is to leave the others hungry enough to reduce their prices at the next negotiating round.) The use of available TV program or time positions may be presented to a company for a last-minute rapid decision (with little or no preparation or prior analysis) as part of a complicated web of negotiating relationships between the agency and the network.

Until the mid-1960s, advertisers bought program time from the networks from a rate card that provided for volume discounts, and they bought sponsor-ship rights to programs supplied either by the networks' own production staffs or by independent producers. Few advertisers today want to risk the cost of full sponsorship of a regular weekly prime time program, which was typical of television's early years, as it had previously been of network radio in its heyday. Most advertisers buy participation in a "scatter plan" offered by a network, with commercials placed in a number of different programs on various days of the week and at various times. An effort is generally made to select programs with audience "profiles" or characteristics that match the attributes of the product's consumers. But contracts must be signed well in advance, and programs are now selected and replaced right up to the last minute—beyond that, even in mid-season. Time buyers must therefore rely on their familiarity with viewing habits and their conjectures about competitive network attractions, to estimate the audiences and efficiency of alternative scheduling possibilities.

Before the buying for the season begins, the network decides the cost-per-thousand for each program; agencies submit their requirements, and the networks set the price. (Commercial time on "specials" is generally priced higher than on regular programs in prime time, while on early evening news shows it may cost two-fifths as much and late at night [11:30 p.m.–1:00 a.m.] about a fifth as much.) Networks guarantee their advertisers a minimum level of clearance (generally 85 percent) for programs, since not every affiliate station will automatically carry the national feed in every time segment.*

Network television can be bought "up front" in advance, with a commitment for a full broadcast year and a choice of the full array of programs, or it can be bought quarter by quarter on a "scatter" basis or opportunistically on a last-minute basis. The networks argue that "up front" buying of commercial time for a 39- or 52-week season provides better prices than the opportunity buying that takes place in the course of the broadcast year.

During the early 1970s, the networks began offering informal guarantees to major purchasers of scatter plans. When network rates soared at the time of the 1976 Olympics, agencies wanted assurances to justify the huge investments their clients were making.

Advertisers insisted that they be "guaranteed' a certain minimum level of audience (usually expressed in Gross Rating Points or GRPs) for their investment, with the networks supplying additional commercial positions to make up for any deficiency. If the subsequent ratings reports show that audiences of the desired sizes and demographic characteristics have not been achieved, the advertisers receive compensation in the form of "make goods," or additional spots at off-peak times. This has increased dependence on the ratings services as arbiters of the value of what is delivered at a given price. (The practice of guaranteeing characteristics was abandoned by CBS in 1982 after drops in network audience share.)

Full sponsorship of regularly scheduled weekly programs virtually came to

---

* Networks also offer regional buys to advertisers who want 30 markets or more, and these can be more economical than spot buys if other advertisers can be found with complementary coverage needs.

an end with the development of scatter plans. Major advertisers who wanted to make an impact and who realized the value of identification with a particular program turned to spectaculars and to special events—the Super Bowl games, the Academy Awards, space launchings, and the like.

Apart from sports events, network television has continued to make use of major entertainment programs, of "specials" that preempt regular programming. They encompass made-for-TV movies, previews of forthcoming regular programs, and opportunities for a star or troupe to be featured. The series, "Roots," which ABC broadcast in 1977, was the prototype because it permitted advertisers to achieve enormous total audiences through their participation. A number of similar successful efforts have followed.

For the advertiser, specials provide the opportunity to be associated with a particular kind of program or performer, to broadcast an intensive series of commercials to a particular audience, and to anticipate, or in some cases even influence the content of the program itself.[3] But the proliferation of specials reduces viewer loyalty to regularly scheduled programming and commensurately takes the edge off the "special" designation.

In another development, independent station networks were introduced in the early 1980s, as network share of total audience dropped and specials and spectaculars preempted weak regularly scheduled weekly programming. Since the programs that start a broadcast season are likely to be reviewed after the first six weeks, it became more attractive for advertisers to put their own individual station networks together for special series—for example, those imported from Great Britain.

Participation in a new network show is commonly sold on the basis of a pilot tape (or sometimes even a mere outline of intention), and agency and advertiser may be under pressure to move fast before the big opportunity is snapped up by someone else. The network is motivated less by its aspirations for any particular program than by its desire to maintain a large and stable audience from segment to segment of the evening lineup.

The changing media buyer

A striking transformation has taken place in the agency media function. Until recently, the media department was made up of people who might be classified as either "bookkeepers" or "diplomats." The former kept the files on rates, circulation, program ratings, and other statistics and used them to work out estimates on schedules pretty much specified by the account groups. The "diplomats" were the media relations people whose job it was to listen patiently to competitive sales pitches and, when the time came, to wangle an ad into a far-forward position or a commercial into a better time slot.

The new breed of media specialists see themselves primarily as marketers. Their planning starts with the consumer product the client is trying to sell and not with the media products the agency is going to buy.

There are a number of reasons for the New Look in agency media departments:

1. The internal complexity of the advertising business has grown to vast

proportions. The job of riding herd on media practices and innovations can be handled by nothing less than an agency's best minds.

2. Research has grown several times as fast as advertising billings. There is a vast new reservoir of knowledge about products, consumers, communications, and audiences. To be intelligently used, these data require a new kind of specialized know-how, skill, and training.

3. The computer has emerged as a major influence on decision making, not so much because it has forced new kinds of decisions as because it has demanded a new discipline on the part of the decision-makers. It has attracted a different kind of technician to the agency media department and has stimulated a whole new wave of technical training.

4. Today it is generally understood that no area of advertising is an island unto itself. The new kind of media specialist must be an advertising generalist who understands consumer motivations, merchandising tactics, and principles of copy and layout. Just as an ad communicates through its total content—copy theme, illustration, and headline—so the kind of schedule a budget buys within a medium cannot be separated from the decision about what to put in the space or on the air. And what goes into an ad or commercial cannot be divorced from its size or length. So the media buyer has to think in terms of the total advertising plan.

The researcher is a natural ally for the media planner.* He turns to him for the data he needs to help him arrive at his more sober judgments and to justify and rationalize his more subjective ones. To many advertisers, in fact, the distinction between the·media planner and the market researcher is not altogether clear; in many smaller agencies both hats are worn on the same.head.

Among the innumerable petty civil wars of jurisdiction that rage intermittently in every advertising agency, the struggle over media research is an old one. Some large agencies place this function in the media department, others in research; still others give it a separate and independent status altogether. The skill most commonly associated with media research is statistics, for the media analyst's principal task has always been to estimate numbers that do not exist out of numbers that do: the duplication of audiences, the turnover of viewers from one program to the next, the reach of a schedule of different magazines over a cycle of weeks or months.

To be sure, the analyst can prepare such estimates only if he knows how to distinguish good numbers from bad ones, so he has always been (more or less in individual cases) a methodologist probing and passing judgment on the studies made by the media for their own selfish purposes.

The media planner has traditionally made use of only a small part of the

---

*By contrast, a natural enmity pervades the relation of researchers and creative people, but it exists almost entirely on the side of the latter. As for the researcher, it is the creative output, laboriously ground out or spun of sudden inspiration, on which he is called to pass his objective judgment. He bears the creative group no grudge. In fact, he may secretly sympathize with the writer's impatience at literal interpretations of his ratings or scores, for he knows that these are the weapons that account executives use to defend and rationalize their own plans and convictions when they present them to the client.

research spectrum. He is unlikely to be much of a psychologist. This is a serious deficiency, since more and more his job entails passing judgments on the comparative communications capabilities of different media, different vehicles, and different units of space or time. He has dealt primarily in the statistics on media costs, circulation, and audiences. For years, circulation data were looked at in relation to the coverage of households in cities and counties. Audience data were dealt with in aggregates rather than in terms of their component parts. As more and better information became available on the different characteristics of consumer markets and media audiences, the media planner's job expanded beyond the task of maximizing coverage and cost efficiency. It became one of matching media and markets. Broadcasting, with its volatile, constantly shifting public, made him concerned with the duplication of media vehicles and with the accumulation of audiences. In all these assignments the media planner relied on the help of the survey technician, the statistician, and the marketing expert. Rarely, if at all, did he feel the need to call in the psychologists for help.

This changed, to a degree, in the era of motivation research, which was all the rage in the 1950s but whose traces are still apparent in all current research on the creative aspect of advertising. The media themselves, like advertisers and agencies, called in psychoanalytically oriented psychologists to explain the attraction their products had for the ultimate consumer. Some of these projects were undertaken for reasons of internal planning by the media operators; in this category were Herta Herzog's classic studies of the daytime serial and the Professor Quiz show,[4] and also the extensive efforts by CBS, under Frank Stanton's leadership as research director, to find out how various programs worked, and the roots of their audience appeals. Only a few years later, when W. Lloyd Warner was commissioned to study the daytime serial,[5] the intention was to discover a way of explaining to advertisers that soap operas were *good* for the housewife—that they lessened her anxieties and taught her to cope with her daily lot. By inference, advertising on such programs would be respectable and wholesome.

Continuing in the tradition of qualitative media research, Burleigh Gardner did a series of studies for MacFadden Publications that documented the helpful, prestigious role of *True Story* and its sister magazines in providing readers with models of proper behavior. The lowly confession books could now be seen by the advertiser in a new and warmer light, as the blue-collar housewife's indispensable guide and companion.[6] Gardner did a study for *Good Housekeeping* in 1956 that had a similar objective.[7] It demonstrated to the advertising planner a dimension of readership that ordinarily had to be conveyed over martinis by a space salesman: the emotional feeling that readers had for a publication, its meaning in their lives, their confidence in it, its editorial vitality.

But studies of this kind were early casualties as motivation research retreated from the scene. They were replaced by the more familiar, conventional, and hence more comfortable compilation of statistics on audience size and composition just as suitable to the new jet-age all-purpose plans of electronic data processing as it had been to the pencil and paper calculation of readers per dollar in an earlier era.

For years, marketing research was dominated by a concern with what has always been the principal task of field intelligence—the collection and ordering of data. This descriptive tradition took a considerable buffeting with the advent of social scientists in advertising, for they took the position that the numbers one collected on the facts of marketing life were less important than the analytical interpretation of those numbers. The arrival of the computer was greeted with jubilant cries from the nose-counters. Operations research (O.R.) had, in their view, the merit of being based on numbers, and it arrived on the scene with impressive credentials: a mathematics unfamiliar to most marketers and hardware so expensive that no one who had invested in it could afford to deny its authority. As advertising research developed in the computer era, it produced ever more descriptive, ever more up-to-date compilations and recompilations of similar data. Media research studies were produced essentially to provide raw material for the agency's statisticians. The humanistically oriented social scientists and clinical psychologists faded from center stage and the model builders took over.

In some of the largest agencies, media planners were actually far ahead of their counterparts in the research departments in mastering the new technology of the computer.* Historically, the rapid acquisition of proprietary interest in electronic data processing on the part of media departments took place during the years when market and opinion researchers were floundering about, trying to debug their computer programs to make them more efficient than the conventional IBM counter-sorters on which tabulations had traditionally been done. Thus the first major applications of computers tended to be achieved not by agency researchers but by their better-heeled counterparts in the corporations, whose work with large masses of sales records lent itself to more straightforward techniques of mathematical analysis.

While the media planner has become more of a figures man than he used to be and these days may even be thought of as one of the Big Brains of his agency, his day-to-day job continues to require cunning, good judgment, and intimate acquaintance with the devious ways of organizations and individuals who can help him get things done.

Media presentations are commonly made at group luncheons, often with the aid of an imposing battery of audiovisual devices. Those on the receiving end are presumably lulled into a state of euphoric acquiescence by the libations that traditionally precede the first spoken word. The canny media buyer listens and applauds politely and customarily witholds all judgment until he or his "research expert" has had a chance to study the "leave-behind" booklet that sets down in writing everything that was said in the presentation itself.

---

*As will be described in Chapter 13, computers entered the agency via accounting and billing, an area closely allied to the media department and in some cases under its direct control. The automated handling of media accounts opened the way for media cost estimating by computer. This relatively simple operation ate into one of the traditional tasks assigned to media department manpower and in a number of instances caused the estimating function to be shifted from media to accounting. From computer cost estimating for different schedules there was only a small step to computer comparison of value received in terms of reach, frequency, and other criteria.

For the media director who is really in the big time and gets involved in television programming decisions, the glamorous atmosphere of show business may present even greater enticements. Media strategy has been changed as much in the swimming pools of Beverly Hills as in the counting houses of Madison Avenue. (The networks and package producers have long ago learned to include the client's advertising specialists in this part of the act!)

Decisions, reasonable and unreasonable

How much are advertising decisions swayed by emotion rather than by evidence? One could have quite an argument defining emotion and evidence in this connection. It is not surprising that a large part of the research that is done for any medium is designed to demonstrate its virtues rather than its limitations. But the media themselves are not alone in using facts selectively. A substantial part of the workload of any agency media research department has always been to marshal data to support a strategic decision already made on intuition. And much of marketing research generally, including the studies made by large corporations, has the hidden or acknowledged aim of proving somebody in management right— or wrong!

A well-known broadcasting and show business personality was a leading stockholder in a major drug firm, going back to the early days of his relation with the company's current management. Long after his program had lost much of its audience and had ceased to be an efficient buy, it represented a major advertising commitment for the drug corporation.

The television schedule for a major appliance concern was set up to include all cities in which the company had manufacturing plants and in which principal distributors were located. This was true even though the schedule was otherwise set up to cover a limited number of markets, and even though the cities in question rated low in relation to others on the list.

The world of media buying and selling is governed by strong interpersonal relationships, just like the relations of agency and client. Buyers like some media representatives and dislike others, and few people have enough insight to know when their presumably objective judgments are influenced by this fact.

Even in the computer era, the media planner must spend a part of his time holding court, like a medieval baron, for the troops of salesmen who fill his reception room. They call him to offer new statistics, presentations, research reports, creative suggestions, demonstrations, cocktails, lunches, good fellowship, and all other possible forms of persuasion and influence.

In some quarters of the advertising business, a media sales presentation is met with resistance, or even resentment. Most advertising practitioners, particularly media specialists in agencies, assume that they already know the qualifications and characteristics of the various media.

However, no intelligent media planner ever refuses to see a media salesman or representatives, who purvey information that occasionally can be applied directly to the marketing problems of an account. In every campaign, the buyer runs into highly varying standards of performance from every medium he uses. He never knows when he will next be involved in negotiations over rates, position, timing, exclusivity, or compensation for some dereliction of quality control. On such occasions, it is the media salesman who is the buyer's friend in court, who must plead his case with his own superiors or production people. It is to the salesman that he must go for help and service on matters that sometimes have no bearing at all on the use of his medium.

Media salesmen are the honeybees of the advertising world; they get around from agency to agency and from one dukedom to another within the big, sprawling, impersonal agency empires. They help people find jobs, and they provide invaluable reports and rumors of competitors' activities. They carry tidbits of personal gossip on the impending moves of accounts and individuals, tidbits which give the lowliest agency man a sense of having his ear attuned to the most powerful forces in the world.

This particular function both stems from and feeds the illusion that advertising is just one big happy family business. Partly this is in the good old American tradition of Kiwanis, Elkdom, and Odd Fellowship. Partly it reflects the high rate of job mobility among advertising people, which gives them a broad acquaintance. And partly it reflects the first-naming that is almost universal in American marketing. The man with whom I once shook hands at a brief meeting is forever Jim to me. The junior account executive who is called Joe by the president of the agency responds by calling him Bill. This makes the trade gossip about Jim or Bill *personal* gossip, involving my own acquaintances, my *friends!**

E. Lawrence Deckinger recalls that while he was at the Biow Company he conducted some research for a client which suggested that certain ads would be better if the type were run at an angle. Later, during a meeting in the client's office, the firm's fabled president sat calmly thumbing through a newspaper. All at once he came upon one of his ads with the type set at an angle. He turned purple. "What's this?" he demanded, starting up. Hurriedly it was explained to him that research had been done that demonstrated that the type should be displayed at an angle. "———— the research!" the president shot back, "I want it straight!" Thereafter, "straight" it was.

The client's wife has long symbolized irrationality in media decision making. No one in the agency business is without his own stories about her, or about her equally terrible spouse (he is the one who used to oppose TV advertising on Sunday afternoon because everyone is out at the polo matches at that time). I know of one such wife who had an aversion to a certain national magazine which, folded in its brown wrapper, she always confused with one of her favorites and then was disappointed when she opened it. She was married to a top executive in a major firm. Although the company was a wide user of magazines, this publication was never included in any of its media lists.

The wife of yet another executive, this one in a giant automotive firm, was particularly fond of Dalmatians (dogs, not people). The order went out to include such an animal in all future truck ads. One day the boss was asked to approve a double-page, four-color spread that showed the heavy-duty line of trucks en-

---

*The Madison Avenue practice of first-naming people was adopted by television, which brought the world's great into every living room on a basis of intimacy with every talk show host and thus, by implication, with every member of the family. From there, first-naming has permeated politics and business life.

gaged in heavy construction work in a sand-pit setting. It was a very busy ad, trucks coming and going, a flagman directing traffic, and so forth. The executive took one look and said "N.G." "Why?" cried the ad man. "No Dalmatian," said the client. "My wife will kill me."*

In another little-known incident, the copy chief and art director of an agency spent 16 sleepless hours polishing up the agency's recommended fall campaign for a client meeting. After a two-hour presentation, replete with comps (ads ready for reproduction), finished copy, and media programs, the president leaned back, reached in his jacket pocket, and pulled out a piece of paper. "Here's a little thing my wife happened to scribble down last night," he said to the shocked agency group. "Now for a layout." He proceeded to draw some lines on a yellow pad, and concluded the meeting by saying, "Here's how it should look." The agency had to go along with his wife's copy and his layout.[8]

All of these stories are not really about wives, of course, but about the irrational element in business decisions, which occurs in realms other than advertising. Why does the agency generally go along with the client's decisions even when the client seems to be out of his mind? The answer may have been supplied by Bill Day, a former plans board chairman at J. Walter Thompson, who once proclaimed, "I'll never sacrifice my principles on the altar of poverty."[9]

Notes

1. This study by the Newspaper Advertising Bureau was reported by Frank E. Orenstein, "Are Automobile Dealers Good Judges of Media Allocations?" *Journal of Marketing*, 26, 1 (January 1962): 76-78.
2. "Stewart Deplores Bureaucracy That Entangles Ad Programs." *Printer's Ink.* October 2, 1964, p. 9.
3. For recent examples of a long-standing practice *cf.* Todd Gitlin, *Inside Prime Time* (New York: Pantheon, 1983).
4. "On Borrowed Experience," *Studies in Philosophy and Social Science*, 9 (1941): 65-94. "Why People Like the Professor Quiz Program," in Paul F. Lazarsfeld, *Radio and the Printed Page* (New York: Duell, Sloan and Pearce, 1940).
5. W. Lloyd Warner and William E. Henry, "The Radio Daytime Serial: A Symbolic Analysis," *Genetic Psychology Monographs*, 37 (1948): 3-71.
6. *The Meaning and Function of True Story for Its Readers* (Chicago: Social Research, Inc., 1955).
7. *The Meaning of Good Housekeeping and Its Advertising to Its Readers* (Chicago: Social Research, Inc., 1956).
8. David North supplied me with this story.
9. This profound remark is recalled by Sidney Dean.

---

*Dalmatians were, for years, also featured in Texaco advertising as part of a "Fire Chief" theme. On one occasion, the Texaco agency's creative group conceived of a television commercial in which a clever Dalmatian performed back flips and similar acrobatics. Scripted and storyboarded, the idea went over big with the client. Valentine Appel recalls, however, that a nationwide search among animal trainers failed to turn up a Dalmatian who could do the necessary tricks. Eventually a remarkable Spitz was found in Germany who did back flips with ease. With the help of a body stocking and a little white and black paint, he was transformed into a Dalmatian long enough to make a commercial to the client's satisfaction.

Chapter 5
Persuasion and the Marketing Plan

A great deal of confusion and error always result when people are asked to report where they saw or heard a particular advertisement, no matter how vividly they remember the words of the message or the pictures associated with it. This very disregard for the media involved well serves the advertiser's purpose, which is to give his product unique overtones of meaning, rather than to connect a particular slogan or sales argument with a certain media environment. However, it often leads to distortions in the popular view of advertising.

If the success of an advertising program depends on the overtones of meaning with which it endows the product, then the question of what advertisements should say is just as critical as the questions of how heavy an expenditure should be used to disseminate them and how those expenditures should be allocated. What elements of meaning make messages persuasive? What techniques make them compelling? And what research tools can the advertising strategist employ to make his ads even more persuasive and compelling?

Motivation research revisited

When advertising is discussed by people who are not themselves involved in the buying, selling, or creating of ads, the talk usually centers on an ad's content, rather than the medium through which it is presented. The tendency is to focus on the strategy of what to say rather than on the strategy of when, where, and to whom to say it. Most popular books on advertising reflect this emphasis on consumer motives and how to play on them in copy.

For a number of years, the layman has been told to equate advertising psychology with a subversion of the public will. This evokes an image of experts armed with mysterious weapons to probe and control the mind of the consumer. After first opening his unconscious weaknesses to the cunning manipulations of "Hidden Persuaders" who prey on secret fears and fantasies, the advertisers then sell him what he does not need and does not really even want. This view of advertising psychology has attained such wide currency that it may now be taken to represent an integral part of the public view of both advertising and psychology.

Fear of advertising's sinister power to manipulate its audience rose to a height following an innocent experiment by market researcher James Vicary in

1957. Ingeniously, Vicary flashed tachistoscopic urgings to drink and eat during intermission time at a drive-in movie, and the concessionaire delightedly reported that sales went up (though there was no comparison with what openly readable promotional lantern slides might have accomplished).* The resultant flap over "subliminal advertising" provided material for sermons from coast to coast and eventually drove the hapless Vicary out of business (and into a temporary shelter at the Newspaper Advertising Bureau).

It is by now clearly established from psychological experiments that communication of some kind can take place below the threshold of conscious awareness.[1] Flashing the word "beef" for an imperceptible five milliseconds a couple of times during a movie seems to make people more hungry, but it does not make them hungrier for beef.[2] However, the evidence is also clear that weakly presented messages below awareness cannot begin to·have the communications effects that stronger, overtly presented messages do.[3]

Vance Packard, in a best-selling book,[4] described advertising research as a kind of occult practice providing irresistible powers of control over the public mind. Packard identified Madison Avenue as "the chilling world of George Orwell and his Big Brother." The public is being "treated like Pavlov's conditioned dogs. . . . Nothing is immune or sacred . . . [A] Chicago ad agency has used psychiatric probing techniques on little girls."

David Ogilvy's man in the Hathaway shirt and Leo Burnett's Marlboro cowboy have both been presented as creatures of the Hidden Persuaders, even though there is no indication that they were the products of psychological investigation rather than advertising inventiveness.

To provide an eyepatch for the man in the Hathaway shirt was inspiration, but it was also inspiration that led a researcher to suggest that baking a cake is comparable to having a baby. Both were imaginative and provocative ideas that arose from insight rather than from research. There have always been some practitioners who are remarkably skillful at sparking such ideas but who are less concerned with the unglamorous task of putting them to the test of evidence.

In reciting his case histories, Packard drew no distinction between marketing decisions based on research and others which simply reflect creative ingenuity. He offered the following example:

> An Indiana supermarket operator nationally recognized for his advanced psychological techniques told me he once sold a half ton of cheese in a few hours, just by getting an enormous half-ton wheel of cheese and inviting customers to nibble slivers and cut off their own chunks for purchase. They could have their chunk free if they could guess its weight within an ounce. The mere massiveness of the cheese, he believes, was a powerful influence in making the sales.[5]

To Packard's readers this represented psychiatric depth probing, Big Brother, and Pavlov's dogs, but maybe it was nothing more than smart cheese mer-

---

*A tachistoscope is a device used in the psychological laboratory to flash extremely brief images before the eyes of an experimental subject.

chandising! Is it dangerous and immoral for manufacturers with goods to sell to employ the services of experts who can help them do an effective job? It is hard to·see how they could fail to take advantage of the twentieth century's improved understanding of human behavior. To ask today's advertisers to leave psychology out of their ads is like asking them to dispense with photography or with the rules of good layout and design.

In a competitive economy, researchers, like advertising people and business-men, work for different ends. They are not in conspiracy. The real job of persua-sion rests with the experts in the arts of persuasion. Research does not write copy, redesign packages, or change distribution methods. However, more intel-ligent decisions on how to persuade may be made with an understanding of consumer motivations, as well as with knowledge of the basic facts about who and where the customers are.

The qualitative advertising research of the 1950s and 1960s typically used a modest number of intensive personal "depth" interviews in which open-ended questions were used to extract verbatim comments and mental associations re-garding products that typically lacked salience or significance for the people being interviewed. The samples were generally small (since such interviews are costly) and often unrepresentative (sometimes deliberately so).

In its heyday the concept of consumer motivation was sometimes broadly applied. The psychologist Herbert Kay refers to an advertising agency research report that included a "motivation type question" which read as follows: "Why do you use this product occasionally?" The most commonly given answer was "because I don't like this product," and the next was "because I just use it occasionally."[6]

Many of the research reports of the motivation era were brilliant essays, in which assertions and psychological insights of varying plausibility or validity were woven together in a tissue of supporting quotations from the words of interviewed consumers. At their not-so-best, the reports represented a distilla-tion of what went on in the mind of the analyst rather than a synthesis of the data actually collected.

One leading motivation researcher was retained to review ads at the Leo Burnett Agency and to explain their deep psychological meanings. "He was, of course, a very bright man," remarks John Coulson, "and he knew well enough not to knock Leo's personal favorites. One day an account man came to the meeting early. The ads were all racked up, and the researcher was looking at them. He turned to the account man and asked: 'These are all interesting ads, but tell me, which ones are Leo's favorites?' And he kept coming back for years."

The more flamboyant practitioners of "motivation research" did nothing to discourage the myth that there is only one door to the study of buying motives and only a handful of keys. As shrewd businessmen, they were enchanted by the idea that they were shamans endowed with other-worldly knowledge of the secret working of the mass mind. After all, with this magical gift, their patrons could mold and control the popular passion to consume.

One of the best known practitioners of motivation research, Ernest Dichter, argued that "each individual represents a motivational universe. . . . To record scientifically how the population is motivated with respect to a specific phenomenon, we must fully understand why each individual as a member of this group behaves the way he does.''[7]

But our understanding of one individual's motivation has to be based on principles of behavior that can only be deduced from the systematic study of large populations. To be systematic, some kind of counting is called for, and then there is no choice but to obey the rules of good statistical practice.

Fortunately, or perhaps unfortunately, the secrets, such as they are, of research were and are readily accessible to all who will pay for them. Qualitative research methods had an established place in the armory of social scientists long before they were adapted, glamorized, and publicized. The special advantages won by the firm that was first to apply imaginative new research techniques were quickly lost as competitors hired equally competent consumer psychologists (or often the same ones) to unlock the mysteries on their behalf.

In the 1970s, another type of qualitative research rapidly moved to the forefront: the so-called focus group interview in which a half-dozen to a dozen people are assembled and engaged in a discussion. (The term *focus group* is a barbarism that confused sociologist Robert K. Merton's technique of an unstructured but "focused" interview—in which a skillful interrogator keeps the respondent's attention from wandering off the subject at hand—and the traditional sociological techique of talking to a homogeneous or related group of people who stimulate each other under the interviewer's practiced guidance.)* A group interview can be conducted with little more expense than an intensive interview with one individual, but since everyone in the group gets counted, a respectable number of respondents can be toted up in the sample.

The most beguiling aspect of focus groups is that they can be observed in action by clients and creative people hidden behind a one-way mirror. Thus, the planners and executors of advertising can be made to feel that they are themselves privy to the innermost revelations of the consuming public. They *know* what consumers think of the product, the competition, and the advertising, having heard it at first hand. The trouble is that people who can be enticed into a research laboratory do not always represent a true cross-section of potential customers. A cadre of professional respondents are always ready to volunteer, and loud-mouths can dominate and sway the discussion. While useful and provocative ideas emerge from groups just as they do from individual qualitative interviews, it is dangerous to accept them without corroboration from larger-scale survey research.

Consumer psychology and the making of ads

Advertising research has had some very striking personalities as its spokesmen. They popularized the social sciences and social theory and gave everyday currency in the realms of business management to terms and concepts that were ignored or disdained by the first generation of market survey technicians.

---

*Paul F. Lazarsfeld and Frank Stanton first combined these techniques in the radio Program Analyzer. Groups of people pressed buttons to record their moment-by-moment responses to what they heard. The interviewer, examining the tape, questioned them as to why they reacted as they did. CBS still uses this technique to evaluate television programs.

The market research pioneers of the 1920s and 1930s were essentially business statisticians who collected consumer data through sampling surveys as an afterthought to their sales and distribution analyses. They were largely preoccupied with the description of the market rather than with an understanding of the forces within it.

This emphasis on description reflected the defensiveness of these early practitioners. They had to protect their discipline from the know-nothing school of hard boiled business judgments characteristically suspicious of the egg-head in a world where know-how comes from direct exposure to field conditions, impatient with long-winded discussions of method and concerned with conclusions rather than with how they were derived.

The early market researcher was strongly concerned with methodology; the doubts of the know-nothings required that he keep justifying himself by proving that his findings really were valid, that he really could generalize from a few thousand interviews to the buying habits of a whole population. He had to concentrate on producing descriptive data that looked hard and accurate.

Along with the statisticians, occasional psychologists drifted or were pulled into market research. Some, like Daniel Starch and George Gallup, bear names that have become household words (at least in the households of advertising practitioners).

The initial preoccupation of advertising psychologists was largely with the evaluation and testing of advertisements rather than with the systematic examination of consumers' "hidden desires." The use of qualitative techniques of interviewing and data analysis, along with projective methods of psychological testing, did not become prevalent in advertising circles until after the upheaval of World War II.

The subsequent boom in the university output of clinical psychologists and applied social scientists brought into being a cadre of people with more eclectic views and greater tolerance for psychoanalytic theory than had been exhibited by the advertising psychologists of the prewar period, who came out of a tradition of laboratory experimentation.

The flowering of advertising research during the decade following World War II, a period in which U.S. advertising investments doubled, represented an effort to achieve a mutual accommodation between science and art in advertising.

"Science" in this case was represented by the learned doctors who could speak with authority on why people rejected prunes or were psychologically "threatened" by Brand X's new slogan. "Art" was represented by the creative people, the writers and art directors who instinctively felt (and feel) that the "Great Idea" is the secret of successful advertising. In many cases they were (and are) convinced that the Great Idea would come to them more quickly and in purer form if not for the inhibiting interference of clients, account executives, media specialists, and factfinders telling them what to do.

For the "creative" individual in advertising who judges ads or commercials according to whether or not they "send" him personally, motivation research was more readily acceptable than copy research that compared consumer reactions to different advertisements and told him, *after* he had knocked himself out, that his creations were good or bad.

Qualitative research methods carry their own special risks and dangers. The interpretations that are given the data depend very much on the skill and talent of the individual analyst, and brilliant but idiosyncratic interpretations have been known to be just as brilliantly wrong in their implications for action as brilliantly right in their subtlety of insight.

According to Arthur Wilkins, a veteran copy researcher, "If you have a lot of qualitative data about an ad that you know on good authority to be great, you will be ingenious enough to recognize, in the welter of diagnostic data at hand, the reasons why it was so great. But with the *same data* at hand, if you had been told on good authority that the commercial was a 'bomb,' you would see that material in a different light, and would emerge, I am sure, with a no less plausible analysis of the *weaknesses* of the advertising."[8]

Leo Burnett, one of advertising's greatest copywriters, used to circulate a saying he misattributed to Benjamin Franklin: "Nothing is more pitiful to see than a beautiful theory destroyed by ugly facts." John Coulson, who used to head Burnett's research department, remembers an occasion when a top-flight copy researcher made a presentation to Mr. Burnett showing examples of high-scoring and low-scoring ads:

> The research man opined eloquently about why they were good and why they were bad. Leo was enthralled and wanted to use the research service immediately.
>
> Dick Heath, the president of the company, who was well aware of Leo's enthusiasms, suggested to the researcher that he come back with some Burnett ads and make the same kind of presentation. The researcher did. He lined up the Burnett ads and told why the good ones were good *and* why the bad ones were bad. Leo became glummer and glummer. He abruptly left the meeting and said, "I don't ever want to see that contentious bastard again."*

The advertising researcher, when he functions well, can play the part of a benign Muse, stimulating the writer to more exuberant efforts in the direction most persuasive to the consumer and most rewarding to the advertiser. A trained specialist in consumer behavior can contribute deep psychoanalytical understanding that would never be apparent to a mere layman. I know, for example, of an agency group that worked on the account of a synthetic fiber used in tires. Since construction with this fiber eliminated the slight sag that some tires acquire when they remain in one position for a while, the creative department came up with the copy theme, "No Morning Thump." The agency's researchers vetoed this because of "negative sexual connotations!"

Some of the most memorable advertising slogans, as Charles Winick reminds us, employed double entendres: Chateau Martin's "Had any lately?" Clai-

---

*But not all creative potentates have this impatience with readership research. David Ogilvy, another great copywriter who founded a major agency, credits at least some of his success to his early apprenticeship with George Gallup. David Ogilvy, *Ogilvy on Advertising* (New York: Crown, 1983).

rol's "Does she or doesn't she?" Brut Cologne's "After a shower . . . after a shave . . . after anything."[9] But sex in advertising rears its pretty little head in other ways. Winick observes that "No one knows if advertising copywriters or their audience are fully aware of or respond to the sexual symbolism of lakes or rivers or oceans. . . . That is why cigarette advertising often shows a couple walking or running hand in hand near a body of water." He also suggests that the eye patch on David Ogilvy's Hathaway man was a symbol of impotence, giving "many a man . . . the subconscious feeling that 'I have sexual problems, too, but perhaps I can look as distinguished as he does in spite of my disability if I wear a Hathaway shirt.' "

Subconscious feelings were barely sufficient as advertising copywriters followed the swing of television and magazine entertainment to become more sexually charged during the 1970s. In an ad for Paco Rabanne Cologne, a woman tells her lover, "I'm going to take some and rub it on my body when I go to bed tonight. And then I'm going to remember every little thing about you . . . and last night." This could hardly be termed "soft sell."

Typically, the efforts of advertising psychologists have been diverted from the study of product purchase motivations, considered independently, to the study of how those motivations are reflected in reactions to advertising itself.

While the worth of various advertising ideas can be compared, most of them cannot be evaluated by pure judgment or by instinct. The Great Idea is not likely to be in the sheaf of first sketches that the copywriter submits to his art director; in fact, it is not likely to be out there at all. The free-form consumer interview, qualitatively analyzed by a competent and insightful professional, remains a predictable source of inspiration for those who create advertisements. But inspiration must still be put to the test.

Evaluating advertising

The evaluation of advertising ideas and executions essentially takes two forms: (1) the pretesting of advertisements through artificial exposure of a number of alternative themes, approaches, treatments, or versions, and (2) the posttesting of advertisements after they have actually been run. Each of these subjects is complex and interesting enough to deserve a treatise of its own.

The growth of expenditures on marketing and advertising research has outpaced the growth of advertising billings. In 1983, nearly half a billion dollars was being spent on advertising research alone.

It has been calculated by Du Pont's Irwin Gross that three to five times as much money should be budgeted as is customary to create a wider variety of advertising ideas for testing before any media expenditure is made.[10] But Gross points out that the agency commission system militates against this kind of expenditure of creative effort on the agency's part as long as there is no additional compensation for it.*

The cost of testing a commercial ran between $4,000 and $8,000 in 1983.

---

*Historically, the agency has kept 15 percent of media billings to cover all its expenses and earn a profit.

Thus, an advertiser who believes in testing has a substantial sum at stake in his research budget, which he might well be tempted to add to his advertising allocation. However, if a measurable proportion of advertising is counter-productive, the sales losses it generates would easily justify the research bill.

The 1982 PACT statement by leading agencies[11] set forth nine principles of a good copy testing system: (1) measurements relevant to the advertising objectives, (2) advance agreement on the use of the results, (3) multiple measurements, (4) covering reception, comprehension, and response to the advertising "stimulus," (5) considering more than one exposure, (6) favoring finished executions, (7) controlling for bias, (8) defining the sample, and (9) demonstrating reliability and validity.

Print advertising copy pretesting has for years generally used some variant of the "portfolio" technique, in which different ads are presented for comment in a random order. In exceptionally elaborate versions of this technique, ads have been printed and bound into an actual copy of a magazine. It is rare to conduct such tests on layouts in a rough or preliminary sketch form. More commonly, ads are set in type and photography or art is carried to a level of execution that falls somewhat short of a final finished state without looking unprofessional to respondents. Television commercial testing is far more complicated and expensive, both because commercials cannot be shown as conveniently as a portfolio of print ads and because producing alternative versions of ideas for commercials can be a very costly proposition.

A variety of procedures are used by many different organizations engaged in pretesting commercials. Cable facilities (like AdTel's) are used to send certain commercials into some homes and other commercials elsewhere, with respondents asked in advance to watch. People are assembled (by Audience Studies, Inc., and other research companies) in theaters and subjected to different assortments of commercials under the guise of previewing new television programs.

The same "operant behavior" principles that behaviorist B. F. Skinner used in training pigeons have been employed to pretest commercials since the 1960s by DuPont.[12] In their CONPAAD system, a foot pedal had to be pressed continuously by experimental subjects to keep a TV picture from fading. The frequency of pressing the pedal was automatically recorded, both for an unmotivated showing of a program in which the test commercial was embedded and then for repeat showings of the commercial, with the subject motivated to learn everything he wanted to know about it. (A Lucite commercial tested by this technique was found to have a high unmotivated attention level, but was less successful in conveying the main points about the product.) CONPAAD was only one of a number of technical innovations that have been applied to advertising evaluation, as I shall show in a few pages. But essentially, most copy research continues to depend on questions and answers.

While research is widely used today to help in the preparation of ad campaigns and the evaluation of advertising ideas at every stage, a substantial part of this effort appears to be done pro forma or by methods that would not stand up to searching criticism.

The best evidence on this point comes from an ANA investigation of copy research practices. Sixty of the largest advertisers and 39 of the largest agencies responded to a questionnaire on television copy research methods sent out by Benjamin Lipstein and James Neelankavil.[13] Nine out of ten advertisers and all of the agencies claimed to do "strategic research" that broadly described the market and provided a basis for their creative approach. Nine out of ten agencies and seven out of ten advertisers evaluated copy ideas. Virtually all the agencies and advertisers evaluated commercials at both a rough and finished stage and went on to evaluate complete television campaigns. Two out of three tested competitors' commercials. One in four said they did studies of commercial "wearout" (the loss of effectiveness as a result of repetition).

To generate copy ideas, virtually all agencies and advertisers were using focus group interviews, while one-on-one interviews were used by nine out of ten agencies and two out of three advertisers. Half the agencies and a third of the advertisers also conducted "small exploratory field studies" (though these were not further defined). Most of this qualitative research was used to test campaigns as well as individual commercials, and in about half the cases it was used to evaluate as well as to develop ads (in spite of the obvious impossibility of generating projectable findings from the small and unsystematic samples typically used).

Interviewing was almost universally done in shopping malls, while the traditional door-to-door interviewing was done by only 18 percent. Seven out of ten tested copy ideas in the form of "concept statements," but nine out of ten tested rough executions in the form of "animatics" (crudely animated drawings), and three out of four tested them in "photomatics" (simulated motion pictures using still photographs). (There is also another form, "live-amatics," a cheap production of a live commercial.) The evaluative measures used almost universally were playback of copy points, reactions to the commercials, mentions of product attributes, and persuasiveness (generally defined as the shift in brand choice before and after exposure).

As for finished commercials, while almost all the advertisers and agencies tested them, only a fifth of the advertisers and 3 percent of the agencies tested all of them routinely, and few of them provided any systematic explanation of the method used to select the ones they tested. As with the testing of roughs, the most commonly used evaluative measures were recall, playback of copy points, and shifts in purchase preference.

How valid are the commonly used pretesting methods? That is, how accurately does a score that reflects an advertisement's memorability predict its power to move people to buy? From the evidence, it appears that while there is more than a random relationship between recall and persuasion, it is not all that much better than chance.[14]

This conclusion could also be drawn from a large-scale field experiment that Stuart Tolley, Frank Orenstein, and I conducted in 1968 and which will be discussed in some detail when we come to the broader subject of advertising effects.[15] For 31 ads, we measured a number of indications of effectiveness, as well as recognition and proven recall (accurate playback of the ad's copy or features). The rank orders of the ads by these last two measures were closely correlated, just as they were shown to be (at the +.92 level, or almost perfectly,* between recognition and aided recall) in the ARF's 1955 study of "Print Advertising Rating Methods" (PARM).[16] But neither measure showed any correlation with sales performance.[17]

Proven recall of commercials was not significantly related to subsequent buying activity, according to yet another analysis by Harold Ross. He compared the purchase rates for advertised brands among 2,241 viewers who had participated two weeks earlier in Mapes and Ross on-air tests of 142 different commercials in 55 product categories.[18] However, his analysis validated the testing procedure used by his firm, which measures brand preferences before and after commercials are shown, to compare residual effects. The actual brand purchase rates among those buying the product were three times higher among those originally persuaded to change preference than among those whose preference in the test did not change.

Far less encouraging results regarding the validity of television pretesting methods emerged from on-air tests of 633 commercials run on BBDO's Channel One experimental cable facility under the direction of Lawrence Light. Of these, 106 were tested on two occasions, with an average of 6.4 percentage points difference between the first and second tests, against an average awareness level of 33.4 percent. On seven different measures of communication and persuasion there were comparable variations, suggesting that half the scores fell below acceptable standards of reliability and were, therefore, useless.†

Where the identical commercial was evaluated both through an on-air test and in a theater test, Light found that in 24 (or 77 percent) of 31 cases, the commercials would have been judged differently by one system than by the other. A similar comparison of yet another eleven commercials produced a correlation of .06 on recall levels, little better than chance.[19]

The perfect copy testing system, Horace Schwerin once declared, would be to throw ads or storyboards down the stairs and know that the one that landed on top would produce the most sales. Such a system would be "fast, inexpensive, and predictive." Unfortunately, it has not yet been perfected.

Sweaty skin and brain waves

Psychologists interested in the subject of emotional arousal have developed a variety of nonverbal methods of measuring the unconscious autonomic responses of the body when it is confronted with new stimuli. Advertising psychologists have for many years borrowed such laboratory devices to ascertain the power of ads to stir an audience.

The psychogalvanometer, which measures skin conductivity, has been offered as a means of tracking response to commercials. On one occasion, the media research director of a large agency was asked to place his hand in a box.

---

*A perfect correlation is +1.0, while a completely random one is 0.

†Reliability as a statistical term refers to the ability of a measuring instrument to produce the same measurement time after time.

It rested on a plate that would register his reactions while he listened to a sales presentation on behalf of a new service that offered to evaluate commercials by this method. A sensitive needle tracked his record on a tape resembling that of an electrocardiogram. Unfortunately, the record came out as a straight line, with barely a wobble.

The pupillometer, a form of eye camera that measures pupil dilation, operates on the same principle of detecting arousal. In the mid-1960s, the University of Chicago's Eckhard Hess, consulting with McCann-Erickson, used such a device to pretest both print and television advertising. At least two research organizations, Telcom and Perception Research Services, were still using this method in 1983. No one can quarrel with the premise that eye pupil dilation and changes in skin conductivity and the pulse rate all provide evidence that emotions have been engaged. But it is not always clear what the nature of those emotions is.* The pupils enlarge with horror as well as with ecstasy, and it still takes questions and answers to probe the meaning of a reaction.

The same general comment may be made about the interpretation of brain wave data, which has recently been in vogue among philosophers of advertising. Computerization has made it possible to conduct more sensitive and sophisticated analyses of the several varieties of electrical emissions that accompany different brain functions. (Alpha waves characterize brain activity among people who are awake but not engaged in any particular activity, while beta waves characterize arousal and attention. Delta and theta waves reflect still other states.)

Physiological psychologists have had a growing interest in the distinctive operations of the two sides or hemispheres of the brain. The observation of brain-injured soldiers in wartime developed striking indications that in most people the left hemisphere controls the processes that involve language and logic, while the right hemisphere controls the handling of spatial relationships and the emotions. If the left rear (temporal) lobe of the brain is impaired, verbal memory suffers; a corresponding impairment of the right side hinders the memory of visual images. Of course, there are few people actually walking around with only half a brain. Nor are there "left hemisphere" and "right hemisphere" people, as Michael Corballis concludes from a far-reaching review of the technical literature: "Hemispheric differences have to do with the verbal or nonverbal nature of the creative enterprise rather than with creativity itself."[20]

The two sides of the brain work in tandem. As Marcel Kinsbourne points out:

People differ in their habitual patterns of thought because of different temperaments and different life experiences. As a consequence, some will use certain parts of the brain more frequently and intensely than will others. . . . But most of the time, people do not appear to confine themselves to just one of these polar opposites of thought. They range

---

*A small pilot study of 21 people by Don Bowdren for *Life* compared the verbal responses to photographs with pupil dilation measurements. Not only did the pupillometer records fail to jibe with the ratings; they changed completely when four of the subjects were subsequently retested.

freely across and between them, integrating the products of diverse mental operations into their overt behavior or covert mental activity. They use areas on both sides of the brain as the situation demands. . . . There is no reason to assume that this dichotomy in the brain represents the most important polarity in human behavior. There are many polarities around which useful constructs about aspects of the mind can be formulated.[21]

Marshall McLuhan made the valid observation that reading engaged the left side of the brain and television the right side. However, McLuhan, an erudite professor of English Literature, paid scant attention to the physiological psychologists when he began to popularize the notion that people could be classified, as though into blood types, by their hemispheric proclivities: "The effect of television is certainly to turn off the left hemisphere, and insofar as it is being used by mainly left hemisphere people, that is sort of against the grain. TV itself cries out for right hemisphere programming. Yet we have a left hemisphere establishment. They are the people in control of bureaucracy."[22]

Even though it may be hare-brained to classify human beings as either right-brained or left-brained, it makes perfectly good sense to apply brain activity measurement techniques to the study of communications effects. Herbert Krugman, who became interested in the phenomenon of arousal through his work with the Hess pupillometer, was the first advertising psychologist to become intrigued by the idea of studying cerebral activity among people looking at ads. In 1970, he engaged Sydney Weinstein, a distinguished neuropsychologist, to compare the EEG (electroencephalographic, or brain wave) record for a subject who was reading a magazine and for the same subject while watching television.[23] While reading produced in this sample of one (Krugman's secretary), a pattern that suggested intense mental activity, the televiewing pattern was almost somnolent in character. Krugman proposed in a later paper that interruptions to reading are "more refreshing than frustrating," while TV interruptions are frustrating because they activate the left hemisphere and frustrate the right hemisphere's tendency to relax. "It is the right brain's picture-taking ability that permits the rapid screening of the environment—to select what it is that the left brain should focus attention on."[24]

In another brain wave experiment conducted by Weinstein in 1972 in association with the Newspaper Advertising Bureau (and in consultation with Krugman), an eye camera record was also obtained to measure what type of print or video content was being looked at, and the three subjects were interviewed later to get their reactions to the content. The EEG records varied greatly among individuals in relation to neutral stimuli that were used to calibrate the equipment. There was great similarity in the response to content that the subjects considered significant, whether in the newspaper or television, but no apparent difference between material that was regarded as pleasant or unpleasant. And no indication emerged of a consistent difference in the pattern of brain activity for newspaper reading and television viewing.

Several years later, Weinstein was engaged by the Simmons Market Research Bureau to conduct similar research on behalf of the magazine industry, which was excited by the prospect of demonstrating that readers were actively chewing away intellectually at what the advertiser presented, while viewers remained in a semi-catatonic state of hibernation. However, this effort (among 30 women exposed to 20 different commercials three times each) produced "no evidence to support the belief that TV viewing is a right-hemisphere activity."[25] In a casebook illustration of how controversy advances science, Krugman persuaded Weinstein to reanalyze his original brain wave data. He concluded that the results confirmed his theory, since they showed that the dominance of left hemisphere (thinking) activity in response to the first exposure declined progressively in the second and third exposures. Thus, he called them "the most compelling evidence to date that *natural* TV viewing is indeed a relatively right-brain response."[26]

Although the debate is by no means concluded, it is quite clear that brain waves vary with real sensory experience. However, no one has yet been able to relate them to subjective changes of imagery in the mind's eye. Apart from their ability to characterize different activities, brain waves seemed to hold the promise of providing a highly indicative moment-to-moment record of changing reactions to media content and especially to advertising.

Intrigued by these commercial possibilities, Weinstein left New York Medical College and set up NeuroCommunication Laboratories, Inc. By comparing activity in the two brain hemispheres during exposure to advertising, Weinstein sought to determine whether the response was primarily emotional or intellectual and further to evaluate whether the type of arousal corresponded to the advertiser's objectives. For example, a suntan lotion commercial used logical arguments on the sound track but supported them with visuals showing women in bikinis. This resulted in "right-hemisphere arousal processing and left-hemisphere interest processing," which turned out to be quite effective. In another commercial, a tender scene between a father and daughter was followed by product information in the form of a "super" and voice-over. "This would not be the ideal time to present the product information, since the right hemisphere still was highly active emotionally, and this right (brain) activity would decrease the probability of linguistic processing," Weinstein commented.[27]

Other investigators have had less luck in applying the electroencephalograph to copy research. In an experiment conducted at Rutgers Medical School for Gallup and Robinson, a dozen men and a dozen women saw twenty 30-second TV commercials for eight different brands arranged in five clusters or "pods" and scattered through a 90-minute TV pilot film.[28] Their brain waves were recorded while they watched, and standard reaction questions were asked in a telephone interview three evenings later.

Different individuals saw commercials (for the same brands) that had previously been tested as "high" or "low" by the usual Gallup and Robinson technique. Commercials that registered an emotional response were better remembered. But although both interest and emotional response differed between commercials and programming, there was not much difference in the brain wave records for high- and low-scoring commercials. It appears that new techniques, like old ones, still have a way to go before they can predict perfectly whether or not an advertisement will be persuasive.

Product familiarity as a goal of advertising

The advertiser must make his product acceptable before he can persuade the consumer to buy it. It can be acceptable only if it seems familiar. To "know" a product may be compared to "knowing" a personality; the single verb may cover a broad range of varied experiences. We may say we know someone who is not even a proper acquaintance because we can recognize and place him or can identify him by name, by his general position in life, or by some trait of character revealed to us through observation rather than interaction. And from there on we move through all the shades of mutual recognition, association, friendship, and intimacy.

We regard it as a commonplace that on some critical occasion we may discover in a loved individual—a spouse, child, parent, sibling, or close friend— characteristics, qualities, or defects that many years of close familiarity have not revealed to us.

Knowing someone is a continuous process. People whom we "knew" in the past are not necessarily among those whom we "know" today. People whom we know in certain well-defined roles or situations are not necessarily recognized, placed, or greeted when we see them out of context.

We feel we "know" political or entertainment personalities who do not know us because the mass media give us an illusion of insight into their lives and because we have vicariously shared some of their private dramas, if only as anonymous spectators.

The nature of our knowing a person reflects not how often we meet or observe him, but the quality of those meetings and the kind of interaction which takes place. We may be physically in the same room with someone many, many times and yet not feel we know him. Or we may briefly meet someone once and yet recognize this as a significant experience. His salience for us may reflect who he is, how he behaves toward us, or the intensity of common experience.

Sociometrists (those sociologists who study the patterns of human relationships) have been intrigued by the problem of how we come to rank each other in the hierarchy of familiarity that ranges from nodding acquaintance to intimacy. Many things come into play that arise from personal compatibility: common occupational or family role; mutual acquaintances; common social, ethnic, religious, or cultural background; similar intelligence; and compatibility of temperaments. But in large part the quality of acquaintance will depend on purely material factors: the physical location or propinquity of the parties; the frequency, duration, and circumstances of their contact; and the degree of privacy or impersonality in contact, a reflection of the number of other people present.

All these factors could be set forth in a schematic diagram that would look very plausible and nonetheless utterly fail to capture the uniquely qualitative element in interpersonal relations, the cues and signs that people present to each other, the complex interplay of the elements that make up each personality, and one human being's mysterious interaction with another.

The manufacturer of a product is, at great remove, engaged in a complex process of communication with the product's eventual customers that is in some ways comparable to interpersonal relations. The haggling of buyer and seller in a Levantine marketplace illustrates the most direct confrontation of personalities in the economic process; there the joy of bargaining may be of far greater importance to the eventual transaction than the utility of the goods exchanged. In our society of impersonal mass marketing and mass consumption, the relationship of buyer and seller is greatly attenuated, yet in a sense the advertiser is still constantly trying to establish a relationship with prospective customers or to deepen a relationship which already exists. The reputation of his company or brand is as complex and subtle a product of events and forces as is the impression one human being has of another. That reputation is built from many bits and pieces of personal experience,* conversation, and symbolism of name; packaging, pricing, and product attributes; and channels of distribution. But above all, it emerges from the mass media and the way advertisers use them.†

For consumers with low brand loyalty, increased advertising can result in brand switching, but among the brand-loyal consumers, it can actually increase purchases of the product (and thus of the preferred brand).[29] The importance of brand identity is shown in a study made by P. E. V. De Bruin and J. H. van Lonkhuysen of Philips Lamp in Holland. They compared a split-run of a full-page, two-color ad for a photo cell in a Dutch industrial publication, "The Engineer." The copy and illustration were identical in both ads except that one carried the logotype symbol that identifies "Philips" and the other a logotype for the mythical brand "TAG." The Philips logo created *five* times as much unaided recall, "action scores" which were four times as high, and aided recall which was over twice as high as created by the unknown brand name.

Brand loyalty seemed to be waning in the 1970s as retailers supplemented their private labels with "generics" sold strictly on price. In 1980, 64 percent of the men and 56 percent of the women in a national cross-section interviewed by Needham, Harper & Steers agreed, "I try to stick with well-known brand names." In 1975, these proportions were 80 percent and 72 percent.

But whether or not they consciously "try to stick with" them, people tend to buy the advertised brands they know. In a 1982 study sponsored by DuPont and the Point of Purchase Advertising Institute, 781 shoppers were interviewed as they entered 12 high-volume drugstores and reinterviewed as they left. For

---

*Never underestimate the importance of personal experience. A 1982 Bruskin study among former users of 24 well-known branded products found that some (Campbell's Soup, Crest toothpaste, Heinz catsup) were still regarded favorably by people who had switched to a different brand, while others (Arrid deodorant, Prell shampoo, and Campbell's Swanson brand of TV dinners) had a substantial minority of former users who were unfavorable.

†Paul Lazarsfeld and Elihu Katz have described the "two-step flow" of communication by which mass media content is transmitted by word of mouth and thus acquires the more vivid character of interpersonal contact. This process works with advertising as well as with other types of messages, but only rarely can an item of conversation be traced back to any specific ad as it might be to a specific news story or TV program. More usually it is a whole ad campaign, particularly one with some highly distinctive slogan or illustrational flair which, as it gathers momentum, gets talked about and is gradually absorbed into the stream of social currency. Cf. *Personal Influence* (New York: Macmillan, The Free Press of Glencoe, 1955).

the average item purchased, 41 percent of the purchases were planned specifically in advance, by brand; in 22 percent of the cases, the product purchase was planned, but the brand decision was made in the store. For 5 percent of the purchases, another product was substituted for the one originally intended. One purchase in three represented a decision made in the store without any prior intention (and this proportion ranged from 80 percent of the jewelry and automotive supplies down to 20 percent of the alcoholic beverages and 24 percent of the cigarettes).

Not surprisingly, preselection by brand differed considerably from one product category to the next. For cigarettes and other tobacco products, 68 percent of the purchases were planned, by brand, and for only 9 percent the brand was selected in the store. For hardware and housewares, only 17 percent of the purchases were planned by brand, while 41 percent were planned by product. And consumers do differentiate among various classes of products when their brand attitudes are probed. Among 221 interviewed by BBDO in 1982, 80 percent thought there were "too many" brands of cigarettes. (There were actually 225 available.) But only 24 percent thought there were too many brands of canned vegetables (and 11 percent said there were too few).

Gerard Cavallo and Lewis Temares found 19 percent of shoppers switching brands for three product categories within the store. The higher the shopper rated a brand she intended to buy, the less likely she was to switch brands in the store or to substitute another brand if it was unavailable.[30]

The reputation of the store may be just as important to the consumer as that of the product. Louis P. Bucklin of the University of California surveyed 506 women shoppers in Oakland.[31] He found that where *no* brand was known and *no* particular store preferred, 31 percent of the women had made more than one shopping trip for the (unidentified) product in question. Where *no* brand was known but a particular store was preferred, 21 percent of the women made more than one shopping trip. When a brand was known but *no* store preferred, 16 percent of the women made more than one shopping trip. When the brand was known *and* a particular store preferred, the proportion who made more than one trip dropped to 15 percent. Of those women who preferred a particular store and were familiar with all the brand features, only 7 percent made more than one trip. This proportion was 35 percent for those familiar with only some of the features. Apparently, familiarity with *both* the brand of merchandise *and* the store that sells it reduces the uncertainty that causes people to shop around before they buy. This sense of familiarity and trust is what every advertiser seeks to establish.

What makes a brand name familiar?[32]

Brand names are the visible, symbolic expression of a competitive economy, and product advertising is virtually inconceivable without them. To say that a brand is reputable implies that it is familiar. Indeed, a great deal of advertising is designed to reinforce the public's sense of brand familiarity on the assumption that familiarity is translated into acceptance and preference when the brand is juxtaposed with less familiar ones at the point of sale. Where products are very similar, brand identity—based on the name, packaging, or advertising themes and techniques—produces the illusion of difference that is vital to competitive selling.

Familiarity is not in itself an index of a brand's market position. The leading brand of any product usually enjoys both familiarity and salience out of proportion to its market share, if only because at least some who accept it as the leader will pick a secondary brand for price or other reasons at the time of decision.

Although brand familiarity is never an end in itself, most marketers consider it a desirable objective. The difficulty and expense of accurately measuring advertising's effects on sales often make it expedient to substitute changing levels of brand awareness for exact records of purchase or consumption trends within a product field. A typical question from such a survey is, "When I mention mousetraps, what brand comes to mind first? What other brands can you think of?" As a last step, one may move from active to passive familiarity, from recall to the larger realm of recognition: "Have you ever heard of 'Mighty Mouse Traps'?"

But a brand's identity can also be considered as part of a wider universe of consumption symbols. One usually knows many more brands than he has used. In the kaleidoscopic tumult of advertisements in all media, brand names are not sorted into product bins.

In one study made at the Newspaper Advertising Bureau, we examined the brand awareness that arises from the large, heterogeneous, and haphazard outpouring of diversified advertising messages. Brands, we reasoned, exist as psychological symbols that compete with other brands in totally different product fields. How do names rank in this wider world of brands? Do their positions reflect the comparative levels of affect or involvement that different products evoke? Or do they reflect the comparative visibility of the individual names and their particular aura of associations? To what extent can brand familiarity be explained by frequency of use or purchase, or by the pressure of advertising behind it?

About 29,000 different brands are advertised on a national or regional scale in the United States. We would hardly expect anyone to know all of them, and we would expect even fewer to be at the top of anyone's mind. To determine comparative awareness of brands, personal interviews were conducted with 400 housewives offering a "brand new nickel for each brand name you can recall" in a four-minute period. Respondents typically visualized the shelves of a supermarket arrayed with merchandise. Sometimes the shifts in product fields were rather abrupt, as when one lady's train of thought went from Ex-Lax to Joy and another's from Ex-Lax to Waring Blender. An average of 28 brand names were mentioned. Eight brands were mentioned by more than one-fourth; 18 by at least one-fifth. In general, brands that enjoyed an outstanding position in overall familiarity also ranked high in the number of first mentions they received. When brand mentions were grouped into product categories, food products accounted for over one-half; 16 percent were soaps, detergents, and household supplies; 11 percent were toiletries, cosmetics, and pharmaceutical products, and 9 percent were big-ticket items—appliances and household furnishings.

A typical food advertiser has ten times as much chance of having his name on the tip of the housewife's tongue as does a nonfood advertiser, probably because of the frequency with which food products are bought and used.

The percentage of brands recalled ranged from 82 percent for instant coffee to 10 percent for deodorizers and was in no way related to the number of brands available and on sale. Inherent product differences determine the visibility of brands. It is simply harder to get consumers to think about deodorizers than about coffee, quite apart from comparative levels of promotional expenditures or advertising-to-sales ratios.

Products whose brands were familiar usually had a lot of advertising behind them. However, brands familiar in a product class were by no means familiar in proportion to the advertising pressure backing them up: food and soaps, with 38 percent of the total national investment, produced 67 percent of all the brand mentions, while appliances and household furnishings, with 5 percent of the national advertising dollars, got 10 percent of the brand mentions.

It is difficult to compare advertising investments across product fields because advertising-to-sales ratios differ widely. However, it is possible to compare specific brands within a product category, so we compared advertising expenditure data for 73 brands with the number of mentions these brands received relative to others within the product category. With a typical brand of staples, for example, where the correlation was high, the more a brand advertises, the higher its familiarity; with a brand of toiletries, where the correlation was low, the connection was not much better than that expected by chance. In 5 of the 7 product categories, however, there was a substantial (+.50) correlation between advertising and brand awarenesss. There was, however, no apparent relationship between brand visibility and the proportion of the ad budget that goes into television.[33]

Recency of exposure to advertising (in any medium) did not readily explain a brand's salience for consumers. Fourteen percent remembered seeing or hearing any advertising "yesterday" for the first brand mentioned.

Of the 106 brands named by at least 5 percent of the respondents, not one had been introduced within the past five years. It obviously takes a long period of exposure before a brand enters into the consciousness of any significant number of people.

Media strategy, motivational strategy, and brand distinction

Researcher Alfred Politz once said most advertising people accepted the following syllogism:

> Major premise: My advertisement has to compete with a tremendous number of advertisements.
> Minor premise: My advertisement must stand out from the crowd.
> Therefore, my advertisement must be different.

The true syllogism should be:

> Major premise: My *product* has to compete with a great many other products.
> Minor premise: My product must stand out from the crowd.
> Therefore, my product must be perceived as different.[34]

And that, of course, is where advertising comes in.

National advertising includes many product categories in which different brands have virtually identical physical characteristics. In such product fields as soaps and detergents, soft drinks, cigarettes, beer, liquor, and gasoline, objective tests indicate that many consumers are unable to tell one brand from another when labels are removed. As we have seen, these are commonly referred to as "parity" products.

As a result of research, advertisers of such products long ago became aware that in making the choice among relatively undifferentiated brands, the consumer buys mainly the satisfactions arising from a brand's unconscious symbolic meanings and associations.

This makes the task for advertising quite distinct from what it is for cars or appliances, where there are large and self-evident differences in the design of various makes and where the commodities are invested with considerable emotion because they represent major expenditures.

The planning and strategic thinking of a number of large advertising agencies is dominated by the package-goods clients whose products are of low interest to the consumer and closely resemble those of his ever-vigilant competition. Because these big advertisers are both powerful and unusually thoughtful and exigent, the theoretical assumptions that underlie their kind of advertising may tend to be carried over into the deliberations of agency account groups and plans boards when they deal with less sophisticated and demanding clients.

One objective for any low-interest product is to get a top-of-mind or tip-of-the-tongue association between the generic product category and the individual brand (not "soft drink" but "Coke"; not "facial tissue" but "Kleenex"). Such an identification makes it more likely that the customer will ask for the brand by name or reach for it on a shelf arrayed with identically priced and apparently similar items.

The advertiser wants the customer to feel that his item is a widely advertised, well-known (and therefore respectable) product manufactured by a big company. The company is assumed to be "big" because it is well known. Because it is big, the customer further assumes it cannot afford the risk of distributing merchandise that is not good.

The advertiser must break through the barrier of inattention that confronts a low-interest product. If people are not interested in what he has to sell them, they are not likely to pay attention to the messages that review his points of product superiority.

Behind the widespread use of television to promote low-interest products is the assumption that sheer repetition can break through the inattention barrier, that a message repeated often enough to the senses of sight and hearing in a time dimension simply cannot be ignored.

However, competitive brands in such product categories often start out with very similar assumptions and from them derive similar media strategies. The effect of this is the proliferation through the same medium of an enormous array of competitive messages that are frequently repeated and that reiterate product claims that may be virtually indistinguishable from each other.

This tremendously complicates brand decisions for the consumer, who must distinguish meaningful demands on his attention from the surrounding sea of noise that washes over him constantly through all the mass media. In the midst of this clamor, the exact repetition of a message no longer adds to a brand's ability to break the consumer's resistance. It may merely add to the confusion.

When we compare brand share and brand awareness in many product fields, we find that there is no consistent relationship. This fact must be kept in mind in considering the assumption that, for an advertiser to win the market share he wants and expects, he must make a far larger proportion of the product's potential purchasers aware of his brand's name. In practice, for a widely used commodity he may have to take as his goal making "everybody" aware of it. He must assume that product quality, pricing, distribution, and merchandising efforts will all work at a peak level of efficiency to translate advertising awareness and successful transmission of product claims into actual share of market.

To make a brand stand out from its competitors may require a unique appeal to consumer motivations, but it also requires a media strategy that can make that unique appeal universally familiar to all those who might be persuaded to buy.

Which comes first: creative theme or market strategy?

"Promise, large promise, is the soul of an advertisement," said Dr. Samuel Johnson. Many of the most astute practitioners and articulate theorists of advertising seem to agree that the advertising plan should start with a creative spark.[35]

Creative advertising types were seeking out new accounts through ads of their own at least as far back as 1885, when Francis I. Maule solicited "correspondence from any who think I might be of service to them." His ad in the *Century Illustrated* was headlined "Genius," and the copy announced that "I formulate 'things' not easily definable." He was drawn, he said, to "subjects that seem to have been long since exhausted by reason of their having had all there was to say about them thoroughly ventilated. I take a genuine pleasure, when treating these matters, in the occasional unearthing of new ideas from such presumably unpromising sources." Today's "creative boutiques" still sell their services on this principle.

The foundation for a successful campaign, wrote the late Rosser Reeves,[36] former chairman of the Ted Bates agency, is the "Unique Selling Proposition," the embodiment of those qualities (real or putative) that distinguish a brand from its competition and offer the consumer a unique benefit. Marion J. Harper, Jr., the legendary former chairman of Interpublic,* had long used a similar concept, that of the "purchase proposition," as the starting point of the advertising plan.

David Ogilvy, that master copywriter, places similar stress in his *Confessions of an Advertising Man* on the importance of beginning with the right creative touch to set a product apart from its competitors. Ogilvy puts it this way: "What really decides consumers to buy or not to buy is the *content* of your advertising, not its form. Your most important job is to decide what you are going to say about your product, what benefit you are going to promise."[37]

In more and more product fields (runs the argument of both Ogilvy and Reeves) the consumer cannot easily tell one brand from another, regardless of

---

*The Interpublic Group of Companies, Inc., formed after McCann-Erickson began to acquire other agencies.

whatever minute differences really exist. Every advertiser of beer, gasoline, filter cigarettes, or toothpaste must begin his planning by defining how he would like his brand to be considered "different," either in those tangible attributes that the consumer experiences and tests first hand or in its "personality." We may note in passing that it is one of the main tasks of consumer research to assist, at this stage, by describing the personality characteristics that people already associate with a brand and its competitors and by indicating the directions of possible change and improvement.

One of Reeves' concepts is that everything that an individual learns from an advertising campaign forces out awareness of other advertising campaigns, even those for different products.

He cites a Ted Bates study of the campaigns of 78 major advertisers, which found a range between 78 percent and 1 percent in "penetration" levels (the percentage of people who remember the ads).

Reeves insists that frequent change of the advertising campaign message results in a loss of penetration. "Changing a story has the same effect as stopping the money, as far as penetration is concerned. Thus if you run a brilliant campaign every year, but change it every year, your competitor can pass you with a campaign that is less than brilliant—providing he does not change his copy."

It follows that "unless a product becomes outmoded, a great campaign will not wear itself out." This conclusion in part reflects Reeves' assumption that "the consumer tends to remember just one thing from an advertisement—one strong claim, or one strong concept."

Reeves attacks "originality" as the most dangerous word in advertising. He chortles over the fact that when an advertising magazine asked top creative people to pick the three worst television commercials of recent years, they included two of the most dramatically successful. (The fact remains that in few major agencies is the choice of what ads or commercials are to run made by the creative people.)

Unfortunately, the evidence that Reeves introduces falls considerably short of proving his point that establishing awareness of the slogan is the mark of success in an advertising campaign. In fact, some of the evidence seems contradictory. He himself points out that not only do brands differ widely in public familiarity with their current slogans, but there are similar wide variations in what he calls "usage pull"—the degree to which knowledge of the slogan makes any *difference* in actual product use. One is left with the uneasy feeling that consumer confidence in General Electric or Pillsbury may reflect a long-established, advertising-influenced corporate reputation rather than the Unique Selling Proposition of the current year.

In essence, Reeves' emphasis on the USP is an appeal for a return to advertising's first principles—simplicity and concentration of effort. This makes great sense when the product is a toothpaste whose special claims to superiority, or even to a separate identity, are circumscribed within a narrow sphere. Yet how useful is the USP to a manufacturer who sells his product to different kinds of people who buy it with different motives?

Reeves asks, "Is it better to reach a smaller audience, to reach it more times? Or is it better to reach a bigger audience—and reach it less often? The answer is, buy dispersion. Try to reach more homes, not the same homes. Try to reach more people, not the same people."

Implicit in Reeves' position (although he does not come out and say it) is the notion that one must start first of all with the right message, theme, or Unique Selling Proposition and then figure out the right means to get this message around to as many people as possible.

In spite of Reeves' disparagement of "originality" (which he, as a great copywriter, can afford to make), the assumption that governs this sequence of steps is that the key to successful promotion is the Great Idea concerning what to say about the product. *How* to say it best can be learned through copy research, which tests different methods of giving expression to the Great Idea. The job of media selection comes last and entails, first, a judgment about the suitability of each medium to the creative approach already chosen, and, second, a matching of media audiences to the demographic or psychological characteristics of prospective customers.

Herbert Maneloveg, one of advertising's top media practitioners and theorists, also believes that the copy approach is paramount. "In the final analysis it's what you have to say that counts. ... When an agency or client puts media selection before copy and lays most emphasis on media, it is usually because the product's appeal is low, very low, and the only way to penetrate through the boredom screen of today's tumultuous cacophony of sound and messages is by pounding away with a slogan, any slogan, often a mediocre slogan, but pound, pound, pound."[38]

This strategy demands that the advertiser start with an introspective look at his own reaction to his product. From such introspection may come (if he is lucky) insight into the right thing to say. Once he is saying the right thing, how can people fail to listen?

There are, however, other possible starting points for advertising strategy. For instance, the planner may start by looking at the customers rather than at the product. If he begins with the marketing data, he must first ask where—in what sectors of society—his customers or prospects are, and next how—with what media—they can be reached. Only then will he consider the media context or auspices that promise to find them in the most receptive mood. These considerations would lead him to select a medium or a mix of media. Creative strategy and style would then have to be developed in the terms most appropriate to the medium selected and the audience desired rather than on the basis of fantasy, speculation, or research about the product in an abstract setting.*

If media plans were developed in this sequence, it would reduce the problems that arise whenever a campaign successfully developed in one medium is carried over to another. Too often the resulting ads or commercials are mere adaptations that fail to account for the essential differences in form between media, the varying possibilities for attracting (or even overwhelming) attention,

---

*One qualification should be made here: Practical economy reasons as well as the desire for creative coordination may require that the same background sets and models be used in shooting for television and taking still photographs for use in newspapers, magazines, and outdoor ads.

the emotional effects of color, the audience's frame of mind and expectations, and the editorial or entertainment context of the advertising message.

In actual practice, few advertising plans are developed exactly in either one of the two sequences described here. Just about every plan submitted is derived from the plans that preceded it and there are generally starting points both on the creative and media sides that modify and shape strategy as it evolves. The Great Idea is often visualized in the context of a particular medium or with a particular audience in mind. And the media plan that emerges in mechanical projections from marketing statistics may be irrelevant to the real communications problem of the product.

Advertising and the decision to buy

In a simpler era, buyers and sellers were part of the same community, knew each other's habits, and worked within a very restricted range of opportunity and choice. But even in our present society, with its complex distribution system, manufacturers and retailers alike commonly talk of "their" customers, as though these were specific individuals who constituted a particular and exclusive preserve. In fact, everyone engaged in the sale of goods and services knows that consumers are at least somewhat unpredictable.

Marketing and advertising strategy is almost inevitably (and understandably) devised from the perspective of the seller. The person who has a product to sell generally starts with the idea of placing the message before prospective customers. These may be heavy users of the product or simply people susceptible to persuasion for one reason or another. Generally he hopes to convert or persuade them to try his product the next time they are "in the market" or ready to buy.

The marketer may urge these prospective customers to "rush right out and buy it now." Some of the time this may just be hyperbole, but in the case of the retailer or of a national advertiser with a new or promotional item, there may be an honest expectation that a certain number of people will be persuaded to "rush right out" because of a special incentive or deal that the advertising proclaims.

Implicit in the mind of the advertising planner is the notion of an audience of consumers, real or potential, with varying degrees of propensity for using his product, frequently or in substantial quantities, and in various stages of predisposition to buy it. His ads are placed before customers in the context of messages for products that compete either directly or indirectly with his own. They are intended to persuade or *pull* people toward his product who might not otherwise be receptive to buying it at all or who might be impelled toward a competing brand.

However, the real function of advertising looks very different when seen from the standpoint of the *buyer* rather than the seller. We might start by thinking of the degree to which people in our advanced commercial society live with a constantly changing set of internal and external pressures to consume a great array of products and services. These pressures vary in intensity from moment to moment, from day to day, from week to week. They jostle and compete with each other for the consumer's available resources of disposable income and shopping time. They reflect changes in life circumstances, family relationships, the seasons, the weather.

Considered from this vantage point, advertising must, of course, be numbered among the influences on people's consumption values. But an ad's short-term influence cannot be described, as it is so often, as sensitizing people to the merits of a product or making the product seem more desirable and important. This kind of effect on the way people position products and brands occurs only over the *long* term. Advertising is really inseparable from all the many other long-term economic and cultural influences on personal values.

Few consumer *needs* stem from an individual ad for a particular product. The direct short-term effects that an advertiser may expect from a specific ad are those from the few people who already want the product and who are so close to the act of purchase that the ad *triggers* their decision by reminding them of a brand or style or store. The extent to which conscious readiness to buy is converted to an actual purchase depends on a myriad of accidental factors involving the daily time budget and the pressure of competing interests, activities, and purchase desires.

Most advertisers think of the "pay-out" or yield for an ad or commercial in terms of the carry-over of favorable familiarity into a future purchase period. Our perspective must be quite different when we think of it in terms of the immediate or short-run sales potential that it activates or generates.

When we look at advertising from the perspective of the buyer, it is apparent that most advertising messages are wasted. They *have* to be, because at any given moment only a fraction of even the best customers are on the verge of buying the product. Nevertheless, a correspondence school may use matchbook advertising very efficiently even though only a very small proportion of the people to whom matchbooks are distributed have any conceivable interest in taking a correspondence course. It is still worthwhile to put the message in the hands of a great many uninterested people if in the process it reaches the handful who may write for information.

The return to an advertiser from his media investment must be calculated in terms of the very, very small numbers of people to whom he really wants to talk at any moment.

This theory of the "necessary waste" in advertising must work differently for products that are bought infrequently, like refrigerators or cars, and those that may be bought daily, like cigarettes or bread. For a product whose frequency of purchase varies from one individual to another, obviously the frequent (or heavy) buyers will be found "ready to buy" in disproportionate numbers at any given time.

This theory also implies that there is value in exposing customers to the message as close as possible to the time they decide to buy. The point of decision often occurs well before the actual purchase. It is reflected in the timing and direction of the shopping trip, as well as in the composition of the shopping list.

A further implication of the theory of wasted messages is that high frequency of exposure is valuable not so much for the purpose of accumulating reach or for building a persuasive impact by message piled upon message, but simply because it maximizes the probability that the story is being told to people who are close to the buying decision.

Introducing a new product

Consumer goods marketing in a competitive economy depends on a constant infusion of new products, of which a surprisingly large proportion win acceptance. Of 13,311 new products recently introduced by 700 manufacturers, 65 percent were successful while the remainder failed.[39] (One reason for the high success rate is that new products rarely reach the stage of a national introduction today without having undergone testing of the underlying concept, of actual field performance, and of market acceptance.)[40]

In making the first major announcement or delivering the first major message for a new product, it is desirable that there be some prior subconscious sense of familiarity or acceptance. Thus even before a large investment is made some kind of minor preconditioning is often called for.

A heavy push for a product that no one has ever seen or heard of before may tend to create a degree of disbelief, rejection, or resistance. If the product name has already been placed before the public, such resistance might be diminished.

How can one quickly build up such a sense of familiarity? One way, obviously, is to scatter small unobtrusive messages before the public in a variety of different contexts. For instance, in newspaper advertising, small-space units lend themselves very well to this objective. The first such ad may capture the conscious attention of a very few readers. But when the same ad or a variation of it appears again in a very different context, the very *incongruity* between the second appearance and the first, along with the *similarity* of the basic story, may produce a kind of low-level shock effect. This may jar into awareness readers who might otherwise skim by the same item if they were seeing it for the first time.[41]

A spectacular initial drive may succeed in making a product well known to a high percentage of the public. It is fair to assume that there would be a very rapid attrition of that awareness, particularly among people who are not at the moment in the market for the product advertised, even though those who enter the market in the ensuing weeks may have their familiarity refreshed when they actually go into the store and encounter the merchandise on the shelf.

A major objective for a new product must, therefore, be to maintain the level of familiarity or awareness for a continuing period *after* the introductory wave of heavy advertising. The rate at which people are being reminded has to compensate for the rate at which they would otherwise forget because of their disinterest in the product category itself.

This argues for the consistent use of reminder advertising to keep alive the memory of both the brand name and its product characteristics. Ideally, one would always wish this reminder advertising to take the form of messages delivered in unit sizes large or impressive enough to assure the high level of attention that was achieved by the initial effort, but this is only rarely feasible within budget limitations. The advertiser thus perennially faces the problem of balancing greater frequency in small doses against less frequent messages strong enough to revive the memory of his whole product story.

When is the right time to give a new product a second big push? A low-key continuity campaign may maintain awareness at a desired level, but beyond a certain point there is apt to be a strong need for full restatement of the product's basic story. This commonly calls for a change of pace within the existing media mix, or a radical, usually temporary, shift of media balance. The timing of such a move is often governed by merchandising requirements, but it may also be influenced by traditions such as spring and fall promotions.

The advertiser is always fighting a losing battle over a period of time. Unless he repeats an ad of the same powerful dramatic quality he used originally, there will be fewer and fewer people every day who spontaneously associate his brand with the product category.

He can try to offset this attrition by periodically introducing a more powerful message unit in the form of a bigger ad or by adding to the string of commercials in his current "pool" or available assortment. This might restore awareness in people who have become oblivious to the ads for reasons that have to do either with their lack of interest in the product or with the creative themes.

The function of advertising is often merely that of a catalyst. Two men with identical buying wants and capacities may pass the window of a store in which shirts are offered for sale. If one of them has seen an ad for these shirts that day, he may be more impelled to walk into the store and buy the merchandise. In practice, however, it is hard to tell whether the positive decision of any one customer reflects the influence of advertising, of greater immediate needs, of purchasing power, or of a private affinity for the styling and color patterns of the shirts in the window.

The consumer decision: a minor purchase

How does the persuasive power of advertising fit in among all the forces that influence the consumer's buying decision? The answer to this question varies, as is illustrated by the case histories of two strikingly different commodities we studied at the Newspaper Advertising Bureau. The first is a product category with a broad market, low consumer interest, and high purchase frequency. Interviewers stationed outside supermarkets in Modesto, California, questioned 613 housewives who had just bought one or more paper products—kitchen towels, facial tissue, toilet tissue, wax paper, and napkins.

Eighty-four percent of the purchases were reported by the shopper to have been planned or thought of in advance. In half these cases she had actually written the item down on a shopping list.

The study indicated that nearly 3 women in 5 believe that one brand in particular is outstanding. While in general they buy that brand, if a price or premium offer is available, it may easily deflect them. Yet only 7 in 10 said they had looked around in the store to see the prices of other brands.

Four out of 5 shoppers reported that the item they had just bought was a brand they usually use. When asked why they preferred that brand, the percentage referring to a price advantage ranged from 9 percent for facial tissue to 40 percent for napkins, and there were notable differences among individual brands. Of the switchers who did not just buy the brand they "usually buy," between 40 percent and 50 percent reported that they had made their purchase on the basis of price.

During the period of the study, a record was kept of actual sales and of changes in shelf facings and displays. In one period, a brand of facial tissue was selling at its regular price in a certain supermarket and was bought by only 2 out of the 35 women who bought facial tissue. A few days later, it went on sale. On two sale days, 13 out of 25 facial tissue purchasers bought it.

When another leading brand of facial tissue was on sale and was prominently displayed in the store, 25 of 33 tissue buyers chose that brand. Its share dropped to 7 purchasers out of a total of 15 when its leading competitor also went on sale. When only the competitor's product was on sale, the leading brand was bought by only 3 out of 10 facial tissue purchasers.

In another supermarket, a brand of paper towels attracted a total of 22 purchasers with a premium offer. In another period, with the premium offer plus a sale price, it got up to 14 out of 16 purchasers. When this brand (with a premium offer only) had the same number of shelf facings as its leading competitor (which had no premium), it was outsold, 11 packages to 16. But when it was later offered at a sale price as well as with a premium, it sold 10 packages to every 5 for the competitor.

Where does advertising fit into such a volatile mix of marketing forces? Paper products as a group are consciously missed when the household supply runs low or out. If the need has registered, the housewife automatically plans a purchase; she even writes it down.

It is not that the subject is of any particular interest to her. Despite the enormous volume of advertising in this category ($68.6 million in 1982), only one woman out of four spontaneously recalled any advertising during the past week for the product she had just bought. Yet that advertising, sustained over the years, helps her to make quality distinctions among brands, so that when she comes into the store she has both a preference (not a clear-cut one, but a general tendency perhaps) and also a range of acceptability for other brands, with definite outer limits on how far she can be lured by a premium or price advantage. (In 1982, over half the public, in a survey by the Opinion Research Corporation, said they would switch brands of paper towels to take advantage of a 25 cents-off coupon.)

When 3 women in 10 say they did not look at the prices of brands other than the one they bought, this does not necessarily mean that they are oblivious to price. It merely indicates that they perceived the pricing of their brand relative to its competition to be within the bounds of expectation and tolerance.

Advertising thus serves the primary function of placing a brand within the spectrum of what is acceptable.

As a second function chronologically, advertising's stress on specific product advantages or its symbolic overtones give the consumer a rational or an emotional inclination that is reinforced by actual purchase. An imperceptible advantage on a continuum of preference for one brand versus another becomes an absolute yes-no advantage when the consumer must decide in the store on purchase or non-purchase. Once the affirmative act of purchase has been made, the consumer is psychologically committed to support the brand she chose with her preference, and advertising gives her the reasons.

Finally, advertising may alert the consumer to a sale or special offer. This is important in reaching the extremely economy-minded customer or the one who uses advertising as a reference in making up her shopping list. But to many more customers, the notice of a sale serves as a preliminary cue to be activated at the point of sale or as a trigger that sets into motion the cumulative effect of much previous promotion.

The consumer decision: a major purchase

If the purchase decision on paper products represents the low end of consumer interest and involvement, the automotive purchase decision, next to that of a home, is usually the biggest and most important one that a family makes.

To understand how people go about buying a new car, we asked the Oxtoby-Smith research firm to conduct intensive interviews with nearly 200 recent purchasers. With the help of some searching questions, the purchasers were asked to retrace the steps they had taken in arriving at the decision to buy. On the basis of their responses, it would seem that the process of buying a car can be visualized in two separate stages, each of which starts in a vague fuzzy way and ends at a hard, sharp focal point.

The first stage is one of "preliminary exploration." It may be described as the gradual evolution of a state of readiness to buy. It culminates in a definite decision, expressed in verbal commitments, to enter the market. This exploration is set in motion almost imperceptibly, in response both to external events and to internal psychological changes. An individual arrives at this state, for example, when his car has passed a certain age (which he defines as "old" in comparison with the model year of cars owned by people he considers significant). Or he may be impelled from the stage of unconscious sensitivity to one of active readiness by a change in life circumstances—a marriage, a change of job or residence, the birth of a new child, a death in the family—anything that alters his functional or status requirements. A buildup of tension takes place gradually over months for most people. During this period, anything that goes wrong with the prospect's current car assumes an importance it did not have before. If the car burns oil or gets less mileage to the gallon of gas, or if minor parts have to be replaced, this now becomes a matter of family conversation. (Family discussion, in fact, accompanies all of the subsequent stages in the process of decision-making.)

As the car owner finds himself talking more about cars, he also becomes more sensitive to advertising and editorial matter dealing with automobiles. He pays more attention to new models he sees on the road. New model introductions intensify the process by creating fresh occasions for conversation and reflection.

As this "preliminary exploration" goes on, the car buyer comes more and more to think of himself as being actively in the market. He may define his interest now in terms of a target date for his purchase. This may be related to the introduction of the new models, to the end of winter, or to the anticipated lowering of prices at the end of the old model year.

Often some decisive incident or event (a major repair job, or an occasion to celebrate) forces the prospect to begin his active shopping. Even before he reaches the point of decision to buy, he has become highly conscious of the different makes and models and of the dealers in his area of residence.

Once he has made up his mind to buy a car, the customer starts to look into showroom windows and even to browse through floor displays. He starts studying the ads to compare features and prices. He consults the "experts" of his acquaintance. He chats with friends about his own past experience. At the final stages he talks to dealers about features, prices, and trade-ins and, on the basis of comparison, closes his deal. In a majority of cases he makes up his mind within a matter of weeks after he has made the decision to buy.

Throughout these crucial weeks, the prospect's feeling about the reputation of a make is buttressed now by what he sees in the advertising to which he has suddenly become sensitive. But the ads he sees with new interest produce their effect by reactivating all the other advertising—not to mention all the news and rumor—that has reached him over the years.

This description of the automotive purchase decision holds up nearly universally, but the actual form and timing of the various stages in the process show considerable variation from one individual to the next.

Brand advertising in perspective

In two examples of the purchase decision as disparate as those for a paper product and a new car, the differences are far more striking than the few common elements—the awareness of a need, the decision to buy, the shopping process, and the choice among brands on the basis of both general reputation and specific price value.

But the two studies together lead to certain conclusions. They force us to place advertising in a realistic perspective among all the forces that influence a purchase. Whereas in both cases advertising proved to be an important element, its importance lies not in having elicited a specific purchase response to a specific ad. The real significance of advertising is its total cumulative weight as part of the culture—in the way in which it contributes to the popular lore of ideas and attitudes toward consumer products. The information and impressions that people have about branded goods represent folk wisdom: they are part of the landscape of symbols with which people are familiar from childhood on, and which they play back to each other in the discussions that precede a major purchase.

Advertising forces the consumer to recognize the values in a product, or it may create artificial values in the form of a symbolic aura. But these values, material or psychological, are constantly being weighed against the reference point of price. Advertising may limit the range of choice to a number of acceptable brands. But the scales can easily be tipped by a price advantage.

Both the studies force us to differentiate among customers according to the way they go about buying. No realistic model of the purchasing process can apply equally well to all people, whatever the degree of their price motivation and whether or not they pursue novelty or whether or not they are brand-loyal.

Timing, repetition, dominance, reach, and frequency represent strategic considerations of quite different dimensions for advertising that is going to be actively consulted and for advertising whose main purpose is to lay a foundation of imagery or information to which a prospective buyer will subconsciously refer.

The timing requirements are different for a purchase decision in which months have been spent in reflection and one made in a matter of hours or minutes, starting merely with the customer's observation that she is running short on a needed item.

Except in the case of sales or specials, when the advertiser can induce a sense of urgency, the problem of timing his messages may be likened to the management of a municipal water system. The relationship is tenuous indeed between each drop of water that trickles into the reservoir and each drop of water that trickles out through a faucet at the other end of the system. Whether any particular drop gets into the reservoir, or whether any particular drop flows out of the faucet makes little difference to the system as a whole. But should the water stop coming in, there would eventually be nothing to come out at the other end.

In advertising we are, in effect, trickling drops, spoonfuls, or buckets of persuasion into the reservoir of product information and opinion from which consumer actions are drawn. We can rarely trace the flow from any one message put into the reservoir to any one purchase act, and any connection between the two exists almost outside of a time dimension.

Wanted: the great creative idea

Although most advertising messages may lose their individual identity soon after they go forth, no advertiser fails to expect from his agency the unique advertisement that will endure forever; and rarely will an agency refuse this assignment. The struggles to complete it become particularly painful in the case of those low-cost frequently purchased packaged goods that constantly face new competitive brands and product changes. Often the old brands are kept faintly alive as the manufacturer puts new ones on the market, until a fresh infusion of promotional effort returns them to the ranks of the effective contenders, freshly baptized as "new and different." William Weilbacher, former vice-chairman of Dancer Fitzgerald Sample, once reported to me the case of just such a product, scheduled for re-introduction:

> Always willing to be convinced, the manufacturer had designed a market test, complete with a fully-produced ad campaign (to be limited to the test areas). At a meeting with the client, the agency presented the comps for the test campaign. The agreed theme was to be centered on convincing consumers that the re-born product is *changed*. The agency man rolled back the cover sheet from the mounted comp [comprehensive or final] layout. The layout was an orthodox four-color bleed page, dominated by a Gallup-Robinson formula illustration area, a formula copy block size, a formula logo size—but a *non*-formula headline running diagonally across the illustration. The head read, "'Ooh, Boppo! How you've changed!"
>
> "Not bad," said the client ad manager. "Let's see the others."
>
> After a few exchanges of blank looks, the agency men explained that the "others" were eliminated by the account group back at the

shop, and that *this* was their concerted choice of their best effort.

"Won't do," admonished the ad manager. "Please bring us some alternative approaches to consider."

After an interval, the same characters met in the same place. The agency man had several veiled comps standing in the chalk trough, leaning against the board. After proper introductions of why the meeting was called, he ceremoniously rolled back the cover sheets on the alternate layout approaches the creative group had produced. As he progressed, a look of disbelief came across the face of the ad manager. All of the layouts were identical to the original one in every respect save one: the headlines. On one layout, the head said, "Ah, Boppo! How You've Changed." Another said, "My Boppo! How You've Changed!" Another, "Goodness, Boppo! How You've Changed!"

Why does the output of extraordinary ads not increase in proportion to the increased volume of advertising? Works of genius are inevitably individual creations rather than the products of collective effort. But the process of producing advertising today is a group activity, both in the initial effort and also in the bureaucratic reviews which are part of the system.

In Albert Lasker's heyday, he could jot a slogan on a piece of paper, show it to a client, and put his advertising in print, just about in that order. Today's creative ideas are discussed in committee, reviewed with account groups, and traipsed before a series of plans boards within the agency. When they pass this ordeal they are subjected to further scrutiny at the client level.

At every stage of the review process, suggestions and additions are made. The final product is subject to further modification based on copy research. Is there any wonder then that innovation in advertising today must often beat the system to find expression and that Great Creative Ideas are something less than universal?

Among the hurdles that such ideas must leap are the restrictions and obstacles presented by copy research. While the principal issues that are involved in *pre*testing have to do with the applicability of the experimental (and hence artificial) results to the real-life competitive marketing environment, the principal issues involved in *post*testing relate to the validity of the measures. Economical measurements like recall and recognition (of which I shall have more to say in Chapter 7) are widely used because they are relatively inexpensive, while measures of persuasiveness and sales effectiveness (as I shall discuss in Chapter 13) are costly and difficult to employ.

Posttest scores can satisfy the curiosity of individual advertisers or agency creative directors as to how a particular advertisement "did" compared to the averages. Apart from this, posttest scores have provided a large pool of information that can be analyzed in relation to the content and style of advertisements. Thus they provide tips that may be related to future performance. For example, the Newspaper Advertising Bureau sponsored the Continuing Study of Newspaper Advertising through Carl Nelson Research between 1939 and 1961, collecting recognition scores on thousands of ads and disseminating the secrets of success derived from comparing those that scored high with those that did poorly. Although similar analyses have been made for other media, with the resulting lore embodied in generations of introductory advertising textbooks, there is no indication that today's ads and commercials are any more persuasive than they used to be before the vast accumulation of posttest data. Measuring services continue to show a tremendous gap between the best- and worst-scoring advertisements in any medium. All of which provides welcome reassurance that there is still room for creative ingenuity in the advertising business.

Expressed in terms of noting scores, the best-read magazine ads yield double the average, while the poorest read ads yield only 27% of the average. What are the magic ingredients that bring advertisements to the top of this incredible range in productivity?

Henry Brenner, now chairman of NPD Research, began his career as a copywriter in a small agency, where his boss, John Ward, took a shine to him and promised, "I'm going to make you into a great patent medicine copywriter." "Oh, I'm willing to work hard," said Brenner. "You don't have to work hard," explained Ward. "Just remember the secret: 'Good for what ails you, if what ails you is what this is good for.' "

Innumerable recipes have been offered for success in advertising, but admonitions on what to avoid are generally more constructive than advice on what to do. And periodic attempts to establish a taxonomy of advertising appeals and techniques are generally not of too much practical help to a creative director confronting a specific marketing assignment. For instance, Julian Simon has identified ten creative strategies, including "command," "obligation," "symbolic association," and "repeated assertion." But these turn out to be unrelated to the performance of magazine ads, as measured by noting scores.[42]

After examining a large number of relevant studies, Charles Atkin groups the factors that affect response to advertising under the headings of "source" and "messages." Among effective persuasion strategies he lists fear appeals, comparative brand claims, explicit recommendations to buy and "stylistic hooks, such as humor, sex, and music." Trustworthiness (established by the use of credible actors in a commercial or ad) is more important than competence (or expertise) or dynamism, reflected in the use of celebrities, attractive models, or unique trade characters.[43]

The venerable Daniel Starch described the readership of ads as determined by "inherent human interests," but when he spelled this out they seemed like truisms: Men have high interest in sports and automobiles and low interest in fashions and food preparation. According to Starch, ads that win high noting scores "have dominant attention stoppers, present people in action centered around the product, have pictures and headlines that provoke curiosity and interest . . . present buyer benefits, are specific, concrete and factual, and are believable."[44]

David Ogilvy and Joel Raphaelson find above average recognition scores for newsworthy ads, ads with story appeal, before and after illustrations, and ads showing the product in use, along with the end result.[45] Long headlines of 13 words or more seem to work better than short ones; blind headlines that are not self-explanatory are below average; headlines that quote somebody are high in memorability. Corporate presidents are more effective spokesmen for their companies than nameless announcers or speakers.[46]

Testimonials by well-known people are as old as advertising itself. Dr. Johnson remarked that "To know that our wine (to use an advertising phrase) is 'of the stock of an Ambassador lately deceased,' heightens its flavour." Ronald Reagan delivered commercials for Chesterfield cigarettes and Van Heusen shirts before he became the corporate spokesman for General Electric between 1954 and 1962. A Gallup and Robinson study in 1979 found that commercials featuring stars scored 35 percent above average in memorability and 10 percent in persuasivenes. However, an Ogilvy & Mather study (with a different group of stars) found that although product recall was 22 percent higher than average, persuasive power was 21 percent below it.

A similar disparity between two criteria of performance surfaced in a study by Herbert Krugman. He compared the responses of 90 people to a Timex watch ad that showed virtually nothing but two watches and to a Pan American Airways ad showing a picturesque European village scene.[47] The more "structured ad" (as Krugman describes it) for Timex produced fewer thoughts than the less structured, more evocative Pan Am ad. It yielded a narrower, more product-oriented range of thoughts and far fewer thoughts expressing a desire for the advertised product. Krugman concludes that "a highly structured or controlled response, while it may be most communicative or informative, may be least motivating or persuasive."

The range in performance is just as enormous for television commercials as it is for print. In a theater test situation, the typical 30-second commercial has an unaided recall level of 51 percent a half-hour after exposure, but the range is from 1 percent to 97 percent.[48] Commercials score differently when tested after multiple exposures than they do with a conventional single-exposure test.[49]

One leading packaged-goods advertiser who has conducted hundreds of tests of his own commercials and those of his leading competitor has found that though they produced the same scores on average, there are wide disparities between the two brands at any given point in time. The essential thematic content remains the same for these two close competitors, so the execution is all-important.

How 200 women watched 17 television commercials was studied with an eye movement device by Cunningham & Walsh in 1977. The analysis concluded that the first second of a commercial is critical to capture attention, while in the closing seconds attention is often dispersed. Viewers often ignore superimposed text ("supers") and closeups of labels, while "packages get visually lost when displayed by spokesmen." Fewer than half the viewers look at the product when its use is demonstrated while an announcer is talking. (Mouths get most of the attention when people talk.)

Social psychologist William McGuire has summarized the list of "body language" cues that make personalities attractive and believable: pupil dilation, smiles, forward body lean, head nods. Confidence is built with low eye contact while speaking but full eye contact when listening, relaxed posture, strong gestures, and an avoidance of questioning intonations.[50] But knowing all this does not necessarily equip a professional actor or nonprofessional corporate spokesman to put it into effect in front of the TV camera.

DuPont researcher Robert Grass reports that for about nine-tenths of the commercials tested by the CONPAAD technique (which I mentioned on page 86), "there is a straight-line relationship between attention and learning. . . . How much the viewer learns from a commercial depends directly on how much attention he pays to it."[51] People seem to carry away about seven points or "message links" from a commercial, no matter how simple or complex its content. Grass concludes that "we'd better be careful about cluttering up our commercial with extraneous information, because the viewer is going to learn what is easiest for him to learn, not necessarily what *we want* him to learn."

In 809 commercials tested by Mapes and Ross, brand preference change (as a result of exposure) was associated with certain techniques: problem-solving, humor, relevant characters, "slice of life" (involving the conversion of a skeptic), news, "candid camera" testimonials, and demonstrations. Celebrities were memorable, but unsuccessful in influencing brand preference. Commercials that started with a key idea were most effective. Cartoons and animation worked well with children but not with adults. "Supers" added to effectiveness if they reinforced the main point. Changes of scene produced below average effects and so did commercials that failed to show the package or that ended without showing the brand name.

As we saw earlier, some of the most controversial aspects of advertising involve the balance of reason and emotion: facts vs. puffery, hard sell vs. soft sell. There is little indication that generalities apply in this area. In the context of other similar messages, the effects of a hard-sell message decay rapidly, while a soft-sell message in the same context has less initial impact but builds up over time.[52] Emotional or "feeling" commercials are less well recalled the day after exposure than those that are more cerebral in content. (But this difference does not hold for magazine ads.)[53]

Magazine automobile ads containing puffery produce readership scores no higher or lower than those that don't.[54] A newspaper supermarket ad was more effective when it compared prices and mentioned the store's own weak points than when it simply knocked the competition.[55]

Ogilvy & Mather, in a 1975 study of 450 women, found comparative ads more confusing than the norm and more likely to produce incorrect brand identification from TV viewers. And comparative advertising is not regarded as more informative than other kinds of ads. An analysis of 524 television commercials by David Aaker and Donald Norris found that those perceived to be informative are considered convincing, effective, and interesting and quite distinct from commercials that are disliked or that are regarded as either entertaining or "warm."[56] Informativeness turns out to be unrelated to mentions of price, reports of government tests, discussion of product components, or expert testimonials. In short, viewers appear to consider advertising informative when they like it as well as the other way around.

Communication and persuasion are matters of substance and style: What to say and how to say it. The study of substance concerns the public's motivations and how they can be aroused, appealed to, or even manipulated and exploited. The study of style concerns the technique with which advertisements are designed.

It is never possible to separate the two in practice, because technique is itself a matter of managing motivations. But technique also involves a great many factors that have little or no connection with the symbolic overtones of the advertising art or copy, with the skillful selection of themes, models, and sets. Technique has to do with the eye's or the ear's ability to distinguish the essence of the message from the background. It is connected with the readability of type, the visibility of the package, the audibility of a jingle's lyrics, with the esthetic balance of the layout, with the ease of visual or aural access to the various elements of the ad.

Principles of good advertising technique are easier to derive from theories of perception and cognition than the principles of effective substance from theories of motivation or persuasion.

Just as there are valid and established principles to copywriting, ad layout, and commercial production, there are tricks of the trade in every craft that contributes to finished advertising.

One can follow all the shibboleths of good technique—prominent product identification, dominant headline, central focal point, avoidance of distraction—and yet when all is said and done, the success with which those principles are executed always depends on how the individual ad's substance is presented. There are infinite possible combinations, so each new effort must be tested from scratch.

We know a lot more than Aristotle did about specific mechanisms of communication, but we have not improved our ability to communicate or to persuade. This is because every message is unique, and the art of forming it has to be learned all over again every time it takes shape. The reason why every message is unique is that it always occurs in a different context.

Even though the creative individual knows exactly what he wishes to express and knows all the technical tricks for achieving his expression, the nuances of communication are such that he can never be sure of success. And this is why, no matter how much we know or how much we learn about what makes an ad memorable or persuasive, the rules have to be bent or revised every time to accommodate the real article. There is no single truth in persuasion. It has to be found out over and over again to suit each task and each occasion.

I doubt whether anyone has ever written great advertising copy as a result of reading a book by Claude Hopkins or David Ogilvy on how to do it. Studying the work of such established masters is part of the basic training in any craft, of course. The copy cub who dissects the latest output of this year's Hot Creative Agency is (properly) picking up pointers that he will put to good use later on, but this kind of study can not evoke the copywriting Muse, just as no amount of reading Tolstoy or Proust will train anyone to write a great novel.

Advertising is different from fiction, you may be thinking, and indeed it is, for so much of it is written and forgotten every day. For a writer of routine reports, training can make the difference between copy that is acceptable and copy that gets rejected. But the textbook rules of advertising are constantly being violated by the copywriters who have a Great Idea.

Promise a strong consumer benefit! Don't confuse copy claims! Keep the headline short! Have one dominant illustration! Don't use long sentences or big words! Be specific! Avoid cuteness and unusual references! All of these rules vanish into the air when we look at individual campaigns. The Great Idea that catches the public fancy never comes by the book and never comes from perusal of what worked well in the past.

Does this imply that the advertising novice can forget about principles of persuasion and trust only his own inner light to guide his path? Not in the least. Perhaps the first two basics of salesmanship are to show people what you want them to buy and to ask them to buy it. And yet a lot of advertising fails to do either.

Of 150 commercials for nationally advertised products analyzed in 1974 by Arthur Bellaire, two out of three failed to ask the consumer to try or buy the advertised product. The product was visible for an average of 16 out of the 30 seconds, with the brand logo visible for only six of those seconds.*

Every creative man in an advertising agency has the goal of the Great Idea before him every time he confronts a blank sheet of white paper or a fresh storyboard pad. And yet as a practical matter he is rarely convinced that he is going to achieve it.

Look at and listen to the advertising around you today. What proportion of it is fresh, inspired, or unusual? There is a good reason why the proportion is so small. Unusual ideas carry a strong risk of being unusually bad as well as unusually good.

Advertising plans are made by businessmen, they involve large sums of money, and there is a strong conservative resistance to the off-beat, to breaking with the formula. Why shouldn't there be? Off-beat ideas, especially untested off-beat ideas, have a long record of failure.

There are a number of reasons why Great Ideas are as rarely visible in ads as they are in the fine arts. Much of American advertising is placed by retailers cataloguing their wares and offering specific factual descriptions of features and prices. The most brilliant retail advertisements rarely penetrate beyond their own home markets and thus for the most part are invisible to the country as a whole.

Many fine national advertisements also have a highly restricted audience because they are aimed at minor segments of the market and confined to media that reach special small groups of potential customers.

Finally, the Great Idea itself wears out in practice. It is embellished and varied in subsequent repetitions of the same campaign; it is adapted from one media form to another and always loses something of its original vitality in the process. And it is likely to be imitated to the point where it appears overly familiar and hackneyed and generates ridicule or resentment.

Needless to say, the Great Idea invariably has some functional relationship to the product advertised. Even when the Idea involves a gimmick, this becomes meaningful only in relation to the fantasies it releases with regard to the product.

---

*Advertising Age, December 30, 1974. In terms of technique, 36 percent of the commercials involved an on-camera spokesman, 31 percent employed a demonstration, and 23 percent showed a "slice of life" (a mini-story suggesting the value of the product. Typically, a commercial showed two principals on camera). Nine percent used humor, and 5 percent animation, but 44 percent had some kind of music.

Advertising ideas misfire when the gimmickry buries or overwhelms the product or contradicts its appeal. People are attracted to what's funny. Two-thirds of all humorous magazine ads measured by Starch between 1976 and 1979 scored above the norm in recognition and four out of five in readership.[57] But one of the hardest elements to introduce successfully into advertising is humor; when it is too robust it threatens or blanks out the product, when it is too gentle or intellectual it carries the risk of being ignored altogether. Examining the evidence from a variety of laboratory experiments and field studies, Brian Sternthal and Samuel Craig conclude that while humor may get attention, it may also interfere with the understanding of the advertiser's message by distracting or confusing the audience.[58] Humor may facilitate persuasion by creating a good mood and putting the advertiser in an agreeable environment and making him appear more believable. But its power to persuade is no greater than that of a serious approach. Context is all-important here; the serious reader is not prepared for levity on the facing page, whereas the entertainment-minded listener or viewer is equally unprepared to change his mood to deadpan earnestness when the commercial comes on.

If Great Ideas in advertising are few and far between, there are even fewer that are considered great by marketing men and copywriters alike. A great advertising campaign is, by definition, one that advertising professionals admire aesthetically or intellectually, and not necessarily one that sells the client's product line. A creatively undistinguished advertising campaign may sell a lot of merchandise as part of an overall effort that involves far more than the copy theme or execution. (For one thing it probably involves a good product as well as a substantial advertising investment.)

Hard-nosed marketers are fond of expressing disdain for campaigns that win awards but fail at the cash register. They merely choose to ignore the fact that an even higher percentage of campaigns that don't win awards *also* fail at the cash register.

A Great Idea in advertising has coherence, simplicity, and unity. For this reason I think it is inconsistent with the growing tendency to define advertising goals in highly specific terms that can then be used as yardsticks for scientific evaluation.

This harks back to the tired businessman's ancient lament (maliciously attributed to John Wanamaker) that half his advertising budget is being wasted but he doesn't know which half. The preoccupation with assessment is, as I shall point out later, at odds with the great difficulty of making a meaningful evaluation of advertising's unique contribution to sales. It causes the goals of advertising to be redefined, shifting attention away from sales or market share statistics (the playthings of competitive action) and focusing on goals involving changes in awareness, information, and opinion of Our Brand—changes that *can* be measured and compared under different conditions or at different points of time.

Alas, advertising agencies are often in business to make the client happy, and many can stay in business only by keeping him happy over the short run. Many a bad commercial or ad has been approved by an agency plans board simply because pretests show it will get a good score from Burke or Starch or Gallup and Robinson (if these be the idols whom the client venerates). By similar logic, why cannot advertising campaigns be designed to raise "unaided recall of Our Brand's slogan" from 4 percent to 6.5 percent in a three-month period, or to raise its share of mentions as "one of the best" from 23 percent to 31 percent?

The Great Idea does not lend itself to such petty and transitory goals, however amenable they may be to measurement. It belongs to the realm of lore and fable, which measurement can only distort and falsify. How can one measure the effects of the Three Bears and Goldilocks, or of Red Riding Hood and the Wolf? Why then measure the effects of Rinso White! Rinso White! Jell-O again! Burma-Shave, Burma-Shave! Lucky Strike Green has gone to war! I can't believe I ate the whole thing! or any of the more recent additions to the mythology of American commerce?

The Great Ideas in advertising are indistinguishable from the other elements of popular culture that are deeply embedded in our collective experience of the mass media. In the minds of all who grow up and participate in a world of half-real, half-fictional personalities and symbols, the presence of the Marlboro cowboy, Colonel Sanders or Frank Perdue is to be taken for granted as much as Frank Sinatra or Donald Duck. All alike are regarded as universally known and surrounded by a set of universally understood associations.

The Great Idea in advertising gives a product this kind of commonly known, clearly defined character. It keeps its identity vivid and positive. It gives it new overtones of freshness when it threatens to become tired.

Whatever the unique requirements of the product, the creative idea becomes persuasive only in an appropriate media environment. In a brilliant marketing plan, the message, the medium, the target audience, and the product attributes all fit together like pieces in a Chinese puzzle.

Notes

1. Robert B. Zajonc, "Feeling and Thinking: Preferences Need No Inferences," *American Psychologist*, 35, 2 (February 1980): 151-75.
2. Lloyd H. Silverman, a Veterans Administration psychologist, reported in 1981 that schizophrenic patients respond differently to the "tachistoscopic flashing of the message 'People arguing' than to 'Mommy' (or in the case of women, 'Daddy') and I are one." (This implied that the message was coming through.) His report aroused a mixed reaction from other experimenters who tried, in some cases unsuccessfully, to replicate them.
3. Timothy Moore, "Subliminal Advertising: What You See Is What You Get," *Journal of Marketing*, 46, 2 (Spring 1982): 38-47.
4. *The Hidden Persuaders* (New York: David McKay Company, 1957).
5. Packard, *The Hidden Persuaders*, p. 2.
6. Herbert Kay, "How To Get False Media Audience Figures Without Really Trying," address to the Media Research Directors Association, October 19, 1966, New York, N.Y.
7. *The Strategy of Desire* (New York: Doubleday & Company, Inc., 1960). For a more recent statement from another leading practitioner of motivation research, cf. Burleigh Gardner, *A Conceptual Framework for Advertising* (Chicago: Crain Communications, Inc., 1982).
8. Unpublished communication.
9. Charles Winick, "Sex and Advertising," *Sexual Behavior* (April 1971): 36-79.
10. Irwin Gross, "Should the Advertiser Spend More on Creating Advertising?" Paper

presented to the Advertising Research Foundation Conference, New York City, November 14, 1967.

11. See the earlier reference on p. 49.

12. Robert C. Grass, "Prediction of Commercial Field Performance Using Laboratory Techniques," Paper presented to the Association of National Advertisers, New York City, October, 1972.

13. Lipstein and Neelankavil, *Television Advertising Copy Research Practices.*

14. An early review of 23 studies by Jack Haskins found virtually no relationship between persuasion and recall. (*Cf.* Jack B. Haskins, "Factual Recall as a Measure of Advertising Effectiveness," *Journal of Advertising Research,* 4, 1 (March 1964): 2-8.) Similar findings were reported by Calvin Hodock for studies done at Benton & Bowles and at BBD&O (Calvin L. Hodock, "Predicting On-Air Recall from Theater Tests," *Journal of Advertising Research,* 16, 6 (December 1976): 25-32.) and by Shirley Young for studies done at Grey Advertising. Her correlation was .05. (Shirley Young, "Copy Testing Without Magic Numbers," *Journal of Advertising Research,* 12, 1 (February 1972): 3-12.) Roy G. Stout of Coca-Cola reported similar results. (Roy G. Stout, "Some Things We've Learned from Experimental Advertising Testing," Presentation delivered to the ANA Advertising Research Workshop, New York, 1980.)

15. Leo Bogart, B. Stuart Tolley, and Frank Orenstein, "What One Little Ad Can Do," *Journal of Advertising Research,* 10, 4 (August 1970): 3-13.

16. Advertising Research Foundation, *A Study of Printed Advertising Rating Methods* (New York, 1956).

17. For recognition the rank order correlation was .13; for recall .03.

18. Harold L. Ross, Jr., "Recall versus Persuasion: An Answer," *Journal of Advertising Research,* 22, 1 (February/March 1982): 13-16.

19. Cited by Thomas Dillon, "What I Don't Know About Television," Paper presented to the ANA Television Workshop, New York City, February 25, 1975.

20. Michael C. Corballis, "Laterality and Myth," *American Psychologist,* 35, 3 (March 1980): 284-95.

21. Marcel Kinsbourne, "Hemispheric Specialization and the Growth of Human Understanding," *American Psychologist,* 37, 4 (April 1982): 411-420.

22. Quoted in *Atlas World Press Review,* May 1977, pp. 23-26.

23. Herbert E. Krugman, "Brain Wave Measures of Media Involvement," *Journal of Advertising Research,* 11, 1 (February 1971): 3-9.

24. Herbert E. Krugman, "Memory Without Recall, Exposure Without Perception," *Journal of Advertising Research,* 17, 4 (August 1977): 11.

25. Valentine Appel, Sidney Weinstein, and Curt Weinstein, "Brain Activity and Recall of TV Advertising," *Journal of Advertising Research,* 19, 4 (August 1979): 7-15.

26. Herbert E. Krugman, "Media Imagery: Perception After Exposure," Paper presented to the AMA Attitude Research Conference, Carlsbad, CA, March 4, 1980.

27. Sidney Weinstein, "A Review of Brain Hemisphere Research," *Journal of Advertising Research,* 22, 3 (June/July 1982): 59-63.

28. E. A. Rockey, W. F. Greene, and E. A. Perold, "Attention, Memory, and Attitudinal Reactions to Television Commercials Under Single and Multiple Exposure Conditions as Measured by Brain Research," Paper presented to Advertising Research Foundation Conference, New York City, 1980.

29. S. P. Raj, "The Effects of Advertising on High- and Low-Loyalty Consumer Segments," *Journal of Consumer Research,* 9, 1 (June 1982): 77-85.

30. Gerard O. Cavallo and M. Lewis Temares, "Brand Switching at the Point of Purchase," *Journal of Retailing,* 45, 3 (Fall 1969): 27-36.

31. *American Druggist,* June 6, 1966.

32. The following section is adapted from Leo Bogart and Charles Lehman, "What Makes a Brand Name Familiar?" *Journal of Marketing Research*, 10, 1 (February 1973): 17-22.

33. The aggregate correlation was −.05. In fact, the heavy weight of brand advertising on television was not reflected in a higher level of brand awareness among women, who receive the lion's share of television advertising impressions. Those who viewed four or more hours "yesterday" mentioned an average of 27.6 brands; medium viewers (2-4 hours) mentioned 29.0 brands; those who watched fewer than two hours named 28.1 brands.

34. This bit of wisdom was recalled by Rosser Reeves at Politz's memorial service in 1982.

35. Cf. "How to Build a Creative Strategy" in the opening section of the first-rate primer by Ogilvy & Mather's Kenneth Roman and Jane Maas, *How to Advertise* (New York: St. Martin's Press, 1976).

36. *Reality in Advertising* (New York: Alfred A. Knopf, 1961).

37. *Confessions of an Advertising Man* (New York: Atheneum, 1963).

38. *Advertising Age*, August 23, 1965.

39. The proportions found by Booz Allen & Hamilton were essentially unchanged since 1968, when a similar survey had been made. (*Marketing and Media Decisions*, May 1982, p. 48.)

40. An analysis by the European Industrial Management Association of 97 technical innovations showed that the failure rate among those picked by top management was over 80 percent; for those picked by the technical staff, it was 74 percent. But among those picked by the commercial staff (the marketers), the failure rate was only 45 percent.

41. These considerations suggest the desirability of using a number of small-space ads on different pages within the same issue of a newspaper. If all the ads were placed before the reader at the same time, i.e., on the same page, the likelihood of intriguing him would be less. If the same ads were scattered over a longer period of time, the normal processes of memory attrition would reduce the probability of this kind of carry-over of attention. If they were spread out over a very long period of time, the probability would also be less. Putting them together within a period of 44 minutes (the average newspaper reading time) heightens the possibility of getting the message across. In the newspaper, the use of small-space units has another advantage: it permits the placement of ads in sections known to have particularly high traffic among men or women. Thus the copy, illustration, and headline can appeal to different segments of the total audience reached. (Comparable strategic considerations would obviously apply in introducing a new product through other media.)

42. Alan D. Fletcher and Sherilyn K. Ziegler, "Creative Strategy and Magazine Ad Readership," *Journal of Advertising Research*, 18, 1 (February 1978): 29-33.

43. Charles K. Atkin, "Television, Advertising, and Socialization; The Consumer Roles," in David Pearl, Lorraine Bouthilet, and Joyce Lazar, eds., *Television and Behavior: Ten Years of Scientific Progress and Implications for the 80's*, Vol. 2 (Washington, D.C.: Government Printing Office, 1982).

44. Daniel Starch, *Measuring Advertising Readership and Results* (New York: McGraw-Hill, 1966, p. 176).

45. David Ogilvy and Joel Raphaelson, "Research on Advertising Techniques that Work—and Don't Work," *Harvard Business Review*, 60, 4 (July/August 1982): 12-20.

46. Vicki Reuben, Carol Mager, and Hershey H. Friedman, "Company President versus Spokesperson in Television Commercials," *Journal of Advertising Research*, 22, 4 (August-September 1982): 31-33.

47. Herbert E. Krugman, "Processes Underlying Exposure to Advertising," *American Psychologist*, 23, 4 (April 1968): 245-53. Krugman showed both magazine ads and television commercials to respondents at home and asked what thoughts they evoked. He reports

0.5 "connections" per ad exposure. (As will be described later, "connections" represent verbal linkages to the individual respondent and may be taken as an indication of personal involvement.) Negative thoughts were reported for about a third of the television exposures, but to none of the print ads tested except those for cigarettes.

48. Ray Tortolani, "Testing Your TV Spot? Once is Not Enough," *Advertising Age*, November 15, 1976. A research firm, McCollum-Spielman, reports similar results.

49. McCollum-Spielman & Co., Inc., "Multiple Exposure Test Needed to Evaluate Commercials," *Marketing News*, September 31, 1979, pp. 13-14.

50. William J. McGuire, "New Developments in Psychology as They Affect Advertising," paper presented to the Advertising Research Foundation Conference, New York City, 1982.

51. Robert Grass, "Prediction of Commercial Field Performance Using Laboratory Techniques."

52. M.R. Leippe, A.G. Greenwald and M.H. Baumgardner, "Delayed Persuasion as a Consequence of Associative Interference: A Context Confusion Effect," (Unpublished paper cited by William J. McGuire, "New Developments in Psychology").

53. Hubert A. Zielske, "Does Day-After Recall Penalize 'Feeling' Ads?" *Journal of Advertising Research*, 22, 1 (February/March 1982): 19-22.

54. Bruce G. Vanden Bergh and Leonard N. Reid, "Puffery and Magazine Ad Readership," *Journal of Marketing*, 44, 2 (Spring 1980): 70-81.

55. William Swinyard, "The Interaction Between Comparative Advertising and Copy Claim Validation," *Journal of Marketing Research*, 18 (May 1981): 175-86.

56. David A. Aaker and Donald Norris, "Characteristics of TV Commercials Perceived as Informative," *Journal of Advertising Research* 22, 2 (April/May 1982): 61-70.

57. Thomas J. Madden and Mark G. Weinberger, "The effects of humor on attention in magazine advertising," *Journal of Advertising*, 11, 3 (1982): 8-14.

58. Brian Sternthal and C. Samuel Craig, "Humor in Advertising," *Journal of Marketing*, 37, 4 (October 1973): 12-18. Another study of 2,056 television commercials found that 15 percent used humor, related to the product in half the cases. *Cf.* J. Patrick Kelly and Paul J. Solomon, "Humor in Television Advertising," *Journal of Advertising*, 4, 3 (1975): 31.

Chapter 6
Understanding Media

In the cryptic words of the late cultural historian, critic, and oracle Marshall McLuhan, "the medium is the message."[1] The content of the medium communicates only in the manner that the form dictates, and symbolic meanings are inseparable from the unique kind of sensory stimulation that the medium employs.

In McLuhan's words, "Our conventional response to all media, namely that it is how they are used that counts, is the numb stance of the technological idiot. For the 'content' of a medium is like the juicy piece of meat carried by the burglar to distract the watchdog of the mind. . . . The effect of the movie form is not related to its program content."

For McLuhan, the "Gutenberg Galaxy" of communication through print, the impersonal symbol, and the individual's eye are giving way to a new era. Broadcasting brings mankind back to an earlier epoch of communication through the direct contact of speech.

Advertisers have long appreciated that each medium puts its characteristic stamp on the messages it disseminates, although they would be reluctant to admit that there isn't a little something of the message left to work just for their benefit!

When we refer to "messages" in advertising, we customarily have in mind communication units in the major media—newspaper and magazine ads, television and radio commercials, outdoor or transit posters; we rarely consider window displays and promotion devices, or the brand names and labels emblazoned on products and packages. Such casual reminders represent a very large proportion of the total number of product messages presented to people each day, though few of them represent direct attempts at persuasion in the sense, say, of a "hard sell" TV commercial.

The influence of conventional media advertising can best be understood if we consider the consumer's response to packaging, store displays, and sales promotion devices. A consumer may remain oblivious, for all intents and purposes, to the advertising message on the wall calendar, the ash tray, or the matchbook, however often he looks at it. He accepts such messages as part of the environment. The subtle penetration of these messages is demonstrated when the consumer encounters the product or brand in another context. The familiar name encountered in an unfamiliar setting may produce the little "shock of incongruity" that trips it into conscious awareness.

Unfortunately, the word "message" applies equally to a brand name on a soup label seen on the pantry shelf and to a 30-second television commercial or a six-page blockbuster gatefold ad in a magazine. The advertising lexicon contains no intermediate terms to differentiate the varieties of communications experience embodied in advertisements of different dimensions in different media. In spite of this, advertising plans characteristically compare media messages by such criteria as coverage, frequency of exposure, and cost per thousand—just as though the units being compared weighed equally in the balance.

Distinguishing media capabilities

Which medium is best? No question in advertising is easier to answer, the answer being, "it all depends." It depends on the product, on the marketing target, on the budget available. Many experts would also say it depends on the copy theme and creative approach, and in practice it often does. But there are few copy points, to judge by my own experience, which cannot be well expressed in a variety of media, even though each may make its own special technical demands in expressing the story best.

Perhaps the best evidence that no particular medium is indispensable to an advertiser comes from the experience of the cigarette companies after their broadcast advertising was banned by the Federal Communications Commission in 1971. In the preceding year, television and radio had accounted for 74 percent of cigarette advertising budgets. Subsequently, advertising was switched into print and outdoor advertising and budgets reduced. (There was also a shift to assorted promotional efforts, like sponsorship of stock car racing.) Per capita consumption of cigarettes has been adversely influenced by the health warning label on the product and by antismoking campaigns and positively affected by the growing number of working women who have become smokers in response to a changed daily environment. But there is no indication that the sharp change in media policy made it any harder to sell cigarettes, nor did it shake up brand shares (which in any case were being shaken up by the proliferation of new brands).

In the selection of media, advertisers may be powerfully influenced by corporate rate discount structures devised to lure them into placing all or most of their eggs into the basket of a particular publication or publishing house. Still, the larger the advertiser and the more diversified his product line, the less likely he is to think of which one medium to spend his money in and the more likely he is to think in terms of a combination of media to accomplish all the tasks he has in mind. There are exceptions to this rule, of course. Procter and Gamble habitually (and most successfully) puts over 90 percent of its advertising dollars into television in support of a wide array of new and established products. But most of the time, the big advertiser has to use a number of media simply because his advertising objectives are apt to be complicated.

The small advertiser may also have complex marketing problems, but his ability to spread out among a number of media is sharply limited by his budget. In many media his dollars do not buy him as much as do those of his big competitors, in quantity or in quality of position. If he markets his wares in only a restricted area, he can turn to city magazines or to magazines that issue regional editions. Through the sectional editions now offered by 205 magazines, in up to 111 segments (for *Newsweek*), the regional advertiser now has an extraordinary degree of flexibility, but he will have to pay a premium over the national rate per reader and the distribution of the edition may or may not coincide well with his own sales territory. Above and beyond any financial disadvantages, the small advertiser who divides his budget among the media is apt to be spreading himself too thin to make any substantial impact with any one of them.

In evaluating a medium, the advertiser must think in terms of what *he* will get out of it in terms of position, timing, scheduling, and public attention, rather than of the medium in the abstract. In practice, glamorous media vehicles or the advertiser's own favorites may find their way on to a list because of their aura rather than their inherent suitability.

Comparatively little of the total effort expended to research, promote, and sell media is made on behalf of media as the advertiser and agency consider them. Such efforts are made by the advertising bureaus that every medium has set up to serve its collective interests. Most media research, promotion, and selling are used by one vehicle within a medium in its competitive struggle to win an advantage over other vehicles in the *same* medium—to get on a list ahead of their confreres. Yet rarely (except in network television) is a decision made to use a vehicle until *after* a basic decision has first been made to use the medium of which it is a part.

Advertising planners are strongly tempted to think of media in the idealized and highly differentiated way that is fostered by the media themselves in their promotion and selling. Because each media communications environment is thought of at its prototypical best, the qualitative or psychological differences among the media may be exaggerated.

The true difficulty of sharply differentiating between the qualitative environments of one medium and another appears if we accept two principles: (1) for most people the mass media represent a relatively trivial pastime rather than significant aesthetic or cathartic experiences; (2) much advertising is incidental to, or actually at odds with, the audience's primary purpose in reading, viewing, or listening.

This latter principle must be refined to distinguish between print and broadcasting. Advertising is perceived differently in the heterogeneous visual context of print than in the one-dimensional flow of broadcasting. The audience does not make the same kind of clear distinction between advertising and other content in the newspaper that it makes in the case of television.[2]

In broadcast media, commercial messages are dispersed in time and station position throughout the day. Even though commercials get an excellent response when they are unusually humorous, dramatic, informative, or attractive, it is not ordinarily conceivable that a viewer or listener might tune in to a program for the purpose of hearing or watching a commercial.

By contrast, advertising in print media may be as avidly consulted and sought for as editorial content. Classified advertising sections in the newspaper are based on this premise. Newspaper readers, especially women, use the paper as a daily catalogue of merchandise, comparative prices, sales, and style information. Advertising in specialized magazines and industrial publications serves a similar function of keeping the reader informed about products and services in which his occupation or avocation give him a direct interest.

Media may be differentiated in terms of the size and characteristics of their audiences, their communications capabilities, their cost and flexibility of usage by the advertiser, and the environment they provide the advertising message. Today all U.S. media are mass media, although individual media vehicles are not. Ninety-nine percent of all American households have a radio, and 82 percent of the adult population are reported to listen, on the average, 3.3 hours per day. Ninety-eight percent of the households have one or more TV sets, and 84 percent of the adults watch TV for an average of 3.3 hours on a given day.[3] Seventy-five percent of the households receive at least one newspaper on the average day, 77 percent of these home-delivered on a regular basis. Over the course of five weekdays, 89 percent of all adults read a paper, and 67 percent read one on an average day (an average of 1.2 per reader). At least one single weekly or monthly issue of the current magazines is read by 90 percent of the adults.

Beneath the surface of these general averages lurk great differences in the audience sizes of individual media vehicles. On a single TV network in prime evening hours (7:30–11:00 p.m. EST) one week in September, 1983, the range of Nielsen ratings was from 22 to 6. Magazines range in size downward from *Reader's Digest* with 18.3 million circulation in 1983 to those with only a few thousand subscribers. The New York *Daily News* had a circulation of 1.5 million in the same year, but the median U.S. daily paper was in the 14,000 circulation bracket.

Along with this variation of size goes a considerable variation of audience composition. Generally speaking, the print media make their greatest appeal to those of highest education and social status, while broadcasting's appeal assumes the reverse direction. (In the heaviest TV-viewing fifth of the adult population, according to SMRB, the median household income in 1981 was $14,277, while among the lightest viewing fifth it was $23,748.[4])

Of course, such generalizations may cut no ice as far as any particular advertiser is concerned, for within any medium he can seek to be selective in choosing those vehicles that give him the kind of audiences he wants to reach. An exception occurs in single-newspaper or single-radio station towns, where he has the sole option of using the medium or not using it. Another exception occurs when he buys spot television without current information about viewership for his program/adjacency positions. In that case, the people he is most apt to reach, and reach most often are the people who in general watch TV most. And of course with such media as billboards and car cards, the advertiser has only a limited option—by selecting poster locations—to concentrate his fire on less than the whole population at once.

How media define markets

"Market" may well be the most popular word in advertising circles, and yet it is used to mean a number of different things. A market is a place, but it is often also a state of mind that characterizes people of common tastes and buying propensities. As such, it is apt to be made by—and be defined in terms of—the mass media of communication and advertising.

Markets have traditionally been thought of in geographical terms, as focal points of a distribution network. We have always had to define them in terms of the accessibility and availability of various forms of transportation along which both customers and goods could conveniently and economically be brought together.

Historically, markets (like towns) developed at breaks in transportation which became the logical stopping and crossing points for travelers with different types of merchandise and services to exchange. When we think of markets in today's terms, we normally think of towns or cities which, as agglomerations of populations, are reservoirs of buying power and central points of distribution for the goods and services to be bought and consumed.

A broader definition of the market probably found its first expression in the concept of the "retail trading zone"—the area surrounding any population point within which people tend to do the bulk of their shopping. By extension, a market may be defined not only as a town or town trading zone, but as a region with some geographic homogeneity (held together by a web of transportation and communication or by a common historical and social heritage) like the American South. Markets are also limited by political boundaries. Thus Fort Worth and Dallas make up a metropolitan agglomeration although they are by no means a single market in an economic sense.*

A market may correspond to something existing in nature (like an island) or constructed by man's artifice (like a railroad line), but it may also exist in terms that no one can describe in any physical sense at all. It may have to be defined— and increasingly *is* defined—in terms of the spread of advertising media rather than in terms of distribution areas. When an advertiser gears his planning to "the New England market" or "the Southern California market," he is actually conjuring up something that acquires reality only because his particular objectives require it.

The old geographic definition of the market, as a town and its hinterland, has been shaken in this century by two parallel developments: one is the enormous expansion of world population, reflected in highly developed countries by the growth of metropolitan regions and the expansion into vast semi-urban areas along the main lines of transport (exemplified by the English Midlands, the Ruhr Valley, or the almost continuous series of towns that stretch from Portland, Maine, to Norfolk, Virginia). The isolated communities of another period have been replaced by the growth of these vast interurban belts.

The second major development has been the tremendous improvement of systems that permit the movement of people and goods over vast areas with greater speed and less effort. This development carries with it an important

---

*The government-defined Metropolitan Statistical Area (MSA) consists of a central county with a city of 50,000 or an urbanized area of that size (and a total population of 100,000), together with adjacent counties closely connected by economic and social ties. (In New England the definition is modified.) Contiguous metropolitan areas are known as Primary MSA's, and grouped as Consolidated MSA's.

implication for the definition of a market. It means that the most effective and economically practicable distribution range for almost any commodity (including even the most perishable) can be extended far beyond the area surrounding the point of production.

Another force is working in the same direction. Modern machinery and mass production techniques make possible the fabrication of identical standardized products not only at different points in time, but at different points in space. It is possible to produce virtually identical cars or tubes of toothpaste or bottles of Coca-Cola working with identical equipment in different towns of the same country or even in different countries.

All this has meant that the problems of distribution for any fair-sized manufacturer are less and less apt to be matters of logistics, shipment, and warehousing. More and more they have become problems of retail penetration—getting goods into the right kinds of outlets and displayed in the right kind of way. Paralleling this change, the problems of advertising have become less and less those of reaching the people who live where the goods can be bought and more those of pin-pointing efforts to reach the people who want the goods or who can be persuaded to want them. Accordingly, markets have increasingly tended to become defined in the minds of manufacturers in terms of consumer characteristics rather than in terms of geography—in terms of what kinds of people the potential customers are rather than where they happen to live. Concepts like the "youth market," the "black market," the "Hispanic market," or the "senior citizens market" are examples of such nongeographical market definitions. When large heterogeneous sectors of the population are lumped together in this manner, the word *market* might just as well be dropped out of the designation altogether.

In the big city, human relations are impersonal, and people do not necessarily know their next door neighbors. Friends are apt to be people who share the same field of work, church, school, political preference, or hobby, rather than the families next door. In the suburbs, community life is re-established, but on a much different basis than in the towns of the horse-and-buggy era.

By 1980, the small towns of rural areas were growing faster than cities or suburbs, reflecting the spread of a service-oriented economy. Central cities were fast losing their commercial dominance, their purchasing power, and their civic health. With the growth of shopping centers and the diffusion of industry to the fringes of metropolitan regions, it becomes possible for people living on the outskirts of the great city to live their lives without ever venturing to its center. And yet, though they tread their way gingerly around the edges, their lives are still part of that fantastic web of tangled human and business relationships that is the modern metropolis.

It is apparent, then, that the bonds that connect people and make them similar as customers are increasingly less apt to be bonds of place than bonds of common character or common interest. An advertising director of a company in New Orleans has more in common with the advertising director of a company in Denver than either has with, say, a baker, a brick layer, or an insurance salesman in his own city.

The modern community can no longer be delimited by the artificially set municipal boundaries drawn with a surveyor's rule a century or more ago. People in complex modern industrial society live segmented lives in which they are simultaneously members of different communities corresponding to different kinds of activities or interests. We all go through life playing the different roles appropriate to the different situations in which we find ourselves and the people we are with. Similarly, we are members of audiences for different mass media and respond appropriately to each type of media exposure. I am a different person, in effect, when watching television with my family than when reading the newspaper on the bus, and I am a different (though not necessarily a better) man when I read the editorial page than when I read the comics.

To say that media make markets means nothing more than that they create common interests and set common standards of taste. They tend to attract people who are alike socially or culturally or in certain dimensions of personality. The same psychological elements may help to dictate or influence a person's choice of a medium as help to define his use of a product or choice of a brand.

Every advertising medium tries as hard as it can to define a market for itself by making advertisers and audiences alike conscious of something which, for practical purposes, may never before have existed. A radio station may establish itself as "the Voice of Northeast Lower Something," in order to carve out for itself a lucrative area of doing business, even though the people living in that area may have no sense of common identity other than that created by the medium itself. A magazine like *Vogue* or *Sports Illustrated* may actually create in the minds of its readers a feeling akin to that of membership in some kind of secret order. And it is in terms of these characteristics that make for a common life style that advertisers themselves often tend to define their marketing objectives. The choice of a medium thus may influence not only an advertiser's perception of what he has to say to his customers but the whole orientation of his business. This is by no means true of all advertisers, and even among those who depend on selective publications, the term *market* continues to be used with geographical or demographic meanings as well as to refer to markets made by media.

Newspapers have long distinguished their circulation in the concentrated "City Zone" from that in the larger "Retail Trading Zone" from which the central city stores were traditionally expected to draw customers; a great deal of information has been assembled to conform to these areas.

But no medium has had the impact on market definitions that television has had. Each of the two major television ratings services divides the country into "coverage areas" made up of aggregations of counties. Nielsen calls these Dominant Market Areas (DMA's) and counts 205 of them, while Arbitron calls them Areas of Dominant Influence (ADI's) and has 210. (Except for a handful of markets, the definitions exactly agree.) The areas represent counties in which more of the households, over the course of a week, watch the stations located in a particular metropolitan area than stations in other locations. Where metropolitan areas lie close together, they are either considered to be part of a single television coverage area, or the counties in between are assigned to one or the other, according to where most of the viewing is oriented. In this way, every county in the United States, and all its households, is located in one area or another.

As television became the principal medium of most packaged-goods advertisers, and as spot TV became a more significant part of their total media budgets, the television coverage areas became an increasingly common tool of their media and market analysis and planning. In the case of companies whose television expenditures represented a good chunk of their total operating expense, there was a logical progression from market tests that analyzed sales within TV coverage areas to the redefinition of sales districts in terms of these territories. Other media came to be evaluated in terms of their coverage of the television markets, when their function was considered to be one of complementing the basic TV buy.

In this process, the other media were progressively disadvantaged, inasmuch as their content was geared to constituencies that had been defined at other times and on other assumptions. Within a large television coverage area, for instance, there are commonly dozens of newspapers and radio stations serving communities with distinctive identities and distribution networks. Such distinctions are obliterated when the media buyer sets up the worksheets for his facts and figures on the basis of a homogenized DMA or ADI, which ignores the reality of real people traveling down real roads to shop in real stores in markets with names and some sense of boundary.

However, the diffusion of broadcast signals has become a more dubious basis for defining markets as cable continues to spread, carrying a variety of signals obtained by satellite or community antenna from distant points of origin as well as programming confined to the small locality served by a single system. Low-powered television, with a coverage radius of only a few miles, will further subdivide existing market areas. It appears inevitable that markets will have to be redefined in terms that run closer to the patterns of marketing movement as well as to the channels of communication.

Local markets and national coverage

Media exposure and advertising pressure are not evenly distributed against the entire population. At the very bottom and very top of the socioeconomic scale people tend to insulate themselves from the mass media experience in which advertising is embedded. The welfare client may not be a reader of anything much and may not have the cash to repair the TV set. The Brahmin prefers the companionship of books and stereo to that of mass culture.

But there is another kind of unevenness in advertising pressure that reflects both the distribution system in marketing and the pattern of media costs. The bigger the media vehicle, the more economical its rates are apt to be in terms of impressions or exposures delivered. Big local media—television and radio stations, newspapers, and outdoor plant operations*—are in big markets. Exposure

---

*The outdoor "plant operator" is one who owns or leases a number of billboards in an area. No substantial advertiser uses a single poster; he buys positions in aggregates or "plants," and aims at a certain "showing" that represents a proportion of the total traffic in the area.

to all media is bound to be higher in urban areas where there are more competitive media choices among stations and papers. In the rural hinterlands, the educational level is lower than it is in the metropolis and people read less. They are also less likely to be within the effective same-day distribution range of a newspaper and less likely to get many TV channels with full strength.

To plan his schedule in any medium, the media planner is apt to work from the top of the list down. Whether he ranks markets in terms of population, aggregate disposable income, purchase of the generic product or of his own particular brand, or by any other measure of sales potential, he almost invariably puts the big ones on top and the little ones at the bottom. There are strong reasons for him to follow this course of action, apart from the fact that media in the bigger markets offer him a greater economy in cost per thousand. The big-town consumer has more brands available to him when he shops. Economies of scale operate in big markets in warehousing and in the logistics of handling merchandise as well as in advertising. The advertiser's own distribution centers are apt to be in the bigger markets; so are his regional offices and his biggest customers. He has to start where his people are, where his own business is concentrated.

When you start at the top of a list of markets you always have to stop somewhere down the line in making up a schedule. Media lists are not only limited in length, they are also commonly subdivided into A, B, and C components that attribute disproportionate weight to the A markets, sometimes with the rationale that the potential sales volume there is higher, sometimes on the grounds that the media cost efficiency is higher.

It is true, of course, that income in the United States is not evenly distributed. The 20 top metropolitan markets, with 30 percent of the population, had 34 percent of the purchasing power in 1982. All metropolitan markets, with 75 percent of the population, had 80 percent of the purchasing power. Wealth and purchasing power have concentrated to an even greater degree within the very largest markets. In the big markets, a higher proportion of the work force is engaged in better paying jobs of higher skill than is the case in small cities and rural areas. Family incomes are bigger and spending on consumer products is greater. Thus, advertisers have been encouraged to concentrate their marketing and sales promotional pressure on the major areas that account for so heavy a proportion of their total sales. An even higher proportion of all advertising messages go into these same markets than the superiority of their wealth and spending would seem to justify. It is in the development of neglected small town sectors of the market that some regional brands have their strength.

It might appear logical to advertise most where public acceptance of a brand, as reflected in sales, was high. Yet, rarely does a brand's sales preeminence coincide exactly with the manufacturer's facilities for physical distribution. There is a tendency for a company to want to support its product with advertising wherever it has distribution, regardless of its share of a given market or of the market's importance in the total sales picture. Thus the mere fact that the product is distributed creates consequences for the planning of advertising and sales promotion. If a product is in the stores, has salesmen calling on dealers, and has wholesalers or distributors who handle it, this means that there are people who must be placated, whose enthusiasm must be aroused or maintained. The manufacturer must convince them that he is backing up the product with advertising support. A similar phenomenon occurs in areas where the product's market position is weak or where it faces stiff local competition; there may be strong pressures to overadvertise, if only to maintain the "presence" of the brand in the market.

Few advertisers distribute their products evenly on a truly national basis, i.e., so that one may be 100 percent sure of finding them in even the smallest crossroads general store. Nevertheless, the advertiser frequently aims at national coverage.

Via television, national coverage can be achieved with a standard network hookup of about 195 stations whose signals can be heard in most of the households in the country.* (A network guarantees advertisers that its programs will be "cleared" or carried by stations that cover 85 percent of the country and provides a rebate if they deliver less. But the advertiser may have to supplement his network buy to get into the missing markets.) National coverage of a kind can also be attained through the use of magazines whose dispersion and distribution are national, even though it is not likely to be consistent. Even the biggest national magazines show thin spots in many rural counties on the coverage map. *Time* magazine's circulation per thousand households ranges from 12.6 in Ann Arbor, Michigan to 1.7 in Danville, Virginia. To cover the *whole* United States with a newspaper campaign would require the use of hundreds if not thousands of dailies and weeklies in cities and towns and villages, but the 100 biggest daily newspapers can deliver about 43 percent of total newspaper circulation.

Why do advertisers commonly think in terms of covering the whole country? One reason is that professional marketing and advertising people move in circles where facts, figures, and concepts tend to be expressed in broad national terms.

Partly this is because United States government statistics are among the best available in the world and represent the yardsticks used by most industries and corporations. The distribution territories of the advertiser rarely coincide exactly with the standard territorial categories of the statisticians (state or county boundaries, Census divisions, or regions). Salesmen's districts are apt to follow the snaking of highways across the landscape and these in turn may be delimited by rivers or mountain ranges, and have very little to do with the standard political boundaries on which Census data are based. (By the same token, sales districts can by no means coincide with the coverage area that represents a TV or radio station's effective signal strength, or a newspaper's circulation.)

Postal ZIP code areas (which vary enormously in population size) are in-

---

*The network connection remains vital to the independently owned stations. In 1960, a typical network-affiliated TV station received about a third of its income from its network as its share of advertising sales. By 1982, this had been reduced to about 7 percent. However, by that time, the station was deriving nearly half its income from the sale of up to 500 or 600 commercials in slots between and within network shows. (The remainder of its income came from the sale of commercials within and between its own shows.) *Advertising Age*, April 26, 1982.

creasingly used as a unit of market analysis, especially by retailers, since census information is available on this base. Direct mail and (in many cases) newspaper insert advertising can be distributed to conform to the ZIP codes. But the postal areas themselves are defined arbitrarily by criteria other than those that marketers would employ.

Advertising people in big companies express themselves in national terms simply because general conversation usually focuses on prototypes, on "good examples," on averages. When we think of marketing in the United States, we are likely to have in mind the most *typical* patterns of distribution and consumption rather than the full range of patterns.

Another reason why advertisers often think in national terms is that the changing character of the American public has tended to break down the old distinctions among urban markets or trading zones. America has a highly mobile population, thanks to wars, the automobile, long vacations, and years of affluence. Nearly a fifth of the households move each year, and two of every three young adults (18-24) have moved at least once in a five-year period. Regionalisms of speech, dress, manner, and custom tend to become more and more obscure.

The very growth of the mass media has in itself become a factor of profound importance in creating national cultural unity. The advertising carried by these media, like the editorial or entertainment content, has offered the same model of The Good Life, with identical artifacts and appurtenances, to households from Maine to Hawaii. It has helped create a common marketing climate in the suburban housing developments and shopping centers that present much the same sight from coast to coast.

Local community boundaries might appear to have less and less importance in an era in which downtowns have deteriorated and the motorized housewife looks increasingly to the city's periphery to fill her buying needs. In the typical interurban complex midway between large urban centers, people have a number of focal points to which they can turn for shopping and recreation, but they by no means lose their sense of identity with the community.

In a market that Frank Orenstein and I have called Intercity, we interviewed 500 people regarding their shopping habits, their media exposure, and their total pattern of work and movement.[5] Intercity is a town of under 30,000 that lies within easy access of a dozen other towns and cities, including some major markets. We selected it because it has no daily newspaper or broadcasting station of its own. People read daily newspapers that emanate from half a dozen or more surrounding towns and can watch TV channels from four of those towns.

We found a strong correlation between the towns where people travel to work, to shop, or to visit, and the town where the newspapers they read are published. The relationship held, both with regard to general shopping and visiting patterns and to the specific facts of where people made their last major purchase of certain items of clothing or furniture. Those who shop in a town were apt to read the newspaper published there, while their next-door neighbors who did their shopping somewhere else were likely to read the newspaper published in that other town. Thus even in a period of growing urban complexity, each daily newspaper sorts out a market by attracting as its audience those who look to its home community as a place to visit and buy.

Local news of familiar people and places is a strong part of the newspaper's appeal. Independent radio stations, particularly those in smaller towns, very often have this same strong identity with their home towns. In the case of television, however, we found no correlation between the location of the station that people watched most and the town where they were most likely to visit or shop. These findings are easy to understand when we recognize that television is perceived by its viewers as entertainment in the main line of show business from New York to Hollywood. Television programming is big time and national, and the local station often has little identity except as the outlet for a network.*

In spite of the tendencies toward homogenization in American society, powerful regional differences still exist, some on a scale which marketers and advertising planners rarely recognize. The habit of talking in terms of national averages unfortunately disguises enormous regional and local market differences in shopping habits, in competitive brand distributions and brand standings, in consumer tastes and preferences, and in the actual characteristics of consumers themselves.

In 1980, the 327 metropolitan statistical areas (SMSA's) of the United States ranged in population between 57,118 and 9,120,346 and in land area from 23 square miles to 27,279 square miles. Yet these metropolitan areas are often lumped together in marketing and media plans as though they represented a common set of conditions and way of life!

The median ages of the population in the separate SMSA's ranged from 22 to 50 years, the median household incomes from $11,275 to $29,239, two-car homes from 30 percent to 79 percent.

In a 1982 study of the top 10 U.S. markets by Mediamark Research Inc., ownership of Chrysler-made cars ranged from 3.4 percent in Cleveland to .8 percent in San Francisco. Ale consumption in Philadelphia was 309 percent of the 10-city average; in Los Angeles it was 44 percent. Bourbon consumption in New York was 42 percent of the average; San Francisco 148 percent. Vermouth consumption ranged from 205 percent of the average in New York to 70 percent in St. Louis. Use of sleeping pills was 122 percent in Washington; 64 percent in Cleveland. Vitamins were 134 percent in Los Angeles and 79 percent in St. Louis.

Solomon Dutka points out that between 20 percent to 30 percent of the total market for most product categories is made up of local or regional brands. Comparing nationally marketed products, Dutka finds strong variations in the regional distribution of their sales. One food brand has 56 percent of its sales in the East, another 19 percent. Of two competing cigarette brands, one has 19 percent of its sales in the Central region, the other 44 percent. One of two competing appliance brands has 26 percent of its sales in the West and the other 3 percent. Yet the management of both companies think of themselves as "national brands" and are apt to require national coverage in their media schedules.

These kinds of striking local variations provide a rationale for the use of local media by national advertisers, either as a flexible primary force in promo-

---

*The exception to this is provided by the station's own newscasters.

tion or to supplement national media with extra pressure in the places that need it.

Media attributes and contrasts

Consider two of the most disparate forms of advertising—the classified newspaper ad and the outdoor billboard poster. The newspaper reader who turns to the classified section and looks for a particular kind of ad may be eager to buy or sell. The person who passes the outdoor poster or painted bulletin is exposed to it on a more or less random basis, since the message is displayed to the world at large.

The **outdoor** or transit advertiser is not interested in everyone who passes by his sign. There may be some relationship between the location of the billboard and the point of sale for the product, as when a gasoline advertiser places a poster on a highway within a mile of a service station.

Usually the mass media advertiser starts from the premise that the potential customers for his product are widely scattered. He uses a mass medium rather than a specialized one precisely because he assumes that the tastes or interests expressed in the demand for his product or brand do not correspond to those appealed to by any particular advertising medium.

The task of outdoor advertising is to create a quick impression, a reminder that the product exists. The outdoor advertiser seeks to maintain a reference point in the consumer's mind for possible future action, but he can normally do this only by reinforcing the effect of previous impressions from other sources.

In some of its applications, radio has taken on these characteristics of billboard advertising used as a reminder of other contacts between advertisers and customers. In its Golden Age, **radio** linked the advertised product to the show-business glamour of program personalities whose activities were avidly followed by the mass audience. When a popular program host like Arthur Godfrey spoke of Chesterfields or of Lipton Tea, he spoke as a convinced and enthusiastic user anxious to pass on his enthusiasm as a matter of public service. These advantages of broadcast program sponsorship have been largely usurped by TV. Even though today many radio disc jockeys seek to preserve the tradition of personal testimonials in their recitation of commercials, how many listeners accept this as more than the merest convention?

Radio messages often resemble buckshot in being widely scattered in their impact. However, wise advertisers do not place their radio spots in a random pattern. As music became the dominant element in radio, and as the number of stations multiplied, stations became differentiated and specialized in terms of musical styles and formats that were generally accepted as identical with those of the cultural tastes of clearly defined social class, ethnic, and age groups: country and Western music, punk rock, "beautiful" music, soul music, classical music, jazz, progressive rock, etc.[6] (The average listener to rock is 24 years old, for "talk" stations, 48.) A handful of stations went to an all-news format. But comparatively few changed styles through the course of the day.*

---

*By 1984 there were no less than 18 national radio networks servicing stations with different formulas.

In short, few radio stations any longer try to provide the entertainment needs of the entire family as they did in the pre-television era. Radio's current role is that of an intimate personal companion. The spectator at the baseball game whose transistor is tuned to the broadcast of the game is seeking an affirmation of his own sensory experience, as well as a better understanding of it.* (Presumably, if, as is often the case, the radio is tuned to the account of another game, he is extending his horizons!)

As a source of information and instant orientation, radio, with its ubiquity and mobility, has carved out a new and indispensable place for itself in the communications system. Forty percent of all radio listening takes place outside the home. As a purveyor of "background" music, radio permits each individual listener to move about always surrounded by his own wave length of personal sound (occasionally to the annoyance of others). It is the most widely accessible source of instant news.

Precisely because radio is now an individual rather than a group listening experience, it offers special values for the advertiser whose product—accident insurance or athlete's foot remedy—may represent too delicate a subject for TV. The familiar announcer or disc jockey may take the tone of a buddy offering direct personal advice. And radio commercials stand out in their environment. Using a technique known as "volume compression," the average volume level of a commercial can be raised without exceeding the allowable maximum. The effect of this is to make commercials louder than they once were.

The advertiser who echoes the musical theme of his TV commercials on radio may evoke the original visual image as well, at a much lower cost than by added frequency on television. "One method by which music helps to communicate value is closure," says advertising music-maker Sidney Hecker. "Music may be left incomplete, or known commercial music is played without words, and the listener fills in what is missing. Because the consumer becomes a participant in the process, the message often makes a deeper, more lasting impression than if he or she were merely a listener."[7]

Television has three great advantages for the advertiser: (1) of all the media, it comes closest to the intensity of interpersonal confrontation; (2) it generates huge audiences at the same moment in time; and (3) it permits the advertiser to encounter the consumer in a relaxed frame of mind, ready for whatever light entertainment the magic box will bring him, eyes and ears simultaneously engaged.

To a viewer in a passive, receptive state the advertiser can show his product in use, he can evoke empathy with the personality who is his spokesman, he can perform all the tricks of film editing and montage.

The television advertiser can employ animation and special effects which give fantasy a form of expressiveness it can rarely achieve in print. He can get

*He is also, incidentally, more apt to read a newspaper account afterwards to review his recollections.

the viewer to project himself into remote realms of the imagination, and have the fantasies taken literally.*

Color is an important ingredient among television's attractions, and in 1982 89 percent of TV homes had color sets. The quality of television color is assured by cable transmission, so while the future spread of cable may change television programming and economics, it is unlikely to lessen the communications impact of television advertisements. Such impending refinements as high-definition and large-screen projection television will give the medium still more power.

Television has the unique capacity to create vicariously the illusion of personal experience, of "being there." Millions of people who watched the funeral of President Kennedy or the first moon landing were bound together in a sense of common participation in a momentous event and in a universally shared emotion. But this kind of rapt involvement, in which even a slight interruption is intolerable, represents one extreme of a long continuum of TV communications experience. At the other end of the attention scale, television programming may be no more than a casual accompaniment to other activities—a drone of sound and a flicker of light at the far periphery of perception.

The solitary viewer is engaged in essentially a different type of activity than the shared experience of watching (and talking about) a program in the company of other family members.† The television audience can comment, criticize, and participate in what it sees; within the home environment it is stimulated to the kind of conversation about content that is not permitted in the theater or the movies.

It is precisely the capacity of television programming to arouse audience involvement that makes the commercial break an interruption. In living room viewing, the commercial break provides the occasion for the kind of remark on what has come before that is inhibited by the theatrical convention of silence at the time the program is on. To this extent, the advertiser may lose as well as gain from the very strength of the medium.

The advertising planner is normally not concerned with such matters as the difference between situation comedy and gag comedy as environment for his commercials. In comparing television with other media, he often tends to think of the advertising tasks to which each medium most typically lends itself. To do this he must deliberately ignore the variations that exist among programs. Yet, programs with different kinds of internal structure (dramatic or episodic) provide settings that are propitious for the advertiser's message in varying degrees.

The integrated commercial, in which the performers stop their antics long enough to tell a product story, is today a rare phenomenon on American television, found only on locally originated live programming and virtually vanished from network shows, with their reliance on film and tape.

This alienation of the commercial from the immediate entertainment envi-

---

*A fresh problem arises, of course, when the technique takes attention away from the subject, when the advertising becomes so cute that the viewer misses the point.

†The greatest amount of individual viewing occurs in multiset households, which by 1982 accounted for 55 percent of the total.

ronment is by no means an unmitigated loss. With integrated commercials (which are still encountered on overseas television), the audience is sometimes more absorbed by technique than by substance. Their interest in a known personality may make them less attentive to his words about a product than to his style of talking or to the incidental stage business. And if the performer is a comedian, his serious advice to buy may not always be taken seriously.* But such problems of technique are minor indeed in the light of television advertising's unique capacity to capture and hold the viewer's attention and interest.

In contrast to TV, much **magazine** advertising is predicated on the belief that an integrated mood or tone between the ad and the editorial environment is desirable. Most people reject the idea of magazines and newspapers without ads. Many others who claim that they would prefer to see publications without ads would probably find them most uninviting. Ads are part of the total configuration of what the reader expects to find.

Four-color advertising in magazines affords the advertiser an opportunity to picture and describe his product faithfully and attractively. He encounters the reader in a situation where useful information can be savored, where appealing pictures and inspired text can set off fantasy, where the reader can be spoken to as an individual in a leisurely reflective mood.

However, the reading situation is not always the rapt, deep-in-the-club-chair type idealized in the promotional literature of magazine publishers. It also encompasses the casual skimming that occurs in a barber shop or dentist's waiting room, where the reader picks up the publication in the expectation (and even the hope) that his perusal will be quickly interrupted.

Just as some types of TV programs leave viewers less prone to distraction, so certain types of magazines demand more intense reading. Text magazines are read longer and picked up more often than picture books. Monthlies are kept around the house longer than weeklies are. (An Audits & Surveys study for *Newsweek* found that the weekly news magazines capture 60 percent of their total audience within the first week after publication; 80 percent within 10 days; and 90 percent within two weeks.)

It is easy enough to visualize the woman who studies and clips the ads in *Good Housekeeping* to get recipe ideas or food service suggestions, or her sister who buys *Vogue* for the fashion ads, or the man who pores over the pages of *Popular Mechanics* as much for the advertised gadgets as for the how-to-do-it articles. These same people may be in a quite different frame of mind when they go through the *Reader's Digest* or *TV Guide*. Reading *Good Housekeeping* may have more in common with reading the women's page of the newspaper than it does with reading *The New Yorker*.

The big magazine success stories in recent years have been those of specialized publications, like *Money, Omni* or *Discover. The deaths of the weekly Life, Collier's,* and *The Saturday Evening Post* and the biweekly *Look* directly reflected the com-

---

*This works differently for adults than for small children. Among four-to-seven year olds questioned by Charles Atkin and Wendy Gibson, a third thought that cartoon characters Fred Flintstone and Barney knew "very much" about which cereals children should eat.

petition of TV as a general entertainment medium.* The accepted wisdom of
the moment is that any magazine can handle its assignment best if it attracts a
homogeneous hard core of readers who can be clearly defined for the advertiser
and whose expectations as to advertising content are directly related to the
editorial formula.

Theodore Peterson has written in his historical study of magazines:

> The influence of the minority magazines could not be measured by
> their circulations. Men accustomed to reaching vast audiences some-
> times found their power a little puzzling. Frank P. Walsh once called the
> *Nation* the greatest mystery in American journalism. He had written an
> article about railroads for it in the days when its circulation was about
> 27,000. He had done a series on the same subject which was syndicated
> by the Hearst newspapers, which then had a total circulation of about
> 10,000,000. Soon after the *Nation* appeared, he got phone calls from
> senators, lobbyists, persons of importance. But never, he later recalled,
> had he ever met a person who mentioned his articles syndicated by
> Hearst.[8]

TV Guide and the *Digest* cannot present a sharp audience profile any more
than the CBS Television Network can. Such general media seek to be all things
to all men, women, and children and, accordingly, the nature of their editorial
offerings is both varied and diffuse. The advertising content of great national
magazines parallels their editorial matter in its attempt at universality. Ads and
articles together give these magazines their flavor; they mirror the variety and
complexity of the contemporary world. They would be quite different without
their miscellaneous ads, which form a succession of striking visual *non sequiturs*
in keeping with the flow of the articles and features.

Big or small, a great magazine has *character*, a unique personality that sets it
apart from the others that resemble it. The vitality and force a magazine exudes
can have great value for the advertiser if he can harness the tone of his message
to the large editorial force around it. But few magazine ads are prepared with an
individual touch for each publication on the schedule. The typical campaign is
designed to be run in the "women's books" or the "shelter magazines" and the
expensive engravings are put to multiple use.

Some publishers display genius in making their magazines appear unique in
the eyes of the advertiser. Others are less successful. On one occasion a quarter
century ago, three associate media directors and eight buyers from the media
department of a large advertising agency stood through several rounds of drinks
and sat through a dinner of rare roast beef in a private room over an expensive
midtown New York restaurant. The magazine which was paying for this luncheon—as it had done and would do again for dozens of identical luncheons in the
same setting—was now about to have its innings. One of the agency men excused
himself and hurried off immediately after the meal, pleading an urgent meeting

---

*Life and the *Post* eventually resurfaced as monthlies with a small fraction of their
former readership.

back at the office. The publisher of the magazine stood up to express his appreciation to those still present for their attendance. He had no new research, no facts or figures to report. (This was a good thing, too, because the facts and figures on his particular publication showed a steady decline by every criterion advertisers might consider.) But he did want to talk about the editorial character of his publication which made it unique and gave it a mandatory position on every magazine list. "The *American* magazine," he said gravely, "is everything the name implies." It died soon afterwards.

Newspaper **supplements** represent a special form that many media planners find hard to classify. The Sunday magazine is often considered as part of a magazine budget and evaluated as such in terms of cost and coverage. For many years, the major syndicated Sunday magazines fostered the concept that they were part of the magazine medium, in spite of the fact that the audience reads them as part of the big diversified Sunday newspaper itself. Supplement ads are commonly adaptations of magazine ads, even though the editorial environment and audience expectations are somewhat different.

The nationally syndicated supplements (*Parade* and *Family Weekly*) increasingly compete with locally edited ones, which most major newspapers have introduced. While some, like *The New York Times Magazine*, maintain total independence, national advertising in others is sold jointly through the Metropolitan Sunday Newspapers group. As a medium, the supplements offer the advertiser vast circulation at low cost. They also offer him the opportunity to expose his message at a highly concentrated time, as opposed to the much more attenuated and longer life of a magazine issue's readership.* The supplements have also made much of the relaxed and leisurely home environment of Sunday reading and suggest that on this day of rest the buying plans for the strenuous week to come are discussed in family council.

The daily **newspaper** offers the advertiser great flexibility, both in timing and creative technique. A given quantity of newspaper space can be divided into a very large number of units and shapes, and these can be scheduled to fit the advertiser's needs. While the broadcast spot on the desired channel and time slot must generally be wangled well in advance, the advertiser can almost always get his ad in the paper on the day he wants and with very short notice.

However, Val Corradi remembers the year when Oldsmobile won an unexpected double victory in the fabled cross-country Mobilgas Economy Run. The result was furious copywriting, editing, clearances with officialdom, and wiring copy to papers overnight. The multipage wire from the agency included type sizes for headlines and body text and was signed by S. P. Costan, chief newspaper buyer. The full page that appeared in one major newspaper the next day carried the ad in all its glory, shouting the news about the twin victory. And the logo—in bold two-inch high "war" type—read, not Oldsmobile, but S. P. COSTAN.

Small space units in the newspaper can be scattered and directed at different buying interests. Large space can be used dramatically with the aid of R.O.P. (Run of Paper) color. High-fidelity color can be obtained through inserts pre-

---

*As with the rest of the newspaper, only a small part of supplement readership is "pass along."

printed in rotogravure or offset. Ad headlines, copy and art can be localized.

The newspaper represents a regular part of its readers' daily experience, with a habitual place and time of reading. This gives it an intimacy and sense of identification on the reader's part as the voice of his home town.[9] Although daily and weekly newspapers represent the original medium of local news and advertising, the technology of satellite transmission has made national dailies into powerful elite advertising vehicles.

Because the newspaper is perceived as the comprehensive daily directory or encyclopedia of information, no one reader reads it all, nor is he expected to. To be successful, newspaper advertising should reflect the here and now of today's paper and carry the same sense of immediacy that is reflected in the news columns. Although retail advertisers understand how to achieve this effect, the manufacturer and his agency find the task more difficult if they believe their product to be of low interest or have nothing new to say about it.

For such an advertiser, the chief merit of the newspaper medium is akin to that of the billboard; a single message (in most markets) can be put in front of a high proportion of potential customers, and—unique to the newspaper—it can be put in front of them when the advertiser wants it there.

Direct Mail offers advertisers extraordinary flexibility, both in creative technique and in distribution. Occupant-addressed mailings, extensively used by chain retailers and in coupon promotions by national advertisers, can saturate any desired geographic area and thus be tailored to distribution requirements. The extensive sorting of census population data by postal zip code designations makes it possible for marketers to concentrate occupant-addressed mail to residents of areas that appear to offer a high concentration of prospective customers. Retailers also commonly send catalogs and other promotional matter to charge account customers with whom they are already linked. Thousands of mailing lists permit individual-addressed mailing pieces to go selectively to individuals who fall into some predesignated occupational or consuming category. Computer-driven ink-jet printing makes it possible to address individuals with sales letters that refer to them in personal terms.

Mailing pieces range in kind from elaborate and expensively printed catalogs sent out by mail order houses, through the colorful sales promotion rotogravure tabloids mailed by the millions by Sears and K-Mart, to the simple flyers sent out by the local laundry. High income people are on more lists and get far more mail advertising than poor people do. The average household receives about 1.6 pieces a day. People discriminate sharply among the advertising mail they get and screen it immediately for potential interest, as with any other form of print advertising.[10]

On comparing media

Every advertising medium has been used successfully by someone, in some way, and every media salesman has a portfolio full of success stories that can be pulled out at the right moment to convince the wavering prospect.* There may be a case history of failure for every one of success, but these are the ones that are rarely publicized.

Horace Schwerin, whose career was devoted to testing commercials, concluded from a series of comparative studies made by his firm in Germany that the relative merits of print and television advertising vary substantially from one product field to the next. So cautious a statement can hardly be called into question. However, when advertisements appearing in various media are compared in the aggregate, strong advantages do not usually emerge for one medium over the others.

The 1974 AAAA study of consumer attitudes toward advertising found wide variations for the individual media,[11] with TV and newspapers contributing most to the direction of opinion toward advertising in general. Eighty-eight percent expressed generally favorable opinions about advertising in newspapers, 81 percent to magazine advertising, 73 percent to radio, 60 percent to television, 52 percent to billboards, and 28 percent to direct mail. Similarly, a 1977 national survey by Franklin Carlile and Howard Leonard (already cited on page 7) ranked newspapers, magazines, radio, and television, in that order, in terms of the truthfulness of their advertising.

The "perceived utility" of advertising was studied by Garrett J. O'Keefe, Kathleen Nash, and Jenny Liu through a survey of 1,049 adults in Buffalo, Denver, and Milwaukee in 1979.[12] Newspaper ads were rated as "very useful" by 28 percent and "somewhat useful" by 46 percent, while magazine and television advertising received lower ratings. Fifty-four percent described radio commercials as "hardly useful at all." There were comparable ratings given on the attention paid to advertising, except that television emerged in second place. Deeper analysis indicated that appraisals of the advertising in each medium were related to the amount of exposure that people have to it. Newspaper ads appeared to have comparable utility levels in all socioeconomic groups, magazine ads were slanted toward upper levels and broadcast commercials to lower ones.

In a study for ABC Radio, Daniel Yankelovich selected 25 matched sets of advertising messages in radio, television, and magazines. These were exposed to and evaluated by matched groups of 50 respondents each, about 500 in all. Yankelovich had each of the ads ranked on 46 measures of "impact" as well as measures of the degree to which they stimulated "buying interest" or favorable brand attitudes. The criteria included such characterizations as "useful," "honest," "informative," "real," "believable," "clear," "sociable," and "intimate."[13]

---

*The resourcefulness of media representatives is legendary. Mac Morris recalls a memorable sales trip to Detroit in which a magazine salesman was called on at the last moment to substitute for his publisher. Whiling away the hours in a bar at LaGuardia Airport, he forgot one set of slides for a two-projector presentation. He spent the night rewriting his script to fit the remaining slides and put the revised presentation on the following morning to the proverbial "great acclaim." When he returned to New York, his publisher, pleased by his success (and ignorant of the near-catastrophe), asked for a private showing of the presentation. His only comment was, "I thought we were going to use those shots of cars on the Merritt Parkway!" The fast answer was, "Too many old models."

Remarkably, on 42 of the 48 measures, radio, TV, and magazine ads all performed equally well.

For reasons I shall develop more fully later, research experiments comparing media are almost always comparing other things at the same time, and the results are apt to be inconclusive. Such research generally proves highly frustrating to sponsor and user alike, because the findings are always specific to the individual ads and commercials tested. There is always room for argument as to whether the creative adaptation of the advertising for a second form is honestly comparable to the original ad. Moreover, no matter in what way the residual "impact" of the advertising message may be defined in experiments of this sort—by awareness, information, opinion change, or purchase behavior—the research is commonly done under laboratory conditions of enforced exposure in which people agree ahead of time, for a consideration, to expose themselves to the advertising. This has several consequences: it makes the exposure situation an artificial one, and perhaps the abnormality is more to the advantage of one medium than to the other. It ignores the normal scope of coverage of the two media under comparison, against which the "impact" figures must be projected. And it is not generally concerned with the comparability of costs for real-life usage of the media being evaluated.

An illustration of the difficulties of this kind of comparison may be seen in a study by Robert Grass and Wallace Wallace, who created six magazine ads to be comparable to television commercials for six different products.[14] (Comparability was tested by ascertaining that the same number of information points were registered in a "forced-exposure" situation.) The ads, transferred to slides along with magazine editorial matter and nontest ads, were shown to 84 subjects, and commercials were similarly shown in the context of programming and other commercials. Following what the researchers describe as this "unmotivated exposure," the magazine ads conveyed 56 percent of the facts that they registered in the pretest, while the television commercials conveyed 81 percent. The commercials were nearly twice as effective in teaching the advertiser's message, and the advantage was especially marked among people who had a very low probability of using or buying the advertised product. The researchers conclude that this was because the television commercial imposed itself on viewers' attention. However, the unnatural transference of print onto slides may also have had something to do with the results.

An earlier attempt to equate the residual impact of print and television advertisements was made by W. R. Simmons & Associates for *Life* magazine in 1966.* In metropolitan San Francisco, Pittsburgh, Miami, Omaha, and Boston, interviews were conducted with people who had watched prime-time television the preceding evening. Separate interviews were held with people who had read the current issue of *Life* within the past 24 hours. Viewers who had watched a program the previous evening were shown a series of 18 commercials on a

---

Life was at that time a weekly with an audience of 30,000,000 readers per issue and in its most successful years a great innovator in advertising research. Willard R. Simmons, a notable survey researcher and statistician, was at that time head of the company that still bears his name as SMRB (the Simmons Media Research Bureau).

portable projector and asked to identify the ones that appeared on the show in question. Similarly, people who had just read the current issue of *Life* were shown 30 full-page advertisements and asked to identify the ones in that issue.

When all the data had been collated, Simmons calculated a "net retention curve" (the difference between the number of commercials or ads that an individual *correctly* identified with the program or magazine and the number *mistakenly* identified). The television commercials received a slightly higher retention score—17.6 percent, against 15.3 percent for the magazine ads.[15]

Life also sponsored, in 1969, a three-phase 24-hour recall study by Grudin/ Appel/Haley of television commercials and ads for the same brands in a specially prepared issue of the magazine.[16] In all but two cases out of fifteen, the magazine ad had higher recall, the average being 18 percent for the *Life* readers and 11 percent for the TV viewers. There was no significant difference between package goods and hard goods advertising. The recall level was identical (on average) for 30-second and 60-second commercials.

A study done by Teleresearch in 1971 for the three television networks was designed to counter these magazine studies of comparative sales effectiveness.[17] Unlike the large scale field investigations conducted by the magazines, this study used 4,039 shopping mall interviews in Los Angeles. Shoppers were shown either magazine ads or television commercials in a mobile van and then given coupons that could be used in a nearby supermarket to get a reduced price on the advertised brands. On the average, the magazine ads added 9.6 sales per 100 shoppers, and the television commercials 17.5, or nearly twice as many. However, the sales added ranged between 3.1 and 22.5 for the individual magazine ads and between 4.8 and 33.5 for the commercials (the most successful one being one minute long compared to 30 seconds for the others). Both the print and television messages performed better when they were shown in isolation than they did when shown in the context of a magazine or program.

The advertiser who attempts to project such results to his own problems in comparing media is still faced with the differences between magazines and TV in cost, coverage, and communications capacities other than those involved in ad recall. If he is really sophisticated, he may also ask himself whether a publication, which accumulates its full readership over weeks, should really be compared with a broadcast, which exists at a moment of time.

Electronic and print media

For Marshall McLuhan, space and time are not the most useful dimensions for classifying media. He prefers "hot" and "cool." "Hot" media like radio and newspapers, McLuhan believes, are active, aggressive, crammed with information. A "cool" medium like television must be activated and participated in by the viewer to suck out information and meaning. Such intriguing and arbitrary statements contradict the more conventional distinction made between the broadcast media (to which the audience is passively exposed) and the print media (from which the reader must actively extract information).*

Gestalt theory in psychology teaches that if we see an incomplete circle we tend to complete it in our minds. The expenditure of energy required to make it seem whole makes us *more* aware of it than we would be if it really *were* whole. The work of the eminent psychologist B. F. Skinner leads to the conclusion that conditioning is most successful when it is only partially reinforced. We tend to lose interest when a given act always results in predictable consequences. We learn best when there is an element of uncertainty in our learning, when we have to work hard and participate actively. Just these conditions exist during the reading process when the reader himself is an active participant.

The key distinction between space and broadcast communication is often described in terms of the time dimension.[18] But though it takes time to read a magazine or newspaper, this time is under the reader's control and he can scan vast quantities of information very rapidly in order to absorb what he needs. For this reason, the total time spent reading and time spent viewing or listening are simply not to be compared (as they sometimes are) as measures of communication.

The real difference between electronic and print media starts at the point where the message is physically presented to readers or viewers and where the attrition of interest sets in.

Any medium that flows in time begins with a higher probability of dominating the senses on behalf of a given message than does a static medium in which the printed word is scanned and assimilated selectively. This gives broadcast advertising its quality of intrusiveness.

Broadcast advertising demands a higher level of conscious awareness than print. But broadcast messages are for the most part randomly scattered and not (to the same degree as with print) selectively perceived by those who are predisposed to be purchasers of the product.

Several different advertising tasks may be lumped together loosely under the heading of "getting the reader to think about the product." He may use the advertising as a reference point to absorb factual information, or he may use it as a starting point for revery or fantasy, imagining that he owns the product and considering the utility it might have.

In the case of print, revery can set in the moment the reader stops at the ad. When his scanning is interrupted and he stops to read the copy or look at an illustration, he is already, in his own mind, building up an appropriate set of symbolic associations for the interpretation of what he sees. The more physically dominant an advertisement is, the better able it is to attract attention long enough for the reader to become involved in this type of speculative revery or fantasy.

---

*It almost appears as though McLuhan is contradicting his own major premise about the preeminent importance of media form over content. What makes radio and newspapers "hot" may be less the sizzling immediacy of their communications technology than their news informational content. (News items *are* aggressive, when one stops to think of it.) The entertainment *content* of TV seems "cooler" than its steady flow of lighted dots across the sensitized surface of the picture tube.

_ bound broadcast advertising, we expect speculation or revery to last _ ine actual duration of the commercial and to end abruptly when the next commercial or program comes on. Demonstration in a television commercial mobilizes the viewer's fantasies about the use and ownership of the product, but ordinarily, when the demonstration ends, the viewer must cope with the new images and ideas that follow it on the screen.

The media mood

How does the emotional response of audience to medium redound to the advertiser's benefit? It has long been understood that a product can borrow prestige from the media in which it advertises, and much media merchandising has been based on this. The small regional manufacturer who runs space in *Newsweek* can proclaim his product at the point of sale "as advertised in *Newsweek*" much as he can display the Good Housekeeping Seal of Approval. On television, "magazine concept" shows like "Today" and "Good Morning America" have used much the same technique. (Of course, a personal testimonial delivered by a local radio or television showman expresses par excellence the product's opportunity to borrow authority from the medium.)

That editorial context is important finds corroboration in a number of studies relating advertising to its environment. A study conducted for *Life* magazine on "The Effect of Media Context on Advertising" by Nowland and Company in 1962 placed identical ads in *Life* and *Look* magazines and an unmarked portfolio. Each respondent was shown three different advertisements, one in *Life*, another in *Look*, and a third in the portfolio. The respondent was asked to choose one of the three advertisements for each of six different criteria (including interest, believability, and choice of product). The study concluded that "selections of the advertisements when they appeared in *Life* were significantly higher than when the advertisements appeared in the portfolio, on five of the six criterion questions. . . . *Life* selections exceeded *Look* selections by significant amounts on four criterion measures." Each magazine's readers chose the ads in that magazine significantly more often than readers of other magazines.[19] People who give high ratings to the editorial content of a publication are also more apt than other readers to say that they usually look at most of the ads in the publication and find them enjoyable, informative, believable, and creative.[20] The people who read both mass and selective magazines give higher ratings to the advertising in the selective ones.

In television, TvQ—a syndicated service that periodically measured program popularity—consistently found that people who like a program more than average are also most likely to recall commercials and advertisers. In a series of studies TvQ made for the International Latex Company, 42 commercial tests were conducted for brands in four product categories over a period of a year, with a total of 8,800 respondents. Housewives were interviewed on their choice of brand before and after each new program came on the air. People who liked the program when it appeared switched to the advertised brand 40 percent more than those who felt the show was "average" and 200 percent more than those who did not like the show.

In another study, TvQ compared reactions to commercials for "favorites" and "nonfavorites" among the premier telecasts of new programs at the opening of the 1962-63 season. This approach permitted the investigators to get reactions to programs that did not have a history of prior exposure and existing attitudes. The percentage recalling one or more commercials was 27 percent in the case of those who termed a new program their "favorite," compared with 22 percent for the "nonfavorites." The advantage was even more substantial for the "favorites" with regard to recall of the commercial highlights and key selling points.

In England, two studies—one conducted late in 1964 and one conducted in the Spring of 1965—measured both presence and attention during commercial breaks. Those who liked a program best were most apt to be viewing attentively, without other distracting activity. Liking the *preceding* program had more influence on determining attention than liking the *following* program, suggesting that a receptive mood carries over but is not necessarily anticipated.

A similar finding comes from a series of studies made by the Newspaper Advertising Bureau (in 1965, 1974, and 1981) in which people watching television were interviewed about the advertising on the program they were actually watching. Remarkably little difference was found in the spontaneous recall of the last in-program commercial between those with above-average interest and those with average interest in the program they were watching, but recall fell off in the case of those with less than average interest.

This same research also demonstrated that within television a distinction between primary and secondary audiences could be drawn much like the distinction long recognized as making a difference in attentiveness to magazine advertising. Viewers were separated first into those who were watching alone and those who were watching with others in the family. Then each group in turn was subdivided—the solitary viewers into those who had planned in advance to watch the program and those who merely kept the set on from the previous show or twirled the dial, and the group viewers into those who themselves selected the program and those who were merely along for the ride as part of the family viewing situation. In both cases, the viewers who had exercised conscious choice of the program were better able (by a two-to-one margin in 1981) to recall the last commercial or to name any advertiser on the program.

These planful viewers are, almost by definition, the ones who are most likely to return to the same program week after week. They are thus the most likely to become familiar with the commercials and to recognize them wherever they appear. Such a regular viewer is most likely to be the one who has a spontaneous and favorable association between program and product at the point when he makes his purchase decision.

Under these conditions, to paraphrase McLuhan, the program *is* the product; the aura of favorable association with the media vehicle is a significant part of the brand image itself. The housewife standing before an array of packages in the supermarket is subconsciously comparing the appeal of TV programs or magazines as part of her comparison of the attributes of the products themselves. This is not at a high level of deliberation; it is simply part of the whole complex order of comparisons that confronts her at that moment and out of which she makes her spontaneous choice. This kind of automatic identification takes place for all brands whose advertising habitually occurs in a certain context. The more concentrated the advertising is on a particular vehicle, and the more exclusive its dominance of that vehicle (full sponsorship on a TV program, as opposed to spot participation), the richer and more vital will be the texture of associations that carry over from the program to the product.

In 1982, no evening network shows were under a single sponsorship, but special events (mostly sporting and political) are still often sponsored by just one company. The benefits of such full sponsorship appear to be obvious. The program sponsor is able to select the kind of environment in which he wants his message to appear. His commercials will occur at "natural breaks," when the audience is least likely to be irritated by the interruption. And he can echo the theme and sometimes use the personalities of the program in the commercials.

Full sponsorship involves hazards as well as benefits, particularly when the sponsored program is considered controversial or has political overtones.

The prevailing desire of most American corporations is to remain inoffensive to any group of potential customers. An executive of the Coca-Cola Company stated this viewpoint succinctly when he was queried some years ago about the company's position on racial matters: "Our problem is to walk a very fine line and be friends with everybody. I've heard the phrase 'Stand Up and Be Counted' for so long from both sides that I'm sick of it. Sure we want to stand up and be counted, but on both sides of the fence. For God's sake, why don't they let us go on selling a delicious and refreshing beverage to anybody who's got a gullet he can pour it down."[21]

On one occasion, the Xerox Corporation underwrote a series of 90-minute spectaculars on the United Nations. As soon as the news was announced, protest mail started to come in. The letters ran at a rate of 100 to one against the forthcoming shows. An analysis of the letters found that 61,000 had been written by about 16,000 people. As the management of Xerox became concerned about this project, pro-UN organizations rallied to the support of the company. They stimulated 14,500 letters of approval from 14,500 separate individuals. A Roper survey made for Xerox among a national cross-section of 1,500 adults found that more than one out of four had seen, read, or heard about one or both of the first two UN shows, and one out of five had actually watched at least one of the shows. Three out of four called the program "good" or "outstanding," and among those aware of the programs, 31 percent identified Xerox as the sponsor, in spite of the fact that the corporate identification had been limited to an opening and closing institutional credit. Only 5 percent termed the series "not a particularly good idea." But a more timorous management might have rushed to cancel the show when the first barrage of hostile letters began!

When the advertiser is merely a participant in a network show, he no longer enjoys the prerogatives of sponsorship. This is even more the case when he buys a network package, with his messages spread over a number of different shows. And when he buys spot TV on a local basis—no matter how courageously his agency's time buyers may negotiate for the best positions next to the highest-rated shows—he has altogether lost his special privileges to control his ad's environment.

The print advertiser rarely has any such special privileges. If he is a regular advertiser on a long-term continuity schedule, he may win a special position on the back cover or inside front cover. In newspapers, advertisers may specify that they want their ad in the sports pages or the financial section, but they cannot specify that the Giants are to win or lose or the Dow-Jones stock averages are to go up or down, even though this coloration of the surrounding editorial matter may have a profound effect on the way people see their messages.

Media concentration or media mix?

The major argument for concentration of an advertiser's budget within a single medium is that it provides him with an opportunity to dominate that medium relative to his competition. This dominance applies at least to those prospective customers who are likely to be exposed repeatedly to the medium.

The advertiser who pursues this course expects that his strong impact on a part of the market is translated into greater familiarity with his brand—and thus to actual preference. This reasoning seems particularly cogent in the case of those packaged goods for which the consumer cannot detect material brand differences. When it is hard for him to distinguish brands in actual use, he is likely to select the brand he perceives as most familiar and acceptable. He may identify the brand's apparent popularity with public approval, which in turn he associates with successful performance. It must be the best if it's the favorite! The sharply concentrated use of a single medium can give a brand this aura of mass acceptance in the eyes of people whose restricted orbit of media exposure coincides with the advertiser's scheduling strategy. There are also several contrary arguments in favor of a mix of media. The principle of "synergism" has often been invoked by media planners and media salesmen alike to justify the advantages of a media mix. The idea is that the communications effect of two media working together is greater than that of either alone. The use of two channels of persuasion working together improves the odds of breaking through the defenses that people erect against irrelevant communications. Thus presumably the same effort or investment distributed over two media can work more effectively than it can in a single medium.

German laboratory experiments reported by Otmar Ernst found that awareness of advertising grew at a faster rate when magazine readers were exposed to it in more than one magazine.[22] But he also found that ads created especially with a given magazine in mind showed a stronger effect on advertising response.

Valentine Appel of SMRB has suggested the concept of "media imperatives" as a way of looking at the audience for advertising.[23] He classifies respondents into groups according to the amount of their exposure to each major medium and considers it "imperative" to balance the light exposure of some people to a particular medium (like television) by using another medium (like magazines) that is complementary in its coverage pattern. This restatement of the familiar argument for a media mix entered the advertising vocabulary when the magazine business took it up in sales presentations and demonstrations for individual product categories, supported by SMRB's syndicated research analyses.

A media mix has another advantage that goes beyond its coverage pattern. It permits the advertiser to segment his audience by delivering different forms of the message with different copy themes or psychological appeals through different media to different kinds of prospective customers. An advertiser can use one approach in *Town and Country* and another in *Woman's Day*, or he can address himself to teenagers on the radio and to sports-minded men or house-wives in the newspaper (depending on the section in which he places his ad).

Another advantage of the media mix is that it permits the same individuals to be contacted within different psychological contexts. This presents the possibility of attracting attention in one environment for a product that might not be noticed in another. And by presenting a familiar message in an unfamiliar or different context, it creates possibilities of capturing fresh interest for an otherwise tired subject.

The chances of winning attention increase if there is a touch of familiarity about an ad, with a touch of uncertainty as to why it appears familiar. This is like seeing someone who looks familiar and stopping to speculate as to where one has seen him before. The mind will dwell longer on the person's identity than it would if he were an acquaintance whom one had expected to see. A man may pass the office receptionist ten times a day and each of those meetings will have very little effect on his impression of her. But if he sees her at the theater, dressed to kill and smiling at her boyfriend, she suddenly appears in a different light and becomes a more interesting subject of speculation.

The basic principle here is that of the poetic metaphor, in which the sensibilities of the audience are aroused by an unexpected juxtaposition of familiar images. One of the virtues of the media mix is that a product message received in an unaccustomed media context arouses this kind of small shock of recognition. The product familiar through its radio commercial which is suddenly seen on a billboard will create greater awareness in us than if we hear another commercial for it.

On the other hand, an advertised product must follow the characteristic style of advertising technique for every medium it uses. The constant shifting of creative techniques within a medium, or among media, can create inconsistencies and confusion in the product image and actually inhibit attention.

Notes

1. *Understanding Media* (New York: McGraw-Hill Book Company, 1964).
2. Gerald L. Grotta, Ernest F. Larkin, and Bob J. Carrell, Jr., "News vs. Advertising: Does the Audience Perceive the 'Journalistic Distinction?' " *Journalism Quarterly*, 53, 3 (Autumn 1976): 448.
3. This estimate of viewing hours comes from an SMRB report of audience composition, based on the diary method.
4. When only prime-time viewing is considered, the difference between heavy and light viewers is greatly narrowed, with the heaviest viewing fifth having a household income of $17,330 and the lightest viewing fifth $20,581.
5. Leo Bogart and Frank Orenstein, "Mass Media & Community Identity in an Interurban Setting," *Journalism Quarterly*, 42, 2 (Spring 1965): 179-88. The field work for this study was done by Ilse Zeisel.
6. The predominance of music and the growing popularity of stereo prompted a shift from AM (amplitude modulation) to FM (frequency modulation), with its higher fidelity sound (but shorter range). Although FM accounted for only 28 percent of total radio usage in 1973, it was up to 63 percent in 1982. An analysis of Arbitron 1980 radio ratings data shows wide differences in the distribution of total radio listening (in met-

ropolitan areas) for FM and AM by programming format types. For example, 23 percentof the FM listening, but only 3 percent of the AM, goes to stations with an "easy listening" style of music; 28 percent of the AM but only 17 percent of the FM was for stations with an "adult contemporary" style; 6 percent of AM and 31 percent of FM went to stations specializing in rock or "album oriented rock." Only 6 percent of all listening time went to all-news stations. Cf. Edward Papazian, "Radio: The Revitalized Ad Medium," *Ad Forum*, June 1982, pp. 44-45.

7. From a paper presented to the Advertising Research Foundation conference, Chicago, 1982. Hecker suggests that good jingles should have a clearly defined objective, which might be entertainment, "nurturance," warmth, or empathy; they should offer the listener an emotional reward and exemplify a brand personality. Needless to say, this advice applies to TV as well as to radio jingles.

8. *Magazines in the Twentieth Century*, 2d ed. (Urbana: University of Illinois Press, 1964): 439. The article by Walsh was written in 1921.

9. A surprising number of people have direct contact with the newspaper as a local institution. Fifty percent have placed a classified ad at one time or another; 13 percent have written a letter to the editor.

10. Newspaper Advertising Bureau, *National Study of Direct Mail; an Inventory of Household Mail and How it is Treated, 1983.*

11. Differences in attitudes toward advertising in various media more or less reflect differences in attitudes toward the media themselves. A 1981 survey conducted by Brehl Associates for the Newspaper Advertising Bureau in Pittsburgh, Pennsylvania, and Lubbock, Texas, found some striking differences in the perception of television and reading by people at different age levels. Among those 18 to 34, 86 percent called watching TV a "waste of time." Among those 65 and over, the proportion was 36 percent. Among the younger adults, 55 percent described reading as "hard on the eyes," while only 34 percent of those 65 and over did! The percentage who found either watching TV or reading dull dropped with age. Curiously enough, the percentage who said TV was "a good escape from everyday routine" rose from 38 percent of those 18 to 34 to 48 percent of those 65 and older; whereas the percentage who described reading this way fell from 56 percent to 29 percent. The percentage who say watching TV "keeps your mind active" was 16 percent among the young and 29 percent among the old, whereas the percentage who said that reading "keeps your mind active" went from 82 percent to 45 percent.

12. Garrett J. O'Keefe, Kathleen Nash, and Jenny Liu, "The Perceived Utility of Advertising: A Cross-Media Analysis," *Journalism Quarterly*, 58 (Winter, 1981): 535-42.

13. "The Yankelovich Report, A Media Research Program," Fall 1965. "Brave," "clean," and "reverent" were omitted from the criteria used.

14. Robert C. Grass and Wallace H. Wallace, "Advertising Communication: Print vs. TV," *Journal of Advertising Research*, 14, 5 (October 1974) 19.

15. In keeping with the usual pattern, magazine ads scored significantly higher among people of high income—18 percent—against 12 percent for those in the lowest income group. The tendency was reversed in the case of TV (15 percent versus 19 percent). Curiously enough, there was no such consistent pattern when the retention scores were analyzed by educational level. The margin of difference was very slight for women— 14.9 percent for TV and 14.3 percent for magazines. For men, the difference in favor of TV was greater—20 percent compared with 16 percent for *Life*.

16. The first and second phases among women in Yuma, Arizona, and suburban Pittsburgh, were run with both personal and telephone interviews. The third phase, conducted entirely by telephone in four other cities, included both men and women. Each test used parallel samples of *Life* readers and TV viewers. (The first two tests used

commercials, both 30 and 60 seconds, inserted into a cable TV movie; the third used commercials appearing in five regular prime-time network programs.) "Verified recall" was established by asking for each ad or commercial, identified by brand, whether the respondent recalled it and then probing for a description of everything that was remembered about it.

17. "Action Speaks Louder Than Words," New York: Teleresearch Inc., 1973.

18. Actually, visual perception does not exist outside of time. A figure must be exposed for 0.003 seconds before it is "seen" with a complete contour, according to H. Werner, cited by William Dember, *Psychology of Perception* (New York: Holt, Rinehart, and Winston, 1960).

19. Before this—in 1956—*Good Housekeeping* had engaged Burleigh Gardner's Social Research Inc. to demonstrate that the same ad directed to the housewife was more warmly received and better attended to in a woman's magazine than in *Life* or the *Post. Cf.* "The Meaning of Good Housekeeping and Its Advertising to Its Readers," *op. cit.*

20. *Subscriber Attitudes Towards Editorial and Advertising in Five Magazines* (Harper-Atlantic Sales, Inc., 1966).

21. E. J. Kahn, Jr., *The Big Drink* (New York: Random House, 1960), p. 153. The Coca-Cola Company has changed its corporate position in this area dramatically since that time.

22. Otmar Ernst, "New Evidence on how Advertising Works," *Admap*, February 1978, pp. 80-89.

23. Valentine Appel, "Magazine/Television Audience Segmentation Analysis: The Media Imperative," Address before the Advertising Research Foundation Conference, New York City, 1975.

Chapter 7
Getting the Message Through

"Advertisements are now so numerous that they are negligently perused," said Samuel Johnson in 1758. Today, too, a large proportion of observed ads are not recorded as noteworthy in any way, as we saw earlier (pp. 10). But even more striking is the small number of advertising messages counted under conditions of hypersensitivity to advertising, i.e., sensitivity artificially induced by the research plan. What a minute proportion the count of 76 observed ads in 12 hours represents in light of the tremendous daily outpouring of messages from all sides and through all media!

Is there a practical physical limitation on the number of messages that the human senses can absorb? There is good evidence to the effect that a constant input of fresh stimuli is essential to our mental balance. During every waking moment we are bombarded by an enormous array of sensory impressions. Yet we do not ordinarily lose ourselves in contemplation of the design of the fabrics and furniture around us, the play of light and shadow, the beating of our pulses, the itching of our skins, or the varied sounds that reach us through the open window. We can at any moment selectively concentrate our attention on any of these many stimuli, or we can ignore them. In the same way, the proliferation of communications in our visual and aural environment forces us to be selective in what we recognize and register. To use the terms of Gestalt psychology, we learn to separate "figures" from "ground." We place certain stimuli within the forefront of our attention, while others of equivalent intensity are relegated to the background.

The film historian Siegfried Kracauer refers in his *Theory of Film* to "the blind spots of the mind."

> The role which cultural standards and traditions may play in these processes of elimination is drastically illustrated by a report on the reactions of African natives to a film made on the spot. After the screening, the spectators, all of them still unacquainted with the medium, talked volubly about a chicken they allegedly had seen picking food in the mud. The film maker himself, entirely unaware of its presence, attended several performances without being able to detect it. Had it been dreamed up by the natives? Only by scanning his film foot by foot

did he eventually succeed in tracing the chicken: it appeared for a fleeting moment somewhere in a corner of a picture and then vanished forever.[1]

The "blind spots of the mind" may be experimentally located in the psychological laboratory. When, through the use of a stereoscopic device, an upright face is presented to one eye and an upside down face to the other eye, the individual does not see two super-imposed faces; he sees one face right side up. Similar results are obtained when a nude and a clothed figure are presented simultaneously. When a baseball picture and a bullfight picture are shown at the same time to different eyes, Americans see the ballgame, Mexicans the bullfight.

How we perceive

What makes us perceive things as meaningful to us so that they register in our minds? In the words of W. H. Ittelson and F. T. Kilpatrick,[2] "perception is never a sure thing, never an absolute revelation of 'what is.' Rather, what we see is a prediction—our own personal construction designed to give us the best possible bet for carrying out our purposes in action. We make these bets on the basis of our past experience."

According to the perception theorist James J. Gibson, "perception involves meaning; sensation does not. . . . Sensations are not the cause of perceptions. . . . Conscious sensory impressions and sense data in general are incidental to perception, not essential to it. They are occasionally symptomatic of perception. But they are not even necessary symptoms inasmuch as perception may be 'sensationless' (as for example in auditory localization). Having a perception does not entail the having of sensations."[3]

The processes of visual perception are extraordinarily complex. J. Bronowski writes:

> The brain asks the eye for information not about points but about objects: their boundaries, their movements and their contrast against the background. This is a much more recondite system of information than we, who are used to television pictures and graph paper, would expect. Moreover, in higher animals it is relayed to either two or three different parts of the brain, which have evolved at different times. In short, the brain (and the retina, which in origin is part of the brain) is concerned from the first moment with integrating the impressions it receives from the environment; it *begins* by discriminating. What it treats as units of information are far more complex assemblies and contrasts than we would think of feeding to a machine.[4]

Within the retina, the greatest concentration of photoreceptors is in an area called the fovea. We move our eyes in order to get the maximum information we need to this very small area. These eye movements are so rapid that they take up only about 10 percent of the time we spend "seeing."

Derek H. Fender describes the changing of the eye's focus in visual search as a matter of feed-back controls or servomechanisms. One such servomechanism, for example, controls the eye muscles "to position the image of an object on the fovea. Each pair of muscles receives signals proportional to the displacement of the interesting part of the image from the fovea, and the muscles then act together to move the eyeball in such a way as to reduce the displacement to zero."[5]

Through still another servomechanism, the eyes are brought to the correct angle of convergence, making depth perception possible. Similar changes occur in the thickness, and therefore in the focal length, of the lens. The accommodative mechanism of the eye has what Fender refers to as a steady "hunting motion . . . superimposed on it that continually lengthens and shortens the focal length of the lens."

Depending on the location of the object being viewed, a change in one direction will improve an out-of-focus image, and a change in the other direction will worsen it; this information is fed back to steer accommodation in the direction of the sharpest focus. Once the correct lens thickness is found, information about it is fed across to the convergence mechanism. The two systems exchange information but are separate and distinct in their modes of control.

In a second, we normally experience two or three saccades, movements that carry our focus to different points in a visual field. We also fixate our vision at a particular point when it holds our attention. What we see is translated into neural activity in the visual cortex of the brain, and when we recognize an object we are in effect matching that pattern in the visual cortex with a corresponding pattern in our memory system. Images stored in memory are imprecise. We recall a building without being able to visualize the number of stories it has because we cannot change our fixation and count them as we do in actual perception.

Perception is a matter of probability, a probability that increases as the intensity of the stimulus is changed. Change is experienced as a "shock of transition," to use William James' term. Thus we normally think of perception as an activity that involves a reaction to stimuli *above* the threshold of consciousness or awareness.

The geometric relationship between stimulation and experience is expressed in Weber's Law, one of the landmarks of perceptual psychology. The stronger or more intense the existing stimulus, the greater the real change required to produce the sensation of change. William Dember points out that Weber's Law deals with variations in the intensity of a given stimulus against a constant background. If the Law applied *regardless* of the original intensity of the stimulus whose strength is being varied, then its detectability would depend only on the relative contrast of target and background. But when the background has high intensity, it is harder for a stimulus target to be distinguished. Conversely, when the background has less intensity, it is easier for a stimulus to be noted. And the bigger the visual target, the easier it is to distinguish it from the background—this holds true up to a critical focal point beyond which it becomes harder again.[6]

A similar relationship of message to background appears to apply to hearing as well as seeing. John Cohen proposes that the apparent duration of a brief interval is influenced by the intensity of the stimuli that delimit it. "The more intense the stimuli are, the shorter the interval seems to be. . . . A reverse effect occurs, however, if the interval is defined by a continuous stimulus and the subject is asked to compare two equal intervals made up of stimuli of unequal intensity. The interval with the more intense sound seems to last longer than the interval with the less intense sound."[7] In short, our perception of what we hear and see is inseparable from the environment of the message.

Our perception is also inseparable from the categories through which we define experience. In the Eskimo languages there are dozens of words for snow to describe the innumerable forms and consistencies it assumes under different conditions. We see what the Eskimo sees, but we find it unnecessary to differentiate, linguistically or perceptually. What for the Eskimo is a very complex, densely informative set of perceptions, we reduce to a sweeping summary.

In English, we commonly use eight names for colors, although there are about 7,500,000 just-noticeable differences. Yet as Gordon Bower points out, "our color-naming does not force us to judge, when remembering, that green peas are the same color as green Christmas trees."[8]

Another psychologist, Henry Helson, has applied the concept of "adaptation level" to describe the neutral perceptual state of an organism at the moment a fresh stimulus is received. Thus a new sensory impression is always perceived not merely in terms of its own physical strength, but in relation to the stimuli that have preceded it.

We bring to most experience a "set" of expectations about what is to come next. We interpret new stimuli in terms of these anticipations and see, in effect, what we expect to see. People who are hungry or thirsty are more likely to recognize words that pertain to hunger or thirst. When we look for more than one thing at the same time, it is harder to detect *any* of the things we are looking for. Experiments have shown that we recognize familiar words more easily than unfamiliar ones, but that unfamiliar words are detected more rapidly when we are prepared to expect them.

Our minds are endowed with unconscious mechanisms by which they avoid processing unneeded and unwanted information. It is these perceptual defenses that make consumers oblivious to the blandishments of most of the advertising to which they are exposed.

When we look at a crowd, our attention picks out among the faces the ones that look familiar, or whose appearance is striking, or appealing, or repulsive, while the rest remain undifferentiated. Just so, we focus our attention selectively on advertising messages that emerge from the surrounding blur because they resonate in some way to our interests and predilections, either because of their subject or because of their superb technique.

Our very ability to pay attention presupposes an ability to differentiate. It is impossible to be attentive to all the signals that are constantly reaching our eyes and ears. Just as unwanted sounds fade into background noise when we listen to a speaker, so the voice of the speaker may become background noise if our attention is caught by an attractive member of the opposite sex, or if boredom with what the speaker is saying leads us into reverie.

Most of what is before our eyes, most of the time, may be considered the visual equivalent of background noise. And most of the advertising to which we are exposed, in all media, must be put under that heading, for most people. Our ability to shut out most of the advertising messages that flash by us accounts for their ephemeral nature.

G. S. Blum has shown that at low levels of awareness "the individual would be sensitized to threatening impulses and impulse-related stimuli; but if the stimuli were close to awareness, defense would occur. Thus both vigilance and defense are predicted depending on the level of awareness."[9]

Blum demonstrated his point by showing to his experimental subjects both anxiety-producing and neutral pictures; the subjects were then asked to identify the pictures under two different conditions of exposure, one much briefer than the other. On brief exposure, the anxiety-producing stimulus was identified more often. It was *less* easily identified when the exposure was long enough to permit some awareness of the content.

This finding has interesting implications for advertising dealing with subjects that are essentially unpleasant (like headache remedies, for instance). The suggestion would seem to be that product identity might be more readily established in print (where the reader could abbreviate his contact with the message) than in a TV commercial where the message could not be avoided. Successful experiences in television would seem to belie this.

Scanning and reading

When we read, we rapidly go through a succession of very short visual exposures, each of which covers a large and complex amount of information. Fast readers process more of that information with each visual fixation than slow readers do, but regardless of how fast or slowly one reads, about a quarter of a second is required to perceive and process the meaning from a word (the same amount of time that is required for storage). As the eyes focus on a new portion of the reading matter, the visual image of the previous fixation is erased. Thus, the interval between fixations (which is under the individual's control) can be used by efficient readers to make sense of what they have been looking at.[10]

Ulric Neisser has observed that "reading" is an ambiguous word that covers many levels of comprehension. Scanning is a kind of reading that involves a relatively low level of cognitive analysis and that takes place at a rate that seems independent of the quantity of information to be processed. Neisser describes scanning as it is exemplified in the daily work of people who are accustomed to looking for several thousand targets at once:

> The readers in any newspaper-clipping agency. Such a firm may have hundreds of clients, each of whom wants a clipping of at least any newspaper story in which he or his firm is mentioned; beyond this, many clients will be interested in an appreciable number of different trade names and titles and others will specify their clipping needs in a more general way. . . . It takes a year or more to train a clipping reader to scan newspaper type at well over 1,000 words a minute, keeping watch for all the agency's targets. Error rates are said to be in the neighborhood of 10% for the best readers, and neither the error rate nor the speed seems to change as an agency gradually acquires more clients.[11]

Neisser concludes that "visual search can involve a multiplicity of processes carried out together." He points out that "perceptual analysis, then, has many levels. It seems to be carried out by a multitude of separate mechanisms arranged in a hierarchy, the more complex mechanisms receiving as their input the information that has been assimilated and predigested by more elementary ones."

Eye movements may actually be "anticipations" rather than "responses" to stimuli. "The eye's control system must be doing something more than reacting to a motion; it must be predicting."

The psychoanalytic concept of repression helps to explain at least one aspect of the scanning process. Ordinarily, the term "repression" refers to the subjugation, below consciousness, of an unpleasant experience or emotion. A newspaper reader sees a photograph of an atrocity and then "forgets" that he has seen it. At a far less intense level of emotion, he represses his perception of an ad for a product with unpleasant brand name associations.

But this psychological mechanism is distinct from the kind of rejection that takes place automatically in the normal reading process. Most of what is seen or heard but not perceived does not represent an active repression of information for which there is an actual aversion. It represents rather an economical response to an oversupply of stimuli. As the reader scans, he inhibits not so much the unpleasant as the merely irrelevant.

The newspaper represents a large, complex array of visual stimuli, and studies of how it is read can tell us a good deal about the general process by which advertising messages come through to us.

Since the eyes are always in motion, the reader constantly confronts new cues that stimulate new interests on an open spread of pages in a magazine or newspaper. His focus of vision is attracted to those areas of potential interest that are glimpsed in the periphery of the visual field.

In the reading process, our systematic scanning is arrested and concentrated when we find something we want to examine more closely. To some extent the reader is engaged in a purposeful search for useful information. But he also appears to be in a state of hypersensitivity or susceptibility to relevant information that he is neither looking for nor expecting to encounter. All this, moreover, occurs in the twinkling of an eye.

The reader, as he scans, unconsciously tends to simplify things for himself by fitting material into context. To use a concept from Gestalt psychology, the reader seeks for closure: he tries to reduce the environment to the most easily manageable terms; when he looks at the page, he interprets it in terms of its *overall* meaning.

What attracts our attention

As we go from a small ad to a big one in print, or as we add color to black and white, we increase the probability that the reader's eye will physically alight upon the message in the normal course of the scanning process. We do not comparably increase this probability as we go from a brief I.D. to a longer commercial on TV, although the opportunity for the absent-minded or diverted viewer to return his gaze to the screen is greater if the message is extended in time.

Novelty and complexity attract our attention. However, as William Dember points out, even complex stimuli "should lose their attractive power once they have been thoroughly investigated. The most interesting painting, for example, cannot be viewed interminably. The finest symphony, if repeated often enough, becomes banal and commonplace. The best novel cannot bear continual re-reading."[12]

In an experiment conducted at the University of Manchester, a group of people exposed to a concert of recorded music were asked to signal when they became aware that their minds had been wandering away from the program. As reported by John Cohen, the percentage of inattentiveness rose from 19 percent after five minutes to 66 percent after 10 minutes and to 82 percent after 20 minutes. When a similar experiment was run with a lecture instead of music, the proportion rose from 27 percent inattentiveness after five minutes to 52 percent after 10 minutes and 61 percent after 20 minutes. Curiously enough, the lecture audience became *more* attentive after a half-hour had elapsed.[13]

Curiosity, the sheer zest for exploration, appears to be an essential human attribute. Human beings (and their brethren, the apes) go "stir-crazy" in a dull monotonous environment. Experiments in "sensory deprivation"—in which extraneous stimulation is kept to a minimum—show that people lose many of their normal attributes and capacities under such circumstances. They even create their own excitement through hallucinations.

On the opposite side, extreme stimulation (pain, for instance) can also interfere with the normal workings of perception and intelligence. The optimum condition is stimulation short of the extreme. To quote Daniel Berlyne, a psychologist who has specialized in this subject, "novel stimuli attract more inspection than familiar stimuli. Similarly, human subjects will spend more time looking at more complex or more incongruous pictures, unless complexity becomes extreme."[14] Stimuli that produce conflict also produce arousal and readiness for action. Attention is stimulated by the presence of the unexpected and the uncertain.

For the advertiser, there is a fine shade of difference between the degree of conflict that produces attention and interest and the degree that people perceive as unpleasant and seek to avoid. No one can state in advance and in general terms where this fine shade of difference occurs, because it is always peculiar to the product and to the advertisement. The "shock effect" of seeing a familiar figure out of context (a well-known sports personality with a bag of potato chips) represents a quite different kind of "conflict and arousal" than a grisly photograph of an automobile wreck. Insurance companies that show wrecked cars inevitably show them only slightly wrecked, and the casualties have only superficial wounds. (In its "Kill or be Killed" training films, the Army taught World War II infantrymen the technique of hand-to-hand combat. One film showed the soldier emerging from his gory first battle with his arm in a sling. For the trainee this device created attention rather than utter panic and abhorrence.)

It is quite clear that there are limits beyond which one does not normally want to go in scaring people with the threat of "body odor" or foul breath. Filter cigarette ads do not mention lung cancer or heart disease; they don't have to because it is tacitly understood by advertiser and customer alike that the thought is present in every line of copy that deals with filter action. So they stress fine tobacco and great taste.

The incongruity that whets attention may be created by media scheduling, as well as by the creative theme. It may be done through a media mix in which the product appears in different contexts. Or it may be created by the use of different spatial or time units that make the advertising look or sound different when it is encountered on different occasions.

Norman Mackworth, a psychologist who studies perception with the aid of a camera that photographs eye movements, makes a key distinction between "looking" and "attending," activities that he considers closely related but *not* identical. Mackworth points out that the hockey player who must look ahead of him at the other players still manages to attend to the puck at his feet. He sees without looking, through his peripheral vision. The reverse, looking without seeing, is a common phenomenon of everyday life—and the cause of many traffic accidents.

When people look at pictures they tend to concentrate their gaze on a small part of the total area (usually less than 10 percent). Their eye movements cluster around the edges, especially the angles, and more especially around the areas of high informational content, especially those with unusual details.[15]

The amount of information acquired about a picture depends on the number of separate fixations and not on how long they last. The "informative" area to which attention is directed also tends to be the most easily recognized part. A whole scene can often be interpreted or identified from only a small part of it. Because pictures represent more complex visual phenomena than words, Mackworth concludes from his evidence that pictorial information is processed more slowly than words are by (literate) adults.

The "useful field of view" in which visual information is actively being processed varies in size according to the complexity of the information within it. When the material being presented is crowded with irrelevant or unwanted details or when there is less time to process information, the useful field of view is narrowed, much as the eye's pupil contracts in the presence of too much light.

Mackworth stresses the importance for perception of internal factors that help direct the line of sight. "Every time an individual uses his eyes to perceive, he is making a choice." There is a constant "interplay between external sensory stimuli and internal schemata." He distinguishes two kinds of exploratory behavior in which the individual selectively changes what comes before him. A person can *modify* what he sees through short eye movements—"visual steps." Through longer movements—"visual leaps"—he can bring in new stimuli from sources previously *outside* his field of vision.

Although they tend to get similar information, different people examine pictures in a different sequence, and the same people look at them differently on different exposures. Mackworth compares the eye movement tracks to a "random walk." "The fixation point is really an area of regard. Therefore an apparent near miss with the fixation point will often represent a successful attempt to locate a region rich in information."

Mackworth notes how an unexpected incongruity can affect perception: "In reading ... a visual anomaly such as a misplaced letter may force itself on attention after the eye has moved on and then cause a backward checking glance. This indicates that somewhere the visual pattern has been stored and examined."

Symbols and perception

There is a basic physiological element at work in perception that arises from the tendency of the central nervous system to avoid unnecessary fatigue and to seek equilibrium. Attention is most likely to be attracted to a visual field that can be apprehended with a minimum expenditure of energy. This occurs when there is adequate framing, good design and layout, and sharp contrast. Attention is harder to get when there are fuzzy gray areas or different units of illustration or text that fight for attention, as they do in a cluttered advertisement or poorly made-up page.

The appearance or sound of an ad makes it clear or complex—and hence more or less easy for the eye or ear to absorb its meaning. The essential principles of good design apply to TV as they do to print. The "no-clutter" principle is expressed not only visually, but also in the cardinal rule of producing commercials: video and audio should reinforce each other.

Purely physiological reactions to physical stimuli are only partly responsible for the way we perceive advertising or any other form of communication. Perception is also a matter of symbols and the meanings they convey in relation to existing reference points.

Form always carries symbolic associations and meanings, intended or unintended in the case of man-made forms. The interdependence of purely physical and symbolic forces in perceptual attraction is illustrated in a description by Rudolf Arnheim of a Renaissance painting that shows St. Michael weighing souls on a balancing scale:

> By the mere strength of prayer, one frail little nude figure outweighs four big devils plus two millstones. The difficulty is that prayer carries only spiritual weight and provides no visual pull. As a remedy, the painter has used the large dark patch on the angel's dress just below the scale that holds the saintly soul. By visual attraction, which is non-existent in the physical object, the patch creates the weight that adapts the appearance of the scene to its meaning.[16]

We see and hear things because our eyes and ears are sensitive to light waves and sound waves that the central nervous system is able to organize into meaningful patterns. This can happen because new sensory input can be related to previous significant experience. The constant and instantaneous comparison of new sensation to the meaning of what has happened before makes it possible for us to discriminate one event or thing from another and to separate messages from their backgrounds.

Like any other vehicle of communication, an advertisement is made up of symbols on many different levels. The shape and contrast of dark and light areas represent letters that individually, in our Western alphabets, stand for sounds and in combination are words that symbolize objects, actions, or properties.

Headlines, slogans, text, and logotypes convey symbolic meanings. So do the illustrations of products, people, and backgrounds that evoke whatever associations the advertiser has in mind—and often many that he hasn't.

The sociologist Erving Goffman observes that in print advertisements "a scene can be simulated in which figures are captured in those acts that stereotypically epitomize the sequence from which they are taken." The way in which figures are positioned in ads "whose meaning can be read at a flash" reflects positioning in real life. Thus, when men and women are shown together, the man is typically in an "executive" role, physically placed higher than the woman. Women are often shown in a recumbent position, suggesting at the same time their low status, their vulnerability, and their sexual availability.[17]

Advertising for any product will arouse a more intense response from prospects (however these are defined) than from nonprospects. But every ad or commercial uses verbal and pictorial symbols with overtones of meaning that have nothing to do with the product at all and to which different kinds of people are especially sensitive or responsive. This is particularly true of television commercials in which the announcers or models and the background situations lead the viewer into realms of fantasy that do not necessarily support the sales message.

Horace Schwerin reports that commercials that use maximum exaggeration are preferable to milder "half-way houses of hyperbole." The most effective commercials for a men's grooming product were those in which girls actually swooned when the wearer approached. The most effective commercials for children's sneakers showed a child traveling at a speed faster than sound when he wore the advertised product.

It is obvious that a brassiere ad showing a shapely model will arouse different kinds of product- and non-product-related reactions and fantasies for men than for women. Similarly, though less obviously, an automobile ad that shows a car on a rugged mountain road carries different meanings than an ad showing the same car in the driveway of a stately mansion. Moreover, the relative weight of car fantasy and irrelevant fantasy in each case will vary for people of different temperaments with different life styles and car-using patterns.

The significance of nonproduct symbols in advertising art and theming is often discussed in the context of copy or qualitative research, but it is seldom treated as a significant factor in media planning. The use of a baby, an animal, or a pretty girl to capture the reader's or viewer's attention is a trick way to realize the full potential of the audience. The objective is no different from that of the media planner who tries to maximize attention by using an unusual shape for his ad in the newspaper or by spotting his TV commercial in a particularly favorable adjacency.

Remembering print and TV advertising

When we separate the elements in perception that are predominantly physical from those that are predominantly symbolic, certain innate characteristics of print and television can be better distinguished.

The act of paying attention to a print ad is different from the act of paying attention to a commercial. The broadcast viewer may show inattention by being physically absent (as when he walks out of the room to get a drink of water), by being selectively inattentive (as when he picks up a newspaper or a deck of cards or converses with someone without changing his position in front of the set), or by being mentally absent when, to all intents and purposes, he continues to look at the set but fails to register the message because it does not concern or interest him.

When the reader of a magazine or newspaper opens to a page, however briefly, he can ignore an ad only by being selectively inattentive in the latter sense. He is not going elsewhere. He is simply rejecting the content of the ad as meaningless or inappropriate for him, but this takes place as part of an instantaneous and largely subconscious registration of the ad upon his field of vision.

In broadcasting, we consciously tune in the programs we like and tune out those we do not like. But on the mental level we also psychologically "tune in" those messages that are of relevance, interest, and concern to us and "tune out" those that are irrelevant. (In terms of everyday life, "tuning in" is like hearing one's name mentioned by someone at the other end of the room in a crowded cocktail party; "tuning out" is the typical male's obliviousness to the display in a dressmaker's window which he passes each day on the way to work.)

In advertising research we usually assume that an advertisement registers an impression that, together with an accumulation of other similar impressions, and interacting with other *non*advertising influences, will imprint itself on the minds of the audience and condition the ultimate buying decision. We generally assume that the strength of these impressions is primarily a matter of *conscious* impact, so that recall and recognition are widely used as indicators of an important intermediary step in the process by which advertising works. Along with the particular impact of a given message, our research methods tend to measure the accumulative impact of all similar preceding messages.

We use measures of recall (in which we ask people to tell us what was in an advertisement) or recognition (in which we actually show people the advertisement) because they are available in a standardized form from readership research services, even though we know that recall of both broadcast commercials and print advertising represents not an accurate report of actual attention at the moment of exposure, but rather the residual capacity to identify the advertisement after time has elapsed. Tests of recognition yield higher scores than tests of recall (which place greater demands on the memory).* Recognition scores also

---

*We are most apt to recognize people we barely know when we see them in the familiar setting in which we have come to know them than when we encounter them unexpectedly. In listening to a foreign language, we recognize unfamiliar words most readily when they are spoken in the context of a conversation. Recognition obviously covers a greater spectrum than recall. Recognizing the right answer to a multiple choice question is easier than recalling the answer spontaneously without a reminder. We recognize more words in other people's vocabulary or in reading than we normally employ in our own speech or writing. The same principles apply to measurements of advertising. A variety of experimental studies show that readership scores can be boosted to much higher levels by reducing the time lag between the original reading and the interview or by providing the respondent with incentives to remember advertising messages that at first do not come easily to mind.

show a more gentle rate of forgetting than do measures of recall. They have been common currency in the advertising world since the turn of the century, when Walter Dill Scott asked his students at Northwestern University to recall ads in magazines they had looked through in class and asked Chicago street car riders to recall the car cards they had seen. Daniel Starch began his studies on the recognition of ads in 1922 and kept doing them for nearly 60 years.

The memorability of television commercials is commonly measured by techniques that require the person interviewed to recall some features of the commercial from memory. Print ads are generally assessed by methods that give the ad every possible benefit of the doubt. All anyone has to do in some kinds of interview is nod his head (which comes very naturally for some people). Even by these generous standards, readership scores for individual ads vary all over the lot both in newspapers and magazines, though research on both these media shows that most readers open about four out of five pages and are thereby physically exposed to the advertising.*

Reports of reading editorial matter are uttered with significantly less confidence than reports of reading ads. In a 1971 study of 41 readers of a British women's magazine, the longer the time that had actually been spent in looking at the page (as recorded by a hidden motion picture camera during the experiment), the greater the confidence in the report of reading. More confidence was expressed for the noting of color ads, compared to black and white.[18]

Readership scores are a curious amalgam of psychological projection ("This interests me so I must have seen it"), original attention value, and the persistent memory of the ad itself. When recognition (noting) scores are projected against audience figures, the resulting numbers reflect product interest as much as or more than advertising reach or efficiency. We remember what makes sense to us better than what we merely try to remember.

In everyday advertising parlance, television is described as an "intrusive" medium. This reflects the psychological truth that learning takes place as a result of attentive arousal to information and the need to respond to it, whether or not the individual *intends* to learn. In an experiment by J. Richard Barclay, one group of people listened to sentences describing relationships among animals, men, or cars, and were told that their assignment was to line them up in proper order. Another (control) group heard the same sentences and was given the task of memorizing them. While virtually all in the first group could reconstruct the order of the objects, virtually none of the second group could. More important, the first (or "comprehending") group could accurately recognize the sentences when they were presented along with false ones, while the second group failed the test miserably.[19]

Commenting on this, James Jenkins concludes, "We should shun any notion that memory consists of a specific system that operates with one set of rules on one kind of unit. What is remembered in a given situation depends on the

---

*Studies by the Newspaper Advertising Bureau have found that awareness of inserts holds at a steady level even when there are as many as a dozen in a copy of the paper. However, readership of the pages within an insert is higher for customers of the advertiser than it is for noncustomers.

physical and psychological context in which the event was experienced, the knowledge and skills that the subject brings to the context, the situation in which we ask for evidence for remembering, and the relation of what the subject remembers to what the experimenter demands."

We remember by fitting new experiences into the framework of what we already know. We do this by the *selection* of only relevant information to be encoded into memory, by the *abstraction* of underlying meanings, and by the *integration* of what remains into our existing knowledge. Finally, *interpretation* enriches what is remembered by adding inferences and details derived from prior experience. Thus, what we remember represents an interaction between (1) what we encode and "rehearse" (or consciously strive to remember) at the time of our initial exposure to an event and (2) the conditions, cause, and motivations that prevail at the time we are trying to retrieve the information.[20]

There may be one kind of memory for pictorial images and another kind for linguistic matter. The former kind may be almost limitless, but the second type is definitely not. For that reason, faces are more easily recognized than names recalled. Ralph Haber and an associate presented subjects tachistoscopically with 2,560 pictures and an hour later showed them 140 again, interspersed with 140 similar but new pictures. Nine out of ten were correctly identified as previously seen.

Although people remember whole pictures much better than details, some of those details are reflected in their associations with what they have seen, though on the surface they cannot be remembered. Haber points out that "since the pictures are not stored in words they cannot be recalled in words either. . . . If techniques could be found to facilitate an attaching of words to visual images, recall might dramatically improve."[21] Printed words are not stored in memory as a collection of letters but rather as ideas. "A road sign is not remembered as a brightly colored panel with an arrow or a warning on it but as a message to stop, slow down, or turn."

The memorability of an advertisement reflects only one of the tasks it set out to accomplish. Advertising may function (1) as a way of creating initial awareness of a product, (2) as a reminder of a product, (3) as a source of information about a product, (4) as an argument on behalf of a product, (5) as a stimulus to create an emotional climate auspicious to a product, or (6) as a means of establishing an aura or image of a product. Measurements of the ad's memorability provide no means of gauging the intensity of qualitative performance for all these functions.

Readership studies invariably find that men remember noting ads of interest to men more than those of interest to women and vice versa.* In one such study,[22] readers of the *Des Moines Register* were shown two facing pages, one a woman's

---

*This selectiveness also holds true for recall of television commercials. In the 1965 Newspaper Advertising Bureau survey mentioned on page 144, women recalled 19 percent of the woman's product commercials and 12 percent of the men's. Men recalled 24 percent of the men's product commercials and 19 percent of the women's. For a typical television commercial, users of the product have an average Burke "day after" recall of 25 percent, while nonusers have an average recall of 21 percent.

page and the other a general-news page; practically everyone, men and women, reported opening the general-news page. And practically all the women reported opening the woman's page. Yet only three out of five men reported that they had opened that page, even though it was physically impossible for them not to have had it open when they opened the opposite page. This sort of mechanism reflects more than selective forgetting—it suggests that the initial perception was selective. It was hardly surprising to find that women remembered more of the advertising directed at their sex than men did. But they also actually *saw* more such advertising. As items of interest were seen out of the corner of the eye, the reader's focus of attention was more likely to move toward them.

A full-page ad appealing to women was remembered by far fewer men than reported having opened the page (in the context of the opposite page). Yet since there was nothing else on the page with the ad on it, it is inconceivable that a reader could open the page without "seeing" the ad, however briefly.

In research conducted at the University of Minnesota's School of Journalism, people were re-interviewed after an ordinary readership interview and asked to explain why they had not reported seeing certain ads. The readers' most frequent answer was a kind of acknowledgment that the ad had been seen but simply filtered out of conscious awareness: "I'm not interested in that product" or "I don't shop at that store." (Part of the creative problem in retail advertising is exactly this—to intrigue the reader's interest in a store she has never thought of as being "for her.")

In another small-scale experiment, Mackworth's eye camera was used to make a filmed record of what people actually *focused* on when they read the newspaper in a laboratory situation.[23] This actual record of the changing focus of the readers' vision could be compared with what they reported later in a conventional Starch-type readership-recognition interview (in which they were asked what they remembered having seen or read).

In the past, studies using "confusion controls" have shown that some reports of recognition of ads in any medium are false. (That is, some ads are claimed to have been seen or heard even though they have never appeared.) This reflects not so much outright distortion as "yea-saying" (agreeableness) or psychological projection, arising from interest in the product or familiarity with the brand. In some cases, of course, what appear to be false claims of recognition actually reflect sighting of the same or similar ads on past occasions.[24] In the eye camera experiment, the number of ads focused by the eye and then forgotten by the reader was about thirteen times greater than the number falsely reported though not actually seen.

The readership process was further explored in the Des Moines experiment mentioned previously. Five different versions of the same day's paper were prepared and delivered in the usual way to matched samples of reader households. In four of these versions (on the same page), blank space was substituted for a different size advertisement. Telephone interviews were made the same evening by Eric Marder Associates and personal interviews the next day. Thus there were measures of performance for the empty space of each size and for an ordinary advertisement in the same space.

This research corroborated the eye camera evidence that we see things out of the corner of the eye and then redirect our attention accordingly. A reader who has once stopped at something on the page is more likely to stop and look at other things—including those he would otherwise screen out as irrelevant in his initial scanning.

When the experimental page was altered by substituting white space for the various ads, the page as a whole was reinterpreted as being of greater interest either to men or to women, depending upon what material now stood out in the changed visual array.

People who opened a page on which a large white space appeared in place of an ad often "saw" and interpreted it as part of the normal advertising environment. Just as bigger ads are noted by more people than small ones, so the bigger white space got more attention than lesser spaces. But the study found that a good advertisement with a good layout for a product of interest to readers could command an attention level many times greater than that which was par, so to speak, for the empty space. A good dishware ad got nearly four times the level of recognition from women that it got from men. This level was also four times as great as recall (by men or by women) of the same space unit when it was left blank.

The space in the medium merely provided a base on top of which the advertiser's creative treatment determined the level of reader attention. Recognition, in effect, appears to be mainly a measure of interest in the product and of responsiveness to the way in which the product is presented creatively.* It is not really a measure of the probability that the message will actually be seen by the reader's roving eye. Page opening appeared to be the only measure of readership that remained relatively stable.

Big ads and ads for interesting products start out with a better chance of catching the reader's attention. So do ads in certain key positions. (In magazines, Starch noting scores for back cover ads average 65 percent higher than inside ads, while inside cover ads run 30 percent higher.) But the Des Moines findings suggest that the task for both the advertising agency and the advertiser really begins at the point where the reader's eye is caught. From then on, memorability varies with the individual ad.[25] It seems to reflect the ability of the individual advertiser, starting with whatever advantages or handicaps his product gives him, to do a creative job in the space he buys.

Print: opportunity, exposure, registration

The Des Moines experiment suggested that not only does an ad win a certain amount of attention in its own right, it also appears to enjoy an added element of attention derived from the power of other ads and editorial items on the page.[26] The study demonstrates, in sum, how the environment provides cues that

---

*The relationship of the advertising message to its immediate editorial environment was examined in a study made in Eugene, Oregon, by Galen Rarick with the support of the Newspaper Advertising Bureau. Ad position was varied above and below the fold, from right- to left-hand pages, and from the front to the back of the paper. No major changes took place in recognition scores, even though the surroundings of each advertisement were obviously different under these different circumstances.

can either help or hinder the observation of any particular unit of space.

The Des Moines experiment illustrates an essential principle of Gestalt psychology: that we perceive things always in relation to other things. We see or hear advertising in the context of other advertising, of editorial matter, or of entertainment.

The editorial environment does not seem to affect the noting of print ads, according to the Starch organization, which measured recognition of some 90,000 magazine ads between 1967 and 1969.* Ads designed especially for a particular publication get 30 percent to 40 percent higher recognition than those that remain unchanged across a schedule of different magazines. In any given magazine, the best read ads in a particular product category get nearly 7.5 times as many noters as the least read ads.†

Both in magazines and in newspapers, Starch noting scores are no different for ads on right and left-hand pages and not much different for ads at the front and back. However, ads generally get lower recognition scores when they appear in a publication thick with advertising than they do in a thin one. (Partly this is because the thin publication takes a shorter, less demanding interview; partly it may reflect the fact that there is less competition for attention.) Ads in an experimental August 1980 issue of *Esquire* fattened with 47 additional full-page ads received claimed recall levels that were 26 percent less and proven recall levels 22 percent less than they did when measured in a regular issue.[27]

Another controlled experiment used 20-page dummy issues of the *Saturday*

---

*This observation carries with it some implications for newspaper makeup. Would it be advantageous to lump together all the advertising for a particular kind of product in one part of the newspaper, as is commonly done with financial ads on the business pages or with food ads on the women's pages? One must answer this question cautiously. Such a grouping makes it convenient for the advertiser to attract that minority of readers who, on any given day, start out in an active search for a particular kind of product information. But it makes it harder for him to attract readers who are not "looking," who might at first glance not consider the subject of interest but who might be held as a result of a second glance directed at something else nearby.

A study made by Million Market Newspapers in association with the Milwaukee *Sentinel* compared ads with a medical or health subject under two make-up conditions. In one version they were spread throughout the paper, in the other they were concentrated on a single page with a number of articles and features on health. This concentration on a single theme added somewhat to the noting scores of the individual advertisements. How much of this represents a real shift in initial attention is hard to say. There is no question that the grouping of related ads and articles made the page as a whole more memorable to the readers and produced better recognition of its components.

†This flat statement demands a qualifier. Retailers welcome the presence of their competitors on nearby pages, since it generates comparisons of values and shopping excitement. Contrast this with the identity crisis faced by cigarette advertisers when broadcast media were barred to them. A single issue of a magazine may contain ads for a dozen different competing brands of cigarettes. The Sunday supplements limit the number of pages of cigarette advertising they will accept in any week to avoid domination by this single type of product. Over two out of five billboard ads in major markets advertise cigarettes. No one concerned welcomes the resulting opportunity for total confusion.

Review and *True Romance*, each containing a different set of six ads. Recall levels were unrelated to the individual magazines in which the ads were shown, although those drawn from one magazine were recalled substantially better, both in their own publication and in the other.[28]

Recall and recognition are not, of course, the only meaningful criteria of advertising performance. When the identical ad was shown to matched samples of people who were told that it came from different magazines, the believability of the ad varied, reflecting attitudes toward the vehicle.[29] But people seem to accept advertising in the publications they read themselves, regardless of what others may think. Thus, a 1982 study by SMRB's Valentine Appel found that test ads tipped into issues of the *National Enquirer* were rated the same on believability and product quality by *Enquirer* readers as they were by readers of *McCall's*, *People*, and *Reader's Digest* when placed in those magazines.

Perception Research Services used an eye camera record to track 150 responses to ads in five different magazines, represented by pages projected two at a time on a screen. About 15 percent of the ads were overlooked entirely (a proportion roughly congruent with page-opening figures in other studies), and subjects did not directly focus on 45 percent of the advertisers' names. Ads on right and left pages performed equally overall, but the same ad often performed differently in different magazines. Ads facing dull subject matter on the opposite page performed better than when they were placed against strong editorial content.

In broadcasting, as in print, the advertiser confronts innumerable unexpected elements: inappropriate editorial matter or programming in the immediate environment, competing demands or clashing symbolism in other nearby advertisements or commercials. (When unpredictable events have a known probability of occurrence, an advertiser can use them to advantage. Thus, in 1982, J. Walter Thompson had an agreement with an all-weather cable network to show commercials for a Quaker Oats hot cereal whenever the temperature fell below 40 degrees.)

The advertiser may write into his contract certain demands that eliminate the most obvious and painful contradictions of his aims. He may refuse to share space or time with competitors. Airlines generally specify that their ads or commercials should not appear on the same page or news broadcast that reports an airplane accident, and liquor advertisers ordinarily specify that their ads should not be placed next to reports of accidents caused by drunken driving.

But unanticipated problems may arise out of the advertising context. Subtle incongruities crop up in the language or pictures, in the choice of models, or in the copy themes when ads are juxtaposed even though the products appear to be perfectly compatible. Accordingly, there are elements of uncertainty and risk in the placement of every ad or commercial. In short, the degree and quality of attention actually paid to the message bears a variable and unknown relation to the physical opportunity for exposure provided by the vehicle.

In a series of national studies by the Newspaper Advertising Bureau, the relationship between the physical *opportunity* for exposure and the *actual* exposure to advertising has been measured for a cross-section of weekday readers of the American press.[30] These studies obtained not only a conventional recognition measure of the ads and articles, but also a record of whether or not they were adjacent to other items the reader remembered. These data, together with other information, were handled so as to deal with the readership of advertising as a series of probabilities rather than in the either-or terms of conventional research on ad noting.

The physical opportunity for exposure to advertising, represented by the opening of the newspaper page, remains constant regardless of what products are advertised and regardless of the size of the ads. Interesting and uninteresting products have much the same chance of being within range of the readers' vision, as determined by the proportion of people reading something on the part of the page where the ad was located (and allowing for differences in the size of the typical ad and for different types of products). Yet the *performance* of the advertising, in terms of reported readership and active search for the ads, varies widely depending on the levels of interest that the products themselves arouse in the readers. (In the first of these studies, these levels were determined in a separate series of interviews with the same people.) By every criterion used, the best prospects were about twice as likely to remember the ads as nonprospects.[31]

Thus, for a product with a thinly spread-out market, the use of small-space print ads would appear to be warranted: the ads would be within the physical range of exposure to a broad cross-section of the public, yet a high degree of selectivity would separate the prospects from the nonprospects in terms of actual readership.

Of the ads for products that consumers rated of *high* interest in the 1964 survey, 24 percent were reported seen by the frequent purchasers who opened the pages on which the ads appeared. The proportion was only slightly lower (21 percent) for the group that included less frequent purchasers and nonusers. However, ads for *low* interest products showed a strong contrast between heavy and light users. Twenty percent were reported seen by the frequent purchasers and only 10 percent by the other people who opened the page.

In short, the frequent purchaser is only slightly less likely to pay attention to an ad for an intrinsically uninteresting product than for an essentially interesting one.[32] An interesting product will draw nearly as much attention to its advertising from light users as from frequent users. But a low-interest product draws only half as much attention from the nonprospect and the occasional or rare purchaser as from the heavy user.

Over 50,000 reader evaluations of individual ads were obtained in 1979 in yet another study by the Newspaper Advertising Bureau, in cooperation with 27 newspapers. For each paper, 150 readers of a particular issue were interviewed on the telephone by Admar Research about 10 to 15 display advertisements. The percentage interested in the average ad was 76 percent among people who expected to buy the advertised product and 18 percent among people who would not.[33] This research began with the premise that "interest" is a fair equivalent of the recognition or "noting" conventionally measured, without the misleading connotation that only the "noters" actually saw the ad. (Noting or readership scores may be misleading when their averages are taken literally.) The tasks, objectives, and strategies being pursued by the ads run on the newspaper pages by different types of local merchants and national manufacturers vary greatly.* Ads for different products differ in their creative appeals and their use of space.

But for every kind of ad, national or retail, and regardless of the type of merchandise being advertised, there are always a proportion of readers who report that the product involved is one whose advertisements they are actively seeking. For any particular type of ad, in the 1964 study, this proportion was always a minority of the total readership of the newspaper, ranging anywhere from 1 percent to 15 percent, depending on the ad size and product. Projected against the total population, however, such percentages represent an enormous number of customers actively in the market and searching for information about values, prices, and features on the merchandise that they need.

TV: attention and inattention

Getting the message across in broadcasting involves different hazards than accomplishing the same task in print, where the dangers of reader inattention are self-evident. In judging the performance of television advertising, the advertising planner is more apt to deal with program audience ratings than with estimates of how many *people* have seen his commercial. Some advertisers are naive enough to equate commercial and program audiences on the grounds that, in the face of TV's intrusive power, no one can fail to get the message. Yet not everyone tuned to the show can be on hand when the commercial comes on; some of those who "see" the commercial will always have their defensive blinders up, and of those who are receptive to the message, some, as in print, are bound to forget it.

On March 12, 1961, at the height of the rivalry between two reigning variety show hosts, Jack Paar and Ed Sullivan, De Forest Television placed an advertisement in the Chicago *Sun-Times* for sets with two or three screens in the same cabinet:

> The great networks are sharpening their weapons—competitive performances at the same hour—you simply can't jump all round the dial and take a small bite—there's too much to miss. But De Forest's double or triple screen TV lets you see all—all the time—when you like what you see better on one, you touch your remote button and switch sound only, or flick the super magic infra-red remote for channel changing: head phones for the stubborn. It's more fun than you dreamed about— try it tonight. Enjoy it up to 1 year if you like without paying anything.[34]

The multichannel set has proven to be less versatile than the multiset household. The advent of color and all-channel receivers accelerated the rate at which people acquired new TV sets even before the old ones were worn out. By 1983, 59 percent of all TV households had more than one set. Thus TV has been taking the route that radio went before it, changing from a home entertainment center in the living room to a more personal medium, often located in bedroom

---

*Retail and national ads of the same size perform about equally, overall.

or den for the convenience of the individual viewer.

Still, viewing remains predominantly a family activity. In 1981, a three-city Newspaper Advertising Bureau telephone survey by Burke Research found 44 percent of the viewers watching television alone. Nineteen percent were in single-person households. Eliminating these, 31 percent of the total viewers were watching by themselves, 39 percent were watching along with one other person, and 30 percent were watching in the company of at least two others. The program viewed was chosen by 60 percent of the respondents individually, and another 25 percent said it was chosen jointly by them and someone else in the household. Fifteen percent were watching a show that someone else had selected. (The comparable figure in 1965 was 29 percent.)

People seem to be more easily persuaded when they receive communications individually than when they receive them as part of a group.[35] They are most apt to pay attention to messages that are congruent with their existing mood. Happy messages are best attended to by happy people.[36] Thus, the way they watch television has a great deal to do with what they get out of television commercials as well as with the way they watch them.

In our three-city study, 40 percent of the viewers were doing other things as well as watching TV. (Among these, 12 percent were working, 6 percent reading, 5 percent eating, and 5 percent engaged in a hobby.[37] This suggests that there has been a generational change in the usage of television. (In another 1981 study of 495 respondents in Pittsburgh and Lubbock conducted for the Newspaper Advertising Bureau by Brehl Associates, 28 percent of those under 35, but only 11 percent of those over 65, report they often "use TV as a background for other things. . . . [They] turn on the set and leave it on without paying much attention to it, or even go into another room and do something else part of the time.")

For a number of years, SMRB has asked viewers whether they are fully attentive, partially attentive, or absent from the room. The results have been consistent over time. The greatest attentiveness recorded between 1977 and 1980 was for "Roots" (a special series on the black American experience), which had a score of 88 among men and 93 among women. By contrast, the popular domestic comedy "All In The Family" got an attentiveness score of 68 for men and 83 for women. Although there are variations among individual programs, they seem relatively minor by this measure, and, on average, 74 percent of prime-time viewers report themselves to be fully attentive to what they are watching. However, these reports come from those people who are willing to record their viewing in a research diary and who might therefore be described as attentive almost by definition.

By contrast with the SMRB report on attentiveness, a 1975 study by the Broadcast Bureau of Measurement in Canada found that of people who were aware that the TV set was on at home, 79 percent were in the same room, 73 percent were noticing the content, and 55 percent were paying attention.[38]

If programs receive something less than 100 percent of viewer attention, can commercials do any better? A 1980 Audits and Surveys study of 2,265 households for *Newsweek* found that, on the average, 62 percent of the adults watching prime-time TV remain in the room during the entire commercial break. Two percent switch channels. However, only 22 percent remain in the room watching the commercials without engaging in any other activity. Among the remainder, 13 percent read, 8 percent talk, 4 percent engage in household chores: a total of 39 percent distracted by other activities.[39]

Comparable figures come from a "near-coincidental" telephone study among 1,615 viewers in the Springfield, Illinois, ADI in June 1981. Forty-nine percent were engaged in some other activity while viewing television, and 38 percent were engaged in "a distracting act," excluding eating and drinking. Forty-four percent of the viewers did not leave the room at all, 13 percent left it during the program, 20 percent just during commercials, and 23 percent during both commercials and the program.[40]

Perhaps the most famous study of TV commercials ever made was the notorious Toledo toilet study in which it was demonstrated that water pressure all over town went down significantly at the time of the station break. Over the years much more persuasive evidence has been marshalled to demonstrate that not everyone who is watching a TV program stays on hand for the commercial. It may be that the absences are not randomly distributed and that people of a given psychological or social type are more apt to leave the room or divert their attention during the commercials, just as some people are likely to read the financial pages of the newspaper or the front-of-the-book section in *Time* magazine, while others habitually miss those sections altogether.

The 1966 Alfred Politz Media Studies report, which was the last major study that used a "personal coincidental" measurement (of the number of people actually watching at the time the interviewer knocks on the door), showed that during prime evening time there were about 64 viewers watching during the station break for every 100 watching the program. Politz also found that in about 10 percent of the cases, when the television set was on in prime time, no one was watching it.

As an indication of the volatility of the audience at the time of the station break, only about half the households are tuned in to the same station at both the first and last commercials in a series of spots at the time of the break.[41]

Many other studies have documented the gaps between tuning and viewing, between viewing the program and viewing the commercial, and between viewing the commercial and remembering later what it was all about.[42] One of the most ambitious of these studies was made among housewives by two ad agencies, Foote, Cone & Belding and Needham, Louis & Brorby.[43] In St. Louis, with evening interviews only one hour after the broadcast, content was recalled by women in 19 percent of the homes tuned to opening and closing network commercials. Spot commercials did just as well on recall of content as mid-program network commercials of the same length.

This research found interesting differences in response to commercials for different program types.[44] There were also important differences by product categories. In the daytime, food and beverage commercials were far less well remembered than commercials for soap products, which also had excellent recall in evening hours. One can only speculate as to whether the high frequency of repetition for soap and detergent commercials may have influenced this result. In the evening, automobile and cigarette commercials did particularly poorly (perhaps because they are addressed more to men than to women).[45]

Gary A. Steiner[46] studied the behavior of 183 Chicagoans (mostly women) while they were actually watching television commercials, in the days when those were a minute long. The viewers were observed and recorded by college student members of their families. The study ranged over one week's television viewing and covered nearly 48,000 observations, but only of the commercials *within* programs. Just before the network commercial came on, 70 percent of the viewers were paying "full attention," in the judgment of their observers, 22 percent partial attention, and the remainder were not watching television at all.[47] When the commercial came on, 5 percent of the viewers expressed some form of annoyance, 4 percent showed some pleasure or relief, and 90 percent showed no reaction at all. During the commercial, 47 percent of the audience were reported to have paid full attention, 37 percent partial attention, 5 percent were not in the room at all, 6 percent left the room in the course of the commercial, and 5 percent stayed in the room but got up and diverted their attention.*

In general, commercials following other commercials had less of the audience's full attention to begin with. Better educated and younger people showed a lower attention level during commercials. This fits in with the evidence from other studies, which show that the better educated are most resistant to TV and its advertising. However, since better educated people may also be more adept at learning, they may be able to "get the message" at a lower level of attention. Since the first commercial in the body of a program begins and continues with higher viewer attention than a commercial that follows another commercial, Steiner wondered whether it might create greater annoyance on the part of the viewer whose program had been interrupted. This was indeed so, but only to a very small degree.

Charles Allen went one step farther than Steiner in actually observing TV viewers during commercials.[48] He used a stop-motion camera called a Dyna-Scope to provide a film recording of what goes on in front of the TV set. The camera (in an unobtrusive black box with a one-way mirror) took pictures at intervals of a quarter-minute whenever the set was turned on. It photographed everything in the room and, through a mirror reflection, the program on television at the time. The participating families were conditioned for a week to the presence of the camera before any recordings were made. Although only 100 households in Oklahoma and Kansas were in Allen's sample, the analysis of the thousands of individual frames of film was a major research job.

Allen found that during prime evening hours 35 percent of the sets in use

---

*Eighty percent made *no* spontaneous comments on the content of the commercial, 7 percent made some positive comment, 6 percent a negative comment, and 5 percent only neutral or ambiguous comments. Curiously enough, long commercials (over a minute) aroused more positive spontaneous comment from the viewers than shorter ones. (A full 21 percent of those watching a two-minute commercial made favorable comments.) The nature of the comments very much depended on the product, rather than the artistry, technique, or personalities employed in the advertising. However, individual brands of the same product varied widely in the amount of favorable or unfavorable comment they elicited.

had no one watching during the average minute and that 36 percent of the persons viewing were children. This latter proportion went up to 43 percent children during the average commercial minute (it was 58 percent in morning hours). Neither Allen's findings nor Steiner's can be projected nationally, but they both are of interest because of the unique observational methods used.

Unfortunately, most of the evidence we have comparing the attention-getting abilities of commercials of different length, position, and subject matter is not a matter of systematic observation, as in the studies of Steiner and Allen. Mostly it represents a reconstruction by inference from what people remember afterwards. This kind of recall is highly prone to variations that arise from the technique of asking questions, and it inevitably reflects selective processes of memory that may have nothing at all to do with the original level of attention a commercial aroused.*

Gallup and Robinson showed in 1971 that the main or "featured" idea of a typical magazine or TV tire ad was recalled after 24 hours by 8 percent; for television set ads it was 6 percent, for autos 6 percent, for insurance 3 percent, and for aftershave 8 percent. However, these averages covered enormous variations. The range for tire ads ran between 0.8 percent and 29 percent, for autos between 0.3 percent and 40 percent, and there was a similar range in the other categories.[49]

The heavy viewer who relies more on television and enjoys it more than average not only sees more commercials but is more tolerant of them. He is in fact more apt actually to enjoy them. This would add to the already existing probability that the heavy viewer will be better able to recall particular commercials than the light viewer just because he is more likely to find them familiar.

From a series of experimental studies, Michael Ray and Peter Webb conclude that when viewers are familiar with a program and know when to expect the breaks, they appear to be able to avoid commercials.[50]

Apart from the natural wanderings of bodies and minds, technology is finding new ways to increase the gap between program and commercial audiences. Channel switching during the commercial break is facilitated by remote control devices, with which 30 percent of all television sets sold in 1982 were equipped (compared with 5 percent of those sold in 1976). A 1982 study by Statistical Research, Inc., found that cable subscribers with remote control devices were three times as likely to switch stations to avoid commercials as were people who would have to get out of their chairs to get to the control knobs on their sets. Most "zapping" occurs in the first five or ten seconds of a commercial, and advertising for personal hygiene products and deodorants is more likely to be turned off than advertising for computers or chewing gum, according to a 1983 study by Information Resources Inc.

---

*Comparable figures of unaided recall for print advertising do not exist for the simple reason that normal magazine or newspaper reading behavior cannot be interrupted by a telephone interview with the same facility that can be done with a broadcast message. Thus measurements of print advertising readership are generally based on aided recall techniques which jog the reader's memory and produce higher scores. They are also usually made at rather long intervals (like 24 hours) after the original reading took place.

The advent of video cassette recorders also threatened to reduce the impact of television commercials, even though television spokesmen pointed to its possibilities for increasing program audience size by permitting delayed viewing. A 1979 Nielsen study found that 60 percent of viewers who could use their VCR's to eliminate commercials did so during the 25 percent of the time broadcasts were being monitored while they were recorded. (By 1983, 6 percent of the households had VCR's.) In addition, 31 percent of VCR viewers said they used their "fast-forward" control to eliminate commercials.

The programming context

Because broadcast advertising flows in time, it is always perceived in relation to what comes before and after. An analysis of day-after Burke recall scores for over 1,000 commercials found that the characteristics of viewers, defined in the traditional demographic terms, at least, did not explain differences in recall.[51] Only 7 percent of the variance in recall could be explained by the content and style of presentation. Far more (18 percent) could be explained in terms of the programming environment.[52]

Context is always critical to the evaluation of communications in two respects: (1) the expectations the audience brings to a message; (2) the way in which messages relate to each other. Oscar Lubow, a former president of the Starch organization, once concluded that although "editorial adjacency does not seem to affect the scoring of print ads . . . types of programming seem to have an effect on the noting and association of TV commercials."[53] (At that time, Starch was measuring recognition for TV commercials as well as for print.)

Similarly, Sonia Yuspeh (formerly of J. Walter Thompson) reports that viewer responses to commercials (recall, purchase intentions, playback of content, and brand evaluations) are influenced by program context.[54] On-air recall scores for the same commercials vary depending on the surrounding program, and may even vary for different episodes of the same program. Recall can be affected by such extraneous elements as channel selection, time of broadcast, program preemptions and cancellations. It must be added that within any type of program, viewers' reactions among individual programs can be greater than they are between different types. (In a 1980 study, Burke reported that recall scores in late evening newscasts were 27 percent lower than they were for the identical commercials in prime time.)[55]

Commercials get better than average recall on the following day by people who rate the surrounding program "one of my favorites" and below average recall by those who rate the program as poor.[56] Familiar commercials are better recalled on the following day than they are shortly after exposure.

Gary Soldow and Victor Principe have theorized that "as viewers become more involved in a program, there is reason to think they become less attentive to and receptive to commercials."[57] By experimentally manipulating the placement of commercials within programs, they found that people who were "most involved with the program were least likely to want to buy the product." This tends to support the idea that commercials are objectionable when they interrupt an interesting program. Actually, it is now commonplace for program scripts to be written to provide for "natural" breaks for commercials. However, General

Electric commercials that interrupt programs produce more favorable attitude change than commercials in shows with natural breaks, Herbert Krugman reports. He concludes that "when an interesting show is interrupted by an interesting commercial, the momentum of aroused interest does carry over."[58] This jibes with the results of a small-scale experiment by W. R. Simmons and Associates in 1968. Viewers paying full attention to a program were twice as likely to recall an advertised product as those paying less attention and more than twice as likely to recall the brand, and they recalled three times as many products and brands.

Attentiveness and involvement in programming can obviously take many different forms, and this probably accounts for the difficulty of generalizing from the few studies that have dealt with the subject. Thus, J. Walter Thompson has found that more violent shows create more viewer involvement and greater commercial recall. But Robert Grass of DuPont reports that recall is lower for commercials in stressful shows.

In an experiment involving 133 students at the University of North Carolina, the aggressive response to two violent feature films (*The Wild Ones* and *Attica*) was heightened (in comparison with a nonviolent film, *The Mouse that Roared*) when they were interrupted by commercials.[59] But "while the commercials served to anger and make subjects more tense (as expected), they also made subjects happier and less tired (not as expected)." Perhaps this was because they provided a welcome break and because they were light and entertaining.

In violation both of common sense and psychological principles, advertisers can always be found who will place commercials on programs that can only arouse disagreeable responses from the audience, like NBC's "Holocaust" in 1978. This is done on the premise that if a large audience is available at an economical cost, the message will somehow penetrate and achieve the desired favorable effect. The premise is wrong, as I shall indicate later, because when advertising fails to work positively it is not necessarily neutral; it can have a negative effect as well. This negative effect can result from the context as well as from the content of the message.*

In reading, we are accustomed to accept incongruities that would never be tolerable in a broadcast sequence. No one would consider it strange that on the front page of the same paper whose banner headline announced, "Men Walk on Moon," the local weather forecast appeared in its usual little box in the upper right-hand corner. However, in broadcasting, strange incongruities can occur when messages are divorced from the surrounding programming.

In February 1968, at the time of the Viet Cong's Tet offensive, I tuned to a television news broadcast in which film clips freshly flown over from Saigon vividly showed the agony and devastation of war in images that must have shocked and distressed any normal viewer seated comfortably in his living room. The

---

*Commercials appeared only *before* the nuclear holocaust scenes in the 1983 telecast, "The Day After" (nuclear war), though the large viewing audience was well aware of what was to follow. A Bruskin telephone survey, sponsored by ABC, found that two-thirds of the viewers said their feelings about the sponsors had not changed, 13 percent were more favorable and 4 per cent less. These responses do not, however, tell us what reactions really occurred.

final part of the sequence showed Colonel Loan of the South Vietnamese National Police killing a civilian-clad Viet Cong prisoner in cold blood. As the victim sank to the ground, the television screen suddenly switched to the commercial. The beaming face of an actor dressed as a filling station attendant cheerfully greeted the audience, "Hi there, I'm your friendly Phillips 66 dealer!"

Another example: In 1975, a special public affairs documentary on poverty was televised in New York City. Scenes of hunger and despair were interrupted with ads for chocolate candy. At one point, a commercial for cat food was followed by an episode in the program that reported that some poor people were buying pet food for their own consumption because of its low price. Such an unexpected juxtaposition is, of course, horrifying to all concerned, but it illustrates the risk in evaluating advertising without regard to its environment.

Before tobacco advertising was banned from the air, there was a period in which antismoking public service commercials were extensively shown. Within the tobacco industry there was even some concern that these commercials would reduce smoking, so the broadcast advertising ban (which caused an end to the counter-propaganda as well) was not a total disaster from the industry's point of view. However, during this period, the cigarette companies were perfectly willing to have their commercials appear on comedy programs in close proximity to antismoking skits. The premise was that the quantity of exposure was more important than the context.

Recall in the changing TV environment

Advertisements are ordinarily evaluated in limited batches, often just one at a time. When advertisers spend money on research they usually have very specific questions in mind concerning their own campaigns. The very nature of controlled experimentation means that the environment for advertising must be regarded as a constant. Yet the decisions made by individual advertisers, in many cases with the aid and guidance of research, interact with each other to change the advertising environment and thus to produce unexpected effects on the performance of individual ads.

An illustration of this process may be the "speeded-up" broadcast commercial, a by-product of progress in data transmission technology, which puts a premium on the compression of intelligible speech. The text of a 30-second commercial can be compressed into a 24-second length, without a reduction in comprehensibility.[60] Even before this development, some leaders in advertising were urging the reduction of standard commercial length to 15 or 10 seconds, on the grounds that this was sufficient to efficiently register the main point in a typical advertiser's message.[61] And in 1983, all of the television networks announced that they would accept 30-second commercials split to advertise two different products of the same advertiser, reviving the "piggy-backs" of an earlier era.

The value of a given quantity of commercial time to the broadcasters' revenues is obviously enhanced if advertisers are persuaded that a short message is almost as good as a long one. (In 1979, the price of a 10-second ID [actually nine seconds of air time in most cases] ran at 50 percent-70 percent of the price of a 30.)

The precedent for this type of argument was the research that preceded the substitution of the 30-second unit for the one-minute commercial that for many years had been the U.S. television standard. A widely publicized laboratory study made in 1967 for Corinthian Broadcasting by Daniel Yankelovich demonstrated that 30-second commercials produced 92 percent of the brand-name recall of their 60-second counterparts. *Broadcasting* (October 23, 1967) headlined its report on the study, "30-second spots good as minutes." (The 30's tested actually produced slightly higher percentages of people who rated the brand "at least average" and who would consider recommending it. Since none of these differences were statistically significant at the .05 level, the report concluded that "there is no real difference in the communication value.")

This study and many similar ones[62] were used to spearhead a sales drive that in a few years transformed the advertising content of television. Rates for 30-second commercials were set at about 75 percent of the former one-minute level, thereby enormously increasing the potential profitability of both TV networks and stations. Countering this, the inventory of available commercial positions vastly increased, thereby in the short run affecting the buyer-seller relationship and encouraging a substantially greater use of spot television by local advertisers. (They represented 15 percent of all television billings in 1965, 25 percent in 1974, and 26 percent in 1982.)

But the switch from 60's to 30's had another effect that was more important than its immediate economic consequences. By adding greatly to the number of commercials broadcast, it transformed the total advertising communication system, with consequences that could not be predicted from experiments that compared a handful of individually paired 30's and 60's in a laboratory setting.

Between 1967 and 1981 the number of network commercials rose by 119 percent, from 1,856 to 4,079 a week. The number of spot commercials also increased by 119 percent, from 2,413 to 5,300 a week in the average of the top 75 markets. As commercial length switched from 60's to 30's, the networks placed a limit of four consecutive commercial announcements in each program interruption. However, a third pod of commercials could be placed back to back with the station break position in a network program, and spot advertising in station breaks and locally originated programs added to the "clutter." The increase in the number of commercials was paralleled also by an increase in "promos" (promotional announcements for programs or stations) and in public service announcements. In 1977, a study of the three network affiliates in New York City for prime time in three evenings found that nonprogram material ranged between 10 and 14.1 minutes per hour, although the NAB Code set a limit of 9.5. But 23 percent of the average 13.5 minutes of nonprogramming time (with 35-40 different communications per hour) was devoted to promotional announcements, including public service material. (In daytime, the 12-minute limit on nonprogramming material was also exceeded.)

How did these developments change the productivity of a typical commercial for the advertiser? Light was shed on this question in three studies by the

Newspaper Advertising Bureau, of which the first (with field work by N. T. Fouriezos Associates) was conducted in 1965, when the isolated 60-second commercial was still the norm.* Similar studies were done through Burke Marketing Research in 1974 and 1981. Each of the three studies was done in several cities with a total of about 1,000 telephone interviews. People who had been watching a network television station when the phone rang were asked about the product and brand advertised in "the very last commercial" on the program they were watching, and this was checked against a monitored record of what was actually on the air, with the timing carefully coordinated. Although "the very last commercial" stood alone in 1965, it subsequently became one of a pod within a program or a whole series during a station break. Therefore, in 1974 and 1981, a response to the "last commercial" question was coded as correct if it referred to *any* commercial broadcast in the last cluster. By this criterion, correct recall fell from 18 percent in 1965 and 12 percent in 1974 to 7 percent in 1981. The proportion of viewers claiming "no recall" increased from 60 percent in 1965 to 80 percent in 1981.

The percentage of correct responses in all three surveys is highest when the shortest time interval has elapsed. However, a remarkable number of confused, erroneous, and null responses are offered even by viewers who had watched the last commercial less than two minutes before the phone rang. It is no reflection on television's fantastic power of communication that most of the people who have just seen a commercial within the past few minutes are unable to remember it spontaneously. This fact merely serves as a dramatic illustration of the "looking without attending" that characterizes *most* advertising exposure.

In all three surveys, men show a higher level of correct recall than women do, a point worth noting since men spend less time in the aggregate watching television and are presumably exposed to fewer commercials. The findings seem to suggest that women, being exposed to more commercials, strengthen their perceptual defenses.[63]

All three surveys indicate that recall is adversely affected when the viewer is also working, reading, talking, or engaging in some other activity, as an increasing proportion are doing. Recall is also lower among those who say they just happened to be in the room where the TV set was on.

In 1974, 21 percent of the viewers correctly recalled at least one brand name or advertiser in the last half hour of viewing, with 4 percent naming two or more. In 1981, 13 percent could name a brand, with 2 percent mentioning more than one.[64]

Burke scores show that an average commercial is recalled after 24 hours by 23 percent of the people who have watched a program, and this has not changed appreciably.[65] The ability of people to recall messages appears to be constrained by the capacities of short term memory, so that as the number of messages increases greatly, the number recalled shows only a slight increase. But Burke normally asks people whether they remember a commercial for a specific product or brand. Viewers' ability to remember advertising has not changed as much as their ability to use that memory actively. (The contrast is roughly between the

---

*Some findings from this research have already been mentioned on page 144.

ability to describe the characters and plot of a movie and realizing, once one is in the theater, that one has seen it before.)

Recall represents the cumulative effects of all the previous exposures to a commercial rather than just the unique residual memory of the last time it was seen.[66] Of the viewers who recalled a "last" commercial, 31 percent in 1965 remembered having seen it previously. By 1974, after the switch to 30's, the proportion was 52 percent. In 1981, it had grown to 58 percent.

The public's increasing sense of *déja vu* reflects the reality that more and more commercials have in fact been *déja vus*. Advertisers moved in television's early days from live commercials to films and kinescopes and eventually to tape. As "scatter plans" replaced the program sponsorship of network television's pioneer days, repetition of commercials became essential to accumulate the levels of audience "reach" that advertisers required, just as it had been from the start in spot buying. Commercial production costs mounted steadily, so that costs of $250,000 for a single 30-second commercial were not unheard of in 1983, and at least one is reported to have cost a million dollars. Although advertisers became increasingly convinced of the necessity of pretesting commercials at an early stage, it appeared that they were driven by production expense to make greater use of a smaller pool of finished commercials. Thus it seems quite likely that contemporary viewers are seeing more commercials more often than was true in 1965.

As we shall see in Chapter 9, repeated exposure to a given commercial (as opposed to repeated exposure to different but related advertisements from the same advertiser) creates the likelihood of "wearout," or progressive attrition of memorability and communications effectiveness. And it is precisely the phenomenon of wearout that is manifested in our own data in the decline of recall.

The evidence indicates a change in (1) the level of attentiveness of viewing in general, reflecting the maturation of television and its acceptance as part of the scenery, and (2) the increased fractionation of the commercial environment, which has reduced the memorability and presumably the communications value of any individual message. Thus the transition from 60's to 30's carried with it consequences for the whole system of television advertising. These were unanticipated by advertisers who accepted the initial experimental evidence that treated commercials as isolated fragments of communication.

Positioning and "clutter"

I have stressed the importance of the context for advertising, but context is created by other advertising as well as by the programming or editorial environment. In television, commercials now rarely stand by themselves; they occur in a sequence, either within a program or during a commercial break. The effects of positioning within that sequence have been intensely studied ever since the mid-1960s, when advertisers first began to break their one-minute units into two half-minute units for two different products—a practice known as "piggybacking."

By the mid-1960s, the demand for television network time by national advertisers passed the limits of available one-minute commercial positions during peak viewing hours. One solution that was found to this situation was the "piggyback commercial," in which the minute was divided into two entirely separate 30-

second units, each devoted to a different product of the same manufacturer. Since both the products and brand names were different, no connection was drawn except by that rare viewer who knew that Crisco shortening and Crest toothpaste were both made by Procter & Gamble or Sanka and Jell-O by General Foods. The effect was to add substantially to the number of separate messages that were crowded into a given length of air time and to initiate concern with the problem of "clutter," a term applied to the proliferation of disconnected reminders and exhortations that succeeded each other before, during, and after the station break.

Piggybacks were a transitional phenomenon before the switch from one minute to 30 seconds as the standard commercial length. In his observational study, which I mentioned earlier, Gary Steiner found that the second part of a piggyback commercial received slightly less attention than the first part, but the difference was no greater than between the first and second commercials in an unrelated sequence. Steiner concluded that attention waned mostly because of the absolute length of a series of commercials and not because of the number of different products advertised: "One minute is one minute whether devoted to one or to two products."

However, BBDO reported that too close a relationship between the products advertised might be distracting to the viewer. As reported by *Broadcasting*, "An acute similarity of products (coffee and cream, for example) may tend to confuse the audience, while dissimilar but not completely unrelated products (pie and cheese) may heighten the awareness and performance of the commercial by providing a rub-off—that is, by mutually assisting each other." (Note how in this instance as elsewhere, the existence of a tolerable incongruity appears to heighten awareness.)

The importance of the environment goes beyond the messages that are immediately adjacent. When two commercials for competing brands are scheduled within 30 minutes of each other, recall drops by 18 percent; within 10 minutes it drops by 42 percent, according to a 1972 Gallup and Robinson study for Benton & Bowles.

By now, advertisers generally accept the fact that it really does matter whether their commercial comes first, in the middle, or last in a sequence, though there is generally very little they can do to get into a preferred position; stations and networks must shuffle the order all the time to avoid favoritism.

Day after recall scores measured by Burke between 1965 and 1971 were lower (61 percent) for commercials within a string than they were for those at the beginning (71 percent) and end.[67] But replication of the Burke study in 1976 found that recall declined steadily from the beginning of the cluster until the end. Scores were lower for commercials at the station break than for those embedded within programs. Gallup and Robinson found that commercials in a short cluster of less than two minutes did 7 percent better than those in longer clusters.[68]

In a series of experiments, the same commercials were shown by Michael Ray and Peter Webb under varying conditions of "clutter" (ranging between 16 and 38 commercials and promos—"nonprogram elements"—and between 8 and 18.3 nonprogram minutes out of the hour).[69] They found that increased clutter reduced attention, recall, and registration of the messages but had little effect on attitude and purchase intention. Curiously, the number of commercials correctly recalled ranged only between 2.9 and 3.3. (This meant that a typical commercial in a low-clutter condition had a higher chance of being recalled, at least under the conditions of this kind of test.)*

Increases in the number of promos and public service announcements produced slight negative effects on the recall of the commercials themselves. The first commercial in a string scored best, the last one next best, and those buried in the middle did poorest. Earlier commercial positions in the longer string were more effective in stimulating purchase intention as well as in producing recall. The first commercial (apart from the 10-second commercials) also had the highest attention score in 28 out of 40 cases. A schedule with six breaks and two commercials per break yielded the highest response per commercial.

There were substantial differences among individual commercials in their ability to withstand the effects of clutter. One commercial was recalled by 58 percent of the viewers in the least cluttered condition and by 18 percent in the most cluttered condition. However, another commercial scored twice as well under maximum clutter (40 percent) as under the minumum (20 percent).

An advertiser must be concerned not only with whether his message is delivered and remembered, but with whether the point of it has been registered and understood. It seems that a substantial volume of advertising fails this test, even under conditions of forced exposure, with learning conditions far more favorable than they normally are.

The miscomprehension of commercials was investigated by Jacob Jacoby, Wayne Hoyer, and David A. Sheluga in a study supported by the AAAA Educational Foundation.[70] They interviewed 2,700 people at testing rooms in shopping malls. Each respondent was exposed to 2 out of 60 communications, one of which was selected to represent image, "cause," or conventional product and service advertising and one of which was selected from various kinds of programming, speeches and editorials, or public service announcements. All these communications were selected from a large scale monitoring and videotaping of over-the-air output and were coded in terms of their complexity. Unaided recall of the "main idea" and "other ideas" in the communications were obtained from the respondents immediately after they were shown. Next, they were given a six-item quiz on the information content of the communications they had just seen.

The immediate playback of the "main idea" and "other ideas" of the communication yielded "disappointing results." Eighty-three percent of the viewers gave at least one incorrect response on the quiz for a given communication. Overall, 30 percent of their answers were wrong. Among the 60 communications tested, miscomprehension ranged between 11 percent and 50 percent. The level of error was not significantly different for product commercials, other kinds of advertising, and program excerpts. There were only negligible differences in the miscomprehension scores for different kinds of people, with better educated doing slightly better than average. There were also only slight differences in the

---

*As I suggested earlier, this reflects the limitations of active memory rather than those of television.

miscomprehension levels for facts and inferences. However, inaccurate statements aroused far more miscomprehension than accurate statements did.

Apart from the question of attention level, the proliferation of commercial messages on TV has a much more serious aspect for the advertiser. This is the problem of maintaining clear individual identity for his product in the face of competitive messages that the viewer can hardly distinguish from his own. For example, during the third week in April, 1983, the five commercial channels in Chicago carried 259 television commercials for 25 brands of packaged soaps and detergents, the total air time being 129 minutes and 30 seconds. The Colgate brands accounted for 26 percent of the total time. The Lever brands accounted for 12 percent and Procter & Gamble brands accounted for 62 percent.

Here is a series of product claims for nine detergent brands, as aired in 1983:

1. "Claim your spot. . . . gets it clean."
2. "Gets clothes deep down clean, fluffed up soft."
3. "For a white that compares to new."
4. ". . . . is a change for the better."
5. "For clothes that actually are as clean as they look."
6. "Gets your clothes so clean they smell clean."
7. "A little detergent, a lot of clean."
8. "Saves energy and money."
9. "Penetrates deep for a dynamite clean."

The housewife is expected by the advertiser to distinguish his claim from the others. An analysis made by Million Market Newspapers found that the heaviest viewers, who indeed see the most commercials, are best able to identify brand slogans. But their choice of brands is not much different from that of the lighter viewer.

Horace Schwerin says that "it is possible in some product fields to find imitation, borrowing, and conformity create an almost incestuous similarity of execution shared by every brand's advertising."[71] Schwerin points out how the unique vitality of a copy claim may prove to be of transitory advantage:

> Let us postulate an advertiser with a simple and demonstrable vital promise of great strength. He mounts a highly successful campaign, varies the basic idea, and carves out his projected share of the market. Time will generally breed two worms in this rose: one the gradual wearing out of the original vital promise, the other the appearance of competitors who imitate, encroach on, and vitiate the uniqueness of the vital promise—turning it into a generic product story available to all brands. When *this* happens—when, to oversimplify, we observe the phenomenon that "all brands are saying the same thing"—the time is ripe for our hypothetical advertiser to consider the so-called "creative" approach: the *execution* that is sufficiently arresting to revivify (or, if necessary, supplant) the basic vital promise. This could take myriad forms—optical hyperbole, humor, slice of life, mood, powerful analogy, and so forth.

Thus the Great Creative Idea moves away from the product and into pure gimmickry in order to break through the barrier of inattention.

Notes

1. New York: Oxford University Press, 1960, p. 53.
2. "Experiments in Perception," *Scientific American*, August 1951, p. 55.
3. "The Useful Dimensions of Sensitivity," *American Psychologist*, 18, 1 (Janury 1963): 1-15.
4. Review of Michael A. Arbib, "Brains, Machines and Mathematics," *Scientific American*, June 1964.
5. "Control Mechanisms of the Eye," *Scientific American*, July 1964.
6. "Ricco's Law," cited by William W. Dember, *Psychology of Perception* (New York: Holt, Rinehart, and Winston, 1960), p. 359.
7. "Psychological Time," *Scientific American*, November 1964.
8. Gordon H. Bower, "Mental Imagery and Associative Learning," in Lee W. Gregg, ed., *Cognition in Learning and Memory* (New York: John Wiley & Sons, Inc., 1972).
9. "An Experimental Reunion of Psychoanalytic Theory with Perceptual Vigilance and Defense," *Journal of Abnormal and Social Psychology*, 49, 1 (January 1954): 94-98.
10. Ralph Norman Haber, "How We Remember What We See," *Scientific American*, May 1970, pp. 104-12.
11. "Visual Search," *Scientific American*, June 1964.
12. December, *Psychology of Perception*.
13. Cohen, *Psychology and Time*.
14. "Conflict and Arousal," *Scientific American*, August 1966, pp. 82-87.
15. Our memory of what we see may be constructed from our memory of the pattern of eye movements required to assemble the whole picture from its various features and details. *Cf.* David Noton and Lawrence Stark, "Eye Movements and Visual Perception," *Scientific American*, June 1971, pp. 34-41. *Cf.* also Norman H. Mackworth, "Ways of Recording Lines of Sight," and "Stimulus Density Limits and Useful Field of View," in Richard A. Monty and John W. Senders, eds., *Eye Movements and Psychological Processes* (Hillsdale, NJ: Lawrence Erlbaum Associates, 1976), pp.307-21.
16. *Art and Visual Perception* (Berkeley: University of California Press, 1954) p. 11.
17. Erving Goffman, "Genderisms," *Psychology Today*, August 1977, pp. 60-63.
18. Robert Fletcher and Bill Mabey, "Reading and Noting Revived," *Admap*, December 1971, pp. 422-28.
19. Unpublished doctoral dissertation, University of Minnesota, 1971, cited by James J. Jenkins, "Remember That Old Theory of Memory? Well, Forget It!" *American Psychologist*, 29, 11 (November 1974): 785-95.
20. Joseph W. Alba and Lynn Hasher, "Is Memory Schematic?" *Psychological Bulletin*, 93, 2 (March 1983): 203-31. *Cf.* also Norman E. Spear, *The Processing of Memories: Forgetting and Retention* (Hillsdale, N.J.: Lawrence Erlbaum Associates, 1978).
21. Haber, "How We Remember What We See," p. 105. The process of placing words into memory begins with "iconic" or visual storage. It takes less than a second for an image to be scanned and classified before it is stored in short-term memory (along with up to three or five other items). It is passed on to long–term memory by recoding or translating from its name to its meaning.
22. Leo Bogart and B. Stuart Tolley, "The Impact of Blank Space: An Experiment in Advertising Readership," *Journal of Advertising Research*, 4, 2 (June 1964): 21.
23. Leo Bogart, "How Do People Read Newspapers?" *Media / scope*, January 1962, p. 53. Another small experimental study using Mackworth's eye camera was made in 1966 for the Newspaper Advertising Bureau by Donald Payne and Herbert Krugman. The research suggested that advertisements that are sufficiently complex in structure or content to require a good deal of their area to be scanned are actually not as well remembered as simple ads that receive fewer eye movements.

24. In 1961, W. R. Simmons showed people who claimed to have read a magazine "yesterday" a selection of ads, some of which had actually appeared in that issue and some of which had not. The claimed readership for the fake ads was about half that of the real ones. Commenting on this study nearly 20 years later, Simmons points out that respondents are unable to distinguish between pages seen "yesterday" and those seen on preceding days in the case of a magazine that is typically picked up repeatedly over a period of time.

25. Ads that are recalled vividly also stay in the memory longer, according to a study made for *Look* magazine by Audits & Surveys. Print ads and TV commercials that rated high (over 30) in verified recall were compared with relatively low-rated ads. The recall scores for the high-rated ads were just about the same on the third day as on the second and first days after original exposure. On the lower scoring ads, recall dropped by about a third from the first 24-hour recall period to the 48-hour recall period and held at that level after 72 hours. Here, from my own experience, is a specific illustration of how two advertisements with a comparable capacity to win attention may have varying degrees of memorability: on December 10, 1963, the Studebaker Corporation announced that it would cease manufacturing automobiles in the United States; a few days later, Studebaker's Mercedes Benz distributorship in New York placed a full-page newspaper ad reassuring customers that normal service would continue. A full-page ad for another automobile make appeared in the same issue of the paper. Twenty people who were informally interviewed the next day all spontaneously remembered seeing the Mercedes Benz ad, and all recognized it when it was shown to them. Only one or two remembered having seen the other car ad, but they all recognized it and agreed they had seen it when they were shown the paper.

26. Reported by Oscar Lubow, then president of Daniel Starch and Staff, in "The Critical Confrontation," an unpublished paper, to the Magazine Advertising Bureau of Canada, Montreal, October 20, 1970.

27. *Marketing News*, June 1981. Characteristically, it is the fatter, more successful magazines that are measured most often.

28. Richard F. Bromer and David B. Learner, "Effect of Magazine Context on Ad Recall," unpublished paper, 1967.

29. Charles Winick, "Three Measures of the Advertising Value of Media Context," *Journal of Advertising Research*, 2, 2 (June 1962): 28-33.

30. Audits & Surveys Company, Inc., *A Study of the Opportunity for Exposure to National Newspaper Advertising* (New York: Newsprint Information Committee, June 1964); Newspaper Advertising Bureau, *A Million Miles of Newspapers*, (New York: 1971); Newspaper Advertising Bureau, *The Measure of a Medium*, 1983. These studies show that page opening does not change very much from the front to the back of the paper, except that sections of special interest either to men or to women tend to be toward the back and lose some exposure among the opposite sex.

31. *Cf.* also Stewart A. Smith, "Factors Influencing the Relationship Between Buying Plans and Ad Readership," *Journal of Marketing Research* 2, 1 (February 1965): 40-44. Smith concludes from an analysis of many readership studies made for the Philadelphia *Inquirer* that prospects (by his definition, persons who claim to be "planning to buy or who might buy" a product) read 30 percent more newspaper ads than nonprospects.

32. The gap would, of course, look greater if interest had been classified into more than a simple dichotomy.

33. After establishing whether or not they had opened pages containing the test ads (86 percent had), the readers were taken back through the pages and asked about each ad in turn, "Do you expect to buy this type of item within the next year?" and "If you were to buy, would [the advertiser] be your first choice, possible choice, or an unlikely

choice for that type of item?" Finally, respondents were asked, "Does the ad itself have any interest at all for you?" Among the best prospects (those who expected to buy the advertised item within the next year and for whom the advertiser would be the first choice), 90 percent expressed interest in the ad. For those probable purchasers for whom the advertiser was a possible choice, the figure was 78 percent. It dropped to 48 percent among those probable purchasers for whom the advertiser was an unlikely choice. It was 48 percent among the nonprospects who were inclined toward the advertiser, 33 percent among nonprospects for whom the advertiser was a possible choice, and only 11 percent for nonprospects who considered the advertiser an unlikely choice were they to come into the market.

34. Quoted by Daniel Boorstin. *The Image, or What Happened to the American Dream*, (New York: Atheneum, 1962): 128-29.

35. William McGuire, "New Developments in Psychology as They Affect Advertising," cites a number of psychological experiments to support the conclusion that persuasion is facilitated if people are eating or drinking. (In contrast to this "benevolent" environment, the frustrations of sitting in rush hour traffic don't seem to reduce the persuasive impact of radio commercials.)

36. Gordon H. Bower, "Mood and Memory," *American Psychologist*, 36, 2 (February 1981): 129-48.

37. Women are somewhat more likely than men to combine TV viewing with other pursuits (46 percent versus 34 percent). The larger percentage of women who say they are tending to some household chore (17 percent versus 7 percent for men) accounts for most of the difference. This may be related to other research findings that even though women are more likely than ever before to have outside employment, working women tend to have as many household responsibilities as full-time housewives. Cf. *Women, Work and Markets of the 80's* (Newspaper Advertising Bureau, 1980).

38. Reported to the 1975 ARF Conference, New York City. In the case of radio, of those aware that the set was on, 82 percent were just hearing the set, 54 percent were noticing the content, and 38 percent were paying attention.

39. *Newsweek*, "Eyes on Television 1980: A National Benchmark Study of Prime-Time Television Audiences Conducted by Audits & Surveys, Inc.," New York, 1980.

40. Elizabeth J. Roberts and Peter H. Lemieux, *Audience Attitudes and Alternative Program Ratings*, (Cambridge, Mass.: Television Audience Assessment, Inc., 1981).

41. A.S.C. Ehrenberg, "Media Men Don't Want to Know," *Journal of the Market Research Society*, 10, 1.

42. In 17,470 telephone interviews conducted by the Richmond Newspapers between 1956 and 1964, 80 percent of the respondents were able to identify the program then playing on their sets; 25 percent could (correctly or incorrectly) identify at least one commercial, sponsor, or product on the program being watched. Studies made by BBDO show that the average television commercial can be identified by about 35 percent of a program's viewers and that 24 percent can play back at least some of the commercial points. Gallup and Robinson figures show about the same ratio. F. Wallace Knudsen of Audits and Surveys analyzed 2,100 interviews with viewers of hour-long evening programs that had an average of six to eight commercials and found that 21 percent of the viewers could remember *no* specific commercial. 19 percent could remember one, 17 percent could remember at least two, and 9 percent could remember every commercial on the program: *cf.* his "Is 'Clutter' Too Narrowly Defined?" *Printers' Ink*, March 20, 1964, pp. 42-43.

43. A first study was conducted in Queens, New York, in March and April 1961, and recorded over 9,000 completed interviews from 17,000 telephone dialings. A second study was made in St. Louis in October and November 1962, with over 10,000 com-

pleted interviews from 20,000 calls. Still a third study conducted in Chicago by Needham, Louis & Brorby showed parallel results. In homes tuned to a program the proportion of housewives who 23 hours later remembered exposure to the commercial was slightly less in the evening than in the daytime. Recall of the content was about a fifth lower (16 percent for the typical evening commercial and 20 percent for daytime). These levels were slightly higher for women's interest products and those advertised on women's interest programs in the evening.

44. For example, among women viewers of Western programs in St. Louis, 10 percent could remember the average commercial. But that proportion went up to 28 percent of those watching a general dramatic, detective, adventure, or suspense show. This raises interesting, but unprovable, speculations that the average woman viewer of the Western is merely "along for the ride" with the male members of her family and that her attention level is correspondingly less.

45. Eleven percent of women watching a program in St. Louis advertising cigarettes could remember the commercial. This proportion increased to 29 percent when the product advertised was a food or beverage. Many of the nonsmoking ladies had "turned off" the commercial without touching the dial.

46. "The People Look at Commercials: A Study of Audience Behavior," *Journal of Business,* 39, 2 (April 1966):272-304.

47. In the case of non network commercials, which often follow other commercials rather than programming, only 58 percent of the viewers were paying full attention immediately before the commercial came on, and a smaller proportion (42 percent) paid full attention to the commercials themselves as compared with network commercials.

48. Charles L. Allen, "Photographing the TV Audience," *Journal of Advertising Research,* 5, 1 (March 1965): 2-8.

49. *Advertising Age,* April 12, 1971, pp. 51-52.

50. Michael L. Ray and Peter H. Webb, "Advertising Effectiveness in a Crowded Television Environment," Cambridge, Mass.: Marketing Science Institute, 1978.

51. Burke Marketing Research, Inc., "Day-After Recall Television Commercial Norms," Cincinnati, 1978.

52. In this respect, different research services have drawn different conclusions from rather similar kinds of evidence, perhaps because of variations in the samples of commercials they test. Thus, Burke finds that among women viewers, movies and dramatic programs produce higher commercial recall than situation comedies or variety formats. However, Gallup & Robinson finds that commercials in movies rate *below* average among women viewers, while recall of viewers for comedy, variety shows, and situation comedies is slightly above average. Both Gallup & Robinson and Burke agree that medical dramas and television movies score well above average and musical variety shows below. It should be noted that day-after recall of "emotional" commercials is understated (since it elicits verbal responses) according to a 1981 study by Foote, Cone & Belding of 400 women cable TV subscribers in Grand Rapids and San Diego. A masked recognition test produced results 19 percent greater than the standard day-after recall technique on three commercials classified as "thinking," by 68 percent on three "feeling" commercials.

53. Oscar Lubow, "The Critical Confrontation." Lubow reported that the range in Starch recognition scores for TV commercials was comparable to that for magazine ads: 8 percent-44 percent for 10-second commercials, 12 percent-54 percent for 20 seconds, 13 percent-55 percent for 30 seconds, and 19 percent-65 percent for one-minute commercials. About one viewer in four who remembered a commercial could correctly identify the brand. Correct (as opposed to incorrect) brand association was higher for one-minute commercials than for shorter ones.

54. Sonia Yuspeh, "The Medium versus The Message," in G. B. Haffer, ed., *A Look Back, A Look Ahead* (Chicago: American Marketing Association, 1980).

55. Alan R. Nelson Research has reported that the same commercial rated 15th in "empathy" on an early evening news show and 32nd or 33rd on an early morning or late evening news show.
    A Burke survey for the Association of Independent Television Stations in 1979-80 found that the same commercials received a 19 percent higher recall score in nonnews programming on independent stations than they did on early evening newscasts on network affiliate stations. In the late evening (when scores were lower over all) the nonnews programs had a 25 percent advantage. Overall, there was no difference in recall, believability, persuasiveness, attitude, or perception between the same commercials on network and independent stations.

56. David Leach, "The Reliability, Sensitivity, and Validity of Burke Day-After Recall," paper presented to the ARF Key Issues Workshop on Copy Research Validation, New York, 1981. This finding is based on 105 tests among 18,000 program viewers. Leach points out that the effects are minimized when the results are based not on the total program audience but on the "commercial audience." The less involved viewers tend to leave the room when the commercial comes on.

57. Gary F. Soldow and Victor Principe, "Response to Commercials as a Function of Program Context," *Journal of Advertising Research*, 21, 2 (April 1981): 59-65.

58. Herbert E. Krugman, "Television Program Interest and Commercial Interruption," *Journal of Advertising Research*, 23, 1 (February/March 1983): 21-23. Commercials appearing in specials sponsored by General Electric were more effective than those appearing in variety shows, documentaries, or newsmaker interview programs.

59. Stephen Worchel, Thomas W. Hardy, and Richard Hurley, "The Effects of Commercial Interruption of Violent and Nonviolent Films on Viewers' Subsequent Aggression," *Journal of Experimental Social Psychology*, 12 (1976): 220-32.

60. James MacLachlan and Priscilla LaBarbera, "Time-Compressed TV Commercials," *Journal of Advertising Research* 18 (August 1978): 11-15; James MacLachlan and Michael H. Siegel, "Reducing the Costs of TV Commercials by Use of Time Compressions," *Journal of Marketing Research*, 17 (February 1980): 52-57. The unaided recall scores of compressed commercials were 36 percent higher, and aided recall 40 percent higher, perhaps because they were harder to follow and thus required more unconscious attention.

61. In 1973, Alberto-Culver launched a move to split the 30-second commercial into two 15-second units. In a headline-making speech in 1974, the late Andrew Kershaw, president of Ogilvy & Mather, predicted that "ten years from now the 10-second commercial will be the basic length." Five years later, the same agency's research director, Jennifer Stewart, told the Association of National Advertisers that "compared to 30-second commercials, 10-second commercials are able to hold 40 percent more viewers throughout the entire commercial." (*Television / Radio Age*, January 15, 1979, p. 36) Data from about 100 tests conducted by Mapes and Ross showed that 10's were 78 percent as effective as 30's in producing changes in brand preference and 60 percent as effective in generating recall. However, Burke found in 19 tests of 10-second commercials that next-day recall averaged 13 percent compared to 24 percent for a typical 30. Earlier (in 1970), Starch conducted some 100,000 telephone and personal interviews over a period of 30 nights during prime time, regarding commercials broadcast over four Atlanta stations. Ten-second commercials were correctly identified by 10 percent, on average, and wrongly attributed to another advertiser by 8 percent.

62. In the same year (1967) Audience Studies Inc. compared 30-second and 60-second versions for 37 commercials in nine product categories. On the average 30's scored at

94 percent the level of 60's on brand name recall and 96 percent on sales point registration. Similar results were obtained for other commercials tested by ASI and analyzed in separate batches by Benton and Bowles and by Foote Cone and Belding. On pre/post scores, the performance of 30's ranged between 75 percent and 93 percent in the three summary averages. Benton and Bowles also reported on fourteen matched pairs of day-after recall scores, in which 30's averaged 72 percent the level of 60's. A 1970 analysis by Foote Cone & Belding of 400 sets of paired commercials found 30-second commercials to be typically 38 percent-54 percent as effective as 60's, but the range was between 14 percent and 183 percent in specific cases.

Horace Schwerin examined 79 abridgments of 60's to 30's and found that they retained about 70 percent of their effects, on average. Experiments by BBDO using its testing facility in Utica, New York ("Channel One") found that for 130 commercials, 30's created 78 percent the awareness of 60's, and 62 percent of their ability to register sales points. Gallup and Robinson's Proved Commercial Registration from 16 paired comparisons showed 30's averaged 67 percent of 60's—the lowest level found in any of this research. (These data are digested from "A Summary of Available Information on the Relative Effectiveness of 30" vs. 60" Versions of the Same Commercial," Chicago: Foote Cone and Belding, 1970.)

William D. Barclay, Richard M. Doub, and Lyront McMurtrey, who made nearly 12,000 telephone calls in the Chicago metropolitan area in 1963, found a striking difference in "unaided proven recall" between 20- and 30-second commercials but only a small difference between 30's and 60's. For a 20-second commercial, roughly a *third* of the people who believed they were watching it could really remember it, but the proportion rose to about *half* of those reportedly watching half-minute and full-minute commercials. (*Journal of Advertising Research*, 5, 2 [June 1955: 41-47].) *Cf.* also John A Martilla and Donald L. Thompson, "The Perceived Effects of Piggyback Television Commercials," *Journal of Marketing Research*, 3 (November 1966): 365-71. They found that 60-second commercials did not create significantly more product recall than 30-second commercials, but they did create more favorable attitudes.

63. Starch TV commercial recognition scores were also 10 percent-15 percent higher for men viewers than for women, and correct brand identification was higher (though the opposite is true for magazine ads). *Cf.* Oscar Lubow, "The Critical Confrontation."

64. These findings conform with those of a study made in 1973 for Golden West Broadcasters by W. R. Simmons and Associates. This involved 1,583 interviews with viewers of the six commercial television stations in Los Angeles, between 7:30 a.m. and 9:00 p.m. Station logs and monitored records showed an average of 19.8 commercials per hour, exclusive of promotional and public service messages. The viewers were asked, first unaided and then aided, about the products and brands advertised in the past hour on the station they were watching. Eighty percent could recall no advertised brand, even with reminders for 10 product classifications. Only 5 percent remembered more than one brand. (The figures were almost identical among those interviewed between 7:00 and 9:00 p.m.) Earlier, a 1970 Gallup and Robinson study had found that prime-time TV viewers could recall the last commercial accurately 10 percent of the time compared with their 1967-69 average of 8 percent for radio listeners.

65. But another study by Lewis Winters reports the same trend we have found. The norm for commercial recognition (the percentage of viewers who could correctly identify the sponsor in in-home interviews done at the conclusion of a campaign) dropped from 67 percent in 1974 to 56 percent in 1981. Lewis C. Winters, "The Relationship Between Advertising Pretesting and Tracking Studies of Awareness and Attitude," Paper presented to AMA Attitude Conference, Scottsdale, Arizona, February 8, 1982.

66. "Familiarity with past advertising is the most influential factor contributing to high

recall scores," according to Elliott Young of Perception Research Services, which tracks eye movements during commercials: *Marketing News*, November 27, 1981.

67. Burke Marketing Research, Inc., "Viewer Attitudes Toward Commercial Clutter on Television and Commercial Buying Implications," paper presented to the ARF Conference, November 14, 1972. There is at least one contradictory bit of evidence. A study by Baker Advertising tested nine 60-second commercials and found that when three were shown at a time (and their order rotated), the first position produced highest recall, the last position the lowest. Unaided recall, aided recall, and brand name recall were higher when only two rather than three commercials were shown at a time. (Correct recall was not signficantly different.) ARF *Verb-Item*, January 1968.

68. Peter J. Spengler, "TV Clutter. . .Enough Already?" Paper presented to the ANA TV Workshop, March 1, 1978.

69. In these experiments, viewers in groups of four watched a crime drama and a comedy program in a laboratory setting designed like a living room, where they were observed through a one-way mirror, and their attention level was recorded. They also filled out questionnaires afterwards. The respondents were first divided into three subgroups, one subjected to a standard format (three commercial breaks within each program, each of two 30-second commercials and one with an additional 20-second promo plus a between-program break with four messages), a "heavy" format (with three commercials in each break) and a "very heavy" condition (with four commercials each time). Three additional subgroups were added to the experiment: A no-promotion version of the standard format, a "high-promotion" version of "very heavy" clutter (adding two announcements), and a variant of the standard format in which three 10-second announcements substituted for a 30-second commercial in each of the two half-hour programs. *Cf.* Michael L. Ray and Peter H. Webb, "Advertising Effectiveness in a Crowded Television Environment," Cambridge, Mass.: Marketing Science Institute, 1978 Peter H. Webb and Michael Ray, "Effects of TV Clutter," *Journal of Advertising Research*, 19, 3 (June 1979): 7-12; Michael L. Ray and Peter H. Webb, "Experimental Research on the Effects of Television Clutter: Dealing with a Difficult Media Environment," Cambridge, Mass.: Marketing Science Institute, 1976; *Cf.* also Robert Liddell and Gordon Young, "TV Clutter: What's the Problem? What's the Answer?" Paper presented to the ANA TV Workshop, New York, February 2, 1977.

70. Jacob Jacoby, Wayne D. Hoyer, and David A. Sheluga, *Miscomprehension of Televised Communications* (New York: American Association of Advertising Agencies, 1980).

71. S.R.C. Bulletin, Vol. 13, No. 7, July 1965.

Chapter 8
Reach Versus Frequency, and the Third Dimension

Media scheduling is essentially a matter of balancing two objectives, reach and frequency,* within an available budget. *Reach* is the extent of coverage, the percentage of people brought within exposure range of the advertising over a stated period of time. *Frequency* refers to the number of times this exposure takes place. Should we scatter our messages in such a way as to contact the largest possible number of people or concentrate them to deliver repeated impressions to the same people? (By *people* we usually mean prospective customers rather than the public at large, though that distinction, I shall point out, is not always easy to make.)

No advertiser—not even a Procter & Gamble or a General Motors, spending many millions of dollars—can get the maximum of *both* reach and frequency. One must always be sacrificed in the interests of the other

Media scheduling may be planned in relation to two characteristics of the product advertised: the breadth of the market and the intensity of the consumer's involvement or interest.† These two elements (each of which represents a separate continuum) are sometimes mistakenly lumped under the same heading of consumer interest. A moderate overall level of consumer interest might reflect the strong concern of a relatively small group of customers. Only a limited number of people suffer from psoriasis or wear false teeth, but for these people any ad (however small) that deals with their problem presumably has compelling interest. By the same token, it would be rather difficult to attract a person who does not wear false teeth to study an ad for a denture cleanser, regardless of how large a space unit was used to command initial attention.

---

*Foote, Cone & Belding's Frank Gromer prefers "freak and recency."

†Other variables may be brought into the picture. A third might be the degree to which brand differences are perceived as important in the product field, but this would probably affect media scheduling only insofar as it affects overall product interest. A fourth variable might be the product purchase and usage cycle, but since different consumers are generally at various points of that cycle on any given day (except for products with seasonal use), this is easier to take account of in theory than in practice.

When the marketer is able to define his target in narrow dimensions, he must pursue a strategy of concentration. If his best customers are located in a particular segment of the population that corresponds closely with the audience profile of a particular medium, then it obviously makes sense to concentrate his budget with repeated messages in that medium. This is essentially what industrial advertisers do; they know that if they want to reach purchasing agents they must put the message in *Purchasing Week*. The consumer goods advertiser who sells ten-bladed pocket knives to Boy Scouts knows he can reach them in *Boys' Life*; if he sells skin-blemish cream he may use *Seventeen*.

Many products with an essentially narrow market cannot be defined in clean-cut demographic terms. The market may reflect idiosyncrasies of personal taste. The psychological traits that lead to consumption may be scattered throughout the population. They may not necessarily be associated with the basic personality structure of any particular social group.

No single mass medium can single out people who are receptive to product innovations. No medium can zero in on the users of auto seat covers or the anxious people who respond to snob appeals in automotive copy or the "oral optimists" likely to respond to certain symbols in a cigarette's name or package design. Mass coverage may be the only way to reach a narrow market embodying a combination of demographic traits to which no medium quite corresponds. There are magazines that are read by rich women and others that have particular appeal to older women or to small-town women. But to reach rich old women in small towns, the advertiser must spread himself thin.

When he must use a mass medium to reach a narrow target, the marketer assumes that the audience will be to some degree self-selective. Whether he uses broadcast or print, he expects the potential customers to pay more attention to his messages than the average consumer, even though both groups will be exposed to them at the same rate.*

The use of broad mass media may be called for with four very different kinds of marketing targets. Major appliances typify products with a broad market and high consumer interest. Detergents represent a product with a broad market but low interest. Air travel has a relatively narrow market and high interest. Nail polish remover is a product with a narrow market and low interest.

In all four instances, the advertiser must spread his messages to a wide audience. His need for frequent display of his message and brand name may be less in the case of high interest products, regardless of how broad their market is. High-interest products arouse more attention for their advertising and presumably can get along without the constant reinforcement that low-interest items need. The product with a narrow market may require substantial or dominant space or time units to make sure that the message does not fail to come across to any of the relatively few potential customers. To balance these sometimes contradictory requirements takes shrewd and subtle assessment in each particular case.

---

*This is *generally* true, although, as we saw in Chapter 3, there may be substantial variations in advertising pressure for different products that sell at the same price.

The third dimension

The third dimension in any discussion of media reach and frequency is the size or length of the message unit and the character of the media vehicle in which it is embedded. Within any given budget, the smaller the unit, the greater the number of different vehicles that can be used in the schedule and the more often each can be used.

In print, the size of the ad affects its ability to achieve actual exposure. It is therefore a determinant of true reach (as opposed to potential reach). Although it is still possible for broadcast advertisers to buy shorter or longer units, they are generally limited to the 30-second commercial on television and 60 seconds on radio. But in principle, there is a communications value that accrues to longer commercials as compared to shorter ones. (As cable offers an assortment of commercial lengths, including even extended "infomercials," the question of how much time the unit should take will assume a revived importance.)

The larger or longer the message, the more likely that the reader or viewer will be stopped in his tracks long enough to get the point.* A larger unit appears to be more important; it can carry more information about the product, it can incorporate more elements of a multifaceted product appeal, it can use more elaborate devices to capture the interest of the audience, and (in broadcasting) it is better able to evoke empathy with the company spokesman. But if the message can be put well in a smaller unit, it can be run more times for a given sum of money. Thus the smaller unit carries all the advantages of frequency.

Within a given budget, one of these three dimensions (reach, frequency, and the size of the message unit) must always be sacrificed in order to improve the others. To run a campaign of ads or commercials of a given size or length, we may plan our expenditure to maximize reach, or we can maximize frequency within the limits of certain reach. If we want to look important by increasing the size of the message unit, we must reduce either reach or frequency.

Maximum reach of potential prospects is always desirable in and of itself—provided that a particular advertising unit in a given media vehicle is adequate to the task of persuasion. (This latter restriction can be extremely important; below a certain minimum, a unit may no longer convey meaningful information, and the advertiser paying for it will actually be running reminder ads when there is nothing in the prospect's mind of which he can be reminded.)

In print an advertiser can sacrifice attention value for the sake of repetition, or vice versa. A four-color, double-page magazine spread dominates the reader's attention, but it costs the same as a number of half-page black-and-white ads that

---

*Larger ads hold their advantage even when the environment changes. In a 1982 Audits and Surveys study among a national sample of 2,000, we analyzed the recognition of ads on pages where half or more of the space was devoted to advertising and on pages that were predominantly editorial. Ads of a given size maintain the same average levels whether they are positioned with other ads or with news articles. The larger ads also generated greater interest among nonreaders of yesterday's paper who were taken through a similar assortment of pages.

might be exposed to his attention repeatedly.* The print advertiser must decide whether to buy the large space necessary to control his own environment or whether to take his chances, with smaller space, on appearing in an environment where random and uncontrollable influences are at work and are bound to affect the performance of his ad.† (Such random environmental influences are, of course, present in any medium.)

In the case of a product for which nearly everyone is a prospect, but which has mediocre or low interest (shoes or cereal), large space insures the maximum possible traffic and scanning and thereby enhances the likelihood that potential purchasers will be stopped long enough to get the message. A small space unit might be expected to be more likely to win the attention of the reader to whose interests the message is directed, whereas a larger unit might seem to have a better chance of being sighted by less interested readers in their random progress through the publication.** A small ad next to others for related products may stand a better chance of attracting the reader who has reached the stage of the purchase cycle in which he is actively searching for this kind of information. However, when a small advertisement appears out of context, cheek by jowl with unrelated ads and editorial matter, there would appear to be more likelihood that it will be seen, however briefly, by people who are not "in the market" but who might be nudged a little in the right direction.

One problem in evaluating the relation of ad size to standard readership scores is that different kinds of advertisers (with products of different interest to the consumer) habitually use different ad sizes. Thus average readership scores for different items reflect comparative product interest as well as the attention value of different size units.[1]

In the Des Moines study described in the previous chapter,[2] we examined the ratio of recall to recognition as a clue to the persistence of the message's initial impact in the reader's memory. We reasoned that although the size of an

---

*The evidence suggests that a tabloid-size ad in a tabloid newspaper is perceived in relation to the total size of the page and that an ad in a magazine of *Reader's Digest* size communicates in much the same way as a full-page ad in a regular-size magazine. However, it does not follow that the communication capacities of full-page ads are the same whatever their absolute size simply because their capacity for winning attention may be comparable in relation to their environment.

†Consider, for example, two adjacent pronouncements, the first by the United Lutherans: "Faith Gives You Power!" and "Gulf Gives You More Power!"

**In print, the shape as well as the size of the advertising unit may affect attention value. Daniel Starch has compared single-column, quarter-page magazine ads against square-shaped ads of the same space: Daniel Starch, "How Does Shape of Ads Affect Readership?" *Media/scope*, July 1966, pp. 83-85. Both noting (recognition) and reported readership of the single-column ads proved over a fourth higher than for the square ones. When Starch compared Lucky Strike ads that appeared sideways with those in which the type ran horizontally on the page, he found noting to be about the same but readership to be higher in the case of the regular ads. However, a similar analysis made on Botany tie ads found no difference either in noting or reading, and an analysis of full-page Jarman shoe ads with a large illustration found a decided advantage for the sideways ads. Thus it would appear that the positioning of the ad may affect readership in relation to the layout itself.

ad would affect its ability to win attention, it should have no bearing on whether a message is effectively communicated and remembered once the reader's attention is on the ad. (Two ads with identical *recognition* scores presumably are equivalent in their capacity to win the reader's initial attention. But if they have different recall scores, this means that one registered its message more durably.) Our hypothesis was supported by the results.

Clearly, an advertisement's performance reflects the product it advertises as well as the form the message takes, and its ability to arouse attention is at best a crude index of its ability to sell the product.

Message size and performance

"Which gives the better results, a small number of large advertisements or a large number of small ones?" This question was asked in 1914 by E. K. Strong and it is still being asked today. Strong showed 39 people dummy magazines once a month for four months.[3] At the end of that time, the bigger ads got better recall. But recall did not increase in direct proportion to the increase in space; it grew by the square root of the increase. When the time interval between repetitions was later shortened, Strong found that it was more efficient to use small ads. When the time interval was long, large advertisements were better. (Brian D. Copland of the London Press Exchange reported in 1949 that "the square root law" had indeed applied in England before World War II but that since the War, no doubt owing to the stress and strain of those gallant years, attention increased by the cube root!)

The square root law appears to hold for other indicators of performance, apart from remembrance of the advertisements themselves. In 1936 H. J. Rudolph reported that a half-page ad produces 70 percent as many coupon returns as a full page, and Daniel Starch produced identical findings in 1959.[4]

The Yakima, Washington, *Daily Republic and Morning Herald* ran a one-and-a-half-inch ad buried down near the bottom of the paper with the statement, "there are 17 universities in France." When people were called on the following day, 8 percent had read the ad the night before and remembered the answer. When the ad was increased to two columns by five inches, 12 percent remembered correctly. A nearly sevenfold increase in the size of the message added only 50 percent to the memorability of the message, suggesting that there might be a limit to the extent of potential interest in the subject.

In broadcasting as in print, advertising performance does not go up in proportion to unit size, as we saw in the last chapter. Although commercials occasionally still run up to two minutes in length, and 10-second ID's have not totally disappeared, the advertiser does not normally have much opportunity to depart from the 30-second standard on TV and 60 seconds on radio. But he expects to pay a price that varies according to the time of day and the character of the program and the station, apart from the size of the audience. Just as in choosing one publication over another because it offers a better environment for his messages, he may be trading impact, within a given budget, against reach and also against frequency. Most advertising strategists recognize that (1) generalized findings do not necessarily apply to specific cases and (2) the communications values that signify greater impact are not necessarily reflected by the single criterion of recall (the registration of specific points of information, the solid identification of the product with certain desirable attributes, the imputation to the advertiser of a serious purpose in his message).

Repetition to build reach

The advertiser is ordinarily concerned with the size and environment of his individual ads or commercials only because these factors relate to cost and because he must deploy his limited resources to best effect. What any one ad can accomplish is usually significant only in relation to a continuing chain of messages in the campaign of which it is a part. Because such campaigns must often be fully planned and developed before they are actually in print or on the air, the advertiser may get tired of his own advertising long before the public is aware of it. E. Lawrence Deckinger remembers the following episode:

> The Detroit office of J. Walter Thompson once worked on a new campaign for nine months under Henry Ford's close personal direction. At the final meeting, final proofs of magazine ads, billboards, and what-not were stretched all about the room. Mr. Ford entered and said without looking around, "Boys, I think the public is getting tired of this campaign." Not a single ad in the campaign had yet been run.

The term *repetition* in advertising means different things from the standpoint of advertiser and audience. An advertiser may repeat his message in order to add to the total number of people he reaches. He can do this because most media vehicles accumulate new audience members with every successive issue or broadcast at the same time that they lose an equivalent part of their old audience.

As long as a given selection of media vehicles is being used, reach can be extended only by adding frequency, since people predisposed toward a particular publication or program are likely to turn up in the audience again with greater than chance probability. This phenomenon is particularly true of broadcasting because of the great variability in the time that different kinds of people devote to viewing and listening. When the television advertiser repeats his messages to accumulate reach, he correspondingly steps up the frequency with which his messages are exposed to the people who spend the most time with the medium. This creates what is often referred to as a "skew," with a highly disproportionate number of impressions delivered against a small minority of all those reached at all, and only one impression or two (or even none) exposed to a substantial part of the public over a defined period of time. (This becomes a powerful argument for using a mix of media, not only to extend reach and to even out frequency, but to balance the characteristics of the people reached.)

It is common practice to measure media performance in terms of Gross Rating Points.* Thus, each opportunity for exposure is given equal weight, regardless of whether it represents the first or the tenth in a given household. Although the term GRP originated in radio and was adopted for TV, it has been taken up by print media as well.

---

*These have already been defined on page 43.

Young & Rubicam's Joseph Ostrow remarks that "Using average frequency is like talking about the man who drowned in a lake that had an average depth of two feet." He suggests instead that the planner adopt a minimum frequency goal "and then maximize reach at that frequency level." But reach is always a by-product of frequency in a complex media schedule, and when an optimum frequency goal is set, the considerations of selecting media to reach a particular target group may become overwhelming.

To produce an exaggerated illustration, a print schedule with two insertions might reach 50 percent of the public with an average frequency of two (assuming that all the people who read the first issue of the publication also read the second and no new readers are added). A broadcast schedule with 20 spot announcements might also reach 50 percent with an average frequency of two, but half of those reached may have seen or heard one commercial, and 1 percent may have received 20. So average reach and frequency tell us nothing about the shape of the exposure pattern.

The various media differ in their characteristic exposure patterns and thus in their ability to expand the accumulated audience when messages are repeated. A magazine with a large pass-along audience (including many casual and occasional readers) adds proportionately much greater reach through repetition than a magazine with a total audience of equal size made up largely of loyal primary readers.*

In general, media whose audiences are accumulated mainly as a matter of regular habit (like daily newspapers or technical publications) have a low capacity for extending reach through repetition compared with media to which exposure takes place on a somewhat irregular and random basis, as in evening television. As prime time schedules get larger, according to Nielsen's William S. Hamill, reach increases "and eventually achieves a flat trajectory at the 500 to 600 GRP level."

The retailer puts most of his advertising in newspapers which reach the readers over and over again each day. By contrast, the national advertiser is not out to sell a product, at a particular price, on a particular day, so much as he is trying to get across some points of information and build an image that will serve him well in the long run. Therefore, he compares media not in terms of a single message but in terms of continuing schedules. Most advertising research on television and radio deals not so much with the one-time audience for a program or for a spot position as with the cumulative reach of that program or a schedule of spots over a period of time.

Today's typical television or radio advertiser scatters his messages over the time and program spectrum in an attempt to achieve broad reach. He either buys television time on a spot basis (41 percent of all national TV advertising dollars went to spot commercials on local stations in 1982) or through participation on network programs, typically along with other companies, and with his messages

---

National Geographic and *Family Circle* both had the same total audience, about 30 million in 1982 according to MRI, but 50 percent of the *Geographic's* audience was classed as primary compared with 35 percent of *Family Circle's* audience. The *Geographic* inevitably accumulated fewer new readers than *Family Circle* from one issue to the next.

spread around through a number of shows. As a practical matter, this kind of scheduling often must be bought with little regard to the nature of the programming in which the messages are to be embedded.

The spot TV advertiser must assume that his messages either will go repeatedly to the same people or will extend his reach to different people in proportion to the total amount of viewing done by various segments of the audience. When a commercial is repeated to an audience of the same size it reached the first time, the probability that it will reach new people is directly proportionate to the probability of reaching those people with the first broadcast. (People who watch TV a lot, and who missed the commercial the first time, have a higher-than-average probability of catching it when it is repeated; light viewers who happened to be on hand the first time have a lower-than-average probability of viewing the repeated message.)

"Vertical" and "horizontal" scheduling of prime-time TV spot announcements have been compared by Gallup and Robinson using a system they have called "Total Prime-Time Television" research (TPT).[5] This system is based on recall of the advertised brand on the following day and "registration" (the ability to play back—or describe—the commercial accurately). They define vertical scheduling as the alignment of station-break commercials within a given station's schedule on a given night. Horizontal scheduling refers to the alignment of station-break commercials *across* all stations in a market at the same time on a given night.

The conclusion of the TPT research was that performance depended essentially on the total number of times a commercial was repeated. With a horizontal schedule on different stations, the advertiser can expect a high cumulative audience but a low frequency, since his messages are concentrated in time. A vertical schedule on a single station produces a low cumulative audience but gives a high frequency of exposure. (The term *exposure,* as used by TPT, refers to what we might prefer to call the opportunity for exposure.) Gallup and Robinson conclude that exposure may be multiplied against reach directly, without regard to frequency. Their analysis argues that a given number of gross rating points on spot TV produces the identical yield in communications effect (measured by recall of the advertised brand and "registration" of the sales message), regardless of whether they stem from repeated messages on one station at different times or parallel messages at the same time on different stations. However, the advertiser who sticks to a "vertical alignment" on the same station gets more for his money than if he spread his budget over a number of stations.

In practice, the prime-time spot TV advertiser can rarely buy the identical time position for his commercial on all channels in a market. If he uses a number of stations, his scheduling is apt to be "diagonal" (at different points in time) rather than horizontally broadcast (at exactly the same time). If his campaign continues for any substantial number of weeks, the constant flux of the TV audience inevitably must give him approximately the same ratio of reach to frequency with a given number of messages broadcast on one station or on several with the same size audience. And the ultimate effect of the advertising must be the same by any standard.

The "campaign"

In the advertising world, media performance is customarily measured with reference to arbitrary benchmarks. Where actual audience data are not available on the basis of the arbitrary benchmark period, statistical simulation techniques are generally used to develop estimates of what has been achieved in reach and frequency of exposure within the allotted time. Some of the benchmarks arise from the calendar, some from the contractual practices in buying and selling media. Still others have arisen artificially out of the report-scheduling habits of media research services.

The year has four seasons. Even for products with a seasonal sales pattern, few advertising schedules are designed to follow the calendar exactly except for the vacation months of July and August. Broadcast advertising contracts are often expressed in 13-, 26-, 39-, or 52-week cycles. The advertiser who buys time outside this framework often incurs a cost penalty.

In the magazine field, rate structures are based on the 12 annual issues of a monthly magazine or the 52 annual issues of a weekly. To encourage continuity of usage of the publication, the publishers of a weekly magazine usually offer an advertiser a more economical rate scale if he orders 13 ads (one-fourth of a year, or 1 issue in 4). He is not likely to order 11 or 12 insertions when the cost of the thirteenth is nominal. This simple fact makes 13 a magic number and forces the advertiser and his agency to calculate the reach and frequency of his advertising in terms of the 13-issue period.

The word *campaign* is often used in advertising to describe the advertiser's contractual obligations. A 26-week commitment to co-sponsor a television program is referred to as a "campaign"; a commitment to run an ad in every other issue of *People* for a year is a "campaign." Implicit in this military nomenclature is the illusion that the advertisements encompassed by such a contract are also perceived by the public as a coordinated and concerted effort. The advertiser often encourages this illusion by publicizing such "campaigns" to his employees and distributors. He "merchandises" them to his dealers.

The word *campaign* may also be used to describe the introduction of a new product, and here the term is normally more appropriate because it suggests a carefully timed convergence of distribution, promotion, and advertising through a number of media. If the product and its promotion are strong enough to catch the attention of the public at large, they may indeed be aware of a "campaign" to impress and interest them.

In estimating advertising performance for an established product, the benchmarks used are often based on practices of the syndicated media measurement services. Although "overnights" are available in a few major markets, network television ratings are released on a biweekly basis. Data on audience accumulation and duplication for different programs have, by custom, been analyzed over a four-week period. This has carried over from the relatively simple era of network radio programming to the much more complex epoch of spot TV. The four-week period has thus become another magic number for media analysis. With the development of the intermedia syndicated services based on diaries or self-administered questionnaires, the four-week period has been extended into print media.

The rise of spot television has enormously spurred the tendency of the advertiser to think in terms of the four-week period. This period not only corresponds to the TV measurements that are customarily available, it also has a great practical advantage. The television advertiser may reach only a small percentage of the total public with any given spot announcement, particularly in daytime. He relies on the repetition of announcements to give him the reach he desires. What point in time, then, should he consider to be the outermost limits of that reach? Theoretically, he will keep accumulating additional audiences *ad infinitum* as long as he advertises. He will never put his message before *everyone* because, for a variety of reasons, not everyone is accessible. Yet every message that is printed or broadcast will add something both in reach and frequency to the messages that have gone before.

By the end of four weeks, numbers have accumulated that look large and respectable enough for the agency's media planner to show to a client who dreams of "total coverage" and who might be overwhelmed with anxiety if he were confronted with figures that showed the reach from a single commercial or a single ad.

A time period of 4 or 13 weeks may be convenient or politic to use; it may be the way media research data are most often reported; but it represents no reality at all in the psychology of communication or in the world of consumption. People do not customarily buy products in 4-week cycles or 13-week cycles. In the rare cases where they do, the timing of those cycles can hardly be expected to correspond with the sequence of messages in an advertising campaign. In tracing the effects of a series of advertising messages (except those for new products), the planner must always begin his calculations at one point in a chain of events and end them at another point. Both these points may be reasonable and wisely selected, but both must also be arbitrary in relation to the ongoing process of communication between the company and its customers. This is true even when the advertiser embarks on something that *he* considers to be new, as when he goes into a new media schedule or begins the use of a new slogan or new creative approach. If the same commercial is broadcast repeatedly over a 4-week period, we generally assume that with each broadcast its effect on those people who have seen it before reinforces or "builds on" all previous exposures.

But what of the effect the first time the commercial is broadcast? Does it start from scratch, with nothing to build on? Quite the contrary, it reflects and builds on the accumulative impact of *all* the audience's previous exposure to the product: their exposure to its advertising, to in-store sightings of it, to conversations or news about it, to its actual performance through personal experience with it.

Simon Broadbent refers to the sum total of advertising exposures as the "ad stock," in which previously received messages are constantly decaying in a "half-life" analogous to that of atomic particles.[6]

When the media planner summarizes the cumulative audience reach and frequency of a series of messages, he perforce performs his calculations as though each message existed by itself. It does, of course, from the standpoint of the advertiser who has to pay for it or the planner who has to schedule it. But from the standpoint of the consumer on the verge of seeing or hearing a new advertising message (but just before it is presented to him), the effects of all the previous messages have, in most instances, already faded and fused into a single image, a composite of mental fragments from all the impressions and imagery to which he has been exposed. The individual messages of the past are undistinguishable.

This is not to say that individual messages may not have had an impact. Let us consider the smoker who saw, and was startled by, the very first ad that showed a Marlboro Cowboy. When he saw a different cowboy in another Marlboro ad, he must have had a feeling that he had seen this very ad some place before. The third time he saw such an ad, he might still have had a specific recollection of each of the two previous occasions. But as the years went by and the reader saw 20, 30, or 40 similar ads, he could only be left with a residual impression of the slogan and of the product rather than of the individual ads.

The fusion effect in no way weakens the positive achievement of the advertising. The Marlboro advertising I cited was, after all, one of the most highly memorable campaigns in history because of the brilliant attention-getting device it used.

Within an ongoing series, a single ad may also be highly memorable. Needless to say, the ad that creates individual identity through a technical trick may entail the danger of psychologically submerging the product. (The housewife may be amused by the blinding dazzle of the wash in the TV commercial and may vividly remember details of the action, but she may have her doubts as to whether the clothes were whitened by Tide, Bold, or Fab.)

If the consumer were to be asked to recall advertising for Green Giant vegetables, she would be likely to play back an accurate description of the figure symbolizing this product—the Jolly Green Giant. Apart from this general recollection, she might even be able to think of specific advertisements or commercials she had seen during the product's advertising life. But more likely the memory of all the individual ads would have been collapsed into a single composite impression independent of the media background in which each message was originally placed.

As every new advertising message is presented to the consumer, it evokes and reinforces, however faintly, the effects of all the other messages that preceded it. The extent to which this happens reflects specific content, verbal and visual. (There are, of course, instances where it is desirable that there be a minimum of continuity and a maximum of incongruity between an old advertising campaign and a new one. Such instances may arise, for example, when a product faces a radically different competitive marketing situation during which its packaging or ingredients undergo modification or replacement, or when a copy theme is "tired" to the point that further repetition may actually produce a negative effect.)

The residual effect of a message always reflects the preconceptions that the consumer brings to the product and brand. Therefore, the history of earlier exposure to repetitions of the *identical* message is impossible to divorce from the history of prior exposure to all *other* messages for the product, including those that occur not through advertising channels but through product usage, display, news reports, or word of mouth, etc.

The concept of accumulation in advertising properly describes a process: every message works on the base of all the other messages that have preceded it. But this process of accumulation can be measured only in relative terms, never in absolutes. Accumulation must be measured within time limits, and these must be arbitrarily determined. When different media schedules are compared over a given time period, a "natural" time unit for one medium must be equated with an "unnatural" one for another.

Advertising planners find the concept of accumulation too convenient a crutch to discard it merely on the grounds that it has no basis in valid communications theory. Under "laboratory" conditions it may be possible to measure the communications effects of an individual message in a series, in isolation from the effect of all the preceding messages. In real life it cannot be done. Campaigns in advertising exist only in the dreams and schemes of advertising generals.

Dominance

In the mind of every advertising planner is the goal of achieving dominance for his product relative to his competition. He wants dominance in the mind of the consumer, dominance in the total volume and impact of his messages, and dominance in the position of his ads within every medium he uses. Each of these types of dominance involves different strategic problems, although the advertiser often confuses them.

The message that is delivered most often might be expected to be the one that creates the biggest return, by whatever criteria the advertiser chooses to use. But rarely does a brand's share of all advertising messages for the product turn out to be exactly the same as its share of the market. The obvious reason for this is that many other forces besides advertising go into the creation of a market share. A not so obvious reason might also be present, even if advertising were the only force and even if all advertising messages were exactly equivalent in persuasive power. There may be a point of diminishing returns when we increase the number of messages, just as there may be a minimum threshold below which advertising may be too weak to make its mark.

Market reserach studies generally show that the biggest selling brand in a field (General Electric or Coca-Cola) or the most prestigious brand (Cadillac) has greater "top of mind" share of mentions as the first brand that people think of than it has of the market. However, a fascinating study suggests that beyond a certain point of dominance in its advertising volume, a leading brand no longer gains in its level of public awareness in proportion to an increased output of messages.

The inference can be drawn from a series of experiments made by William D. Wells and Jack M. Chinsky,[7] using college students as subjects. In each experiment the student was seated in front of a keyboard containing two rows of numbers (1 through 5 and 6 through 10). Numbers were read to him through earphones attached to a tape recorder. After each series of numbers, the student was asked to register one of the numbers by pressing a key on the machine. In an ordinary sequence, each number's share of "choices" coincided almost exactly with its share of "messages." When a given number occurred more often than others, it continued to be chosen in proportion to its share, up to the point where it was mentioned three times as often as the number with the lowest frequency. This pattern changed when a number became completely dominant. The number with a "dominant" share of 50 percent of the messages got less than two-fifths of all the choices. A number with only a 5 percent share had about a sixth of the choices. The intermediate numbers had a share of choices corresponding to their share of messages.

The authors put a great many qualifications on their findings, modestly pointing out that "they have nothing to say about the product characteristics that produce or prevent a repeat sale." They do indicate that "perceived salience, as denoted by choice, can be increased by increasing a message's share of the total message stream. Up to a point, an increase in share of messages produces a proportionate increase in perceived salience, but at some point further increases in share of messages become inefficient and do not produce commensurate returns."

The Wells and Chinsky findings refer to messages received within the framework of a given "message stream" (or medium). But in real life many message streams are flowing at once. An advertised brand may dominate its product field within a particular medium and still remain weak within the total market. This can happen if the audience for the medium is small or substantially duplicated by other media which carry a large amount of advertising for other brands of the products.

There are substantial benefits for an advertiser who, by his consistent and dominant presence, creates an identification between his product and a vehicle that has a unique significance for its public. This is well known and much played upon by "little magazines" or by radio programs that boast of their small bands of loyal and devoted followers. The implication is that to the reader or listener this is *his* magazine or program in a sense that others are not, because others are for "everybody."

Thus the advertiser is presumed to reap a double dividend, both from the greater intensity of interest and attention with which the audience comes to his message and from the audience's conscious loyalty to the advertisers who support their medium. ("Mention our name when you buy from our fine advertisers!")*

There are two separate components in the notion of dominance within the medium. One relates to the short-run experience of a day's TV viewing or radio listening or the reading of a particular issue of a magazine or newspaper. The other refers to the ongoing and accumulative force of advertising in the medium as a whole within one magazine issue or broadcasting day. The dominant advertiser is the one who by sheer expenditure of effort or brilliance of execution manages to make his voice heard above the din. His ability to make his message stand out from all others seen or heard in the same media context will have much

---

*This is only a step away from the ads extracted from local merchants for the high school yearbook or the fireman's ball program: essentially a ritualized form of tribute rather than a means of promotion.

to do with the nature of what he is selling and the content of what he is saying.

The concept of dominance must assume that throughout the industry everyone is trying as hard as he can. Talent and the coming of the Great Creative Idea are unpredictable—part of the luck of the game.* Where control *can* be exercised is over the money to be invested and the strategy of investing it. One can outspend the competition, if only in the obscure and neglected wedges of the market, and thereby achieve dominance (if only dominance of effort) in selected places and times.

The more advertising messages that are placed before us at the same time, and the more that are presented to us in the same context, the bigger the job becomes of using the interesting and relevant ones and screening out the ones we interpret as meaningless "noise."

This screening process takes place in terms of perceptual units that may or may not coincide with the media units in terms of which the advertiser thinks and by means of which he hopes to dominate the market. The advertiser may want to dominate today's paper, but if I read the paper on three separate occasions and open different sections or pages each time, he may be "dominating" my second reading but not the first or third, which for me are separate media "events."

The advertiser who buys an outsize gatefold ad in a magazine is willing to pay a premium because his advertisement will dominate the medium in a direct, tangible, physical sense. People cannot pass it by as part of the scenery. Whether or not the message is convincing, it is bound to stand out. This is dominance of the media unit. The reader's attention has been arrested.

The typical television or radio advertiser defines dominance in terms of the volume of GRPs he delivers in a given period of time. Most characteristically, he believes dominance to be a matter of repetition, rather than of physical format, in his messages.

The aim to win dominance rarely is limited to an issue of a publication or to a single sequence of programs on a particular network. It means being the biggest air conditioner advertiser in magazines or the most heavily advertised detergent brand in daytime television. When the advertiser defines the problem of dominance in this broadened way, he is no longer concerned with the job of breaking through the barrier of inattention. He is under no illusion that anyone puts down a finished copy of *Reader's Digest* with a sigh of pleased recollection of his great ad. He asumes that media experiences fade into one another and that few people carry full awareness of the original context with them from one advertising exposure to the next.

The advertiser who seeks to maintain dominance in a whole medium may start with a number of possible assumptions. One is that the medium is exactly right for the product; it has the right audience profile to match product usage.

---

*This does not contradict the ability of advertisers to improve their chances by pretesting ads and commercials before they are run. Pretesting reduces the risk of making bad mistakes, but most substantial advertisers now do it routinely, so it is hard for any one of them to have a competitive edge. And while research may stimulate ideas, it is not a substitute for inspiration.

He may also assume that the medium provides the right emotional climate: the housewife consults the newspaper when she makes up her shopping list; her mind is on the subject when she's reading a "shelter book" like *Better Homes and Gardens*; it takes the right kind of beloved, smooth radio talk show host to kid her into trying this product; the product cries for demonstration on TV.

The advertiser may also start with a wary look at his own resources and those of the competition. No matter how extensive his funds may be, they are rarely big enough to dominate everything. This may cause him to redirect his attention to two different kinds of opportunity for dominance.

First, there are sectors of the market that the competitors are not reaching: the housewives who barely scan the newspaper, never look at *Better Homes*, hate talk shows and don't watch much TV. Our advertiser might concentrate his fire on these neglected people and capture their attention (and undying brand loyalty!).

A second opportunity is often provided by the fact that certain copy points can be made better through one medium than through another, with the result that all the competing strategists have rushed in the same direction and are operating from the same premises. The ensuing clutter of similar claims, the succession of cheerful smiling satisfied housewife models, may have left the public utterly confused on the subject of brand identity. If Our Brand moves to a different medium, the same copy points may stand out with greater individuality; or perhaps different copy points can be used to further differentiate our product from its competitors.

In short, a given dollar expenditure in a minor or secondary medium may win a brand dominance in one area of the consumer's mind, whereas the identical number of messages delivered in the context of a medium dominated by the competition might fail to establish a substantial identity for it.

The advertiser who makes use of this second opportunity is after the same body of potential customers that his competitors want; instead of bucking into the center, he is going around left end, so to speak, and reaching his target in an environment where the competitors ain't. Reach and frequency should never exist as objectives for their own sake; they are meaningful concepts in advertising strategy only in relation to where the customers are and how the competition is getting to them.

Notes

1. Verling Troldahl and Robert Jones found that size alone explained 40 percent of the readership of newspaper advertisements, type of product 19 percent. This left 39 percent to be explained by the creative elements of the ad itself. *Cf.* Verling C. Troldahl and Robert L. Jones, "Predictors of Newspaper Advertisement Readership," *Journal of Advertising Research* 5, 1 (March 1965): 23-27.

2. See page 163.

3. E. K. Strong, "The Effect of Size of Advertisements and Frequency of Their Presentation." *Psychological Review*, 1914, pp. 136-52.

4. Cited by Julian L. Simon, "Are There Economies of Scale in Advertising?" *Journal of Advertising Research* 5, 2 (June 1965): 15-20.

5. *Cf.* Morris J. Gelman, "The Search for Marketing Efficiency in TV," *Television*, 22, 5

(May 1965): 30.

6. Simon Broadbent, "One way TV advertisements work," *Journal of the Market Research Society* 21, 3 (1979).

7. "The Effects of Competing Messages: A Laboratory Simulation," *Journal of Marketing Research* 2, 2 (May 1965): 141-45.

Chapter 9
The Uses of Repetition

To many an advertising planner, telling his story over and over again seems an essential part of persuading the consumer, much as repeated association of food and a bell was essential in the conditioning of Pavlov's dogs. Thomas Smith gave classic expression to the theory in his "Hints to Intending Advertisers," published in 1885, which still represents the premise on which many advertising schedules are constructed.

The first time a man looks at an advertisement, he does not see it.
The second time he does not notice it.
The third time he is conscious of its existence.
The fourth time he faintly remembers having seen it before.
The fifth time he reads it.
The sixth time he turns up his nose at it.
The seventh time he reads it through and says, "Oh bother!"
The eighth time he says, "Here's that confounded thing again!"
The ninth time he wonders if it amounts to anything.
The tenth time he thinks he will ask his neighbor if he has tried it.
The eleventh time he wonders how the advertiser makes it pay.
The twelfth time he thinks perhaps it may be worth something.
The thirteenth time he thinks it must be a good thing.
The fourteenth time he remembers that he has wanted such a thing for a long time.
The fifteenth time he is tantalized because he cannot afford to buy it.
The sixteenth time he thinks he will buy it some day.
The seventeenth time he makes a memorandum of it.
The eighteenth time he swears at his poverty.
The nineteenth time he counts his money carefully.
The twentieth time he sees it, he buys the article, or instructs his wife to do so.[1]

The advertiser's objective in repeating his message may be quite different from that of merely extending his reach. He may want to deliver messages repeatedly to the same people in order to reinforce a message already delivered.

His objective may be (1) to remind the audience of a previous message which might otherwise be forgotten; (2) to reinforce or give added emphasis to such a former message; (3) to break through a barrier of psychological resistance that may have inhibited effective communication of the earlier message; (4) to approach the task of persuasion from a different perspective (that is, by varying the creative approach) and thus to exploit more than a single opening to the consumer's consciousness; or (5) to add to the residue of all the advertiser's previous communications and thus to amplify the consumer's existing fund of information or favorable opinion.

Convincing evidence on what happens when the same message is repeated to the same people comes from coupon advertising, where the pull of the ad is directly traceable in the number of orders or inquiries. As early as 1912, William Shryer[2] analyzed thousands of keyed coupon advertisements soliciting mail responses. His conclusion was that "the first insertion of a tried piece of copy in a new medium will pay better, in every way, than any subsequent insertion of the same copy in the same magazine."

According to Julian L. Simon, "virtually all published mail order data corroborate this finding." He cites Victor Schwab's 1950 estimate that if a full-page ad is repeated within 30 to 90 days the second ad will pull 70-75 percent as many mail orders as the original ad; the third insertion within a short time will pull only 45-50 percent as much.

However, the national advertiser must hesitate before he infers that mail order ads present a pattern that also applies in his own case. Typically, the mail order advertiser sells to only a restricted minority of the market. He may use up the potential of interest long before most national advertisers do. And for any given time, he is less likely to be after the repeat sales on which any packaged goods manufacturer relies to maintain his business.

National advertisers repeat their messages in the hope that consumers will "learn" them and be persuaded by their knowledge. But advertisers also expect repetition to work in quite another way, by simply impressing the advertised name upon the consumers' consciousness and making them feel comfortable with it. When an individual comes across a familiar object, wrote the noted psychologist Edward Tichener, he experiences "a glow, a sense of ownership, a feeling of intimacy."[3]

As a general rule, familiarity is a prerequisite for acceptance and preference, but it is familiarity with the product and its brand name that is desirable rather than familiarity with any particular message promoting it. Repeated exposure to a particular label on a can of soup or a package of macaroni may give the consumer the feeling that it is a comfortable and trusted symbol, but repeated exposure to an advertisement for that product may give rise to what psychologists label "perceptual defense," to irritation, or even to outright rejection.

Sally's Studio, a Fifth Avenue fur storage salon, once ran a memorable series of commercials concentrated on a single radio station in New York, the idea being to inundate the particular breed of listeners who kept it on all day. One commercial began with the sound of a fire engine siren, followed by the sound of breaking glass, a woman's shriek, the cry, "I'll save you, lady!" and then the reply, "Wait, I have to go back for my furs!" The announcer broke in with the doleful admonition, "Don't let this happen to you!" Another commercial, with the same tag line, began with bellowing dogs and cries of "Stop, thief!" After a few days of this saturation schedule, says Henry Brenner, a flood of calls, letters, and bomb threats forced the station to cancel the campaign.

Exposure to nonsense words or photographs induces favorable attitudes, but additional exposure has little room to make people more favorable when they are already familiar with a subject.[4] Robert Zajonc and Don W. Rajecki "advertised" nonsense words like "kadirga," "iktitaf," "afworbu," and "jandara" in column inch boxes in the student newspapers of the University of Michigan and Michigan State University. In subsequent classoom tests, students expressed the greatest liking for the words that had appeared most often and were most likely to think they meant something good. In a subsequent comment, Zajonc notes that "saturation is caused not by an excessive number of exposures of the object but by exposures that are too repetitive, that is, those that do not allow the person to confront other objects or prevent him from experiencing some minimum of stimulus change. . . . Exposure creates stability, while over-exposure produces a capacity for change."[5]

Zajonc points out that in campaigns of persuasion, people are exposed not only to positive arguments but also to the name that is the subject of persuasion, pro or con. The two positive effects reinforce each other.[6] When a persuasive campaign is negative, it can boomerang. This seems to have happened in the case of the American Medical Association's campaign against Medicare, simply because of the high visibility given to its target. (As politicians say, "I don't care what you say about me; just spell my name right!")

Rats could "choose" to listen to recorded music by either Mozart or Schoenberg, depending on where they sat in an experimental chamber.[7] The rats reared for 52 days listening to Mozart preferred previously unheard Mozart works after a two-week rest period to works by Schoenberg, while rats reared with Schoenberg preferred *his* music. However, rats reared without any musical exposure tended to prefer Mozart!

Discussion of the effects of repetition in communications usually assumes that the *same* message is repeated. However, no message, inside or outside the laboratory, is ever perfectly repeated. In ordinary experience, its context of editorial matter or entertainment (and other advertising) on one occasion, even within the same media vehicle, is not the same as its context on other occasions. Context may affect the likelihood that a message will be perceived, but it also affects the likelihood that it will be perceived as meaningful, interesting, or relevant. The people who get the message are also different at different points in time; their mood, needs, and circumstances are never exactly the same from one exposure to the next.

Because the advertising practitioner tends to think of repetition from the standpoint of what he is doing rather than of what the public is getting, he is apt to view repetition in terms of a media schedule in which he may put repeated insertions in the same vehicles. But from the standpoint of the audience, getting messages for a particular product in the same magazine or radio program may or may not really mean getting the same message twice.

Changing the visual or symbolic form of a message within the framework of the same unit and media environment (as when we run a series of magazine or newspaper ads or television commercials) is qualitatively different than repetition of the identical message.

When the form of the message changes, we no longer have perfect reinforcement (the same direct reminder of a previous experience). Of course the memory trace of that initial message may be evoked by retaining certain visual, verbal, or symbolic continuities from ad to ad throughout a campaign. By changing the outer form of the message we can add to the information or appeals we stressed the first time. We can do this either by aiming at a different class of prospective customers or by arousing a different array of psychological motives on the part of people who have already been approached by another tack. In the former instance, we extend the reach of effective communication, since succeeding messages may be caught by people who were not receptive to the first one. In the latter case, we add to the persuasive effect on people already reached by giving them new reasons or incentives to buy the product.

A message may change character completely, depending on its environment. An ad in *Good Housekeeping* may have a completely different effect when seen again in *Better Homes and Gardens* than it would if repeated in *Good Housekeeping* a second time. The second time the reader comes upon the ad in the same magazine, it seems part of a familiar environment. To the degree that she "expects" it, it may not register at all; but when she sees it in a new publication, there is a sense of incompleteness or uncertainty about the familiar look of the ad itself in a changed environment.

Real time must also be a factor in determining the level of incongruity and the extent to which it can force perception of the message up to the level of conscious attention. If an ad is placed in the same week's issues of *The New Yorker* and *Time*, the reinforcing effect on the reader who sees both within the space of a few days is bound to be different than if the same ad is repeated in *The New Yorker* after a week or a month.

Advertising themes usually do have a limited life span in popular expectations, and an ad repeated after a fairly long time interval is bound to evoke a different kind of response than one which appears at the time when it is "supposed to."

The effect that can be achieved with repetition varies with the specific marketing problem. No two brands of the same product are identical, either in character or in sales objectives. Each brand faces a unique set of tasks that arise from its competitive environment. Each has its own symbolic overtones that reflect its qualities, its packaging and name, its past history of advertising and promotional themes, its established position in the marketplace, and its reputation with consumers.

"Teaching" the advertising message

Regardless of his specific objective, the advertiser is always engaged in "teaching" people something about his product. He repeats a message to the same individual both to make certain that his "lesson" has sunk in and to offset the processes of decay in memory.

The most frequently cited student of repetition is the great nineteenth century psychologist Hermann Ebbinghaus, who studied the processes of memorizing meaningless things like nonsense sequences of three letters. Ebbinghaus' findings take the form of a decay curve that is "negatively accelerated" (becoming less steep as it goes along). The Ebbinghaus curve is often called the "forgetting curve." Actually, the amount and rate of forgetting are different for remembering exact words and for remembering general sense or content.

"Overlearning" occurs when there is continued practice and exposure to information after it is already perfectly recalled. A small amount of overlearning is valuable because it permits longer retention of the already learned material. There is, however, a point of diminishing returns, beyond which further overlearning fails to produce additional results. A critique of the familiar memory curve has been made by Harry P. Bahrick[8] on the grounds that it does not make allowances for such "overlearning." Bahrick observes, "We cannot demonstrate a classical retention curve by the recall measure for the words in the Lord's Prayer or the National Anthem for most adult Americans."

Bahrick points out that measurements of recall may fail to reflect changes that take place in the quality of thoughts that people associate with overlearned information. Thus people may continue to "remember" advertisements a long time after they have forgotten a great deal of their meaningful content. (The great advertising campaigns of the past, whose slogans are still vividly remembered, reflect this kind of overlearning.)

Much of the information we acquire in daily life has no value to us beyond the immediate moment and is retained only long enough to serve its immediate purpose—e.g., dialing a telephone number or responding to a casual social introduction. Short-term memory varies according to the type of material used as well as with the age and general intellectual ability of the individual. It is notably vulnerable to obliteration by distractions, as when we look up a phone number and have to speak to someone before we dial.

Immediate forgetting is a great blessing, since most of the information we acquire is only of momentary value. If we were to retain every minute detail of the things happening around us, says Ian M. L. Hunter, "this would deprive us of freedom to consider the detailed requirements of the present moment."[9] Because of immediate forgetting, it is hard to compare in minute detail two events that are separate in time. However, the vulnerability of memory presents a particularly difficult problem in advertising because of the furious pace with which messages succeed each other.

Short-term memory becomes more fallible the greater the number of elements or "chunks" that have to be remembered. It is also hindered by the number of similar messages received just previously. The longer the interval between such extraneous messages, the less the interference. But interference from other messages is the prime reason for short-run forgetting. Messages that have really been learned (and are in long-term storage) do not weaken or decay with time, but short-term memories do, even when there has been no interference from earlier messages. One student of the subject, Lloyd Peterson, observes, "Perhaps the decay should be considered a perceptual phenomenon rather than an element in what is traditionally called memory; it occurs before the subject has had time to process the message."[10] Repeated, brief presentations of the same visual stimulus do not create "increasingly clearer percepts," but they do permit an individual to aggregate or combine successive observations that are "perceptually independent."[11]

For a given number of messages, a slow rate of presentation makes for better learning than a fast rate. When one or two extraneous pieces of information are introduced between a message and a test of memory, learning is better in those cases where the message is presented twice in rapid succession. However, when the amount of extraneous material is increased, learning is improved if the messages are repeated after a spaced interval. The paradox, in Peterson's words, is that "in order to remember something better you should allow some forgetting to occur."

Explanations for this phenomenon remain for the moment in the realm of conjecture. As Peterson puts it, "Perhaps there is a charactertistic of the retrieval process that enables it to work more efficiently after an interval of irrelevant activity. A related possibility is that recall itself is a disrupting process, tending to interfere with storage activities."

There is a great danger in analogizing from the kind of induced learning that takes place in laboratory experiments to the much more casual way in which we learn advertising messages in the ordinary course of events. However, there is some implicit support in Peterson's work for the principle of reinforcement which—wittingly or unwittingly—plays an important part in advertising scheduling.

When we repeat commercials for the same product within a given television or radio program or on different pages of the same issue of a newspaper or magazine, we may profit from the extra measure of learning that comes because extraneous information (entertainment or editorial matter, or other ads) has been interjected between the messages we want to deliver. The advertiser may benefit from this kind of short-run repetition insofar as those he reaches with the particular media vehicle learn his message more thoroughly. However, he accomplishes this at the expense of an opportunity to reach additional people with the same message delivered on an entirely different occasion or with a different vehicle.

Typically, the curves that graph the results of experiments in learning have an exponential shape. Each increase adds a little less than the one that came before. This might lead us to believe that it is more efficient for advertising to strive for maximum reach on a one-time basis than to accept the progressively reduced effect of repeated messages.

But things are not that simple, unless the advertiser's sole objective is to communicate the name of his product once. Normally, his tasks are more complex; he has much more to say, in words or pictures.

B. F. Skinner, some of whose most remarkable psychological experiments have involved training pigeons rather than people, has shown that learning takes place most rapidly when the learner has to "work" at it, when there are gaps that he has to bridge himself—by chance, guesswork, or reasoning—and when he has the opportunity to test his experience again and again in varying contexts. Repetition reactivates the traces of earlier messages. The individual on the receiving end has to "work" by searching his memory and "feeding back" the associations with his past experience. After a certain number of repeated exposures there is a breakthrough in learning: the message has been delivered. (This notion has been applied in programmed learning, in which information is broken up into a number of components, each small enough to be absorbed readily and each representing a logical development from what is already known.)

Essentially, the idea is that we progress in knowledge by *bursts* rather than in a steady stream. It may take a certain number of repetitions to break through the veils of resistance to disinterest. A logical conclusion from this might be that breadth of reach in an advertising campaign is highly inefficient if it is not supported by sufficient repetitions to register a message forcefully.

"Bursts," "flights," and "pulses"

A fascinating experiment by Hubert A. Zielske[12] of Foote, Cone & Belding produced findings that at first glance might appear to contradict the "burst" theory. He mailed the same 13 ads to two matched samples of women in Chicago, in one case at weekly intervals, in the other at four-week intervals. At the end of thirteen weekly exposures, 63 percent of the women could remember the ads, but forgetting took place rapidly when the messages stopped and virtually no recollection remained nine months later. By contrast, the monthly messages provided continual reinforcement and built gradually up to a 48 percent recall level at the end of the year. Zielske thus demonstrated *both* the need for continuity *and* the efficacy of using bursts of messages to penetrate awareness.

Zielske's study has been interpreted to mean that "a frequency of one simply is inadequate." This is what Michael Naples, president of the Advertising Research Foundation, told his constituents in 1982 at a workshop on effective frequency. But this inference was contradicted by a number of other speakers at the same meeting, including ARF's (then) research director, Ira Schloss, who noted that a single mailing of the workshop program had produced a sellout attendance.

In another study, Zielske and Walter A. Henry have found that different allocations of the same number of TV rating points over time produce radically different patterns of recall.[13] Concentration in time produces a higher recall level than spreading the same number of rating points over a longer time period.

Edward Strong replicated Zielske's pioneer study with two experiments in which direct mail pieces were sent to housewives at one-week intervals and recall was measured on the telephone.[14] The results were embodied in a computer program (delightfully named Skedaddle), which took into account the seasonality of demand for the advertised product. The findings suggested that monthly exposure was best, biweekly next best, and weekly least effective. For some ads, the repetitions appeared to have little value, since it was the product and the creative treatment that determined the effects. The output of Strong's statistical model supported the proposition that ads should be scheduled closely together and presented in "flights" to maximize their effectiveness, but he cautioned that "putting too many ads in a flight is also wasteful."

"Flighting" was also studied by Wells and Chinsky in their research on "The Effects of Competing Messages" (see page 202). A number was withheld from the stream of messages for the first part of a series and then fed in at a double rate in the second part. This "flighted" number was chosen at a rate about 50 percent greater than its share of messages, strongly suggesting that concentrated repetition makes a communication more memorable than the same number of repeated messages strung out at even intervals.

This study offers support for the theory of scheduling advertisements to run in concentrated bursts separated by substantial time intervals, rather than in a continuous series. This is particularly true if the advertiser has a new sales point, and a real one, rather than a mere restatement of the established virtues of his product. Such a message might have a considerably greater effect if it is repeated after a short interval rather than after a long one, simply because the original impression may be more vivid—and thus more readily reinforced. (William Katz proposes that flights of advertising should be gradually spaced out in a "sliding" schedule, so that the initial "burst" of awareness generated by a strong initial effort is evenly maintained through the duration of a campaign.)[15]

Nearly 3,000 housewives in three areas were interviewed by William Moran about their TV advertising awareness and purchase intentions for brands in four product categories, and then reinterviewed after four weeks.[16] In addition, the women kept a diary record of their TV program viewing. Advertising on all the channels in the three markets was independently monitored. Altogether, 240,000 advertising messages for 38 brands were transmitted on programs that the respondents reported viewing. In all four product categories, brand awareness levels were identical at the beginning of the four weeks and at the end. But the position of individual brands varied considerably as a reflection (at least in part) of the different scheduling strategies that they used.

To begin with, the study verified the principle that awareness of advertising increases with its weight. Women who received three messages for a brand over the four-week period gained in awareness at twice the rate of those who received only two messages. Regardless of whether their initial level of awareness was high or low, advertising produced similar effects relative to the potential for improvement. When messages were received in a concentrated period of time (that is, to use the jargon, when they were "flighted" or "pulsed"),* the net gain in awareness was greater than when they were spread out. The more effective the creative treatment, the greater was the advantage of flighting.

Extending these findings through a mathematical model, Moran suggests that brands that have an initially high awareness level benefit less from flighting over an eight-week period than they do in four weeks. Thus Moran concludes that the value of flighting depends on the characteristics of the advertising vehicle, on audience turnover patterns, on the purchase cycle for the product, on the initial level of advertising awareness, on the creative treatment, and on the size of the advertising budget. Apparently, it all depends.

Repetition and interest levels

The value of repetition is often debated in terms of the marketing characteristics of the advertised product: how many people buy it, how often. It is rarely thought of in terms of *what* is being communicated. With a message of extremely

---

*Pulsing is generally used to refer to messages broadcast at very short intervals.

low interest to everyone, no amount of repetition may be sufficient to force the point through the audience's protective internal censorship. Conversely, if an advertisement says something vitally significant to the audience, there is no particular value in repeating the message, since almost everyone interested will remember it anyway. (When Crest toothpaste won the endorsement of the American Dental Association in 1960, a single press advertisement announcing this fact created a recall level of 42 percent among women two weeks later, a phenomenal level of retention for a single advertising message.)

This does not mean that people will not forget; they do very rapidly. But reminding people of something they already "know" presents the advertising planner with problems quite different from those he faces when he wants to make sure they are learning the message in the first place. Repetition enriches *understanding*. When we have occasion to use information often in different kinds of situations, we have mastered it more thoroughly than if we know it only in a given setting. (This is an important argument for the media mix.)

Repetition also serves a *maintenance* function, since repeated use of what has been memorized favors later remembering. The sooner the repetition follows the original learning the better, since this repetition serves as a review of the originally exposed material. Ian Hunter observes that "the best rehearsed actor never gives two performances which are identical in every respect." In the simplest task of memorization—memorization of all-digit telephone numbers, for example—individuals assimilate information and remember things in completely different ways. People do not remember even a mere sequence of random digits simply by rote; they note relationships among them and further try to relate them to sequences (like dates) that are personally significant as numerical reference points. We reproduce memories by reconstructing their context or the series of events that led up to them. Thus we can best recall those things that can be visualized as part of a pattern of associations.*

The more complex and the longer the information that is being mastered, the more time it takes to learn it proportionate to its length. (In one experiment a passage of 100 words required a learning time of nine minutes, 200 words required 24 minutes, 500 words 65 minutes, and 1,000 words 165 minutes.) The greater the spacing between periods of study, the less time has to be spent in the actual learning periods, although, of course, there is an increase in the total time required before the learning is completed.[17] This would appear to suggest that with a given amount of advertising effort, short messages that are dispersed and separated might outperform those that are highly concentrated into single long units—provided that the short messages reinforce each other as parts of a single learning experience. However, there is a profound difference between the process of learning as a purposeful task and the kind of incidental learning that advertising messages represent.

Our memory is hindered most by interference from messages that closely resemble what we should remember.[18] Different processes are involved when we

---

*"Anticipation" is the aspect of memory in which we respond, often at a subconscious level, to stages in a familiar pattern of events. When we anticipate something, we are in effect extrapolating a certain outcome from similar experiences we have already had.

memorize information by rote than when we try to learn it selectively from amidst a body of incidental or extraneous material. The incidental learning of "unwanted" information interferes with the "selective" learning of useful information. The more such incidental or unwanted information is present, and the more it resembles the wanted information, the more interference occurs with useful learning.

The extent to which useful information is retained in the memory depends on how little interference there was in the original learning process.[19] The implication for the advertising planner is that even the best prospects, those who are interested in the message, can be effectively distracted from getting the point because of the vast amount of irrelevant advertising to which they are simultaneously being subjected in the same context.

Behind much advertising theory lies the psychological assumption that there is a kind of reservoir or pool of attention that consumers reserve for advertising messages within the time span they devote to a given publication or to a given block of listening or viewing. Competing brand messages in the same product field naturally crowd and cancel each other out; but apart from the contradictory effect of directly competing messages (for no one is going to switch both to Winstons and Marlboros at the same time), there is another, more subtle, negative effect that derives from the accumulated pressure of *all* other advertising messages. The idea is that the poor human mind can comprehend so much and no more. The theory holds that in effect every advertising message must crowd out some other message; any attention devoted to a message for one product hastens the forgetting of all other messages for all other products.

An analogy could be drawn between the consumer's capacity for information and his limited purchasing power. He can buy either a new alarm clock or a bottle of Scotch; he may not be able to afford both. If he holds the Schenley ad in mind, how can he remember the one for Arnold's Bread?

These propositions have a core of truth but suggest a great many false corollaries. Interference does occur in short-term memory when ad messages succeed each other in rapid succession, but messages that have been learned and assimilated are not ordinarily vulnerable to the same kind of interference. There is no evidence from the students of learning and memory to support the notion that new information is acquired at the expense of old established knowledge. One of the most amazing features of human intelligence is its virtually unlimited capacity for acquiring new experiences and new ideas. Old and important memories often have greater vitality than recent ones. So the concept of a pool of product and brand information truly constant in size simply makes no sense at all. Advertising is also only a part, and in some cases only a small part, of the total amount of information we have about consumer products. (How well we remember dad's old car, the brand of shortening mother used, the brand of cat food that the cat wouldn't touch!)

As we become aware of a new brand on the market, we do not forget the old brands—forget in the sense of not being able to recognize them. If the new brand captures our interest and patronage, the old ones may, however, become less salient for us. We may be less likely to think of them spontaneously, or to recall their particular virtues or slogans. But such a switch is not likely to happen unless the new brand succeeds in out-advertising its established competitors from the standpoint of effort, skill, or both.

Although new messages can be learned without our forgetting old ones, this doesn't contradict the principle that all messages are in competition for our interest in the first place, in getting to the point where they *might* be remembered.

It stands to reason that advertising that is useful for any one individual may represent interference for another. The constant progression of advertising messages through all media represents a realistic and significant barrier for the learning of any new message. The presence of similar messages leads to especially strong interference. However, from the standpoint of the consumer, similar messages may be those that are similar in style or technique of presentation, i.e., layout, artwork, models, melody, etc., rather than necessarily those that advertise the same product.

Krugman's theory of how repetition works

Herbert Krugman, a leading theorist in consumer psychology, has pointed out that our emotional response to repetition depends on what is being repeated.[20] He finds that six or eight repetitions of a certain style of music make it more acceptable as it becomes more familiar, but that liking does not increase beyond that point. However, with a simpler subject (packages of a washday product) there is no increase in liking after a single repetition of exposure to the design.

Krugman refers to the work of the social psychologist Eugene Hartley,[21] who observes that at the onset of a series of repetitions "we contend with the effective significance of new stimuli, the pleasure of novelty or the gratification of curiosity." As repetition continues, the object benefits from a feeling of conscious familiarity and the reponse to it improves. But a time comes when the object is thoroughly familiar and where further repetition "leads to a loss of associative power, a dedifferentiation of perception, and boredom, satiation, or negative adaptation." In short, one mint after dinner is fine, two are better, and the twentieth creates disgust.

Krugman observes, "Marketers would like to think that their products were indeed better and/or that consumers believed them to be better. What is often the unrecognized case, however, is that their products are neither liked nor considered better but chosen only because they are adequately good *and* for the pleasure of their recognition, i.e., sheer familiarity."[22]

According to Krugman, advertising represents "information which the consumer recognizes as present but to which he makes no personally relevant connections, i.e., he remains uninvolved." He defines "involvement" as the number of conscious "bridging experiences, connections or personal references per unit of time which the viewer makes between his or her own life and the stimulus."[23]

He postulates that with low-involvement material there would be an absence of "perceptual defense." In other words the unconscious psychological mechanisms of self-protection are not aroused by communications that people consider unimportant. Thus the repetition of low-involvement stimuli "can alter the salience aspects of perceptual structure without accompanying changes in verbalized attitudes." When an unimportant message is repeated, the content may seem more *familiar* even though it is not any more consciously *acceptable.* Repeated exposure to ads for a brand builds a potential for seeing it in a new light. "The change process may be over before the customer heads for the store, shopping list in hand."

The potential may be activated at the point of sale when the customer recognizes the brand on the supermarket shelf as something that is already familiar through advertising. Its familiarity may "trigger the actual shift in perception, this shift followed by behavioral change." The behavioral change in turn might give rise to new attitudes consistent with the individual's actions.

Krugman suggests that the television stimulus is "animate" while the observer is "inanimate." Since the rate of "stimulation" (the pace of the communication) is out of the viewer's control, there is a relatively low opportunity for personal "connections" with the advertising message.

In the case of print, however, the quality of the stimulus is "inanimate," while the observer is "animate." Krugman argues, therefore, that print advertising may lead to a shift in opinion at the time of *actual* exposure. Being active, the individual is busy establishing personal "connections" with what he reads, and any psychological defenses that may be called forth are aroused *before* he enters the store. Krugman contrasts this with the "low-involvement" nature of stimulation through TV advertising, which must be activated when the product is seen at the point of sale.

Krugman tested his hypothesis by analyzing the descriptions people give of television commercials and magazine ads for the same products. Looking for the personal "connections" that relate the message to the reader's own interests, he concludes from the data that "direct attention to advertising materials produces fewer and slower connections than when attention is focused on something else, in this case the more natural focus on editorial matter." The very strength of print advertising may therefore arise from the fact that the reader must be *distracted* from his main line of search in order to get the advertising message.*

In Krugman's view, the process of "gradual shifts in perceptual structure, aided by repetition, activated by behavioral choice situations, and *followed* at some time by attitude change" characterizes low-involvement products. High-involvement product choices might well be made on the basis of *conscious* opinion change based on a conflict of ideas.

Krugman's intriguing hypothesis has stimulated a substantial amount of new research. Of course, products cannot be neatly separated into low- and high-involvement categories, each with its own different mechanism of consumption behavior. What is a low-involvement product to one person may be a matter of fairly high involvement to another (soap, for example, is one thing to the slovenly housewife and another to her compulsive neighbor).

It seems plausible that there is a continuum of involvement from low to high, with both conscious changes of attitude and unconscious changes in perceptual behavior taking place to some extent at both extremes. Curiously enough, the classic example of how purchase behavior results in rationalization of attitudes

---

*This line of inquiry into the differences between print and television communication led Krugman to the investigation of brain wave data that was reviewed in Chapter 5.

after the fact comes from the automotive field, the very prototype of high involvement. It has long been an accepted dictum in automobile advertising circles
that the most intense readership of new car ads is on the part of recent purchasers who wish to reassure themselves that they made a wise choice.

In an influential series of papers, Krugman turned his attention to the
question of what happens in the mind of the television viewer when he sees the
same commercials over and over. His work with Eckhard Hess's eye pupil dilation
measuring equipment indicated that the peak of arousal to a television commercial occurs four to ten seconds after it starts.[24] When the same commercials are
shown repeatedly, there is in some cases a dramatic increase in arousal on the
second exposure, in some cases a small increase and in other instances an actual
decline. But on the third exposure there is never an increase, and in most of the
cases the arousal level is lower.

Krugman went on to suggest that the first response to a message is a "What
is it?" response, which attempts to classify and understand the nature of the
stimulus and therefore requires an intellectual effort that guarantees initial attention.[25] The second exposure is a more personal "What of it?" response, in
which the viewer asks himself whether the message has any personal relevance.
The second exposure arouses a recognition response that is itself startling and
thus engaging. The third exposure is merely a reminder, and the viewer with-
draws his attention. However, if he should at some time later be in the market for
the advertised product, the twenty-third exposure to the commercial might
produce a response as though it were the second.

As we shall see shortly, there is a variety of theories as to how many repetitions of a message are "enough," and an assortment of contradictory data as
well. But as I stressed earlier, repetitions from the standpoint of the public mean
quite a different thing than repetitions from the standpoint of the advertiser.
Howard Kamin infers from typical reach and frequency patterns that it may take
up to twelve *potential* exposures to attain Krugman's optimum of three contacts
at the level of *perception.* [26] This assumes that what is true of an average viewer is
true of everyone the advertiser wants to reach (which is impossible). And it begs
the question of whether the ideal number of three exposures holds constant
regardless of how much time elapses between the first contact and the third.

Field experiments in repetition

Outside of the psychological laboratory, studies involving repeated exposure of
the same advertising content to the same people have been done most often on
print media because of the greater ease of conducting controlled experiments
with print. In general, advertising studies of repetition duplicate the findings of
academic research, though most of the experiments are at the same time less
rigorous and on a much larger scale.[27]

In its purest form, repeat exposure to an advertisement means seeing or
hearing it again in the *identical* context. This can never happen in radio or
television. It *may* happen when a magazine or newspaper is picked up for a second
time if the reader had not finished it on the first occasion. A typical newspaper is
picked up on two or more occasions by 48 percent of its readers.[28] And the
average magazine page is opened 1.7 times by an average reader.[29]

Daniel Starch reported that ads repeated in different issues of the same publication maintain the same level of readership, through at least six successive insertions in a monthly publication. He inferred that this "obviates the necessity of preparing additional copy and plates."[30] Few advertising strategists today would agree with him.

Do advertising messages lose their power to persuade as they become familiar through repetition? The evidence suggests that they do, and many advertisers behave on that assumption. (Lee Weinblatt of Telcom believes that when television commercials are discontinued because of fear of wearout, 60 percent still have plenty of life left in them. Great old advertising slogans like Alka-Seltzer's "I can't believe I ate the whole thing" retain better top-of-mind awareness than those of current campaigns.)

What really happens when ads are seen or heard repeatedly? Horace Schwerin analyzed tests of 118 TV commercials and of print ads in which measurements were taken both before and after high-frequency repetition in the normal course of their respective campaigns (in England and Germany).[31] The time interval between the first test and the repetition ranged between one and eighteen months. (Unfortunately, the exact degree of respondents' prior exposure to the advertising was not measurable in this research.)

In 91 of the 127 cases, the results of the second test (after the message was already generally familiar to the public) were less favorable than on the first occasion, when the message was brand new. (In 27 of the cases, the decline was statistically significant.) In only *one* case were the results significantly *better* for the oft-repeated message.

Aaron J. Spector of National Analysts studied 127 magazine subscribers, each of whom was shown every page in an advance issue of the publication.[32] Half were exposed only once and the others were shown the same pages again on the following day. A variety of recall measures was used in an interview two days after the initial contact and exposure period. Repeat exposure created 30 percent more unaided recall, and comparable improvement occurred by some other criteria. This appeared to be true whether memory of the ads was checked one day later or two.

To compare the effects of two magazine advertising exposures with one exposure in the same issue, Charles Swanson of the *Saturday Evening Post* commissioned Alfred Politz in 1959 to interview 150 subscriber-readers of the *Post* in Rochester, New York. (Since a copy of the *Post*, a text magazine, was picked up on more occasions than its picture-book competitors, *Life* and *Look*, there was an obvious advantage to demonstrating the value of repeat exposures.)

In each household, an interviewer hand-delivered a specially prepared copy and asked the reader to go through it in the usual way. Questions about the advertising and the brand were asked two days later, and another specially prepared copy of what appeared to be the same issue was left with the reader at the end of the interview. By rotating 12 ads in the specially prepared issues, 4 were exposed once, 4 twice, and 4 not at all to each reader. The final interview was conducted three and a half days afterwards. Which pages were opened was determined by the use of a glue spot that stuck the pages together.[33]

Familiarity with both the brand and the advertising claims and the degree of willingness to buy the brand increased at about double the rate for two exposures as for a single one. Belief in the claim increased three times as much with two exposures as with one.

Some years later, Politz made a somewhat similar study of "Repeat Exposure Value,"[34] this time for *Reader's Digest*, which has a long-standing sales strategy of stressing the advertising value of its long "life" and repeated pickup. He interviewed a national cross-section of 361 adults, divided into four equal groups. Two of the groups were given one day to look through a new copy of *Reader's Digest*. The other two groups were given a second one-day "exposure" after a three-day interval. The magazines left with the respondents were specially doctored, with half including one set of six test ads and the other half a different set.

When the interviewers returned, they checked the readers' familiarity with each brand and its sales points, their rating of the brand's quality, and their interest in buying it. (Of course, they asked this not only about the "test" brands whose ads were included in the text magazine, but also about the other six "control" brands.)

A single day's reading added 12 percent to the top-of-mind familiarity, comparing the average brand "advertised" with those not in the magazine received by the reader. With two days' reading, the advantage rose to 21 percent. Similarly, among those familiar with the advertising claims, the percentage who correctly associated claims and brands went up 15 percent among those with one exposure and 25 percent with two. The proportion rating the brand "very highest quality" was 11 percent higher with one exposure, 17 percent higher with two. The proportion who said they "would buy" the advertised brand was 15 percent greater after one day's reading and 26 percent greater after two.

In another (1966) study, Politz found that familiarity with a brand rose 19 percent after one exposure and 34 percent after two. The two-thirds or three-fourths margin of improvement resulting from a second exposure is thoroughly congruent with other studies on the effects of repetition. However, the findings are hard to apply to the effects of repeated exposure in *different* issues of the same publication. They still leave the media strategist with the problem of whether it is worth doubling his delivery—and thereby his expenditure—of the same messages to the same people, in order to get less than double the residual communications effect.

Unfortunately, the research did not compare the value of repeated exposure for the same issue of the same magazine (as measured) with the possible value of similar repetition with different issues, or with different magazines altogether. It can only be conjectured whether the "shock" of receiving the same magazine after a three-day interval prompted the readers to look at it with a degree of bemused curiosity quite different from their normal interest in an unfinished magazine lying around the house and picked up for a second time.

In another experiment, readers of *Look* magazine were interviewed by Politz' Universal Marketing Research in 1964 on their recall of advertisements and then re-interviewed about a month later on the ads in a second issue. The recall of advertisements accumulated at a faster rate from issue to issue than the audience for the magazine itself. Because of this, an increasing proportion of the audience potential was translated into recall as the campaign progressed.

For example, four issues of *Look* had 24.1 million readers (including those who read several issues) compared with 14.7 million reached by one issue. But while a single ad in one issue might have a recall level of 25 percent (or 3.7 million of the 14.7 million readers), with four repetitions the number remembering it rose to 11.6 million readers, nearly half of the gross audience. Ads with low recall scores tended to accumulate readers slightly faster than high-scoring ones (since their "potential" for conversion was greater). Presumably—although the published reports of the research do not offer the evidence on this point—the rate at which the ads were remembered grew faster than the rate at which the magazine accumulated readers because of the weight of the repeated advertisements on the regular readers who saw several issues.

In another experiment, housewives were sent advertisements under weekly, biweekly, and monthly schedules. Michael Ray, Alan Sawyer, and Edward Strong measured their recall of the advertising, their mentions of the brand, and their preferences for it.[35] Repeated exposures apparently overcame previous consumer ignorance. Repetition of color ads increased recall more than black and white, but more detail was recalled from the black and white ads. The effects of repetition were greatest for ads that were designated as "grabbers" (distinctive in their format to attract attention).[36] The experimenters observed that "there are so many variables that might influence repetition effect in each situation, there will never be enough general guideline research to make adequate predictions in each specific advertising situation." Amen.

How many repetitions are enough?

"Wearout" has two components: the decline in *attentiveness* to a repeated advertising message and the attrition in *memory* of the information in the ad or in the perception of the advertised brand. How do these two phenomena interact? How many times does an advertiser want to place his message before the same prospective customer? When does a message begin to "wear out?" The short answer to these questions is that there is no one answer. A variety of interesting studies produce an assortment of somewhat contradictory conclusions that reflect the individuality of advertising tasks and creative approaches. Using the AdTel "split cable" facility, which permits different advertising schedules to be fed to two matched samples of households, an experiment was run in 1974-75 on five brands of a major advertiser. Viewing data were obtained for three two-week periods and related to purchasing behavior before and during the test. Although the results of the study showed a different pattern for each brand, they showed a positive response to advertising in every case. In households that used each brand, purchases increased sharply and kept increasing as there was greater exposure to the advertising. This was especially true when the brand had a high share of market (which of course increased the probability that its advertising would be reaching users). In non-user households, there was an initial increase, but it was not followed by significant gains as advertising exposures were added.[37] The implication seems to be that most non-users have a penchant for tuning out the advertising for the brands they don't use.

In an analysis of 38 brands, Michael Naples reports that awareness leveled off after three exposures. But gains continued for up to five exposures when the proportion becoming aware of the brand was measured relative to total competitive changes in brand awareness.

In 1976, tests run by Rosenfeld, Sirowitz & Lawson indicated that a typical spot announcement had to be seen *six* times before the average person could recall it.[38] But there are a lot of other opinions on this point.

The British Market Research Bureau's Colin McDonald has linked frequency of exposure to the purchase cycles as determined from consumer diaries.[39] McDonald examined TV commercials in nine product categories. He found that "one exposure has a below average effect, because it is not strong enough to overcome the competitive weight of other brands on the housewife's list for which she has seen two or more exposures at the same time." People who had seen two or more ads for a brand were 5 percent more likely to switch to it than from it, especially if the repeated exposure occurred within a few days of the purchase. However, with both print and television, three or more exposures were no better than two. McDonald's findings were corroborated by a major advertiser who used brand advertising awareness, rather than purchasing, as a criterion of effectiveness.

By combining results for 39 different German magazine studies, Otmar Ernst concluded that active knowledge about the product increased at a steady rate up to three exposures to an ad, then rose sharply in response to four exposures, and showed very little change between the fourth and fifth exposures.[40] (Unfortunately, these exposures were not controlled within any particular period of time.) However, other experiments by Ernst differentiate the effects of repetition for new ads and ads that are already known. While repetition of familiar ads showed a diminishing effect on recall levels and no effect at all after nine exposures, recall of new ads started out at a much lower level, grew at a slow pace, and showed a jump between six and eight repetitions. Predictably, repetition added more to recall levels when the advertising changed theme than when the same theme was used throughout.

The concept of "effective rating points" has been introduced as an alternative to GRPs to describe advertising impressions delivered within a range of optimum frequency (thus eliminating the people who receive too few impressions and those who are oversaturated). Alvin Achenbaum has argued that only those messages that represent between 3 and 10 exposures to a prospect are effective and that advertisers should therefore measure their media coverage in those terms.[41] Schedules would concentrate their messages within the optimum range, avoiding both inadequate and excessive frequency of exposure. While this proposition reformulates a tactic that most national advertisers have probably always followed by sheer instinct, it is difficult to see how it can be achieved in practice, at least in broadcasting. (It is the inherent variability in viewing habits, as I mentioned earlier, that always destines some viewers to receive fewer than three exposures and others more than ten.)

The value of repetition looks different depending on what criteria of effectiveness are used. Harold Spielman, in a study of nine often-repeated television commercials, found that unaided brand awareness built for a year before it plateaued, while registration of key sales points built for a year and then declined. However, persuasive influence gained only slightly during the year and then declined sharply. Spielman concluded that commercials of equal initial effectiveness did not always wear out at the same rate and that those that were well-liked had longer-lasting effects.

More than 8,000 commercials have been studied since 1968 by McCollum/Spielman. Summarizing them, Spielman observes that "the vast majority of total movers to the test brand came to it after the second exposure. Similar ratios held up in all other product categories tested." In some cases, a particular campaign enjoys an edge after one exposure while another campaign is stronger after two. In several cases, two exposures of a commercial did not add much to the level of recall, but they added significantly to the registration of copy points. In one instance, the visual aspect of the commercial overpowered the product claims on a first exposure but not on a second.

A series of experiments by Robert Grass and Wallace Wallace has suggested that repetition may be advantageous in some respects but not in others. When the same commercial is shown twice within a half-hour program, recall is increased, but purchase intent is actually reduced. The copy points that are learned after multiple exposures are sometimes different from the points played back after a single exposure.[42]

Grass provided four matched groups with different levels of exposure to a TV campaign. Brand awareness increased over two times among those heavily exposed, then leveled off and declined. The more lightly exposed groups took longer for awareness to build. The most interesting finding was that while awareness levels built up and subsequently declined, attitudes toward the brand became more favorable and held at a plateau without declining. In short, advertising is an instrument through which perceptions are modified, and they remain modified after the ads themselves have been forgotten.

Repetition's effects depend on the persuasive quality of the message, on its prior familiarity, and on the initial acceptance that the advertiser already enjoys. In another experiment, Ohio State University students were asked about their liking and familiarity with 27 brand names, of which eight were included in a series of 28 ads shown on slides.[43] Ads for very familiar brands were better recalled than those for less familiar ones. And a study by AdTel suggests that the value of frequent exposure is different for dominant and lesser brands, since a brand that is already well-known and highly visible requires relatively less reinforcement of its position and thus can maintain its established share with less switching from other brands.

Naturally, the memorability of commercials reflects their ability to make a favorable impression in the first place. Valentine Appel conducted 96 24-hour recall retests of 81 different commercials for 31 brands.[44] Overall, they were better remembered after they had been on the air for a few months than they were after several years. However, there were distinctly different wearout patterns for TV commercials that had initially scored high or scored low on copy tests. With the low-scoring commercials, wearout began immediately; additional exposures actually resulted in less recall. But the commercials that initially scored high registered significantly higher levels of recall with each additional exposure. In short, a good ad is worth repeating; repeating a bad one is counter-productive.

Similar thoughts emerge from a laboratory experiment at Purdue University, where 490 housewives were exposed repeatedly to television commercials for several different products.[45] Their changes in attitude toward the advertised brands were found to reflect their previous familiarity, attitude, and exposure to the brands. However, the relationship turned out to vary for different brands and products. For familiar brands in low interest product categories, additional exposures to advertising may have little opportunity to influence brand attitudes.

I have said (repeatedly) that (except for a brand-new brand) an advertising message does not start at ground zero. Even a totally new theme in a totally new format evokes echoes of the previous advertising for the brand. The effects of repeating any particular advertisement thus must depend on where it starts in the consciousness of the public. This point can be drawn from a major study of advertising effectiveness done in 1981 by Lieberman Associates for Time, Inc., and Joseph E. Seagram & Sons.[46] All advertising for two products was blanked out in Milwaukee and the state of Missouri except for *Sports Illustrated* and *Time*. Some people received copies without ads for a particular brand, some received copies with one ad, some received two, and some received four. The ads were changed every 13 weeks in the course of a 48-week period. Altogether, 16,500 people were interviewed, with subgroups asked each week about their use of the test brands.

Of the eight brands tested, four were categorized as having high initial awareness and four low awareness. For the first group, awareness jumped after a single week of advertising. The low awareness brands did not show the same kind of improvement immediately, but they registered a greater overall gain. Awarenesss levels continued to rise, even after 48 weeks. Whether brand awareness started high or low, there was very little difference in reported purchasing between people who had the opportunity to see either one ad or two ads a month; both groups increased 35 percent. But with exposure to four ads a month, purchasing was 170 percent greater.*

The time dimension

Repetition has two aspects: frequency and time. Ernest Rockey and William Greene of Gallup and Robinson reviewed 24-hour "Proved Commercial Recall" for 123 TV commercials appearing one or more times within a three-hour time span on one evening.[47] The greater the total commercial exposure time, the greater the recall. (Frequency *per se* was not recorded.) The recall for two minutes of exposure was nearly twice as great as for one minute, thus suggesting that the third and fourth exposures (of a 30-second message) were almost as effective as the first repetition. (Some of these case histories involved several different commercials for the same brand, while others were repetitions of the same commercial. However, the pattern was no different for these two situations.) Whatever the explanation, there is a discrepancy between these findings and those of most repetition studies conducted over a longer time span. This would seem to support the conclusion that the length of the interval between exposures makes a tremendous difference in the results.

---

*In 1980, 67 percent of Seagram's measurable ad expenditures were in magazines. In 1982, the proportion was 61 percent.

Messages repeated at different intervals of time may reinforce each other with varying degrees of effect. Timing on the calendar becomes significant for some advertised products if it relates to the purchase pattern. (There are rather subtle aspects to this, as one of the incidental objectives of advertising is to create demand for seasonal products out of season.) For products that are bought evenly throughout the year, the advertiser customarily assumes that if messages are evenly spread, the more often they are repeated, the greater the likelihood that they will hit their target at a time close to the individual purchase decision, when their effect is presumably greatest.

The literature in psychology does not suggest that opinions are most likely to change in response to the latest word on a subject. In purposeful learning, the first items in a sequence are mastered soonest, then the very last items, and the middle items are learned most slowly. This is the famous so-called inverse "J" curve which favors the first message that comes along. (We saw on page 180 that this applies to TV commercials in a cluster.)

The advantage of being first or last depends on the nature of the argument and varies according to the competitive pressures on opinion. The world would be a strange place indeed if everyone were always convinced by the last argument heard. We would all be incapable of consistent action, and our behavior would change constantly in response to the pressure of incoming information and appeals.

Studies of "the order of presentation in persuasion" by Carl Hovland[48] and his associates indicate that when conflicting or competing messages are presented to an audience in an effort to influence their thinking, there is not necessarily a permanent advantage for the message that is received last. Any such advantage is dissipated within moments, if the message is one of a long series.

This should be all the more true when messages are, as in the typical advertising campaign, part of an interminable series to which the consumer has been subjected over many years in a highly competitive field. Each advertising message in such a product category has a slight reinforcement effect that offsets the slight decay in cumulative effect since the previous message. The timing of the message last exposed to the customer may be of far less importance than the persuasive effect of some earlier message that he perceived as informative or significant.

The closeness of the message to the purchase act can hardly have any significance if the major purpose of repetition is reinforcing the original communication. From the standpoint of delivering cumulative effects, the process of persuasion is really almost independent of the purchase cycle; it exists in a different time perspective.

Except for that minority of advertisements that directly solicit telephone or mail orders, the main object of most advertising is not to clinch a sale, but to qualify a product or brand for purchase in terms of the consumer's definition of utility. This may mean defining a brand as one that falls within the range of acceptability as a well-known, nationally distributed product. It may mean getting the consumer to believe that the brand has special features that add to its values and distinguish it from its competition. It may mean persuading the consumer to think of the product in terms of some time-bound sense of urgency

("Available only while the supply lasts." "This week only $8.99"). This feeling of immediacy, of short-lived opportunity, is, of course, the secret of most retail advertising.

The time factor in consumer decision-making involves two separate dimensions: (1) the *actual* sequence of events, and (2) the *perception* of events.

Certain events in life require corresponding changes in consumption habits. Immediate changes in a family's distribution of its income follow a rise in the wage earner's salary or his loss of employment, but changes also follow the birth of a child, the death of a spouse, the departure of a son for college, the wedding of a daughter. On a much more trivial scale, buying decisions result from circumstances that have little to do with conscious desires: things we use wear out or are consumed and have to be replaced.

The man who has to buy his wife an anniversary present confronts this situation with a different degree of earnestness on the date of the anniversary than he does in the previous weeks during which he may be more or less in the market. The housewife who knows that she is low on meat for the freezer is in a different situation than the one who suddenly finds she has company coming for dinner that night and knows she must buy a roast to cope with the situation. A car owner who has been thinking about getting a new automobile because the old one is starting to burn oil faces a less urgent decision than the one who finds that his rear axle is broken.

A great deal of advertising seeks to create an artificial sense of urgency about the purchase, on the premise that the chance of making a sale is greater in the face of an implacable deadline. This may take the form of a deal, special, bargain price, tie-in offer, or coupon. Or it may take the form of an appeal to changing taste, fashion, or styling, or to the consumer's urge to be first to try a new product. In either case, the aim of this advertising is to force the subject to the forefront of the consumer's consciousness. The assumption is that the consumer is already a potential prospect—one who is either vaguely in the market or who might be brought into the market though he would not otherwise be motivated to buy.

Such advertising seeks to create new demand, rather than to improve a brand's share of market. There is no logical relationship between the timing of the advertising contact and the "normal" time of purchase. Naturally, the advertiser would like to reach people at a time and in a setting where they are most easily persuaded, but the interval between the message and the impulse to purchase will reflect the effectiveness of the message itself.

A different case exists where people enter the market for a variety of reasons and where the decision to buy stems from circumstances that have very little or nothing to do with advertising. In this case, the advertising message is important as a reminder of the product's utility for the user or of the brand's distinctive merits. The advertiser wants the greatest possible likelihood of exposing his message to those people who at any given moment are faced with the need to buy. This means the broadest possible coverage of the prospects that is consistent with high frequency within a given budget.

The philosophy of the soap companies in their use of daytime TV is to use high frequency for the purpose of achieving dominance rather than to extend reach. At any given point in time the housewife's awareness of Bold detergent versus Fab is only slightly influenced by the accidental fact that a Fab commercial or a Bold commercial happens to be the last one that she saw. The purpose of advertising to her with high frequency is not to increase the chances of having the last word before she departs for the supermarket. It is rather to increase the chances of breaking through the wall of her indifference to learning anything more about a product about which she feels she already knows as much as she wants to know.

To the extent that advertising is actively sought or consulted, its timing is critically important. Theoretically, it is possible for a car manufacturer to concentrate his whole advertising budget in the week of new model introductions. If he did this, he might have a tremendous impact in distinguishing the make both from the previous year's models and from the competition. But as the model year wore on, there would be no way for the prospective purchaser to refresh his memory of this announcement, and the manufacturer's initial advantage would be lost. No car maker could afford to advertise in this way, because car owners are apt to enter the market at any time, and the message must reach them when they are susceptible to influence.

The timing and spacing of messages is one of the most vital strategic problems in the preparation of an advertising schedule, but it involves different considerations in print and in broadcasting.

Consider the problem that remains once we have made the strategic choice between ten large dominant units within a publication and a hundred small units at equivalent cost. Whichever solution we choose, we are still faced with the problem of how to distribute the units we select. We can disperse them evenly one at a time or we can cluster them in groups succeeding each other at short time intervals. We can even place a number of ads within the same publication, reducing the time interval between exposures to a minimum—typically, less than the interval between commercials in successive pods on a TV program.

Clustering ads may give us an advantage in creating immediate awareness. Yet we lose the advantage of continuity that we get by spreading ads over time, and we reduce the likelihood of any given message reaching the maximum number of purchasers close to the moment that is psychologically ripe for each.

The broadcast advertiser must concern himself not only with the *number* of occasions his messages are diffused, but also with the *distribution* of these messages in real (clock and calendar) time. He must compare the relative value of scattering messages over an entire broadcast season or concentrating them in brief intense bursts.

A large concentration of commercials within a short period of time adds to the chances of catching the viewer's attention. A special program, sportscast, or spectacular may have the sponsor's three, four, or five commercials periodically interrupt the entertainment. The recurrence of commercials is expected to have the same overwhelming effect on the viewers that the print advertiser hopes to achieve by the massive use of space. Within such a framework of intensive exposure, the repeated commercials are intended to produce different results than if they were scattered through an evening on several different networks or spread in the course of a week over different programs on the same network.

The length of the real-time interval between repeated messages is critical to the subject of broadcast repetition. An advertisement repeated in a print publication may be exposed to the same people after a substantial time interval. Even if the same ad is inserted in the newspaper every day for a week, a twenty-four hour lag separates one day's reading and the next. With magazines, the interval may be a week or a month.

Even in a 24-hour period, random exposure to a vast number of other messages and experiences occurs, and the residual impact of any single advertisement can be expected to be small indeed unless it vitally touches the reader's material interest, aesthetic sense, or private symbol system.

But on television or radio, if several commercials for a product occur within the same program, each one starts only slightly below the level of awareness created by the last one. Among those viewers who are attentively viewing when the first commercial comes on, comparatively little of what comes through will have been forgotten by the time the second one comes on. (This sidesteps the point that for the typical commercial, communication is far from perfect, even with the attentive viewer.) Repetition used in this way creates high conscious awareness of the advertising message. (It probably also creates strong awareness of the advertising technique being used or of the mechanics incidental to the main sales purpose.) Scattered spot TV messages lose this advantage.

Varying the content

Repeating the identical message in the same media context involves different psychological mechanisms than the repetition of messages that differ in their style or substance. When an advertiser repeats a message in a given media environment, he hopes to recreate some of its original impact and to reinforce its effect on those who saw or heard it previously. He also expects to deliver the message for the first time to those who had missed it before because they were not exposed to the medium, not in physical range of the message, or simply inattentive to it in its original context.

When the same space or time unit in the same medium is used for a new advertisement or commercial, it combines an element of the familiar (e.g., the medium, context, product name, and advertising theme) and the unfamiliar (new art and layout; a new spokesman or setting).

Several variations of the same ad or commercial are commonly repeated in a particular publication or program. The process works somewhat differently when the same message, with slight variations, comes to the consumer from several media. A reinforcing effect may be produced when a television jingle is sung on radio. Or there may be carry-over from print to TV (or vice versa) because of the copy, the visual symbolism, or the models used.

In 1916 a pioneer advertising researcher, Henry Adams,[49] prepared a dummy magazine in which a given ad appeared either once, twice, or four times. The second repetition added about 50 percent to the recollection of the ads, whether it was a quarter-page, half-page, or full-page unit. The four appearances of the same ad represented about two-and-a-half times the value of a single ad. On the other hand, when *different* ads for the same brands were used, instead of repetitions of the same ads, the value of two ads was two-and-a-half times the value of a single one, and the value of four ads was about four times as great.

Many years later, Grass and Wallace of DuPont found that interest (as measured by the CONPAAD technique discussed on p. 86) fell rapidly when the same commercial was repeated six times within a program. However, interest could be revived by interspersing other commercials. If six *different* commercials were shown, there was no significant loss of interest.[50]

An ambitious study of repetition in advertising was directed by John Stewart (with the sponsorship of the Newspaper Advertising Bureau and the Newsprint Information Committee)[51] and involved the experimental introduction of two new products: a frozen chicken dish (Chicken Sara Lee) and a pre-packaged bleach (Lestare) in Fort Wayne, Indiana. The full advertising campaign for each product was a thousand-line newspaper ad once a week for twenty weeks.

Matched sections of the city were blanked out from exposure to the ads for varying periods. In a control area, no advertising ran at all; in another matched section, advertising ran for four weeks, in another for eight weeks, and in a fourth for twenty weeks. Over a 23 week period, interviews were conducted with matched samples totaling nearly 6,200 respondents.

The design of this research posed a dilemma right from the outset. Since the objective was to study the effects of repetition, it was necessary to repeat the same unit of advertising space. But above and beyond that, it was necessary to repeat the identical ad each time. Any variation in layouts, copy themes, or illustrations of the sort we would normally expect in this kind of campaign, would have changed the very thing which was being measured—repetition of the *same* message.

By any of the measures used (awareness of the new product, information about it, or attitudes toward it), a certain number of successive repetitions (between half-a-dozen times and ten) clearly continued to have an incremental effect. Beyond that point, the major value of repetition was in maintaining the product at the level it had previously attained and protecting it from the immediate attrition that sets in when advertising stops. The more often the ads were repeated, the slower the rate of decay in the effects of the advertising. But the exact point at which the favorable effects of repetition started to wear out appeared to vary with the individual campaign. For one product, the second four ads added more net effect than the first four; the advertising campaign had an accelerating effect as it continued. For the other product, the pattern was reversed; the second four repetitions had a diminished effect.

Clearly, this vital difference must be accounted for by the particular creative strategy used in relation to the product in each case, since the media vehicle, the space unit, and the time interval were the same in both instances. In the first instance, the correct procedure was to repeat the same ad as long as it continued to build up to its maximum effect. In the second case, different ads might well have been used in successive insertions. Some readers seemed to have reached a threshold of psychological resistance when the same ads were shown to them again and again and again. After a certain point, the advertising (in its particular theming and appearance) no longer appeared to register with those who were not potential customers. They had seen it before; it fell into context; it simply did not have to be perceived as the eye scanned by it.

What would have happened to the shape of the curve of net favorable effect if the ad copy and layout had been changed periodically? There is reason to believe that it might have shown accelerated growth with each change. Each new format would have won the attention of some readers who were responsive to the new approach even though they had become oblivious to the old one.

A combination of familiar and unfamiliar elements in a campaign reinforces the original message, but at the same time it creates attention and awareness because of the audience's need to close the psychological gap between the expected and the unexpected. The reader is stopped by the incongruity between familiar and unfamiliar elements that he must resolve himself.

The same copy line and visual scheme can be effectively repeated through a variety of media in an effective advertising campaign. Each variation on the same creative theme arouses at the same time a sense of the familiar or *déjà vu* and of the unfamiliar. There are many devices for doing this: a common headline or slogan with different subheads (or vice versa), similar artwork with varied subjects, steady use of the same models in different settings (or of the same setting with different models).

A Great Creative Idea acquires a momentum of its own when its motif becomes common currency. Imitation and parody, which are possible only when it can be assumed that the original is well known, begin, and the caricatures evoke all the original meanings. A relatively unfamiliar brand thus enters the realm of universal familiarity. When the consumer sees it on the shelf, it is a known quantity, "a friend." All the connotations created by advertising are now inseparable from the name of the product itself.

Notes

1. Thomas Smith. *Hints to Intending Advertisers.* London, 1885. Quoted by James Playsted Wood in *The Story of Advertising* (New York: Ronald, 1958), p. 241.
2. Cited by Julian L. Simon, "Are There Economies of Scale in Advertising?" *Journal of Advertising Research* 5, (June 1965): pp. 15-20.
3. Edward B. Tichener, *A Textbook of Psychology* (New York: MacMillan, 1910), p. 411.
4. Robert B. Zajonc, "Attitudinal Effects of Mere Exposure," *Journal of Personality and Social Psychology*, Monograph Supplement, 9 (June 1968): 1-27.
5. Institute for Social Research Newsletter, Winter, 1973, p. 2.
6. Robert Zajonc, "Brainwash: Familiarity Breeds Comfort," *Psychology Today*, February 1970, pp. 33-63.
7. This research, by H. A. Cross, C. G. Halcomb, and W. W. Matter, is cited by Zajonc, "Brainwash."
8. "Retention Curves: Facts or Artifacts?" *Psychological Bulletin* 61, 3 (1964): 188-94.
9. *Memory*, London: Penguin, 1964, p. 79.
10. *Cf.* Lloyd R. Peterson, "Short-Term Memory," *Scientific American*, July 1966, pp. 90-95. In the article, Peterson describes short-term storage of information as an "activity mechanism" in the nervous system which dies out if there is no occasion to repeat the experience. He distinguishes it from the long-term storage that takes place in real learning, where a structural change actually takes place within the nerve cells.
11. *Cf.* Michael E. Doherty and Stuart M. Keeley, "On the Identification of Repeatedly Presented, Brief Visual Stimuli," *Psychological Bulletin* 28, 2 (August 1972): 142-54.
12. "The Remembering and Forgetting of Advertising," *Journal of Marketing* 23, 3 (January

1959): 239-43.

13. Hubert A. Zielske and Walter A. Henry, "Remembering and Forgetting Television Ads," *Journal of Advertising Research* 20, 2 (April 1980): 7-13.

14. Edward C. Strong, "The Spacing and Timing of Advertising," *Journal of Advertising Research* 17, 6 (December 1977): 25-31.

15. William A. Katz, "A Sliding Schedule of Advertising Weight," *Journal of Advertising Research* 20, 4 (August 1980): 39-44.

16. William T. Moran, "Does Flighting Pay?" Paper presented to the Advertising Research Foundation Conference, New York, 1976.

17. This observation is based on experiments made by A. P. Bumstead in 1940 and quoted by Hunter, *Memory*.

18. In a study made in 1931 by J. A. McGeoch and W. T. McDonald (cited by Hunter, *Memory*), university students received a list of adjectives to be memorized, and different kinds of activity were interpolated between memorizing and the test recall. Forty-five percent of the adjectives were recalled when the interpolated activity was reading jokes. When numbers were shown in between, recall of the adjectives went down to 37 percent. With nonsense syllables, recall of the adjectives went down to 26 percent. Learning adjectives unrelated to the originals reduced the percentage to 22 percent. Adjectives opposite in meaning to the originals brought the score down to 18 percent. When the students had to learn a list of adjectives synonymous with the originals, they remembered only 12 percent of the original list.

19. Eugene Burnstein, "Some Effects of Cognitive Selection Processes on Learning and Memory," *Psychological Monographs*, 76, 35, Whole No. 554 (1962).

20. "An Application of Learning Theory to TV Copy Testing," *Public Opinion Quarterly* 26, 4 (Winter 1962): 625-34. Krugman concludes in this article that some individual television commercials are more susceptible than others to an impairment of effectiveness through heavy and long exposure.

21. E. L. Hartley, "The Influence of Repetition and Familiarization on Consumer Preferences," Paper presented at the Convention of the American Psychological Association, September 6, 1961, quoted by Krugman, "Application of Learning Theory."

22. Herbert Krugman, "The Learning of Consumer Likes, Preferences and Choices," unpublished paper delivered July 1966 at Purdue University. *Cf.* also Krugman's "The Impact of Television Advertising: 'Learning without Involvement," *Public Opinion Quarterly* 29 (Fall 1965): 349-56.

23. "A Low Involvement Model of Mass Media Impact," a paper delivered before the 1966 Conference of the American Association for Public Opinion Research. Swampscott, Massachusetts. *Cf.* also "The Measurement of Advertising Involvement," *Public Opinion Quarterly*, 30, 4 (Winter 1966): 583-96.

24. Herbert E. Krugman, "Processes Underlying Exposure to Advertising," *American Psychologist* 23, 4 (1968): 245-53. *Cf.* also Herbert E. Krugman, "Why Three Exposures May Be Enough, *Journal of Advertising Research* 12, 6 (December 1972): 11-19; Herbert E. Krugman, "What Makes Advertising Effective?" *Harvard Business Review* 53, 2 (March-April 1975): 96-103; Herbert E. Krugman, "Sustained Viewing of Television," Paper presented to The Conference Board, New York City, February 1980.

25. Herbert E. Krugman, "How Potent is Television Advertising? Some Guidelines from Theory," Paper presented to the ANA Television Workshop, New York City, October 11, 1972.

26. Howard Kamin, "Advertising Reach and Frequency," *Journal of Advertising Research* 18, 1 (February 1978): 21-25.

27. Much of the literature on the declining return from repeated advertising messages has been reviewed by Michael J. Naples, *Effective Frequency: The Relationship Between Frequen-

cy and Advertising Effectiveness, Association of National Advertisers, 1979, and in the Proceedings of the Advertising Research Foundation's Conference on Advertising Repetition, *Effective Frequency: The State of the Art*, 1982. Unfortunately, many of the experiments on repetition do not control for the different effects produced at different time intervals, nor do they make the critical distinction between repeating the same advertisement and repeating a variant creative treatment of the same theme.

28. From the Newspaper Advertising Bureau's 1982 national study by Audits & Surveys.
29. From a 1982 study of 31 magazines by Audits & Surveys for the Magazine Publishers Association. The study showed that the average magazine is looked at on 3.2 different days by each reader, with 52 percent of its pages opened on each reading day.
30. Starch, *Measuring Advertising Readership and Results*, p. 97.
31. *SRC Bulletin*, 14, 8, September 1966.
32. *Media / scope*, September 1960.
33. This "glue spot" technique has been used in a number of experiments to verify the accuracy of reader reports of page-opening. In a 1966 study conducted for the British Institute of Practitioners in Advertising, people were filmed and observed as they read publications, or newspapers treated with glue spots were used in home reading situations. The next-day reports on page openings were found to be understated on the order of 25 percent. (Michael Brown, "Average Issue Readership Measurement in Britain," in Harry Henry, ed., *Readership Research: Theory and Practice* [London: Sigmatext, 1982]).
34. Alfred Politz Media Studies for *Reader's Digest*, January 1966.
35. Michael Ray, Alan Sawyer, and Edward Strong, "Frequency Effects Revisited," *Journal of Advertising Research* 11, 1 (February 1971): 14-20.
36. This conclusion is contradicted by Bobby Caldwell and Brian Sternthal, who observe that "wearout is not likely to be eliminated by strategies designed to enhance attention." ("Television Commercial Wearout: An Information Processing View," *Journal of Marketing Research* XVII (May 1980): 173-86.
37. Summarized in Naples, *Effective Frequency*.
38. Reported by Gene DeWitt in *The New York Times*, June 22, 1976.
39. Colin McDonald, "What is the Short-Term Effect of Advertising?" in Naples, *Effective Frequency*, pp. 83-103.
40. Otmar Ernst, "New Evidence on how Advertising Works."
41. Alvin Achenbaum, "Effective Exposure: A New Way of Evaluating Media," Paper delivered to the Association of National Advertisers, New York City, February 3, 1977. *Cf.* also, "Superman Has Effective Reach: Can Advertisers Duplicate It?" *Advertising Age*, April 2, 1979, pp. 67-69.
42. Robert C. Grass, "Satiation Effects of Advertising," Paper presented to the Advertising Research Foundation Conference, New York City, 1968. *Cf.* also Robert C. Grass and Wallace H. Wallace, "Satiation Effects of TV Commercials," *Journal of Advertising Research* 9, 3 (September 1969): 3-8, and Wallace H. Wallace, "Predicting and Measuring the Wearout of Commercials," Paper presented to the American Marketing Association, Kansas City, April 1, 1970.
43. C. Samuel Craig, Brian Sternthal, and Clark Leavitt, "Advertising Wearout: An Experimental Analysis," *Journal of Marketing Research* 13 (November 1976): 365-72. This study also found that a very high level of repetition produced greater recall a week and two weeks after exposure, but it did not show this advantage over lower levels of repetition when recall was measured after a few days or after more than a two-week interval.
44. Valentine Appel, "On Advertising Wearout," *Journal of Advertising Research* 11, 1 (February 1971): 11-13.
45. Frederick W. Winter, "A Laboratory Experiment of Individual Attitude Response to

Advertising Exposure," *Journal of Marketing Research* 10, 2 (May 1973): 130-40.

46. Robert J. Schreiber, Clark Schiller, and Marvin Belkin, "The Effects of Frequency in Magazines on Attitudes and Purchasing Behavior—A Large-Scale Experimental Study," Paper delivered to the Advertising Research Foundation Conference, New York City, 1982. This study found that changes in buying habits did not always follow a change in advertising recall or in attitude. For Time, Inc.'s Robert Schreiber, who supervised the study, the findings suggest that it is not necessary to change attitudes in order to change buying habits.

47. Ernest A. Rockey and William F. Greene, "TV Commercial Effectiveness Under Multiple Exposure Conditions," Paper delivered to the Advertising Research Foundation Conference, New York City, October 1978.

48. *The Order of Presentation in Persuasion* (New Haven: Yale University Press, 1957).

49. *Advertising and Its Mental Laws* (New York: Macmillan, 1916), cited by Simon, "Are There Economies of Scale in Advertising?" Corroborating this proposition many years later, Samuel Craig, Brian Sternthal, and Clark Leavitt concluded from several experiments that "wearout is attributable to the audience's inattentiveness to stimulus materials and loss of motivation for retrieval of brand names when repetitions are substantial," which means that "there is some optimal level of repetition" and that "the nonbeneficial effects of high-frequency campaigns can be mitigated by varying the execution of the same theme." ("Advertising Wearout")

50. Robert C. Grass and Wallace H. Wallace, "Advertising Communication."

51. John B. Stewart, *Repetitive Advertising in Newspapers* (Boston: Harvard University, Division of Research, Graduate School of Business Administration, 1964).

Chapter 10
Defining the Target

Who was the genius who first discovered that rich people buy more things than poor ones? Or his equally anonymous successor who discovered that smokers buy more cigarettes than non-smokers, among rich and poor alike? Let monuments be erected in their memory, for every year these startling discoveries are made anew!

The concept of marketing implies a national market. We have become a culturally more homogeneous nation, entwined in an intimate web of transportation and communication. This makes it possible to think of market segments made up of drinkers of imported liqueurs, compulsive cleaners of pots and pans, one-time users of razor blades—people scattered across the continent but linked together by common attributes. In a society of greater complexity, affluence, and education the citizen-consumer's avocational interests multiply, as well as the means to indulge them.

"The Consumer" is a mythical creature. He exists in only one aspect and has only one function: to consume whatever we may happen to be making or selling. He is part of the same simplified abstraction of human behavior that has given us the concepts of an advertising "impression" and of "cost-per-thousand," which we will be discussing later.

The chief executive of a large packaged goods company, in a recent address, referred to "the female market segment." He meant women. In a period of media specialization and of "scientific marketing," it is perhaps inevitable that human beings should be reduced to such one-dimensional terms and that sales plans and marketing models deal with them as though they were identical specimens stamped out of a mold, like lead soldiers. By contrast, the old-fashioned word *customer* defines a person in a specific role with respect to a specific product. It suggests that he has a multiplicity of other roles that make him complex and unique.

Every advertiser wants to use media that will bring him straight to his marketing target. Unfortunately, there is no general agreement on how marketing targets should be defined. The U.S. Information Agency's policymakers in a South American country once defined three target groups for a big public information campaign. The first was "all literates." The second was "all illiterates," and the third was "all others."

John W. Burgard, an advertising director of the Brown & Williamson Tobacco Corporation, commented years ago, "Some advertisers either do not have very good information on audience composition, or else ignore it; otherwise right now I don't think we would see a cigar commercial on a show that has a very definite skew to older women."

The question of how many *people* could be reached by a medium for a given cost is commonly rephrased to inquire how many *customers* can be reached. Gail Smith, a former director of advertising of the General Motors Corporation, put the proposition in these words: "I think the advertiser will be able to buy a pound of people or a pound of territory as today you can buy chicken breasts or legs without getting stuck with the whole bird."[1]

The development of mass marketing in the United States has been accompanied by an enormous amount of research designed to locate the best prospective customers for different commodities and services or the most likely shoppers at different stores. The relationships between market and media audience characteristics were readily seen as a problem of matching, and the ability to put messages in front of prospects with minimum waste and at minimum cost is often considered to be one of the chief skills of the advertising planner.

Elementary to the alignment of media capabilities and marketing requirements is the concept of market segmentation. Wendell Smith, a distinguished marketing theorist, may have been the first to use the term, which he applied to "developments on the demand side of the market . . . a rational and more precise adjustment of product and marketing effort to consumer or user requirements . . . viewing a heterogeneous market as a number of smaller homogeneous markets in response to different product preferences among important market segments." He saw market segmentation as a distinct strategy from product differentiation, which "is concerned with the bending of demand to the will of supply."[2]

The concept of segmentation is, in effect, being implemented by any company that systematically seeks to describe its customers and potential customers and to distinguish them from the public as a whole either with regard to their personal characteristics or in terms of the way they use the product.

Like markets, media audiences can be divided into segments. People have always defined themselves by their media preferences and habits. I noted in Chapter 6 that the more restrictive the medium, the greater the sense of kindred spirit among those who share it. (Business and professional publications are the prototype of the specialized, narrowly targeted media vehicle.)* There are half

---

*Trade magazines are commonly promoted by free distribution at meetings and conferences. On one occasion, the publisher of *Beef*, a magazine of the meatpacking industry, flew from Chicago to Dallas to attend a convention of cattlemen. He shipped 15 cases to the convention hotel, each box containing 100 copies and appropriately labeled. The airline's freight service put them aboard a refrigerated compartment, and in Dallas they were taken in a refrigerated truck to the hotel, where they were promptly put in the freezer. The anguished publisher, who had been pounding the desk and calling Chicago for three days, did not locate them until the last day of the convention, by which time the cattlemen were returning to their ranches. He was presented with 15 frozen cases of *Beef*, and ultimately with an $8,000 bill for shipment and storage.

a dozen magazines for joggers alone, and over 10,000 magazines and periodicals altogether. Radio has become a medium of specialized audiences. The spread of cable television has been hailed by advertisers as a means of permitting them to zero in more efficiently and selectively on particular interest groups.

In their selection of media, advertisers have long attempted to match the particular profile of their own consumers with comparable media profiles. A manufacturer selling a product to high-income professional families looks for "class" media. An advertiser selling to young mothers tries to find a medium directed at their interests.

In one of its sales bulletins, NBC once said, "If income were the sole criterion of a medium's value, advertisers of such products as laundry soap and toothpaste would be concentrating their budgets in such media as *The New Yorker* and *Saturday Review*."[3]

A media vehicle may have an audience that is highly concentrated in a certain income or age sector of the population and still fall far short of giving the advertiser adequate coverage of that sector. It may be more efficient for him to use a vehicle that has a more diversified audience yet also covers his desired specialized target more completely.

In their eagerness to get to the most rewarding segments of the market, advertisers often succumb to the tendency to use standard definitions, regardless of whether they coincide with the proper target—those who are ready to be persuaded.

"Positioning" the brand

The counterpart of any effort to describe probable purchasers of a product is to describe whom a product is designed to please. Just as Molière's bourgeois gentleman was delighted to find that he had been speaking in prose all his life, many marketers in recent years must have been heartened by the discovery that they had been "positioning" their products without even being aware of it.

"Positioning" is another of those catchy terms that speechwriters invent to embellish the banal thoughts of marketing executives forced to make statesmanlike utterances on ceremonial occasions. It refers to the practice of trying to carve out a distinctive niche for a brand (or store) in a competitive market by slanting its promotion toward a definable group of consumers. This target group may have certain social attributes or personality features in common, or its members may share a particular set of motives for using the product or a common pattern of use.

Pets are owned by young people and old ones, by rich people and poor people. But a dog may fill a need for companionship or for protection; it may be a surrogate child or a surrogate mate. The themes used by different dog food advertisers may be oriented to the personalities and motivations of these different kinds of pet owners.

The practice of directing appeals to a selected portion of the potential purchasers is probably as old as advertising itself, and certainly as old as brand name advertising. In the pre-deodorant era, Lifebuoy soap aimed its messages at those vigorous but insecure types who feared that body odor might destroy their attractiveness to the opposite sex, while Camay offered women a restoration (or affirmation) of their virginal purity. Lucky Strikes soothed the well-founded anxieties of the heavy smoker by promising "not one cough in a carload." This kind of targeting has always combined psychological selectivity in the theme and execution of the advertising with a selective use of media. (Camay soap has never, to my knowledge, advertised in *Esquire*, nor Lucky Strikes in *Bride's*.)

What is of relative recency, however, is the practice of developing products from scratch to occupy what is perceived to be a gap in the market. The most striking and costly example was the Edsel, which was created to round out the Ford Motor Company's product line in the hope that rising young executives would move up from Fords to another Ford product instead of turning to Oldsmobile or Pontiac when they couldn't afford a Ford-made Mercury. The Edsel, mostly for design reasons, was a notable failure, but success has come to innumerable other new products similarly produced to specifications set by analysis of the existing market structure. This kind of analysis inevitably starts with consumer research that examines the strengths and weaknesses of the brands currently on the market and determines the areas of vulnerability in which a new entry might carve out a niche or in which an existing brand can refashion itself to expand its share of the business.

For example, research by McCaffrey and McCall found that although Ben-Gay had traditionally been advertised as a reliever of muscle aches, about a third of its users, accounting for half its volume, used it to fight arthritis pain. This led to a "repositioning" of the brand with two separate advertising strategies.

Kraft positioned its Breyers brand of ice cream with an "all-natural" appeal that stressed the absence of artificial flavorings and repositioned its other premium-priced brand, Sealtest, as "The Supermarket Ice Cream with That Ice Cream Parlor Taste." To attract customers unwilling to pay the price of a premium ice cream, they developed a new brand of ice milk under the Light 'n' Lively name, which had already been made familiar through a line of dairy products. In a five-year period, Breyers' sales increased by over 50 percent, Sealtest's by 23 percent, and Light 'n' Lively's by 45 percent at a time when the overall market for ice cream and ice milk remained flat.[4]

However a brand is positioned in terms of the consumer benefits it offers, the advertising strategist must still develop his marketing plan to bring the message to the most promising targets. How are they to be defined?

Trapping the heavy user

Who is the elusive prospect that every advertiser seeks, the one whose defenses will melt and whose deep-rooted purchase habits change immediately, if only our message can reach him?

For many knowledgeable marketers, the best prospect can always be defined as the heavy user, the one who buys more of the product in question, faces the purchase decision most often, and is thus, presumably, most sensitized to advertising. In almost any product category it can be demonstrated that a large percentage of the sales volume comes from a minority of the total public, often from a minority of the product's users. How logical, then, to seek media whose audiences are made up of just those very same heavy users!

One illustration of this approach comes from an analysis by Dik Warren

Twedt[5] of data taken from the Chicago *Tribune* consumer panel on eighteen product categories. (The 402 families in the *Tribune* panel kept a continuing record of their purchases which made possible the comparison of their individual product and brand selections over extended periods of time.)

The heavy-using families were different for different product categories. Twedt therefore inferred that demographic characteristics are not good predictors of heavy usage. It seemed to follow that it is more efficient to measure consumption of each product directly—in direct relation to the media habits of the heavy users—than to assume that they fall into any particular population bracket with known media exposure patterns.

Twedt tested this hypothesis and concluded that "the media vehicles used to optimize our reach among heavy bacon users are not the right ones for reaching heavy instant coffee users. . . . A television program, for example, may have as many ratings as it has potential sponsors."

While this conclusion is intriguing to anyone prepared to recognize the complexities of the market, the evidence on which it rests is somewhat incomplete. As in a great many similar attempts to match market and media profiles, the unit of Twedt's analysis was the household. This makes sense when we analyze consumption because for the most part families consume together, whether or not they buy together. We know, however, that media experiences are, to a large extent, individual within the family. The individual who does most of the buying for a particular item in a heavy-using household is not necessarily the same one who does most of the reading, viewing, or listening to the media vehicle that has heavy exposure in the same family. The products analyzed were all grocery items whose use varied substantially, not merely with income but with family size, composition, and ethnic background (since persons of Italian and Polish descent eat differently even when they have similar jobs and housing).

We are left wondering whether a demographic analysis that used more variables at once might not come up with far better yardsticks of prediction than those that Twedt tried and rejected. The widespread tendency to make measurements in terms of households rather than in terms of people is a by-product of the accidental fact that the Nielsen Audimeter—the most widely used instrument in broadcast audience research—measures set-tuning rather than the actual process of communication, which is always on an individual basis.

It goes without saying that a family's consumption characteristics do not necessarily apply to all of its individual members. In some households, the husband has three beers a day and the wife has none; this is a heavy-using household. Similarly, there are patterns of household *media* consumption that do not apply to individual members. The paterfamilias may remain oblivious to the women's magazines his wife leaves all over the living room; his household is "heavily exposed." In large families, TV viewing is higher than in smaller ones, but the housewife actually watches TV *less*. The kids watch TV while she is slaving over a hot stove to get their TV dinners ready.

A 1980 Benton & Bowles study found that over a two-week period, a third of the men said they had cooked an entire meal, and four out of five had done the main grocery shopping. Sixty-three percent of married men helped choose the brand of cereal, 40 percent toothpaste, 44 percent soap.

The advertiser often faces a tactical question as to whether to aim at the ultimate consumer or at the purchasing agent. His problem is compounded by the fact that when several members of the same family are interviewed, they often disagree as to who controls the brand decision. (Men make a third of the brand selections in supermarkets on products they use personally. The husband's brand choice in personal and health care products differs from the wife's in three out of five cases.)[6]

In developing any advertising plan, it is of course essential to know who the heavy users are and to determine whether they buy the product for reasons that are in any way different from those of other people, in which case they would demand a different copy approach. However, the most effective advertising is not always that which provides the most concentration on users of the product in general, or even on heavy users in particular. Often the advertiser's problem is less to hold on to his existing share of market than to expand the market as a whole by attracting new customers or increasing consumption on the part of light or moderate users. Or, by contrast, in a mature market where there is "saturation usage," like the soap and coffee markets, the advertiser's main marketing task may be to attract customers away from his competition at *every* level of use.

In many product categories, usage is governed by strictly objective material considerations like family size, income, or position in the life cycle, and advertising serves largely to shuffle brand shares rather than to expand consumption per se. The extent to which people can be induced to increase their consumption of soap as a result of advertising is small relative to the increase in consumption that takes place when a new member is added to the family.

There is also a serious technical problem in relating consumption patterns accurately to media use. Most survey data today are subjected to a constant process of adjustment and weighting. The numbers that are ground out of the computer no longer represent straight answers to questions asked of individual people. New techniques of sampling give us more accurate projections for the whole population, but at the same time the sampling error is harder to calculate.

This becomes more of a problem when we compare smaller and smaller subgroups, like heavy users of a given product who read a particular publication or listen to a certain radio program. At this point, any comparisons we make, even when we start with a big sample, are based on a small number of interviews, which means the results may show a large statistical error. This problem gets even more serious when we compare surveys at different points in time. How far should we pursue the heavy user through this jungle of statistical questionmarks?

Who is the target?

Paul Klein, a former NBC executive, once visited an advertising agency handling a large margarine account and delivered a presentation which showed that a particular schedule on his network would reach a very large concentration of the heavy margarine users. After he had finished his presentation, complete with numerous statistics, the account executive told him plaintively, "But we want to reach the heavy *butter* users."

In defining the target, every marketer must decide on the probabilities of converting the people who do not use his product. His tactics must necessarily be different for a broad market than for a narrow one. If he goes after current users only, he may lose the chance of winning new customers to the product field. If he goes after heavy users only, he loses the chance of convincing the light users to buy more. If his is the dominant brand in the market, expanding total sales for the product field will redound directly to his benefit. If he has a minority position, his success in getting people interested in the product may either carve out a unique new position for his brand or merely benefit his competitors. Thus the interrelation between defining the target and plotting the advertising strategy can clearly be seen.

Colin McDonald distinguishes (1) committed major users of a brand (whom advertising cannot convert), (2) uncommitted users, (3) minor users committed to a competitor, (4) uncommitted non-users, and (5) non-users who are committed elsewhere (and with whom "it may well be unproductive to make too much effort").[7]

The advertising planner must weigh the productivity of converting existing users to his own brand at the same time that he keeps his present customers safely within his camp against the blandishments of the competition.

Like many other marketing buzzwords, the phrase *brand loyalty* suggests emotional overtones that rarely exist in reality. The tendency to repeat purchases of the same brand indicates preference or habituation that should not be confused with the attachments that dogs have to their masters, fans to their teams, or old grads to their alma maters. How much brand loyalty actually exists? Whatever the answer, there seems to be less of it. Between 1975 and 1981, the proportion of people telling a Needham, Harper & Steers poll, "I try to stick to well-known brand names" fell from 77 percent to 62 percent.

A typical brand of packaged goods gets about 80 percent of its annual sales volume from between a fourth and half its buyers who make six or more purchases of it in the course of a year.[8] (Normally, the proportion of people who buy the same brand in successive periods of time is the same as the proportion who buy it repeatedly over non-consecutive periods.) In some instances, over 90 percent of a family's purchases of a specific product over a three-year period are concentrated on a single brand.[9]

Repeat-buying represents only one of the ways in which brand loyalty has been defined and in which it varies from one type of product to another. A 1982 survey by Leo Shapiro Associates for *Chain Store Age / General Merchandise* found that 96 percent of the people who might buy a pair of designer jeans have a specific brand preference, but 7 out of 10 have no brand preference when it comes to athletic shoes or motor oil; 6 out of 10 have no brand preference for electric blankets or microwave ovens; and 4 out of 10 have none for cookware. Similar variations are found in the number of grocery shoppers who will go to another supermarket if their favorite brand is unavailable. This ranges across product categories from 23 percent to 67 percent, according to Procter & Gamble's Jack Gavin.

A 1978 study by J. Walter Thompson among 2,500 consumers found a wide range in the proportions willing to switch brands in response to a price saving.

Fifty-three percent of cigarette smokers would stick with their favorite brand, even if they could buy a different one at half price, but only 16 percent of the users of aluminum foil would remain loyal in the face of this temptation. Commodity-type products understandably arouse the least loyalty and products involving health and safety the most.

An analysis of SMRB 1980 data by Edward Papazian shows that two out of three users of hair tonics, oven cleaners, and vitamins claim to use only a single brand, but such loyalty is found among only 2 percent of the users of cold cereal, 8 percent of the users of household cleansers, and 10 percent of the users of toilet soap. Papazian points out that "many categories have relatively low brand loyalty because of the interaction of various household members. Thus, the man of the house may prefer Dial soap while his wife likes Dove and his daughter favors Zest." (Apart from that, none of them may have very strong feelings about soap brands in the first place.) Not only does brand loyalty differ from one kind of product to another; it also differs among competing brands. The leading brands in any category generally command the highest rate of repeat purchase. One analysis showed that brand loyalty for toothpaste has ranged from a low of 32 percent for Listerine to a high of 74 percent for Crest.[10] A comparably broad range of variation occurs in many product fields.

Older people and people of lower income and education have the highest rates of brand switching, whereas those of higher income and education are most brand-loyal. However, the brand-loyal people of lower income switch from one *established* brand to another, while the higher educated have the greatest propensity to switch to new products and brands.[11]

Does this mean there is a certain kind of brand-loyal customer whom the advertiser should seek for his very own? Ross Cunningham observes that there is no significant proportion of families who are *consistently* loyal across all types of product categories. Those loyal to a brand of one product may have very little brand loyalty in the case of another product. Cunningham found the highest brand loyalty for headache tablets, margarine, and scouring cleansers and the lowest for canned peas and toilet soap. He noted that many families apparently have a favorite second choice but that this makes less difference the more loyal they are to a single product.

Cunningham discovered "secondary" loyalties that carry over from one of a manufacturer's brands to his other brands. Brand loyalty appeared to be almost impervious to price offers and deals and showed no truly significant relationship to store loyalty or to the size of the consumer's purchase. In the case of the low-priced, frequently purchased items measured, brand loyalty appeared to be unrelated to socioeconomic characteristics. In essence, Cunningham tells us that brand loyalty is real and important, but it is specific to the product category rather than to any particular type of consumer.

Reviewing the evidence on brand-switching behavior, Frank Bass concludes that it is essentially "stochastic," or randomly determined.[12] This does not mean that "it is not possible to find causal relationships which will discriminate among the probabilities of choice for various consumers." But, says Bass, "It will never be possible to provide good predictions of individual consumer choice behavior for separate choice occasions." In short, with brand choice, as with so many other aspects of advertising's influence, it all depends.

This does not, of course, imply that buying patterns cannot be classified in a meaningful way. Our own studies at the Newspaper Advertising Bureau have found that people of higher income and education are most likely to buy private labels.[13] They also make the most active use of advertising as an adjunct to the shopping decision and are most receptive to new inventions and products. Low-income people tend to shop around in order to hunt bargains regardless of whether they actually like shopping per se. The higher-income person who doesn't enjoy shopping can afford simply to stick with the store he knows and trusts. Bargain-minded people are more skeptical of the truthfulness of advertising. The most skeptical people are those who consider shopping a chore, but in spite of this, because they tend to be of lower income, they do more shopping around among stores.

Women enjoy shopping; men regard it as a chore and are therefore much more likely to shop at a single store for any particular major purchase rather than to shop around as women do. Men are less bargain-minded than women are; they are more apt to buy on impulse and are less resistant to credit purchasing. Women are more conscious of consulting advertising for information than are men. In general, people enjoy shopping less as they grow older, and this is reflected in the decreasing number of stores they visit on a shopping trip. Facts like these make it clear that the marketer can hardly expect to find all the customers of a certain type clustered together in one place and available to him through any particular advertising medium.

Related conclusions are reported by Herbert Kay from a pilot study[14] among 300 women. Kay defined "prime prospects" as people who use a product, who can be persuaded to switch brands, and who are susceptible to advertising appeals. By his definition, prime prospect status is not related to the volume of usage or to conventional demographic classifications. In one product category, 33 percent of the prime prospects he surveyed were in the lowest income bracket, compared to 13 percent of the other users, but in another product field, the proportion of prime prospects and other users with low incomes was the same (about a fifth).

Comparing two products with the same proportion of users who are over 35, Kay showed that one has virtually identical proportions of prospects among both younger and older women, whereas the other has twice as high a percentage of younger women users as older ones who might be persuaded by advertising to switch brands.

Comparing two women's service magazines with an identical four-week cumulative audience, Kay found that the percentage of heavy toothpaste users who read at least one issue of each was identical with that of all the women interviewed (35 percent). However, one magazine reached 24 percent of all those users whom Kay classifies as the "prime prospects," the other 44 percent. Among prime prospects who were also heavy users, the disproportion was even greater.

Kay provides other examples of media vehicles that appear to be evenly matched in terms of audience size and even in the proportion of product users and heavy users who are reached. Yet when he adds in the extra dimension of willingness to switch brands, he finds striking differences in the proportion of magazine readers or program viewers who are prime prospects for conversion. The explanation has to be that certain media vehicles, because of their content, manage to attract more of the persuadable than others do. The evidence is slim, but the concept is appealing.

There is no *perfect* case of media and market matching. Any medium, no matter how selective, will reach some people other than the ones who are prospects for a manufacturer's product. Any market of heavy users, no matter how concentrated, will include many people beyond the reach of a selective medium.

In any attempt to correlate media and consumption habits, some very important simplifications have to be made. To the extent that there is a relationship at all, it is rarely a *direct* relationship between the two. Instead, it usually arises because of the intrusion of a third element that reflects such things as the consumer's age, education, or income, or more subtle matters of personality and taste.

Exposure to any one advertisement is not, of course, randomly distributed among those exposed to the medium that carries it. Within the audience for any medium there is selective sensitivity to different types of advertising content and technique. Not only the media plan, but the very nature of the message, determine whether or not the advertiser reaches his target. Who that target really is is something he must judge for his own unique product; no easy formula can define it for him.

Locating the "interested" prospects

Every advertiser hopes to strike a responsive chord among the people exposed to his message. But how can he decide who will be interested?

A number of propositions emerge both from common sense and from a variety of consumer studies:

1. An expensive item is more likely to arouse the consumer's emotional involvement than a less expensive one.
2. A product about which the consumer feels deeply is most likely to arouse an active, purposeful search for information when he is in the market.
3. A product category in which the customer perceives brands as being very different creates a more purposeful selective interest in advertising than one in which the customer assumes that all products are pretty much alike.
4. Most products that are bought arouse comparatively little involvement. They are likely to be inexpensive and they demand rather effortless or routine decision-making. (This is not true of products that are consumed daily but that serve as symbols of social position or of individual personality or taste—cigarettes are the best example.)
5. The more expensive an item is, the more money is normally expended on promoting the sale of each unit and the greater the total advertising pressure that influences each purchase and seeks to raise the level of consumer interest.

6. The more differentiated the product from others of the same kind, the more informative the function of advertising and the more actively the prospective buyer consults and uses it in making up his mind.

The people interested in a product are not always the best prospects. Some products, like insurance or weed killer, may carry a rather high degree of emotional involvement, and yet this may be a negative feeling. Product interest and frequency of usage were both considered in the national study we conducted in 1964.[15] To follow up on a survey of daily newspaper readership, a sample of approximately 1,600 people representing a national cross-section was interviewed about a variety of consumer items.* It was assumed from the start that the attitudes and actions that defined an individual as a prospect in one product category might be substantially different from those that defined him as a prospect in some other field. Frequency of purchase was recorded rather than the volume of use (with which it would closely correlate but which is harder to estimate accurately). However, it was not assumed that the frequent buyer could always be considered the best prospect. The survey questionnaire also measured (1) the degree to which the consumer found the product pleasant or unpleasant to use, (2) the degree of his interest in reading and hearing of new developments in the product field, and (3) his willingness to talk about the product.

For the typical product, the largest proportion of people interviewed reported that they found it pleasant to use. (A few categories—liquor, cigarettes, air travel—elicited rather sharply differentiated responses from users and non-users.) The next highest proportion of the respondents liked to read or hear of new product developments. Finally, a much smaller proportion liked to talk about the products. (Air travel is an exception, because people are interested in reading or talking about it as much or more as they find it pleasant.)

All three of these measures (pleasantness, interest, and discussion) were combined into a single score of the consumer's involvement with the product. The variation from product to product was striking. For men, the proportion with a "high involvement" score ranged from 75 percent for new cars down to 8 percent for women's make-up. For women, canned vegetables and packaged mixes got a "high involvement" score of 66 percent and vodka a low of 7 percent. Even though advertisers often aim their messages only at men or only at women, the study found that the opposite sex often showed a high level of interest in the product. Bread and some other food products aroused high involvement scores from men, while cars, tires, and air travel received high scores from women.

In addition to the questions about "involvement" with the product, people were asked whether they considered the brands in the product field to be all the same or different, and their "brand loyalty" was also investigated. These data were related to the readership of advertisements for the same products, obtained in a separate interview two weeks earlier. The highest level of readership oc-

---

*The items about which questions were asked varied from one interview to the next. They reflected the incidence of newspaper advertisements for the products in question and were not a representative selection of *all* advertised products relative either to consumption or to the total amount of national advertising.

curred among people who were brand-loyal, but not among the *most* brand-loyal. (Since their minds were already made up, they did not want to be confused with the facts.) Those who think most brands in a given product field are really different pay more attention to advertising for that product than people who think the brands are all alike (and therefore not worth learning more about).

Soft drinks and coffee are among those product categories where blindfold taste tests customarily show that differences among individual brands are difficult to detect. Yet these two categories were tied for second place (after new cars) in the percentage of men who believed that there were important differences among brands.

The extent to which people feel there are important brand differences in a product field has very little to do with their attitudes toward the product as such. For example, 9 out of 10 men and 8 out of 10 women considered bread extremely pleasant to use, but only about 1 in 3 people liked to talk about bread and only half thought that there are important differences among brands of bread. Only 1 man in 4 believed that there are important differences among airlines. Yet, next to automobiles, men reported talking about air travel more than about any other measured product or service.

How does the frequency of using a product relate to attitudes toward it? Different patterns appear to emerge in different categories. For example, in the case of blended whiskey the most frequent purchasers were also those who were most likely to find the product pleasant to use, who were most interested in new developments, most inclined to talk about it, most convinced of differences among different brands, and who showed the highest proportion of brand loyalty.

In the case of bread, a product that almost everyone uses, frequency of purchase appears to have no bearing at all on either brand attitude or purchase behavior or on involvement with the product. This merely reflects the fact that the user of bread is not necessarily the purchaser. His feelings toward the product may have no opportunity at all to be translated into buying behavior.

In the case of airlines there is still another pattern, for the key difference in attitude appeared to be between flyers and nonflyers, rather than how often flyers fly.

The results imply that the most efficient advertising campaign may be the one that reaches not the highest proportion of heavy users, but rather the highest proportion of people who are susceptible to persuasion to use the product more often, or to shift brands. As we have seen, product usage, product attitudes, and brand attitudes do not relate to each other in the same predictable way for every product.

The problem of classification

Media researcher Alfred Politz pursued a regimen of vigorous exercise and confined his diet to proteins and vitamin C, especially avoiding starches and fried foods. On one memorable occasion, after an especially exasperating day, he ordered potato pancakes for dinner. His associate, Paul Chook, pointed out to him that he was violating his dietary code. Politz replied that he did not place potato pancakes in either the fried food or the starchy categories.

It is still not unusual in American advertising and marketing for the public to be classified in terms of categories that have long outlived their usefulness. In the early years of marketing research, it was standard practice for interviewers to be assigned quotas of people to contact in what were euphemistically known as A, B, C, and D neighborhoods. How these social classes were defined varied in description from one interviewing organization to the next and each interviewer made her own interpretation, depending on which side of the railroad tracks she herself had been raised.

During the mid-1940s and early 1950s, the concept of social class developed by W. Lloyd Warner and his school of social anthropologists became widely familiar.[16] Studies made by Warner's disciple, Burleigh Gardner, of Social Research, Inc., were widely popularized by Pierre Martineau, the gifted promotion director of the Chicago *Tribune*.* Warner and Gardner related consumption styles to social class position, of which income was a component but not necessarily the sole determinant.

The classic sociological analysis of social classes, begun by Karl Marx and continued by Max Weber, dealt primarily with power relationships. Warner stressed the idea that prestige, as both a cause and derivative of power, had much to do with an individual's worldly display of possessions and manners of conduct. Warner's scheme of description began with the social class to which a person was assigned by others. In his system, class position was related to the *source* of a person's income as well as its amount. It was further affected by the type of his occupation, his level of education, his racial or ethnic origins and church affiliation, and the type of house and neighborhood he lived in.

Social mobility also loomed large in Warner's outlook. A competitive economic order places a high premium on striving for promotion and achievement. The marketing system and the pressures of advertising all work to arouse appetites for the joys of consumption as the fruit of personal achievement. Warner showed that the way a person spends his income, including his product and brand choices, might in many cases have far more to do with the symbols of social class toward which he aspires than does his original social background.

Although Warner defined six social classes—ranging from Upper-Upper to Lower-Lower—in his famous study of Yankee City (Newburyport, Massachusetts), Gardner preferred to simplify the contrast into that between upper-middle class values and those of the "Middle Majority," which linked the petite bourgeoisie and the solid working-class in banal conformity to conventional virtues.[17]

The influence of Warner and Gardner's social class analysis waned with that of motivation research. The main line of marketing and media data still uses the traditional demographic comparisons based on income, education, age, and city

---

Motivation in Advertising (New York: McGraw-Hill Book Company, 1957). Martineau once explained what was wrong with beer advertising (as recalled by Don Grasse): "You agency people spend the day digging into the demographics of the heavy beer drinkers, desperately seeking the hot button that will boom beer barrelage, immersing yourselves in beer the entire day. At five o'clock you are worn out and ready for refreshment. So you go across the street to the watering hole. And what do you order? Beer? No. As you chatter inanely over what's wrong with the beer business you sip martinis."

size. These necessarily lump into a single category individuals who are highly different in their characteristics, outlook, habits, and values. For example, the common practice of classification by education lumps into a single bracket a man with a Ph.D. from Harvard and one who has spent a year or two in a junior college. Such individuals probably differ totally in their income, outlook, habitat, and lifestyle, and yet they are lumped together as "college-educated" in many studies that analyze consumption.

Lifestyles reflect the great complexity of roles that individuals play in an increasingly segmented society. No man is just of middle income and over 35. He may also be a father, churchwarden, union member, Mason, medical patient, and Republican. It is precisely at the intersection point of these varied roles that we find the most interesting deviations from expected patterns of buying.

These roles are not fixed for any individual. As young people leave the dependent world of childhood and become consumers, job-seekers, club members, taxpayers, car owners, and heads of families, their media habits change as well as their activities as consumers. All this has profound implications for the advertiser. He must "teach" each generation of consumers all over again what its parents know.

A consumer's buying style does reflect his measurable demographic traits, but it is also—and in some cases to an even greater degree—an expression of highly individual personality attributes.

One of the problems with consumer surveys in general is that they are seldom made with samples large enough to allow us to classify people in terms of more than one or two dimensions (like income, education, age, etc.). When we compare people in terms of three or four of these characteristics simultaneously, even though we may start with a very large sample, we usually end up with far too few in any one subgroup to make the results statistically conclusive. Thus the market analyst chronically settles for comparisons that are far less sophisticated than those he wants and needs.

When we meet a stranger, we automatically make very complex and subtle assessments that allow us to position him in terms that are meaningful in the sense that they provide us with cues as to how to communicate with him. We make instantaneous judgments from his appearance and manner about his age, social position, urbanity, ethnicity, regional origins, intelligence, and personality. We make all of these judgments simultaneously and in relation to each other. They are subject to testing by our further observation or experience with him.

This kind of delicate differentiation comes as close to the heart of the marketer's problem as anything could. The marketer is always dealing with people's consumption tastes, with their vulnerability to certain kinds of persuasion, and with their media exposure patterns. All of these phenomena correspond to the kinds of highly individual attributes that enter into a first-hand, everyday, informal assessment of personality. Yet the marketer rarely gets his research data in a form that allows him to look at people in terms of these dimensions. He is forced to work with crude generalizations, and with variables that are not sensitive enough to distinguish among key elements in the market.

Consumers are today increasingly differentiated, not merely with regard to the traditional types of demographic characteristics but also in terms of psychological attributes that are not automatically related to such conventional measures as age or income. This may be true in the case of widely used products (like cigarettes or white bread) where brand choice reflects response to symbols rather than to any objective or overt product differences.

Some personality traits do seem to have a relationship to social class and distinctive practices of child rearing. But any such relationship is unpredictable for large populations and certainly of less significance than so simple a matter as whether one is a first-born or middle child.

The importance of individual personality differences in consumption may be suggested by some of the findings from the study of car buying that I described before (page 106). Consumer decisions to purchase automobiles appear to cluster into three major patterns that we termed the repetitive, emotional, and logical. People who follow these different purchase patterns seem to differ more psychologically than in demographic terms.

In the repetitive pattern, advertising mainly fills a supportive function. The purchaser really knows all along what he is going to do and the advertising is a way of reassuring himself that he is correct in staying with his present make and dealer.

In the emotional pattern, advertising is a strong stimulus to fantasy. The symbolic aspects of car ownership are important to this kind of buyer, and advertising differentiates his image of the various makes.

In the logical buying pattern, advertising has little to do with the decision to buy, which is essentially utilitarian, but advertising is actively consulted as a source of information on particular makes and models.

All these people are prospects for a car manufacturer, since they buy cars, yet advertising has different tasks for each group. For the repetitive buyer, advertising serves to create a feeling that the time to buy is right now. It keeps the public informed of new automotive developments, relates the make to the local dealer, and assures the potential purchaser of the value he is getting. For the emotional buyer, the main task of advertising is to build a brand image consistent with his own aspirations or values. (At one time, social status was preeminent; then the reverse snobbery of simplicity and fuel economy took over for some car buyers.) Image also creates the feeling that new important improvements are constantly on the way to support this type of buyer's feeling that the car means pleasure, excitement, and adventure. For the logical buyer, advertising must provide the specific factual information needed for reference to compare different makes.

Like users of consumer products, media users may also be distinguished on grounds that go beyond the more conventional classifications. In those cases where the standard demographic characteristics yielded no points of particular distinction, attempts have been made to differentiate media audiences in psychological terms.

Readers of *Harper's* and the *Atlantic*, matched against nonreaders of identical income, age, and other attributes, have been shown to engage in more foreign travel, drink more Scotch, and write more letters to their Congressmen. Media also have turned an apparent handicap into an asset, for example, by extolling the marketing virtues of the blue-collar housewives who read "confession" magazines.

On one occasion the media director of an advertising agency pitching for a new business account kept talking about the blue-collar market. He couldn't understand why his colleagues were silently grimacing until he suddenly realized that the only man in the room wearing a blue shirt was the president of the company whose account was being solicited.*

Personality and market segments

The catchword *psychographics* has come into vogue among marketers to denote not only uniquely individual dimensions of personality but also descriptions of lifestyle and life cycle position. As I commented in Chapter 5, psychographics introduces standardized, uniform descriptions of personality and values in an attempt to go beyond the sociologically oriented categories that have long been traditional in survey research.

An early example of the psychographic approach to market segmentation was a study we made at the Newspaper Advertising Bureau in 1972 through the Consumer Opinion Research Panel.[18] A national sample of about 4,000 men and women filled in questionnaires that included, in addition to questions about buying and media activity, 150 different self-descriptive items for each sex. Rating themselves from 1 to 5, men most often agreed that they wanted "children who turn out well" and least wanted "more time to take part in demonstrations and protests." Women most often agreed that they wanted "a very good relationship with my children" and disagreed that "holding public office would appeal to me." Fewer women wanted a boat than agreed that "I think most people don't realize how much our lives are controlled by plots hatched in secret places." Fewer men wanted to be a clergyman or an astronaut than to be a successful gambler or to be on a professional sports team.

The self-assessments covered personality, aspirations, and social roles or lifestyles. Thus, under the heading of personality, women described themselves in ways that were reduced by factor analysis† to terms that might be described as "affection-seeking" and "phlegmatic" (among quite a number of possible attributes); men as "cynical" or "thrill-seeking." Under the heading of aspiration, women rated themselves on traits like "feel more alive" and "tension free"; men on "acts of physical daring" and "religious salvation." Women's social roles included "capacity for status" and "prudent shopper," and men "dining out" and "escape from work."

A further set of statistical computations made it possible to classify all the

---

*Richard Baxter reports this poignant tale.

†Factor analysis is a statistical procedure originally developed by the statistician Charles Spearman, in which correlations are computed among a considerable number of variable items (which may be attributes or answers to questions). These are progressively distinguished and reduced to a limited number of factors, each of which is largely independent of the others, but each of which closely relates to some of the original items.

men into eight mutually exclusive groups and to do the same with all the women. Each group was then provided with an appropriately catchy name (for women, the "conformist," the "puritan," the "drudge," the "free spender," the "natural contented woman," the "indulger," the "striving suburbanite," and the "career seeker"; for men, the "quiet family man," the "traditionalist," the "discontented," the "ethical highbrow," the "pleasure-oriented," the "achiever," the "heman," and the "sophisticate"). For example, the conformists believe "children should always obey their parents" and don't want "to live abroad for a while." The puritans "believe in a life hereafter" and disagree that "when I see something I like, I want to buy it right away."

The most distinctive psychographic profiles were found for products and services whose use was limited: air travel and alcoholic beverages, for example. For universally used products like toothpaste, there was little difference among the various groups, but even with such products, there were sharp distinctions among users of individual brands. In the case of paper towels, the heaviest using psychographic group was only 7 percent ahead of the lightest using group, but there was a 40 percent spread between the usage of one leading brand by the "puritans" and the "career-seekers."

To what extent were the differences we found in consumption and media behavior a reflection of inherent psychological differences and to what extent were they merely refractions of underlying characteristics? I observed at the start of this chapter that an intelligent classification of consumers for any commodity requires that they be separated by sex, age, income, education, ethnicity, city size, and other standard demographic descriptions. Differences in reported behavior (usage of a product) or attitude (preference for a brand) between men and women, between young and old, or between rich and poor allow us to infer how consumption choices correspond to social role. The differences may be biologically determined, as they often are by sex or age, or they may express differences in lifestyle and values. The conventional social categories are synoptic summaries that encompass substantial variations in individual behavior. In using them, we tacitly assume that, other things being equal, a person with higher income not only has more money to spend but also has a distinctive outlook that governs the way he spends his money. We assume that, other things being equal, a person in a particular age bracket is at a point in his personal development that produces distinctive needs and motivations and that subjects him to distinctive interpersonal influences. For instance, SMRB's (1971) data show that young men (ages 18–24) are twice as likely as older ones (over age 65) to describe themselves as "venturesome," and nearly three times as likely to describe themselves as "influential." The richest and best-educated men are also above average on these attributes.

A BBDO poll found that high school graduates are happier than grade school or college graduates; young people are happier than older ones. Another study found that wealthy people perceive themselves as amicable, stubborn, dominating, intelligent, sociable, and refined, while professionals describe themselves as broad-minded, efficient, and trustworthy.[19] It is not surprising to find that rich and poor or young and old not only differ in their outer characteristics but that these summary social descriptions carry with them different clusters of personality traits and different patterns of perceiving and knowing the world.

The specificity of these personality attributes becomes even more meaning-ful in relation to consumer behavior when the standard demographic classifica-tions are related to each other. This process inevitably reaches a point of no residual return when the subsamples become too small to permit additional variables to be isolated and held constant. Yet within any demographically ho-mogeneous cell of a sample survey, there are always variations in product con-sumption and use, in shopping habits, brand choices, and resistance and attrac-tion to different promotional messages. This leads to a search for personality variables that might predict consumption patterns within demographic compart-ments or that might turn out to be even stronger determinants than the demo-graphics.

But the distribution of personality traits is not independent of social class, sex role, age position, and the other conventional cutting points. As an illustra-tion, consider birth order, which for a decade and a half has been widely studied as an influence on personality development and thus, presumably, on consumer behavior.[20] In a national survey of 1,800 adults,[21] there was only a slight indica-tion of differences between older-, middle-, and younger-born individuals. How-ever, only children turned out to be markedly more conformist and conservative.

The experience of being an only child does not arise by chance, nor is it perpetuated by chance. More of the only children are in households in which they themselves are the only members. They have fewer children of their own. More of them are in households headed by someone with a professional or managerial job, and more of them have completed college.

This merely documents something that is already well known: Higher social status is associated with smaller family size, and smaller family size is a way of perpetuating higher status because it reduces the financial barriers to upward mobility. Birth order is important as a determinant of behavior. But when we look at it in relation to social class, how are we to interpret evidence of its influence on personality? This question should also alert us to the difficulty of drawing intelligent generalizations from large studies in which psychological indicators are divorced from their social context.

Unfortunately, attempts to classify market segments by personality type often end up merely as restatements of age or social class differences. The results can appear naive or irrelevant, and a cautious critic looks for the random caprice of statistical error. Thus, one study reported that people who own auto-rental credit cards have a self-image that is "more spontaneously decisive, less self-controlled, and more domineering." Users of pain-relieving rubs are "more pragmatic," while users of laxatives are "egocentric." Volkswagen owners are "less anxious" than average, while Cadillac owners are "more anxious" than average, but both of them are equally "happy and outgoing."

Another study revealed that "Republicans are probably good customers for cartridge-loading tape recorders"—a spurious correlation involving several var-iables.[22] It was solemnly reported that viewers of "Daniel Boone" (a television show) were concerned over trade-in values in cars. "Venturesome" people liked late-night talk shows and disliked the "Beverly Hillbillies." Viewers of "Laugh-In" liked beer with body, while viewers of "The Lawrence Welk Show" liked it light. But these are tautological observations. To vastly oversimplify, "venture-some" people are smart, and educated people do not go in for cornpone humor. Viewers of "Laugh-In" were young, rich, and urban, and viewers of Lawrence Welk were old, poor, and rural. What additional psychological dimension has been added beyond the obvious symbolic linkages to lifestyle?

The answer is that the personality dimension adds value when it is used in combination with the more conventional ways of distinguishing people. In a series of studies of the television audience, ABC's Alan Wurtzel used 31 questions to divide the public into eight psychographic groups. Two of them (the "family oriented" and the "rigid and resistant") had almost identical age, income, and educational profiles, and yet they differed sharply in their television program preferences.[23] However, not all programs have an appeal to different personality groups. The audiences of the three network early evening news shows, in spite of their well-known and distinctive teams of newscasters, have identical psychographic profiles.

Another instance of the segmentation approach applied to television audiences was a large-scale study conducted by Ronald Frank and Marshall Greenberg.[24] They asked their nearly 2,500 respondents 139 questions that reflected their interests in such activities as house cleaning and horse racing and in such subjects as managing money and mathematics. They asked another 59 questions on personal needs ("to understand myself better, to lift my spirits"). With extensive use of the computer, they classified the people into 14 segments, described in terms like these:

> *Detached*. Low socioeconomic profile. Extremely few interests and activities and few psychological needs satisfied by them. Low scores on needs related to both intellectual stimulation and interpersonal contact and support.
> *Cosmopolitan Self-Enrichment*. Extremely high socioeconomic profile. Diverse pattern of intellectual and cultural interests. Physically active. High needs for intellectual stimulation, unique/creative accomplishment, and understanding others. Low needs for status enhancement and for escape from boredom.

It is better, in short, to be rich and healthy than to be poor and sick. (And if wealth and health tend to be associated, there is no mystery as to which comes first.)[25]

The authors set out to compare their "interest-based segmentation of audiences" for specific types of television programs with the "more traditional demographic-based" approach. Their report stated proudly that "adding the interest segmentation scheme to the demographic one already in frequent use (which was represented by only the two variables of sex and age) results in an increase of explained variance of 3.1 percentage points." The fact is that it still left 91.5 percent of the difference in audience profiles unaccounted for.

One explanation may be found in the study's finding that 71 percent of television viewing is done in the company of someone else. Thus, it is only to be expected that prime-time network audiences for different kinds of programs are not sharply distinctive and that viewing patterns do not necessarily mirror the respondent's own interests. And since television viewing is a pastime activity, inertia keeps many viewers on the same channel from program to program, across the gamut of content. Market segmentation as embodied in this kind of a study would have been inconceivable in the precomputer era when statistics were ground out by the sweat of the brow. Technological progress has provided the social sciences with an instrument for making the complex simple. It also makes it possible to do the reverse.

Sonia Yuspeh and Gene Fein have reported that when people were classified into "benefit segments," the resulting classification had no predictive value for subsequent research and that the underlying demographic factors provided a far better basis for segmenting the market.[26] A dozen years earlier, Harold Kassarjian looked at dozens of studies that sought to link personality to consumer behavior and described the results in a single word: "equivocal."[27]

But that is not the last word. In a far-ranging review of all the studies done through 1975, William Wells noted that the correlations between psychographic measures and consumer behavior are generally low, "with many close to zero." Still, he concluded that "the predictive validity of psychographic variables is likely to be substantially higher than the predictive validity of the demographic attributes that have long been accepted as good, true, and beautiful in marketing research."[28]

But the sensitivity of a full-scale investigation of personality is a far cry from the use of a handful of psychological items on a questionnaire devoted essentially to other subjects. This can yield at best only hazy intimations of a respondent's personality. And yet the practice has found wide use.

The VALS (Values and Life Style) scale developed by the Stanford Research Institute and adopted by SMRB typifies recent methods developed under the heading of psychographics. Thirty self-descriptive questions (partly demographic and partly psychological) are used to separate the population into nine segments: "need-driven" people "who buy more out of need than choice" and who are subdivided into "survivors" (4 percent of the total) who are "distrustful" and "struggling for survival" and "sustainers" (7 percent) who are "hopeful for improvement over time." There are "outer-directed" people "who buy with an eye to appearances and include 'belongers'" (35 percent) who are "preservers of the status quo," upwardly mobile "emulators" of the rich and successful (10 percent) and "materialistic, comfort-loving" achievers (23 percent). Then there are the "inner-directed, who buy to satisfy their self-expressive, individualistic needs" and are divided into the "very individualistic," "I-am-me" (5 percent), the "experiential" (7 percent), who have "intense personal relationships," and the "societally conscious" (9 percent) who are "socially responsible" and indulge in "simple, natural living." In addition to these groups, which add up to 100 percent, there are the Integrated: "rare people who have melded power of the Outer-Directed with sensitivity of the Inner-Directed. Their lifestyle is one of tolerance and self-assurance; their buying style is oriented to ecologically sound, esthetically pleasing, one-of-a-kind products."

The astrological cadences of these descriptions are echoed in the oracular "imperatives" that VALS presents for media selection. For example, "Radio-television combinations are best adapted to Emulators, but they will also reach I-am-Me cost-effectively. Survivors, Sustainers, and Belongers are better approached through television alone. The Inner-Directeds and Achievers are exposed more to radio alone."

Michael Jones of the New York Telephone Company told an AMA conference in 1982 that the VALS typology had been useful in the reexamination of the company's product line of decorator sets. By evaluating each design, it was determined that some "segments" already were being offered several alternatives, while others had none. In telephone sales training, personnel were instructed to be sensitive to certain key words that would permit them to "type" their customers. According to Jones, "Belongers" are "very sensitive to high prices and discounting, so for sets that appeal to belongers, we considered offering discounts." Since they have a "strong family orientation," the "Reach out and touch someone" campaign was developed to appeal to their emotions.[29]

And *Dun's Review* reported that "Merrill Lynch & Co., Inc. changed the thrust of its 'Bullish on America' campaign when VALS indicated that its prime customers were achievers, while its bull-herd had greatest appeal to belongers. It kept the bull, but deftly shifted the focus by showing a single animal, with the slogan, 'A breed apart.' " Apparently the advertising business always has room for more bull.

Demographic categories and social change

The realities of a fast-changing American society have made the classic structural definitions of the social order more and more suspect—or even irrelevant. The advertising strategist who recognizes that a person's choice of both media and products reflects his particular social environment must also recognize that the meaningful distinctions between one environment and another are not limited to such classical determinants as city size or household income. Anxieties over crime, schools, and taxes may be the most pertinent considerations.

Marketers today must advertise, distribute, and sell their wares against a background that seems hardly the same from one day to the next. Consider the implications of just a few important factors: age, mobility, education, women's roles, family structure, suburbanization, ethnicity.

Age. The changing age composition of the population has created new self-conscious interest groups of people in the same age bracket who have been shaped more by a common historical and social experience than by family income. The post-Vietnam War generation of adolescents represents a community of interests, values, and heroes, and a certain community of consumption styles just like the Vietnam War generation before it. Much the same might be said of the growing group of aged people with considerable remaining life expectancy who are modestly affluent as a result of social security and company or union retirement plans. The emergence of such age-interest groups, with their own special product interests and symbolic focal points, represents a major new development. But the visibility of an age group changes along with the age mix of the population itself. In 1970, 4 out of 10 Americans were under the age of 21. In 1990, the proportion will be 3 in 10. The actual numbers of those under 21 dropped from 81 million in 1970 to 75 million in 1983.

Mobility.   In the past 30 years, the number of cars has grown 2.5 times faster than the number of people, and the car today is typically a personal rather than a family utility. Thus shopping goes on over a wide orbit, affecting the retailer's advertising requirements.*

The "baby boom" generation was on the move. (Among those in their twenties, 68 percent moved in a four-year period in the mid-1970s, half to another part of the country.) This great increase in personal mobility reduced the sense of rootedness in the home community, changed the relative position of local and national media, and presented retail advertisers with the need to reassert their identity to the many prospective shoppers who had not grown up with their stores. The mobility of the population was creating a national buying public that was increasingly cosmopolitan in outlook and less differentiated by regional styles of consumption (even though chicory-flavored coffee is still popular in Louisiana). The dispersion of retailing to shopping centers and the concentration of retailing in chain-owned stores tended to give the American landscape an increasingly uniform appearance.

Education.   The rise in the average level of schooling has been phenomenal, initially spurred by veterans' benefits after World War II and the wars in Korea and Vietnam. This was carried forward by the economic boom of the 1950s and 1960s and the student loan programs of the 1970s. In 1952, 17 percent of the civilian labor force had attended college. By 1981, the proportion was 36 percent. This trend upgraded tastes, modified media habits, and increased the public's capacity to absorb information. Increased education moves people away from broadcasting and toward print. They also move in the direction of more sophisticated content and specialized media that meet broader interests. They become information *seekers*.

There are ample causes to complain about the deficiencies of the American school system. (In New York City, half of the students drop out from the ninth grade on.) Complaints about the schools seem to reflect higher levels of aspiration. But what is commonly regarded as a decline in reading skills may actually represent a decline of reading interest. The average reading and writing abilities of American students did not change significantly during the 1970s.

The rising level of education and the functional demands of a complex industrial society have fostered secularism and a weakening of the traditional moral code. They have also raised the level of public tolerance for racial minorities, for nonconformity, for idiosyncracy in belief and in personal habits. In an incredibly heterogeneous and urbanized country, there is more room for variety than on Sinclair Lewis's "Main Street." The shift in attitude is most dramatic when young people are compared with older ones. Tolerance for homosexuals,

---

*Out-of-store shopping of all kinds—by catalog, mail, and phone—has shown a steady increase, and the Sears catalog is already on videodisc. Even a minor shift of, say, 10 percent of general merchandise purchases out of stores can have a dramatic impact on retailing and on advertising.

unmarried couples, people with beards and long hair, and employees who wear sneakers to work has accelerated the differentiation of lifestyles and thus has had interesting marketing implications.

Women's Roles. Perhaps the most important long-term trend that has changed the marketing environment is the rising participation of women in the work force. The proportion went from 43 percent of those between the ages of 18 and 64 in 1960 to 62 percent in 1983. (Among those 20-44, it was 70 percent.) This movement added substantially to family purchasing power, since households in which both the wife and the husband work have 22 percent greater average income than those with a full-time housewife and a working husband. Apart from having more money to spend, women who work have a greater variety of consumption needs and wants than those who don't. By their own reports, they lead far more stimulating lives, go out more, and enjoy greater esteem both in their own eyes and in the eyes of their sisters who stay at home. In 1971, 63 percent of full-time housewives described themselves as living "a full life." By 1979, this had dropped to 45 percent.[30]

Working women retain major domestic responsibilities; 59 percent of the mothers of children under 18 held jobs (or were seeking them) in 1983. And although women continue to be concentrated in less skilled and less remunerative jobs than men, a growing percentage have entered management and the professions. This reflects their improved level of educational attainment. What had been a substantial gap between women and men in years of schooling typically completed was virtually eliminated during the 1970s. The number of women enrolled in colleges actually passed the number of men.

Although all this had immediate effects on patterns of living, consuming, and buying, it had other important effects of a more subtle kind. As career inspirations became the norm for young women, their relationships with men underwent a change. Household routines were altered as men assumed more of the domestic chores, including child care. This meant that men as well as their working wives were under more time pressures, leaving less time available to be spent with media and other leisure pursuits and enhancing the value of informative advertising that saves time and steps.[31]

Intertwined with these changes in women's role was the sexual revolution. It followed the widespread adoption of the birth control pill and the loosening of traditional reverence for authority in the revolutionary mood of the Vietnam war period.

Family Structure. And home itself is a different place than it used to be. That picture book family of a working father, a mother at home, and two school-age children accounted for only 7 percent of all U.S. households in 1981. More families had a handicapped child than had two children with a mother at home. Marriage takes place later; the divorce rate doubled in the 1970s, and there are fewer children in the average household. In that same decade, the number of singles went up 16 percent; female-headed households 49 percent; there were more households of two or more unrelated individuals living together. (Yet to keep this in perspective, 97 million Americans lived as married couples in 1981;

only 2.7 million as unmarried ones.) One- and two-person households grew to 55 percent of the total. All this affected buying habits. Convenience foods and single-serving packets represented a manufacturing response. The demand for household furnishings and appliances kept pace with the formation rate for households, which grew 115 percent more rapidly than the number of people between 1970 and 1983.

Changes in family structure not only affect consumption patterns. They also affect communications media and vice versa. Television intrudes into the time that previous generations spent in conversation, play, or common projects. This has weakened the mutual allegiance of family members and the emotional bonds that are the basis of trust and understanding. The impersonal communication of the media substitutes, to a degree, for the close interpersonal family communication of the past. Members of a household are less likely to share the same reading matter and the same broadcast programming. And all this influences the way people perceive advertising.

During the 1970s, the pathological manifestations of social strains were seen in rising rates of drug use, youthful suicide, and illegitimate births. The "youth movement" of the Vietnam War period and its "counter culture" produced a variety of new forms of self-expression in religion, the arts, and personal adornment. Among children of an affluent upper-middle class, there was a widespread rejection of many of the strivings for social status and material possessions that had been a dominant feature of American life since the day after the Pilgrims landed. This affected the content of advertising and even the design of products. It gradually dawned on corporate brand managers and agency copywriters that commercials could no longer be addressed to women who had been slaving over a hot stove all day or to householders whose main concern in life was keeping up with the Joneses.

Suburbanization.   Another development reflects the rapid shifts in the American population and the crumbling (by court decree) of the rural political dominance that traditionally kept state legislatures under the control of a conservative and often benighted minority element.

The urgent needs of urban areas in housing, transportation, and recreation have profound implications for marketing. In 1980, 68 percent of Americans lived in the metropolitan areas, a growing majority of these in the suburbs. The growth of the metropolis went hand in hand with the deterioration and population losses of central cities. Suburbs spread into exurbia, housing white working-class refugees from urban cores inhabited in increasing proportions by minority groups.[32] Population shifted to Southern and Western states, creating problems for those areas as well as for the aging cities of the North.

These developments have shattered traditional community identifications that formerly gave some cohesion to the social order. Not many Americans can just walk down the village street to their jobs, their shopping, their bank, their dentist, and their friends. The result is a vastly increased volume of communications to sustain these widely scattered relationships. In 1980, there were 200 billion telephone calls made in the United States and 100 billion pieces of mail handled by the Postal Service. The effect of social changes on the distribution system is generally understood by merchants concerned about the future of "Downtown" and by newspaper publishers faced with the loss of both retail advertisers and subscribers. Today, nearly half of all retail business is done in shopping centers, as distinct from the traditional urban centers or shopping districts or streets.[33] But social changes have had an equally great effect on people's values and on what they do with their money, as well as with where and how they buy. Yet the impact of significant social change on individual consumption patterns is rarely encompassed by consumer surveys.

The Ethnic Factor. Ethnicity may make tremendous differences in consumption style even in a country where egg foo yung, pizza, and matzo-ball soup are all part of the priceless national heritage. In an analysis of liquor consumption in Ohio, Frederick W. Williams, Jr.[34] demonstrated that bourbon predominates in the rural and small-town counties where the population is of native American stock, while blended whiskey (everybody's type, with its "neutral spirits") is favored in the big cities with their diversified population of more recent immigrant ancestry.

Only rarely have media analyzed their own audiences along ethnic or religious lines, although it is obvious that differences exist that parallel the different occupational, educational, and political complexion of different ethnic groups in the United States. Foreign language media are not (except in Spanish) any longer the best way to cover any ethnic group. When the advertiser does go after particular ethnic segments, he most commonly uses a creative approach that also has an appeal for the rest of the market he must cover to reach his target. A 1970 study by the Newspaper Advertising Bureau demonstrated that black models in ads added to their effectiveness among black readers, without reducing their effectiveness among whites.

Race and ethnic origin (with its religious associations) may have profound importance for the marketer. Blacks and the several distinct Hispanic minorities have won attention as unique marketing targets, with specially designed products and promotions. In addition to special requirements in cosmetics and special tastes in food, the average black does have some buying habits that are different from those of the average white at his own socioeconomic level. But the average black household's income is 44 percent lower (since there are fewer wage-earners), and it must be spent on a different array of purchases. (To illustrate: a four-week analysis of warehouse transfers to supermarkets made by *Progressive Grocer* found that stores in black neighborhoods sold only 14 percent as many olives as the average store, but over twice as much canned milk and 76 percent more canned peaches.)

The psychological disadvantages that blacks face seem to account for their heavier than usual reliance on prestige brands. The reputations of particular manufacturers for good or bad race relations have also influenced the position of their brands in sales to blacks.

By and large, the advertiser reaches far more blacks through the mass media than he can through *Ebony* or *Jet*, the black press, or black radio. But his advertising in minority media can build an identity for him that gives his messages in the mass media greater force with his target audience.

The civil rights movement of the 1960s brought about dramatic changes in the social position of blacks (and ultimately of other minorities). Blacks had virtually been nonpersons on the American media scene in general and were totally absent from advertising, except for ads in black magazines and newspapers and a presence on "soul music" radio stations usually owned by whites. Political pressure, followed by governmental actions, succeeded in integrating television advertising with nary a ripple.

Advertising surely has played a part in raising the aspirations of impoverished minority groups. No one can say to what extent the constant procession of commercials promoting the good things of life may actually have helped inspire the frustrations that found expression in riots and looting in the black neighborhoods of Los Angeles, Detroit, New York, and other cities during the 1960s and 1970s.

Redesignating market segments

The tremendous changes on the American scene compounded the differences that normally exist among people of different ages and social origins who live in different kinds of communities. Thus marketers were increasingly drawn to the use of shorthand rubrics to describe groups that, in an earlier period, might have been designated in strictly demographic terms.

"Swinging singles" conveyed a more colorful impression of lifestyle and attitudes than "unmarried and childless adults under 40 employed in white collar occupations, in metropolitan areas, not residing with their families of origin, and with at least some college education." It took just another small step to go on to describe such people as gregarious, actively interested in the opposite sex (and therefore in their own appearance), fun-loving (or "hedonistic," to use the prevailing expression), interested in entertainment and travel. Another step and one could point out that they were above average consumers of wine, running shoes, movie admissions, and health foods in small packets.

This procedure of fleshing in the demographic bare bones became popular as more and more syndicated research produced detailed marketing data and as electronic data processing made it possible to establish statistical linkages that "clustered" attributes so that these could be appropriately named. Some of the designations were derivations from "ideal types" popularized by the media: "Archie Bunker" represented a rough and ready, street-smart, tavern-centered urban working class milieu; "Dogpatch" conveyed an instant snapshot of an impoverished Appalachian backwater; "Blondie and Dagwood" symbolized the fast-disappearing traditional family of plodding lower-middle-class suburbia. But while comic strip characters have always vividly typified certain well-known personality traits and social settings, no one has ever confused these with the complexities of real human beings. The practice of market segmentation, based on factor analysis, has sometimes applied comic strip sociology to consumer behavior, with dubious results.

The 1980 Census spawned a considerable interest in "target marketing," involving the computer application of demographic data to small geographic areas in a way that permitted highly selective concentration of promotional pressure. Between 15 and 20 companies provide services that reanalyze Census data in terms that can be used for geo-demographical analysis.

PRIZM ("Potential Rating by Zip Markets"), a "Geo-demographic market segmentation and targeting" system developed by the Claritas Corporation, has rated all 35,600 zip code areas in terms of their population characteristics as counted by the Census and assigned them to 40 "zip-market clusters" and 10 cluster groups on the basis of a multivariate factor analysis of 535 measures of education and affluence, family structure, mobility, ethnicity, and urbanization. Taking a leaf from the Barnum and Bailey terminology of psychographics, each of the 40 clusters is assigned a memorable name like "Pools and patios," "Tobacco Road," "Shotguns and Pickups," "Sun-Belt Singles," "Furs and Station Wagons." (Some of the titles are less colorful, like "Hispanic Mix" or "Blue Collar Catholics.") The PRIZM classifications were adopted by SMRB and applied to the media and marketing data in its sample. Later, SMRB and Donnelley Marketing Services jointly introduced Cluster Plus, which similarly classifies ZIP code areas into 47 different clusters.

ACORN ("A Classification of Residential Neighborhoods") similarly offers a geographic subdivision of the population based on the 256,000 census tracts or block groups, which have been classified into 44 clusters bearing no-nonsense titles like "college areas," "low income, older population," and "middle income." ACORN designations have been included in the syndicated research produced by Mediamark Research Incorporated (MRI). (The data base for both MRI and SMRB was available through IMS, Telmar, and MSA, three media time-sharing networks.)*

Marketers are able to use this type of information in relation to their own sales figures on a neighborhood-by-neighborhood basis to obtain profiles of their customers.

Apart from the obvious applications to direct mail distribution, ZIP code information has been used to set up selective target marketing programs for magazines and newspapers so that advertisers can deliver messages only to the customers in areas they want to reach. ZIP code data have also been used to choose new site locations for fast food outlets and for automatic teller machines in banks, as well as to plan the introduction of new products. At least one magazine, *Apartment Life*, which had changed its name to *Metropolitan Home*, demonstrated to advertisers that its readership was changing by a ZIP code analysis of its updated subscriber list.

Customers in motion

Upon the concept of market segmentation has been constructed a rather substantial edifice of market research, data analysis systems, and selective promotional and distribution programs. Originating with manufacturers of national brands, the doctrine of target marketing has made a substantial impact in retailing as well, with its adoption by the major chains. Retailers' acceptance of the idea that promotion should be focused on the key customers is shown in the rise of direct mail catalog merchandising and the increased use of zoned distribution of newspaper inserts and of small-circulation neighborhood "shoppers" and

---

*We shall be saying more about these in Chapter 13.

weeklies. But in essence, market segmentation remains a theory and practice of national advertisers.

The national advertiser often thinks of himself as being in direct communication with the customers and takes for granted the retail environment in which the sale must actually occur. So let us think for a moment of the setting in which the buyer actually confronts the product whose advertising she has been seeing or hearing about.

The very first point to be made about this contact is that it is very transitory. Shoppers are constantly in motion, within a store and from store to store, and they are being continually stimulated and importuned by the sight of things to buy, quite apart from all the stimulation of their buying needs by advertisements.

Merchandise is perceived, compared, and purchased in context. This means that the salience and attractiveness of different potential purchases are highly susceptible to influence from the prominence and character of their display in the retail store. As customers move from one shopping location to another and from one store to another, new buying interests are aroused.

What the customer buys is not separable from when and where she buys it. The selection of goods available in a specific retail location, their juxtaposition and display, present options and influences that govern the ultimate choice.

Customers gravitate toward stores that are convenient and familiar, but customers also shop around for values and to satisfy their tastes. One-third (35 percent) of the grocery shoppers go to more than one food store on their major shopping trip of the week, and 28 percent visit different stores for their main food shopping on consecutive trips.[35]

For food and drugs, three out of four shopping trips are made within the home neighborhood or area, but 23 percent are made to locations at least 5 miles from home, and 9 percent are made to locations 10 or more miles away. For general merchandise, people are willing to travel much farther.* For inexpensive items, about half (47 percent) went to a location 5 or more miles away from home and 22 percent traveled at least 10 miles. For big ticket items, 60 percent traveled 5 miles or more, and 30 percent went 10 miles or more.†

Both among men and among women, a car was used in 1974 on over 9 out of 10 shopping trips for general merchandise to shopping locations other than downtown. In the preceding month, over half the women (52 percent) interviewed had shopped for general merchandise only or mostly outside their own neighborhoods, and another 15 percent shopped equally in their neighborhoods and elsewhere.

Why do women happen to go to a particular shopping area? Forty-four percent mention factors directly related to the location: closeness to home or to work, convenience, or the fact that they were already drawn to the area for another non-shopping reason. Eighteen percent express attitudes related to the character of the shopping area itself, its range of stores and services. Twenty-

---

*This merely verified a commonplace of retailing theory known as Reilly's Law.

†In our 1982 study, reported below, this last figure was 36 percent for the last purchase costing over $300, and two out of three customers who went this far indicated that price was the reason.

nine percent refer primarily to the assortment and quality of merchandise in the particular store to which they went. And 15 percent say they went where they did for reasons that might be connected with advertising, such as a sale or an advertised special. When questioned directly about the influence of promotions or sales, 17 percent of the women indicate that these might be an influence on the choice of the shopping area they visited.

The decision to go to a particular shopping area is usually made on the same day, often just shortly before the trip takes place. The spontaneity of the expedition, in a majority of cases, helps explain why a substantial proportion of all the purchases made are not planned or thought of in advance. That they are not, at least with respect to general merchandise, has been documented by two similar Newspaper Advertising Bureau studies. The first (in 1965) was conducted among women in five metropolitan areas.[36] In the second (in 1982), a national cross section of about 4,000 men and women were interviewed on the phone by Response Analysis Corporation about their shopping and buying of general merchandise (excluding grocery and drug store items and liquor) in the preceding seven days. They were also asked what purchases they were planning to make within the *next* week. A week later, they were called again and asked the same questions. In addition, most of them also returned a questionnaire we sent to obtain additional information about their buying habits. (Grocery and drug items were deliberately excluded from the questioning because of the sheer number of purchases and the great frequency with which such items are bought.)

For 85 percent of the general merchandise items planned for purchase "soon" in 1965, consumers had one or more particular stores in mind. The proportion was lowest (three out of four) for big-ticket items like upholstered furniture and major appliances. For low-budget items like children's clothing, more than 9 out of 10 prospective purchasers had a particular store in mind.

Where fashion, taste, styling, and color scheme enter into the decision, there is more shopping around. Big-ticket purchases are more likely to take place as a result of needs that have been perceived well in advance; the amount of money involved is apt to call for reflection, family discussion, and comparison-shopping before any action occurs.[37]

The fantasy that surrounds such merchandise can wax and wane in intensity and even in consciousness over a long period of time. As a lady told us in another study, "I'm very seriously thinking about buying a dishwasher, and I must say I've been seriously thinking about it for quite some time. For several years."

By contrast, an inexpensive article like hosiery may be bought when a woman sees it on sale or gets a run in her stocking. Certain merchandise has an almost inflexible demand: infants' wear, for instance. When baby needs new shoes, mama will get them—and quickly; the buying plans will not be dropped. When the expenditure is small, where gadgetry can exercise an appeal (as in the case of housewares), the consumer is more likely to make what is commonly labeled an "impulse purchase."

Even "impulse" buying usually arises out of a predisposition, a latent interest, an existing need ready to be triggered into consciousness. And in accomplishing this, advertising can play a part. An unplanned purchase may be made in response to a sudden need, as when the refrigerator breaks down or the car battery is stolen or a friend announces that she has gotten married over the weekend. Buying impulses are also created by all the consumer goods that people see around them—attractive clothes on passers-by in the street, furnishings in the homes of acquaintances, articles in shop windows.

Advertising is an important and continuing source of such direct stimulation to purchase. (In our 1982 study, 45 percent of those making an unplanned purchase in the past month said that the purchased item was brought to their attention by an ad, generally in the newspaper.) A store in a good location and with an established reputation might be able to generate a substantial amount of traffic without any advertising at all, but an ad that brings in even a few additional customers may be sufficient to make the difference between profit and loss. Many unplanned purchases are made as a result of the fact that people are already in the store shopping for something else and are reminded or stimulated by what they see. That means that for the retailer, advertising serves not only to sell what is advertised, but to generate traffic for the store itself.

How this works is shown in a 1976 study that measured the side-effects of [newspaper] ads for particular items of merchandise.[38] In seven different stores in different cities, 1,347 shoppers were interviewed at the sales counters where they were examining advertised merchandise, and 451 were later called at home to find out what they had bought in the store. Of all the people looking at the advertised items in the store, 60 percent said they had seen the advertising, and 34 percent said they had come to the store that day specifically because of it. Three-fifths of this group (61 percent) actually bought the item. (By contrast, of all other shoppers looking at the merchandise, only 20 percent bought it.) The proportion buying was very high for motor oil (where the customer was pre-sold) and low for dresses (where the ad's promises had to be measured against the merchandise itself).

Only one customer in five bought nothing at all in the store that day. Among those people who shopped for an item because they had seen it advertised, an additional dollar was spent for other merchandise (as I mentioned on page 40) for every dollar spent on the advertised item. Of all those customers who had seen the advertising and had bought what was advertised, 45 percent said they had decided to come to the store after seeing the ad. Three out of four had not looked for the merchandise in any other store. If this is true of the more focused shopping trips occasioned by a particular piece of merchandise news, it must be all the more true when customers visit a store with less urgent motives in mind.

Among all the shoppers who looked at the advertised item but did not buy it, 70 percent were in the store for reasons that had nothing to do with advertising (either for the item in question or for something else). But among those who bought the item, only 36 percent were in the store for other reasons. So while this study added another modest bit of evidence that advertising sells what is advertised, it also suggests a more interesting conclusion. Advertising churns up latent buying interests and thereby stimulates the movement of customers that is essential to assure the manufacturer of a continuing active demand for what he makes.

Most purchases are purposeful and practical rather than impulsive and frivolous. So is most shopping activity, in spite of the elements of play and recreation that undoubtedly infuse much of it. The degree to which search or shopping is converted into actual purchasing varies substantially from one type of article to another. For every actual purchase of a woman's coat or suit, shoppers visited an average of 3.6 different stores in 1965. For every purchase of furniture or a bed, 3.5 stores were visited. But only 1.4 stores were shopped relative to every purchase of small housewares, men's furnishings and footwear, boys' furnishings, girls' and women's undergarments and lingerie. In 1982, 72 percent of those who shopped for a major appliance within the past week bought one, compared to 97 percent of those who shopped for infants' or children's wear.

There are also substantial variations in the rate of conversion from shopping to purchase for different types of stores in different markets and also for individual stores of a particular type.[39] For example, of three department stores in Cleveland, one converted 40 percent of shopping trips for all items into sales in 1965, while its two major competitors closed the sale in 49 percent of the cases. In another city, one of the national chains converted 60 percent of the shoppers in its stores into purchasers for the average item; in the same market, another competing chain converted only 46 percent. This difference may be attributable to better use of floor space, better merchandising or merchandise assortments, or more or better trained sales personnel. Whatever the explanation, the fact is that it translates into a tremendous difference in sales and profits, with equivalent store traffic. (It also documents the difficulty of evaluating advertising, whose mission it is to attract the customer, but which can rarely clinch the final sale.)

The distribution of shopping among different types of stores (specialty shops, discount stores, national chains, traditional department stores, etc.) varies from item to item. Unlike many other aspects of consumer behavior, it also varies from market to market. This reflects the historical reality that markets have developed in different ways, each with a unique mix of retail establishments. Although many types of stores today carry similar merchandise lines and compete directly with each other for the patronage of the same customers, different types of stores are able to convert shoppers into actual buyers at a different rate for the same articles. Specialty stores, which still put a high premium on direct personal service, are best able to make a sale to people who are "just shopping around."

The tremendous spatial mobility of today's shopper as she darts from one store to another creates a psychological mobility reflected in constant revision of purchase intentions with respect to the goods themselves. A very high proportion (85 percent) of the purchases reported in 1982 were unanticipated; at least they had not been articulated as conscious intentions in the first interview a few days earlier. Of those who bought housewares and household supplies, 95 percent had not planned their purchases in the preceding week. Even 79 percent of the purchases of furniture were made by people who did not mention this intended purchase on the first interview.

Conversely, most buying intentions remained unconsummated, at least over a one-week period. Of every hundred who planned to buy women's shoes within a week, 44 actually shopped for them in the next seven days, and 31 bought a pair. Of the remainder, most continued to be in the market, but 19 had dropped their plans a week later as other buying interests moved into the forefront or as the purchase seemed less urgent for one reason or another. Of those who were planning to buy a major appliance, stereo, or TV set, only 30 percent actually went out and shopped for one in the following week, and 15 percent bought one. But only 7 percent dropped their plans. Of those planning to buy an item of automotive supplies, 55 percent shopped and 52 percent bought.

It is remarkable that, in spite of all this volatility, the percentage who planned to buy any given item and the percentages who shopped for it and bought it were practically identical in the first and second interviews, both in 1965 and in 1982. The apparent stability in the size of the market and in the extent of consumer activity actually masks a constant shifting of buying intentions and interests. The substantial number who drop their buying intentions must be replaced by new people coming into the market.

In both of the studies I have been citing, our interviews were conducted one week apart. But the same principle applies also when there is a much longer time interval between interview and reinterview. For example, of those planning to buy a car within the next year, only half had actually bought one a year later. Two-thirds of the cars bought are sold to people who had not stated an intention of buying one a year earlier.[40] And the same volatility is noticeable when people are interviewed at two time intervals that are only briefly separated.

Does the turnover in buying intentions for general merchandise also take place with respect to packaged goods? After all, 65 percent of all shoppers take along a shopping list when they go to the store.[41] This suggests rather planned, purposeful behavior. Still, the evidence clearly shows that a good many intended grocery purchases are never made and that many unanticipated purchases are. As I have pointed out earlier, supermarket shoppers are responsive to price promotions and specials featured in advertisements or by displays inside the store.[42]

Once within the store, the shopper may decide to use substitutes for some of her originally planned purchases; she may postpone others. And she is stimulated and attracted by items seen on the shelf that would otherwise not have come to mind.

The DuPont Company for many years interviewed supermarket shoppers just after they entered the store and re-interviewed them again after the checkout to compare their original buying intentions with what they actually bought. In the most recent of these studies, done in association with the Point of Purchase Advertising Institute in 1977, 2,000 shoppers were interviewed. Of all the items they bought, 35 percent were specifically planned in advance, and another 15 percent were "generally" planned, but not in terms of a particular variety or brand. Three percent of the purchases represented substitutes for what was originally intended, and 47 percent were totally unplanned and represented decisions made in the store.

A wide range of variations among product categories was found in an earlier DuPont study among 7,147 shoppers in 345 representative supermarkets. To illustrate: 48 percent of the purchases of soap flakes and detergents were unplanned. Impulse purchases accounted for 82 percent of the magazine and book sales, 80 percent of the toy sales, and 74 percent of the soft goods purchases. Three-fourths of the white bread purchases, it was found, were planned ahead of time, but only two-fifths of the rolls. In the fruit and vegetable department, half of the purchases of oranges were planned, but only a fourth of the berries. Three-fourths of the meat buys are planned, but only half the fish. For branded packaged goods, the variations are just as striking.

One customer enters the store with a shopping list and a set of product decisions in which brand choice is already involved. The other customer makes her selection when she is confronted with an array of packages, each with its own connotations and memories, vivid or faint. Is the function of advertising the same for both? The constant turnover in the market merely pinpoints the problem faced by the national advertiser in determining who his customers are and how he can reach them. The target he faces is a shifting target.

Who is ready to be persuaded?

Like the atom, the market is in constant flux, and it may be described as "thin." The prototype of a "thin market" is one that represents a relatively small proportion of the total population but that is distributed among all types of people in all walks of life (the prospective customers for a denture cleaning agent or a dandruff cure might be collectively considered prototypes of this sort of market).

Markets that are huge in their annual volume are made up of buying decisions made by very small numbers of people in a given period of time. For example, in a typical week in 1982, American retailers sold over $365 million worth of shoes. But during that week (as shown in our study that year) only six persons in 100 bought shoes for themselves or their children. Similarly, only 28 adults in 1,000 bought any kinds of women's slacks, jeans, or shorts in the course of a week, and only 21 bought a dress. Fourteen in 1,000 bought a small appliance; 18 in 1,000 bought furniture; 3 in 1,000 bought an article of luggage.

General merchandise represents, on the whole, more substantial and less frequently purchased items than packaged goods of the grocery and drug store variety. But a number of studies confirm the principle that even the most commonly used products are salient for only a minority of consumers on any given day.

The Bureau of Labor Statistics' 1973 survey of consumer buying habits shows that (except for bread and bakery products, beef, and milk) even the most basic commodity food items are *not* purchased by a majority of households over a one-week period. There is some repeat purchasing of staples in the course of a week. However, on even the most active shopping day of the seven (Saturday accounted for a fourth of the dollar volume in 1976, according to the Food Marketing Institute) only a fraction of the active consumers buy each item.[43]

In a 1969 study among 2,438 housewives in six markets, only 27 percent bought bread in a period of about a day and a half ("so far today or yesterday"), and only 38 percent planned to buy it in the next day and a half ("today or tomorrow"); 11 percent bought cigarettes, and 17 percent planned to buy.[44] Seven percent bought laundry detergents, and 17 percent expected to buy them. Only 1.6 percent reported buying instant coffee and 3 percent toothpaste. Although these percentages may seem incredibly small, they can be verified by taking the total annual sales volume and dividing it by the number of shopping days in a year. (Dollar volume can be translated into unit sales by taking the average price of an item into account.)

As with general merchandise, the proportion with buying intentions generally is considerably greater than the proportion actually purchasing over an equivalent period of time. But these ratios vary, and for some categories (e.g., coffee, dog food, and canned or prepackaged meals) there is more buying than planning, suggesting a high degree of in-store response to special promotions.[45]

In the case of grocery products, the amount of advance planning, reflection, discussion, and fantasy that precedes purchase is, of course, negligible compared to most general merchandise items. Even for products that we normally consider to represent a big, broad market, the proportion of people who are sensitive, alert, and interested in the subject is extremely small. Yet to the advertiser there is nothing more precious than the few people who are in the market and ready to buy right now. This brings us back to the problem of matching the characteristics of marketing targets and media audiences, because it forces us to question the utility of the concept of the heavy user. That is because the few people in the market for any item at any given moment are apt to be widely scattered throughout the population. We are not likely to find them all clustered in one place.

The established doctrine in marketing says that if 30 percent of the people buy 60 percent of the product, they should get 100 percent of the advertising targeted to them. Every brand manager worships at the same altar and studies the same divinely inspired computer printouts. The result is that we move closer and closer to a situation where 100 percent of the advertising would go against 30 percent of the consuming public, and the remaining 70 percent get the gleanings, and those begrudgingly. Across the country, billions of dollars' worth of goods and services are consumed by vast sectors of the public who are increasingly scorned by advertisers because they fall below the averages. The disparity will accelerate as we move further in the direction of pinpoint marketing.

The best possible example of sensible targeting might be by sex, even though it is widely known that 60 percent of the shopping at supermarkets is by men, alone or accompanying women. There is no good reason why a pantyhose manufacturer should waste advertising messages on men, although our 1982 shopping survey found that in no case are all the purchases of any type of item made by members of one sex. Women account for 24 percent of the purchases of men's wear, men for 24 percent of the purchases of household supplies.

But the degree to which the customers are dispersed is obscured by market analysis in which percentages are based on the "independent variable" (like sex or age) on which consumer actions or attitudes are assumed to depend (rather than the other way around). This technique aims to establish cause-and-effect relations. If we think rich people buy more of a product than poor ones, we look at purchases income group by income group, so that the percentages are based on 100 percent of the rich compared with 100 percent of the poor. When this is done, comparatively small differences between the profile of users and that of the general population blow up into what appear to be large differences.

For example: usage of frozen vegetables goes up directly with income. In a month, 24 percent of the families with high incomes ($40,000 and over) buy seven or more packages. That proportion is half, 12 percent, among those with low incomes of $10,000 and less. This is a substantial difference. But let's consider the actual distribution of heavy users in relation to total population. Seventeen percent of the heavy users are in the high income category compared with 11 percent of the total population. At the other end, 19 percent of the users have low incomes compared with 25 percent of the population. Now the differences in profile look far less overwhelming.[46]

To a certain degree, purchasing patterns can indeed be explained by the social or personality characteristics of the consumer. Better educated customers, for example, are more likely to read labels, note unit prices, buy private label merchandise, and switch brands. Individual stores, by their pricing policies, merchandise choice, and style of presentation and service tend to attract customers of a certain kind.

But a great deal of shopping activity simply cannot be explained in these terms. It rather reflects the enormous volatility in the market itself and the complex and partially random interaction of customer movement and merchandise offerings.

In 1982, 27 percent of adults were in households with incomes over $30,000. They accounted for 29 percent of all the purchases of women's wear in our own survey and 41 percent of the purchases of men's wear. (Obviously, they also bought more expensive dresses and suits, so their dollar value to the retailer was even greater.) But the 73 percent of adults with household incomes under $30,000 made 71 percent of all women's wear purchases and 59 percent of all men's wear purchases; they accounted for 66 percent of all the furniture buys, 69 percent of all the small appliance buys, 65 percent of all the hardware buys. So while it is true that rich people are especially worth having as customers, few advertisers would be able to survive very long on their business exclusively.

A similar point can be made when shoppers are separated by age. Many marketers today regard young adults as an especially desirable target. People under 35 make up 32 percent of the adult population and make half of the purchases of books and records and (being young parents) of infants' and children's wear, of toys and games. But even in those categories, half the purchases are made by people over 35, who account for the lion's share of sales in virtually every other product classification.

In the very thin market as it exists on any given day, the actual buyers are very widely scattered through the income, age, and educational spectrum. And they are not easy to pinpoint.

When the advertiser aims his effort at heavy users, he tries to match their profile against the profiles of various media audiences to deliver as many messages as possible against the most rewarding targets. The assumption is that if he can only get to these people, he can use all the powers of *persuasion* to get them to buy his brand. He must keep pounding his message home so that he attracts their attention and pulls them over to his side. But we have seen that at a given moment in time only a very small number of people have a potential interest in what he is trying to sell them, and these few people are usually not clustered together within easy reach.

Some of these people are looking the other way. They have lowered the iron curtain of indifference. Almost nothing the advertiser can say to them can possibly rouse their attention, much less persuade them. Some of the people out there have cautiously turned their heads. They may have some faint flickers of responsiveness or interest in the product. But within that cold and abstracted crowd, there are a few, a precious few, who right at this moment have turned around. Some are actually coming his way. Be they heavy users or light, they *are* actively in the market; they *are* ready to buy; they *want* to know what he has to tell them. The marketers might well be more sensitive to the mood of these real prospects, and to their desire for information, and not try quite so hard to *persuade* the many others who are simply not to be persuaded on the day he speaks to them.

Notes

1. Speech before the Magazine Publishers Association, June 4, 1964, White Sulphur Springs, West Virginia.
2. Wendell R. Smith, "Product Differentiation and Market Segmentation as Alternative Marketing Strategies," *Journal of Marketing* 21, 1 (July 1956): 3-8.
3. *What Is The Marketing Value of the Heavy TV Viewer?* NBC Research Bulletin No. 273 (G-R-TV), Marketing Studies, March 18, 1965, p. 1.
4. Samuel R. Gardner, "Successful Market Positioning—One Company Example," in Earl L. Bailey, ed., *Product-Line Strategies* (New York: The Conference Board, 1982).
5. Address before the Advertising Research Foundation, October 6, 1964, New York City.
6. Time, Inc., "Changing Roles of Men and Women in Brand Selection," New York, 1980.
7. Colin McDonald, "Individual Respondent Analysis Made Better with Complete Single Source Records," Paper delivered to the ARF Effective Frequency Workshop, June 4, 1982, New York City. *Cf.* also Colin McDonald, "What is the Short-Term Effect of Advertising?" Marketing Science Institute, Special Report No. 71-142, February 1971.
8. A. S. C. Ehrenberg, *Repeat-Buying: Theory and Applications* (London: North-Holland Publishing Company; New York: American Elsevier Publishing Company, Inc., 1972).
9. Ross M. Cunningham, "Brand Loyalty—Where, What, How Much?" *Harvard Business Review* 34, 1 (January-February 1956): 116-28.
10. Brand Rating Index for a six-month period between December 1964 and May 1965. (Brand loyalty was defined by BRI as mention of a brand as the one bought most often at both points in time.)
11. *Ibid.*
12. Frank M. Bass, "The Theory of Stochastic Preference and Brand Switching," *Journal of Marketing Research* XI (February 1974): 1-20.
13. Newspaper Advertising Bureau, "The Emerging New Food Shopper," 1982. *Cf.* also Louis E. Boone, "The Search for the Consumer Innovator," *Journal of Business* 43, 2 (April 1970): 135-40.
14. Private communication.
15. This study, conducted by Audits & Surveys, has already been mentioned on page 168.
16. *Cf.* W. Lloyd Warner, Marcia Meeker, and Kenneth Eells, *Social Class in America* (Chicago: Science Research Associates, 1949).
17. *Cf.* Lee Rainwater, Richard P. Coleman, and Gerald Handel, *Workingman's Wife* (Chicago: Social Research, Inc., 1959).
18. Newspaper Advertising Bureau, "Psychographics: A Study of Personality, Life-Style, and Consumption Patterns," New York, 1973.
19. Timothy Joyce, "Personality Classifications of Consumers: A New Approach to Measuring Self-concept." Paper presented at the meeting of the American Psychological Association, Honolulu, Hawaii, September 5, 1972.
20. C. Schooler, "Birth order effects: Not here, not now!" *Psychological Bulletin* 78 (1972): 161-75.

21. This was a 1971 study by the Newspaper Advertising Bureau.
22. Motivational Programmers, Inc., "The Creative Consumer Study Conducted for *Holiday Magazine*," New York, 1969.
23. The other groups are "organized participants," "community leaders," "other-directed traditionalists," the "alienated," "aimless and dissatisfied," and "liberal cosmopolitans." *Cf.* Alan Wurtzel, "People and Programs: The Application of Segmentation Techniques in Television Research," Paper presented to the Advertising Research Foundation Conference, New York, 1983.
24. Ronald E. Frank and Marshall G. Greenberg, *The Public's Use of Television: Who Watches and Why* (Beverly Hills and London: Sage Publications, 1980).
25. The relationship between social status and the sense of well-being is thoroughly documented in an analysis of national survey data from the Institute of Social Research of the University of Michigan. *Cf.* Joseph Veroff, Elizabeth Douvan, and Richard A. Kulka, *The Inner American: A Self-Portrait from 1957 to 1976* (New York: Basic Books, 1981).
26. Sonia Yuspeh and Gene Fein, "Can Segments Be Born Again?" *Journal of Advertising Research* 22, 3 (June/July 1982): 13-21.
27. Harold H. Kassarjian, "Personality and Consumer Behavior: A Review," *Journal of Marketing Research* 8, 4 (November 1971): 409-18.
28. William D. Wells, "Psychographics: A Critical Review," *Journal of Marketing Research* 12, 2 (May 1975): 196-213. *Cf.* also, William Wells, ed., *Lifestyle and Psychographics* (Chicago: American Marketing Association, 1974).
29. *Marketing News*, November 12, 1982, p. 10. For a full description of the VALS typology, cf. Arnold Mitchell, *The Nine American Lifestyles: Who We Are and Where We Are Going* (New York: MacMillan, 1983).
30. From two national surveys conducted for the Newspaper Advertising Bureau by the Response Analysis Corporation. *Cf.* also Rena Bartos, *The Moving Target* (New York: Free Press, 1982).
31. Between 1965 and 1975, working women reduced their time spent on housework by 3.5 hours a week, and working men increased the time they spent on it by 1.5 hours a week.
32. Between 1970 and 1980, cities of 250,000 and over lost 5 percent of their population. This tells only part of the story. Blacks and Hispanics became a majority in a number of cities; they represented half of the central city population in all metropolitan areas of over a million.
   An authoritative study by the Brookings Institution concludes with a pessimistic forecast of the possibility that urban decline can be reversed in the near future and finds that the problems of central cities are linked to a lack of real growth in their metropolitan areas. *Cf.* Katharine L. Bradbury, Anthony Downs, and Kenneth A. Small, *Urban Decline and the Future of American Cities*, Washington, D.C., Brookings Institution, 1982.
33. Estimated by the International Council of Shopping Centers.
34. Unpublished research report, Newspaper Advertising Bureau, 1964.
35. Unless otherwise noted, my data on shopping mobility come from "Shoppers On The Move," a 1974 Newspaper Advertising Bureau study sponsored by the Newsprint Information Committee. In five markets, 5,900 female heads of households were contacted three times each, twice by telephone and once with a mail questionnaire, by the Response Analysis Corporation. They also kept a diary to record all their shopping over a three-day period; 2,700 of their husbands also filled in a mail questionnaire.
36. *The Retail Customer: How, When, and Where She Shops and Spends* (Newspaper Advertising Bureau, 1966). This study was conducted by Opinion Research Corporation and spon-

sored by the Newsprint Information Committee. There were two series of interviews, seven days apart, with some 10,000 women in five markets ranging in size from Cleveland, Ohio, to Rutland, Vermont. The respondents were asked about all their shopping and purchases in the previous week for all general merchandise items. Similar questions were asked about shopping intentions for the following week.

37. In a 1980 study of 157 married women under 30, 27 percent reported they had purchased an article of new furniture the first time they shopped for it, 55 percent made two or three shopping trips before they bought, and 18 percent made four or more trips before settling on the purchase. This national survey was conducted for the Newspaper Advertising Bureau by R. H. Bruskin Associates.

38. The field work for this study (already mentioned on page 40) was conducted by Response Analysis Corporation.

39. Different types of stores draw different types of customers. For example, among shoppers at traditional department stores, 29 percent were college graduates in 1982; among shoppers at chains like Sears, Penney's, and Ward's, the proportion was 23 percent; for K-Mart shoppers it was 16 percent.

40. *Consumer Behavior of Individual Families Over Two and Three Years*, Studies edited by Richard F. Kosobud and James N. Morgan (Monograph Number 36, Survey Research Center, Institute for Social Research, Ann Arbor: The University of Michigan Press, 1964).

41. Fifty-eight percent make up a shopping list before they go to the supermarket; 30 percent check a list they keep; 66 percent check the refrigerator and cupboard; 41 percent check needs with other members of the household. Based on a national survey of 828 food shoppers conducted for the Newspaper Advertising Bureau in 1978 by Response Analysis Corporation.

42. Sixty-eight percent "always" or "almost always" compare prices when shopping; 41 percent go to more than one store to find the best food buys.

43. Similar findings were obtained in a 1974 study of 2,373 wives and 1,767 husbands in a national sample of 2,480 households made by Haley, Overholser and Associates. In the course of seven days, only the following packaged grocery products were purchased once or more by over a fourth of the households: margarine (30 percent), ice cream (29 percent), packaged luncheon meat (27 percent), laundry detergent (27 percent), paper towels (25 percent), packaged American cheese (25 percent), nondiet carbonated soft drinks (25 percent). On any one shopping day, of course, these percentages are sharply reduced.

44. The field work for this study was done by Opinion Research Corporation for the Newspaper Advertising Bureau.

45. According to the 1977 DuPont study, cents-off coupons were brought to the store by 24 percent of the shoppers and were used by 19 percent. Advertising and in-store displays had a mutually reinforcing effect on sales. In the case of canned vegetables, sales increased 91 percent with an in-store promotion, 149 percent when there was newspaper advertising, and 301 percent when both were present.

46. SMRB, 1982.

Chapter 11
The Concept of "Audience"

For a number of years the term "audience" has been essential to the vocabulary of media and communications research. The measurement of media audiences has absorbed vast effort and expense; the findings obtained have become an indispensable component in every advertising plan. The fundamental validity of the audience concept is rarely called into question. Yet can it be taken for granted? There are in fact five good reasons to be wary of this concept.

1. The word *audience*, in the vocabulary of today's advertising, means something quite different from its original meaning and has been applied for quite different reasons to the consumers of broadcasting and print.
2. Audience measurements represent far-from-certain estimates that are in no sense comparable among media.
3. Audience data are intangibles and abstractions but are often dealt with by marketers as though they corresponded to real "things" or physical objects.
4. The preoccupation with audience size has led to erroneous decisions in the management of media content.
5. The energy devoted to audience measurement has deflected concern from more useful research into the communication process.

Until modern times, the term *audience* was associated mainly with the theater. Recently, however, by a process of gradual extension, it has come to be applied in connection with those mass media that interest the marketer. Drama exists only in relation to the audience. Murmurs, rustles, coughs, and laughs communicate reactions back to a cast long before the curtain provides the signal for applause. Such an audience has collective characteristics, apart from those that characterize its members as individual spectators. An audience, in the classical tradition, must be conscious of itself, of its presence and purpose in being where it is, and of its own reactions. There is a social cohesion among the members of the audience, but this arises out of the spectacle. Drama arouses the Aristotelian feelings of awe and pity only to the degree that it can play on those universals in human experience and aspiration which are intensified in a collective setting.

It was only with the motion picture that the term "audience" began to be applied generally to a mass medium. The cinema theater is, after all, superficially identical with the legitimate theater in its seating arrangements, its fixed spatial relationship between spectacle and public, and its rule that the audience must sit in darkness and silence. But in the motion-picture experience there is no feedback, except for the long-run effects of box office receipts, fan mail, and articles by the critics. Essentially, the communication flows in one direction.

Audience and the mass media

It was logical for the term *audience* to be applied directly to radio and (later) to television, which, like the movies, reach people who cannot play back their reactions directly to the performers. As in the movies, there is often a time lag between the original performance of a program and the time of exposure. The listeners to a particular broadcast (and, in a different way, the regular listeners to a series of broadcasts) share a common experience and a certain consciousness of each other's presence. Quite early, the studio audience was introduced as a device to promote empathy on the part of the scattered listeners.

Audience as a *measurement* concept for radio evolved some years after the term *radio audience* had become a conventional part of the broadcaster's vocabulary. At a time when broadcasts were on the air for only a few hours a day and only a few people owned wireless sets, it was indeed logical to assume that anyone with the equipment to experience the miracle would naturally put it to use each evening. But when networks of stations (connected by telephone lines) were formed in the United States in the early 1920s and programming developed on a regular basis, it became imperative to distinguish the audiences of individual shows from one another.

The number of letters received by a broadcasting station provided only a crude indication of the number of its listeners. The volume of mail varied from program to program depending on whether it was solicited, whether attention was focused on individual performers, whether these were strong or popular personalities, and whether there was any departure from an established or conventional pattern of listener expectations.

As more and more radio stations crowded the airwaves, it could no longer be possible for a station to reach every listener within its signal range. Stations began to vie with each other in their claims of listeners, just as newspapers or magazines vied with each other in claims of circulation.

The units of air time that stations and networks sold to advertisers appeared to be fixed in quantity. Actually, they varied greatly in the size and character of the listener groups they yielded. The advertiser was not really buying an hour of time so much as the opportunity to present a sales message to a certain number of listeners. He knew that the number would vary according to the signal strength and popularity of the station and the timing and appeal of the programming in which his message was embedded.

Thus the survey method—to which advertisers had already grown accustomed in marketing research—became the source of listener estimates. As advertisers made larger investments, the need for accurate measurement of what they were getting led to greater innovation in research techniques, larger samples, and more frequently repeated surveys, not only on a national basis but also for individual markets. The "ratings" industry became big business. Measurement now consisted of estimating an intangible—"the listening experience"—rather than making a count of tangible objects—radio sets or letters to the station.

Uncertainties in audience measurement

What was encompassed in the term *audience*, as it now came to be used in relation to the modern media, could only be defined pragmatically in terms of statistics yielded by particular research methods. Thus, *audience* could be the number of people who said they "ever" listened to a particular show, the number who said they had listened to that show last week, or the number who reported they were listening at the very time they were interviewed. It could be the number who selected the show from a roster, or who listed it in a radio-listening diary.

Audience could encompass not only the respondents who were the source of information but other members of their families—on whose listening the respondents also reported. *Audience* could be the people who listened to *any* part of the program, those who listened to at least five minutes, or only those listening during the average minute.

Paradoxically, the most widely used and most objective broadcast audience measurement instrument available today, the Nielsen "Audimeter," is the furthest removed from the reality of communication. Since this device mechanically measures set-tuning, it leads to audience data expressed in terms of households (or "homes," as Nielsen somewhat sentimentally puts it), rather than in terms of the individuals who are actually listening or viewing.

But the very ubiquity of Nielsen ratings based on the audimeter—their undisputed place in the whole power structure of advertising—has led to widespread use of the household concept in other media-audience measurement (even marketing surveys). The use of the household as the unit of coverage becomes particularly open to question when household audiences are treated comparatively as "duplicated" (reached by more than one media vehicle) or "unduplicated" (reached by a single vehicle only), when the media vehicles in question may reach different members of the family.

Over the years, an enormous range of ratings statistics has been produced by a variety of definitions and research methods. Yet all these statistics represented the *same* thing, not only to laymen but to most nonresearch people in broadcasting and marketing. The true practical value of the measurements lay not in the absolute numbers, but in the program-to-program comparisons obtained by *any* given measure, regardless of its validity.

Each measurement assigned a single quantitative value to the term "audience"; yet what was being measured represented more than a single kind of listening experience. When the manager of a theater counts the house, he knows that there are a certain number of people in the auditorium. He also knows that they are, with few exceptions, present from the beginning to the end of the play.

In broadcasting, the count of the house may also be treated as a simple matter, but this does violence to reality. The members of the audience are unknown to each other; they are continually drifting in and drifting out; some of them are more attentive than others. In short, "audience" measurement requires that a rather considerable variety of media-exposure patterns be lumped together only for the sake of convenience.

All this had a profound effect upon the study of print media, where the established criteria of measurement involved that most tangible of yardsticks, paid circulation.

Until the establishment of the Audit Bureau of Circulations (A.B.C.) in 1914, circulation was a nebulous term that reflected the claims that rival publishers made in order to assert their own importance and prestige.

In 1869, Rowell's *American Newspaper Directory* employed the following symbols to designate the reliability of its data:

> The so-called Z attachment indicates that the paper finds it impolitic or impossible to make a circulation statement that will hold water; a Y means that the publisher finds it better to make no statement at all; the double question mark means that the rating is unsatisfactory, but facts to warrant a better rating cannot be got at; the plus and minus sign, indicating that two statements of circulation received from the office, covering the same period, give different figures; the double exclamation marks indicate that there is something about the paper that the advertiser ought to know before he spends too much money in it; the double daggers indicate that the publisher is a kicker from whom little information can be extracted; the white pyramids indicate that the paper may be dead; the black spheres indicate that the paper says it ought to have a higher rating, but is shy about furnishing facts to warrant the accordance of such a claim; the so-called doubt-marks, not to put too fine a point upon it, indicate that the publisher has been putting out circulation statements that were false, and got caught at it.

F. C. Goodin, business manager of the Spokane *Spokesman-Review*, wrote to its publisher, W. H. Cowles, in 1895, "Rowell & Co. are still pushing for an itemized statement of circulation. I told Mr. B. that I considered it a species of blackmail that should not be tolerated. He confessed that almost all metropolitan journals looked at it in the same light and refused to comply with the demand."[1]

The A.B.C. represented a great milestone in media research simply because it replaced an intangible criterion with a tangible one. The tangible criterion was a verified, audited, checked-out count of actual copies of publications that people had paid money to buy.

When radio audiences came to be measured in terms of people listening, rather than by the possession of sets, the resulting figures were of an order of magnitude that few newspapers or magazines could match in circulation. There was an immediate competitive need for a measure which acknowledged that a newspaper or magazine normally had several readers for every copy printed and placed in circulation.

The evolution of marketing concepts made advertisers and agencies more and more conscious of the need to direct advertising to the best prospects for their products. Questions about the kinds of people various publications reached were conventionally answered through subscriber surveys, but for widely circulated magazines and newspapers it became possible (during the 1920s and early

1930s) to use a sampling survey of the general population to locate readers and then to compare the total numbers from one publication to the next.

The application of the term *audience* to the readers of a periodical probably had its origins with the formation of the Magazine Audience Group in 1937. *Life*'s Cornelius DuBois wrote, "The term *audience* is used for convenience. . . . Since there were no philologists on the committee, it was decided that it was better to use the familiar word *audience* than to try to create a visual equivalent."

Life and *Look*, as picture magazines, had much to gain from the use of a measurement concept that incorporated the "pass-along" readers, giving them equal value with those who had subscribed or paid for the publication. But text magazines like the *Saturday Evening Post* and *Collier's* also benefitted from a media yardstick that produced figures in the millions, rivaling those projected by the radio rating services.

Not all magazine publishers recognized the advantage of the new concept with equal speed. The following advertisement, a full page spread in the New York *Herald Tribune* of Wednesday, December 7, 1938, is worth reproducing in its entirety for its sheer quaintness:

To Advertisers and Advertising Agencies
_____A CORRECTION!
Data from a survey purporting to show the number of readers reached by the four leading weekly magazines are now being shown to advertisers and agencies.

This survey credits Collier's with an amazing average of 15,900,000 people "who see, open, and read some part of each issue. . . ."

Despite the flattering total of readership found, we wish to make clear that Collier's had no part, financial or otherwise, in the conduct of this survey.

Nothing in our experience, during the nineteen years we have owned Collier's, in any way justifies an assumed readership of 15,900,000 people per issue.

A national survey recently made by our own circulation department among 166,600 people indicated that Collier's might have as many as 7,032,454 readers for every issue.

We believe, however, that any rating of magazine values by readership estimates, no matter how conscientiously compiled, is unsound and confusing; and harks back to the dark ages of advertising before the Audit Bureau of Circulations was established as the quantitative appraiser of circulations.

And until some standards better than those of the Audit Bureau are available, we will continue to claim for Collier's only its net paid A.B.C. circulation—2,633,878 average for the third quarter of 1938; and an intimacy and influence with the most Active Audience in the national market.

THE CROWELL PUBLISHING COMPANY
Publishers of: COLLIER'S • WOMAN'S HOME COMPANION • THE AMERICAN MAGAZINE • THE COUNTRY HOME MAGAZINE

It was only a few years before *Collier's* also leaped on the bandwagon, too late to save its life. (Sadly, not one of its sister publications has survived either.)

The first studies that applied the term *audience* to magazine readership were concerned primarily with the evolution of techniques to validate the reader's claim that he actually had read the magazine in question.[2]

As more audience studies of print media were completed, rival sets of data emerged measuring what appeared to be the same thing. In part, this was because different methods were used. Variations also resulted from a combination of ordinary sampling errors, differences in statistical adjustment procedures, and divergences in sampling and interviewing techniques. For some time, they also arose from different limitations placed on the universe to be sampled in terms of geography or age (for example, all individuals over 10, over 15, over 18, or over 21). However, since the early 1960s, surveys of the adult audience have conventionally been conducted among persons of 18 and over.

In most readership surveys of magazines and newspapers, the publications that order and pay for studies have different objectives than the people who ultimately use the findings. This contrasts with the common practice in market research, in which the survey specialist works directly for a client who has certain questions he wants answered. (It also differs from the practice of the broadcast ratings services, to which the advertiser and agency must subscribe, even though the broadcasters pay the lion's share of the cost.)

Advertisers and *agencies* are the ones who eventually put print media research to work in preparing plans and allocating budgets, but it is the *publisher* who picks up the check—both because it is expected of him and because he hopes to promote the findings in such a way as to demonstrate the desirability of his publication. There is, of course, just one magazine that can claim the largest number of readers, but it is only an exceptionally unimaginative advertising manager who cannot discover or define some criterion of readership or some category of magazines in which his publication will rank first, whether in terms of circulation or of size or quality of audience, "accumulative audience," "primary readership," "cost per page," "cost per thousand," "cost per ad readership opportunity," "time spent in reading," "reading days," "length of time in the household," "number of times picked up," "ad page exposures," or in terms of "reader heat," "depth of reading," "reader impact," and "reader loyalty," as demonstrated by either the *high* percentage who buy it on the newsstand, or by the *low* percentage who buy it on the newsstand.

The highly competitive character of the publishing business was for many years reflected in its research. Each publication has its strong and weak points, and in the era of customized surveys, it was likely to order the type of study most likely to produce a good case. At the very least, a duplication of effort resulted when separate surveys used slightly different methods to measure readership of the same magazines. Sometimes the sampling or analytic techniques contained a built-in bias that reduced the value of the results.

Thus, there were surveys of high school students claiming to be "nationwide" that were based on a sampling of 29 high schools (only 1 in a major metropolitan area). There were studies based on panels of "1000 *typical* readers selected from women who have written the beauty editor for help and advice." A magazine that ranked seventh in circulation and fifth among magazines with a preponderantly female readership once advertised a new survey of 3,500 women shoppers that placed it second among "magazines received in the home" and first among "magazines read regularly." The 14 stores at which shoppers were interviewed were not representative of anything except themselves, but the statistics looked very impressive.

The "validation" of samples was sometimes as spurious as the sample selection itself. In a report that once reached my desk the researchers had apparently selected a sample from their returns to conform with the circulation distribution of their magazine—an admirable procedure. Their statement read: "Well over 3,700 questionnaires were filled out and returned from all parts of the nation, but only 2,600 were used in this report. How closely the returns paralleled the actual circulation distribution by geographic divisions and city size groups is shown in the comparison on the next page." Thus the very method employed to overcome the biased response to their survey was quoted as evidence to support its validity.

With the passing of the great mass magazines (*Collier's* in 1957, the *Saturday Evening Post* in 1969, *Look* in 1971, and *Life* in 1972), the market dried up for large-scale audience research sponsored by an individual publication. In the newspaper field, local market studies continued for a longer period, often combining audience measurement with questions on shopping habits and reading interests. In 1969, the leading organizations concerned with newspaper advertising agreed to standard measurement methods, following the procedures developed in the Newspaper Advertising Bureau's 1961 national audience study.

During the 1960s, custom-tailored magazine audience studies were largely replaced by a number of new syndicated research services that periodically offered data on a variety of media and products, based on a single set of interviews. These intermedia services provided what to the layman could easily appear to be essentially the same information, although they were (and are) conducted by substantially different methods.*

---

*A combination of methods was used by the Nielsen Media Service, which was disbanded after several years of operation. Among the other syndicated offerings that came and went in the 1960s was the Politz Media Service, which relied entirely on personal interviews for TV as well as magazines. By contrast, the American Research Bureau conducted local experiments with an all-media diary and Sindlinger with all-media telephone surveys. Standard Rate & Data Service's Data Inc. used personal interviews to obtain all its data on product consumption and print media, but added a roster to measure audiences for a selected list of TV programs. (A "roster" is a list of programs, usually arranged by time periods and identified by channel or network, which the respondent looks at as an aid to his memory.) Brand Rating Index used a self-administered report form to measure newspaper and magazine readership and the viewing of a roster of TV programs. The great success of BRI arose from its extensive reporting of product use and brand choice in many merchandise categories. The service folded in 1970, soon after Willard Simmons demonstrated to an Advertising Research Foundation Conference that the BRI audience figures for magazines bore an uncanny resemblance to his own and the TV figures to Nielsen's.

All of the syndicated services, successful and unsuccessful alike, have solicited audience data on a great variety of media vehicles, more than was previously considered feasible for inclusion in a single omnibus survey. In addition, they incorporated a considerable number of questions on product usage and brand choice for a wide array of packaged goods.*

"Through-the-book" and "recent-reading"

Through the growing influence of the Advertising Research Foundation, the prevailing standard of readership validation in the United States eventually became the "through-the-book" method. This is a disguised readership test in which the reader is asked to leaf through a copy of the publication, asked his opinion of the different articles or features, and only at the end confronted with the question of whether he happened to read that particular issue. The method was originally developed by the Magazine Audience Study Group, which included such eminent figures as Cornelius DuBois, Paul Lazarsfeld, Raymond Franzen, Darrell Lucas, Elmo Roper, and Archibald Crossley.

The "through-the-book" method requires an actual copy of each particular magazine issue to be measured. This wily way of avoiding "yea-saying" (or respondent agreeableness) and innocent exaggeration worked very well as long as interviewing was confined to just a handful of major, highly competitive magazines, which was the case for a number of years. But with the advent of syndicated magazine audience research, it clearly became impractical for interviewers to walk around carrying full copies of all the measured publications, so slimmed-down issues were used instead, incorporating just a few major articles. This procedure is still being used in an annual survey of 19,000 adults by SMRB to measure 40 leading magazines. But for 100 other magazines, SMRB uses the "recent-reading" method, which the other principal syndicated research service, Mediamark Research, Inc. (MRI), employs exclusively for all the 190 magazines it measures among 20,000 adults each year.

The recent-reading method is standard in Europe and was first widely used in the United States for a research subsidiary of the J. Walter Thompson agency called Target Group Index (TGI).† This method uses a deck of cards, each bearing the logotype title ("logo") of a different magazine. The respondent shuffles the cards into different decks, according to whether or not he is sure he has seen the magazines they stand for in the past six months, and then is questioned further about the issues he claims to have read within the past week (for weeklies) or in the past month (for monthlies). In addition, MRI and SMRB both obtain broadcast and product information from a self-administered questionnaire that respondents are asked to complete and mail in afterwards. SMRB conducts two interviews, a month apart, with each respondent to provide esti-

---

*The implications of this omnibus questioning are developed in Chapter 13.

†TGI's founder, Timothy Joyce, formerly headed the agency's research operation in the United Kingdom, where the recent-reading method had been used for some time. In 1979, TGI was merged with SMRB, thus giving rise to that company's hybrid measurement. Joyce subsequently founded MRI.

mates of audience accumulation, reach, and frequency.*

Even when two organizations use what appear to be identical research methods, their findings are apt to look dissimilar because of their differing field forces, sampling procedures, and interviewer instructions. Needless to say, if they use different questioning procedures and timing, as MRI and SMRB do, the variations in their results are apt to be even larger. Unexplained differences in media audiences often appear from one survey period to the next, even in the reports of the same research organizations. When the data are expressed in their original form as percentages of the total population sampled, the variations in results obtained by the different methods are often fairly small.† However, the same variations are exaggerated—in terms of hundreds of thousands or millions of customers—by the practice of making statistical projections from survey results.

The 1982 SMRB report showed *TV Guide* with a total audience of 36,334,000 while MRI showed 47,236,000. *Family Weekly* had 25,520,000 readers according to SMRB, but 20,239,000 according to MRI. *Better Homes and Gardens* had 21,045,000 readers in the SMRB report and 34,231,000 in MRI's.

The variations in these figures, arrived at by different organizations at about the same time, are matched by the variations in the figures found in successive surveys by the same organization. Although circulation figures showed little change between 1981 and 1982, MRI's readers-per-copy average fell from 5.0 to 4.3, and total audience fell 15 percent. Asked about this, MRI's president, Timothy Joyce, "shrugs, and blames most of the changes on the recession, lower newsstand sales, and a troubled automotive market."[3]

Discrepancies in magazine audience estimates have made big advertising news. Magazines that have continued to sell the same numbers of copies have been reported in readership surveys to have widely different numbers of readers per copy in successive years. For example, *Esquire*'s paid circulation remained at 1.25 million copies, but its male readers, according to Simmons, fell 50 percent, from 5.45 million in the 1973-74 report to 2.75 million the following year. The Simmons report also said that *Time* had lost 14 percent of its readers from the year before, while its paid circulation stayed the same. It showed *Time* and *Newsweek* with an almost identical audience size, although *Time*'s circulation was nearly half again as large as *Newsweek*'s.

The repercussions of this survey were felt on Wall Street as well as on Madison Avenue. *Advertising Age* (December 16, 1974) reported: "Wall Street analysts concerned with threatened *Time* ad revenue losses have also noted *Time*'s poor showing on the new Simmons. Some have put cautionary notices on Time, Inc. stock in their customer recommendations." In the first quarter of 1976, *Esquire*'s advertising revenues were down 29 percent.

The year-to-year changes in the overall figures on magazine audience size are magnified when specific subgroups are examined. Salesmen for *Harper's* and

---

*Another service, Mendelsohn Media Research, covers 77 consumer magazines in a sample of 15,000 adults with household incomes of more than $40,000. Mendelsohn uses repeated mailings of questionnaires to come up with average issue exposure data.

†This lack of major variation might be interpreted as giving an advantage to the least expensive method.

Atlantic were pleased when the Simmons report showed they had the highest incidence of passport ownership among all magazines. The following year they had the lowest.

Between 1966 and 1967, *Time* showed a 26 percent increase in the number of readers who were managers of companies with over 1,000 employees and a 4 percent decrease among those employed in small companies with less than 100 employees. In the same period, *Business Week* lost 36 percent of its managerial audience in middle-sized companies, but had a 145 percent increase among government employees. *House Beautiful* lost 46 percent of its readers in households with children under 18 and 53 percent whose house was worth between $20,000 and $30,000.[4]

How can such differences occur? Willard R. Simmons has suggested that at least part of the variation may arise because "the fact that a magazine sold about the same numbers of copies in two successive years does not mean that the copies were sold to the same people in both years. Many publications have a turnover of thirty percent in their lists of subscribers from one year to the next. . . . A picture of Mickey Mantle on the cover of *Sports Illustrated* would lead to a somewhat different audience than a picture of Cassius Clay, a hunting or fishing scene, or perhaps a golf champion."[5]

But a better clue may be found in an experiment run by the Advertising Research Foundation on the 1964 Simmons study. Telephone interviews were made 10 days later with a subsample of those originally interviewed. The breakdown, by percentages, of those in the group who had different answers to various questions in the two interviews could be projected into enormous figures. For example, car ownership figures changed by 7 percent among the same people, which projects to 4,000,000 families nationally. In the second interview, 5 percent of the answers on smoking were different from those given in the first, which is equivalent to "switching" on the part of 6,000,000 adults. This kind of variation reflects the standard problems of interviewing people at two points in time.

Variations that are within the normal range of chance sampling error,[6] when they are projected, can look frightening to anyone who assumes that the estimates produced by surveys represent reality. When we recognize not only that these estimates are approximations subject to human error but also that at best they mirror phenomena that are constantly changing, we must be far less willing to take the term *audience* at its literal meaning.

To reduce the shock of inexplicable variations, some syndicated research services follow the practice of averaging the data from each new survey with that of the previous year. But the differences that a particular research organization shows from year to year are small compared with those between one organization and another.

The substantial discrepancy in the audience sizes reported by the two principal syndicated research services has created continuing consternation. This was not diminished when SMRB released the findings of its first survey after merging with TGI and adopting the recent-reading method for 33 small magazines previously measured by the more elaborate through-the-book system. For these magazines, the number of readers per copy rose by an average of about 90 percent. SMRB's response was to adjust the statistics by eliminating people who claimed to read fewer than two issues in four.

The Magazine Publishers Association, the AAAA, and the ANA raised $450,000 for a major examination of audience research methods, which was conducted by SMRB in 1979 under the auspices of the Advertising Research Foundation. In three parallel samples, with a total of 4,600 respondents, magazines were measured either in an interview using the traditional through-the-book method or by a combination of that and the recent-reading method.[7] Individual groups of magazines were presented in a rotated order, sometimes by one method and sometimes by the other. As in SMRB's own report, the smaller circulation monthlies came up with audience figures 96 percent higher by recent-reading than by through-the-book; the larger monthlies were 80 percent higher and the weeklies 27 percent higher.

Curiously, the through-the-book method produced scores that were about 10 percent higher for monthlies (though not for weeklies) when it was used in the context of an interview in which other magazines were being measured by the recent-reading technique. Since the research explicitly avoided any attempt to determine which method came closer to the real truth of what had been read, the exhaustive analysis of the data led to no conclusions as to which method was preferable. Moreover, nothing came of an elaborate effort to develop a system of "calibration"—by which each technique might be systematically adjusted to produce results compatible with the other.[8] Nonetheless, SMRB has lately been lowering its recent-reading figures with formulas based on "calibrated frequency."

To determine the level of magazine reading, Mediamark Research Inc. conducted 1,000 telephone interviews in 1980 in which people were asked about all of their reading of newspapers and magazines for each part of the preceding day.[9] The total number of readers for each major category of magazines was very close to the numbers projected from MRI's syndicated survey, so the report concluded that the through-the-book method understates readers of weeklies by a fourth and readers of monthlies by almost one-half. MRI's Timothy Joyce suggested that the method's screening procedure wrongly eliminated readers, that the interview was fatiguing, and that the "issue-specific" methodology prompted "memory failure" and did not capture "late pass-on reading."[10]

Countering such argument, SMRB's Valentine Appel pointed to experimental evidence of his own from a telephone survey of 700 New Jersey women in 1980-81. Appel's argument was built around the principle of "telescoping," which holds that the longer ago an event took place, the less accurate one's memory of when it took place and the greater the exaggeration of its recency. Applied to the field of audience measurement, it would imply that the recent-reading method would exaggerate the audience for monthlies relative to weeklies (since more past issues would be mistakenly credited to the past four weeks). When 700 New Jersey women were interviewed by phone about their viewing of 20 weekly television programs, the average rating (obtained in interviews spread out over a week) was 30 percent higher than in interviews conducted on the following day. The same procedure was then applied to nine weekly magazines, producing a 26 percent advantage for "recent-reading" as opposed to "yesterday" recall. Noting that this was in line with the 27 percent higher level of magazine audiences obtained by the recent-reading method in the ARF Comparability Study, Appel concludes that "telescoping" is responsible, since respondents are unable "to judge whether or not a particular event has occurred within the publication interval." Thus, "not only does the recent-reading method produce spurious audience estimates, it does so in such a way as to seriously disadvantage weekly publications relative to monthlies."

Yet another critique of the recent-reading method came from Time, Inc.'s Clark Schiller in 1980 after 510 interviews in Long Island shopping malls, using the technique with fictitious or defunct publications included in the roster. Projecting the results on a national scale, *Look* was found to have a current issue audience of 6,690,000; the *Literary Digest*, 1,220,000, and *Collier's*, 1,410,000. Among the imaginary titles, *Popular Sports* had 2,780,000 readers and *Newsevents* had 2,340,000.[11]

Michael Brown, a British researcher, also found audience levels for a defunct publication at 75 percent of its former level by the recent-reading method. From a 1979 experiment, he concluded that readership reports were highly sensitive to the positioning of magazine titles in the interview. "A woman's monthly shown to an informant within a group consisting only of women's titles obtained a higher level of readership claims by women—and a lower level of claims by men—than when it appeared among a group of titles appealing to both sexes."[12] But these are hardly the first times it has been found that some people can give confused or mistaken replies to an interviewer's misleading questions.

To balance the indications that print audience figures may be overstated, other studies suggest that they may be too small. In 1958-62, William Belson, a leading British survey research methodologist, used intensive interviewing about the circumstances of reading. He demonstrated that conventional methods produced both substantial underclaiming and overclaiming of readership. However, the underclaiming was by far the greater, especially as the frequency of publication decreased. (For daily newspapers, the intensive interviews produced levels that were 21 percent higher than the normal interview; for Sunday papers they were 18 percent higher; for weekly magazines they were 12 percent higher; for monthlies 61 percent higher.)

Newsweek's Stephen Douglas used Audits & Surveys in 1983 to investigate what magazines had been read for the first time "yesterday" and found that among 300 people, the reported readership levels ran higher than those reported by SMRB or MRI for an average day.

Three tests of reader "certitude" were conducted between 1977 and 1979 by Audits & Surveys for the ARF Magazine Development Council. In the first test, 208 people were recruited into a research laboratory with a one-way mirror, ostensibly to participate in a soft drink taste test. While "waiting" 15 minutes for the test to begin, they had the opportunity to read prepublication copies of six magazines, with their reading under observation. They were interviewed at home one day to two weeks later by interviewers who knew nothing of the initial phase. Not surprisingly, recollection of the issues read was related to the time originally spent with them, and it was much lower after two weeks than after one day. Even one day later, 15 percent of those who had been observed reading an issue were missed by the recognition technique and 39 percent by the recall method.[13]

Studies using the "recognition" or "through-the-book" method employ a preliminary question to filter out those magazines the respondent never or rarely sees. The statistician Jerome D. Greene points out that "regardless of home-office instructions, irresistible pressure builds up on the interviewer to keep down the number of magazines that 'pass the filter': he or she knows beyond a reasonable doubt that a respondent will not take the time anyway to examine 20 issues page by page."[14] (Audience figures are larger when respondents are asked about ten magazines than when they are asked about 60, as Audits & Surveys found in a study sponsored by Time, Inc.)

And Willard Simmons suggests that the problems of projecting from one day's reading to a monthly figure are compounded by the fact that "the same respondent who spent five minutes reading the issue yesterday may well have also spent an hour with the same issue one day last week or vice versa."[15] Simmons points out that the very times when people are available for interviewing may be the times when they might otherwise be preoccupied with reading (or viewing), so that their reports of the previous day's activities may represent an understate-ment of their real exposure. In the case of a working woman, "any day on which she can be found at home and interviewed must follow a day and evening she spent away from home with little chance to read magazines."

Why audience estimates vary

What is to be made of this continuing controversy? If the problems of valid measurement seem almost insoluble, this has to do with the inherent require-ments of syndicated research rather than with the deficiencies of either the through-the-book or recent-reading methods. The limitations of this kind of research reflect the economic constraints of the marketplace—somewhat more accurate research is very much more costly—but they also stem from the char-acter of research procedures. In the face of rising research costs, syndicated services have offered an economical way to pool information of common interest. As the demand by advertisers has grown for media information related to their own specific marketing needs, services have added more and more questions, covering such topics as chewing gum consumption and car rental habits. This has produced even more discrepancies in media research statistics, even more inexplicable jumps and dips from one study to the next, as attention shifted from the general population to the small subsamples of heavy chewing gum users and car renters. The most accurate research concentrates its inquiry to maintain the interest of those being interviewed. As the amount of miscellaneous information extracted from a single respondent has grown and grown, interview question-naires have grown longer and more tedious, reducing the number of willing respondents and weakening the quality of the results.

An additional factor in reducing respondent cooperation has been the grow-ing sense of personal insecurity throughout the United States, the suspicion of a stranger at the door, coupled with an increased volume of survey research. There have also been occasional abuses of the survey method to sell everything from encyclopedias to political candidates.

To try to overcome some of the problems of nonresponse, there has been a great shift toward interviewing by telephone, although personal contact with respondents has unique advantages for going deeply into a subject. Telephone interviewing brings new technical problems in designating respondents, in limiting the length of interviews, and in distinguishing residential and business phones in random digit dialing (a procedure for including unlisted phones in the sample).

In the human error department, media research takes its place as a subdivision of consumer surveys. Over a one-year period, the Advertising Research Foundation conducted over 7,000 interview verification checks on a variety of market studies. Although 95 percent of the original interviews could be verified, no more than 63 percent had been done correctly, meeting all specifications without error.[16] Statistical weighting techniques improve sampling by mathematically adjusting for various subgroups in the population. But when the computer is used to compensate for interviewing problems, new elements of statistical variance and new possibilities for error are introduced. It was only a step from justifiable "massaging" of the original data in the interest of improved accuracy to allegations that numbers were actually being fabricated (by services now deceased) in imitation of standard and acceptable sources.

The percentages in most media research no longer represent real people whom somebody actually questioned; they are percentages of magnetized impulses on computer tapes. This is, to be sure, in the interests of greater accuracy. In one national survey I supervised in 1982, using personal interviews with a probability sample of 1,979, the necessary "sample balancing" (to compensate for different completion rates in different population groups) inflated the computerized sample to the equivalent of 163,867 cases.

The use of elaborate statistical weighting schemes inevitably leads to bizarre disproportions in the value assigned to a single interview. The 1980 ARF evaluation of the SMRB service found that some respondents were weighted to represent 700 people, others 70,000. This procedure qualitatively transforms the relationship of the research analyst to his data. At any rate, most of the people who deal with media research statistics are not analyzing them; they are quoting them, either to sell advertising or to justify their purchases of advertising to their clients or employers. Users of the numbers don't want to be bothered by what they regard as trivial technical matters, and so, for a quarter of a century, since the beginning of regular syndicated research, they have been sweeping the details under the rug.

There is a routine acceptance of error when there is no firsthand feel for the fragility of survey data. When advertising buyers compare one report with the next, changes that may be the results of human mistakes and random probability can become the subject of endless preoccupation and concern. Thus, meaningless, often chance differences between percentages based on tiny subsamples can become the basis for allocating millions of dollars of advertising investments.

William S. Blair, publisher of *Blair and Ketchum's Country Journal*, believes that "the more money a magazine spends on the (syndicated) services, the greater the probability that it will go out of business. (Because the data are usually out of date by the time they are published . . . what you get is not a diagnosis but a post-mortem . . . one of the few postmortems that have been largely financed by the corpse.)" Blair argued that the services "have not been of great value to the magazine industry as a whole; have been of value to very few individual maga-zines; are not valid for small magazines, which may be the wave of the future, and have had one very unfortunate effect: the budget drain has been so great that the flood of innovative research that used to typify the magazine industry has simply dried up."[17]

Yet the services continue, because their data comfort the advertiser with assurances that his messages are reaching the right targets. In the real world of magazine space buying, agencies make their own judgments regarding the merits of one syndicated service or the other and commonly make their own arbitrary adjustments of the numbers to rationalize their choice of particular magazines for a schedule. The sophisticated user of research recognizes that "readership" is itself an arbitrary definition that covers everything from intense study to a casual glance and that the reader's relationship to a publication and its advertis-ing is not automatically determined by the fact that he has been counted in the audience. But how many of the users *are* sophisticated?

Syndicated newspaper research

Syndicated research on local newspaper audiences was also launched with a few abortive attempts in the 1960s, but received its first major test with the launching of the Three Sigma study of 34 markets by Willard Simmons in 1979. Simmons sold this service to his old firm, SMRB, in 1982; their survey that year met new competition from Scarborough Research, which was surveying papers in 50 markets.* Moreover, customized newspaper audience studies continue to be done by Belden Associates, Market Opinion Research, and more than a dozen other well-qualified firms, all of them following the standardized procedures.

Since the majority of U.S. newspapers are far too small to afford the expense of an audience study, the Newspaper Advertising Bureau devised a computer system, CAN DO ("Computer Analyzed Newspaper Data On Line"), to estimate audience size, composition, reach and frequency for schedules involving such papers. Circulation and population data, along with the figures from national read-ership studies, are used in these estimates along with the actual audiences reported from surveys done by 201 papers, representing 50 percent of total circulation.

In competitive newspaper cities, audience studies have been used with even more bitter rivalry than in the magazine field. The competition has been com-pounded by the inevitable disparities in what the audience figures show, not only as between the research services, but between studies produced by the same service.

Apart from the fact that the two syndicated newspaper audience research organizations produced figures for the same papers that were not always in agreement, their aggregate figures were also out of line with those from national studies of newspaper reading. For example, while the national SMRB report for 1982 showed that the average paper had 2.14 adult readers per copy (a figure

---

*The two firms merged their newspaper survey operations in 1984.

consistent with that from other sources), the papers measured by SMRB's 34 local reports and Scarborough's 50 reports showed an average of 2.7. Naturally, the disparity arose partly from differences between personal and telephone interviewing* but mostly from the fact that only papers in larger markets were covered in the local surveys. (Big city papers, with lower penetration levels, have more pass-along readership.) But as with other inconsistencies in media research, the glutinous reality is forgotten in the face of impressive-looking arrays of tables, converting reports of readership into hard "impressions" at so many dollars and cents.

Measuring broadcast audiences

The widely publicized discrepancies in print media research are often compared invidiously with the apparent consistency of the broadcast ratings. But this difference is illusory. Over a period of time, the ratings services produce parallel rankings of programs. But the absolute levels of audience size reported are to a considerable extent functions of the individual measurement techniques used.

Radio provides a good example of this. In 1966, several different methods were compared by the All-Radio Measurement Survey (ARMS), partly in response to questions raised by a Congressional Committee and partly because of a widespread conviction in radio circles that the medium had been shortchanged by inadequate measurement of out-of-home listening. The most accurate method of establishing the size of a program's audience at any given point is generally considered to be the "coincidental" interview in which people are caught in the act of listening to radio or watching television by a telephone call or a personal visit.[18] The ARMS committee, consisting of a group of distinguished broadcasting researchers, took as its standard a coincidental telephone measurement, which showed the average in-home quarter-hour radio audience between 7:00 a.m. and 10:00 p.m. to be 11 percent of the adults in the homes called. The comparable figures generated by other measurement techniques ranged from 7 percent with a telephone-solicited four-media diary† mailed in every week, to 14 percent for a personally placed radio-only diary mailed in daily. The total "all-

---

*Telephone interviews produced audience levels 21 percent higher on weekdays and 25 percent higher on Sunday in a 1983 SMRB study for the Los Angeles *Times*.

†A "diary" in broadcast rating parlance is a seven-day record of viewing or listening by quarter-hour period, kept by families who agree to cooperate with the research, usually for a period of several weeks. The diary method of rating television programs is used for local ratings by Nielsen and Arbitron (the American Research Bureau). Diaries are sometimes amplified to include consumer purchases and to cover newspaper and magazine reading as well as radio and TV. In the area of local television, the Nielsen Station Index in 1983 was using diaries to cover household and individual audiences in over 220 television markets. In addition, there were six markets measured by audimeters in which daily (overnight), and weekly reports were also available. Cumulative household audience was also available on a weekly and four-week basis by day part. Arbitron collected between 200 and 2,300 diaries in all but four of its 210 local TV markets. It used meters in four major markets with 350 to 500 in those samples and reports available on a daily and weekly basis. While Nielsen had over 2,000 clients for its local service, Arbitron had 3,350 and released its reports through four sweeps a year.

places" quarter-hour listening figures found by these two methods ranged between 18 percent and 10 percent, and the daily net-reach-of-radio figures (the percentage listening at all on a given day) ranged from 90 percent to 63 percent.

The Hooperatings of radio's ancient times were the last regular ratings service to use the telephone coincidental method. The Nielsen audimeter and the program diary or log are the two devices in most common use. Meters measure the time when a television set is on and tuned to a particular station; they cannot automatically record the presence of individuals in front of the set or their attention to what is being presented. Viewer diaries require cooperating respondents to record who is watching a program, and since diaries are filled out with varying degrees of conscientiousness and completeness, and often well after the actual viewing period, their accuracy has often been questioned. Even when diaries are filled out perfectly, they reflect the total audiences for programs to which viewers are constantly tuning in and tuning out, rather than the audiences at a given average moment, which must inevitably be smaller (on the average by 15 percent).

Since diaries demand a fair amount of effort, they present special sampling problems. Even though the major ratings services precede the mailing of each diary with a personal telephone call soliciting cooperation, some of those originally solicited refuse to cooperate. Others fail to return diaries as promised (even though they are prodded with an additional phone call). Moreover, of the diaries returned, some are unusable or incomplete. This means that the ratings services must project to the total universe of American adults from records submitted by only about one-half of those originally designated. For obvious reasons, these people differ from the noncooperators in many ways, including their television viewing habits. A good deal of effort has been devoted to the analysis of this problem, by comparing diary-based ratings with those obtained from meters and telephone interviews. This has led the ratings services to the conclusion that the discrepancies, on aggregate, are small ones.

The essence of the ratings system is that there must be a way of getting comparable measurements day after day and week after week. When the objective is to get figures on a program's or station's *share* of audience, a different kind of measurement method must be used than if the objective is to get the most accurate figures possible on a one-shot basis.

For television, the Nielsen Television Index, which provides the only available ratings on a national level, has the great merit of measuring set tuning on a continuing basis. It does this with a sample of 1,700 households, which yield under 1,500 usable audimeter records on an average day. (The A. C. Nielsen Company had long sought to increase its 1,250 household sample, but its clients refused to pay the necessary costs until 1983.* The network program ratings measure the audience at the average minute.

---

*The Nielsen Television Index measures the three commercial networks, the Public Broadcasting System, and WTVS, Ted Turner's "Superstation" headquartered in Atlanta. In 1983, Nielsen served about 300 national clients with 24 primary reports covering two-week intervals and cumulative information for up to four weeks. Nielsen also offered a Home Video Index that covered cable-originated programming, videotex, teletext, VCR, VDP, computer games, and interactive services. This was done with a quarterly report to

There are obvious difficulties in making and keeping a permanent sample or panel representative of the whole population. Not everyone is willing to let a gadget be attached to his set. (For that matter, not everyone is willing to keep a diary of viewing for several weeks, as Nielsen's local ratings and other services require.) Nielsen replaces 25-30 percent of the audimeter panel every year, but this means that its characteristics are not uniform. For example, in 1974, 51.6 percent were adult-only households; in 1975, the figure was 55.4 percent. Inevitably, this kind of variation had to be reflected in the ratings of children's or child-oriented programs.

Nielsen measures audience composition six times a year based on a special national sample of 2400 households that accumulates four weeks of "Audilog" diary data. These are checked against a sample of 1200 "Recordimeters" that monitor tuning time. In 1983, the company announced plans to introduce a push-button device in its metered homes, through which family members could record the composition of the viewing audience for each program watched.*

Broadcast ratings

Estimates of broadcasting audiences vary even more than those from print media surveys because samples are generally much smaller, and because program ratings are produced on a continuing basis. As usually happens when different measurements are available to describe the same thing, ratings have been raised as banners by rival networks and stations and have often become a matter of claims and counterclaims. For example, in the 1979-80 season, CBS "beat" ABC by one-tenth of a rating point! Such imaginary victories are taken seriously, since a prime-time television rating point is worth $50 million a year to a network. "The image of NBC has been tarnished this season," wrote John J. O'Connor, television editor of *The New York Times*, on April 24, 1976. "'Today' has slipped noticeably over the last year; it is currently down about one full rating point— about two million viewers—from a year ago." Thus are insignificant statistical vagaries translated into momentous judgments.†

While most practitioners of national advertising are familiar with the fluctuations and inconsistencies in magazine audience figures, they generally ascribe a certain sanctity and stability to broadcast ratings. One reason for this is that magazines must live or die on the basis of a single annual number, the percentage of people who claim to read an average issue. By contrast, television ratings are

---

which over a hundred subscribers were in place in 1983. The survey, based on 20,000 households, measured the average quarter-hour household and individual audience and the average minute household audience, along with "day part" cumulative household or individual audiences for up to four weeks.

*AGB, a leading European market research company, was also introducing "people meters" into the United States in 1983.

†In the same vein, the Television Information Office once proclaimed that upper-income households using television in prime evening time had shown "an increase" of half a percentage point. A difference of as much as *eight* percentage points would not be statistically significant (i.e., explicable on the basis of random probability 95 times out of 100) between two separate samples of 200 each. (Nielsen had 201 upper-income households in its panel at that time.)

produced nationally and for major markets for every time of the day seven days a week all through the year. Even for individual stations covered only in a semiannual "sweep" of measurements, ratings are produced for every day and every time period, so that simply by the laws of probability, competitive advantages and disadvantages are evened out.[19]

Hugh M. Beville, then executive director of the Broadcast Ratings Council, has explained the relative invulnerability of broadcast audience measurements to criticism on the grounds that the broadcast audience "is a true assemblage of listeners or viewers," while a monthly magazine's "audience" [the quotation marks are his] covers people who looked at it over a period of seven or eight weeks. Thus, in contrast to magazines, "the structure of the broadcast audience makes it relatively simple to measure effectively."[20]

But in fact, the structure of the broadcast audience is perhaps even more complex than that of print media, because it includes people with varying degrees of attentiveness to what is on the air. A 1975 study by the Canadian Broadcast Bureau of Measurement found that only 55 percent of those who were aware that a television set was on when they were telephoned said they were paying attention to it. For radio, the equivalent proportion was 38 percent. Of course, these figures reflect both attentiveness and availability. Considering only people who were in the same room, 69 percent said they were paying attention to the television set, and 45 percent to the radio.

There are not only predictable differences of attention levels to different kinds of programs, but somewhat unpredictable differences among similar programs. (In 1975, the SMRB report shows that the proportion of viewers claiming "full attention" ranged from 43 percent on the Sunday Sport Spectacular to 58 percent for NBA Today, also on Sunday.)

In short, audiences for radio and television represent a heterogeneous assortment of experiences, just like the audiences for print. This explains why different measurement methods tap different dimensions of the viewing or listening experience and thus produce audience figures of different size. Ratings based on people must always be smaller, for instance, than ratings that show sets in use or households using television, since not everyone in every household can possibly be present at the same time. Data that are gathered while listening or viewing is going on will be less subject to error than data gathered after the fact. Data that require listeners or viewers to cooperate actively (by filling in diaries or questionnaires) will produce more of a response from some kinds of people than from others.

Local ratings measure the "total audience" of those watching a quarter-hour program segment for 5 minutes or longer. By 1983, Nielsen was providing overnight audimeter-based ratings for six major markets as well as in its national ratings. Arbitron (American Research Bureau, or ARB, the leading measurement service for local TV), which first went to a meter of its own in 1958, was also producing local ratings by this method in four markets.

Basically, however, local television ratings are obtained by Nielsen and Arbitron from viewer diaries that are placed in "sweeps" that occur up to seven times a year (typically three or four times, depending on the size of individual markets and the number of stations that can support the expense).

Since the results for the 12-16 "sweep" weeks are applied throughout the entire year, stations often attempt to influence the ratings reports for these "sweep" periods by manipulating the programming at that time or by running contests as inducements to view. A 1975 analysis by a special committee of the Advertising Research Foundation found evidence to support the widely held belief that stations introduce unusual programming and promotions during these measurement periods to raise or "hypo" their ratings. For prime and fringe time half-hour periods, 31 percent of the station audience shares were substantially higher or lower than they were before or after the sweeps. This meant that ratings were inflated for the stations that did the hyping, while their competitors were unfairly penalized.

In the national TV ratings field, the A. C. Nielsen Company has been the "only wheel in town" for a number of years. Since Nielsen adjusts its national audience composition reports to conform with its audimeter data, discrepancies are virtually undetectable. Nielsen's national ratings have been difficult to challenge in the absence of any competitive measurements other than those produced by SMRB and MRI, which are incomplete, cover only a short period of time, and carry the additional taint of being sponsored largely by the magazine business. Still there is reason to believe that Nielsen's projections of people viewing (41 percent of adults at the average minute in prime time during the peak viewing months of the year) may be overstated.

In 1980, Audits & Surveys contacted 2,265 households by telephone on weekday nights during prime time corresponding to 8:30-9:30 p.m. Eastern Standard Time, or when the equivalent programming was being broadcast locally. They found 38 percent of all adults watching television during the average quarter hour of this period and 61 percent of all households using television. (The proportion ranged from 33 percent for those 18-34 to 43 percent for those 50 and over.)

Coincidental telephone studies made since 1956 by Richmond Newspapers indicate that in that market, the prime time TV audience, at the average minute, includes 36 percent of the adult population.

Just as we have seen that the same syndicated magazine research service can produce unbelievable fluctuations in the characteristics and size of a particular magazine's audience from one measurement period to the next, so can the same broadcast ratings service produce disparate reports on the very same program.

In November, 1974, ABC's Wednesday night audience between 10:00 and 11:00 p.m. had a Nielsen rating of 9.7 in households with over $15,000 income. A year later, it was 25.6. Two years earlier, it had been 19.4. This might be explained by changes in program scheduling during this period. But in the same four Novembers, in the same income category, the ratings for M*A*S*H* ranged from 22.9 to 31.7 and for The Waltons from 16.2 to 25.3.[21] Comparable changes occur for different demographic categories and for other programs. Partly, such variations reflect real changes in the competitive alignment of program choices from year to year; partly they reflect the vagaries of sampling. But in any case, they demonstrate the futility of most efforts to buy television audiences to fit specific marketing requirements.

ARF's 1975 analysis of TV diary sweeps, as a by-product, revealed substantial discrepancies in the size of audiences reported by Nielsen's national ratings service (NTI), based on meters, and the local diary measurements made both by Nielsen and by Arbitron. The local ratings were 23 percent lower for late night programs, and local weekend daytime ratings were between 12 percent and 25 percent lower. For all day parts, Nielsen's local service showed TV sets in use 9 percent less time than did its national service.

And when Nielsen introduced meters into four major markets and compared them with diary results for the month of February 1981, there were enormous differences both between the results for network affiliates and independent stations and also for particular categories of programs. Movies, for example, were up by 59 percent in terms of homes using television. Late news ratings increased 58 percent on independent stations, but only 14 percent on network affiliate stations.

On July 12, 1965, CBS broadcast a documentary on the subject of TV ratings, and Arthur Nielsen, Jr., was one of the authorities interviewed. Remarkably enough, this program had a rating of 20.8 in New York according to Nielsen, but only of 11.7 according to ARB! And in an experiment conducted by Arbitron in 1982, diary records were compared with two-way metered feedback from 73 cable TV households. (Only one set was used in each household.) In 23 percent of the quarter-hour segments measured between 8:00 and 11:00 p.m., there was disagreement between the two measurements as to whether the set was on or off. The two sources also disagreed for 37 percent of the broadcast programs, 45 percent of the basic cable programs, and 56 percent of the pay cable services.

Nielsen's local ratings often differ from Arbitron's, in spite of the fact that the two services use virtually identical methods and show almost identical viewing levels, in the aggregate.

A 1975 analysis of the 15 top-rated programs by *Television/Radio Age* found their Arbitron rating less than one percentage point higher than their NSI rating, averaging results for the country as a whole.* However, this great consistency is not apparent when ratings are examined more closely for individual markets. For example, in October-November 1974, in a sample of seven daytime and nine evening network programs, Nielsen's daytime ratings were 15 percent lower in New York than Arbitron's, and in prime time they were 21 percent lower. In Chicago the Nielsen daytime ratings were 8 percent lower, but they were 10 percent higher in the evening. CBS's "All In the Family" was rated at 40 in New York by Arbitron and at 32 by Nielsen.

Peter B. Case analyzed the ratings of five network programs in 41 local

---

*There was a time when the two local TV audience research services differed more than they do now. In February-March 1971, for example, Nielsen showed 26 percent more women viewing in the afternoon than did Arbitron; 37 percent more teenagers watching in the early evening (5:00-7:30 p.m.); and 14 percent more men watching in prime time. Since the broadcast industry foots most of the bill for the rating companies, its displeasure with Arbitron's smaller numbers was expressed forcefully. In the fall of 1971, Arbitron's methods were modified and the ratings quickly rose to a level comparable with Nielsen's. The president of the company (a researcher) was replaced by a television sales executive.

markets where Nielsen and Arbitron had conducted ratings research covering the same time periods.[22] He found wide variations and occasional instances where the difference was almost as large as the average rating of the program. In the case of the "Hallmark Hall of Fame," where the average rating in 28 markets was 13, Arbitron exceeded Nielsen by 5 or more rating points in four markets; the reverse was true in another 4 markets. "The Young and the Restless," with an average rating of 9 in 27 markets, had Arbitron ahead by 5 or more points in five markets and Nielsen ahead by 5 or more points in two. Case concluded that sampling error accounts for many of the disparities but that some minor differences between the two virtually identical research procedures were responsible for some of the variations as well.

Differences of this order might at first glance appear unimportant, until one remembers what the ultimate consequences are in program survival and in the fortunes of individual TV stations.

Electronic Media (December 9, 1982) reported that "discrepancies in tabulations made last month by Arbitron and A. C. Nielsen Company have put the network owned stations in a tizzy." In Chicago, for example, WLS-TV, with a 14 rating and 21 share, "barely finished ahead of WMAQ (with a 13 rating, 20 share) in the all-important Monday through Friday 10:00 p.m. news race, according to Nielsen. However, that late news situation was reversed in Arbitron where WMAQ's 14/23 outdistanced WLS's 13/22." In New York, "the stations were quick to proclaim WCBS-TV winner of the 11:00 p.m. news race." "WCBS averaged a 10.8 rating and 21 share. . . . WNBC and WABC meanwhile tied at 10.5 and 21." "The wide discrepancies between the two rating services perhaps were underscored most profoundly in the 11:00 p.m. news race in which Arbitron listed WABC as the runaway leader with an 11.6/23, followed by WNBC's 9.5/20 and WCBS's 9.1/18." "Sources said that WABC is threatening to sue Nielsen because it wants to include the brief over-run from the Larry Holmes network TV title fight along with its own late starting local news that night, November 26."

These frantic racing metaphors, with all the emotional panic they suggest, are of course based on misperceptions of the meaning of differences that have no meaning, that really don't exist at all.

Measuring radio

Although Nielsen first entered broadcast measurement with ratings of the national radio audience, meters were out of place after the arrival of the transistor. Twenty-four percent of the radios currently in use are battery-operated portables, and 26 percent are car radios. As we have already noted, this means that the home radio audience accounts for only 60 percent of total listening time. Since the radio audience is typically doing other things besides listening, the problems of accurate measurement are even more difficult than they are for TV.

The radio audience can be classified into four components, Peter Langhoff, then president of the American Research Bureau, told the 1966 conference of the Advertising Research Foundation. He found from surveys in St. Louis and Washington that about one in six home listeners could be described as doing concentrated listening; half the audience were "listening with incidental activity" (a routine chore like housework). A small group were involved in some other activity while incidental listening took place. About a fifth of the total were doing only "incidental hearing."

Since the days of the Hooperatings, a variety of research firms have measured radio audiences on a continuing basis through a number of different techniques, but few have survived. The Pulse, for years a leader in the field, used a personal interview with a roster of programs. RAM and Mediastat used diaries. Burke, RADAR, and Audits & Surveys (with its TRAC 7 system) used the telephone.

In 1983, Arbitron was the leader, as it was in local TV. Arbitron uses diaries in 135 markets in the fall, 261 in its spring sweep, 25 in the winter, and 12 in the summer. Radio Marketing Research, Inc., generally known as the Birch Report (after its head man), uses day after telephone recall in over 200 markets. Birch uses a rolling tabulation in which two months' data are averaged, with one set dropped each month and a new one added. (Differences in sample composition may account for the fact that Arbitron ratings for "beautiful music" stations are higher than Birch's, while rock music stations are consistently lower.)

RADAR interviews about 6,000 people a year by telephone and publishes two reports based on moving averages. Each respondent is interviewed about radio listening over a 24-hour period, and this is repeated for seven successive days. RADAR reports both total radio listening and listening to radio network programs on which particular commercials have been cleared for broadcast. There are no local market or station reports.

There is also Quantiplex, a research service of the broadcast representative firm, John Blair & Co. It provides data on television, radio, and newspaper audiences and a variety of consumer information in 21 markets, based on telephone interviews with between 1,000 and 3,000 adults. In each market, local subscribers are permitted to add individual questions.

In radio, where ratings are issued even less frequently than for television, the spot buyer is just that much more painfully subject to error when he assumes that the ratings for one period are applicable throughout the year. The very small samples used in most local markets produce results subject to a wide margin of statistical tolerance (plus or minus approximately four percentage points, 95 times out of a 100, with a rating of 10 and a typical sample of 300). This merely adds to the likelihood that the week in which interviewing takes place, with its own peculiar balance of seasonal, weather, and competitive forces, is not typical of the whole year. Yet the data are used as if they *were* typical.

Safety in numbers?

While buyers of advertising think of television audiences in terms of rating points, broadcasters tend to think of them in terms of "share," since they well know that the potential size and composition of the total audience is determined by the time of day and the season of the year. TV shows can double their share of audience when network lineups change and they are brought up against more, or less, attractive alternatives.

When a prime-time network television program is fed from New York to affiliates in the Midwest and Mountain States, it is broadcast one or two hours earlier, and the composition of its audience may be different in the various time zones. (In the Pacific zone, a separate feed is normally run to conform to the original time schedule.)

Nielsen's "total audience" (sets tuned for six minutes or more) runs from 10 percent to 25 percent higher for half-hour shows than the Nielsen "average audience" (based on the average moment of time recorded on the Audimeter tape, which moves continuously as long as the set is in use). This differential increases for full-hour and hour-and-a-half programs. Since the total audience for a given 15-minute segment, or for a program, is bigger than the average-minute audience, an advertiser's projection from homes tuned in (Audimeter) to people watching (diary) is bound somewhat to overestimate the number of individuals actually viewing (diary) if it is applied against the total audience rather than against the average audience.

Not all the people in a family who watch any part of the program are going to be watching it at the average minute, since family members move in and out of the room while a show is on. And although many laymen think that a Nielsen rating represents the percentage of people watching a program, it doesn't mean that at all—and couldn't, unless all households had television, and everyone in the households tuned to a program were watching. There has been a growing disparity between sets in use and the percentage of people watching a program, as the presence of extra sets in the home has made television more of an individual medium. Declining family size has also affected the numbers. Between the early 1950s and the early 1980s, the number of viewers per home tuned in dropped from 2.85 to 1.80 in prime time and from 2.75 to 1.60 in the early evening. In the daytime, it fell from 2.20 to 1.25.[23]

The confusion is compounded because when Nielsen calculates program ratings based on tuning of sets in multi-TV households, it counts every set that is tuned to a different program just as though it were located in a different household altogether. The disparity between tuning and individual viewing gets bigger at the upper-income level. In 1983, in the families in the highest income bracket ($35,000 and over), there were 81 percent more adults than in low income (under $10,000) families, and 79 percent of the high-income families had more than one set.

Such statistical niceties as these are generally rejected with impatience by advertising people for whom research methodology is a big, complicated bore and who want to deal with research data in simple, commonsense terms. However, the tolerance of inflated numbers may in at least some cases coincide with self-interest and an unwillingness to rock the rather large boat.

The elemental principles of sampling continue to remain a mystery to many intelligent laymen. William Weilbacher reminds us of a Senate investigation of the ratings services in 1958:

> The Founder, Arthur Nielsen, Senior, went down to Washington to tell the Senators all about sampling and sample size. He took with him a monumental Nielsen presentation on this subject. The presentation went on for three hours and covered every conceivable technical subject that might interest the Senators, as well as many that would not. In

addition, all kinds of statistical gods and the Census Bureau were invoked repeatedly during the presentation. Mr. Nielsen finally concluded. Senator Mike Monroney of Oklahoma, who was presiding, thanked Mr. Nielsen profusely for coming down and making such a great presentation, and then made two extended remarks, the essence of which was: "I just do not understand how you can measure the listening habits of the American people with a sample of only 1,050." Mr. Nielsen's reponse was simply, "I am afraid you are reaching the wrong conclusion, Senator."

The last extensive probe of the ratings services by a Congressional investigating committee took place in 1963.[24] These hearings drove several minor ratings companies out of business by showing that they had merely produced reports without bothering to generate data first. Charges of interviewer cheating and improper or inadequate sampling got the headlines and were easy for the major ratings firms to dispel, since their stock in trade is integrity at the level of data collection and processing. One immediate and tangible effect of the hearings came in 1965 with the organization of the Broadcast Ratings Council under the leadership of Hugh M. Beville, a pioneer of broadcasting research. The Council, which includes advertiser and agency representatives as well as broadcasters, employs outside auditing firms to monitor the field work and data processing of all the ratings services and investigate occasional charges of impropriety. (These have generally arisen from overenthusiastic sales efforts by time salesmen from local stations.) But the council's assignment of assuring the quality of execution does not extend to the comparative evaluation of the methods used by the individual services it oversees.

The most interesting revelation in the congressional hearings was that of the ratings services' major point of vulnerability: their stance of certainty. The hearings suggested that the illusion of exact accuracy was necessary to the ratings industry in order to heighten the confidence of their clients in the validity of the data they sell. This myth was sustained by the practice of reporting audience ratings down to the decimal point, even when the sampling tolerances ranged over several percentage points. It was reinforced by keeping as a closely guarded secret the elaborate weighting procedures used to translate interviews into published projections of audience size.[25] It was manifested in the monolithic self-assurance with which the statistical uncertainties of survey data were transformed into beautiful, solid, clean-looking bar charts.

Such practices were derived from the traditions of store auditing, a field in which the A. C. Nielsen Company first established its mark. When measurements are made of the actual movement of goods across the shelf in a store, the figures must be presented in a way that approximates the reality of goods shipped, stocked, inventoried, and sold. The figures have to look "hard." But this way of looking at the figures as "hard" unfortunately has been carried over into the realm of survey research on audience behavior.

Most advertisers in the United States today use television as a means of scattering messages (through local spots or shared sponsorship and scatter plans on the networks). Sophisticated time buyers aim at specific targets defined by sex, age, and income and established in terms of the audience composition of the programs in which (or adjacent to which) the commercials are expected to appear. The reach, frequency, and gross rating points accumulated by a television schedule are often computed for such selected groups of people. But all of these computations ultimately depend on small subsamples of the viewing recorded in diaries—and a good part of this viewing, necessarily, is reported by other household members. Thus the combination of reporting error and normal sampling error gives the ratings for individual subgroups of the population wide tolerances that defy the appearances of exactitude conveyed in computer printouts.

Moreover, in the usual patterns of television viewing, the people who are watching a particular show are in part carryovers from the one that preceded it and in part fleeing from the less tolerable offerings on other channels. Sportscasts and daytime soap operas will predictably yield high proportions of male and female viewers respectively, but most prime-time programming lacks this sharpness of profiling. This means that a typical television advertiser is spreading his messages largely at random, except that the people who watch a lot of television are more likely to catch them than those who watch little.

There is another aspect to this random delivery pattern, on which I have already commented in Chapter 6: The communications context of the message is as much left to chance as it is to the advertiser who runs an advertisement in a thousand newspapers from coast to coast, never knowing what news or advertising will surround it from one paper to the next. Yet the rhetoric of audience measurement, as applied to rating points in a spot TV schedule, arises from the assumptions applicable to network radio in the 1950s.

Narrowcasting

Cable television received less than 400 million dollars of advertising investments in 1983 compared with the fourteen billions in on-air broadcasting. But cable was transforming the economics and audience patterns of television in dramatic ways. Three out of five households were being passed by cable systems, some offering 100 different channels. New applicants for cable franchises were promising to double that choice. By 1984, the proportion of households on the cable was up to 39 percent and 60 percent of these (three-fourths of the new installations) were subscribing to one or more pay channels. It was obviously only a matter of years before cable became the dominant mode of transmission, although many skeptics still insisted that direct broadcasting to the home by satellite was the ultimate solution. Cable was steadily expanding the number of options available to its subscribers, though about 20 percent of cable homes were on older systems that still provided a dozen or fewer channels.

The cable audience had begun as a collection of people in largely rural communities trapped by distances or behind mountains that cut off good reception from the nearest TV transmitters. But this kind of community antenna TV had been subordinated to urban and suburban systems whose appeal lay not merely in picture quality, but in greater programming variety, enhanced by signals from other cities and by cable network offerings, free and pay, transmitted by satellite.[26] By 1983, there was a score of such networks offering specialized free programming like news, sports, and weather. Pay systems without advertising, like Time, Inc.'s spectacularly successful Home Box Office, competed effectively with the networks for rights to new films, Broadway productions, and major sporting events, evoking memories of a statement made a quarter century earlier by CBS's Frank Stanton: "Television cannot exist half free and half fee."

MGM/UA's chairman, Frank Rothman, "drools" (as *Business Week* put it on February 21, 1983) at the prospect that "when 20 million homes are equipped to receive pay-per-view, we could charge $5 a home for Rocky III, split the profits, and make $50 million in a single night."

A hundred newspapers across the country were leasing cable channels to transmit cabletext that included classified advertising. Knight-Ridder's Viewtron experiments with teletext were offering an interactive advertising service in full color, in which Sears and other major advertisers were participating, along with local stores and services. A variety of "shop at home" services were being tested, and every large advertising agency was dedicating the time of some of its most thoughtful advance planners to examine what these developments meant to the future of advertising.

Some of the resulting forecasts were quite imaginative. According to Jerome Ohlsten, a vice president of Cunningham and Walsh, "By the year 2001, most consumers won't be reading. They'll be comprehending visual symbols and cues at much faster rates. Let's take a look at prime time, circa 2001. Dad has just reentered the family module from his computerized office wing. Mom has dispensed the evening meal of soup wafers and concentrated steak cubes, the kids have finished their interactive TV homework, and every one settles down for the weather report, followed by the most popular world network program."[27] It is comforting to know that the family will still be around in 2001, at which time this vision of the future should make interesting reading, except that reading will apparently be a dead skill.

However murky the general outlook, two things *were* clear: The first was that cable opened up the possibility of using television as a highly selective medium to zero in on specific slivers of the market, as could be done with specialized magazines. (In the inimitable phraseology of Madison Avenue, "narrowcasting" was replacing broadcasting.) The second conclusion was that the networks could never again be what they had been, the almost universal source of evening television entertainment.

The networks' share of the prime-time audience had been slowly eroding even before the spread of cable, as the number of independent stations grew and added alternatives for the viewers. Cable accelerated the process. A Nielsen analysis of five markets found that in the five-year period between 1977 and 1982, as cable penetration accounted for a growing percentage of media households, outside stations' share went up from 20 percent to 35 percent in Peoria, from 26 percent to 34 percent in Albany/Schnectady/Troy, from 21 percent to 33 percent in Charleston/Huntington. Where more than 9 out of 10 viewers across the nation were formerly tuned to the networks of an evening, the proportion had dipped to 80 percent by 1983. But the real effect of competition was being felt in pay cable households. There, network affiliates accounted for 59 percent of the prime-time audience, independents 19 percent, and pay cable 19 percent. Other cable channels accounted for 3 percent. (In basic cable households, the network affiliates had 76 percent of the audience compared with an 84 percent share in noncable households.) The impact of pay cable was greatest on the lower-rated programs carried by the networks.

Areas that have had access to cable are somewhat different in their character than other areas. The composition of the cable TV audience reflects this in part, along with the obvious differences between those people who can afford to subscribe (or choose to, whether they can really afford it or not) and the nonsubscribers in cable areas. In the case of pay cable, the differences are sharper still. Families with children and higher incomes are more likely to be on the cable, and especially on pay cable.[28] This has confused ratings analysts who report more viewing in cable households and sometimes attribute this to the additional attractions rather than to the fact that viewing levels have always been highest where there are a lot of children able to watch.

With the spread of cable to nearly two out of four television households by 1983, the measurement of television audiences became an even more complex proposition. Within what had been a single broadcast market (defined by Nielsen as the Dominant Market Area and by Arbitron as the Area of Dominant Influence), there might be literally dozens of cable systems, each offering a somewhat different mix of local stations, distantly originated broadcast signals transmitted by satellite, as well as cable-only channels presenting news and weather, advertising, "Public Access" programming, and "pay-TV" films and sporting events. With 4,800 local cable systems, some of them generating extremely tiny audiences on individual channels, it became expensive and difficult to retain the previous standards of statistical reliability in measuring low-rated local programs. Although there continued to be a serious question as to whether America would eventually become a "wired nation," or whether direct satellite-to-home broadcasting would make the cable obsolete, it was apparent that in either case the traditional definition of the television market in terms of broadcast signal coverage from the central city would have to be reexamined. This in turn would have tremendous implications for the way in which media data are organized and classified, for the selection of media in general (not merely television), and for the way in which marketing and sales plans are laid out.

For those concerned with the measurement of audiences, the multiplication of local systems and channels presented extraordinary new problems. Regardless of whether viewers were counted by meter, diary, or telephone interviews, the difficulty of the count was vastly more complex. This applied to the sampling process, the preparation of program rosters, the checking of errors, the statistical projections. In 1982, Nielsen, Arbitron, and Audience Assessment Inc.[29] all launched large-scale experiments comparing the audience measurements derived from different methods. Eventually, cable operators could be measuring the audience themselves through the use of addressable converters.

Whatever the long-term outlook for advertising both on network and locally originated cable programs, it was evident in 1983 that there were still some serious obstacles to overcome. Audience demand did not appear strong enough to support a large number of advertising-supported networks. The audiences for local programs in individual systems were almost invariably too tiny to measure and thus seemed unlikely to attract serious advertisers. Still, Ogilvy & Mather's

Larry Cole estimated, with unverifiable but admirable precision, that the cable industry would generate $1.744 billion in advertising revenue by 1990, of which 59 percent would be on the cable networks.

Actually, there were some faint indications that the stage was being set for an eventual introduction of advertising into pay television, in the guise of holding down its cost to subscribers. (Of course, all cable TV is pay TV, since there's always a charge.) And surveys suggested that there was at least some willingness on the part of the public to sit still for this.

Two 1981 surveys by Benton & Bowles and by Opinion Research Corporation found that nearly two-thirds of pay TV subscribers expressed interest in a pay TV option, with advertising, at a reduced price. Similarly, a 1982 Gallup poll found that among basic cable subscribers, 54 percent would take pay service, with advertising, at half price, while 29 percent would prefer full-price pay TV without ads. Seventy-one percent would accept additional cable channels with ads limited to the start and close of shows; 50 percent would accept interruptions at any point, and 35 percent would prefer to pay for the service without advertising.

If advertising were indeed to be admitted to pay TV, there would be substantial repercussions in the economics of conventional broadcasting and thus of the entire mass media system. The growth of cable has altered the balance of advertisers' and the public's respective contributions to the support of TV; this could swing it back.

Numbers versus communication

Audience measurement, for all media, has moved further and further away from the kind of first-hand submersion by the researcher into his own data, which characterizes the best of analytical research. In the latter tradition, a sensitive observer conducts his own interviews or observations and then pores systematically over the evidence, refreshing his insights with recollections of the original reporting as he himself gathered or experienced it.

In current audience-research practice, by contrast, a huge apparatus is called into play. The numbers ultimately spewed forth—by a computer usually—no longer represent a straight count of the number of people who answered "yes" or "no" to an interviewer's inquiry. Interview data transferred onto computer tapes may be weighted in accordance with the "nights-at-home" formula in order to produce a projectable probability sample. They may be weighted further in order to make the sampling results coincide with known criteria of validity. They may be adjusted and weighted further to eliminate inconsistencies between bodies of data gathered by one method, such as a diary, and by another method, such as an interview or a mechanical recording of set-viewing time. A research firm's trade secrets may lie in its complex manner of manipulating data to attain projections of greater accuracy.

The preoccupation with audience measurement reflects the status of advertising as a business investment that is expected to yield a sales return much like any expense incurred in product improvement, distribution, packaging, or promotion. For the advertiser who wants to maximize the yield on his investment, media audience statistics are vital for evaluating alternative courses of action.

In literature, the ascription of human attributes to inanimate objects is known as the pathetic fallacy. In advertising, we are guilty of a pathetic fallacy in reverse when we take the process of human communication and reduce it to numbers to which we foolishly ascribe the attributes of things. These "things" go by different names: messages delivered, rating points, exposure opportunities, impressions.

Business executives are accustomed to working with numbers that represent concrete ideas, whether these are monetary units, units of raw materials, or finished products. Media-audience figures are easily imbued with the same degree of independent reality as statistics representing dollars or francs, cartons of cereal, or cans of beans. They are no longer accepted for what they are—projections from surveys—that reflect the vicissitudes of sampling and the basic problems of response validity.

Such uncertainties are, of course, the last thing in the world that the business executive wants to worry about. But the problem of evaluating communication effects is extraordinarily expensive and difficult when it is attacked with seriousness and sophistication. Over the past generation, the research world has been strewn with the bleached skeletons of innumerable unsuccessful attempts to measure accurately the specific effects of a specific advertising campaign.

The very difficulty and cost of accurately measuring advertising effectiveness led to an emphasis on audience measurement as a poor but useful substitute. The underlying and unvoiced assumption is that the sales yield from an advertising campaign is somehow or other in proportion to the number of people it reaches.

Implicit in the use of the audience concept is the assumption that audiences for different media can be isolated, that they can be considered in separate compartments, much as publications or TV programs can be thought of as separate.

Audience data are compared not only as to the extent of exposure to media, but also as to the characteristics of those reached by one medium or another.

The desire to go beyond total numbers was inherent in the very first decision to reject circulation as the criterion for comparing different print vehicles. Common sense led to the conclusion that two publications with identical circulation might attract very different kinds of readers according to their relative emphases on entertainment or information, on subjects of specialized or general interest, and so on.

This distinctiveness of reader profiles was borne out by the first subscriber surveys. Similarly, radio listening studies quickly distinguished the listeners of daytime serials from those of symphony concerts or discussion programs. However, in recent years it has become more difficult to differentiate the audiences of the major American mass media. In the course of one month in 1982, 32 percent of the adult population reportedly looked at at least one of four issues of *TV Guide*, 24 percent at a single issue of *Reader's Digest*. No wonder the readership profiles of these mass-circulated magazines resemble each other remarkably!

Since newspapers are read in three out of four households, it is not surprising to find that, outside of these big cities that have a highly competitive press, there is generally a close resemblance between the characteristics of the general population of a town and those of the people who at least occasionally read the local newspaper.

As already noted, most evening television programming is leveled at the broad mass of viewers, so there are amazingly small differences in the actual audience profiles for programs that run the gamut of formats and appeals. However, *preference* profiles do show differences. (Among people in households with under $15,000 income, "Chips" had a TvQ popularity rating of 22 in December 1982, and "St. Elsewhere" an 18. But among those with over $30,000 income, "Chips" scored only a 5 and "St. Elsewhere" a 41.)

While measurements of program interest are certainly important to television program planners and may be important to advertisers as well, actual viewing is defined by what is available and by family decisions in which people "go along for the ride," as well as by positive preferences.

There are, of course, individual shows that in their timing or content are specifically beamed to children, housewives, male sports-enthusiasts, intellectuals, and other definable groups. But setting such special programs aside, audience composition in terms of age, sex, income, education, and city size shows remarkable consistency on the average for drama, comedy, quiz, audience participation, mystery, western, and other popular programming types, when these are shown at easily accessible times.

This lack of sharp differentiation seems to reflect the role of television viewing as a pastime. Until now (though this is changing), viewing has tended to be a matter of shared family experience in which the wishes of first one family member and then another may prevail in the selection of programs. The desire for a variety of fare reinforces the tendency to "watch TV" as an activity regardless of what happens to be on.[30]

Audience measurements and media content

In an economy in which the mass-communications media are operated privately for profit, measurements of audience size must inevitably be the basis of decisions that affect media content.

"Do you know why we publish the *Ladies' Home Journal?*" its great publisher, Cyrus K. Curtis, once asked an audience of advertisers. "The editor thinks it is for the benefit of the American woman. That is an illusion, but a proper one for him to have. But I will tell you the publisher's reason . . . to give you people who manufacture things that American women want and buy a chance to tell them about your products." That statement probably would be put less bluntly today, but it remains generally true. In our commercial culture the decisions of advertisers not only govern the life and death of media but also affect changes in their character and shape. Thus they help determine what information the public receives and to form the tastes and values that ultimately find political expression.

Let it be granted that American mass media are, by and large, controlled by responsible people who take their civic duties seriously. Such people would properly resent the charge that what they put into their publications or broadcast time represents prostitution to the demands of advertisers. Yet advertisers' demands often coincide directly with the internalized demands that arise from the goal most mass-media operators set for themselves: namely, to provide, within the framework of a given editorial or entertainment formula, offerings that appeal to the greatest possible number of people. Other things being equal, most mass-media operators seek to broaden rather than restrict their appeal. Obviously they would prefer their influence to be greater rather than less.

The cost per thousand of any media vehicle almost always goes down as the size of its audience increases. Advertising decisions are invariably influenced, if not actually determined, by cost per thousand. Thus media operators are sensitive to all indications of shifts in public taste and often follow research findings in adapting their fare to maximize audience size.

As we saw in Chapter 4, the power to make significant advertising decisions has become progressively more concentrated. In advertising, as in any other business, bigness easily leads to bureaucracy, to operations by formula, and to reliance on electronic data processing as a substitute for brainwork. This means that audience numbers are more than ever in demand and that they have an ever-increasing influence on decisions that govern the shape of the whole mass-media system.

The "illnesses" and deaths of great mass media are linked inextricably with advertising decisions—in which both audience data and unsupportable hunches about audiences play important parts. Not long before it went under, *Life* was being read at least once a month by 41 percent of all American adults; *Look* was being read by 32 percent, the *Saturday Evening Post* by 29 percent. Yet in spite of these vast audiences, these magazines could not generate enough advertising revenues to pay for their enormous costs of production, distribution, and promotion.

Caught up in a fierce competition, these mass magazines joined the race to add new readers by cut-rate offers made in extensive—and expensive—direct mail campaigns. The cost of adding these marginal readers overcame the economies of scale in production. (By the time the weekly *Life* folded, it was spending $15 to get a new $8 subscription.) Advertising rates were forced upward as more copies were printed, so that, for an increasing number of advertisers, the cost of a single-page ad began to seem entirely out of line with its value. When the magazines belatedly acknowledged this discrepancy by cutting down on their circulations, advertisers took this as evidence of a weakness with which they did not wish to be associated. Thus the consequences of media audience research were felt in the business decisions that led to their demise.

The mass magazines were major social and cultural influences that were never replaced. Their reportage heralded and facilitated the revolution in American race relations. Consider *Life*'s remarkable coverage of the arts, *Look*'s sympathetic documentaries on mental illness, the *Post*'s celebration of small-town American virtues, and the investigative reporting of *Collier's*. Each was unique.

Many advertisers and advertising researchers mourned the great publications that died of exhaustion in the numbers game, but few would permit sentiment to interfere with what they insisted were sound business judgments.

When the death of *Harper's* was announced prematurely in 1980 (prior to its rescue by the MacArthur Foundation), media directors shed the obligatory crocodile tears. Ed Weiner of Della Femina, Travisano & Partners noted that there was no need for readership surveys of *Harper's*, since "one could tell the quality of readership the magazine had just by looking at its editorial product." Allen Golden of BBDO said that *"Harper's* was a very fine literary product, but one that may have outlived its need to the reader. People are getting that kind of literary fulfillment from other sources right now, such as books and some of the cultural programming on the Public Broadcasting Service." And although the magazine had a "quality" audience, "the numbers of that kind of person are dwindling."[31]

A fate similar to that of great magazines has befallen great newspapers in cities like Chicago, Philadelphia, Washington, Cleveland, and Buffalo. An analysis of the large newspapers that have merged or ceased publication in recent years shows that while all had suffered substantial declines in advertising revenues, on the whole their circulations in the years before their discontinuance had fallen by an average of only 15 percent. (Even this decline may be ascribed at least partially to the effects of advertising decisions, since ads are an attraction to readers and a paper with fewer ads has less value to them. It's a chicken and egg proposition.)

The *Philadelphia Bulletin* had a million readers every day when it ceased publication in 1981. As in the case of other papers that were perceived as being in second place in their home markets, the *Bulletin* was getting a share of advertising that was far less than its share of readership. The reason was that advertisers, operating by the same ground rules, inevitably concentrate their media budgets in the vehicles that they consider to offer the broadest coverage or the greatest efficiency, without regard to the fact that when all their competitors used the same yardsticks, the cumulative effect might counteract their intentions.

It is easy to be philosophical about such changes and to assume that they reflect the same inevitable pressures of the competitive marketing world that are manifested in the life cycle of any consumer product. But should the criteria applicable to manufacturers apply in the field of mass communications?

The perception of the advertising decision-maker as to what the public wants changes far more drastically than the tastes or motivations of the public itself. The public may have gradations of feeling. The media decision-maker responds in terms of either-or. To the extent that he is responsive to changes in the audience, he tends to overreact and exaggerate. If he feels that a medium has lost 5 percent of its vitality or appeal, he does not cut his budget for it by 5 percent; he may cut it by 50 percent or may get out altogether.

Audience response is more than a matter of the number of people "exposed" to a publication or program. Consumers have different kinds of responses to different media, depending on how these media fit into the pattern of their interests and daily activities. They have different degrees of involvement, of identification, of a sense of possession. Subtle shifts in the quality of this response may occur at a level different from those revealed by audience measurements, or at a considerable lead in time over them.

The life-and-death effect of audience estimates is most clearly seen in the broadcast industry. The overall reliance on ratings in policy planning naturally encourages a tendency for tastes to be leveled to a common denominator. Certainly there is no collusion among the TV networks in determining what goes on the air, but all three networks use the same criteria in selecting programs.

David Mahoney, then executive vice president of Colgate-Palmolive, engaged in the following colloquy with one of the House Committee's investigators in 1963:[32]

Mr. Richardson.	If you are going to renew on a show, does, let's say, CBS, bring you a brochure, or someone within your company a brochure, showing you how the ratings have been throughout the year on that show?
Mr. Mahoney.	Yes.
Mr. Richardson.	In other words, they talk ratings a great deal?
Mr. Mahoney.	Yes, they do.
Mr. Richardson.	They sell by ratings?
Mr. Mahoney.	I think so.
Mr. Richardson.	As far as your company is concerned . . . is it the basic sales tool, in your opinion?
Mr. Mahoney.	Yes.

Mahoney also observed, "In my opinion, they base the price of the show on what they think the implied rating is."

Thomas W. Moore, a former president of the ABC Television network, has noted how the three chains have struggled for supremacy in ratings, often ending up each broadcast season in a close heat. "We do resent having the ratings—our own bookkeeping tool—used to carve us up before the public on the very occasions we elect to rise above the competitive entertainment fare."[33] Yet though every network management feels tyrannized by the ratings, none is willing to risk playing the game by any other rules. In 1983, Van Gordon Sauter, president of CBS News, had a plaque above his desk reading, "In Nielsen We Trust."

In 1982, 62 percent of total station operating hours for a network affiliate were devoted to network programming, 21 percent to syndicated material, 8 percent to feature films, and only 6 percent to locally produced programs.* These overall figures are misleading because network hours almost completely take over in the evening, when audiences are biggest.

The scheduling of shows, which has largely passed out of the hands of the advertisers and into those of the network managements, is governed by the desire to build a strong lineup which will hold the greatest possible number of viewers over the longest possible period of time, against the attractions of the competing networks.

In 1982, only 15 percent of evening network shows had been on the air for seven years or more. In the fall 1982 season, 41 percent of the previous season's prime-time programs failed to return to the air. Within the 1980-81 season 28 percent of 48 shows that began in the fall did not survive in the same time slot until spring. Inevitably, the programs that fall by the wayside have millions of viewers, including many who may have a real attachment to the show's personal-

---

*The remainder represented mostly sports and religious broadcasts.

ities or theme. But the ratings have no place for the intensity of viewer involvement or affection, and they are certainly oblivious to the artistic or moral calibre of the programs that are being measured.[34] The remarkable attrition from one season to the next demonstrates the direct application of audience-rating statistics in programming practices.[35]

The interoffice memoranda of television officials produced in evidence before a Senate subcommittee investigating the causes of juvenile delinquency in 1964 offer interesting insights.[36] The evaluation on one script reads, "Not as much action as some, but sufficient to keep the average bloodthirsty viewer fairly happy." Commenting on a script for "The Untouchables," Quinn Martin, an ABC official, wrote, "I wish we could come up with a different device than running the man down with a car, as we have done this now in three different shows. I like the idea of sadism, but I hope we can come up with another approach to it." On another occasion, the same gentleman warned the producer of the program (who was subsequently fired) of the need for "maintaining this action and suspense in future episodes. As you know, *there has been a softening in the ratings*, which may or may not be the result of this talkiness, but certainly we should watch it carefully." (My italics.)

In defense of the policy of using ratings as a basis for programming decisions, the broadcast industry has argued that this makes eminently good business sense. As Sylvester (Pat) Weaver, a former president of NBC, told the Congressional investigators of ratings,

We who are in the business I am sure all know they are estimates, but again, with all the other problems, you do not go around trying to persuade your client that the one reliable thing that looks like it is safe, that you can talk about, is not safe, either. It is not human nature to work that way.[37]

The broadcasters have also raised the cry of "cultural democracy." The programs that prove popular with the greatest number of people are, according to this argument, the ones that most deserve to be on the air. The counter-argument is that there is a two-way process at work and that public tastes merely reflect a preference for what is made *available* and familiar by the media.[38] It is interesting to note that both the *pro* and *con* sides of this "great debate" tend to take for granted both the ratings figures and the underlying concept: an undifferentiated and attentive body of viewers moving from one program to the next.

A vital question raised in the discussion is whether the commercial system of broadcasting is to be blamed for whatever may be wrong with the state of the television arts, or whether the free choice of the viewer is instead responsible. As David Sarnoff, board chairman of RCA, once phrased the case for the media, "We're in the same situation as a plumber laying a pipe. We're not responsible for what goes through the pipe."[39]

Broadcast industry spokesman (and former FCC commissioner) Lee Loevinger calls TV "the literature of the illiterate; the culture of the low brow; the wealth of the poor; the privilege of the underprivileged; the exclusive club of the excluded masses. . . . A demand that popular entertainment conform to the taste and standards of critical intellectuals is mere snobbishness."[40]

Certainly public and educational television have not been able to attain massive audiences in competition with commercial TV. Although 44 percent of all adults tune in to at least one public television broadcast in the course of a week, the average share of prime-time viewing is only 3 percent. Countries with a state-operated system of broadcasting face the continuing problem of balancing programs aimed at social uplift with others that will assure the presence, night in, night out, of a large body of attentive viewers. The task becomes even more complicated when commercial and state-operated or educational channels exist side by side. A kind of Gresham's law of popular preference operates, leaving no more than a minority available for an educational or elite-interest program when it competes with less demanding amusements. The BBC radio's famous "Third Programme" drew 1 percent of the audience. Further evidence of this comes from the sad case history of CBS's venture in setting up a cultural cable network. After an investment of $50 million, it was abandoned in 1982 in the absence of prospects of accumulating adequate numbers of viewers and advertisers to make it economically viable in the foreseeable future.

As sociologist Leo Rosten puts it, "When the public is free to choose among various products it chooses—again and again and again—the frivolous as against the serious, escape against reality, the lurid as against the tragic, the trivial as against the significant."[41]

In 1957, CBS's exclusive first TV interview with Khrushchev was carried by 105 stations, while 220 took the Ed Sullivan show.[42] On the first night of the Six Day War, a rerun of "Alfred Hitchcock Presents" on an independent station outdrew all three networks' broadcast of the special UN Security Council session.

During the first two weeks of the Watergate hearings, the average minute ratings for the three networks indicated an aggregate audience 3,000,000 less than for the soap operas and game shows for which the hearings were substituted.*

When both CBS and NBC televised the 1966 Senate Committee on Foreign Relations hearings on U.S. Asian policy, these two networks lost 55 percent of their normal daytime audience. After four days, the president of CBS Television ordered the return of "The Lucy Show," and the network's great news director Fred Friendly resigned amidst fireworks and a fleeting moment of soul-searching in broadcasting circles. The whole debate over ratings was crystallized in this one episode. Network management took the position that the sheer number of sets tuned in represented a measurement of communication taking place. There was no recognition of the special character of a unique experience, the depth of meaning communicated by it, its memorability, or the chances of its being incorporated into the permanent residue of a listener's life experience. It takes as long to brush one's teeth as to vote in a presidential election, and on election day

---

*These had accounted for some $300,000 of daytime billings each for CBS and NBC and $250,000 for ABC. The networks estimated that their losses would have run to $4 million a week had all three continued to run the hearings simultaneously. (*Advertising Age*, May 28, 1973)

more people brush their teeth than vote. This does not make toothbrushing on that day more important. Who will stand up against the most popular choice?

Audience measurement or communications research?

The emphasis on audience measurement in American media research has deflected attention from the process of communication. Variations in the intensity and character of the reading, listening, or viewing experience have conventionally been ignored by other buyers and sellers of advertising, who prefer "boxcar" figures that show the largest possible potential exposure.

Audience has been used as a term that aggregates units of equivalent value, so that the major research interest has been in counting these units rather than differentiating them. Audience figures for print and broadcast media are dealt with comparatively as though communication in space and time could somehow be reduced to a common basis; and audience figures for each medium have been lumped together without regard to the frames of reference of different people or the different qualities of communication for different groups.

The conventional kind of audience figure for a TV program lumps together the woman who turned the show on because she wanted to see it, the man who stayed in the living room because he had no place else to do his reading, and the son who came in for a few minutes to ask permission to use the car. They might all be classified as part of the viewing audience, but the concept of total audience is meaningless as long as these three people are given equal weight.

Some of the most interesting research on mass-media audiences has represented an attempt to define them in more differentiated terms than those provided by traditional measurements. In 1950, 42 percent of the circulation of ABC audited consumer magazines was in single-copy sales. By 1981, that proportion had declined to 30 percent. How do single-copy purchasers differ from subscribers? A 1976 study of 1,362 adults and 143 teenagers by Seymour Lieberman for the Publishers Clearing House Inc. found that apart from sports magazines, subscribers gave a higher overall rating to the magazines they read than single-copy purchasers did and also rated them as more enjoyable and informative. And spouses were twice as likely to read subscription copies as those bought individually. Although men and women each made up about half of the subscribers, women accounted for 62 percent of those who mainly buy single copies, for which supermarkets are a primary point of sale. The single-copy purchasers were also younger and lower in income and education. They bought an average of 4.3 issues a year.

Subscribers who were sold on the basis of personal solicitations (like the familiar "working my way through college" routine) showed a much lower commitment to the magazines they read. The same research, incidentally, reported that 21 percent of the population who buy nine or more different titles in the course of a year account for about half of all magazines sold. These "heavy readers," being better educated, also were the fastest readers.

The audience numbers include not only the people who actually bought or subscribed to a magazine and other readers in their families but also all those who casually picked it up in dentists' waiting rooms or beauty shops. (Three out of four men who read *Esquire* and *Sports Illustrated* are "pass-along" readers; so are two out of three persons who read *Newsweek*.)

A variety of studies have differentiated these from the "primary" readers, in terms of their relative value to the advertiser. Research by Don Bowdren Associates in 1974 showed that in the first week after a magazine appears, its primary readers are 4.4 times more likely to learn something from the advertising as are pass-along readers. Another study made by Alfred Politz Research for *Reader's Digest*[43] confirmed that the secondary, or "pass-along," readers of a magazine have lower income and education, are less likely to have an interest in the publication, and spend less time reading it than those who paid for it. But at least some part of the casual pass-along readership may never be counted. On behalf of another group of magazines (*Reader's Digest, National Geographic, Harper's-Atlantic*), Eric Marder compared readership as it was observed in a dentist's waiting room with readership as it was pictured by the answers given later in a conventional magazine audience survey.[44] Over half the observed readers of the smaller publications would not have been counted at all by conventional survey techniques—they were screened out on the opening question, "Have you looked into any issue of this magazine in the last six months?" Evidently they answered in terms of their usual reading habits rather than in terms of their actual (and exceptional) experience as pass-along readers.

Since World War II, radio has changed from the major vehicle of general entertainment into a portable, personal instrument. TV has been undergoing a similar transformation. Yet qualitative changes of this kind are not reflected in audience data. Just as readers may be differentiated according to whether they have purchased a publication or have picked it up casually to kill time, so viewers might be differentiated between those who select a program because they want to hear it and others who merely happen to be around when other family members or friends are watching it.

Listeners tend to identify with radio stations whose character is "right" for them. Every parent of a teen-age child is aware that certain radio stations specialize in the music of a particular subgroup in the teen-age spectrum. As the child progresses in age and interests, he moves from one station to another as his 24-hour-a-day favorite.

Any person who has had his normal routine broken by illness, unemployment, vacation, or some other change in his usual daily schedule has had the experience of turning on the radio or television set at an unaccustomed time and, perhaps, to an unfamiliar station. He then suddenly discovers the existence of a world previously unknown—unknown not only in its entertainment formula but also in its advertising pressures. Long-forgotten brand names suddenly spring back to memory. Perhaps it will dawn on him that "out there" is a part of the public for whom this particular station and time is "home," for whom there is a personal identity with the music, the announcer, and also with the advertiser who regularly uses that station and time.

The intensive cultivation of a small sector of the total population such as that discovered by the unaccustomed listener is the basis of much advertising strategy. By a concentration of effort, the advertiser seeks to attract the loyalty of a limited public rather than to spread himself wide but thin.

Audience research in the future must go further in the task of examining the *quality* of media experience rather than the numbers who experience it, and distinguish among different kinds of communications experiences which are now included together under the heading of total-audience figures. A serious attempt along these lines will lead inevitably to an emphasis on analysis rather than measurement as the proper preoccupation of advertising research.

Much of our current understanding about how we acquire information is based on the behavior of the white rat. Indeed, the white rat has much to teach us about ourselves. But the white rat lacks a soul. Since he is not, like us, a symbol-building animal, he lacks a capacity for identification with the thoughts, goals, interests, and motivations of others, which is the basis of all communication among human beings.

While we communicate by gesture and touch, our main means of interacting with each other is through language. Language is a symbolic device by which we can put ourselves in someone else's place and infer what he means to tell us. This process of communication cannot be reduced to stimulus and response. It defies mechanical explanations. And it entails a set of objectives and methods completely different from those which dominate most audience research.

The most telling criticism that can be leveled at the audience concept is that it deals with the process of communication as though it could be broken down into units or bits—which in advertising are commonly referred to as "GRPs," "impressions," "impacts," or "exposure opportunities," as though they were somehow objects that exist in the real world. Behind this choice of vocabulary is a view of human behavior as something that *can* be reduced to stimulus and response. In such a mechanistic psychology the audience becomes the passive recipient of messages; its members are as gray and faceless as Orwell's "proles."

Audiences for different media are thought of as discrete, as though they consisted of different individuals, when in fact they represent different aspects of the same individuals at different points in time and in different contexts.

How remote this conception is from the idea of the audience for the classic Greek drama, who were individually and together as one with the actors and with the heroes whose *personae* the actors briefly assumed! And how remote, too, this conception of the audience is from the theory of communication as a process of symbolic interaction, which entails the uniquely human capacity to empathize and to infer what other people mean.[45]

The measurement of audiences has deflected energy, attention, and resources away from the major unsolved problems with which students of the mass media might more properly be concerned: the processes of perception and learning through which readers, listeners, and viewers filter and acquire information, relieve their boredom, and expand the horizons of their personal experience.

Notes

1. Ralph E. Dyar, *News for an Empire* (Caldwell, Idaho: Caxton Printers, Ltd., 1952).
2. A pioneer study using this technique was the *Life Continuing Study of Magazine Audiences*, Report No. 1, New York: Time & Life, Inc., 1938. For an authoritative defense of the total audience concept, see Darrell B. Lucas, "Can Total Magazine Audience Be Ig-

nored?" *Media / Scope*, November 1964, pp. 64-72.

3. *Media Decisions*, November 1982, p. 112.

4. Margot Teleki, "How Can We Believe the Numbers?" *Media / Scope*, July 1967, pp. 73-77.

5. *Media / Scope*, September 1967, pp. 47-48.

6. William S. Sachs called attention to the differences between an Audit Bureau of Circulations check of respondents interviewed in Politz's 1964 magazine audience survey and the names on the magazine subscription list. Of the people Politz sampled, 10.2 percent reported that someone in their household subscribed to the *Saturday Evening Post*, and this turned out to be exactly the same proportion uncovered by A.B.C. For *Reader's Digest*, the figures were relatively close—21.6 percent for the sample, 22.4 percent for the publisher's statement. In the case of *McCall's* and *Look*, however, there were discrepancies—10.7 percent for the sample and 12.6 percent for the actual subscriber list in the case of *McCall's* and 9.6 percent for the sample and 11.8 percent in the publisher's statement in the case of *Look*. (*Media / Scope*, March 1966, pp. 60-63.)

7. Some years earlier, a study among 1,650 women in six metropolitan markets was conducted for the weekly *Life* magazine by Alfred Politz Research. It compared audience levels for the same magazines as measured by the "through-the-book" method and by the "recent-reading" method. Half the women were questioned on half the magazines by each method. The unaided recall method produced audience figures for weeklies that were 12 percent higher, and the advantage was higher still for monthlies. (Lester Dorney, "Four Probes Into Space and Time," Paper presented to the Advertising Research Foundation Conference, November 14, 1967.)

8. "ARF Comparability Study; A Controlled Field Experiment Comparing Three Methods of Estimating Magazine Audiences," New York: Advertising Research Foundation, 1980. *Cf.* also, Paul H. Chook, "The ARF Comparability Study," in Harry Henry, ed., *Readership Research: Theory and Practice*, (London: Sigmatext, 1982).

9. Sixty percent had read at least one magazine, but this figure fell to 47 percent when *TV Guide* was eliminated.

10. Timothy Joyce, "The Level of Magazine Reading," in Henry, ed., *Readership Research*.

11. Clark Schiller, "A Study of Overclaiming Readership Using a Recent-Reading Technique," in Henry, ed., *Readership Research*.

12. Michael Brown, "Average Issue Readership Measurement in Britain," in Henry, ed., *Readership Research*.

13. This attrition in the reports of readership was further demonstrated by the other two tests, in which people were observed by their spouses at home or in public waiting areas. *Cf.* Richard L. Lysaker, "The ARF Certitude Tests," in Henry, ed., *Readership Research*.

14. Jerome D. Greene, "Optimum Magazine Audience Research," Report to the Syndicated Research Subcommittee, Magazine Publishers Association, 1981.

15. W. R. Simmons, "Measuring the Quality of Media Exposure—How Some of the Problems Can Be Solved," Unpublished paper, no date.

16. Benjamin Lipstein, "In Defense of Small Samples," *Journal of Advertising Research* (February 1975): 33.

17. Address before the Market Research Council, New York City, January 18, 1974.

18. With the "personal coincidental method," interviewers go out to a fresh cross-section of households, ring doorbells, and find out, if people are home, whether they have a TV set on. The last major study made by this method was a November 1965 survey of over 12,000 households by Alfred Politz Media Studies (at a time when it was still feasible to do personal interviews with a large cross-section of the public during the evening hours). Politz found 41 percent of the households with sets turned on at the

average evening minute (between 6:30 and 10:00 p.m.) and 37 percent with someone watching. The equivalent (January 1964) Nielsen figures commonly quoted showed 58 percent of TV households (55 percent of all households) watching. Politz found 24 percent of the adults (over 18) watching TV in the average evening minute. The discrepancy between 24 percent and 41 percent represented a 71 percent difference in audience size and cost efficiency. The Politz interviewers found no one at home in 35 percent of the households. Since this figure was questioned, *Life* supported an ARF-backed Politz study using an electronic device that could detect the presence of a television set in use. This was carried by interviewers calling on 560 single dwellings in the New York and Richmond metropolitan areas in May 1968. The set-detector record jibed closely with verbal reports in the 336 cases where someone was at home. In the remaining homes, where no one answered the doorbell, only 2 percent registered activity on the detector. (Where respondents refused to be interviewed, there was actually less viewing going on than was provided for in the normal sample adjustment procedure.) With the subsequent demise of the weekly *Life* (and also of the Politz organization), this research thrust was never maintained.

19. For a comprehensive description of ratings and their uses, *Cf.* David F. Poltrack, *Television Marketing: Network/Local/Cable* (New York: McGraw-Hill, 1983).
20. *Television/Radio Age*, December 8, 1975.
21. Cited by Ira Weinblatt in *Media Decisions*, May 1976, p. 74.
22. Peter B. Case, "A Comparison of the Arbitron and Nielsen Local Market Ratings of Five TV Shows," Unpublished paper, 1982.
23. *Ad Forum*, October 1981, p. 43.
24. *Broadcast Ratings*: Hearings before a Subcommittee of the Committee on Interstate and Foreign Commerce, Eighty-eighth Congress.
25. As an aftermath of the hearings, the major services now provide full methodological details as appendices to their reports.
26. To illustrate the difference between these two components of the cable audience: In 1981, 26 percent of the households in A and B counties (basically, larger markets) were on the cable, and among these, 62 percent had a pay option. By contrast, 50 percent of the households in the smaller (C and D) markets were on the cable, but only 30 percent of them had a pay option.
27. "How Consumers View Commercials," *Marketing Review* 34, 1 (September/October 1978): 18-19.
28. In 1981, Nielsen reported that 57 percent of the cable households where there were children present had a pay cable option, compared to 38 percent of those where there were no children present. Fifty-three percent of the cable households with incomes of $20,000 and over had the pay option, compared with 38 percent of the others. In the same year, Mediamark (MRI) reported that only 7 percent of the pay cable households, but 25 percent of other cable households, were headed by people over 65. (The U.S. average was 20 percent.)
29. This organization, in Cambridge, Massachusetts, was sponsored by the John and Mary Markle Foundation.
30. Gary A. Steiner, *The People Look at Television: A Study of Audience Attitudes* (New York: Alfred A. Knopf, Inc., 1963); Leo Bogart, *The Age of Television* (New York: Frederick Ungar, 1972); George Comstock, Steven Chaffee, Nathan Katzman, Maxwell Mc-Combs, and Donald Roberts, *Television and Human Behavior* (New York: Columbia University Press, 1978); Robert T. Bower, *Television and the Public* (New York: Holt Rinehart & Winston, 1973).
31. *Ad Week*, June 23, 1980, p. 2.
32. *Broadcast Ratings*, Part I: Hearings before a Subcommittee of the Committee on Inter-

state and Foreign Commerce, Eighty Eighth Congress, p. 376. (Mahoney was chairman of Norton Simon, Inc. 20 years later.)

33. *Advertising Age*, April 26, 1966.
34. An attempt to fill this void was begun in 1980 by Television Audience Assessment, Inc. By obtaining qualitative judgments of programs, it was hoped that broadcasters and buyers of advertising would temper their reliance on the conventional audience ratings. But there was no indication that this worthy effort would or could modify longstanding practices.
35. *Cf.* "Image Builders Go Back to Print," *Business Week*, October 31, 1964, p. 70; and Harold Mehling, *The Great Time-Killer* (Cleveland: World, 1962).
36. "Television and Juvenile Delinquency," Interim Report of the Subcommittee to Investigate Juvenile Delinquency, 1964.
37. *Broadcast Ratings*, Part I, pp. 176-77.
38. Bernard Berelson, "The Great Debate on Cultural Democracy," in Donald N. Barrett, ed., *Values in America* (South Bend, Indiana: University of Notre Dame Press, 1961).
39. Quoted by Harry J. Skornia, *Television and Society* (New York: McGraw-Hill, 1965), p. 54.
40. *Advertising Age*, October 17, 1966.
41. Quoted by *Television*, July 1965.
42. Martin Mayer, *About Television* (New York: Harper and Row, 1972), p. 205.
43. *A Study of Primary and Passalong Readers of Four Major Magazines*, (Alfred Politz Research, Inc., Pleasantville, N.Y.: Reader's Digest, 1964).
44. Reported by William Blair in an address before the Advertising Research Foundation, October 1966, New York, N.Y.
45. Hugh D. Duncan, *Communication and Social Order* (Somerset, NJ: Bedminster Press, 1961).

Chapter 12
Cost Per Thousand What?

Like other business types, advertising people have always been highly cost-conscious. E. Lawrence Deckinger recalls that the late E. J. K. Bannvart, the Biow Company's new-business specialist, once reported to the agency's head about a meeting he had had with the then president of Lever Brothers. "Their president is the smartest man I ever met," Bannvart began. "I resent that," Mr. Biow replied, without a moment's hesitation. Mr. Bannvart insisted: "He's a bachelor. But he earns $400,000 a year." "Of course he's not married," exclaimed Biow. "Who can afford to get married on such a salary?"

The cost of advertising can be defined simply enough when the advertiser thinks in terms of units of *diffusion*, without regard to what goes on at the receiving end. What does it cost to advertise? Here are a few specific figures that appeared on the standard rate cards for 1983.

A four-color page in *Time* cost $94,420, in *Reader's Digest* $103,600. A full-page black-and-white ad in the Chicago *Tribune* cost $17,987 for a national advertiser earning maximum discounts and delivered a circulation of 758,255 copies. A quarter-page (SAU™13)[1] black-and-white ad in newspapers in each of the top 100 markets cost $260,000.

A schedule of 20, 60-second radio spots on WRC in Washington could be bought for $2,600, while a minute of network radio time ranged in price between $2,100 on Mutual to $6,000 on RKO. One minute could be run on a leading radio station in New York for $600. A minute announcement during the peak driving time of early morning or late afternoon in the top 100 markets cost about $100,000.

On television, 10-second fringe-time spots in Los Angeles cost $375, and one-minute participations $5,400. A 30-second spot announcement on a leading New York television station cost about $8,750. A prime-time spot in the top 100 markets cost $87,729. By 1982, the cost of running a 30-second commercial was as high as $160,000 in top-rated network programs like "60 Minutes" and "Dallas," and averaged $75,000 on network prime time.

Engravings, color separations, and other production costs for newspaper and magazine advertising represent, on the average, about 9 percent over the space costs. By contrast, production charges are a significant part of the broadcast advertiser's total expense. A half-hour episode in a television series cost about $350,000 an hour to produce in 1982, and production rights were sometimes granted by network heads to favorite performers who wanted to try their hands at it. The costs of preparing a 30-second television commercial could be as little as $1,000 or as high as $1 million. Packaging on products may have to be especially redesigned so that they look right to the camera. A musical jingle could be bought for as little as $250 out of a stock file, but a specially composed one could cost up to $20,000, and permission to write commercial lyrics for a popular song could cost as much as $75,000. Name stars like John Houseman and Rodney Dangerfield are each said to have received $225,000 for appearing in commercials.

Miner Raymond, formerly in charge of commercial production for Procter & Gamble, recalls that in 1955 a $2,400 commercial was considered "outrageously expensive," while by 1982, "beer commercials routinely cost upwards of $250,000," and the average 30-second commercial would cost $140,000. By contrast, a typical prime-time drama or situation comedy cost $15,000 an hour to produce, a daytime drama $1,000 an hour, and a feature film $90,000 an hour.[2]

Within a generally inflationary economy, the absolute dollar cost of time or space in all media continues to increase. The cost of a four-color magazine page increased 138 percent between 1974 and 1983; the cost of a page in the ten largest dailies increased 216 percent in the same time period.

Costs separate and unequal

Many advertising media, like most other businesses, offer discounts as an incentive to heavy and continuing use. Such discount structures tend to "lock in" the advertiser within specified units. (It may cost him virtually the same to buy 12 monthly issues of a magazine as to buy 11; so of course he will take 12.)

National advertisers who use a magazine's full circulation may pay less than what a regional advertiser would theoretically have to pay if he bought most of the sectional editions on an individual basis. In the average paper in the top 100 markets, a national advertiser pays 60 percent more than the retail merchant for the same space, according to a 1982 study of rate differentials made by the Association of National Advertisers.[3] Part of the differential is accounted for by the fact that the advertising agency's 15 percent commission and a representative's commission of about 5 percent generally must be subtracted from the newspaper's receipts for national advertising. Moreover, retailers can sometimes effectively use only part of a newspaper's total circulation, while the national advertiser is expected to use it all. The historical justification that newspapers offer for the differential, however, is that the local merchant, day in and day out, is their bread and butter and has to be kept in the paper at the lowest possible cost.[4]

Intense competition in the broadcast industry has made it more and more difficult to keep accurate track of time charges to the advertiser. On smaller radio stations, it is not uncommon for merchandise to be bartered for time or for the station to accept a share of the advertiser's take from a direct offer. On network TV, negotiations lead to package deals by agencies and advertisers in which the official rate cards are "simply a beginning point for bargaining."

The television networks eliminated their volume discounts after the Senate Antitrust Subcommittee pursued allegations that these gave an unfair advantage to large advertisers and even encouraged corporate mergers. But in access to the best program packages and time periods, the big advertiser of course still retains the standard advantages of being the best customer—advantages that are hardly unique to the advertising business.

For a media buyer, there is an enormous attraction exercised by a purchase that can be made simply and with a single order. A single commercial on the 1984 Superbowl represented a one-shot expenditure of $450,000 and a much easier way to spend the advertiser's money than a tailored series of buys scattered among hundreds of individual programs and stations.

In the Golden Age of Radio, commercials were delivered live by the announcer for each program, and in variety and comedy shows, the stars often participated in them personally, linking their own authority to the product. This same procedure was followed in the early days of network television, when programs were under the exclusive sponsorship of a single advertiser and two-minute live commercials were not uncommon. As it became more common to prerecord commercials on film, and eventually on videotape and cassettes, the direct link with the individual program was eliminated. Commercial production became more elaborate and expensive, making it desirable to rebroadcast the same commercials in different contexts on different occasions in order to maximize the return on the original investment.

As the length of the broadcast day increased during the 1950s and 1960s, and as the number of independent stations without network affiliations grew, spot television became an increasingly important component of the medium. The same commercials that appeared on network shows were also used by national spot advertisers who wanted to "beef up" the intensity of their coverage in particular market areas. Since prime-time spot on network-affiliated stations was confined to the brief station break between programs, there was an opportunity for commercials shorter than the one-minute length which had become typical on network programs. Half-minute, 20-second, and 10- (or 8-) second I.D. (superimposed on station identification) units were introduced.

At the same time, the escalating costs of program production forced more and more advertisers to share the costs of sponsorship, further hastening the disappearance of the integrated commercial. In television's infancy, programs were selected, developed, and even produced by advertising agencies (and in some cases by sponsors) as well as by the networks. But as the networks became more conscious of the audience flow from one program to another and of the need to think in terms of their overall scheduling rather than in terms of individual programs, they came to insist on full control of what went on their air. Network programming executives, rather than agency television departments, reviewed the proposals and "pilots" submitted by independent producers. Program production centered increasingly on Hollywood and became financially and artistically entwined with the feature film industry. Whereas advertisers had at one time bought air time from the networks and had negotiated separately on program production costs, they were now forced to make "package deals," in which the two components of time and talent were indivisible.

Advertisers were, however, seeking to maximize their exposure by spreading their messages through more than just a single program, and by the late 1960s, as we saw in Chapter 4, networks were offering "scatter plans" that drastically reduced the former relationship between the program and the sponsor. This was not without its advantages to advertisers in an era in which programs came and went off the air with greater volatility than ever. But as advertisers scattered their shots, they became increasingly concerned that their messages reach the intended targets. In the congenial environment of a sponsored show, they generally had a better sense of whom they were talking to than when their commercials appeared on a variety of programs of different types. The networks responded to this concern by offering advance guarantees of specified numbers of GRPs for viewers defined by sex, age, and income. When the ratings services found less than the promised number of GRPs delivered, the networks "made good" for the difference by providing supplementary spot positions. Similar practices were adopted during the 1970s for spot buying on local stations. However, by 1982, the difficulty of basing accurate projections on diary data for population subgroups had become apparent, and the networks were beginning to limit their "make-good" practices.

In 1971, the FCC promulgated the "prime-time access" rule, which took half an hour of network prime time and returned it to the control of local stations. This created a demand for additional programming, particularly for reruns of programs that had already appeared on the networks. It also spurred the development of program syndication.

By 1982, six of the largest advertising agencies were handling syndicated programming through the practice of "tie-in barter" for spot positions. Since 15 agencies control 60 percent of the spot billings, tie-in barter acquired a tremendous importance in the distribution of television commercial time. Under the practice, an advertising agency buys syndication rights to a program from an independent producer and then offers it to individual television stations. In return, the agency receives an allotment of air time for commercials that can be sold to its clients at a 25 to 50 percent discount. In the view of one station manager, "Agencies offer you the dregs of the programming world—otherwise a full-time syndicator would pick the shows up."[5] One agency executive commented, "I hear rumors about all kinds of scams and messes all the time. Anything is possible. Kickbacks and bill paddings and creative accounting are rumored constantly."

Theoretically, in time-banking, a syndicator exchanges rights to a show for time credits on TV stations. The agency backs the program and gives the syndicator an estimate of the time it will buy on each station. The syndicator's time credits are stored in the agency's computer and used up as needed, with clients receiving time-bank discounts of 20 percent or more.

In practice, it is the agency's programming subsidiary that takes the initiative with the syndicator and that pressures stations to carry the programs, using the size of its spot billings as a weapon to have its way. The value of the time credits is adjusted to meet the terms of the deal, so that the client is receiving "discounts" on a rate that is artificially set.

In this tough negotiating world, the fine points of audience demographics, reach, and frequency would seem to take second place. Thus the realities of the advertising world are often in striking contrast to its proclaimed ideology of scientific marketing.

Gregory T. Lincoln, then director of advertising services of Liggett & Myers, told the Media Research Directors Association in 1970 that "In broadcasting, people are stepping aside from demographics and really looking at the bottom line. . . . It has taken us years to develop demographics, and now, when someone says, 'Forget it. I'll save you a million dollars,' some advertisers forget all that pretty fast. You decide you don't have to have age 18-34 on the West Side of Columbus."[6]

The search for a yardstick

Every medium of communication yet invented can inform people, can persuade people, can sell merchandise and services. And every medium has its own file of success stories to prove it. Moreover, every one of our modern mass media can be used in a remarkable diversity of ways both with respect to scheduling and to creative treatment. From this arsenal of options, each advertiser must select the right use of the right media to solve his own unique marketing problem. He must ask himself at every point in his planning what his strategy is accomplishing, how effective it is in meeting his objectives. He may be initially motivated to be concerned with the *cost* of his advertising effort only insofar as this might allow him to calculate the profits or losses involved in generating each unit of additional sales. However, as Robert Weinberg once suggested in an analysis of the cigarette market,[7] in many product fields the effects of advertising can never directly manifest themselves in sales until a certain level of expenditure is passed. A company must, regardless of its size and share of market, exert a certain minimum amount of pressure if only to maintain itself above the threshold of consumer awareness and thereby stay in business.

One additional way of judging media is in terms of their capacity to achieve that irreducible minimum of market coverage and subtle invisible psychological pressure on the consumer.

An advertising investment is a *means* of achieving the desired end of profit; it is not an end in itself. It follows that the efficiency of advertising can never be gauged by any criterion other than the ultimate *effect* it produces, regardless of whether this is accomplished by reaching many people a few times, by reaching a few people many times, or by merely triggering off other reactions within the complex mechanism of distribution and merchandising that ultimately lead to increased sales. The important question is *where* the advertiser gets, not how he gets there.

The measurement of advertising exposure and the determination of advertising costs make perfect sense as long as they are used as part of the description of an advertising *plan*. For a given budget in any medium, the advertiser knows what volume of space or time is at his disposal. In newspapers and magazines, he knows the number of copies printed and he can estimate from research the number of people through whose hands they will pass. In the case of broadcast media, his researchers can make some preliminary guesses regarding the number and kinds of people who will watch or hear his messages, and he can check these guesses afterwards by means of estimates based on the rating services and other surveys.

Why Cost Per Thousand?   Cost per thousand (or CPM, as it is referred to by the cognoscenti) refers to the common practice of calculating advertising costs on a comparative basis by dividing the budget allocation for each media vehicle by the total number of units of its advertising delivery or performance.

Many different units have been used to derive cost-per-thousand figures: circulation, audience, impressions, gross rating points, viewers, cumulative reach, prospects, sets in use per commercial minute. CPM may be expressed in terms of some measurable response, like recollection of the advertising. Agencies have evaluated their ads' creative performance by the criterion of "cost per thousand noters," multiplying commercial recall figures against ratings and applying the results to the cost of an entire campaign. For example, in 1982 Video Storyboard Tests interviewed 4,000 adults to identify users of 25 different products and then asked those users what TV commercials they remembered in that product category. A "cost per thousand retained impressions" was then calculated, based on the percentage of "prospects" who remembered a commercial for each brand. Among the top 25 brands, Oscar Mayer had a "cost efficiency," by this criterion, of $6.37 a thousand, and Budweiser Lite one of $41.67. Polaroid spent $32 million and reached camera owners at a rate of $13.89 a thousand, while Kodak hit them at a cost of $22.22 on a budget over twice as large: $69.1 million.

We can apply cost per thousand three ways:

1. in comparing different scheduling applications of a particular media vehicle (a program or publication)
2. in comparing different vehicles within the same medium
3. in comparing different media.

The use of cost-per-thousand measurements has long been taken for granted throughout the advertising industry. As far back as 1956, testifying before a Congressional subcommittee, Frank Stanton of CBS presented the prevailing viewpoint clearly, as shown in the following quotation:

I do not think that we can legislate an advertiser into an uneconomic purchase, and unfortunately the facts of life are such that on a cost-per-thousand basis—and I believe the advertiser makes his choice on that basis—I think these moves can be justified . . . .[8]

In the world of broadcast buying and selling, "rating points" have acquired a pseudo-reality of their own, bargained over as though they were material objects rather than mathematical abstractions projected from survey data. It has become common to calculate broadcast schedules in terms of "cost per GRP," applied either to a national buy or to individual markets. (The reasoning, however, is identical with that for the usual CPM.)

Cost per thousand is the common coin of the advertising realm, but its convenience and general acceptance should not be confused with true value.

The use of CPM as a basis for comparing media leads to problems in a number of areas:

1. At what level of communication should the performance of a medium be evaluated?
2. Can communications be treated as units identical in impact or quality, as the CPM concept assumes?
3. Is it correct to ignore the large variations, many of them unpredictable, in the performance of any medium at different times and places?
4. Are there any fair generalizations that can be made in advance about equivalent units of communication in different media?

These questions must always be confronted when specific CPM comparisons are made, and CPM has no meaning at all except as a comparative measure.

Levels of Communication: The A.R.F. Model. At what level of functioning should advertising media be measured to provide cost-per-thousand data? Still in wide use is a model of the advertising process described in 1961 by a committee of the Advertising Research Foundation headed by Seymour Banks, an outstanding media theorist who was at that time a vice president of the Leo Burnett Company.[9] This model has six stages, all of which relate to a medium's capacity to present a message to people who will be persuaded to buy the product.

1. On the first level is the *distribution* of the vehicle. This refers to its physical circulation or distribution into households, where it becomes available for communication. In only some of these households are there prospects for the advertised product.
2. At the second level, the *vehicle* must get actual *exposure* to people; it must have an audience of live human beings, some of whom are prospects. If the television set is on, this is considered "distribution." If people are watching the program, this is media "exposure." If a copy of a publication is delivered into the household, this is distribution; when that copy is read by an individual, it has had exposure.
3. At the third level, the *advertising* itself must get *exposure*. The message must achieve an actual physical presentation within the attention range of the individuals in the media audience. Not all the people exposed to a program, magazine, or newspaper are physically exposed to a specific advertising message. They may be out of earshot when a commercial comes on, or they may skip the particular page where an advertisement appears.

    Up to this point, the A.R.F. description primarily concerns the advertising vehicle and its distribution pattern. Media research measurements at the first three stages deal with the capacity to put the message in front of a certain number of people.
4. At the fourth stage, which the A.R.F. committee calls *advertising perception*, the intrinsic capacities of the vehicle begin to interact with what the advertiser and his agency do with the time or space they have bought. There is apt to be a sharp differentiation between the physical exposure

to the message (at stage 3) and conscious awareness of it on the part of people who might have a potential interest in the product itself or in the advertising appeal.

5. At the fifth stage, that of *advertising communication*, the sense of the message is persuasively transmitted to the recipients. Again this effect is selective; more prospects than nonprospects "get the message."

6. At the final stage, *sales response* represents what the individual does as a result of a persuasive advertising message. Since he has been influenced to buy, this defines him automatically as being on the prospect side of the line.

The calculation of cost per thousand can yield different results at each of these six different stages.

The fungibility of impressions. Some years ago psychologist Gerhart Wiebe resurrected a wonderful term, *fungibility*.[10] Something is *fungible* if it is fully replaceable by an identical item; examples might be dollar bills, hamburgers, hogs going through the line in the packing house. When we think in terms of cost per thousand, we must, of course, think of human beings as fungible; we must think of their reactions to advertising as fungible. There is nothing particularly distasteful or immoral in this. We do this sort of thing all the time when we speak of the population of Cincinnati, the readers of *Good Housekeeping*, or any other convenient designation of people in the mass. But this way of thinking is not very useful if we are trying to understand the processes of communication, persuasion, or selling.

There are no available measurements of true "exposures" or of advertising "impressions." These are not things or events with constant properties, but psychological processes that have no exact counterparts in definable behavior. We are forced to rely either on exposure opportunities (as represented crudely by broadcast audience ratings and page opening data) or on recalled or remembered exposure, which is subject to all kinds of inaccuracy, bias, and contamination from other exposures previous to the one ostensibly being measured.

There is no acceptable common impression unit on which to base comparisons even within the framework of the *same* medium, because in evaluating the psychological processes through which messages are received and ingested, we cannot separate the vehicle from the way it is used to transmit a particular idea from a particular source.

Today, few advertising media planners start with exposure opportunity rather than exposure as the unit for the CPM yardstick. The varying nature of communication achieved by the separate media appears to make exposure opportunity an unsatisfactory criterion. Such media as outdoor and transit advertising produce vast numbers of exposure opportunities at very modest costs. (Many of them, of course, represent the same messages repeatedly confronting the same people.) But these media are commonly presumed to promote only a relatively low level of conversion of "opportunity" (the physical presence of the message somewhere within visual range) into actual exposure or conscious perception. Other media, whose exposure-opportunity costs are much higher, are presumed to be much more powerful in their ability to get the message into the consciousness of the audience and are therefore more economical in the final analysis.

As it is conventionally calculated, cost per thousand represents an average that treats all impressions alike, regardless of whether they are delivered to different people or repeatedly to the same people. So long as the value of a repeated message is assumed to be equal to that of a message which is delivered for the first time, cost per thousand automatically gives an apparent advantage to a medium that reaches a concentrated audience over and over again.

The problem is most acute with television. On the average weekday, 20 percent of all adult women in the United States account for 42 percent of all the television viewing hours, according to a 1982 survey by SMRB. At the opposite end of the scale, 20 percent of the women account for only 5 percent of the total viewing hours. However, brand shares among heavy viewers are not substantially different from what they are among the consuming public generally.

The same cost per thousand may represent very different kinds of advertising values. It is possible to arrive at an equivalent CPM (or at an equivalent number of GRPs) with 10 percent of the people reached 10 times, 100 percent of the people reached once, or 1 percent of the people reached 100 times. Yet these three conditions represent very different values for advertisers with different objectives and different problems of persuasion that arise from the very nature of the product.

A low cost per thousand based on an average impression may disguise poor cost efficiency in reaching key segments of the market. It may be far more economical in terms of results to spend more money to present a first message to hard-to-reach potential customers than to spend less inundating the already much-exposed. It follows from this elementary logic that every advertiser must judge media impact in terms of his own unique problems and objectives.

Cost-per-thousand comparisons are often expressed in terms of particular target audiences, like men 18-44 in households with over $30,000 income. When media are compared by such a limited criterion, it is necessarily assumed that any additional audiences they provide are valueless. Actually, it is hard to imagine a situation in which this is the case and in which potential customers are not to be found in groups other than those designated as the primary target. (This objection can be met by constructing a mathematical model in which lesser values are assigned to the other market segments captured within the audience for each of the media under comparison. However, the values will have a subjective component even if they are derived from consumer surveys, and the whole exercise will be statistically unstable because of the small subsamples from which the audience data originate.)

In any case, the advertising planner must be sure that he has defined the target group correctly. One BBDO analysis in 1975 found that TV's cost per thousand male viewers then was $2.37 for sportscasts and $2.16 (or 9 percent less) for daytime quiz shows. But the quiz show viewers (presumably older and dyspeptic males) used upset stomach remedies at nearly twice the rate of the sports viewers.[11]

With a given number of impressions, the advertiser can, of course, concentrate his fire or spread it out, regardless of what media or media combination he uses. However, conventional cost-per-thousand measures give the same weight to every message whether it reaches a consumer for the first time or for the hundred and first. Useful though the concept of cost per thousand may be to advertising executives in a hurry, it can lead to errors of judgment when it causes them to consider communication as something that exists out of context with the media environment.

When we reduce the effects of advertising to quantities of delivered impressions, we ignore the most essential nature of the communications experience. The user of cost per thousand may be quite aware that he can communicate only as well as he is permitted by the *character* of the vehicle which carries his message and by the specific *setting* it offers him.[12] But the logic of events is such that he tends to use this understanding to *qualify* or *rationalize* cost differences between schedules *after* he has done his arithmetic. (This kind of rationalization, incidentally, is quite different from the considered judgment, at the outset of any cost-per-thousand comparison of media, to select a particular space or time unit in one medium as "comparable" with another kind of unit for another medium.)

Variations within a medium.   Tremendous seasonal, regional, and other kinds of variations occur in the audiences of many media but are not always reflected in their rate structures. These enter, but do not ordinarily dominate, the many considerations involved in deciding whether a medium is right for a particular product in terms of the marketing characteristics of the people it reaches or of its psychological suitability as a form of persuasion.

A medium is only a means of communicating with the prospective purchaser of a product. Its value for the advertiser may depend not on the total number of people to whom it is exposed, but on the number of good prospects among them for the product advertised. There is an enormous range in the quality and efficiency of creative use to which a medium can be put. The same space or time may be used to win high attention and to deliver a message that carries strong appeal and conviction, or it may be utterly wasted.

Within any medium there are tremendous variations in cost per thousand by the standards that are commonly used, which are not sales standards. A TV program with a national Nielsen audience rating of 25 commonly has market-by-market ratings as high as 40 in some places and as low as 5 in others. In the case of broadcast media, the creative aspect is further complicated by the fact that there is a wide range in creative efficiency not only in the handling of the commercial, but also in the handling of the surrounding broadcast time. The broadcast advertiser seeks to reduce risk by placing his commercials (whether in a program or in spot) at a time period during which the average number of sets in use is of a known size. But there is no foolproof way to predict network program ratings, and with spot the problem is compounded.

The rate at which television audiences accumulate follows the shape of an exponential curve, with each successive repetition adding somewhat less to the unduplicated audience than the previous one. A commercial with a rating of 20 percent (that is, placed between two shows whose ratings average 20 percent) would have to be repeated twenty times before 80 percent of the households had tuned in to it at least once.

Within print media, translating circulation into total audience produces uneven consequences. Of the total reading of newspapers, 95 percent represents the primary audience of people in families where the paper was actually delivered (as it is in 3 cases out of 4) or bought on the newsstand, and only the remaining 5 percent is pass-along. For *People*, the primary audience is 18 percent of the total, pass-along 82 percent. Newspaper audience figures represent readers reached almost all on the date of publication, while the most commonly used audience figures for magazines reflect a six-week buildup of readership for a particular issue of a weekly.

Print media also accumulate readers from one issue to the next at widely varying rates that reflect differences in their exposure patterns. For magazines, the importance of pass-along readership is reflected in substantial accumulation of audiences over repeated issues. While a single issue of the *Digest* is looked at by 24 percent of the adult population, the proportion rises to 39 percent who see at least one issue in six. Sixty-seven percent of the adults read one or more newspapers on a single weekday, and the five-day accumulation is 89 percent.

Individual magazines differ substantially in the extent to which their readership is concentrated in the days immediately following publication. Weeklies obviously have a higher proportion of their total readership concentrated in the week following publication than monthlies do.* A publication like *TV Guide*, which is used for reference during a particular week, is more likely to be disposed of when the next issue appears than is the case for a magazine like *People*, which can continue to generate pass-along audiences.

The first readers a publication reaches are its subscribers and a portion of the newsstand buyers. The next groups, in chronological order, are the remainder of the newsstand buyers plus some pass-along readers. Since primary readers are higher in income and education than secondary readers, the weekly audience profile of a magazine changes during its issue life.

In short, the variations among vehicles within any one medium are far, far greater than the differences between different media. This merely underlines the importance of attempts to find good measurements of the *end* results of advertising, rather than of the *middle* range of data on audiences and costs.

Intermedia comparisons. As a measure of efficiency, cost per thousand is only as good as the data it is based on, which may or may not be accurate. On one occasion, an executive of a large agency presented to a media research group a comparison of the cost per thousand people in the 18-49 age group reached by two network programs. Based on ratings, Program A had a cost per thousand of $4.17 and Program B had a cost per thousand of $4.11. When the programs were compared on viewer preference TvQ scores, the comparative CPMs were $8.21 and $8.92, respectively.

This comparison was presented to illustrate the dilemma that confronts the media specialist who must decide whether audience ratings or preference ratings

---

*The weekly newsmagazines capture 60 percent of their total audience within the week after publication, 80 percent within 10 days, and 90 percent within 2 weeks, according to an Audits & Surveys study for *Newsweek*.

are a better criterion for comparing programs. Actually, by either standard (ratings or preference scores), the differences between the two shows were trivial. In both cases, differences that fell within the ordinary tolerance limits of random statistical error were made to seem important when they were projected in terms of dollars and cents.

Time, Inc.'s Robert Schreiber recalls a lecture he gave to the media department of a large advertising agency in Los Angeles:

> At the conclusion, I deplored the way cost per thousand—CPM—dominated media decisions in many agencies. I recounted how another agency had decided to buy seven four-color pages in *Sports Illustrated* because our CPM was $21.24 and that of the competitor was $21.45. And, I continued, another agency bought four such pages for another product—in the competitor's magazine— because its CPM was about 40 cents less than ours, on a $45 base. The media director of the agency leapt to his feet and assured me that *his* agency uses its judgment, that it does look at editorial content, and so forth. He expressed disgust at the stories I told. As I was leaving that agency, the media director stopped me and our sales representative. "Rosemary," he said to my associate, "would you step into my office for a moment." We followed him to his office. "Look," he said, "I have to tell you that you will not be on that schedule we talked about yesterday." She asked why. "Because," he answered, "your cost per thousand is 70 cents too high."[13]

When we compare vehicles within the same medium—different newspapers, television programs, or magazines, for example—it may appear reasonable to use the same yardsticks of efficiency. Really serious problems arise when we seek to compare the efficiency of advertising through different media which communicate in different ways. Everyone talks about the impossibility of making intermedia comparisons, and everyone continues to make them nonetheless. Agencies issue dollars and cents estimates of outdoor "impressions" based on traffic estimates, while they use total audience figures for programs and publications, selecting time and space units predestined to yield results that make one medium or another seem more efficient.

Broadcast time salesmen sometimes compare CPMs based on the total audiences of programs adjacent to 30-second commercials and compare them with CPMs based on recognition scores for full-page print ads. Untold numbers of unsophisticated clients and agency executives see nothing wrong with such practices. Comparing impressions delivered by the various media has been likened to the problem of comparing apples and oranges. More often it is like the problem of comparing watermelons and grapes; not only are there differences in size and in kind, but there are different ways in which each can be sliced and served.

Real time represents different relationships in broadcast and print communication. A radio or TV signal lasts a moment. A billboard or car card may be on display for months, gradually acquiring new readers but also exposing the message to many of the same people over and over. Periodicals have the same capacity to put a message in the readers' hands again and again. Each issue of a newspaper is picked up on the average of 1.8 times by each reader; each issue of the longer-lived *Reader's Digest* is picked up on nearly five different days. Almost all the people who read a daily paper read it on the very day it is published. With magazines the audience for any one issue grows over weeks, as we just observed.

The fact that communication works differently in space and in time creates peculiar problems when print and broadcast campaigns are compared. For a given dollar expenditure, the audience levels reached by the media vehicle that carries the message may appear to be far larger for print than for television. But this balance is sharply redressed when value judgments are made about the extent of conversion from "audience" to "exposure opportunity" and then to "actual exposure." The relative cost advantage of a medium at one level may be reversed at the next. It is precisely in the hazy area of value judgment over the rate of conversion that the disparities in cost efficiency between print and television often emerge.

Units of space and time. One familiar approach to advertising media costs is that of the cost accountant who computes the expense of materials and labor in production and of the various services in selling as a basis of calculating the rate of profit on each item that is made and sold. This method is most directly applicable to product sampling. A sample is a unit, it is a *thing*, we can exactly calculate the cost of making and distributing it. If we know what one product sample costs, we know what a thousand samples cost, just as we know what it costs to make a thousand units of the regular product.

This way of thinking (in bookkeeping terms) carried over very logically into advertising as long as the accepted unit was a thing: one copy of a handbill, newspaper, or magazine containing an advertisement. But an advertiser using a publication does not buy *all* of it; he buys particular units of space in particular issues. Not only did he have to weigh the relative merits of alternative ways of using his money to buy space in a particular media vehicle, he also had to weigh the comparative merits of different vehicles. Simple bookkeeping considerations no longer produced automatic answers for his decision. He was no longer working with *things*. He was working with *communication*, with human perceptions, motives, and beliefs. Yet cost per thousand represents a holdover of the bookkeeping method to problems that are essentially *psychological* in nature.

In terms of real communication, does cost per thousand mean the same thing when there are three half-minute commercials on a half-hour program as when the time is divided between a two-and-one-half-minute and a 30-second commercial? Can the cost per thousand for a 30-second spot in late evening "fringe time" be compared with the cost per thousand for the same spot in prime time? Is a double-page spread exactly twice as good as a single-page ad? To all these questions, the answer can only be, it depends.

Cost per thousand, as defined in terms of *audience* size, does not remain constant if we vary the size of the advertising unit. This is true whether we use measures of potential, like page traffic or broadcast ratings, or recall measures, like noting scores or sponsor identification. By the usual methods of evaluating advertising, the smallest unit of space or time almost inevitably appears to have the lowest cost per thousand. Thus, the split 30-second commercial appears irresistibly attractive.

When total audience figures are discounted to get down to measures of residual advertising effect like recognition or recall as measured by Starch or Gallup and Robinson, the results are never in direct proportion to the size of the advertising unit. The *intensity* of communication through different space or time units is not normally reflected in cost-per-thousand measures. Exposure to the medium, opportunity for exposure to the message, actual exposure, and recognized or recalled exposure all bear different relationships to each other in different media.

An expansion in the unit of advertising space or time is not always translated into a proportionate increase in the number of those who remember the message. Its impact may be expressed qualitatively through more effective persuasion of those exposed.

The size of the unduplicated audience is not doubled from a half-hour to a one-hour television program, nor is sponsor identification. Cost per thousand people exposed to the message does not remain constant as between a 30-second spot commercial and an 8-second I.D. We can never double page traffic, and we rarely double the number of noters or readers, though we *do* double our costs as we go from a single page in magazines to a double-page spread, or from a quarter-page newspaper ad to a half-page ad.

When different broadcasting schedules are compared on a cost-per-thousand basis, the time span selected for consideration may determine the results. Consider an hour-long radio program in which an advertiser broadcasts three one-minute commercials for the same product. He would normally calculate his cost per thousand based on the number of listeners exposed to each of the commercials. But if he chose to split his three minutes of allotted time into two 90-second commercials rather than three of 60 seconds, the cost efficiency might appear to be much less even though he would be reaching only slightly fewer people for exactly the same length of attentive exposure time. The same spurious difference applies when an advertiser must decide whether to buy a page of magazine or newspaper space as a single unit or to divide it up into two half-page units in different parts of the publication. Superficially, it would seem that at half the space cost, each of the small advertisements is being placed before the same size audience as the bigger one, even though it may attract the attention of fewer readers.

Any intelligent attempt to compare different units within a medium has to be framed in terms of specific applications, rather than in terms of universal laws or generalities. The numbers have to be interpreted and tempered by qualitative judgment. The efficiency of a medium must be seen not only in the number of message units it delivers, but in its capacity to reach into areas where competitive advertising is weak.

Qualitative judgment enters, for instance, in determining, for a schedule in a given medium, what size of standard space or time unit—and what size of investment—to put into each market on the list.

The spatial distribution of media may affect, or appear to affect, their comparative cost efficiency. In any local medium, certain basic costs of doing business remain much the same regardless of the size of the market or the number of people reached. Therefore, the small-town paper or station cannot possibly provide the same number of readers or listeners per dollar expended on space or time as its big-city contemporaries. Of course, it costs a great deal more to buy a minute of prime television time or a full newspaper page in a city like New York than it does in Rapid City, South Dakota, but this absolute cost is more than compensated for by the far larger audience that the advertiser can reach with the vehicle in a larger market.

The small-town paper or station can legitimately take issue with the advertiser's assumption that it is fair to apply a constant yardstick of cost. For example, the small newspaper, with its fewer pages, may argue that a smaller unit of its space is equivalent to a larger unit in a larger paper, since there is less competition for the reader's attention. Any small-town medium might claim that its advertisers command a special degree of the community's loyalty, attention, and interest. This argument seems to be supported by the conventional advertising practice of using A, B, C, and D schedules in local media, which we discussed in Chapter 6. Such schedules are ordinarily based on the several markets' size or importance to the particular advertiser. In each category the use of the medium can be varied in the length of the commercial or the size of ad or in the total number of messages run.* (In newspapers, for instance, four color may be used in A markets, two color in B markets and black and white in C markets. Thus, if per capita weighting is heavier in the A markets than in the C markets in terms of messages delivered, it may still be kept equivalent in terms of expenditures.)

The difficulties of comparing different units within one medium are compounded in intermedia comparisons. The problem becomes particularly acute when a decision must be made as to what space unit is directly comparable with what unit of time. This type of comparison is conventionally made in terms of common or standard-size dimensions—30 seconds or 60 seconds versus a quarter-page or a full-page black and white or in four colors. It is never expressed in precise terms: 18½ seconds versus 17¾ column inches. But the use of standard units in making value judgments on media impact has a curious consequence. If the judgments are even slightly off, they are perpetuated throughout all of the subsequent arithmetic on cost efficiency.

Cost-per-thousand comparisons made on the basis of any given unvarying units of space or time inevitably work to the advantage of some media and to the disadvantage of others; this is due in large part to the different patterns of physical distribution for each medium. Most newspaper circulation areas do not radiate as far from their central cities as television station coverage. On the other hand, the competition among vehicles is different from one medium to the next; there are far fewer television stations than newspapers, just as there are far fewer newspapers than radio stations. A strong radio signal covers a much larger area than VHF television, which in turn covers a broader area with the same signal

*This additional complication may in some cases help to keep media lists short. The smaller the number of markets in which the agency media department has to buy space or time, the less work and trouble it has.

strength than UHF. The trucks that deliver morning newspapers travel on un-crowded roads at night and generally deliver to a broader area than their evening competitors.

In 1982 the advertiser who bought a page of advertising in *all* the daily newspapers in the United States paid 95 percent more than if he had bought a page in papers that gave 60 percent coverage or better in the top 200 markets.* It is the unusual advertiser who buys a full page in every newspaper. Suppose he buys smaller space units in middle-sized and smaller markets than he buys in the larger ones. On what basis is his cost per thousand to be compared among the various newspapers? And how should he compare the *average* cost per thousand for his varying-size newspaper ads against the average cost per thousand for his standard-length television announcements? Such questions must be answered in daily practice, but the guesswork and judgment that go into the answers are often forgotten when the numbers emerge at the end of the assembly line.

An alternative approach

Several decades ago, an important (but subsequently ignored) report entitled "Evaluation of Statistical Methods Used in Obtaining Broadcast Ratings" was prepared by a very able committee appointed by the American Statistical Association on behalf of the Congressional Subcommittee on Legislative Oversight. According to this report, "The type of measure called 'dollars per thousand' is biased and has a large variance especially if the rating and effective sample size are both small. . . . The question that we wish to raise is whether it might not be preferable, instead of referring to dollars per thousand homes, to refer to homes per hundred dollars, or perhaps even better, audience per hundred dollars and to include not only the estimate of homes but also the estimate of people and the composition."[14]

This recommendation is based on the simple statistical fact that "in computing dollars per thousand homes, the estimated rating" (which is subject to large variance) "is in the denominator of the equation" where it will, of course, carry the greatest weight relative to the presumably more accurate cost figure. But more important, I believe, is the implicit recognition in this observation that one must start with the overall cost of the advertising investment and *then* use judgment in interpreting what he is getting in return.

The media planner who is forced by his unfeeling, dull, and conventional clients and associates to use CPM to compare media should first calculate the cost of exposure opportunity for each medium and message with the reach and frequency needed to make contact with prospective customers. ("Exposure opportunity" can be defined in the terms of the A.R.F. model, with the advertising message present within the individual's range of potential perception by sight or hearing.) Only then, and with the aid of any available evidence, should he make the qualitative judgment of what he can achieve with words or pictures in the appropriate units of space or time in converting exposure opportunity into exposure.

---

*The typical national spot TV list—and the typical newspaper list—seldom goes beyond the top 50 markets.

We can easily calculate what rates of conversion for two different media (each used as we would prefer to use it) would make their cost efficiency come out equal when translated into exposed message units. At this point we are immediately faced with the consequences of any faulty value judgments we may have made on the subject of impact, and we can reconsider our assumptions if we decide we have erred in the direction of greater generosity toward one medium than the other.

A given medium must be judged differently within the overall mix of media than it can be judged when taken in splendid isolation. Media can, of course, reinforce each other in their coverage of the market, in time scheduling, and in their creative aspect. Where a mix of media is used, the cost-minded advertiser should pass judgment on the efficiency of the combination rather than on each medium by itself.

The advertiser who thinks in terms of cost per thousand is like a military strategist who tries to compare the cost of a thousand men, a thousand planes, a thousand submarines, and a thousand guns. We know today that there are military situations in which it is more efficient to use a patrol than to launch a nuclear missile. The military planner must start with an overall budget, but he distributes it among various weapons in relation to the appropriate tasks he assigns each of them to reach his objective, and *not* in relation to any arbitrary cost criteria.

Notes

1. Standard advertising units (SAUs) were introduced by the daily newspaper business in 1981, a first step in the direction of full standardization of newspaper formats. The bewildering variety of newspaper page sizes, column widths, and formats reflected the wide array of equipment in use, as well as newspapers' traditional desire to look distinctive.

2. *The New York Times*, May 6, 1982.

3. By 1983, almost all newspapers were offering volume discounts for national advertisers under a program called Newsplan, but the differential between national and local advertisers was still widely maintained.

4. In a doctoral dissertation on the subject, James Ferguson has suggested that newspapers have held retail rates down because retail ads are informational and offer as strong an incentive as editorial matter to building circulation. Unfortunately, he ignores the fact that retail and national ads of the same size and product type get equivalent readership scores; *cf.* his *The Advertising Rate Structure in the Daily Newspaper Industry* (Englewood Cliffs, N.J.: Prentice-Hall, Inc., 1963).

5. Quoted in *The New York Times*, February 28, 1982.

6. *Media-Scope*, January 1970, p. 35.

7. Robert S. Weinberg, "An Analytical Approach to Advertising Expenditure Strategy," Paper prepared for the Association of National Advertisers, Inc., 1960.

8. Testimony before the Antitrust Subcommittee, Committee on the Judiciary, Eighty-Fourth Congress, Second Session.

9. *Toward Better Media Comparisons*, Report of the Audience Concepts Committee of the Advertising Research Foundation, 1961, p. 15.

10. Gerhart D. Wiebe, "Public Opinion Between Elections," *Public Opinion Quarterly*, 21, 2 (Summer 1957): 229-36.

11. Thomas Dillon, "What I Don't Know About Television," Paper presented to the ANA Television Workshop, New York City, February 25, 1975.

12. A survey conducted by McBain Research among 118 senior level corporate advertising executives in 1981 found that 57 percent *disagreed* with the statement that "programming quality is *not* as important as cost-per-thousand target audience considerations."

13. Robert J. Schreiber, "The Way Ahead—An American View," in Harry Henry, *Readership Research*, p. 463.

14. "Evaluation of Statistical Methods Used in Obtaining Broadcast Ratings, " Report of the Committee on Interstate and Foreign Commerce, 1961, p. 27.

Chapter 13
Advertising Models
and Advertising Realities

Advertising models, as any schoolchild knows, are good-looking people who pose in ads and commercials, usually flashing smiles of ecstasy in the contemplation of whatever merchandise they are displaying. But there are advertising models of another kind that have become equally important. These are the mathematical representations of communications processes that lead to consumer decisions and the projections and extensions of data from media research in ways that facilitate the strategic planning of ad campaigns.

Intelligent advertising planners have probably always had "pictures in their heads" of how a particular advertising approach might influence people to buy their products. For many years, they have used all the data they could get on markets and media to compare alternatives. However, the advent of electronic data processing revolutionized the handling of these data and created a vast appetite for more.

Today, any discussion of advertising media strategy occurs in the shadow of the computer. Computers have won a firm place in automating clerical operations in advertising: calculating rates, estimating, ordering, billing, and the like. In performing these functions, computers are essentially substituting for the mechanical punch-card processing equipment that agencies used for many years.

Since media rates, circulations, and audiences are constantly changing, the use of electronic data processing to store relevant information represents a possibility for large-scale savings of time and money.

The purchase of newspaper advertisements and of television and radio spots entails many hundreds of individual contracts and arrangements with individual newspapers and stations. The average transaction in buying spot TV involves only $10-15,000, in a schedule that may add up to millions. The administrative cost of handling such schedules is substantially greater than the cost of placing the equivalent billings in network television or magazines, so here the savings made possible by the computer are particularly important.

Availabilities have always represented a major headache in buying broadcast spots, since most advertisers want their announcements placed by the same criterion, i.e., in the time spot with the greatest possible audience, at the lowest possible price. When a computer is hooked up by phone to the appropriate data base, it can instantaneously check available buys (by station and time) in much the same way that it can check seat reservations on the airlines. Station representative firms use their computers for this purpose.

Both station and newspaper representatives also use computers in a way that has become routine in any substantial business: to calculate rates and discounts, produce invoices, record payments, and perform miscellaneous paperwork. Such accounting functions also represent the principal use of computers in advertising agencies. BIAS (Broadcast Industry Automation System) is one of the services that handle computerized record-keeping for television stations, keeping a running inventory of spot availabilities as well as arrangements for billing clients.

Donovan Data Services is used by 22 of the top 25 agencies and is linked to all of the broadcast station representatives. It is an automated buying service that uses computer tapes of the Nielsen and Arbitron local ratings. A buyer can enter his own rate estimates, or the rates previously used, for all commercial positions available on a particular station. These can be ranked by audience size or by cost per thousand. Audience estimates can be made for new programs or for commercial adjacencies next to them. When the ratings reports for the individual markets come out, the actual ratings, which are in the data bank, can be contrasted with the original estimate made at the time of the buy. Representatives negotiate price with the agencies or time buying services, and the computer then checks and ranks their choices.

Our interest in computers does not lie in the area of automating routine operations but rather in media planning and decision making. The application of the computer to advertising was no more than an incidental aspect of its adoption to facilitate business management or, for that matter, of its adoption to facilitate scientific analysis. Enormous amounts of information could be assimilated and melded, and relationships could be examined not only among sets of data describing real phenomena but also among sets of artificial data generated to test hypotheses or to check the consequences of various possible marketing actions.

Before the computer, a substantial staff in every media department was devoted to "estimating" the cost of a buy before a final plan was prepared. With the automation of media rate information, the extent of this clerical operation has been greatly reduced. Moreover, the computer can readily produce collateral information on cost per thousand, audiences, and duplication at the same time it shows the total cost of a proposed schedule.

The computer does not itself actually make decisions, about media or anything else. However, it can make more knowledgeable decisions possible by its ability to rank or compare media according to specified instructions and (on the basis of its ability to do arithmetic) to apply logic and to distinguish like from unlike—all with great speed.

Computer models as learning devices

To instruct or program a computer to compare media, we must first have a mathematical model by which our data can be organized. The fundamental assumptions behind such models must be evaluated, not in terms of mathematics, but in terms of how well they actually hold up in the light of what we know about human beings and their actions and about the process of communication. In science the great value of a model is that it permits a systematic statement of the theories or assumptions that bear on the explanation of a set of events in a way that permits those theories to be tested and evaluated against actual experience. The model provides a rationale for giving order and shape to the evidence. But when the evidence turns out to be inconsistent with the model, the model itself must then be reexamined and altered to bring it in closer alignment with reality.

Models in science are essentially, therefore, a *learning* device, rather than a means of explaining phenomena or of deciding what to do. They represent a problem only when they are taken literally, as a true depiction of the real world, rather than as a technique for better understanding the principles that underlie the events that can be measured and observed.

We can look upon a mathematical model as a simplified representation of a highly complex system. By reducing our description to terms that are economical and abstract, we have a better notion of how things work, even though this stripped-down version no longer exactly corresponds to anything that really exists. This is what the sociologist Max Weber described as an "Ideal Type"—an instructional model. It is instructive to design such a model, to put it through its paces, and to tinker with it to make sure it runs right. In the process of doing this, we are forced to take a fresh look at things we take for granted, and thereby we have insights that we didn't have before. In the past few decades, models and schemata of all kinds have become increasingly common. Presumably, their popularity suggests that it is not only intellectually stimulating for the authors to go though the reasoning process, but that it is similarly intriguing to readers who are willing to follow them step by step along the way.

By altering the input into a model, we can chart the implications of change in one element for all the other elements in the system; we can determine the points of greatest leverage, and we can save time and effort by identifying risks as well as opportunities.

A different function for a model is found when we regard it as a device by which alternative courses of action can be arrayed by predesignated criteria in such a way as to generate decisions. The computer has provided the technological capability for this kind of decision-making model, both because of its capacity to store and manipulate large quantitites of data and because of its ability to simulate new data. Since a model represents a simplified version of the world, the information it uses need not be literally and directly derived from research findings but can incorporate hunches or judgments or estimates based on measures of probability applied against actual evidence.

The economist Joan Robinson has delivered a sharp warning of the dangers involved in representing the complexities of economic activity through mathematical models:

> Mathematical operations are performed upon entities that cannot be defined; calculations are made in terms of units that cannot be measured; accounting identities are mistaken for functional relationships; correlations are mistaken for causal laws; differences are identified with

336 Strategy in Advertising

changes; and one-way movements in time are treated like movements to and fro in space. The complexity of models is elaborated merely for display, far and away beyond the possibility of application to reality."[1]

But such criticism has been offset by the self-evident value of models, both to scholars and to managers, in giving a semblance of order to the vast aggregation of statistics that are incessantly being assembled on every aspect of economic and social behavior. The computer simply provided the mechanics required to satisfy an existing need to handle information in an orderly way and to try to make sense of it. In the social sciences, including marketing sciences, increasingly complex multivariate statistical techniques were routinely used as a by-product of the fact that packaged computer programs for them were readily available. The result was a growing disparity between the real world of marketing and advertising research and the domain of theoretical scholarship fostered in university business schools. In 1966, nonacademic authors accounted for 55 percent of the articles published by the *Journal of Marketing*. By 1972, they represented only 10 percent, and they wrote 16 percent of the articles in the *Journal of Marketing Research* (down from 29 percent).[2] By 1982, by my count, they were 4 percent in both journals.

Mathematical models have been introduced into the marketing practice of major corporations, spurred by the initiative of organizations like the Marketing Science Institute (founded in 1961) and a number of research and management consulting firms. The PIMS project has been run since 1972 by the Strategic Planning Institute, on behalf of a number of cooperating corporations. It collects data on 2,000 corporate divisions, which can be used to determine, through mathematical modeling, what factors contribute to return on investment. And about a third of the agencies and a fifth of the advertisers questioned by Lipstein and Neelankavil[3] in 1981 said they attempted to evaluate ad campaigns in terms of mathematical models, usually related to the amount of money being spent on advertising.[4]

Media selection models in advertising, like other models in marketing, have a great value insofar as they force practitioners to make their assumptions explicit and to think through to logical conclusions the guesses, hunches, and estimates that advertising executives generally make as a matter of course but rarely can articulate. This process of making things explicit goes far beyond the problems of media—even beyond advertising—and covers the much broader subject of consumer decision making.

The computer provides the mechanism by which models can be tested in relation to a great variety of evidence and also in relation to various alternative ways of assessing the same evidence. It can force the practitioner to confront the consequences of changing his opinions about the market, the effects of advertising, or the capacities of the communications media. For example, he can be made to realize that the introduction of new ideas into his conceptions of the purchase cycle, the value of repeated messages, and the qualitative impact of one medium versus another can have certain measurable repercussions on his ultimate decision.

Used in this way, the computer is a tool by which the advertising planner can sharpen his thinking and clearly define the areas of his own uncertainty and ignorance so that they may be examined and studied. Like any useful tool, it may be misapplied. This might happen in media planning if the computer is expected to *make* decisions rather than to indicate what the consquences of alternative decisions might be. The few agencies which by now have gained extensive experience with computers in media selection have learned to use them as an aid to judgment. But many of the advertising layman's notions are still defined in terms of the old idea of the robot or thinking machine, which produces infallible judgments all by itself.

In electronic data processing we put certain arrays of information into the machine and expect to get back rearrangements of this information. We start with a certain input in the form of resources. We have a given number of dollars we can spend in a number of alternative ways. We put dollars in one end and out the other end come measures of comparative efficiency. We usually hope that efficiency reflects the comparative sales yields of these differing strategies of investment.

To be sure, we don't ordinarily project the end results in terms of sales dollars (although this too can be arranged); we usually project them instead in terms of "audience impressions delivered," Gross Rating Points, "ad exposure opportunities," or some other fancy term. But the underlying assumption is that communication can be reduced to units and that different types of communication, with different objectives and in different media, can somehow be reduced to comparable units. This means that a communications campaign must be thought of as an assemblage of units that can be arranged in different combinations. We think of these units—"impressions," or GRPs, or "exposure opportunties"—as though they were things because they all have dollar values.

The conception of human communication as something made of inputs and outputs is compatible with the most mechanistic kind of stimulus-response psychology and can be highly useful for certain purposes. But it is quite different from an attempt to understand communication as a *process* involving the exchange of symbolic meanings that cannot be measured. The computer merely compounds the problems that I reviewed at length in the previous chapter.

What assumptions underlie the creation of a computerized media selection model? A great variety of assumptions have been employed, and the whole field has undergone enormous changes just within 20 years. At an early stage in this short history, E. A. Rawes, Manager of Consumer Research of ICI Fibres, Ltd., presented a model of his company's media selection program to the British Institute of Practitioners in Advertising. He used both audience data (which he defined as "opportunities") and readership data (defined as "impacts"). One of his assumptions was "that the probability of an individual noting an advertisement is constant, regardless of whether or not he has already noted an earlier insertion."[5] This kind of assumption, if incorrect, can wreak havoc with many of the conclusions that subsequently emerge with the authority of "The Machine" behind them.

The place of advertising in a model of the total marketing system was described as follows by a British O.R. expert, B. T. Warner:

Advertising has a short-term effect on predisposition to purchase, and a longer-term effect which is measured by cumulative advertising exposure. The magnitude of the short-term effect was assumed to depend on both the cumulative advertising exposure and the purchaser's attitudes toward the brands in the product group. These attitudes arise from both advertising and previous use. It was assumed that only favorable attitudes arise from advertising, but that attitudes from use may be favorable or unfavorable.[6]

Warner's statement of his assumptions illustrates the problems implicit in a model that reduces the actual complexities of consumer response to only a limited and manageable number of dimensions. For example, he does not allow for the possibility that advertising may have no effect on people's attitudes or that it may have a negative effect. Warner illustrates his assumptions with a series of geometrical diagrams illustrating relationships for such things as the number of advertising impacts, short-term effects on the predisposition to buy a brand, and cumulative advertising exposures. He also presents charts simulating marketing situations that might arise from various strategic moves on the part of the advertiser.

The progress of these hypothetical events evolves from game theory and from the "scenarios" used in contemporary military strategizing. The brand manager plays much the same role as the field marshal of an army. The number of opponents is known, even though the extent of their resources may be a matter of conjecture. Not only may competitive counter-moves be predicted (on the basis of survey data), but also consumer responses to a manufacturer's actions. As the model comes more and more to resemble the real world, more and more information must be fed into it. It becomes more elaborate and sophisticated, and the interaction of all the elements becomes more and more difficult to trace without the help of a computer. Real life is seldom as crisp or simple as game theory almost inevitably assumes it must be. Brand X cannot always expect that only its well-known adversary, Brand Y, will be in the picture when it makes its next move. Other manufacturers may enter the field. New developments may cause the whole product category to become obsolete, or it may be bypassed in public interest for other reasons.

However, even though game theory rests on simplified and idealized notions of the real world of competitive marketing, this type of marketing "game" is very useful for the business-school training of managers and future managers. It provides an invaluable discipline to the marketing strategist who wants to anticipate intelligently the consequences of his own moves in relation to the other forces in the market.

Linear programming

The first and most widely publicized system of applying the computer to media selection involved the use of linear programming. "L.P." is an operating procedure that had previously been applied widely to making business decisions in other fields where complex data had to be manipulated and arranged to arrive at the best solution among a great array of possible alternatives. Perhaps its first application to media selection was made by Alec Lee and John Burkart, then of British European Airways, in 1958.

Linear programming is a mathematical technique that permits the comparison of a great many alternative combinations in terms of a single criterion (in advertising, normally cost efficiency). The alternatives are checked through in a logical sequence by a technique called "iteration," which first takes two combinations at random and compares them, then compares the better combination with another random selection and continues to play the game until one particular combination keeps winning. The procedure allows us to limit the number of comparisons actually calculated and to focus only on those that represent likely possibilities.

Linear programming lends itself to the solution of problems in which the elements being compared differ in their characteristics and capabilities and in their inherent restrictions or limitations. L.P. does not provide *ideal* solutions, but only the best solutions possible under the circumstances, given the existing means and restrictions. Although linear programming can be handled mathematically by hand or with ordinary calculating machines, the amount of information that has to be processed and compared in making most advertising decisions is so great that a computer is essential for practical reasons. Because it is a mathematical procedure, linear programming depends on numbers. Qualitative judgments must be translated into mathematical terms that the machine can accept and manipulate. D. H. Philips, media director of S. H. Benson, a British agency, points out that in his own work "large numbers of media selected by the computer for a specific schedule are insensitive to variations in weights used to reflect qualitative attributes—but enough sensitivity remains to require further work on this problem." (The "sensitivity" or insensitivity refers to the degree of effect that the qualitative weights have on the outcome. This of course depends on the design of the model, as well as on the numbers fed into it.)

The first step in the procedure is the bringing together of all relevant information regarding each alternative under consideration. In media planning, the basic data required by the computer might include (1) the available budget*, (2) the number of people that can be reached by each vehicle, both exclusively and in combination with others, (3) the characteristics of these people expressed in terms that reflect their values as marketing targets, (4) the cost of buying a certain unit of space or time (with all of the discount contingencies built in for each vehicle), and (5) a set of estimates that reflects the conversion of gross audience into effective communication, predicated on the use of that particular space or time unit. The purpose of the last set of estimates is to adjust the raw audience figures by judging how suitable the vehicle is for the objective of the particular advertising campaign, the creative opportunities it affords, the compatibility of the media environment, and the communications impact. Since there is not much relevant existing data with wide applications across the board, these

---

*Since two alternative schedules rarely cost exactly the same number of dollars and cents, the computer is programmed to provide a reasonable amount of leeway in making comparisons.

estimates (when they have been attempted) have represented subjective judgments made by experts.

An essential feature of linear programming is that it accepts constraints that may represent realistic outer limits to certain choices. In planning menus, for example, certain foods, however nourishing, may be served no more often than once a day, or even once a week. In media planning, limitations on the use of a vehicle may rise either from the advertiser's arbitrary judgment that he must use certain vehicles and use them only in certain ways or from the inherent requirements of the vehicle itself. It is obviously impossible to buy 13 issues of a monthly magazine in the course of a year or 53 issues of a weekly. The constraints may be self-imposed, for example, by a policy judgment that it would be imprudent to buy a particular weekly publication more often than once a month.

With all of the relevant information stored in the computer's "memory," the program can be activated to successively rank and combine media vehicles in various combinations in terms of whatever criteria are considered relevant. In practice, the key criterion is apt to be "efficiency," which may represent a restatement of cost per thousand expressed in a new language. The objective may be stated in terms of maximum coverage, reach, reach with a certain desired minimum frequency, or the number of impressions or GRPs delivered against a particular target group. These figures are limited by the budgetary constraint on the selection of available vehicles. Thus maximum coverage or impression delivery of predesignated products still has to be expressed at a given price—in cost per thousand.

In the simplest form of linear programming, every repetition of a message through a given medium might be considered to have a value exactly equivalent to that of every previous repetition. But linear programming does not require an assumption of linearity in the way that advertising works. (Linearity would mean that two advertising exposures were twice as good as one, four were four times as good, etc.) Linear programming can be used in a nonlinear way, following any assumption desired about the greater or lesser value of successive exposures of advertising messages to the same individuals. There would still have to be an orderly progression implicit in this description, so that it could be described algebraically; for example, the second exposure might be worth half the first, and the third half the second—ordinarily it could not be made worth *more* than the second.

A media decision model using linear programming need not be written in a simplistic way to provide a single "optimum solution." It may aim for "suboptimization"—something practical, though less than ideal. The computer may be instructed to provide a variety of solutions ranked in order according to predetermined criteria. The computer can be instructed to print out relevant information (on reach, frequency, and cost efficiency) for alternative schedules so that a skillful analyst can inspect them in the old-fashioned, reflective way, holding his qualitative judgment in abeyance until the straightforward statistical comparisons have been made. This can be done by separating the computations that reflect the effects of qualitative weights or subjective assessments of media impact from those that reflect the harder information on costs and audience size and composition. Thus linear programming provides the media planner with a procedure not only for comparing alternative schedules, but for testing his own assumptions and improving his understanding of their consequences.

Simulation

The advent of computers coincided with the growing information demands of market planning and resulted in a great demand for detailed data on media audiences that could be related to usage patterns of particular products. Small newspapers and radio stations were bewildered when they first received letters from big advertising agencies asking for a breakdown of their audience by education and A, B, C, D Nielsen county groups.* Syndicated research services moved in to offer this kind of information that the local media were not equipped to supply.

But not everyone rushed to subscribe to the new services. Some researchers contended that consumer profiles of media audiences could be estimated by statistical simulation without the need for new research.

Simulation is a mathematical technique whose application has been greatly facilitated by the computer's capacity to sift rapidly through vast masses of data. It can be readily used in association with linear programming to provide useful data in the form needed to make intelligent decisions. However, simulation is not in itself a way of comparing alternatives or of arriving at a "decision."

As the word implies, simulation is a way of extrapolating from existing information in order to estimate the shape of an unknown real world. This can be done by utilizing the computer's capacity to relate evidence from different sources in a random way, by what is appropriately known as the Monte Carlo method. One form of simulation occurs in business "games," in which the consequences of various kinds of decisions on pricing, warehousing, and promotion can be traced against imaginary consumer response and competitive reactions.

The kind of simulation that is relevant to media strategy commonly entails the use of survey data derived from many different separate investigations of the same population. (Surveys are, of course, being conducted all the time using somewhat different interviewing and sampling techniques but aimed at describing very much the same universe or population.) Ideally, the media analyst would like to obtain, using a single study of the same good sample of people, full information on consumption patterns for his product and on the rate of exposure of all his prospective consumers to all the media vehicles he might conceivably consider using. In practice, learning this much from one survey is not often possible.

All numbers projected from surveys represent estimates of the true proportions that exist in the population at large. The statistical errors of sampling in any one survey are constant. When marketing and media questions are asked of the same people, the interrelationships between them have a basic integrity that can only be approximated when the data are combined from two separate sources. But the answers do not necessarily have any inherently greater accuracy than

---

*This is a classification that Nielsen uses to differentiate counties by the degree to which they are urbanized.

answers separately obtained from two samples. This fact provides the essential rationale for the use of simulation.

As I pointed out in Chapter 11, the evidence that we get from public opinion surveys becomes less and less valid as we try to get more and more information about different things in a longer and longer interview. This, of course, is a growing problem as the syndicated research services add additional questions and measurements. In compensation for this possible lessening of accuracy, the longer interviews do provide their users with the opportunity to make all kinds of cross-tabulations without the considerable effort and expense of developing a simulation to solve every marketing or media mix problem. Even the best and most brilliantly planned syndicated research service cannot measure every individual media vehicle with exactness. And it can hardly anticipate all of the vast data requirements of different advertisers with different products to sell, different marketing and advertising objectives, and a different array of advertising budgets within which their media selections might be made. Simulation represents a procedure by which the best available information on each useful item can be put together in order to arrive at a conclusion. In other words, if one survey tells us that the best customers for "hard rock" records are girls between the ages of 12 and 15, we don't need to get our media data from the same survey. Instead, we can use other samples of girls in the same age group and find what they watch, listen to, or read. Then we can use statistical estimating procedures to put the marketing and media data together. Needless to say, the validity of this procedure depends on the real relevance of the criteria by which the data are matched.

A familiar use of simulation occurred for years on election night, when each of the television networks was able (generally correctly) to project the winners from the first handful of votes tabulated. This was done by examining the historical voting records for individual counties or precincts, incorporating any relevant pre-election poll data on voting intentions and preferences and applying the appropriate weights to the limited data at hand.*

A pioneer use of this method was a forecast of the 1960 presidental election by Ithiel de Sola Pool, a political scientist. Through the short-lived Simulmatics Corporation, Pool and his associates sought to apply the same processes of statistical reasoning to the realm of marketing and media decision making. Their system put together information from the best available media and marketing surveys to estimate the comparative virtues of various media combinations.

Almost all major surveys classify respondents by sex, age, income, education, and so on. One survey may break people into 3 income groups, another into 4; and one may classify people into 3 age groups, another into 10. Simple statistical procedures may be used to produce estimates that resolve these differences. The computer itself can be used to rearrange data in different intervals than those assembled in the original field survey. Once all the relevant information on markets and media has been sorted into a convenient set of bins, the simulation technique makes it possible to recombine the information as though it had all

---

*Election night forecasts are now made on the basis of "exit polling" of people as they leave the voting booths, but that is another story.

been gathered from the same individuals at the same time. For example, men under 35, with incomes over $35,000 a year and with at least some college education, living in the suburbs of metropolitan cities, can all be regarded as a single marketing group with a characteristic likelihood of using various products and of exposure to different media vehicles.

Early media mix systems

Although none of them have survived, the media mix models of the 1960s have more than historical interest.[7] They attempted to formalize, in the rigorous logical terms imposed by computer programming, the step-by-step process by which media are analyzed and compared. They made explicit many of the tacit assumptions that underlay comparative assessments of media impact and values.

Mediametrics. The first media-planning computer model to receive wide publicity was the "Mediametrics" system developed in cooperation with CEIR, an EDP firm, by Batten, Barton, Durstine & Osborn (BBDO). In the Mediametrics procedure, media and media units were first accepted or rejected by the planners on the basis of their feasibility for a given advertiser. For example, it might be decided that transit car cards should not be used for an institutional advertiser, that 30-seconds are too short to provide an adequate product demonstration, or that a 100-line newspaper advertising unit would be too short for the lengthy "reason-why" copy.

Within a given medium, some units might be considered feasible and some might not, but a number of different feasible units were brought into the comparison for each feasible medium.

The computer was fed a "static input" of (1) data giving a demographic profile of the consumers, based on available market research, and (2) demographic data on the people and households reached by a single exposure of each media unit. The problem for the computer to solve was essentially one of matching and maximizing economical exposures to the best customers. This required detailed data on the characteristics of media audiences on a basis comparable from one vehicle to the next (though in the case of local media it was often not available on any basis at all).

The procedure also required that there be comparability in the message units for each medium under consideration. Here Mediametrics relied on the expert (but subjective) judgment of the agency's media, research, creative, and contact people on the individual account. With the special needs of the product in mind, they judged the appropriate message unit in each medium in terms of its suitability for telling the story of the product, the quality of reproduction, the media environment, and "merchandisibility" to dealers and the trade. The resulting "impact" value was given a quantitative weight.

Thus a weight of 7.5 might be assigned to a 60-second TV commercial on a particular program while a weight of 5.0 might be assigned to a four-color ad in a particular magazine. This would mean that the average person exposed to the TV commercial would be judged to have received 50 percent more impact than the average reader exposed to the magazine ad.

A measure of "exposure probability" was next applied against the results of the previous calculations. In the case of TV, program ratings were projected both to households and to individuals and were then discounted by a measure of "effective perception" derived from BBDO's TV-copy research experimental setup, "Channel I." (For example, effective perception was set at 60 percent of program audiences for a one-minute commercial and 45 percent for a 30-second commercial.) For print advertising, the audience of the publication was discounted with a rule-of-thumb procedure identical for magazines and newspapers. (This credited the ad with an "effective perception" that generally ran 50-60 percent higher than the Starch noting score.)

The end result of the previous calculations was called a Rated Exposure Unit (REU). The computer then extended this single unit value for each vehicle to the full extent of a media cycle. Into this program could now be built restrictions that incorporated such factors as publication frequency and programming availabilities as well as minimum and maximum budget levels within which the medium could be used with each unit under consideration.

The result of these comparisons was to produce an optimum combination of media (which might be different than a combination of the best media). The objective was to maximize the number of REUs that could be bought within budgetary and other constraints. Substitute schedules could now be compared with the optimum to see what advantages they might offer in terms of aggregate reach, frequency, or cost efficiency. Finally, a "sensitivity analysis" made it possible for the media analyst to see how various elements (including the qualitative ones) affected the final combination. In effect, it was possible for the media planner to judge whether a change of 5 or 10 percentage points in his subjective judgment of a medium (or in his assessment of the relevant data) would bring the medium back into the schedule after it had been eliminated.

The original Mediametrics model was widely publicized as the pioneer application of linear programming to the media selection problems of a major agency, and it illustrates the complexity of the operations involved even in a comparatively simple system. Mediametrics did not solve the problem of how media *selection* and media *scheduling* should interact. BBDO moved on to LP II, an even more complex model that took into account the degree of evenness, as well as frequency, with which messages could be delivered to the desired target in a given period of time.

Iteration. Data Inc., the data-processing subsidiary of the Standard Rate & Data Service, made a strong effort during its brief three-year life span to promote the "iterative solution to optimize media schedules." It defined "iterations" as "successive approximations to an optimum mathematical solution in which each successive iteration improves the solution over the results of the preceding iteration." (This is, in effect, the conventional style of optimization used in linear programming.)

Starting with a given list of media vehicles, Data Inc. calculated first the *total* number of "heavy users" of a product in the audience of each vehicle and then the number which each vehicle would reach exclusively, without duplication from the other media being considered. A vehicle was positioned on the schedule when it contributed a substantially unduplicated reach, and at that point the remaining vehicles could in turn be examined for duplication.

The objective was to produce a "combination of the fewest media vehicles which delivers the most comprehensive coverage of . . . the heavy-user market." Coverage, of course, was expressed in terms of the audience reached and not in terms of exposure or impact, so the problem of spreading an advertising budget among vehicles with widely varying communications capabilities remained. The solution to this problem was achieved by means of a technique that boiled down to an affirmation of old-fashioned, intuitive media judgment. Describing the final stages of its "iteration" procedure for one product, by way of illustration, Data Inc. wrote in its bulletin:

> The creative judgments on this product established one-minute com-
> mercials as necessary on TV, four-color pages as necessary in magazines
> and supplements, and 600-line ads as necessary in newspapers. Using
> these creative requirements, detailed schedules for a one-year period
> were established. . . .

Thus, in this instance, the solution prescribed by the computer flowed directly from the subjective assumptions made by the analysts.

Dynamic High Assay. Young & Rubicam's "High Assay Models" incorporated a "Data Breeder," which took existing media and marketing data from outside services and from the agency's own research files and extrapolated new data for the media evaluation. Y & R was concerned with the timing and spacing of advertising pressure as well as with its total distribution to different groups of potential customers.

The Y & R system also made it possible to evaluate how the different subjective value judgments that were incorporated into the media comparison affected the final outcome. As I suggested earlier, this kind of "sensitivity testing" focuses the attention of the media planner on the more questionable areas of his own judgment.

Y & R used a pluralistic approach; they spoke of "models" (in the plural), suggesting that different procedures might apply to different problems. The planning process broke down into four steps; (1) strategy selection, in which objectives were defined; (2) assumption testing, which reviewed the fundamental picture of the brand and the market; (3) one-time media efficiencies, in which media were ranked according to their efficiency on a single exposure, and (4) integrated advertising planning, which looked at consumption behavior and multiple media exposures extended through time.

As this brief description suggests, the Y & R procedure was oriented primarily to the assembly of the best evidence and guesses of all the relevant marketing information on the purchase cycle, brand switching, the value of repeated exposure, and the effect of copy appeals on holding present customers and attracting new ones.

For any given product, the market could be separated into different segments that differed in their value to the advertiser. An estimate was made of the cost of gaining an additional sale from within the prime target segment, assuming that the more repeated advertising exposures the people in this group received in a given time period (up to a point), the more likely they were to buy the product. Media could then be evaluated in terms of the efficiency with which they accomplished the objective. When additional advertising messages no longer profitably yielded additional sales from the prime target segment, the computer repeated the cycle of analysis for the next best segment of the market, and so on.

MIDAS. Interpublic's Media Investment Decision Analysis Systems (MIDAS) also represented a battery of models applicable to different problems rather than an attempt at the single global solution to all problems. The procedures broke down into four steps:

1. Analysis of existing practice and strategy for a product.
2. Generation of potentially superior alternative strategies. MIDAS used a model called FAST (Frequency Aimed Selection Technique) which aimed to deliver "balanced" message frequency at minimum cost in a given time period.
3. Evaluation and modification of the computer's "proposals" by marketing experts who could add their judgments to the computer results.
4. Final evaluation of the modified alternative strategies. A computer simulation of media usage by different population groups was frequently used at this stage.

MIDAS used a simulated sample of the public with individually assigned probabilities of exposure to various media combinations. The MIDAS procedure could be applied to different kinds of marketing targets. It could be varied to produce data based on total audience or on exposures defined in any manner desired with various kinds of weights built in—e.g., distinguishing primary and secondary audiences. The techniques provided for vehicle selection within a medium with or without intermedia considerations.

COMPASS. This system (Computer Optimal Media Planning and Scheduling System) was developed by a group of major New York and Chicago agencies in a cooperative venture. It was a flexible model with broad application, which made use of simulation, decision functions, and "search" procedures akin to those used in iteration and High Assay. The model explored a wide range of feasible media schedules, evaluated each one in terms of stated reach and frequency objectives, and finally arrived at an "optimal solution." Scheduling of the optimal plan was also considered.

The model could employ qualitative media vehicle weights, relative marketing target weights, and media discount structures. Detailed reach and frequency documentation was provided for each target group. The contribution of each vehicle in the optimal schedule and the potential contribution of all other vehicles was analyzed and reported on during the computer run.

In the words of Bernard Lipsky, a prime mover of the project, COMPASS was designed so that "a media planner is given broad options on an extended set of decision points in advance of a computer run. These decisions are expected to vary from product to product as well as from campaign to campaign for a particular product." The "broad options" on which this sophisticated media planner insisted were a far cry from the notion of the computer as a "thinking machine" that might be the planner's replacement.

The new media services

Through the early 1970s, the principals of leading advertising agencies touted their computer-based media selection models in new business presentations to prospective clients, while the boys in the back room tried gamely to make them work on behalf of existing clients. By the early 1980s, these efforts had largely come to an end. Most big agencies still used crude media mix models that permitted planners to get at least first approximations of what a given budget might deliver against a particular target group, in terms of reach and frequency, with different assortments of media. Sometimes an agency would start by setting a communications goal and asking the computer to calculate how much of a budget would be required to achieve it. But such exercises were not used to do the primary job of media selection and planning.

Agencies found that it was more economical to use the services of one of the companies that sprang up to process syndicated research data than to maintain facilities and staffs of their own. In the field of media analysis, two firms, Telmar and IMS (Interactive Marketing Systems) provided an array of comparable services to which most large agencies and a number of advertisers subscribed. A handful of agences still preferred to use their own computers in media planning, but none still pretended to be doing routinely the kind of media mix analysis that had been heralded two decades earlier. The reason was simple: this type of comprehensive model, so attractive in principle, just did not work. Simulation from an aggregation of different data sources was too risky. There was a striking absence of adequate information on the duplication of media vehicles of different kinds on a common base. There was too general a recognition that weights assigned to the impact value of various media were subjective and arbitrary. The volume of data that had to be produced and scrutinized in comparing alternate schedules was too massive for anyone to make sense of it. So the attempt to have the computer assume the overall responsibility for media planning petered out. For example, the MIDAS system was abandoned (according to McCann-Erickson's media research head, Robert J. Coen) when "the media got more complex, and the interactions became more complicated," making it prohibitively expensive to keep the simulations up to date.[8]

The focus moved instead onto the development of schedules within the framework of individual media, looking separately at lists of magazines or newspapers, network or spot buys on radio or TV. Both Telmar and IMS have comparable procedures for estimating reach and frequency for schedules running up to 39 weeks. They use data on audience size and duplication derived from research organizations like Nielsen, Arbitron, SMRB, and MRI.

These standardized formulas are applied against the particular set of research data to which each individual agency client subscribes and are assembled to meet that agency's own specifications and performance criteria. For example, agencies commonly cut back the magazine audience figures shown by syndicated research, based on the best hunches of the media department as to what the readers-per-copy figures "really" should be. (They are in some cases reduced by as much as 50 percent.) The agency may direct optimization in terms of reach, frequency, or a particular combination of the two.

This procedure generally does not work in evaluating broadcast schedules, because of the absence of usable data on the individual respondents represented in the ratings reports. Optimization is more likely to be defined in terms of gross impressions or GRPs or in terms of the net weekly "cume," or accumulated audience. This reflects the fact that by far the biggest use of IMS and Telmar is in the analysis of spot broadcast buys in individual local markets. In analyzing a broadcast spot schedule, a media analyst can examine the number of gross rating points bought and actually achieved in each market and then consider the amount of spillover from one market to another, eliminating or reducing the buys when the desired level has already been achieved or shifting funds from one market to another.

While print media rates are available from standard sources and incorporated in the data base, information on broadcast buys has to come in every case from the agency for whom the analysis is being run, based on what its time buyers report on the constantly changing state of the market for time. This is usually expressed in terms of an average cost per rating point or per spot for a particular "day part"* for an average network affiliate or independent station in the particular market. (In the case of television, this information is assembled by a service named Squad.) Analyses of the local ratings of network programs permit the client to see where individual markets fall below the average, so that spot or other media can be added to compensate for any weakness.

Major agencies use their terminal connections with IMS or Telmar for complex analyses. But they still are likely to use their own media department computers to compare the costs and audiences for specific schedules. Typically, a prototype buy of a schedule in a given medium can be used to produce preliminary estimates of cost and audiences, as a first step in developing more precise comparisons. As microcomputers become more prevalent, complex media models have become accessible to everyone involved in advertising planning, rather than just to specialists. Through an interface with mainframe computer facilities, each desktop terminal can place a massive data base at the disposal of every advertising strategist.

Just as in the original agency media models, the subjective weights assigned to different advertising units in different kinds of media continue to influence the outcome of intermedia comparisons, whether or not these are made with the assistance of computer runs.

In a widely used media planning system developed by David R. Williams, Inc., advertising executives are asked to provide opinion ratings, ranging from 1 to 100, applicable to a particular advertiser or advertising program for a given period of time. The ratings cover the comparative value of various segments of

---

*A day part may be daytime, early fringe time, prime time, late fringe, or night time, corresponding to the different rates applicable to those periods.

the audience in various regions of the country, taking seasonality into account. Relative values are assigned to reach and frequency as well as to the incremental values of additional reach and frequency. Ratings are given to the power of the individual media and to the programming or editorial environment in various types of television programs and magazines. Also rated are different commercial lengths in radio and television, different unit sizes in magazines, newspapers, and outdoor, the added value of color in print, and the effects of position in print and in broadcast time.

This kind of procedure is not limited to agencies. General Foods still uses an optimization model that incorporates the opinions or weights assigned to various media advertising units by key executives. Their agencies are expected to consider, but not required to use, this standardized set of weights.

In setting its specifications for a computer run, an agency may assign differential weights to advertising impressions delivered to different kinds of people. (In one media-modeling example used by William Behrmann, media director of Ogilvy & Mather, prime-time TV was given a "media effectiveness value" of 100, late fringe 90, daytime 70, and magazines of 80.) Occasionally, a kind of reversal can take place, with the agency examining (and accepting) the mix of people reached by a schedule that optimizes reach and frequency within the constraints of its budget.

However, media mix comparisons are the exceptions rather than the rule now. Most use of computer models closely resembles the practice of the precomputer era in that the budget for each medium is generally predetermined before the list of vehicles is drawn up and analyzed.

Another important use of the computer in media planning and scheduling has been in connection with the subdivision of advertising budgets to individual markets. This can be done either in relation to the present sales of a particular brand or in relation to some other criterion, such as the size or purchasing power of the whole population or of a targeted segment.

Doyle Dane Bernbach's media allocation model goes to work after an initial decision as to what percentage of a brand's budget is to be allocated to national media. This is then broken down by individual markets, based on their sales potential. Market-by-market indices are established, based on the brand's overall advertising budget and on its sales within each (DMA) market. Funds for local media are added to markets whose share of the national media budget falls below standard, based on their potential. A cost-per-thousand analysis is then based on alternative media schedules for the selected allocations.

Procter & Gamble uses a system, developed by Marketing Science Associates, which all its agencies have adopted. For each established brand, they set up a network television budget, starting with a national norm based on the major market in which that brand has the lowest per capita index of sales. Every other market gets additional local advertising funds, set by the number of gross rating points required to bring its budget allocation up to the appropriate index and without regard to cost per thousand. The underlying premise is that sales weaknesses caused by distribution problems can not be remedied and that the advertiser should spend his money where the brand is already doing well. Within the market allowances set up by the computer model, budgets are allocated to individual media based on creative requirements and competitive factors—that is to say, by the old subjective criteria.

Cost per thousand and media models

"In the final analysis," said Foote, Cone & Belding's W. A. Joyce, "cost per thousand is the major factor in determining the inclusion or exclusion from a specimen schedule of any one media vehicle." Much the same conclusion emerges from a forthright exposition of the adventures involved in applying computers to advertising written by Frank M. Bass and Ronald T. Lonsdale.[9] They defined the problem of media scheduling by computer as one of selecting the "best" set of alternatives among various media and within media (in terms of page size, color, etc.) with a given budget. To prevent the most efficient vehicles from "running away with the program," the authors introduced the usual operational restraints. In the style of the early media-mix models, they weighted the audience figures by an exposure factor, by a subjective evaluation, and by their congruity with the market distribution of potential customers. They considered a total of 63 media vehicles, using 33 different linear programs. They came up with very similar results regardless of the system employed to adjust audience figures in terms of "quality" or composition, and they concluded that "the weighting system has very little influence on the solution." Thus "sophisticated weighting systems tend to be 'washed out' in linear models. This suggests that cruder models such as cost per thousand will produce media schedules not very different from those produced by linear models."[10]

In sum, the use of the computer to arrive at *solutions* carries with it the danger of perpetuating media selection in terms of cost per thousand. The computer's real value for the advertising planner is its capacity not to supply pat solutions, but to force him to think his problem through to a higher level of sophistication, and thus to arrive at his own solution.

Computers and communication

Computer models of media selection work on the basis of input and output; they work on the premise that an advertising campaign may be thought of as an assemblage of units that can be arranged in different combinations.

Because of its capacity to organize complex data, the computer opens up new possibilities for the analysis of media in relation to known facts about product distribution, consumption patterns, and competitive forces in the market. This very capacity has already pointed out the inadequacy of our present knowledge about how to arrive at a schedule within a media mix; it has forced the advertising business to do more and better research on the effects of repetition, on the effects of varying time intervals in exposure, on the comparative effects of concentration and continuity, and on the effects of changing the size of the message unit. The analyses we get from the computer can be no better than our best estimates, based on the available evidence from research.

The repetition of an ad in *Time* against a given individual might be given a weight of 50 percent, the second repetition a weight of 25 percent, and so on. It might be possible to assume that with *Newsweek*, the respective weights are 66 percent, 44 percent, etc. But what of the man who is exposed to the ad first in *Time*, then in *Newsweek?* The computer can perform all the necessary calculations, but of course it cannot evaluate the assumptions behind them. The computer offers the potential opportunity to compare the outcomes and interactions of many different assumptions and to take into account the vast stores of information that may be relevant to a marketing problem.

In point of fact, a realistic model would have to be even *more* involved. As we discussed in Chapter 9, successive repetitions might reasonably be expected to add increasingly to the value of the first message if they bring the message closer and closer to the point of breaking into the consumer's awareness. Beyond that point, however, further repetitions might have progressively less value. The point at which the curve shifts direction depends on whether the message is repeated in identical form or with variations. As a practical matter, any assumption about diminishing returns would probably be applied to second exposures across the board regardless of whether the initial message was delivered through the same vehicle or through another with quite different communications characteristics. In that case, the model might lose its value as a representation of reality.

The media planner might assume that the repetition of a magazine ad added 50 percent and a 30-second television commercial 75 percent, but at the present time he would have to base any such assumption on *judgment*. He cannot base it on *evidence*, because there isn't enough to apply to his own particular case. And this takes us back to the subjective weighting of one vehicle against another, which has always been the media analyst's stock in trade.

A value judgment based on personal opinion or on an opinion poll of five account executives is no less a value judgment when it is printed out by a big machine, and that value judgment introduces an enormous range of possible error. Let me hasten to add that subjective judgments, quantified, have been widely used in other fields of computerized decision making, and that quantification does have the merit of forcing awareness of the premises on which decisions would normally be based without a computer. But where in the decision process should these judgments enter in?

For all their virtues, computers have one inherent limitation. Their operations are performed in sequence, one after the other, even though they are performed so fast that many things seem to be happening at once. A computer cannot integrate, cannot synthesize, an experience in the way that the human mind can grasp the shape and flavor of an experience all at once. This is a critical point, because decision making in the field of media has one profound difference that distinguishes it from most other kinds of business.

Operations research, as it developed in the military in World War II and through the Cold War period, was directed primarily at the organization and handling of material in such a way as to minimize waste of resources and time. The loading of trucks, the planning of menus, the scheduling of flights, the deployment of munitions stocks, all represented problems to which an optimum, or at least an optimizing, solution could be found with the aid of sophisticated mathematical techniques. This was the tradition of problem solving out of which advertising media models were first derived. It might be argued that media models also deal with the expenditure of the advertiser's material resources, his dollars, which are used to acquire the material resources of newsprint or videotape. But though the dollars set the constraints for his decisions, no advertiser is interested in paper or in air time *per se*, but only as instruments through which he can present his message to prospective customers and induce them to buy.

When we talk about media analysis or any other aspect of advertising, we are talking about communication, which is in no sense reducible to a series of discrete events. An advertising plan is a whole thing in which the choice of media, scheduling, themes, and creative expression can never be isolated from one another. Communication is a matter of symbols, and symbols are of a different realm than science. The basic shortcoming of the computer in media evaluation is really, therefore, the inherent shortcoming of the scientific method applied to the study of persuasion.

Notes

1. Introduction to Vivian Walsh and Harvey Gram, *Classical and Neo-classical Theories of Equilibrium* (Oxford: Oxford University Press, 1979).
2. Donald E. Sexton, Jr., "Scholarly Journals: A Look at the Contents of the JM and the JMR," *Marketing Review* 29, 9 (January 1974): 17-18.
3. Benjamin Lipstein and James Neelankavil, *Television Advertising Copy Research Practices Among Major Advertisers and Advertising Agencies* (New York: Advertising Research Foundation, 1982).
4. An example of how a computer model can be used to set advertising budget requirements is an analysis by Foote, Cone & Belding of 14 new products that were introduced during the 1970s. The agency estimated that it would take 2,500 rating points against a target audience to achieve a 70 percent chance of getting high brand awareness. With an audience of women 25 to 54, the cost of market entry in 1981 was estimated to range from $3.1 million for a 25 market daytime spot TV schedule to $13.5 million for network prime time. *Cf.* also Dennis Gensch, *Advertising Planning: Mathematical Models in Advertising Media Planning* (New York: Elsevier, 1973).
5. *Computers in Advertising* (London: The Institute of Practitioners in Advertising, 1965): 63-66.
6. *Computers in Advertising*: 52.
7. A number of other models were developed in addition to the ones described here. Benton & Bowles sponsored significant research on the simulation of market behavior. In England, the London Press Exchange developed its own linear programming model. N. W. Ayer had a "Media Equalizer Model" in which "gross exposures" and "impression opportunities" could be compared for a 1,000 line newspaper ad, a magazine spread, and a 10-second ID. "An exhaustive study" of relevant research was used as the basis for developing "adjustment factors" through which audience figures could be transformed into "impression opportunities." Frequency of exposure could then be calculated for people with varying degrees of probability of exposure to each medium, based on typical patterns of reading or viewing.
8. *Presstime*, November 1982, p. 25. McCann-Erickson is, of course, the mother agency of Interpublic.
9. "An Exploration of Linear Programming in Media Selection." *Journal of Marketing Research* 3, 2 (May 1966): 179-88.
10. *Op. cit.*, p. 183.

Chapter 14
On Measuring Effects

An automobile manufacturer once took a large sample of the subscribers to a particular magazine (100,000 of them) and, for a period of several years, eliminated all its advertising from the copies these subscribers received.[1] The car registrations for the subscribers in the sample were then compared with those for a similar list of people who had received the normal dose of advertising in the magazine. The results showed statistically significant differences between the two samples in the percentages owning the manufacturer's car. Translated into the dollar value of the additional sales, the difference made it apparent that the advertising had paid off.

This is an extraordinary story, because the experiment was so simple and the results so clear. It stands as a perfect example of what every advertiser hopes for in evaluating his efforts—hopes for, but almost never gets.

There is no one question that management is apt to raise more often, or with better reason, than the question of what return it is getting on its advertising investment. And there is no one question more likely to send cold shivers down the spine of any researcher who has tried before to answer it conscientiously.

William Weilbacher recalls this episode:

A callow advertising agency researcher once completed a ninety-eight page analysis for a packaged goods brand meant to prove conclusively that television advertising expenditures cause sales. This paper created a considerable stir throughout the advertising agency, and in due course it reached the desk of the agency board chairman. Dynamo and statesman that he was, the chairman rarely bothered with research reports, but on this occasion, much to everyone's surprise, he took the report to the farm for the weekend and read it in detail. At 9:15 A.M. the following Monday morning, the researcher found himself in the sumptuously appointed office of his board chairman, who said, "I have read this report from cover to cover and I disagree with your finding. I believe that this report proves conclusively that sales cause advertising, and not that advertising causes sales. Is my interpretation correct?" The researcher replied immediately and without flinching, "No." "Do you walk on water, too?" asked the board chairman, and signaled that the meeting was over.

It is easy enough for anyone to "prove" that advertising pays. All one has to do is compare the brand opinions or choices of people who claim to have seen or heard the advertising with those of people who haven't. The former are always more favorable, and why shouldn't they be? The people who pay most attention to us are the ones who like us in the first place. The point is illustrated in an anecdote reported by Curtis Grove:

> The scene is the dancefloor of a posh country club on the outskirts of a major midwestern city, as the president of a manufacturing firm bounces across the floor almost in time with the Welkian bubbles of music from the orchestra. Another couple bounces by, and the man (a neighbor, fellow-businessman, socialite, and fellow-club-member) exclaims, "Say! I saw your new commercial on TV last night. It was great! And the kids had a *fit* about that fat little character." "Thanks very much. Glad you liked it," glows the manufacturer, warm with the satisfaction that comes only with the conviction that the new $250,000 spot *is* good.

But few business executives are satisfied to evaluate their advertising by what the neighbors say. They want more convincing evidence, expressed in quantitative terms, that their efforts are productive. And agencies generally recognize what Interpublic's founder, Marion Harper, Jr., called their "accountability" to their clients. In response to management's demands, it is always possible for the advertising department or agency to conjure up a series of charts that document the vast numbers of potential customers to whom the messages have been offered. Advertisers use data on their audiences (which are readily available) in lieu of evidence (generally not available) on what their ad investments accomplish. Unfortunately, the more sophisticated the methodology employed, the harder it generally appears to be to find any statistically satisfactory measure of the effect of advertising in a complex competitive market. Furthermore, sophisticated methods are expensive because they require that very large samples of people be checked at repeated intervals and that the resulting data be extensively manipulated and analyzed.

There may have been a time when the effects of advertising were studied to see if they existed at all, or to determine just how large they were. Much of the research that comes under this heading has been done by individual media to demonstrate their selling power. (Perhaps the most ambitious examples of this type were a series of large-scale experiments directed by Thomas Coffin for the National Broadcasting Company, during the early days of television, in which the buying patterns of set owners were compared with those of their neighbors who had not yet acquired TV.)[2] But advertising effects are now generally investigated in case-specific terms to compare alternative approaches to budget levels, media plans, or creative themes, rather than to tackle the broader question of whether advertising really does the advertiser any good. In fact, many findings from this kind of research have been reported already throughout this book.

Most well-done empirical evaluations of advertising effects require considerable time to complete, and the results are carefully guarded. Over the short run, therefore, advertising tends to be judged by its outer appearances. Advertising professionals are excellent judges of whether or not an ad will win reader attention, but their predictions of its ability to produce sales are no better than chance. Art directors bestow awards upon other art directors in terms of the prevailing canons of aesthetics; copywriters and film producers confer prizes upon each other. Assessments of advertising success tend to be based on the criteria of craftsmanship rather than on hard evidence from the market.

In 1976, 143 advertising campaigns were entered in a contest for an award to honor effective advertising. The evidence submitted for 125 entry applications was analyzed. Three-fourths of these cited sales increases, a third referred to survey results, 13 percent to copy research, and 8 percent to approving comments by salesmen or distributors. Of the sales increases reported, only one in seven used hard numbers like: "In department stores, there was a 67 percent sell-through in 26 days on counter. In drug stores, after 27 days on counter, there was a 75 percent sell-through." Six out of seven were expressed in vague terms like this one: "After six months. . . .clearly established as the fastest growing entry."

Advertising, like any communication, does have effects, and these effects *can* be measured. But the expense of proper measurement cannot usually be justified in relation to the cost of the advertising being evaluated. In practice, marketers who want to check effects insist on keeping the cost of doing so in proportion to the advertising budget. This almost always means cutting corners on the research and winding up with frustrating and inconclusive results.

The effect of advertising on sales can be most accurately measured in the case of a unique advertisement that makes a specific offer that could not come to the attention of the consumer in any other way. This description could be true of mail order advertising, or in fact of any solicitation that provokes direct inquiry in person or by mail or telephone. It may be true of a retail ad where the promotion is *not* also supported at the point of sale.

A product that is advertised over a long period of time does not show wide fluctuations in sales in response to changes in advertising strategy, according to a long-term analysis by Kristian Palda of the sales of Lydia Pinkham's Vegetable Compound.[3] At any moment sales of a product are influenced by the whole past history of its advertising and of competitive advertising, rather than just by the current campaigns.

David A. Aaker and James M. Carman reviewed 60 econometric studies, of which 14 analyzed the same set of data on Lydia Pinkham. Altogether, there were 37 separate market situations involving 176 brands that yielded relevant evidence. They found the evidence from these studies "mixed" and "difficult to interpret," and observed that "the long-term effect of advertising on good will is most difficult to measure econometrically. . . . Advertising probably has some impact, but other aspects of the marketing programs, and the consumer's past purchase and use experience, probably dominate in most situations. . . . Looking for the relationship between advertising and sales is somewhat worse than looking for a needle in a haystack. Like the needle, advertising's effects, even when significant, are likely to be small."[4]

Most advertising being evaluated is not an isolated venture, but part of a continuing promotional effort, offset by a similar continuing effort on the part of the competition. Its total impact may be expected to register gradually. It is obviously a much simpler matter to measure the kind of major change in attitude or buying behavior that can be accomplished by an all-out effort.

A fundamental question in measuring advertising effects concerns the length of the payout period. How long after an ad runs can we expect it still to be producing some benefits, however indirectly? Setting the cut-off at the point where 90 percent of the effects had taken place, Darral Clarke (in a review of 70 studies) concluded that the time could range between 0.8 of a month and 1,368 months.[5] For mature, frequently purchased, low-priced products, cumulative effects on sales occur within three to nine months. Nariman K. Dhalla also reexamined the findings of a variety of published studies, and he also found a wide variation from one product to the next.[6] For cigarettes, liquor, gasoline, and proprietary drugs, the cumulative effect was three times the immediate effect. But within these product categories, the results differed from one brand to the next. Again, it all depends.

Measuring sales directly

Manufacturers have always been able to relate advertising to sales directly, but factory shipments to wholesalers and dealers are an insensitive measure because they occur in large chunks at occasional intervals and do not reflect "sell-through" to the ultimate customer in the retail store. Until recently, retail sales have been measured either by the procedure of store auditing (described on page 44, which the Nielsen organization does nationally and a variety of other smaller companies do on a local or customized basis) or by reports of warehouse withdrawals, representing shipments to supermarkets from chain and independent distributor warehouses. SAMI (Sales Area Measurements, Inc.), a subsidiary of Time, Inc., reports these for a sample located in 45 market areas that account for 83 percent of grocery sales.

The measurement of advertising effectiveness was given an important new tool with the development of the Universal Product Code and electronic scanning in the early 1970s. The postage-stamp size UPC symbols that adorn every package of grocery-store distributed merchandise identify each manufacturer, the brand, variety, and size of the product. They are read automatically at the checkout counter by a laser beam, which automatically records the appropriate price. Apart from facilitating the checkout process, improving the store's operating efficiency, and providing the customer with an itemized list of purchases, the UPC has made it possible for supermarket chains to cut costly inventories while they also reduce out-of-stock conditions that result in lost sales. In addition to their value in producing computerized sales information on a current basis for store managers and chain managements, UPC data promised to become a basic source of sales and market share information for national advertisers.

Even in the absence of a widely used sample of scanner-equipped supermarkets (there were a total of 7,300 in 1983), manufacturers were using actual sales figures from selected groups of stores to conduct market tests and to track and compare the results of specific ads. The Nabscan service (developed by the Newspaper Advertising Bureau in 1975 and later an independently owned company) was used extensively to compare sales before and after an advertisement ran. These exact and sensitive measurements show the same variability in advertising performance that is visible in copy testing. One private label brand had a 614 percent increase for the week in which it was advertised, while a similar product, advertised with exactly the same weight and prominence, had a 22 percent increase. In the case of two coupon offers of identical size and typography buried within the same newspaper ad, one was followed by a 782 percent sales increase, another by an increase of 45 percent.

Soaring sales figures for individual brands often could be found after they were featured in supermarket ads, but such ads often stress promotional pricing. To investigate the separate effects of the advertising itself, as distinct from the appeal of price reductions, the Newspaper Advertising Bureau's B. Stuart Tolley examined the unit and dollar sales data in 1981 for 479 grocery items advertised in 20 newspaper ads placed by 17 supermarkets. He distinguished items that were merely listed, with their prices, in a "liner," those that received "promotion" of more than a line but less than four square inches, and "feature" items that got at least four square inches of space. In the week when the ads ran, dollar sales of price-cut items were three times as great, on the average, as their sales during each of the two previous weeks. For the items that were advertised at the regular price, sales doubled, demonstrating that advertising worked independently of the price promotion. The larger the space received by a regularly priced item, the greater the sales increase: by 188 percent for featured items, 88 percent for promotional items, and 34 percent for one-line mentions. And sales of the advertised items in the following week stayed above the pre-advertising levels, contradicting the theory that promotional sales gains are "borrowed" from future sales that would have been made in any case.

While national advertisers are always ready to accept the idea that retail ads have such immediate pulling power, they are generally skeptical that this applies to their own messages, which are assumed to build a disposition toward the brand gradually over time. But scanner data have been used to demonstrate that the sales effects of national ads can also be measured, not only for the period immediately after an ad runs, but for some subsequent period in which delayed effects might be felt.

In another analysis, Tolley examined 24 national newspaper ads for cereals and dog foods and compared average weekly sales for the three preceding weeks with the record for the four weeks after the ads ran. There was little or no television advertising for these brands during the measured period. All of the ads used coupons—a common practice in grocery advertising in newspapers. In 17 of the 24 cases, sales showed an increase. Altogether, for the average of the 24 ads, sales of the brand went up 37 percent in the first week, stayed 35 percent higher in the second, 21 percent higher in the third, and were still 13 percent higher in the fourth week. Thus, each ad generated the equivalent of an extra week's sales in the month after it appeared, in the context of a highly competitive environment involving other brands and other media.

In spite of the tremendous jumps in sales for any particular promoted items, the Nabscan studies show that sales for the whole product category remain roughly the same from one week to the next. We can better understand this phenomenon if we remember that the total market in any given week represents a tiny percentage of the potential prospects. Substantial promotional effects, as defined by percentage increases in sales, reflect the buying activity of only a small number of customers.

Sales in any product category normally exhibit both seasonal fluctuations (which are minor in most cases) and long-term responses to general economic conditions. For established brands, market shares are apt to show only very small changes from one sales measurement period to the next, both in Nielsen's bi-monthly reports and in SAMI's monthly data. Scanner data, collected at the level of the individual supermarket, show that there are turbulent cross-currents below this calm surface. Competitive promotional activity and pricing, shelf positioning, out-of-stock conditions, and a host of other unpredictable factors all go to produce an enormous volatility in product movement at the level of the individual store. Precisely because so many of the influences are unpredictable, they seem to cancel each other out when all the store sales numbers are added up and averaged. All of which simply reinforces the point that advertising should not be judged by its ability to give a brand an advantage, but by its ability to keep it afloat.

How General Motors did it

Although scanner data are highly exact, they measure the immediate effects of advertising (with their mutual interaction often hard to disentangle from those of price reductions and point-of-sale promotions). They do not measure the long-term effects of advertising efforts that are intended to have a lasting influence on the consumer's perceptions of a brand.

A direct response advertiser may run a single coupon ad for a novelty item and determine precisely how much merchandise it sold. But the brand whose advertising runs consistently through many media expects the return on its investment to be brought in over the long haul and to be reflected in more favorable dispositions rather than in immediate buying action. This is especially true when sales are determined by general economic conditions, by distinctive product features, and by strong price competition, as is true in the automotive business. Indications of the effects of advertising have to be inferred from what consumers say rather than measured directly by what they buy. The whole practice is clearly explained by the great Soviet authority on advanced practices in American advertising, V. Tereshchenko:

> "Women, known to be garrulous, are sometimes quizzed in stores, on the streets, or in buses as to why they prefer a certain item to another, why they like this radio set and not the other brand. This method, though expensive and complicated, is the most reliable."[7]

The national advertiser who is both brave and big *can* study the effect of whole campaigns on a national scale. For several years, General Motors conducted a continuing study of advertising effectiveness using the ANA's DAGMAR approach (described in Chapter 2), which begins by "Defining [specific] Advertising Goals for Measured Advertising Results."[8] The questionnaire developed for this purpose by Audits & Surveys dealt with automotive preference levels by make; it went on to investigate product image, advertising message registration, market behavior, and product inventory. All this information could be analyzed in relation to demographic data and media habits.

To illustrate the painstaking detail of the G.M. project, just the product's image alone was the subject of 35 different questions (each using a seven-point scale) for every brand the respondent considered in his buying class. The research encompassed a benchmark wave of interviews each September and five subsequent waves throughout the year. (These were done at irregular intervals because of the bunching up of the advertising investment during the first two quarters after the new models are introduced.)

A second round of interviews was conducted with all those who said they "definitely" intended to buy a car or "probably" would buy one, with a third of those who said they "probably" would not buy, and with 17 percent of those who said they "definitely" would not buy. This made it possible to compute the probability that an individual who gave each type of answer would actually visit a dealer and buy the product. It was even possible to compute the probability of purchase for the very large class of individuals who were not even aware of a particular make.

In the case of one make, 84 percent of the people who considered it their first choice went on to visit a dealer, and 56 percent of them actually purchased the car. Various opinions about the car and its features were related to the preference level. In some cases, an unfavorable opinion did not relate to preference. In other cases it did.

The difference in awareness of a certain car before and after the test period was 15 percent. Nine percent were reached by medium A only and 33 percent by medium B only. Medium A produced a net change of 3 percent, while medium B changed 11 percent. General Motors' Gail Smith observed: "The analysis leads to the conclusion that we would probably have been better off to spend our entire budget in medium B. The conclusion, however, is based on the way we executed this particular campaign and assuming the use of a different creative approach, the results might have been quite different."

Smith's research colleague at General Motors, Donald Batson, pointed out that with a continuing study of advertising effectiveness it is irrelevant to inquire as to the specific contribution (or demerits) of the creative theme or its execution, the media choice, or the scheduling strategy. What is being evaluated is actually the total campaign as the agency produces it, with every element inseparable from the others. Thus, eventually, the only criterion becomes the contribution of the *total* advertising plan to the sale of the product, as measured *over time* by the purchase records of people with different levels of exposure to the advertising. (Differences in the purchase habits of the exposed and unexposed groups may be compensated for by establishing a base period before a change in advertising strategy occurs.)

General Motors' agencies were never overly enthusiastic about the research program, which was funded out of the advertising budget. The company soon discovered the answer to its basic questions about how quickly slogans were learned and found that its own sales figures closely matched the survey results on buying intentions. There was internal opposition to the research conclusions that the trends favored smaller (and less profitable) cars. With the oil embargo of 1973, the research program came to an end.

The question remains as to whether what was good for General Motors is necessarily good for the average advertiser, whose research problems may be every bit as complex but whose total sales and advertising volume can hardly justify the very high expense of a research program like the one just described. Unfortunately, the costs of researching a given problem are the same for a small company as for a big one.

Do retailers know when advertising pulls?

National advertisers commonly labor under the assumption that, while the effects of their own advertising may be very difficult to measure, the retail merchant doesn't face this problem since every ad he runs is tested by the hard ring of the cash register. Alas, this assumption is an illusion. The retailer can indeed judge whether his ad has pulled mail or phone orders, but he rarely knows how much of the sales of an advertised item are due to the immediate direct effect of the ad itself, how much reflects store traffic generated by ads for other merchandise, and how much represents the delayed effect of past advertising for the same item.

In one of our studies at the Newspaper Advertising Bureau, all advertising for women's dresses run by a major department store over a six-month period was carefully analyzed in relation to the sales of the merchandise for three days after each ad ran. The ads themselves were then examined to determine what characterized the ones that pulled best. Sales appeared to reflect the character of the individual advertised item far more than variations in such attributes of the advertisement as the type of illustration, layout, choice of models, or copy.

As we saw in Chapter 10, the retail market is in a constant state of flux, a condition that reflects the interaction of innumerable factors: competitive merchandising and buying practices, seasonality, weather, economic conditions, and obscurely motivated shifts in customer psychology. Even if advertising were not a factor in retailing at all, one would expect variations from week to week in a store's business in particular merchandise categories. Over the long haul, a store's good weeks and bad weeks should work out to an average from which there are no dramatic variations. Taking any two consecutive weeks, one might expect to find a net improvement from the first week to the second in some cases, a net loss in others, and no change in still others. Such might be the sales pattern for small neighborhood retail establishments that do not advertise.

When we look at bigger stores, however, we would expect advertising to provide some measurable net plus. If the store had suffered a loss attributable to factors other than advertising, the net plus from advertising might still leave an overall loss—though one of less severity than if no advertising had run at all. The dimension and origin of the fluctuations in these other factors cannot normally be measured or traced. Thus we cannot assume that retail advertising has had no positive effects even in cases where a store sold less of a given item in a week of heavy advertising compared with a week of lighter advertising.

In these instances, the pay-out period must be clearly defined. This still leaves a large twilight area for the retailer's judgment on what his advertising is bringing in. From a practical standpoint, one would not expect an advertisement today to result in a sale five years from now; yet it might very well result in a sale tomorrow, next week, or possibly even the week after.

The major function of retail advertising is to retain the position of a store in its market, since this reflects a long-standing reputation in which a continuing advertising program is an important component. The relative week-to-week stability of total advertising by most merchants is mirrored in the week-to-week stability of consumers' mentions of individual stores as the places to buy particular items. Where a store does shift its total advertising direction from week to week in terms of the space devoted to individual products, the most immediate effects are felt by the people who are already on the verge of buying.

A two-week analysis of all advertising in five retail categories was made in the 1964 study of women's shopping behavior that I described on page 245. Stores that increased their linage for a given item from the first week to the next produced a 12 percent greater conversion of purchase plans for the items into actual shopping visits to those stores, compared with the stores whose advertising for the same items did not increase. For major stores the conversion rate was 18 percent greater.

In the short run, retail ads appear to be most successful in converting an existing purchase intention into an actual shopping trip. They are next most successful in redirecting a continuing purchase intention toward the store that advertises, especially in the case of substantial and consistent advertisers. It is hardest to demonstrate how retail advertising creates new demand for the products themselves, if for no other reason than that the complex forces of national advertising are at work at the same time.

But while advertising can bring the customer into the store, it cannot make the sale. An analysis has been made of 2,000 cases in which customers walked out of the store without buying the item they had shopped for.[9] It shows that women who may be brought into the store by an ad may fail to buy the item because the styling or sizes are not right, the merchandise does not meet expectations, or the customers cannot get waited on.

The technique of measuring change

The effects of advertising can best be measured when there is no prior history of promotion that might still be having a delayed influence on an existing product in a competitive marketing situation. When we select test markets we can ascertain the cumulative impact of past advertising from research done before the test begins. But it is much more difficult to assess the interaction (the harmony or incongruity) between the messages of the past and the message we are currently delivering.

Sales result from an accumulation, over time, of impulse, opinion, and information in the consumer's mind. This means that under ordinary circumstances, with an existing product, we cannot trace sales back to any one of a particular series of advertising messages. They may in part reflect the impact of previous messages, just as the particular messages that interest us may have a continuing or delayed effect on future sales.

In a great many product fields, the advertising efforts of one brand may be small compared to the competitive marketing forces. Specific sales results are hard to relate to specific advertising causes when there are only small changes in overall sales volume for the whole product category, as measured by factory shipments or store audits. To meet this problem, researchers turn to a different type of study, in which exposure to advertising messages can be related either directly to purchases, or to some measure of product or brand awareness and attitude that is assumed to correlate directly with purchases. The technical problems we face in trying to measure the effects of advertising are analogous to those of measuring the effects of any other form of communication.

When sales effects are inferred from the product usage or purchases reported by respondents in consumer surveys, the relationship of sales to brand attitude generally appears closer than if store or pantry audits are used to measure sales. One reason for this is that questions on product usage and on brand attitudes are asked of the same people at the same time, whereas audits are made at different points in time and by altogether different research methods.

Survey research people are always trying to impress on their managements or clients the fact that one should never draw conclusions from the totals in a survey because detailed analysis may either turn them topsy-turvy or introduce some important qualifications. One cannot conclude that there is a tremendous untapped market for trousers because nearly half of the American adult public does not wear them every day—a finding that can be interpreted a little more intelligently if the responses for men and women are tabulated separately. This is an elementary thought, but the sight of it is lost too often in designing studies to measure advertising effects.

The findings of social research in the area of attitude change all point to the same conclusion: the more specifically one states the problems, the more confidently one can state one's findings.

The simplest way to study the effect of any communication is in the laboratory, using an experimental group of students, soldiers, employees, or any other bunch of people whose opinion or behavior can be measured at various intervals of time and whose exposure to any persuasive effort or communication can be carefully controlled. Suppose, in such an experiment, we find that 50 percent of the people like Our Brand. We show them a commercial. If we come back on the following day and ask identical questions, we might find that the proportion in favor had risen to 70 percent. There would have been a net gain of 20 percentage points.

If we find only 40 percent favorable to Our Brand in the second interview we have encountered a "boomerang effect." Our commercial must not only have been unconvincing; it must somehow have irritated the audience and produced the reverse effect from that intended. The "boomerang effect" is by no means a hypothetical matter. Copy tests of individual ads or commercials often show negative effects when people are unconvinced or when their attention is distracted by technique. In a study for ABC of 75 "roughly representative" radio commercials, Daniel Yankelovich found that 3 out of 10 were doing an effective job, 3 out of 10 might be doing more harm than good, and the rest were deficient in one important way or another. Carefully conducted field experiments of continuing advertising campaigns, such as those reported by the Milwaukee Advertising Laboratory, provided striking demonstrations that specific (in that case, TV) advertisements can be counter-productive.[10] Eric Marder, who has made many studies of advertising's effects on brand top-of-mind awareness and purchase intentions, also finds that some ads seem to alienate more customers than they win over. This finding shocks many advertisers, but it should surprise no one who has encountered salesmen who antagonize the very customers with whom they are trying to ingratiate themselves.

The effect of our message is not necessarily stable and lasting. In the case where our message had a positive effect, we might come back after a couple of weeks have elapsed and again survey the group to find out what has happened to these newly acquired opinions. Suppose we found that 70 percent were still favorable as they were at first. We could thereupon conclude that the effect of the message had persisted. We might find on the contrary, that the favorable proportion had actually increased to 80 percent. This would point to a so-called "sleeper effect": the message took a while to really sink in, and some of the people who did not change their minds immediately after seeing the commercial, on later reflection may have been influenced more than they were at first. Or, finally, we might find that the proportion favorable to Our Brand had dropped to 60 percent. This would still leave a net gain of 10 percent.

This kind of study can be done in the laboratory far better than in the marketplace. Actually, to talk of people as if they all fit into one of two categories—favorable or unfavorable to Our Brand—is greatly simplifying reality, since in life one normally makes choices among many possibilities, not between just two. Apart from the group that has *no* opinion, there may be many shades of favorable or unfavorable opinion, and there may also be many degrees of conviction with which a given shade of opinion is held. To add to the complexity of the matter, it might be possible to go back and survey at repeated intervals of time to find out what further changes, if any, occur, as people are exposed to still more new advertising messages.

Another, more sophisticated way of looking at the effects of a communication is to use comparable matched groups. This is what we normally do in test marketing. If we survey two identical groups of people we would presumably find that both of them are favorable to Our Brand in the same degree, let's say by a proportion of 50 percent in each case. Suppose we now showed Group A our commercial and showed Group B two minutes of Smokey the Bear extinguishing forest fires. Taking our survey afterwards, we would presumably find that the group that had seen the Smokey film (our control group) would not have changed its attitudes toward Our Brand, whereas the group that had seen the commercial might be more favorable than before.*

Such a favorable effect may be the result of various causes besides our commercial, however. Suppose that Our Competitor launches a clever campaign to discredit Our Brand between the showing of our commercial and the second survey. The favorable proportion in the control group may fall from 50 percent to 40 percent. The group that *had* seen the commercial might show the same percentage favorable as before, 50 percent. We should still conclude that the commercial had had a favorable effect, if it offset the unfavorable effects of other messages working in the opposite direction.

Or suppose that we have unexpected good news—an unsolicited endorsement of Our Brand by the World's Leading Authority. We might find on our second survey that the Smokey group is more favorable than it was and that the others are even *more* favorable, 90 percent compared with 70 percent. In this case, we would say that the effect of our message was felt over and above the favorable trend.

The foregoing examples are of course a simplification of reality, in which many competitive pressures and influences are constantly at work. There are endless combinations of residual effects, sleeper effects, and boomerang effects that have to be sifted out in a real-life comparison of groups with different degrees of advertising exposure. Moreover, when we leave the artificial conditions of the laboratory test, we must match groups of people in terms of sex, age, income, and all the many other social characteristics that might by themselves influence brand opinion or buying behavior.

This matching job is important when we conduct repeated samplings of a given population. At the same time, the researcher always works within margins of statistical error, and samples have to be large enough to keep these down to a minimum. To handle this situation, survey technicians sometimes go back a number of times to the same sample of people. (This group is referred to as a *panel,* whether they are questioned only on two occasions or enlisted to cooperate for a lifetime.) Suppose a survey among members of a panel shows 50 percent

---

*The job of persuasion becomes harder as the proportion of already persuaded people grows. If only 25 percent of the population now like Our Brand, then 75 percent of the public remain to be convinced. If half the public already are on our side, then half remain to be convinced. If opinion is 75 percent favorable, then 25 percent represent the potential for persuasion.

Some very important implications follow from this very simple concept. Suppose that our objective is to win over 10 percent of the unfavorable or unconvinced group. If our original "share of mind" or share of market is 25 percent, achieving our new objective means that we move substantially forward, reaching a new share totaling 32½ percent. If our original share is 50 percent, however, a 10 percent rate of persuasion brings in a smaller number of new converts, raising our position from 50 percent to 55 percent. If 75 percent of the public are already on our side, then we move only to 77½ percent if we succeed in convincing 10 percent of the unconvinced. The stronger our brand position, the harder it is for us to make advances in our total share of the market. Gains are always relative to the starting point.

favorable to Our Brand, as in the previous illustration. Then we put our commercial on the air and ask our panel members to watch it. Exposure to it would still be purely optional and voluntary. If we survey the same people tomorrow, we may again find 50 percent who like Our Brand. We could easily conclude that the commercial had no effects. Actually, its effect may have been different with different members of the group, and these changes may have cancelled each other out. Everything we know about the market indicates that people are constantly testing ideas and goods; they are constantly switching loyalties, allegiances, and attitudes. Unless we are aware of the dynamic movement that goes on within the public mind, the fact that repeated surveys show no change may lead us to wrong conclusions.

Analyzing further, we might find, if we considered only the people who on the first wave of our survey had shown themselves to be favorable to Our Brand, that 70 percent were still favorable but that 30 percent had switched to an unfavorable position. We might find, conversely, that 30 percent of those who had been unfavorable before the commercial had switched in a favorable direction. In other words, it might seem that the commercial had convinced 30 percent of those previously unfavorable but at the same time had a boomerang effect on 30 percent of those who previously had been favorable. This again would be a logical, but a wrong conclusion.

People who are already predisposed to take a particular position tend to expose themselves more to messages that favor that position. Ford owners are more alert than Chevrolet owners to Ford advertising. We would expect those who favor Our Brand to be more cooperative about watching Our Commercial. We should therefore compare the proportions that saw the message among those who were favorable and those who were unfavorable on the first wave. We might find that 4 out of 5 of the previously favorable people had seen it. And we might find that 2 out of 5 of those who were previously unfavorable had also seen it. Accordingly, we must look at the matter in still greater detail, dividing up our sample not only in terms of what people thought on the first survey, but also in terms of whether they had been exposed to the message.

We might find that, of those who had been exposed and were originally favorable, 75 percent were still favorable on the second survey, whereas 25 percent had changed their minds. Among those who were previously unfavorable but who had seen the commercial, 50 percent might now be favorable and 50 percent remain unfavorable. We might find the same proportion among the smaller group who were previously favorable but who had not seen the advertisement. Among the group who had previously been unfavorable and who had not been exposed to the message, only 17 percent might have switched.

In other words, there are two proportions that we have to consider. One is the contrasting percentages of change within each group originally holding an opinion for those who were exposed and for those who were not exposed to the message. The other is the percentage that each of these subgroups represents within the total population.

A real advertising campaign program is an extended process, and people can seldom be divided into either/or groups according to whether they have experienced exposure or non-exposure. To come to serious conclusions about advertising effects, we must measure the varying *degrees* of exposure. We must measure exposure not only to our own messages, but to the various competitive messages that work as counterinfluences. Ideally we must measure these changes at intervals of time. Although the use of a panel has technical advantages in this respect, it also has an important limitation. Surveys themselves are communications; they sensitize people to the subjects about which questions are asked and thereby independently influence attitudes or behavior between one round and the next. This is the so-called "panel effect." Thus, in practice, a panel study is often combined with repeated surveys of different cross sections of the public at large.

In sum, it is not easy to measure the effectiveness of a given advertising campaign. It is easy to take measurements, and it is easy enough to find differences that can be interpreted as effects, but to come to conclusions that can be justified by scientific criteria requires elaborate and intelligent research design and large samples. All of this is frightfully expensive, and it is not unusual for an analysis to take so much time to complete that the results, when they come in, may no longer have much relevance to a changed situation.

Profit and peril in market tests

The marketer limits the number of variables that affect his research results when he conducts his studies within the framework of a single market—or a few selected markets—in which he has better control over his own brand's input and is better able to observe what his competitors do.

Such market testing is common enough in introducing innovations in the product itself, in pricing, or in packaging. Different advertising strategies are often compared by the same technique—or even as part of a study with broader objectives—before a national campaign is launched.

In measuring the effectiveness of advertising, four elements must be considered: first is the level of advertising pressure that will yield the greatest volume of profitable sales; second is the medium or media mix that will yield the best results; third is the scheduling of particular units of space and time through particular vehicles within a medium; and fourth is the creative treatment most appropriate to that use of that medium at that level of expenditure. When we embark on a study of advertising effectiveness, we should be clear in our minds as to which of these four elements we are measuring. In practice, most studies of effectiveness are intended to be evaluations of media, but end up measuring everything else at the same time. Therein lies their great weakness.

Different media require different minimum investments. For a given creative approach and a given frequency schedule, there is probably an optimum investment in each medium. Moreover, to do a given job different media might yield different rates of return at different levels of investment. To illustrate: Outdoor advertising might yield $5 of new sales for every dollar of advertising investment regardless of whether that investment was at the rate of $1,000 or $10,000 in a market. Another medium, say, radio, might show a yield of $3 of sales for every dollar of advertising investment when only $1,000 was being expended in the market, but this might go up to $8 of sales per dollar of advertising at the $10,000 investment level. With still another medium—e.g., direct mail—the pattern might work in reverse. It might be that spending at the rate of $1,000 per market on direct mail for a product with very limited appeal will bring in $10,000 in sales. But spending at the rate of $10,000 might yield only $20,000. Such differences, while they seem plausible enough, must be stated as hypothetical examples, because there is no published evidence that covers the range of media uses at different expenditure levels for different marketing objectives.

In practice, most market tests of advertising involve comparisons of media, expenditure levels, or both. But for every expenditure level in every medium there is a great variety of possible forms and strategies, and an even greater number of creative alternatives. All too often the tester is willing to believe that his results measure the media or budget factors that he wants to measure, when his scheduling or theming may have far greater effects on the outcome.

Market tests have another limitation: a change in the existing pattern of advertising creates a certain effect of its own in combination with the previous pattern. The so-called "bicycle theory" of media planning argues for periodic changes of the media mix in order to shake up the consumers and make them more aware of the product. In a famous study of the Hawthorne Western Electric plant,[11] two industrial psychologists (Fritz L. Roethlisberger and William J. Dickson) began by varying the physical conditions under which a group of women were working. They found to their surprise that even when the working conditions were made less pleasant, productivity continued to rise because the experiment was indirectly building the morale of the group.* Something like this often happens in test market situations when the sales force, dealers, and local media knock themselves out in support of the promotion because they are interested in the test. Their level of performance could simply never be achieved on a national scale. Yet the fine results of the test may be attributed to the advertising alone.

Valid market tests depend on proper controls, which must exist not only in space but also in time. Enough markets must be used as tests and controls to wash out the effects of unpredictable local conditions. We must have an adequate benchmark period, and we must consider seasonal sales variations. If the test period is too short, we may miss the long-run sleeper effects. If it is too long, the results we are looking for may be completely dissipated under the pressure of competitive activity.

Actual sales are the only meaningful criterion of success, and every marketer watches his own sales figures anxiously. But factory or warehouse shipments to the retailer don't necessarily reflect "sell-through" (retail sales to the consumer) nor do they generally reflect it within a territory that coincides with an advertising test market. Sales measurement presupposes good controls over advertising coverage, controls in time and in geography, and controls over such nonadvertising elements as the level of distribution, point-of-sale display, and dealer support or other merchandising efforts.

It is easier to design a study to measure the effectiveness of advertising for a

---

*A recent reexamination of the data has raised important questions about the statistical procedures and inferences of this classic study, but the so-called "Hawthorne effect" remains a valid and ubiquitous element in experiments involving human (and sometimes even animal) subjects.

new product than for a product which is already in the market. Too often in this latter type of test, the product itself and the distribution method are being evaluated along with the advertising. In evaluating an advertising campaign to launch a brand new product in a highly competitive market, however, the question of whether or not to go ahead must often be answered on the basis of a qualitative judgment long before the research results are in. The soap companies provide an exception; their decisions about new products are made with great deliberation. But in many cases of less affluent advertisers the decision to pour more money into promotional support of a new product is made fairly early in the game, under the pressure of anxiety about competitive counter-moves. Long before the store audit results have been tabulated, an assessment may have to be based on informal reports of salesman, dealer, and customer reaction.

Where an advertising campaign has the objective of improving the sales and share position of an existing brand in a competitive market, the only conclusive test is the long-run sales curve. But few items are bought by consumers so frequently that store movement shows a rapid response to advertising which is not supported by unusual promotional effort. Most companies do not have the resources or the patience to wait a long time for results to show. Because of the pressure of time, market tests are often conducted on the basis of unrealistic levels of advertising expenditure. There is a strong incentive to overspend in order to get significant measurable effects over a short period. Unfortunately, this kind of concentration of advertising does not necessarily give us a good basis to predict what will happen when advertising is run at a level the company can afford in a wider market.

To promote a particular product, spending $3,000 in a market in one month might be as effective as, less effective than, or more effective than spreading it out over three months. Spending at the $3,000 monthly rate might be more efficient, less efficient, or as efficient in terms of the yield per dollar of advertising investment as spending at the monthly level of $1,000. The problem is different for different products with different consumer purchase cycles. It also varies according to the position of the advertiser in his field and the brand share he begins with.

Market tests often employ a media mix that is very different from any that would be used in a national campaign. Certain media, like newspapers and radio, lend themselves more readily to testing than do others, like network television and magazines, simply because the production costs represent a smaller share of the budget. Can one really generalize (as I have seen done) from the test performance of newspapers as a print medium to the national use of magazines or supplements; or from the test performance of local spot television to the performance of a network schedule?

The mechanics of research can introduce unexpected complications. In one case, store audits showed a brand gaining sales, while sales records showed it was losing. The explanation: the auditing firm was adding stores and thus changing sample characteristics at just this time.[12]

A further difficulty with market tests stems from their character as just one more weapon in the competitive struggle. When Procter & Gamble test-marketed a new Duncan Hines cake frosting in Phoenix, General Mills rushed into the same stores with a test of a similar product. General Mills' Betty Crocker brand did well and was taken out for broader distribution. The Duncan Hines brand was withdrawn. The marketing manager of another company complained about his competitors to a reporter: "They make special price deals on their own products with the stores, they expand their advertising heavily, and they'll even do things like yanking the number one brand off the shelves temporarily just to foul up sales comparisons. One firm even bought up most of the available radio and TV spots when word leaked out we were going into a city for test marketing."[13]

A coffee company raised the price of its premium grade product and put it in a fancy canister for a market test. The canister was copied by a rival firm, which used its cheapest grade and cut the price in the same market, thereby effectively ruining the test. This kind of interference sometimes makes a brand's test-market performance a dubious indicator of its success in general distribution.

In the time interval between test marketing and introduction of and distribution of a product on a national scale, consumer tastes and the competitive picture may both change substantially. For this reason, some companies (for instance, in the cosmetics field) are willing to assume greater risks of failure with a new product if by doing so they can gain a time advantage.

In short, test marketing's principal headaches arise from the often contradictory requirements of being scientific and being practical. A market test run on the timetable and spending level of the national market carries with it the risk of not having significant findings soon enough. And always the question remains whether the experiment is *really* controlled, whether extraneous forces have not intervened!

The pitfalls of test marketing are always surmountable, at a price. A facility designed to overcome all the ordinary problems of matching test markets was set up in 1964 by the Milwaukee *Journal*. This "Milwaukee Advertising Laboratory" made it possible to combine rigorous experimental controls with the advantages of testing in a real-life field situation. The result was achieved by a combination of ingenious techniques: first, the division of the Milwaukee metropolitan area into a checkerboard pattern totaling up to A and B markets with virtually identical population characteristics; second, a controlled pattern for distributing all newspapers and a substantial number of magazine subscriptions in terms of the two areas; third, a "muter" device attached to the television sets in a sample of 750 A homes and 750 B homes. (The muter, silently controlled by a special signal from the transmitter, turned off test commercials on sets in the designated sample.)

Consumer purchases of packaged goods were recorded through a weekly diary record filled out by consumers. The uncontrollable forces of competitive activity, weather, distribution, and the like that plague conventional test marketing obviously did not apply in the Advertising Laboratory, since they were always identical in Markets A and B. This made it possible to measure the direct sales effects of different expenditure levels, media strategies, and creative approaches.

However, the experimenting advertiser for any given product still had to measure the effects of only one strategic variation at a time, whether it was budget, media mix, media scheduling, or creative treatment. This painstaking manipulation of the advertising and measurement of sales was not easy or inexpensive. The Ad Lab was operated at a loss and was closed down in 1971.

The advent of supermarket scanning data has made it possible to conduct copy tests with the aid of actual records of buying behavior subsequent to exposure to one version or another of a test commercial. (In the system used by Tele-Research, people viewing commercials in a trailer are given a numbered card that gives them a dollar off when they go into the nearby supermarket on their regular grocery shopping trip. Their brand purchases can then be related by scanner records to the particular commercials they saw.) AdTel uses a split cable facility that permits different commercials to be played in matched halves of three test markets.[14] Family members in AdTel's test panel of TV households use identification cards in shopping at their scanner-equipped supermarkets so that their actual purchases can be recorded and related to their advertising exposure.

Another advertising testing facility, Information Resources Inc.'s Behavior-scan, assigns each participating household to a particular sample in which television sets are electronically metered to determine whether test ads are being viewed. The supermarket scanner records for members of these households can then be analyzed in terms of television exposure.

A variety of services now offer simulated test marketing models based on laboratory methods. Typically, consumers are intercepted in shopping malls, brought into a test facility where they are exposed to advertising for a new product as well as for established brands and then permitted to make a brand selection from a shelf resembling a supermarket display. Samples of the new product may also be provided to those who picked another brand. In either case, followup telephone interviews are conducted after an interval of time to measure the acceptability of the new product and, in particular, the willingness to make a repeat purchase. This type of research has the advantages of low expense, fairly rapid execution, and confidentiality (a screening interview eliminates the families of people engaged in marketing and advertising). The research results, along with management assumptions, are incorporated into a computer model that estimates sales and market share after specified periods of time. Average market shares projected from these models appear to be reasonably close to actual results in the marketplace, but they disguise a wide range of variations. In a majority of instances they seem to lead to correct decisions as to whether a new product should be launched or aborted. (Good judgment might lead to a comparable rate of correct go/no go decisions, but objective judgments are hard to come by in a company obsessed by the need for competitive innovation and correspondingly inclined to over-optimism.)

Test marketing has innumerable uses and presents the illusion of great simplicity. But it can offer clear answers to advertising questions only when it is carried out meticulously on a large scale. As in all forms of advertising research, the value of information must be weighed realistically against the risks of getting faulty data because of an inadequate research investment.

Beyond this, there is always the question of whether attention will be paid even to the most convincing test market findings if they fail to confirm the wisdom of existing policy or the gut instincts of a key decision-maker. Consider the following episode, which Don Grasse reports:

> In planning the introduction of a line of frozen dinners, the agency proposed that the product be test marketed in Green Bay, Wisconsin, before moving into national distribution. Somewhat reluctantly, the president of the client company agreed. (He was a rare entrepreneur, not much given to caution or research.) About three weeks later, the account man was visiting a store in the test market when he was called to the phone. It was the president. How he found the account executive is still a mystery. He asked what the account executive was doing in Green Bay. "Checking on the movement of the TV dinners," was the reply. "How are they doing?" asked the client. "Fine," the AE said. "Good," replied the president. "Now get back here to Omaha. We're going national next week!"

In an effort to win packaged goods advertisers away from television, *Life*, *Look*, and *Reader's Digest* conducted an elaborate experiment on five products in six major markets in 1969, with the cooperation of General Foods. Each market was used to test magazines for some products. As a control, television was used as usual for other products. At the outset, copy research was done to ensure that the creative treatments were of comparable strength in the two media.

In addition to sales analyses and store audits, altogether 50,000 interviews were conducted on brand awareness, attitudes, and product trial over a 4-month base period and a 12-month test period. For four brands, a third of the advertising in the test markets was diverted from TV to magazines. For the other brand, there was a two-thirds switch. In this last case (packaged, precooked rice), the results were favorable to magazines. In two other cases (dessert topping and ground coffee), the trends also favored magazines. In another case (ready-to-eat cereal), the results differed in different markets. And for seasoned coating mix, television won. The magazines that had sponsored this impressive study at enormous expense considered that their effectiveness had been convincingly shown to be better or at the very least comparable with TV in the package goods domain that television had virtually taken away from them. The three television networks countered with a study by Tele-Research of matched magazine ads and commercials for package goods, using their standard testing method, which I have just described. TV showed an 82 percent sales advantage.[15] In 1981, General Foods was still putting 85 percent of its measured media ad budget into TV and only 10 percent into magazines.[16]

Attitude and action

Every evaluation of advertising effects through consumer surveys must sooner or later come to grips with the question of how the things that people tell interviewers relate to their actual buying behavior.

The relationship between attitude and action has been given considerable study by social psychologists, and it has become a favorite subject of marketing theorists as well.[17] Robert C. Lavidge and Gary A. Steiner hypothesize the existence of a "hierarchy of advertising effects" ranging from awareness, comprehension, and conviction to knowledge and purchase of the product.[18] Brian Copland looks at the hierarchy of effects as a series of probabilities.[19] The higher up people are on the ladder (from awareness to acceptance of the product claim), the greater the likelihood that they will be buyers. The same view is implicit in the assumption of General Motors' Gail Smith that "attitudes and/or knowledge affect behavior."[20] The evidence Smith cites—for an "average brand" of car—relates preferences to actual purchases made within the following six months. Among those purchasers who earlier listed the make as their first choice, 56 percent bought it, compared with only 22 percent of those who "would consider it favorably," 9 percent of those who would merely consider it, and 3 percent of those who said they would not consider it.

"A direct and close relationship between existing levels of preference [for a brand] . . . and their relative purchase by housewives" was reported by Seymour Banks, who interviewed and reinterviewed 465 housewives.[21]

His conclusion that brand attitudes are good predictors of product use was verified by Cornelius DuBois, an ingenious inventor of research techniques.[22] Incidentally, DuBois found how a brand's market share can remain constant at the same time that there is considerable turnover in brand usage. The proportion using the brand was exactly the same in the three interview periods. However, 11 percent of the women stopped using the brand during the period studied, and 11 percent shifted to the use of the brand; only 17 percent were users on both occasions. (The remainder did not use the brand at all during the period studied.)

Summarizing 27 studies made by the Grey Advertising Agency, Alvin Achenbaum reported that the more favorable the attitude toward a product, the higher the incidence of usage; the less favorable the attitudes are, the lower the usage.[23] The more unfavorable people are toward a product, the more likely they are to stop using it. However, people who have never tried a product have attitudes that are distributed in the shape of a normal bell-shaped curve around the average. Achenbaum found that for a beverage brand "the retention of users is extremely high among people who have very favorable attitudes and much lower among those with unfavorable attitudes" and that the brand's ability to attract former nonusers was greatest among those who were most favorable at the outset. Achenbaum analyzed how attitudes on specific attributes relate to the general attitude toward a brand and concludes that "no one set of specific attitudes is universally applicable to all products. Each product category has its own unique set of factors by which people evaluate the desirability of the product."

Not all the evidence, however, is clear cut.[24] Jack Haskins examined 17 studies reported in *Psychological Abstracts* (1954-63) in which knowledge and attitude or behavior were correlated.[25] Thirteen of these studies showed no conclusive relationship between the two, and the other four were evenly divided between positive and negative relationships.

Michael Ray suggests that the learning "hierarchy" (from awareness to comprehension to conviction to action) best applies to relatively new products that are important to consumers.[26] When brands are relatively undifferentiated and products are at a mature phase of the life cycle, the purchase decision may come first, under the pressure of personal salesmanship, followed by a change in attitude and learning about attributes in that sequence. (This would follow from the psychological principle that people rationalize actions once they have taken them.) In the case of mature products, where consumer involvement is low and brands are similar, action can follow directly from perception, with attitude change as a later stage.

Martin Fishbein and Icek Ajzen have reformulated the hierarchy of effects to suggest that what people do reflects their conscious intentions, which in turn are influenced by what they know and feel.[27] Even if changes lower down in the hierarchy of effects usually precede those higher up the ladder, this does not mean they always work that way. Advertising may increase the salience of a product category more than the memorability of a particular brand.

In a presidential address before the Social Psychology division of the American Psychological Association, Leon Festinger reviewed a number of experiments in which attitude was changed by persuasive messages and in which some measure of *actual* behavior was also available.[28] He concluded that "we cannot glibly assume a relationship between attitude change and behavior." As an example he cited a study (made by Nathan Maccoby, A. K. Romney, J. S. Adams, and Eleanor Maccoby) of "critical periods" in seeking and accepting information. Here a group of mothers were experimentally induced to change their opinions about the proper time to start toilet training for infants. Between the first and the second interviews, the mothers who had been "persuaded" did in fact change in their expectations as to when they would start toilet training. By the standards commonly in use, the persuasive effort would therefore be deemed successful. Festinger took a second look at the evidence on when the mothers *actually* started to toilet train their children, however, and found that there was, if anything, a *reverse* relationship between attitude change and behavior. The mothers in the experimental group started toilet training later than they had thought was right before they were "persuaded," but this was also true of mothers in the control group who were never under "persuasion" at all.

Festinger suggests that

When opinions or attitudes are changed through the momentary impact of a persuasive communication, this change, all by itself, is inherently unstable and will disappear or remain isolated unless an environmental or behavioral change can be brought about to support and maintain it. . . . [In] order to produce a stable behavior change following opinion change, an environmental change must also be produced which, representing reality, will support the new opinion and the new behavior. Otherwise the same factors that produced the initial opinion and the behavior will continue to operate to nullify the effect of the opinion change.[29]

Whether or not Festinger drew the correct inferences, a real question remains as to whether the levels of motivation involved in such significant actions as a mother's treatment of her child are qualitatively comparable with the processes involved in brand selection.

Another eminent social psychologist, Milton Rokeach, points out that there is a difference between one's "attitude toward the object" and one's "attitude toward the situation" in which the object is encountered.[30] Thus changes in verbal opinion are not necessarily translated into redefinitions of a situation in which action is called for. From the standpoint of the advertiser, this analysis has a number of interesting implications. It suggests that the measures that researchers conventionally use to gauge advertising "effects" may be in the comparatively abstract realm of brand opinion, which does not necessarily reproduce the competitive environment in which products are encountered in the store and buying choices are made. It helps explain why consumers may be more motivated to change their buying actions when there are real changes in the product than as a result of advertising alone. And it places advertising, which seeks to persuade people to change their opinions, into the framework of the total marketing environment, which includes distribution and shelf-facings and which must be propitious for opinion change to result in action.

One of the most ambitious published tests of advertising media effectiveness was made for Lucite paint and was reported by Malcolm McNiven, a former advertising research director of the DuPont Company.[31]

Before and after the campaign, 10,000 persons were interviewed by phone in 27 test markets divided into nine three-market groups. Each of these three-market groups was exposed to one of five levels of expenditure in either TV or newspapers. For example, one group received no TV and moderate newspaper advertising, and a second had no newspapers and moderate TV. Each of the remaining seven groups had a different combination. McNiven found that in this instance TV advertising best communicated knowledge about Lucite but did not significantly affect its sales. The newspaper ads used in the test appeared to be unsuccessful in communicating knowledge of the product, but increased sales significantly.

In this case, as in so many similar experiments, one is left puzzled as to whether the apparent inconsistency between attitude change and behavior change reflects a real discrepancy or a communications effect that occurs below the threshold of conscious awareness or beyond the measurement capacity of the questions asked.

Commenting on McNiven's study, advertising psychologist Charles K. Ramond[32] points out that attitude change often appears to follow a sales change merely for the artificial reason that an attitude survey commonly occurs after a purchase is recorded in a sales audit:

> The interval between communication receipt and purchase is usually shorter than the interval between the before and after phases of the typical survey. . . . By the time the after survey gets around to the prospect, he may already have become a buyer. And by that time experience with the product has affected his attitudes ten to 1,000 times as much as his exposure to the advertisements or commercials.[33]

Ramond reports the case of a company's advertising director who said publicly that market tests are worthless, because of his experience in two matched markets. The one without increased advertising had considerably higher sales. "Upon investigation, he learned that the entire month's distribution of his product to the test city had been lost in a train wreck." While Ramond cautions against the use of less than three test markets, he does cite the findings of a number of smaller scale market tests that showed significant changes as a result of advertising in only one or two markets. He concludes that "as measures of marketing effectiveness, sales and communication together are preferable to either separately, because one does not always reflect the other."

Qualified findings are also advanced by Valentine Appel,[34] on the basis of an experiment he made at Benton & Bowles to measure the relative effectiveness of two plans involving equivalent advertising expenditures. This research used eight groups of three matched markets each. Within each of the 24 markets, 200 users of the product category were interviewed on the telephone regarding brand awareness, attitude, and usage. Appel concluded that, with either plan, the advertising had only negligible effects in *changing* attitudes toward the test brand, but that the initial *level* of attitude was clearly related to whether the advertising had any effect on usage. Those consumers whose attitudes were least favorable to start with were least affected in product usage by exposure to the advertising. The advertising had its greatest sales effect among people who already were *somewhat* favorable to the brand rather than on those with the *most* favorable attitude who may have had little room for improvement.

The fact that the advertising could not be directly related to an attitude change in Appel's painstaking study does not mean that it wasn't working. Obviously, the people who were favorable to the brand must have been made favorable by something in the past, and this may have been earlier advertising campaigns or actual experience with the product. If advertising does nothing more than remind an already predisposed individual to buy the product it must certainly be having an effect, albeit one which is related to the product's need to "tread water" to maintain its position in the market place.

John Stewart's Fort Wayne study of repetition in newspaper advertising (see page 230) found that information, awareness, and attitude toward the test products did not relate directly to sales at any point in time, although there appeared to be a general relationship. Growing awareness was accompanied by a sharpening of information retained and by more favorable attitudes. More people became aware of the advertised products as the campaign progressed, and those people who were aware of them tended to become better informed and more favorable.

The findings in Fort Wayne suggest that we must think of the effects of advertising as extending for some time after a campaign ends. Thus not merely the *level* of effect, but its *duration* must be considered in any evaluation. Through a gimmick, an ad message may win a momentary but high level of awareness. Another may make a lasting impression on a smaller number of people. A fair comparison of different media strategies requires that measurements be made at various points during a campaign and afterwards.

The attitudes that people form toward products like the ones tested seem to be much more dramatically influenced by actual usage and experience than by any amount of advertising exposure. Consumers in Stewart's study who at the point of sale ran across a product they had not seen advertised and who were nonetheless stimulated to buy and try it became more sharply and favorably aware of it than consumers who perceived and bought it as a run-of-the-mill advertised product.

The Fort Wayne study forces us to consider the function of advertising in perspective along with all the other elements in the marketing mix. New products were deliberately chosen by the researcher so that there would be no preconceptions in people's minds and so that the situation could be controlled as much as possible. Nonetheless, active competitive pressures continued while both campaigns were on. Each of these products was differently priced relative to its competition. Users of the one were more satisfied with it than users of the other. In spite of the best efforts of the two companies involved, the distribution of one product never got up above the halfway mark, while in the case of the other product it was almost complete.

In the face of marketing forces as powerful as these, the influence of advertising is limited. Consider just two marketing variables studied by Stewart: the consumer's education and her general familiarity with brands in a product category. Awareness of one of the test products was 7 percent among consumers in the bottom half of the educational scale who showed low brand familiarity. It was 44 percent for better educated, brand-familiar respondents. Advertising has the task of imposing an influence above and beyond major influences from the life cycle or life style such as these data reflect. When we understand this, we can appreciate the difficulty of isolating its specific effects.*

What one little ad can do

The job hunter reads the classified ads with a purpose and with attention strongly focused. Perhaps at not quite the same level of intensity, the woman who is in the market for a new fall suit will study ads to get ideas on the specifics of style and pricing before she goes on her shopping trip. Most retail advertising is designed to have this kind of immediate effect. Retailers can measure the direct pull of a specific ad from mail and phone orders or from the increased volume of traffic at the sales counter. An ad can pull traffic but not sales if the merchandise does not live up to the promises.

Unlike the retailer, the national advertiser rarely expects that any individual advertisement will produce a visible sales response unless it announces a radically

---

*In the face of massive amounts of advertising, consumption of a product may diminish. For example, between 1962 and 1983, the percentage of coffee drinkers fell from 75 to 55, and each coffee drinker's daily consumption fell from 4.17 to 3.36 cups. The proportion who drank their coffee black also fell. During the same period, milk became less popular, while tea and soft drinks showed substantial gains. Similarly wine consumption increased greatly, while whiskies diminished. Such far-reaching changes in the market for beverages reflect changes in living habits and values. Advertising may serve to delay or offset an unfavorable tendency or accelerate a favorable one, but there is no way of determining exactly what its influence may be.

new product, or represents a special offer of limited duration, or has a strong fashion or fad appeal. Rather, he expects that the individual ad, along with others in the campaign, will produce a cumulative effect when they are exposed repeatedly to the same people.

If the consumer's disposition toward a brand is apt to be built more out of actual use than out of casual, unwanted advertising exposures, an advertisement's duty may *not* merely be to add its trivial mite to the pile of previous trivial exposures, but also to produce an *immediate* effect on the very few people who were already (whether they knew it or not) "ready to buy" and predisposed to attend to the message with more than casual interest.

Because national advertisers generally acknowledge that the impressions created by a single product advertisement are at a low level of intensity, field studies of advertising effects normally try to measure the impact of a whole campaign, rather than that of any one individual message.[35] The more directly one focuses the attention of experimental subjects on the communications being studied, the easier it is to measure responses that disappear in the confusion of the real marketing world. But can traceable effects be measured for a single national ad under *normal* conditions of exposure?

This question was addressed in a large-scale field experiment run by the Newspaper Advertising Bureau in 1968.[36] In six cities of different sizes, in different parts of the country, matched samples of home delivery routes were selected. The subscribers in each sample received copies of their morning newspapers with six specially prepared and inserted pages that included a selection of ads, each averaging a quarter page in size. (The fake pages were undetectable, as it turned out.) For 18 packaged goods brands, half the papers distributed contained an ad for one brand, while the comparable sample got a competing ad. For 6 other packaged goods and for seven durable items (like cars and refrigerators), the substitutions were randomized. Thus each set of ads represented a control for the other.

About 30 hours after the papers were delivered, personal home interviews were conducted with 2,438 housewives. They were asked about all their shopping "today" and "yesterday," with the aid of a series of questions that reminded them of different kinds of stores and products. They were asked also about their purchase plans for "today" and "tomorrow" and then questioned about the product categories and brands covered in the experiment. Only at the end of the interview were they asked specifically about their reading of the newspaper and their recollection of the ad. So the key comparisons were between women whose papers carried each ad and those whose papers didn't.

In the day and a half between delivery of the test paper and the interview, respondents were, of course, exposed to a variety of advertisements in all the test product categories and in all media, but these could be assumed to carry equal weight in the test and control groups. We were interested in measuring the effects of a single ad over and above the normal flow of advertising messages.

How advertising relates to sales and attitudes can be studied by first considering *only* those people who had the opportunity to receive each test ad in their home-delivered newspaper. If they paid attention and absorbed the copy points of an ad, were they also more likely to buy the advertised product?

To answer this question we compared purchases of the advertised brand by people with varying degrees of exposure and memory of the advertising. The group who best remembered the ad were those who could prove recall by playing back a spontaneous description. Of these, the ones who "connected" with it were the ones to whom it communicated best;* others, when the ad was actually shown to them, remembered noting or reading it; still others who had stopped to read something on the page did not remember the test ad. Then there were those who remembered opening the spread but had not read the ad or any other ad or article on the page. Finally, there were the "unexposed" who said that they had not opened the page on which the ad appeared in the paper.

Among those who could prove recall of an ad, 9 in 1,000 bought the advertised brand in the next day and a half. Among those who did not open the page at all, or who opened it but read nothing on it, only 2 in 1,000 bought the brand. Those who could prove recall of the ad, and especially those who played back personal connections with it, were much more likely to say the brand was one they preferred.

These findings would at first glance seem to demonstrate conclusively that advertising communication is strongly linked to sales effects. However, a skeptic might still legitimately ask, "Do they buy the brand because they remember the ad message, or do they remember the message because they are (perhaps for totally extraneous reasons) customers for the product?"

Had the study rested its case solely on people's memory of the advertising they had read, there would still be strong doubt on the subject of cause and effect. Fortunately this question had been anticipated in the experimental research design.

Taking the aggregate of all the ads and brands under study, we found that in comparison with the control group, the test group showed 14 percent more purchases of the advertised brand (a difference that could occur by chance only once in eight times), a 10 percent greater brand share (a difference that could occur by chance only once in six times), 15 percent more sales of any brand of the advertised product for the six cases where this comparison could be made (a difference that could occur by chance only once in 12 times), and 4 percent more first choices of the advertised brand for purchase "next time," about the same for the 24 packaged goods and the 7 durables and for those who were in the immediate market for a product and those who were not (a difference that could occur by chance only once in 8 times). The research also found parallel 30-hour results for a sample of television commercials that were measured as a by-product of the basic experimental design.

There *was* one finding that ran counter to expectations: fewer women said they planned to purchase the test brand. Perhaps a partial explanation is that the ads worked to trigger faster buying action on the part of women who were

*As I described on page 118, personal "connections" between ad content and the reader's own life measure an ad's ability to arouse involvement with the product. The concept was originally defined by Herbert Krugman as ". . . conscious bridging experiences or personal references . . . that the subject makes between the content of the persuasive stimulus and the content of his own life."

otherwise vaguely "in the market." By converting purchase intentions into actual buying, they may have temporarily reduced the pool of potential purchasers of the test brands.

The overall consistency of the experimental findings corroborates the earlier conclusion that advertising communications cause sales, quite apart from whether the reverse is also true.

What one little ad can't do

Apart from the overall results, it was also possible to look at the variability of performance among the advertisements measured, in terms of all the available measurements of readership and sales effects.

The first conclusion that emerges from this analysis is that while on balance and over the long-haul advertising promotes sales and improves reputation, individual ads may not merely fail to produce results; they may produce *negative* results, as was found in the case of three ads in this test.

As I have pointed out, there is no truth in the common idea that advertising pressure always works in a favorable direction, that mere exposure of consumers to the advertiser's message is bound to attract rather than to repel them. An ad may convey unintended communications that arouse irrelevant fantasies. Copy, visuals, models, background, all convey symbolic meanings that may or may not enhance the product message. One might even infer that a bad ad or commercial that might simply disappear down the "memory hole" of the average reader or viewer would arouse more visible negative effects on the part of a real, live prospect whose mind was already on the product and who was really paying attention to the message. On the other hand, a strong advertisement heightens awareness not only of the advertised brand but of the generic product category, so it may add strength to the competition in an inelastic market.

There is always great resistance on the part of advertising practitioners to the evidence that a good deal of advertising fails to do the job or is actually harmful. Null or negative results are commonly encountered in field surveys and are as commonly explained away on the grounds that the evidence is statistically inconclusive. Since single ads may have a reverse effect, the risks are less when the advertising researcher measures a campaign in which, on balance, the results are more likely to show movement in the desired direction.

If some ads work against the advertiser's interests, this should only heighten interest in techniques that might help to distinguish good ads from bad ones. For this purpose, all the ads in our study were ranked in terms of each performance variable on which there were data. The findings indicated that in a pair of competitive ads, one may be superior by some yardsticks of communication, the other by different yardsticks. Recognition and recall rank orders were closely (but not perfectly) correlated, just as they were shown to be (at the +.92 level between recognition and aided recall) in a major comparison of print advertising rating methods conducted years earlier by the Advertising Research Foundation.[37] Brand preference, not unexpectedly, showed a moderate relationship both with sales on the one hand and with proven recall on the other.

But do measures of ad readership tell us whether an ad is serving the advertiser's *sales* objectives? Our data showed almost no relationship between an ad's sales performance—when compared with other ads—and its comparative readership performance, as measured either by recognition or recall.[38]

It is apparent that an ad may arouse widespread attention and high readership without persuading the few people in the immediate market who are ready to buy. Conversely, an ad may rank low in its appeal to the general reader and still have a strong sales effect upon the very few prospective customers in the immediate market. Obviously, it is in the interest of any advertiser to win maximum attention, but his task does not end at that point.

At a time when advertising communications proliferate rapidly, there is a strong temptation for advertising craftsmen to resort to the gimmickry and technical virtuosity that arouse attention through their ingenuity, startle effect, or entertainment value; in the process the brand's identity and the basic persuasive story may be lost.

Evidence in support of this assertion comes from a secondary study we conducted among 83 decision-makers (company brand and advertising managers, agency account executives, creative, media, and research people) in major advertising centers.[39]

The experts did very well in predicting readership performance; their record in predicting attitude change was mixed, and they could not predict which ads would sell more of the brand. The last and critically important finding follows logically from our earlier discovery that sales results had only a chance relationship to the ads' ability to win attention. But it is precisely the prediction of attention value that is the expert's stock in trade and that in effect makes him an expert. Only the pretesting of an ad's persuasive power (as opposed to its attention value) and pretesting among consumers actively in the market can be expected to reduce the level of random error that even the most talented of advertising professionals introduces into his predictive judgments of advertising performance.

Advertisers should be concerned with the cumulative effect of all their advertising, in a mix of media, and in context, rather than with the effects of a single message. Advertisements resonating with each other in our vast marketing system have cumulative effects that are quite different both from their individual effects and even from the marketer's original intention.

Experiments and creativity

There is an imbalance between the amount of laboratory experimentation on advertising effectiveness and the amount done in the field. Most studies of advertising effects are done in the field, and too often they suffer from inadequate design and inadequate controls. For every dollar of research money expended, advertising efficiency can often be increased more by pretesting creative approaches than by studies of completed campaigns in actual operation. Laboratory experiments are more likely to come up with significant differences that lend themselves to meaningful interpretation and that can be translated into realistic action.

The cost of truly scientific investigation of the problems that most advertisers want to research under the heading of effectiveness is very often out of all proportion to the cost of the advertising itself. If such research is to be done, it should be honestly done in the name of science and not justified in terms of its practical utility to the decisions of advertising managements.

However, there is an aspect of advertising whose effectiveness lends itself to extremely profitable research, with a pay-out that is much more immediate than any comparison of media. This is the creative aspect.

Carl Hendrikson, a pioneer market researcher, once told me of an experimental study he made on the comparative effectiveness of print and radio advertising just before the TV era began. An advertising message was prepared for a brand of toothpaste in two forms: a print ad and a recorded commercial. There were two make-believe brands of toothpaste used in this comparison. Each person interviewed saw the print ad for one brand and heard a recording of the commercial for the other brand. He was then offered a tube of toothpaste and given his choice of the two brands in question.

Offhand this sounds a good deal like many of the experimental intermedia comparisons that have been made over the years. But the results were tabulated as soon as they came in, in groups of 25. In the first few groups, the recorded message enjoyed an advantage over the print ad. In subsequent groups, the two were about equal. Later on the print message did much better. In other words, as the study progressed, the print message did progressively better and the recorded message did progressively poorer.

The explanation for this became clear when the recording as it sounded after many playings was compared with the quality of a fresh pressing. It still sounded pretty good. But something of the resonance, the tone values, the subtle qualitative inflections of the announcer's voice had deteriorated with the repeated playing of the record. This new variable completely reversed the position of the two media that were being compared. Minor variations in the creative handling of a message may have more to do with the nature of what is communicated than the difference between media.

The knowing practitioner of advertising is under no illusion that copy tests, whatever ingenious or devious devices they may use, can substitute for talent, taste, or insight. Herbert Krugman points out that ads are tested and compared once, but that in real life we encounter advertisements many times, and our responses change in the process.

Direct response advertisers are constantly evaluating media vehicles and comparing their productivity in the most immediate terms. Coupon returns make it possible to compare the direct power and cost efficiency of different publications with an identical message. Using a coupon for a grocery item involves a small purchase decision, but the U.S. Army used an inquiry coupon in recruitment advertising bound into 44 magazines. (Naturally, there was no way to ascertain the effect of the advertising on persons who enlisted without returning the coupon.) The cost per inquiry ranged from $4.68 for *Teen* to $393.28 for *Motorcyclist,* and the cost per enlistment ranged from $165.42 for *Jet* to $84,050 for *Newsweek*[40]. This may reflect differences in the audience profiles of the publications, but it also reflects the fit between their editorial environments and the creative approach in the particular ad.

The variations in performance within a medium are far greater than those among different media. Any time that several ads or commercials are tested, one is apt to come away with a lion's share while the others creep in with only a small percentage of favorable response. Just as copy tests show how ads and commercials differ widely in their power to persuade and convince, so standard readership and commercial recall services document the variations in the power of ads or commercials to register conscious remembered impressions upon the mind of the reader or viewer.

For instance, the median four-color magazine food ad gets a Starch noting score of 52 percent among women, but it can get as low as 30 percent, or as high as 59 percent. The median liquor newspaper ad, about a quarter-page in size, is noted by one out of five men readers, but some of the ads get only a few percent noting and others get over 50 percent.[41]

Consider two outdoor campaigns with an identical number and quality of billboard displays in the same community. One for Standard Oil showed an 82 percent higher recall than one for Shell.

With a recall measure that demands more of the audience's memory, the gap between the strongest and weakest advertising looks even greater. Gallup and Robinson report that 15 best remembered TV food commercials scored 39 times better than the lowest 15.

Sponsor identification studies show similar variations in the ability of viewers to associate commercials with the programs they view.

An Art Carney TV show and a Bob Hope show some years ago had almost the same talent and network time costs. The rating of the Carney show was 17; the rating of the Hope show was 41. There is no report of a national rating service in which one cannot find fantastic variations in the size of audiences delivered by programs with identical production and time costs.

In a series of studies done by Benton & Bowles, Arthur Wilkins found that in some cases 50 percent of the TV commercial audience was just viewing TV while the program was on, while in other cases fewer than 30 percent were just watching. This type of variation would not be revealed by any rating figures, yet the level of commercial recall in the attentive segment averaged 60 percent higher than in the less attentive segment.

Studies on the creative side of advertising lend themselves far better to exact experimentation of the laboratory type than do studies that compare media. When we make media comparisons in the laboratory, we measure something different from the normal kind of media exposure that takes place in real life. The medium's strong and weak points, relative to other media, are not necessarily in proper proportion. When we confine our comparisons to alternative creative approaches within a medium, the conditions of exposure can be held constant and the planner can concentrate on the variations in the message itself. This is the area in which research investments to improve the effectiveness of advertising can have the greatest leverage on the final results.

Among advertisers there seems to be a widespread assumption that a dollar spent to advertise is always more productive than a dollar spent in figuring out *how* to advertise. There is no standard, accurate measurement of the total investment in advertising research. In fact, it is difficult to judge how much of what companies spend to study consumer behavior and market trends ends up with applications to advertising strategy. In 1983, perhaps half a billion dollars was being spent on advertising research of one kind or another, ranging from syndicated media measurements down to ad concept tests. This figure is modest in relation to the size of the job to be done and the number of questions that remain unanswered. It is also inadequate when considered in relation to the potential opportunity for increasing the efficient use of the vast sums actually invested in advertising.

By any yardstick, as we have seen, there is tremendous variability in the performance of advertising that uses identical space or time budgets in a given medium. Suppose that through research the effectiveness of a given advertisement can be increased by 100 percent; that the sales it generates can be doubled. How much would the research be worth?

Marginal utility theory tells us that a firm should be willing to spend additional money on advertising up to the point where the extra sales it produces yield an additional dollar of profit above and beyond the cost of manufacturing, distributing, and advertising the product, plus the cost of researching and advertising. Is it worth *half* a million dollars of research funds to double the return from a $1 million advertising expenditure? Maybe the value added in sales efficiency is worth only a *quarter* of a million dollars. In any case, it would appear to be worth more than $7,500—but that is roughly what the average advertiser would spend on advertising research—three-quarters of one percent of advertising expenditures![42]

In industry, the R&D function represents a far greater percentage of manufacturing output. In the aerospace industry, R&D budgets are 26.5 percent of sales; in the hardware end of the communications business—equipment and electrical machinery—R&D is 9.5 percent. Even in the automotive and transportation equipment field, it is 3.5 percent. Yet in making material goods, the unknowns are perhaps even less formidable than they are in the field of communication and persuasion. The businessman's riposte to this argument, Lester Frankel has pointed out, is that his investment in advertising research might be greater if he were convinced that it would actually pay off in increased efficiency. But obviously the value of the research investment in turn requires further research. Zero Mostel phrased a somewhat similar problem at the time of the Army-McCarthy hearings in a song, "Who will investigate the man who investigates the man who investigates me?"

Marketing and advertising are characterized by a constant search for cheap research answers to expensive business questions, most of which cannot be answered within the framework of any individual firm's advertising research budget. Perhaps this reflects a subtle pressure on the researcher within a large corporation to emulate his corporate associates and peers by producing assembly-line statistics on a schedule of his own.

Marketers are so obsessed with the compulsion to inventory the latest figures on circulation and audience that they are prone to forget the far more important and fundamental question of what happens to their messages in the minds of the media consumers. Since the structure of advertising research puts the great burden of financing on the media, it is not surprising to find that a disproportionately large amount of the research on advertising represents the dull and repetitive measurement of media audiences, while a disproportionately small amount is concerned with actual content. Yet the leverage on successful advertising performance is vastly greater for creative research than for media research. What goes *into* an advertising message is always more idiosyncratic in content and form than the choice of the medium in which the message is to appear. The capabilities of the medium remain constant over a broad array of messages and campaigns. The content and form of a message are highly specific to the product, brand, and creative approach, hence are less likely to be researched.

In some sense or other, *any* advertising message, or for that matter any communication, may be said to have an effect. Can the effect be measured? I have tried to show that it can be; sensitive instruments in the psychological laboratory can track the changes it sets off in the pattern of brain waves, the pulse rate, the dilation of the pupil of the eye, the electrical conductivity of the skin. People often answer questions after exposure differently than they did before. Their actual purchase records look different. And yet, a true description of the effects of communication is not to be found in such numbers.

Notes

1. Described by Elmo Roper in *Public Pulse*, October 1965.
2. National Broadcasting Company, The Hofstra Study: A Measure of TV's Sales Effectiveness (New York, 1950).
3. Kristian S. Palda, *The Measurement of Cumulative Advertising Effects* (Englewood Cliffs, NJ: Prentice-Hall, Inc., 1964).
4. David A. Aaker and James M. Carman, "Are You Overadvertising?" *Journal of Advertising Research* 22, 4 (August-September 1982), pp. 67-68.
5. Darral G. Clarke, "Econometric Measurement of the Duration of Advertising Effect on Sales," *Journal of Marketing Research* 13 (November 1976): 345-57.
6. Nariman K. Dhalla, "Assessing the Long-Term Value of Advertising," *Harvard Business Review* (January-February, 1978).
7. *Op. cit.*
8. Address before the Association of National Advertisers, Chicago, May 11, 1965, by Gail Smith, at that time director of advertising and market research at General Motors.
9. J.F. Borden and F.A. Brooks, *Store Walk-Outs: What Do They Cost? How Do They Occur? Can They Be Reduced?* (New York: National Retail Merchants Association, no date).
10. G. Maxwell Ule, "The Milwaukee Advertising Laboratory—A Continuing Source of Advertising Serendipity," Advertising Research Foundation *Proceedings, 15th Annual Conference* (New York: 1969), pp. 71-76.
11. *Management and the Worker* (Cambridge: Harvard University Press, 1939).
12. Samuel F. Melcher, Jr., "Management Style, Intuition, and Research; Business Viewpoint," Proceedings, 19th Annual Conference, Advertising Research Foundation, New York, 1973.
13. *Wall Street Journal*, May 24, 1966.
14. To illustrate the versatility of this method, a split cable television system was also used for a nine-month period in 1970 to evaluate a television advertising campaign aimed at increasing automobile seat belt use. Actual observations were made of seat belt usage by drivers whose car licenses could be identified as being either in the group exposed to the advertising or in the unexposed group. Although the advertising was at a level equivalent to $7 million for a national campaign (or $15 million by 1983 standards), "The television messages had no effect whatsoever on safety belt use." Leon S. Robertson, Albert B. Kelley, Brian O'Neill, Charles W. Wixom, Richard S. Eiswirth, and

William Haddon, Jr., "A Controlled Study of the Effect of Television Messages on Safety Belt Use," Insurance Institute for Highway Safety, Washington, D. C., 1972. *Cf.* also Leon S. Robertson, "The Great Seat Belt Campaign Flop," *Journal of Communication*, 26, 4 (Autumn 1976): 41.

15. Tele-Research, "Actions Speak Louder Than Words," New York, 1972.

16. More recently, a study conducted jointly by General Foods and the outdoor industry demonstrated outdoor's effectiveness when used in conjunction with TV. *Madison Avenue* (April 1983) later reported that "the brand researched did not subsequently use outdoor advertising in any markets, nor did any of the many General Foods brands then receiving advertising support."

17. For a comprehensive collection of the academic references on this subject, *cf.* Benjamin Lipstein and William J. McGuire, *Evaluating Advertising: A Bibliography of the Communication Process* (New York: Advertising Research Foundation, 1978).

18. "A Model for Predictive Measurements of Advertising Effectiveness," *Journal of Marketing*, 25 (October 1961): 59-62.

19. Talk to the 1963 meeting of the Advertising Research Foundation, New York, N.Y.

20. Address made on June 14, 1966, to the American Marketing Association, Chicago, Ill.

21. "The Relationships Between Preference and Purchase of Brands," *Journal of Marketing* 15, 2 (October 1950): 145-57.

22. "The Story of Brand XL; How Consumer Attitudes Affected Its Market Position." Foote, Cone & Belding, New York (no date). Dubois interviewed a probability sample of women in April 1958, then reinterviewed half in June and half in October. Among the users who had called the brand "one of the best" at the time of the first interview, 68 percent continued using it. Among users who called it "good" in April, 50 percent continued using it; among the small number who gave it a less favorable rating, only 28 percent continued using it. Among nonusers, those with more favorable attitudes were more likely to become users in the subsequent months. DuBois lays stress on the differences in attitude patterns among different brands and differences in the proportion of users who keep on using it. In another similar study, DuBois interviewed 1,200 women on three separate occasions about their usage of 12 brands. Although again the market position of the average brand did not change, only 13 percent of the respondents used the same brand all three times, 8 percent used it twice, and 10 percent once. People who changed brands tended to keep on changing. Cornelius DuBois, "Twelve Brands on a Seesaw," Paper presented to the Advertising Research Foundation Conference, 1967.

23. "Knowledge Is A Thing Called Measurement," in Lee Adler and Irving Crespi. *Attitude Research at Sea* (Chicago: American Marketing Association. 1966), pp. 111-26, and "An Answer to One of the Unanswered Questions About the Measurement of Advertising Effectiveness." Address before the Advertising Research Foundation. October 1965, New York, N.Y.

24. Reviewing the evidence from a number of studies, Kristian S. Palda concluded that changes in brand attitude are not necessarily directly related to changes in awareness. *Cf.* "The Hypothesis of a Hierarchy of Effects: A Partial Evaluation." *Journal of Marketing Research* 3, 1 (February 1966): 13-24. Horace Schwerin found no consistent relationship between "playback" or unaided recall of TV commercials and "effectiveness" as measured by changes in brand preference as a result of forced exposure. "Commercials that eschew logic in favor of emotion—and in so doing fall into the twilight zone of 'mood sell'—are often impervious to playback analysis. People may be sold by the vital promise but they can't articulate the reasons for this conversion." *Cf. Schwerin Research Bulletin* 13, 5 (May 1965). Arthur Wilkins has described a comparison of an established commercial and a brand new one that got a higher level of recall, but had less effect in

increasing awareness of the brand (private communication).

25. "Factual Recall as a Measure of Advertising Effectiveness," *Journal of Advertising Research* 4, 1 (March 1964): 2-8.

26. Michael L. Ray, "Marketing Communication and the Hierarchy-of-Effects," (Cambridge, Mass.: Marketing Science Institute, 1973).

27. Martin Fishbein and Icek Ajzen, *Belief, Attitude, Intention and Behavior; An Introduction to Theory and Research* (Reading, Mass.: Addison-Wesley, 1975).

28. "Behavioral Support for Opinion Change," *Public Opinion Quarterly* 28, 3 (Fall 1964).

29. Festinger's data were reanalyzed by Alvin Achenbaum, who points out that the conclusions were based on very small samples and that Festinger failed to take into account the substantial evidence from the field of market research that links opinion and behavior. Address before the Advertising Research Foundation, October 1966, New York, NY.

30. Paper before the World Association for Public Opinion Research, September 1965, Dublin. *Cf.* also his "Attitude Change and Behavioral Change," *Public Opinion Quarterly* 30, 4 (Winter 1966-67): 529-50.

31. Speech before the National Industrial Conference Board, September 1963, New York, N.Y.

32. "Must Advertising Communicate to Sell?" *Harvard Business Review* 43, 5 (September-October 1965): 148-59.

33. Ramond, "Must Advertising Communicate to Sell?" pp. 151-52.

34. Valentine Appel, "Attitude Change: Another Dubious Method for Measuring Advertising Effectiveness," in Lee Adler and Irving Crespi, editors, *Attitude Research at Sea, op. cit.*, pp. 141-52. *Cf.* also *Media/scope*, May 1966, p. 59.

35. As a good example of an effort to measure cumulative effects, the Magazine Advertising Bureau used data from the Brand Rating Index and Simmons to classify men's usage of beer and gasoline and women's use of lipstick and shampoo, according to the amount of magazine advertising exposure to different brands in each of these fields. Those people who read the greatest number of magazines that carried a brand's ads used between a third more and twice as much of it as those who read none of the magazines. Magazine Advertising Bureau, *Isolating and Measuring the Effects of Magazine Advertising: An Effectiveness Study Project* (New York, 1970).

36. *Cf.* Leo Bogart, B. Stuart Tolley, and Frank Orenstein, "What One Little Ad Can Do," *Journal of Advertising Research* 10, 4 (August 1970): 3-13.

37. This is the PARM study I mentioned on page 87.

38. The rank correlation with recognition is +.13; with recall +.03.

39. This secondary study was conducted by Creative Research Services.

40. *Media Industry Newsletter*, December 20, 1974.

41. Daniel Starch & Staff, in a 1957 report on "Tested Copy," analyzed 3,395 food ads (of over 50 lines) in 198 newspaper studies conducted in 1952-54. The smallest ads had a median noting score of 9 percent. Ads of 1500 lines and over (30 or more times larger) had a median score which was five times as great—45 percent. However, noting for the smallest size ads ranged up as high as 34 percent, whereas the highest noting score for a big ad was 78 percent. Thus the smallest ads received, on the average, only one-fifth as much recognition from women as the standard large ad, but the best of the small ads received nearly 50 percent as much recognition as did the very large ads.

42. Large packaged goods advertisers do appear to spend at a rate substantially above this average. Among companies responding to the 1982 Gallagher Report survey, 3.9 percent of the 1983 budget was to be spent on research on advertising effectiveness. Among the 57 percent of the companies that did such research, 29 percent pretested advertising with an average of 4.8 percent of the ad budget.

Chapter 15
Communication: Inspiration, not Computation

The cartoon figure on the television screen who pops up from the back of the cereal box is meaningful to a child because it symbolizes emotions, wishes, and needs that are stirred in him but are left unsatisfied by the real persons in his life. The imaginary creature enters his fantasies and dreams, becoming a part— small, perhaps—of the vital experience through which the child defines himself as a unique human being. To reduce the process by which all this happens into a series of "exposures" and "impressions" is obviously nonsensical, and yet advertising practitioners—we great experts in "communication"—go through this nonsense every business day.

Because the mass media are so largely supported by advertising, they cannot help being shaped by the kinds of judgments and assumptions that advertisers make. As long as many of these assumptions rest (as I have tried to demonstrate they do) on the crude mechanistic notion of communication as a series of events, advertising decision makers will be mainly concerned with numbers rather than with meaning. And the search for numbers—for big, demonstrable, measurable numbers—inevitably must be reflected in the attitudes of those who operate the mass media for profit.

The publisher or broadcaster (when he takes off his green eyeshade and slips on his toga) has always proclaimed his responsibility to mediate the complexity of the world for a broad public in the form of either information or art. Some media operators come close to fulfilling this ideal; many don't bother to try. It may be that the very notion of mass media is incompatible with the highest levels of intellectual or artistic achievement—not because of the deficiencies of the mass audience, but because mass media require production on deadlines and in massive quantities. The pool of talent available to the publisher or television producer may be utterly insufficient to permit him week after week to perform at the highest level of his responsibility or of his medium's potential. But if there are flaws in the quality of mass media, far better that they be flaws of inadequacy than flaws of intent. The intentional flaws—which arise from a cynical view of the audience—go with a philosophy that makes quantity rather than character the criterion of success.

Decisions about advertising have important implications for other decisions made by a business organization. They represent a deployment of resources that could be used in other ways; they involve expectations of profit. Business executives want to solve advertising problems as they solve other business problems, using comparable techniques of assessment, evaluation, and research. But while decisions involving evaluation and research are also business decisions, standards of research are essentially a nonbusiness matter.

A good many advertising people are uncertain about advertising research's status as science. But even those who are the most contemptuous of its integrity show no hesitation in using it when it serves their purpose. Advertising costs money, and there is a constant clamor to find out whether that money is being returned with interest. To satisfy this clamor, numbers—any recent and possibly relevant numbers—are in great demand. New ratings, circulation reports, audience figures, noting scores, and innumerable other statistics pour forth each week; they are the staff of advertising life. Who in American marketing refuses to take the importance of these numbers for granted? Who digs into their meanings, questions their usefulness, asks whether the emperor really is wearing clothes?

A century ago, strategy problems in advertising revolved around the question of what to say rather than over the technique of expressing it or the choice of means by which to say it. Advertising skills primarily entailed the manipulation of words and their meanings.

Today the term *advertising* is subsumed under broader headings. For the retailer it is part of merchandising; for the manufacturer it is part of marketing. In either case, the preparation of advertisements is subordinated to a larger objective and is part of a larger planning process in which product design, pricing, selling tactics, and other considerations must enter and may, in fact, predominate.

Marketing (or merchandising) presupposes planning, order, time tables, schedules, and synchronization of activities with other time-dependent business operations—investment, product research, production, distribution.

These requirements of orderly planning are fundamentally at odds with the nature of the creative process. To be sure, creative geniuses (Mozart, for example) *can* work on schedules and meet fixed deadlines. The application of sustained effort over time may result in productivity, but it will not always yield inspiration. And most advertising does indeed represent the productive output of advertising "factories" rather than inspiration.

One of the things that makes advertising an unusually interesting field of activity is that it involves a perpetual state of tension between its aspect as business and its aspect as art. I have suggested throughout this book that in advertising the Idea has *primacy*, whether it be Great or otherwise. But it should not necessarily have *priority*. Just as the Idea must be framed to fit the requirements of the product, so it must often be chosen to reach a particular marketing target and directed to suit the requirements of a medium. The Idea is not merely a matter of *what* is said. Everything depends on the encapsulation of the message in a phrase, a picture, a headline, a juxtaposition of ideas that is unique and memorable.

Communications of exceptional power make up the collective memory of our culture. This collective memory includes great works of music and striking visual images such as the Mona Lisa or Washington Crossing the Delaware. It also exists in written words that are repeated and remembered.

A communication that has entered the cultural memory bank can be evoked instantly. Being universally familiar, it has a life and momentum of its own, regardless of fluctuations in its popularity. This condition has little to do with the number of people who hear it or see it on any given occasion or with any level of frequency. What difference does it make how many people have heard Beethoven's Fifth Symphony or how often?

Advertising messages only rarely achieve this autonomous existence. The term *image* in advertising is, I suppose, a vulgarization of this concept of collective recognition. Like the words "Beethoven's Fifth" or "Gettysburg Address," the names "Cadillac," "Alka-Seltzer," or "Coca-Cola" automatically set off reverberations from an accumulation of past impressions. For this to happen requires a certain minimum acquaintance. The aura that surrounds a product may arise as much from the volume and distribution of its advertising messages as from its own attributes and history. But beyond the minimum of recognition, the connotations arise from the distinctive character of the messages themselves.

In advertising, as in conversation, it is sometimes better to say nothing than to say something not worth saying, either because it has been said before or because it makes no sense. The company that cannot be distinctive in its product field might do well to cancel its advertising until it *does* have something to say.

The reader who has come this far may be somewhat disappointed to find that there is no set of do's and don't's at the end of these pages, no list of guidelines for action on his particular problems. In advertising, as in chess or war, strategy does not consist of rules or principles, for if these existed the opponent would have a predictable counter-move for every move made. Strategy consists rather of a posture (of wariness and guile) and a method of approaching problems.

Advertising planners can indeed call upon a vast body of existing information to help with the decisions they face today, but the way in which past experience may be applied to present problems is always unique to the product, the company, the competition. To say that "it all depends" is not to say that it all depends on chance or faith. While both these factors may influence the way the planner arrives at the solution that turns out to be correct, the solution itself most often consists of the right combination of unrelated principles.

Market analysis, like psychoanalysis, may create sensitivity to the consequences of one's acts. Psychoanalysis may make an individual more tactful, more alert to other people's reactions and expectations, but it cannot endow him with intelligence, charm, or spontaneity. Similarly, market analysis and research may tell a company who its best prospective customers are, what they think, and even what arguments might be most persuasive to them. But it cannot tell the company how to embody this knowledge in great advertising.

A television version of "Hamlet" performed by the Old Vic Company was once run through an audience reaction test, which found the action parts of the play to be more "involving" than the great speeches. The study's author, Jack

Roberts, later reported that "from other test results, we'd probably be told the killing of the king doesn't come soon enough and there's too much talking with all those soliloquys."[1]

Just as a great play is more than the sum of its individual lines, so The Great Idea in advertising is far more than the sum of the recognition scores, the ratings and all the other superficial indicators of its success; it is in the realm of myth, to which measurements cannot apply.

Communication is a process, not a thing. It involves people, not material objects. It embodies in even its most trivial aspects the total outlook, expectations, and values of the protagonists. A company can no more stay in business without advertising today than an individual can exist without communicating with others. By gesture, intonation, rhythm, stance, and style we give overtones to all the words we utter. They reflect our unique personalities. By the same token, every company too is unique because of the people in it. Some are dull and some have flair. Their advertising tells it. We *feel* the difference.

Notes

1. *Schwerin Research Bulletin*, 13, 3 (March 1965).

Index

Federal Trade Commission (FTC), 18,
19, 19n, 20
Fein, Gene, 254, 271
Fender, Derek H., 152
Ferguson, James M., 29, 35, 331
Festinger, Leon, 373
Fishbein, Martin, 373, 386
Fisher, Lawrence, 22, 33
Fletcher, Alan D., 118
Fletcher, Robert, 183
"Flighting," 213, 214
Focus group interviews, 82
Foley, William F., 51, 60
Food and Drug Administration, 20
Food Marketing Institute, 267
Foote, Cone & Belding, 43, 171, 186,
188, 191n, 213, 350
Ford Motor Company, 238
Ford, Henry, 196
Fouriezos, N. T. Associates, 178
Frank, Ronald E., 253, 271
Franklin, Benjamin, 84
Franzen, Raymond, 280
Friedman, Hershey H., 118
Friendly, Fred, 308
"Full disclosure," 19

G
Galbraith, John Kenneth, 23, 33
Gallagher Report, 66
Gallup and Robinson, 91, 108, 110,
115, 173, 180, 185, 186, 188, 198,
225, 328, 382
Gallup poll, 10, 13, 301
Gallup, George, 83, 84n
Gardner, Burleigh, 74, 116, 150, 247
Gardner, Samuel R., 270
Gavin, Jack, 241
Geiger, Joan, 34
Gelman, Morris J., 205n
General Electric Company, 40, 99,
110, 174, 202
General Foods Corporation, 40, 59,
66, 180, 349, 371
General Mills, 368
General Motors Corporation, 51, 59,
66, 191, 236, 359, 360, 372

Gensch, Dennis, 352
Gibson, James J., 152
Gibson, Wendy, 136n
Giletti, Ted, 69
Gitlin, Todd, 78
Godfrey, Arthur, 133
Goffman, Erving, 160, 183
Golden West Broadcasters, 188
Golden, Allen, 305
Good Housekeeping, 74, 136, 210, 322
Seal of Approval, 144
Goodin, F. C., 276
Grabowski, Henry G., 24, 34
Gram, Harvey, 352
Grass, Robert C., 111, 112, 116, 141,
149, 175, 224, 230, 233, 234
Grasse, Donald, 46n, 68, 247n, 371
Great Britain, 28, 72
Green Giant, 201
Greenberg, Marshall G., 253, 271
Greene, Jerome D., 285, 312
Greene, William F., 117, 225, 234
Greenwald, A. G., 119
Gregg, Lee W., 183
Grey Advertising Agency, 372
Greyser, Stephen A., 13
Gromer, Frank, 191n
Gross National Product, 28
Gross Rating Points (GRP), 43, 43n,
71, 196, 204, 223, 298, 311, 318,
320, 337, 348
Gross, Irwin, 85, 116
Grotta, Gerald L. 148
Grudin/Appel/Haley, 142
Guerck, David, 35

H
Haber, Ralph Norman, 163, 183
Haddon, William, Jr., 385
Halcomb, C. G., 231
Haller, Thomas F., 14
Hamill, William S., 197
Handel, Gerald, 270
Hardy, Thomas W., 187
Harper, Marion J. Jr., 98, 354
Harper's, 249, 281, 304, 305
Harper's-Atlantic, 310

TITLES OF INTEREST IN
ADVERTISING AND SALES PROMOTION
FROM NTC BUSINESS BOOKS

Contact: 4255 West Touhy Avenue
Lincolnwood, IL 60646-1975
800-323-4900 (in Illinois, 708-679-5500)

SALES PROMOTION ESSENTIALS by Don E. Schultz and William A. Robinson

SALES PROMOTION MANAGEMENT by Don E. Schultz and William A. Robinson

BEST SALES PROMOTIONS, Sixth Edition, by William A. Robinson

SUCCESSFUL DIRECT MARKETING METHODS, Fourth Edition, by Bob Stone

SECRETS OF SUCCESSFUL DIRECT MAIL by Richard V. Benson

STRATEGIC ADVERTISING CAMPAIGNS, Third Edition, by Don E. Schultz

WHICH AD PULLED BEST? Sixth Edition, by Philip Ward Burton and Scott C. Purvis

STRATEGY IN ADVERTISING, Second Edition, by Leo Bogart

ADVERTISING IN SOCIETY by Roxanne Hovland and Gary Wilcox

ESSENTIALS OF ADVERTISING STRATEGY, Second Edition, by Don E. Schultz and Stanley I. Tannenbaum

THE ADVERTISING AGENCY BUSINESS, Second Edition, by Herbert S. Gardner, Jr.

THE DICTIONARY OF ADVERTISING by Laurance Urdang

THE ADVERTISING PORTFOLIO by Ann Marie Barry

PROCTER & GAMBLE by the Editors of Advertising Age

HOW TO BECOME AN ADVERTISING MAN, Second Edition, by James Webb Young

BUILDING YOUR ADVERTISING BUSINESS, Second Edition, by David M. Lockett

ADVERTISING & MARKETING CHECKLISTS by Ron Kaatz

ADVERTISING MEDIA SOURCEBOOK, Third Edition, by Arnold M. Barban, Donald W. Jugenheimer, and Peter B. Tu

THE DIARY OF AN AD MAN by James Webb Young

ADVERTISING COPYWRITING, Sixth Edition, by Philip Ward Burton

PROFESSIONAL ADVERTISING PHOTOGRAPHY by Dave Saunders

DICTIONARY OF TRADE NAME ORIGINS, Revised Edition, by Adrian Room

HOW TO PRODUCE CREATIVE ADVERTISING by Thomas Bivins and Ann Keding